Withheld

Matt Corton

Cover art by Sarah Cavani
www.sarahcavani.co.uk/

ISBN: 1466466197
ISBN-13: 978-1466466197

DEDICATION

For Catherine. Without you I would not have begun.

For Sue. Without you I would not have finished.

ACKNOWLEDGMENTS

So many people played their small parts in the creation of this book but Catherine and Sue, you stand out above all others. Catherine, when you were going through your toughest time, you found a way to help me get started on what became the biggest project of my life. Sue, your encouragement, love and belief gave me the confidence and drive to pick up that 'pen' again and finish what had become the Golithian task of editing.

Thank you, both, from the bottom of my heart.

FOREWORD

100 YEARS AGO…

'Dear reader

Do not come here. Do not let your brothers come here, nor your sons. I know it is not permitted to speak of such things, but this is hell. Ostracia is hell. There are things in the Forest, things that none of us should know about. There were forty thousand of us. Forty thousand! There's little more than ten thousand of us left. We were only there a few hours.

Do not come here!

We can only hope we have done what we came here to do. They are all here, all the Kings, Emperors, all of them, even the Scythians, though I think they're in a different camp.

They did not come with us. How can such hell be real? How can they be real? We all heard the stories, but they're real! The things I've seen…'

"The note breaks off here, sire. From the charring we believe the good Captain attempted to burn the letter before he was discovered."

The King of Arcadia nodded. The court, such as a gathering of leaders in a tent could be called a court, was hushed. Only the Scythian Emperor was absent, as he had been for the entire campaign. The Archaean Consul and the Kings of Eozoon, Azoia and Caraiza stood to the left of the two thrones, in one of which Daseae, Fifth King of all Arcadia sat.

Finery had been eschewed for the gathering. All were in their battle armour, with the exception of the Scythian emissary, though all, like Daseae, hadn't even set foot in Ostracia let alone taken part in the battle. Daseae's armour outshone the rest, he reflected with pride. Only their cloaks could tell the Kings apart – the Caraizan red, the Archaean blue, the Eozoon yellow and the Azoian black.

Daseae's own gold-plated steel breastplate, worn over chain mail, bore the sign of his reign – mirrored epsilons, one in reverse one true, etched into the thick gold plating. The mail was heavy, but the strapping holding them to the chain greaves took some of the weight.

He would wear the armour as long as he was here, even to sleep in, not that sleep was in large supply for the allies. Daseae had lost ten thousand of his men in the invasion, he was not about to let some small discomfort prevent him from showing his troops he was with him that for this campaign, at least, he was the military leader of the world's armies.

Nor was he about to let one man ruin what had been planned for so long.

"Is that all you have, Castellan Karlner?" he called to the man in plain green robes who held the floor.

"No, your majesty," his friend replied with all the semblance of sincerity the King had ordered him to show. "Our scribes have pieced together some torn fragments, we believe we have reassembled them in the correct order. It reads:

'*I took him where I was supposed to, to where they were being held. Scythian beast that he was. If you ask me they are no better than the Ostracians. What he did…I should never speak of it. I tried to stop him. It wasn't right, I told him they were people not animals, our people some of them, his people, but he just laughed. Laughed while they screamed.*

There isn't any future for me from here. I haven't slept for the two weeks we've been back here at camp. Not because of the battle. There were bodies everywhere, it's true, but I've seen bodies before, often at the result of my own hand. I had even been prepared for seeing them feed, although that caused panic in many. The human body holds so much blood after all, eventually the stomach can't take any more. Unless that stomach is Ostracian.

The woman was the worst. Her face was as red as her robes by the time she'd wiped out one centurion's entire command and still she fed. The more she fed the stronger she got. Those she didn't feed on she…twisted inside with her foul magics. Their artistry, I believe they call it.

Though we were no better. We all knew we knew force was not to win us the day, we knew victory depended on the Scythians. Though if we have won our victory is hollow after what I saw the sorceror do to those poor innocents.

What it was that he did to them I do not know. There was no blood, apart from the wounds where he bit them, nothing. Held in that trance by his weird eyes while they screamed. They went on screaming…

Then the Scythian, he dropped dead. These sores all over him, all over his face, huge boils, horrible smells…'

Castellan Karlner stopped, a wry smile on his lips as he lifted his eyes from the paper to share a glance with the King Daseae, who fought down the pulse that was rising. "It ends there," the Castellan said loudly, holding up the charred paper for all to see, "that is all we have recovered."

The King tried not to smirk. Karlner had performed exactly as instructed, as ever. It was good to have someone one could rely on.

"It proves well that our mission was a success!" the King cried, to much polite applause. He would have hoped for more, but then he was not King in the Scythian tent. "We should never forget the tens of thousands of men we lost here, but they were lost in possibly the greatest cause we shall see in our lifetimes, gods willing."

This garnered a greater round of applause, even some cheering, much to the distaste of the esteemed Scythian seated next to him. That pleased Daseae. It was time to focus on ending proceedings in this hellish landscape. Daseae could not wait to return to Arcadia and forget this place. It pulled at him. Even the jesters were subdued, wives and children had refused to come. There was something here that should not be here. Daseae's sleep was disturbed. The sickly power, the dread force…

"So we have a traitor, this Captain Eric?"

"Yes, your majesty," the Castellan replied, his voice once more grave.

"In my country he would already be dead."

The man to his left leaned over his throne, the unpleasant scent of his foreign food wafting too close, forcing the King to try not to recoil. "We are committed to fair trial in our lands, where you sit, Arimaspi." The named meant one-eyed, the Scythian representative had told him at their thoroughly unpleasant banquet the night before. The King remembered at the time thinking that having just one eye did not restrict the man from being two-faced.

"A foolish concept, I fear, but who am I to judge? But of course the King remembers that whilst this tent may sit on the land that is, I believe still Caraizan for the moment, rather than belonging of his own Kingdom of Arcadia, that this tent, while occupied by me, represents to you the Scythian Empire, but then I am sure that you remember this, yes?" The man drew back, sipping at his revolting horse milk and blood drink, which the King was sure was the source of the foul odour, tucking himself into his fur coat despite the heat.

Daseae despised Arimaspi. He was only the third Scythian Daseae had encountered on a face-to-face basis and he had despised all of them. No wonder the Scythian people were rumoured to be so miserable, they were ruled by despotic tyrants who thought only of themselves. Daseae had had enough of this façade.

"I shall question the prisoner myself," he cried, to the surprise of those around him, but he had grown weary of them. "You will forgive me, Arimaspi, I hope you understand this is too important a matter to be allowed to spread amongst our peoples. I look forward to seeing you at the banquet tonight. I bid the rest of you farewell!"

With what he hoped was a flourish the King strode from the tent. The sun beat down on him instantly, forcing him to squint in a most un-regal manner, but the way his gold armour shone in the sun here pleased him. It was sad that such a beautiful region should be tainted by so much evil.

Daseae paused as he heard the banners of the Kings rustle in the wind behind him, but resisted the urge to turn and look. He was surprised he could hear them over the constant murmuring that always surrounded a battle camp. The shrieks of the wounded at night were the worst. Daseae closed his eyes – he knew their pain only too well.

"Was that wise, sire?" the man hissed at his elbow.

Snapping his eyes open, Daseae resumed walking, his long stride forcing the Castellan to half-run, half-skip to keep up with him.

It had not been wise and already King Daseae regretted his decision to leave. The Scythians were currently loyal, but he knew their loyalty ended when their mission here did. The banquet tonight was crucial and to anger Arimaspi before the negotiations there began was something Daseae had a feeling he would end up paying for.

It would not do to let Karlner see this, of course. "Do you question the decisions of your King, Castellan Karlner? If we are to be believed, the lie must be seen to be true." The Castellan bowed his approval at once, quickly falling behind again and having to rush to keep up.

Captain Eric was dead, of course. Daseae had instructed the Caraizans who had caught him to deal with him quietly and appropriately. The son of a simple Caraizan merchant, having met with the unfortunate Caraizan punishment of having his tongue cut out, would stand trial in Captain Eric's stead then spend the rest of his unfortunate days in the pits. A simple matter of a few gold coins had bought the man's son. A simple transaction for the good of the people.

The King sighed – he longed for these days of peace and cooperation to end, there was simply no end to the politics. In Arcadia everything was simple, nothing needed to be done for the sake of appearance because Daseae was King and his word was law. As soon as these foreign warlords became involved everything had suddenly become much more complicated.

That was why Daseae had ordered parts of Captain Eric's letter to be burnt. One passage in particular, that Daseae kept on him at all times, not that he needed to, it was burned into his memory, must never fall into hands outside of the Arcadian inner circle.

'It was their faces. The ones they kept like cattle, their stock, they called them. They called the big houses they lived in pens. Pens! These were no pig sties, these 'pens' were larger and finer than my house! They didn't want us to come, didn't want us to help them. They fought us too, but they couldn't fight the sorcery. They weren't Ostracians, they had no strength, no weapons, nothing.

What I can't understand is how could they be happy? We were told they suffered greatly, that these hundreds of people, they were kept as beasts, for their masters to feed on, yet they begged us to leave them be, said their lives had never been so good, that the

Ostracians shared everything with them, treated them like Kings. All those that were left behind, the sorceror bit. When he was dead, those that refused our liberation were slaughtered.

We were told we were sent to help them, but they were happy! We should never have come here!'

The thought filled Daseae with disgust. These unfortunate creatures were blood stock, farmed animals for the Ostracians to feed on. Daseae cared not for their happiness. Such practices were evil, were against everything that nature and the gods stood for. They were an abhorrence, a warning from the hells to the rest of the world. It wasn't just the taking of the blood, of course, there were stories of nosferatu in all kingdoms in all times, the Ostracians did something else, something with their black magic, their blood magic, something to – how did his alchemist describe it? – trigger the power.

The Ostracians had grown too strong, their leaders lived too long and they had set their sights on expansion. They had started to trade outside their borders, they had never done that before. When Daseae's envoy, sent to find out exactly what was happening in the strange kingdom, was slaughtered, along with his entire travelling party, the Castellan sent to see Lord North to find an explanation sent correspondence back that chilled Daseae to the bone. It was the last they heard of the Castellan. It was only when Daseae sent envoys to Caraiza, situated much closer to the border of the Great Forest, beyond which Ostracia sat on its cliff top, that he began to learn the true nature of the city.

Nothing that went in came out. More strangely, no Ostracian had been sighted outside of Ostracia itself. So when they had started appearing in Arcadia, Scythia, Archaea, Caraiza and even Azoia, although they did not last long there, Daseae knew he was being plotted against.

As part of the agreement with Caraiza, this land where they stood, the flat, fertile plains, right on the border of the Great Forest, had been given in tithe to the Kingdom of Arcadia, upon completion of this mission. Too many Caraizans were going missing, called into the Forest, called to serve the Ostracians, to feed them. Too many were lured by that sickly sweet call Daseae heard in his own dreams, promising power. So much power…

"How does it happen, Karlner? How can a whole people turn against nature in this way?" His Castellan smiled in an understanding way but said nothing. "They speak a primitive version of Arcadian, did you know that?"

The man nodded. "That is not surprising, sire, considering they were one of the many kingdoms that existed back in those lawless times. Think of the trouble Archaea causes us, sire and that is but one kingdom. Imagine what it was like with over a dozen…"

"My point is, Karlner, that for all our differences, no Archaean and Arcadian have descended into such horrors!" Karlner nodded again, but this time said nothing, his eyes shifting quickly to their right. Daseae shuddered.

The lines of the necromancers' army stood broken, the gaps in their ranks showing their fallen. The Azoian necromancers had alleged no human troops would be needed, that their ranks of animated dead would win the battle without spilling blood and strengthening the opposition.

Daseae had refused the suggestion outright, as had Arimaspi and the King of Archaea. Pursing his lips, Daseae knew they had done the right thing. Azoia was a troubled place, if word got out amongst their people that Azoians had saved the world from the Ostracian threat, then his position in Arcadia would have been greatly weakened, as would that of the other Kings in their own realms. Now they stood there, in their lines, in front of the opening to the Great Forest, just waiting. None of them moved a muscle, if indeed they even still had such things.

"Azoia and Eozoon have their problems, it is true," he said eventually, "but when Caraiza opens its borders to Arcadian rule, I do not think we will find such as we have here." Once again, the Castellan smiled and nodded, but said nothing. "By the gods, man, doesn't this trouble you? Don't you want to find out why?"

Karlner's face set firm in his understanding smile. "The Ostracians have always been thus, sire, that is why we stay away."

The King turned to his Castellan. "But that is not true, Karlner! Not true at all, the Ostracians were a peaceful, kind people once! They were godsless heathens, yes, but emissaries returned from the city with nothing but good words to say about the beauty of the architecture, which was then decades ahead of our own, not to mention the tales of their magics."

"Sire!" Karlner hissed, drawing closer. "We must not speak of such things!"

"There is nobody to hear us, Castellan and may I remind you that treason does not apply to the King!" Daseae smiled at the Castellan as he spoke; there was little need for Karlner to obey court etiquette, they knew each other far too well for that. "What changed? What made them what they are now?"

"I prefer not to think about it, sire."

"But surely, Karlner, this intrigues you? Surely the mystery of how a people, as ancient as our own, and once as dignified, could turn to such black arts as feeding on their own kind? They were not short of food, or materials, so why? They were a pleasant, great people, they were not evil. They were not born like this, Karlner! Karlner?"

He broke off as he saw the Castellan's worried expression. "Sire, please stop."

"What is it?" The man shifted from foot to foot, not answering and the King turned to face him. "I asked you a question, Castellan."

Castellan Karlner looked up at him with an eager, round, smiling face. "It's just, sire, well, how do you know this? We have no records of the

Ostracians, or the emissaries that were supposedly sent, they are simply tales from other nations. Arcadia sent no such emissaries, it did not exist."

The King frowned. "I don't quite..." He realised the Castellan had a point. How did he know? He could not remember, yet he did. He was sure he did. He could see the Ostracians, in his mind now, just beyond. Just beyond the blackness...just beyond the woods, perhaps he should go, go into the black, go to the mouth...

Karlner shook him, with some force, his smile gone.

"I am sorry, Karlner." Daseae's breath felt cold on his lips. "Gods, we must pray that this works."

"Nothing can go wrong, sire! You have done a wondrous thing! No longer shall we be forced to bear this evil in our lands, no longer will our people disappear, taken to feed their demon lusts, you have saved us!"

King Daseae smiled – the Castellan was a good man, for all he was from eastern Arcadia. A loyal man. It paid, even as King, to have some around that he could trust. "You are right, Castellan," he started to say, but as they neared the edge of the camp, where his soldiers were stationed, he could not help but look back and felt a chill.

In front of the necromancers' armies was the Yawning Maw, the mouth of the Great Forest, an opening the size of a war tent in between the trees, beyond which there was only darkness. It was the only clear opening in the Forest wall that was otherwise virtually sealed by twenty feet high impenetrable thicket. They had cut it down when they had arrived, so they could approach the city in a wide line, but the thicket had grown back overnight. It had been impossible. Each time they had cut it down, it grew back.

Daseae realised his mouth was dry.

"Have that sealed up. Tonight."

Castellan Karlner shuffled, nervously. "That may not be possible, sire."

"I want that hole sealed." Seeing the Castellan eye him strangely, he added, "Nothing must get out."

"I understand that, your highness," the Castellan replied, too smoothly, too quickly. Daseae realised this question had been asked before. "I am afraid, however, that nothing will grow on that path, nothing. No stone can be brought here that is big enough..."

"The tunnels were sealed?"

The Castellan nodded. "All we could find, sire."

"What if there are more?"

The Castellan's face briefly showed the slightest of traces of offence – he had handled the interrogation of the informer himself. "We have the highest faith in our informant, sire, everything he told to us has been proven true. We flooded each of the tunnels, all leading to...well, you know where they led to.

We collapsed a good deal of them too, they were poorly constructed, sire, no skillsmanship at all…"

"I understand, Castellan, thank you." King Daseae tried to hide the annoyance from his voice, it did not do for the King to be seen to be anything other than in control. "What of our informant?"

The Castellan coughed. "He has departed, sire."

"Where?"

"I did not ask, sire."

The King breathed a sigh of relief. One Ostracian would not hurt. The man claimed he found the practice of blood magic reprehensible and in any case, one Ostracian would be easily found and killed should he attempt any mischief. Even so, Daseae was glad to have him gone from the camp.

None more would leave, however. "Construct a wall around the Maw," he told the Castellan. "Lay the foundations deep."

"Sire, the plan to encase the Forest is already under way…"

"You have your orders, Castellan."

The little man departed at haste, seeing the look in his King's eyes. Daseae regretted slightly behaving in such a manner with his trusted ally, but that hole, that mouth, gnawed at his insides.

Ostracia should be sealed. They could never return. The evils of the Ostracians went far beyond what the people knew of. The stock was one horrific part of their design. When the first of their spies had been found, Daseae had known immediately what it portended. The Norths were not happy any longer with the offerings they were being given. They wanted more and knew they could take it. Arcadia, for the first time since its establishment, had needed help.

The King remembered the treacherous journey to Scythia, a long month at sea, to reach the only people who could provide that help, only to be met with the insult of dealing with Arimaspi, who, Daseae was assured with much flowery language, was given complete authority in Scythia to speak for the Royal Dahae, the ruling clan, to negotiate the use of their foul sorcerors.

Daseae had been surprised to learn that the Scythians wanted nothing in exchange for the use of their troops and sorcerors. He had been further surprised to learn that they, too, had uncovered Ostracian spies in their midst, but at a far more advanced stage than that in Arcadia. In Sakiz, an outlying Scythian city, they had even been openly taking people from the street to feed from, creating pens, causing fear and panic among the population.

The Scythians were worried. In Daseae's lifetime there had been no trade with Scythia, no diplomatic relations between their countries of any kind and Arcadia was not unique in this regard. They had sent their help for free, as had the Kings and Emperors across the land. The Ostracian plan had terrified the world.

The people need know nothing of the greater plan, of course, thankfully the moral outrage at the farming of people was reason enough for them to send their sons and brothers, as Captain Eric knew they would, to fight. Ostracians in Arcadia were rounded up and disposed of, but even this could not be done quietly. It was hard to kill an Ostracian, but die they had. The fierce street battles with the Arcadian army had, if anything, convinced the Arcadian people that such a threat was beyond acceptance. It also took their minds off the interminable struggle with Archaea – the countries had, indeed, never been more united. Daseae was secretly pleased by that – he was glad to once again have their fine fish to serve at the banquets at his palace.

Daseae forced himself to turn away from the Yawning Maw. Immediately, he felt better. The strange cloud, the feeling that something was sucking at him, pulling him in to the Forest, was gone, as he strode off to inspect the troops. What was left of them.

The sooner that hole was sealed the better, he did not want the camps that were to be set up along the Forest line to suffer from such torment, but even so, he made a note to mention the Yawning Maw at the conference tonight. Perhaps that camp could be set back a little.

The watch would have to be set here for all time. Not even one Ostracian could escape. Not until the curse was lifted. Not until they were cured. Not until the plague had done its work. Arimaspi had said that could take a century. There had been no argument from any side of the table. All had agreed to send men, weapons, provisions, anything the camps wanted. Ships would be provided to watch the bay. They were united against the evil.

King Daseae sighed. When the camps were set up, when the Forest was sealed with earth and wood, he could return to his people and gods willing, need never consider Ostracia again. A century was well beyond his lifetime. Once, Daseae had held ambitions to rule the world. The scribes and soothsayers had told him it was his destiny, yet still the Archaean dispute wrangled on, the Scythian indifference to the wishes of their gods, the Caraizan duplicity, all offended him and his people, but there was no appetite for war within him now, not when they had been faced with such evil as the Ostracians. This was his war, he had led the negotiations, he led the armies of the world. His soothsayers had been correct after all.

"Sergeant-at-arms! Inspection!" he called out, pleased to see the rush of activity that greeted his words. His people needed peace, not war. His people needed good. The evil that was Ostracia could never be allowed to return.

NOW…

"You see anything?"

Antil looked out over the prow, shielding his eyes from the sun. Gods, but this place was hot. Too hot. It was never anything other than hot, hadn't been in the six months he'd been here, moored in the same spot. Six months at sea, watching a dead city.

"I said, do you see anything?"

"No, Iarok, I do not see anything, in a similar fashion to how I have not seen anything this morning, yesterday, nor for any other bloody day of the hundreds I've bloody been here. I see nothing. A bleeding city on the hill, that's what I see."

"Don't mention blood, for fuck's sake, what's the matter with you?"

"They're not going to hear from all the way down here, are they? There's nobody there, anyway." Antil caught his hands as they made to cross himself, for all his words sounded calm.

"One thing they're definitely not doing is bleeding anyway, we've seen to that." Antil heard Iarok chuckle behind him, but he did not join in. "And how many times, it isn't a hill when it's in the sea! That's a cliff. Look, massive sandstone cliff, must be two hundred people high, sticking straight up, that's like no hill I know about. What's matter with you today anyway?" his friend growled, and Antil instantly felt bad for not at least humouring him.

"Oh, I'm just sick of being here, that's all. Merit and the children at home. Can't even send letters from here."

"Well you can't write!"

"That's not even close to being the point! Captain could read letters to me, sure he'd write some for me if I asked him, there's nothing else for us to do."

It was the same for his compatriots on the other galleys. No vessels came to bring them post or provisions, they had to make do with what they had. In truth, they had plenty for just the three of them, barrels of cured meat aplenty, dried fruits and vegetables, pickles and they made their own bread every week from the grain stores which they would need three times their number to deplete. Plus, they were moored at sea, there was always fish. Antil despised fish. Despite that, he had to admit, the likes of him had never had it so good.

"Think the other ships have got any carrots?"

Antil turned at this, incredulous. "What?"

"I said, do you think the other ships have got any carrots?"

"Well I don't bloody know, why don't you swim over there and ask them?"

Iarok snorted. "Well, I'm off to see if I can find some."

Antil nodded, watching his friend depart. Six months they'd been on the Empire with Captain Craik, just the three of them and he and Iarok had become firm friends. In just another six months, when their relief arrived, a crew of twenty would take them home, with three of their number drawing lots to take their place.

The food was a reward. The books, too, if the next shift could read. Their families at home were similarly taken care of, it was a good job, the best job. Yet they had to draw straws for it. Not because of the year away, any sailor had to accept he was going to miss his family, Antil had seen his children for a collective total of about a month in the seven years since the first was born, but he accepted that. After this he'd get two months off paid, then he'd have to find trade work.

No, they had to draw lots for it because it was close. Too close to them.

Antil looked out across the prow again. The city's three spires rose tall above the clifftop. They were magnificent, towering above the rest of the equally impressive white and brown stone city, still immaculate in colour. The steep stone path that had led down the cliff to the harbour that had stood at its base was gone, the catapults had seen to that almost a century ago. Antil eyed them nervously – they hadn't even tested them since they had been used all those years ago and still they stood primed and ready. If the Ostracians weren't gone and they didn't work…what would they do? Every year their numbers had been reduced, from hundreds to barely twenty.

No, they were there just to watch, not act.

The smoke from the city had stopped years ago, or so the older sailors' stories told and since then there had been nothing. No sightings, no smoke, no signs of activity. No signs of life, if Ostracians could be called alive. The empty, broken eyes of the fine houses on the cliff top, beyond the flimsy wall, were ruined. Sometimes Antil saw birds, flitting in and out of the window looking just like flies buzzing around an empty, dead skull, but even the birds seemed to steer clear of the city now.

Antil shivered despite the heat – they could never be allowed to come back.

So they watched. Six ships, large galleys, side by side, covering the bay. Always six ships. For nearly a century now. Two Arcadian, two Scythian, one Archaean and the Empire, the pride of the Eozoon fleet. The Caraizans didn't send ships, said they had too much to do handling the borders of the Great Forest. Antil sighed – at least he didn't have that job. They'd set up towns right along the border, where the Forest met the plains, the Twelve Villages they called them now, all just to keep an eye out for a lot of people who didn't seem to exist. That was a lifelong term, that one. You took the job, you lived in the Twelve, and nobody wanted to live in the Twelve.

Antil took a strip of dried carrot out of his pocket and bit into it. He'd keep watch. He had to. If they came back…no, it was worth the wait. It was worth being separated from Merit and the children. Anything was worth it to make sure they got rid of the evil.

PROLOGUE

In the early days he'd tried to trust people.

He had been full of hope, happy and eager to give them opportunities to aid the cause, to prove themselves, to rise above the persecutions they endured and the mediocrity and tedious repetitiveness of their lives. He'd wanted them to grow with him, to relearn what had been lost since the invasion and to forget the indecencies of their treatment at the hands of their own leaders, his predecessors. He'd wanted to give them the chance to strive towards the freedom of their race, to end the stifling siege of their imprisonment.

It made him laugh now to think of it.

It had to, the alternative was despair and such self-indulgence was not for those entrusted with responsibility. Like self-disgust, morality or mercy, despair was a childishly simplistic concept. Indeed they were all concepts that only those lacking in any responsibility had the luxury to dwell on. Those with responsibility, with power, were entrusted with considerations of the bigger picture and there was no room in that intricate process for personal feelings or childish concepts, there was only the need for that bigger picture to be drawn correctly.

Elder Cairns had learned there was no room for trust.

Of the many occasions he had made misguided attempts to bring others into his confidence, to encourage their learning or even to allot them simple tasks, simple tasks they consistently found excruciatingly complex excuses for not having completed satisfactorily, none pained him more than the case of the unconscious man, or what remained of him, bound to the rack before him.

He had inducted Elder Rime himself, thirty years ago, after Cairns had found the courage to take power from those who had become too weak, too self-interested and too cowardly to wield it, when his pupil had been no more than eighteen years old. Rime had become the youngest Elder on record, the Elders' records being one of the few things to survive the purge after the revolution that followed the invasion and imprisonment. The man had shown such promise, such a passion for learning all of his art that a man could learn, that Elder Cairns had been almost swept off his feet.

Infatuation. Not with the man, but with what the man represented to him. Bartholomew Rime had represented hope. Hope that his people could rise against their captors, free themselves from their prison and redeem their honour. Hope that they could do it themselves, that they could teach themselves, arm themselves against the plague that was eating away at their population, fight it with the arms of knowledge, fight it with science and their power, their artistry – the blood magic that ran through all Ostracians' veins – but their failure had mutated that infatuation into a coagulation of bitter despair and failure.

The plague had begun almost as soon as the invaders had left, almost a century ago now, in the outer pens. Septar and Nemar had been the first to send envoys to make the day-long trek to the capital city to report the news. By the time his predecessors had found the strength to muster their decaying minds to action, the villagers the envoys had been sent to secure aid for were dead. It had only taken two days. Cairns remembered the scene as they had entered Septar. The buildings were intact, remains of fires still burned. Everything looked normal until the screams had alerted them to the pigs, which were happily in the process of consuming their masters where they had fallen. The mess had been cleared up quietly, although as ever with such matters, not quietly enough.

For a time, that was the end of it and talk of a plague sweeping through what stock remained after the invasion soon turned into alehouse banter, at least until the Deathguards, having returned with the dead for their internment within the city walls, began to die themselves.

It was not long before the city dwellers too, the true Ostracians, began to be consumed by the outsiders' vile parting gift.

"The sickness is in the blood, Elder," the chief alchemist had instructed them all, a decade into the imprisonment by siege following the invasion. Cairns had been a boy then, passed into the Elders' tutelage after his parents…well, he couldn't remember what happened to his parents. He had made sure of that himself with a simple Withholding – an artistic suppression of memory long-forbidden in Ostracia.

The chief alchemist had addressed them as they had gathered in the Elders' Council chambers, in the eastern spire, one of the three that stood on each corner of the once magnificent palace. Constructed entirely of marble, they reached hundreds of feet into the sky, each topped by improbable domes, which seemed to the naked eye to be far too heavy for the stone that supported them. Everything was marble, from the white curling stairs that ran inside the structure, to the many-coloured domes. It was the crowning monument of all civilization.

It was the first time Cairns had been granted access to the Elders' seat of power and the eye-melting mix of colour from the forty-feet of stained glass that surrounded the single circular chamber that sat at the top of the spire, the many-coloured marble pillars, seemed to a child to reach to the skies, but actually only reached to the painted mural that spanned the sixty feet square domed ceiling. The Elders, all twelve of them, sat in their simple white robes on gilt thrones, one from each other major outsider cities, a gift to symbolise everlasting peace. The trusted, few now since the revolution, reclined at their feet on scarlet velvet cushions. Even the mix of colour in the vibrant caftans and dalmaticas they wore had been too much to take in for the young Cairns. He could remember none of it as he should, or as it deserved, but then it was ninety-odd years ago now.

Elder Hugo, the council leader and the young Cairns' tutor, sat on the largest of the thrones, although a man his size could make any chair, even a throne, look weak. What was remarkable about his throne was the huge gilt lion's head that rose behind Hugo's own, its mouth open, teeth bared, expressionless eyes somehow still radiating pure malevolent rage. It was a fitting chair for the man, and one thing Elder Cairns did remember was the look on the alchemist's face as Hugo questioned him. He remembered the look because he recognised how the man would feel having experienced it many times over.

"The sickness is in the blood!" The man had been excited. Too excited. He was proud of his findings and Cairns knew from experience that Hugo hated pride.

"If it is a disease of the blood then the outsiders surely suffer from the same affliction, yes?" The thin, wiry man who was leading the discussion, was the astronomer. Cairns could no longer recall his name, although he had been forced to kill the man a few decades later after he had been unfortunate enough to find out too much about Cairns' plans.

"I'm afraid not, sire. Elder. Sorry." The chief alchemist had been sweating profusely, staggering from foot to foot, and mopping his bald head with a shining silk handkerchief that simply spread the unsightly moisture around his face. "You see the barrier, the infection barrier as we are calling it…"

"The what?"

The man faltered under the interruption, as if his voice staggered, tripped, unsteady for a moment before it could steady itself. "Um…the barrier, the gorge, the charred pit that seemed to appear when the outsiders departed, sires. I'm sorry, Elders. No Ostracian can approach the gorge." The man warmed to his topic as the Elders sat quietly. "The sickness takes them even as they walk. Their blood simply burns its way from their veins."

There were murmurings at this. Cairns remembered listening, fascinated, but Hugo had not called the public here to alarm them.

"We are safe here though, yes?"

"For the moment, sire, sorry, Elder, yes."

"If you refer to any of us as sire one more time I shall break your neck with my own hands!" Elder Hugo roared. "There are no Kings here, no Lords, no aristocrats, no priests, no gods, there is only us! Ostracians are born equal it is our skill and heart that sets us apart, you would do well to remember that, alchemist, we are all equal here!"

"Which is precisely the problem, Elder," the man answered at once, though whether warming to his topic or warming with anger against Elder Hugo Cairns could only guess at. "We are all equal, which is why they have chosen such a plague."

"Chosen?"

"Oh yes," the alchemist answered, turning back to the thin, wiry Elder. "This is a construct of sorcery, Elder. There is no doubt. We have had plagues before, we have cured them, or rather you have, Elders, with your artistry, or we have simply resisted them because of the power inherent in our blood, but this time our own blood has been used against us. They infected our stock!"

The alchemist had been executed the next day, faced then dismembered. Cairns had been taken to watch the execution. He hadn't understood why the other children had been so tearful and scared, some so scared that they hadn't stopped shaking for the next week. It was a death, like any other to Cairns, the result was the same as a knife through the heart or even contraction of the plague – Cairns could not see how the manner of it mattered.

The alchemists' guild had worked for a further month on an alternate answer, but eventually they had reached the same conclusions as their late chief. This time the news was delivered behind closed doors, with no members of the public and no scribes. Years later Cairns discovered why. The infection was already in the blood. In all Ostracian blood. It was already far too late.

The plague resisted all attempts at artistic healing. Those who contracted it, although they died more slowly now than those in those days, could not be healed by artistry and Ostracians had no knowledge of outsider medicine. The insidious destroyer resisted all blood magic, all of the old ways, the ways the Elders preserved and nurtured, all that they stood for. Slowly, the plague killed their people.

This was exactly what the outsiders had intended all along. They had never intended to conquer Ostracia, for all of their sheer weight of numbers and strange projectile-firing weapons that cut a man down before he could draw his sword. When the outsider forces withdrew, the Ostracians had thought it over. They thought they had won. Shortly afterwards, the ships appeared in the bay with their catapults.

The short-sightedness of Lord North was brought to the fore. With Elders and powerful artists banished to their strongholds, the palace was first surrounded by the angry, mourning mob before being razed to the ground in a hail of flaming destruction from the ships in the bay, all members of North's ruling council inside.

They hadn't discovered the bodies for days, the palace, its very bricks imbued with artistry, resisting entry until it had rebuilt itself and by then the first reports of the deaths in the outer pens were reaching city ears.

The invasion had been a distraction. The catapults did not stop until the paths down the cliff side to the sea had been destroyed. That was the eastern border taken care of. The only ways out of Ostracia were through the Forest and those very few that in the next few years did make it past the infection barrier the alchemists had warned them about, were slaughtered by the outsiders that waited for them beyond the Forest.

They had cleared acres of land in a circle around the Yawning Maw, the entrance to the main path through the Forest, the northern and western borders the Arcadian empire forces and their allies awaited any venturing from the Forest. The great river to the South was manned by the Scythians. None took prisoners. None ventured beyond the border into Ostracia. They wanted the Ostracians to suffer the slow death they were suffering.

For a few years after they had begun, the deaths had been kept to a minimum. The plague had taken most of the stock by then, so the pens were shut down. As people cried out for blood, most literally, they were brought into the city and by burning the bodies of those who caught the plague they minimised its spread. Elder Cairns had been uneasy, even as a child. They were trying to carry on as normal, but the people were restless. There was no more blood. Feeding from fellow Ostracians did not work, as a few poor souls discovered. They needed outsider blood but their stock that remained was tainted. Slowly, the Ostracians began to become aware of their power draining away and shortly after that they became angry.

Cairns raised a hand to his own face, wincing as he remembered those poor souls from his childhood. With Withholdings he could hide his deformities from the villagers, but with such artistry banned by his predecessors they had no chance. They were ostracised, then murdered quietly, with no investigation, the authorities wanting no reminders of the plight they suffered as they tried to carry on as normal.

It hadn't taken long for the revolution to happen after that. What was left of the old families, the syphilitic, in-bred leftovers of a bygone age that were clinging on to power with their yellowing fingernails, were wiped on in less than a day. Just five years after the invasion and the entire Ostracian system, the way of life they had been true to for centuries, the way of life that had made them the superior force of knowledge, trade and economic power had been swept aside.

The Elders took over. Then the Elders had doomed Ostracia.

Or so Cairns had thought.

He hadn't counted on another rebellion, centuries-old, that had been working in secret against the Norths. In the end, Cairns had seen the underground Tower in which he now stood before he could find it. It had been shown to him as a child by the man of whom he could recall nothing other than the shining scarlet of his clothing. The man had spoken to him for hours. Cairns had been unable to move, unable to speak, so he had sat and listened. He remembered being interested in what the man was saying, there was something about him he could trust, something that was right. Cairns knew the man had spoken for hours, but he could only remember one small part.

"Your own flesh, your own blood, left to rot in what amounts to a box not big enough to stretch out? Gasping for air until its lungs give up? You wouldn't do that to your dog, let alone one of your own blood!"

If Cairns had ever dreamed he would have thought the shadowy, red-eyed, red-cloaked figure to be nothing more than a fantasy in such a dream, but Cairns had never dreamt. He rarely even slept, not since he had found the means to the salvation of his people.

The analogy the scarlet-cloaked man made had been clear. Should one's child be trapped in a box, one would do everything one could to free the child from that box before it ran out of air. Cairns had no child of his own, his people were his charge. His people were his blood. He had to let his blood of out the box.

Then, all those years later, something had led Cairns back here. He had been fleeing Hugo, and through the Forest he had found his way here. The power from the heart of the First Elders called to him instantly and he had eagerly drunk at it, the heart straining to give after so long sealed and Cairns eager to take.

Yet Cairns knew these old places would all die. The first step had already been taken, his blood taken out of the box of the city they had become stuck in. It had been the first stage of his plan, the only plan, the only thing that would save them.

To save the Ostracians, they had to die.

He had been arguing for it throughout his apprenticeship, but Elder Hugo and the others had been fierce to the point of obstinacy in their opposition to the relocation or, indeed, any idea Cairns had. This was partly because of his junior status at the time, but mostly because of their fear of Elder Hugo. Their incessant insistence upon recovery, upon regaining what had been lost to them, had begun to drive Cairns once more to the point of self-indulgent despair.

"You talk of this as if it were nothing!" he remembered Hugo ranting at him once. "You talk of our defeat, of the destruction of the Ostracian ways as if it were a foregone conclusion!"

"We are defeated!" he had cried in return, at sixteen more than ready to face the Council on their own terms. "Our stock is gone, we have no means to feed. We must find other ways, other means to…"

"The infection barrier and the outsiders prevent our connection to other means, boy," the astronomer had said kindly, "there is nothing we can do on that front. We are not strong enough without the blood of the stock to fight the outsiders and alas we have no steel to produce weapons with which to fight them. No, our way is best." There had been several sage, old heads nodding in agreement with him. "We must continue our search for a cure and encourage the stock in the mean time to breed as I believe we have done with some success in those from Nemar…"

"There is no barrier between us and artistry!" Cairns had retorted fiercely, addressing not the patronising, smiling old man, but the red-faced, thickset hulk that was his tutor, Elder Hugo. "If we all took the splints, if we focused our power, we could leave this place, fight the outsiders, regain our freedom!"

"Leave?" Hugo had roared, rearing himself up to his impressive full height, the large belly from over-indulgence that now protruded even through his loose-fitting white robe making him none the less intimidating. "None can leave Ostracia, boy! I regret every day the choice I made in making you my apprentice, your brains have not developed past those of a five-year-old! If we leave, their accursed infection barrier takes us, or the soldiers will! Do you know how many of them there are? We wouldn't get close enough to them to use our power against them. When the invaders came there were so many they were all over us, we could get to them, they were an easy target – these encampments outsider our border are heavily fortified, they are becoming towns in their own right! Twelve Elders and a few apprentices could do nothing against them, even with all our power!"

"That is exactly it, Elders!" Cairns had pleaded, his voice breaking in more ways than one. "We have power! Separate from that of the blood, if we shared it…"

"Our power comes from an older, deeper source," the old one had interjected, in his sugary, patient, infuriating voice, "one which our people do not share and could never share. Their blood magic is a crude thing, borne from a single source for a single purpose, that of strength. What of the subtlety of artistry? What of the blend of nature and man, the dexterity of touch and grace of the words that command it?"

Hugo stood, silencing the room at once, his huge frame towering over the rest of them. "Do you think yourself greater than the long, distinguished line of Elders who have gone before you?" His voice was so soft that Cairns was taken aback. "I assure you, you are not. You talk of sharing our power? You talk of it here, in the Elders' Council? Not only are you the worst student it has ever been my misfortune to be responsible for, you clearly possess the dullest mind ever recruited to our ranks; you are a disgrace."

Cairns inclined his head to show respect, but before he could reply he realised his mistake. Hugo's fist crashed down upon the back of his skull before his could raise his splinted hand to defend himself.

"You never learn do you boy?" Hugo breathed into his ear. The rest of the room were silent; nobody would interfere, it would be them next should they try. "That place was sealed for a reason, they both were. You think it is the likes of you who are ordained to save this city? Simple fool! By the gods I curse the day I chose such an ungrateful ingrate to teach as my own son! You have been nothing but a mistake!"

Cairns had felt his nose crack and split as Hugo's knee was dropped onto his head and he had lost consciousness.

He had learned something from Hugo then though. There was another place. There was a great power there but Lord North and his family had thrown away their chance to harness it.

With Hugo refusing to grant Cairns the status of full Elder, he had turned in the meantime to the older ways, the older writings, making sure to stay out of his tutor's way. The Elder Council's library had been his home for days on end whilst he perfected Domination and the darker artistic devices he discovered in the books there, the forbidden applications of artistry. It was there, aged eighteen, he had perfected the first Withholding performed by an Ostracian since the invasion, completing the methodology himself. It had taken another year to perfect the removal of such enchantments, but it had been there, in the old language from centuries past. He had been right.

There was a way out!

Cairns had made the discovery almost by accident, stumbling upon the answer like the fool Hugo accused him of being. Time after time he presented his evidence. Time after time he was refused and in all that time Ostracia continued to die.

By the time Cairns was thirty there was no more stock. By the time he was forty the blood magic in his people had become exhausted. With no artistry to stop it, the plague finally had its chance and it moved through the city like a fire, taking half the population in just five years.

Cairns had assumed power when he was fifty years old, as he was now, forty years later as he would be in another fifty years. He had been born on the day the invaders came to sack his lands and he would be present on the day he led his people to freedom.

He would be present long after that.

"This task is for me alone," he whispered to himself as he pulled the rope tight once more around the man's wrists.

"Will he suffer?"

Elder Cairns stopped himself from flinching. He had forgotten the girl was there.

"Will he suffer greatly, I mean?" the girl asked again, in her light, interested voice. There was no trace of fear or concern in her voice, simply the interest of an artist studying her subject. Elder Cairns was proud of her.

"He will, Keeper, I'm afraid." He turned to see the girl force the wide smile that had spread when he used her newly-given title off her face. It made him smile in turn – he would be sad not to see her for so long. "I want you to remember this lesson," he said, in as stern a teacher-voice as he could muster, "for you may need it yourself in the coming years. You may be in need of strength."

She nodded, her blonde curls bouncing in the pale candlelight. This far underground, Cairns thought sadly, her skin would lose what pallor it had in the coming years, no natural light would penetrate here. He had left her what candles he could, but she would have to be economical with them. He had instructed her well enough, though. He was sure she was ready.

"Are you ready?" he said to the bound man, raising a giggle from his apprentice.

Elder Cairns didn't expect anything in reply, that was beyond the poor man now and had been for some years. He turned away as a scream once more choked the calm from his nerves. The incision had been quite large. Cairns knew he would have to act quickly before the man bled to death. The procedure was necessary but without the herbs he needed, but hadn't had time to prepare, there was no way to douse the pain for the poor man. It would be excruciating in ways Cairns hoped he never knew of. No blame could be attached to the man for resisting this, but he knew from experience that if he stopped to consider the horror of what he was doing he would be as weak as the rest of them and after only a short while, just as useless. Power didn't come easily nor was it held on to as a matter of course.

He could perform this horror because his people needed this horror. Elder Cairns needed this because his people needed this. His people needed him, therefore his people needed this. The prize for winning the game was for his people, not for him. It was his duty. He had to free them. Elder Rime was but one person, Cairns was doing this for the whole of Ostracia. He had to.

The elongated echo of the man's tortured, pleading scream, unable to form words without his tongue, took a long time to be consumed by the stone eaves far above their heads. The large circular, underground and almost empty stone chamber was not the ideal place for this, especially in its state of decay. Only the rusting iron rack, to which his erstwhile colleague had been tied for the past five years, remained of the furniture and what fixtures there had been in this once great hall had long since submitted to entropy, including the rusted and broken brackets for torches. The flames from the torch licked off the rusted iron frame of the rack, the sound of the blood dripping onto the stone flagging amplified to grotesque proportions in the eaves stone roof some thirty feet above their heads.

The Transept Tower in its current state was not the place it once was. The dust, dripping down the small, perfectly carved mortared bricks like candle wax, kept falling away occasionally in silent, weightless lumps. It had gathered so thick in places that it had begun to obscure the thick fronds of moss that until recently had been its only fellow inhabitant in the underground tower of the Elders. The spongy green and yellow growths were everywhere.

The bound man's breathing had slowed, cracking occasionally as his as his chest rose and fell in bursts, his wounds a throbbing, inviting red glow breaking through the gloom. The doors were the only feature in the huge, semi-circular chamber not covered in dust and Cairns' lungs were already so dry he could almost feel the flesh cracking. The doors had once been impressive, with embossed, but now rusted iron pictograms nailed to the bracings that held the planks of the foot-thick wood together. Any meaning the pictograms had once had was long lost. The arch in which the doors were housed backed onto the Clear Chamber like a mouth, breaking the perfect circle of the Chamber before the walls could meet. Cairns only wished that mouth had sucked the dust and mould from the room.

They were so far underground that neither sound nor smell had anywhere to disappear to and the nature of the Clear Chamber in particular was to concentrate, hold and amplify. Even the large sunken grate in the tiles often spat out the stench and sounds of pain from centuries past into the present.

It was hard to work in the gloom, the glow from the solitary torch Cairns had roughly wedged between the huge, thick wooden door and it's circular iron handle providing the only flickering, soothing light, but work he must.

As the bound man rasped for breath, spluttering blood-soaked, groaned insults, or what Cairns presumed would be insults, or pleadings, Cairns tossed the latest bloody instrument onto the tray with the others and coughed, the dust from the long-sealed chamber beginning to get into his lungs.

"It won't be much longer," he tried to reassure the bound man, knowing even as he said it that he would neither be heard nor would his words bring comfort. Wincing himself as his left arm, now bound to his side, sent shocks of pain up to his shoulder, then back again on an unbroken circuit, Cairns gave himself a moment to recover.

The thin strips of metal, the splints, hammered delicately under each of his fingernails to ensure the flow of blood, had been torn from his left hand. Cairns hadn't looked at it properly yet but he could tell from how it felt that it would be a long time before they could be reinserted. The nails were gone, so they would have to be allowed to grow back before they could be split once more. It wouldn't leave him vulnerable, exactly, the blood that flowed from his right hand would still provide him with more than enough artistic power but it would leave him weakened. The girl had bandaged his hand the best she could, having read something about outsider medicine in one of the books here, but it was time that Cairns' hand needed. The tonic Rime would give him would not hinder his recovery either.

Recover he must, and quickly. The man he had been forced to kill had been powerful, more powerful than he should have been. Cairns could not afford to have his people make any mistakes. There were only three years left; everything had to be perfect this time, there could be no more mistakes. There would be no more chances.

His people knew nothing of this place. It was better that way, knowledge of the Transept Tower would only raise questions they would want answers to and Cairns didn't have time to either answer them or make sure they were not asked. Not only that, it would serve as a reminder to some of them, those who were remembering too much already, of what they, as a people, as a race, had lost since the invasion. The artistry that ran in all Ostracians' blood, the purest of blood magic, far in advance of the outsiders' primitive sorcery, with its archaic potions, possets and prattling chants, was essential to their survival. The power held in the blood could be harnessed at will, once the user had learned how to tap into it, and of course some held more power in their blood than others, but artistry ran naturally through the blood of all Ostracians and as its presence fell away, their blood was becoming diseased. They were all dying slowly, becoming nothing more than the outsiders.

It was all necessary. Their gift would return, given the right stimulus, but Cairns had to make sure they died. They had to die to be free, they had to become powerless.

The bound man made a strangled sound, something between a cough and a retch, Cairns could not tell which. If the blood was clogging in his throat, he would have to be quicker still. He found himself talking as he allowed the man's convulsions to subside before continuing.

"Piece by piece, life by life, our village becomes lost to us even as we lost the old town stone by stone. I carried the first of those stones to the new village myself. The crowning stone of the courthouse! Part of the great stone mosaic arch under which our judges perverted their positions, in the pockets of the old families. I believe that stone now masterfully keeps order in the foundations of Mary Archer's cottage."

In that sense at least, Cairns had enjoyed demolishing the city. Elder Cairns had tried to show them it was the old ways, the old customs that had to die, not their race. He had shown them, but none of them had possessed the vision to see what they had been shown. It was the future that held power, not the past.

"I am sorry for this."

Cairns reached for the tray of instruments and selected the most intricate; a golden hand-sickle, plain in design, but the only instrument not covered in rust, as bright now as it had been when it had been forged. The golden metal felt cool in his hand, but then it had been made for a cold purpose. His eyes took longer to focus these days, but he brought them to rest on what had once been Elder Rime.

It was time for the girl to see.

"Come here and pass me the vessel," he called to the girl, just thirteen years old. Skipping eagerly from her room, she bounded to the tray, noisily clattering the instruments this way and that before handing him Elder Hugo's golden goblet, a gift to one of the Lords of Ostracia by an outsider prince. Elder Rime screamed again as Cairns caught the blood that surged out of the wound Cairns reopened with the sickle. The eaves of the huge circular room, constructed from the purest of artistic stone, seemed to snatch even the slightest of sounds out of the air, sucking the vibrations up and bouncing them around from stone beam to stone beam before the beating heart in the apex absorbed them as it absorbed all of Elder Cairns' actions. Just as it absorbed everything Cairns thought. Everything Cairns felt.

Just as it absorbed everything his colleague felt.

Cairns turned to watch the girl as he waited for the cup to fill. She, in turn, watched the sight before her eagerly, with no fear of the horror of a full Drawing. Cairns smiled – she was a good choice, for all she was the only choice. She would learn more here in the years she would be incarcerated than she would among her people. Still, a pang of guilt at the thought of her alone here, underground, for three years.

The Clear Chamber, the inner sanctum of the Transept Tower, a structure that had taken almost a century of subterranean construction to raze into Ostracia's earth, had been completed a day before the invaders had arrived. It had been immediately sealed and never opened, not until Cairns had been shown the way.

Cairns was dimly aware of a spurt of wet blood on his hands as the cup overflowed and the gagged screams of Elder Rime shot out, his head turned upwards towards the apex of the cavern, the heart of the Transept Tower, the source of the great Clear Chamber's resonance power, in a contorted shrieking plea.

As quickly as he could, he passed the goblet back to the girl, before grasping the golden sickle and twisting the left prong in his hand. The wound sealed shut at once, held together by its ingenious design. No Ostracian today could master such magnificent technique. "Could you dress the wound?" he asked the girl and watched happily as her eyes bulged with delight.

Cairns took the goblet from her again and stepped back, withdrawing from Elder Rime's panting, moaning form, as the girl ran off to find her instruments. Cairns hadn't given her a splint yet, she would have to draw the blood to artistically heal Rime's wound the traditional way, by cutting herself.

The smell of the wet blood clinging to the already pungent and abundant moss in the cracks of the once fine stone flagging beneath his feet was making him nauseous. When had he become so weak? So old. Drawing power artistically was very different to feeding from the stock as he had done as a child. The Drawings meant using the dark arts, ways older even than the old ways, ways Ostracians had turned upon in disgust, yet ways which had been practised throughout the course of Ostracian history. Artistic Drawing meant the subject did not age, at least physically, so was it his mind that was tiring? He knew he should stop this. It was abhorrent, an insult to nature itself, the deformities it wrought upon his face proved that, but there was no choice. He was bound to his course. This was just one man, his people were many.

A phrase he had learned to dread hearing inside his head.

Cairns slowly paced the cracked flagging, now more a garden to weeds, keeping one eye on the man bound to the chair as the girl worked. Rime had once been gifted, after all, a powerful artist. It was why Cairns had chosen him to be Elder alongside him. It was why he had chosen him both then and now.

As Cairns himself had been chosen, what should have been a lifetime ago.

"Three Elders where they should be a council of twenty. A few hundred Ostracians, where there should be tens of thousands. A mere rippling of artistry flowing in our veins where there should be rivers. No, rapids! Torrents of blood magic that should have elevated us to the level of gods over outsiders, but which we have lost."

The girl turned to him, pausing, and smiled. "Almost lost, Elder. We haven't lost it all, not yet." Cairns smiled briefly at her but could not hold it. The girl frowned. "I've forgotten my cutting knife!" she cried in horror, running off back to her room to fetch it.

At first finding the right course had felt like a beginning, even though the coming years would be in fact be the end. There had been nothing comparable in Ostracian history to the huge loss of life during his time as Elder. His mentors would have loved that. He could almost hear Elder Hugo laughing, thinking he'd been proved right. For Cairns, an orphan, or so he had been told, and the Withholding had made sure remember nothing of his parents, there was no trade to follow. He had been an obvious choice.

A choice they had cause to rue. Cairns had known it was his destiny to wrest power from the privileged from the moment he was chosen. It was the conceited inaction of the so-called leaders, the aristocracy, born into that which they thought better stock, which had led to the destruction of the greatest of cities. They and their farms, their *farms of people* were to blame for the invasion, for the plague that had decimated those under his care, not the outsiders. And by the gods had he made them pay for it. The villagers, in their drunken ramblings, constantly called for revenge on the outsiders, but Cairns would brook no revenge. When they were finally free, Ostracia would simply cease to be. The thought pained Cairns deeply, but there was no other way.

He would wrest their freedom, just as he had wrested control, through artistry, through leadership and through blood.

Artistry depended on blood and that meant to effect artistry, physical or airborne contact was required for all except the most Gifted. Very few Gifted Ones had been known to possess the power of artistry of the mind. Only one Ostracian a century possessed that power. Sorcery, as primitive and limited in application as it was, required no such proximity to its prey. What sorcery gained in power and force, it lost in dexterity and finesse; a true artist could manipulate the minds of those less Gifted, cause death with but a touch and force crops to grow in arid soil; turn earth into water and produce fire from the air. Artistry helped mankind. All sorcery did was destroy and subjugate.

The Ostracians had known sorcery, of course. Many Elders before Cairns had blended their advanced artistic powers with primitive sorcery in secret, but Lord North, the aged and paranoid patriarch of Ostracia's first family, had sought them all out. The practice had summarily ceased, dying with Lord North's trials and the Elders who were the subject of those trials. Cairns smiled; if Lord North wanted to come and get him for the crime, he would have to come from beyond the grave.

Far above his head, deep in the stone eaves, Cairns could feel the heart of the Transept Tower, the congealed mass of flesh made up of the hearts of the First Elders, stutter in its beat, which was otherwise in time with his own. The simplest of sorceries, harnessing the power of generations for the Elders' use and he, Cairns, had found it! Found it after they all knew it was there. Hugo, the astronomer, all of them, they had all sat on the secret of Ostracian salvation. The rebel Elders had known, they had travelled beyond the borders in secret, they had seen how others lived, they had learned that what Ostracians did to outsiders, keeping them as feeding stock, was wrong, that there was another way to harness the power latent in Ostracian veins.

The resonant power of the Transept Tower came from the heart, the sorceric artistry flowing from it into the very stone of the Clear Chamber, where he now stood. Cairns could feel the power here. Had the tunnels that were to have been even further beneath the earth than they were now been constructed as planned, the power would have stretched throughout Ostracia, the tunnels its veins, from the city to the borders of the Forest, giving Ostracians the use of the power from anywhere in their borders. The stock could have been set free.

The girl scurried back into the room, still beaming at having been given such an important task. Rime screamed again as she carefully removed the golden instrument from the wound, but the girl did not even flinch, Cairns noted with pride. She was careful to clamp a clean cloth to help staunch the bleeding as it burst forth anew. Placing a poultice of herbs and other things Cairns did not understand onto the wound, she bound it tightly with the cloth. Cairns turned away as she took the knife from the set in front of her.

There was always a moment of weakness, the quelling of one's natural urges that no matter how trained the person, always surfaced. He was covered in the blood. His hands, his last remaining white robe of office and his tattered sheepskin boots were all stained with death. Cairns could feel his insides telling him to go to the bowl now, never mind the rest of the Drawing, just wash it off, get the blood off, that was all that mattered and to do it as quickly as he could. Cairns had mastered his natural urges many years ago and he just pushed them down as he had learned to do from his master. He focused on the thump he could feel inside his own heart, in time with the heart of the Transept Tower, and on the needles of power bursting from the congealed, mummified ancient flesh, secured far above his head its cradle of stone.

As the Keeper's back was turned, he lifted the goblet to his lips and drank deeply, shutting out everything but the artistry and the cauldron. The sweetly pleasant aroma of the blood widened his nostrils, filling him with a hunger and he bit at the goblet, wanting it, desperate for it, the sweetness turning acrid before vanishing altogether and his swollen mouth was filled with the taste of nothing, an absence of all feeling. The taste artistry left on the living. Only this wasn't pure artistry.

He breathed deeply as the blood mixed with his own and his muscles tensed as he felt the energy creep into his body, feeling the very tissues of his being beginning to renew themselves as they gorged upon the artistry being released from the boiling mass. A laugh jumped unbidden from his mouth as if eager to escape.

Another deep breath, then it was time for the words. Slowly, whispering, he incanted the words from the days that were older than the old days and he felt the power surge through his body. Already he felt younger, the blood pumping through his maimed hand feeling alive, not pained and he wanted more. Flinging the goblet aside, he bit at the air, there was blood there, he knew it, he could taste it, it was everywhere and he wanted it, he needed it. He could smell the blood from Rime's wound and he wanted to rush over, to tear at that wound, to rip it apart and drink, to gorge himself until he was full.

There was almost nothing left. *So soon.* Cairns could smell the dust again. *One more. Just one more, please. This will be the last one.* He sucked in the last of the blood-soaked air and felt himself falling, his mind reeling in ecstasy. He felt the stale blast of the Clear Chamber's air against the scars on his face, scalding like branding irons.

Cairns staggered to his feet. Wind that wasn't there rushed through his ears, wind he floated on as Rime's artistry flooded into him. He hadn't felt so good in years, not since the last time! All of his senses were rolled into one beautiful mass of feeling, a rush of release and gods it felt good!

He smelt the blood of the girl. Fresh, young blood, as it fell onto Rime's poultice. *Her blood would be much better. You could drink her. She has* power.

What had been Elder Rime met his gaze with an accusing, empty eye socket. The flames from the torch on the far wall flickered this way and that, though where the breeze was coming from to cause such violent motion in the flames Elder Cairns couldn't fathom. Now the wind of the rush of the Drawing had ceased the air was stale and still, older and thicker than the dust that carpeted everything. The dancing streaks of yellow and gold illuminated the crimson stains streaking across the floor and caked onto the lowest bricks of the wall.

"There," the girl said, startling him, "all done. Is that right? Will he heal?" Cairns looked at her and felt sick. How could he have thought…

"He will be fine. You did well, my child."

She beamed again, sending the pit of his stomach to his throat. How could he have thought of hurting her? This hunger, this rage… this need inside him… the people would say he would burn in the hells.

Cairns almost snorted at himself. The villagers' stories of life after the flesh had died were nothing but dangerous prattle, peddled by ignorant peasants who couldn't even begin to understand the complexities and charms of the world around them, dangerous myths that threatened the rule of science. All life ceased with death. Once the spirit had nothing to aim for, none of the mysteries of the world and its people to unravel, why should it bother to continue existing?

"Your face…"

Cairns turned quickly, looking at the concern on the girl's face. Quickly, he raised a hand, flicking blood from the splints permanently inserted under his fingernails, letting it fall on his face. Words left him and he felt the muscles on his cheek contract, reshape, as the glamour took hold.

"Is that better?" he asked the girl. With her, he need make no attempt to hide his use of artistry. With her he could be himself. It was not only the girl that would be alone in the coming years.

She nodded, noticeably relaxing. "Much. I should like to learn that," she added with a smile.

"You will, Bethlinda, you will," Cairns replied. Rime moaned something that sounded like a warning behind them, but they both ignored him. The complaints of a traitor were not worth considering. "You will learn much in the coming years, more than you could possibly hope to expect. The heart of the Elders will teach you, mould you."

"And then after it's over you'll make me Elder?"

Cairns grimaced. "As much as I can. After it is over there will be no Ostracia to be Elder of. The heart of the Elders will be gone. But yes, I will ordain you."

The girl beamed.

"I must go."

For the first time, he saw concern etch across her face, just for a moment, before her strength returned. His heartbeat pained him. He considered placing a Withholding of her memories of him, just for the three years, but discounted it as soon as he thought of it. He needed her mind clear.

She would only gain in artistic knowledge and skill during her time here. She would emerge a powerful, formidable artist, the most accomplished blood magician of her time. She was the future of Ostracia. She was his daughter in all but blood.

"Remember to feed no more often than three months," he counselled her again, clearly once too often as the girl's eyes rolled.

"I know, or the blood will start to die and we mustn't drink dead blood."

"That's right," Cairns said firmly. "It will sate you, but your source will be gone. It is wrong to kill just for power, Bethlinda."

"I know, Elder. Once every three months, I promise."

They both ignored another groan from Rime. "I will see you when it is time, Keeper. I will be with you in spirit."

He clasped her bloody hand in his own. "Thank you, Elder," she said formally and he could see she was trying not to cry.

"You know what to do?" he asked, but the girl had started to cry, just nodding. Cairns, feeling tears prick behind his own eyes, pulled his hands from hers. "Then I take my leave." As he made for the door, he forced himself to look back. "I consider you to be my hero, Bethlinda." She smiled, as he hoped she would for the last time he would see her in so long, and he left the chamber. The doors swung to behind him with a horrific thud and it seemed to him the key grated in his soul as it grated in the lock.

Then there was just silence.

Cairns found he had dropped to his knees and absent-mindedly allowed his hand to fondle the little pouch of powders in one of the many folds of his greatly oversized white robe as he forced his knees into action. Just one touch of the powders on his tongue would give him the energy, the feeling he needed to get through the night. He had said never again, but perhaps that was a moment of weakness – he had, after all, put the powders in the folds of his robe, had that been foresight that he would need them? Would one more dose really do him that much harm until the Drawing kicked in?

Cairns scowled as he trudged on through the tunnelled maze; this place reminded him of Hugo, it was one of the reasons he didn't like being here. The heart of the Transept Tower beat at him again, forcing his legs down, refusing to let them work, incessantly thumping its message of distaste home into his spirit. He fingered the pouch of powders in his good hand again. *No. The last time was the last time, I don't need them now.*

When he died, Hugo had been dealing out a particularly savage beating to Cairns, combining the twisting, nerve-crunching attacks of artistry, outlawed by the Elder Council but never abandoned by Elder Hugo, with the vicious, clubbing blows to the head from his hammer-like fists. Warding off the artistic assault with what Hugo thought to be his sole splinted hand, he had waited, enduring the pain as Hugo had taught him to do over the years, until the man had ceased, panting, to exalt in his triumph before dealing the finishing blow to drive him into the dreamless black.

"You'll never see this place again, you hear me?" Hugo said, standing over him, wagging a piston-like finger in his face. "I told you to stay away and by the gods away you will stay if I have to plant you in the ground in the middle of Elspeth Wood!"

Hugo paused to marvel at his own words as he raised his fist high above his head for effect, his knee dropping onto Cairns' splint hand. One of them. The look of shock as Cairns had raised his newly splinted right hand to his tutor's neck and twisted Hugo's nerves until they popped, severing his brain from the rest of his body, was a precious memory to him and an event he wished now that he had prolonged. In seconds, Hugo was dead and Cairns had waited for days, unable to move, his right hand broken in two places, too weak to heal himself, a skill he had never truly mastered anyway, to his shame.

There was another memory there, but Cairns couldn't see it. The man in red had come again, had shown him the key part of the Drawing he was missing. He remembered laughter as the wind of that first Drawing had knocked Cairns off his feet, startling before filling him with the bliss and power that was his by right.

So Hugo had become the first; giving him the energy he needed to dispose of the Elder Council's retaliation.

Cairns opened the pouch, took a pinch of the red powder and let it dissolve under his tongue. Those were memories he didn't want. He didn't have time for this. The powders joined Rime's essence in his system and the effect was instantaneous. He hurried upwards. The hatch was past only a few twists more of the maze of phosphorescent corridors he knew by heart, glowing strangely behind the mounds of moss, that cast eerie shadows, passing in a blur, the thumping of the Tower's heart threatening to burst his skull open to let the pressure out.

His mouth was entirely numb. The alchemist must have increased the absorption speed. He was aware of his mind filing away an intention to congratulate the alchemist; already he felt stronger, more alert, faster, as if everything were smaller than a moment before, and not only smaller, but less consequential. He hoisted himself through the hatch with one hand, feeling as good as he had felt in years; the powders gelling beautifully with the essence that was growing used to his system inside of him, filling his blood. Blood. Their freedom depended on it.

He had both keys to the locks of their prison now. Cairns just had to be careful; he didn't want to make Lord North's mistake and miss something that was hidden. And his people were all hiding something. There were so few left he could trust and only one man he trusted with the truth.

Cairns laughed long and loud as the thumping from the heart of the Elders' power died down to a plaintive tap, begging for his return, and he shut the hatch on the Transept Tower and the feeling..

CHAPTER 1

Assundra cried out again, although she knew nobody would hear her. Her voice was too hoarse now, she'd been shouting for too long. She knew she should wait until her voice recovered some strength, but she couldn't. It was too dark down here, too damp. Things whispered to her in the dark, things that couldn't be there, things she couldn't be hearing.

"Sunny..."

Nobody called her that. Nobody. Yet the voice did, always. "Shut up!" she called weakly, but she, Assundra was sure the voice was female even though she felt the words more than heard them, never replied.

She cried out again, even weaker this time and she broke down into sobs halfway through her pleading. Nightfall was a long way off, she told herself. That was her only hope. Galvarin would come looking for her before then. He had to.

The bucket swayed slightly as she adjusted herself. She was about ten feet down the well, not far, but far enough. She had tried to climb up the rope, but had fallen. Her arm was too weak from where Young Crafter had grabbed her. She couldn't see in the gloom but she was sure there'd be welts all round it. In any case, the long, tight dress she was wearing was hardly suitable for climbing.

The well was large – if she reached out her hands from the bucket she couldn't touch the sides. A cold wind pushed up at her in fitful bursts, making the bucket sway again. It didn't add to any feeling of calm she might have. Testing the rope had proved it was strong, but could she be sure?

Assundra didn't understand. Only last week, as with most weeks, she'd fought Young Crafter off, he wasn't a big man, barely even a man at all he was so slight. It had to have been that he took her by surprise, it was the only way he could have manhandled her into the bucket. She was probably remembering it wrong, he couldn't have been as strong as she felt he was. When he'd come for her last week she'd bloodied his nose and snapped a finger, but, more importantly, she had embarrassed him in front of his brothers and Erol Tyson. They'd run like scared chickens when her father had come out of the cottage to see what the commotion was.

Sighing, she was finally thankful for something that day – none of them knew her father was no longer in any fit state to fight. She made sure nobody knew that. They'd only come after her more if they knew Big Tom Franks was barely able to lift a fork to his mouth let alone defend his daughter.

"Sunny, how could you forget?"

No, there was nobody there! There couldn't be, this was a well. There was only a dark, black drop outside the bucket, she couldn't see the bottom, but even if she could, there couldn't be anyone down there. "There is nobody there," she said quietly to herself, "and there is no water lapping against the bucket!"

As she heard the faint trickle of water again, she couldn't stop herself calling out, allowing her body to do what it wanted, it took her mind off the voice. It had been with her for weeks now, she couldn't shake it. At first she thought she had drunk too much cider and was imagining it, but it was getting stronger, not fading. She kept trying to tell herself she couldn't hear it.

Just like she told herself now that she didn't hear the things slithering in the water that wasn't there. She couldn't see any water and she couldn't see them and they definitely weren't what spoke to her. The rope creaked. If it broke she'd never get out.

She cried out again. Then again.

There was no answer. There was nobody to hear, not this far out into the uninhabited old city, there hadn't been an answer for however long she'd been down here and there wouldn't be an answer now.

If only there were water, she thought to herself, it would quench this unbearable heat. If it was hot in the city square, then it was like a furnace down here, even with the bursts of foul-smelling air from below. Perhaps that's what Young Crafter wanted, she thought, to tenderise her for later.

She couldn't understand why he'd done it. The Elders would have Young Crafter's face for this, when they found out. Drunken brawls were one thing and the Crafters always had enough people backing their version of events, saying they were elsewhere, so that they always escaped punishment, but this? He couldn't escape for this. Could he?

Elder Cairns had seemed barely interested when she'd reported it the last time. "Without clear evidence I can do nothing, Assundra," he had said. "You need a witness."

It had been very hard to hold on to her temper. "Last week, Elder, Young Crafter and Erol Tyson were waiting for me when I came out of the alehouse

– they had a sack to put over my head! If Broadside hadn't come along and warned me, they'd have snuck up behind me!

"Then, the week before, Young Crafter grabbed me round the waist and wouldn't let go, he kept whispering things in my ear, horrible things."

Cairns had frowned. "What happened?"

"He was stupid," she shrugged, "he did it right in front of Galvarin's workshop, so he chased him off. But then," she added, "the week before there were five of them, all chasing after me through the village, saying they were going to…do things to me. Captain Bryant saved me that time…"

"Assundra," Cairns had interrupted impatiently, "as far as I am aware, on none of these occasions has anything more than a pursuit occurred! I cannot bring a charge with that, they would have had to commit a crime."

Assundra had been incredulous. "So you mean they've actually got to rape me before I can charge them with it?"

Cairns had pursed his lips. "I do understand how you feel, but at the moment it is your word against theirs."

"But…"

"Against *all* of their words, Assundra. You were very lucky last time that Young Crafter didn't bring charges against you himself for the broken finger! Do you understand?"

She had understood. Broadside, Bryant and Galvarin had all come along too soon as far as the Elder was concerned. They had saved her, but before Young Crafter and his friends could do anything they could be charged for. She had realised then that she was on her own. She had also realised that what her father said about Elders, with that snarl on his face, was true.

"You have to get out, Sunny…"

This time she just screamed in anguish – how could she get out? There was no way out! What was she supposed to do? She had to wait. Wait for him to come back and… "Oh gods, Galvarin, why aren't you here?" she sobbed into her hands, falling back into the bucket.

"You down there, you outsider bitch?"

The rope jerked, swaying the bucket dangerously from side to side, and she fell over into the murky slime that coated its base. The voice wasn't Young Crafter's! It was far too deep for it to be him – someone had found her!

"Yes! I'm here," she cried as loud as she could, her voice managing to find some strength from somewhere, "help me, please! Get me out, please!"

Even as she finished speaking, the bucket began to rise and she heard the creak of the ancient pulley above her as it span.

"Beware, Sunny…"

Assundra stopped the outpouring of thanks that was rising in her throat. What if it was Young Crafter, come back early? Or the rest of his disgusting family, or worse, Erol Tyson? She pulled her sodden hair back from her eyes and readied herself as the bucket neared the top. Surely she'd been much farther down than that…

A strong hand lifted her bodily from the bucket, even as she swung a fist into thin air. Overbalancing, she fell right into the arms of a huge man, who promptly hauled her over the side, dropping her to the ground, knocking the wind out of her.

"Look at you," she heard a gruff, deep voice sneer down at her, "not so high and mighty now are you, you outsider filth? Dress in tatters, face stained, gods alone know what he wants with you."

Assundra forced herself to a sitting position and looked up. The Deathguard looked down, looming over her. The low afternoon sun behind him hid his features and Assundra was glad of that – the lumps and boils on his over-sized head were not pleasing to the eye, any more than his seven-feet, tree-trunk-thick bulk was. The ragged tunica he dressed in hadn't even seen better days, it had always been a brown, tattered mess and living on his own out here in the old city the man clearly didn't think he needed to bother washing. When she was near him she felt like she'd catch something.

"Thank you," she squeaked through her winded chest as calmly as she could. He was her employer, after all, she couldn't show her distaste, but more than that, he wasn't Young Crafter. She'd have thanked anyone for that.

"Was only a joke, he said," the Deathguard boomed. He wasn't capable of being quiet, in the way he moved or in the way he spoke, he was an ungainly, lumbering giant of a man. Assundra's father was a big man, but in her mind there was a finesse, a dexterity to his size – Deathguard Jessop was just a bulk, a mass of flesh. "I told him to fuck off back to his mum and stop playing games on my time. I find him here again I'll tear one of his arms off, see if that persuades his dad to keep him away, though old coot that he is he'd probably do the opposite out of spite. I'll tear his arms off as well, at that, I'd enjoy that."

She thanked him again, but she knew already the reaction she would get. "Ain't for you, you stupid outsider bitch! I'd gladly watch while he used you any way he wanted, but Elder says while you're here you're under my care. Look," he cried, showing her a bloodied fist, "scraped my knuckles bloody on the bollocking well for him and all," He stooped, bringing his face close to hers and she couldn't help but flinch at the stench of raw meat from his breath. "I hope he gets you tonight. I hope he shows you what women like you was made for."

She didn't react. Didn't respond. It was like this every day, she knew enough about the Deathguard by now that to open her mouth just made it worse and, almost on cue, he drew back.

"Elder might actually send me someone who could do the job properly once the Crafters are done with you." He turned again, leering back at her as he shuffled his huge bulk back down the street. "I told him what time you get off, don't you worry your pretty little slutty head about that. Now get back to work, there's someone to stick in the fucking ground before he stinks up my home."

She sat there on the warm stone flagging for some time after the Deathguard had left, looking up at the well above her. She couldn't stop shaking. Breathing felt difficult, her chest felt like it had been crushed in a vice.

Every day she was reminded she was different. She was the 'outsider bitch'. Where most Ostracians were fair, she was dark. Where they were short she was tall. Where the women of the village wore plain, delicate linen smocks, tunicas and stolas, she wore the elegant and vibrant caftans and gowns from her mother's collection. She wasn't going to let their words hurt her, she never had, but it had made for a lonely life. She'd only ever had Simon and his mother for company, besides her father, until Galvarin had noticed her as more than just a child. Until his interest had turned into a different kind of interest. She smiled as she remembered their first kiss had been in his workshop, where anyone could see, his gesture, he said, to make sure they all knew he didn't care what they thought, that he'd show them they were wrong.

That had only been a few months ago and already the villagers were changing. Some of them. People said hello to her in the street. Some people still shouted things to her, called her an outsider, but it wasn't everyone, not any more.

A few months before she met Galvarin, the only reason they'd have paused in the street when they passed was to spit at her. Alice's birthday had been the worst. Assundra often spent the afternoons with Alice helping her make up pouches of herbs for the village, for poultices, or just to make rooms smell nice. Assundra had wanted to thank Alice so she'd made her a special bouquet of fragrant herbs. She'd spent hours over it, making sure the scent of one sprig complemented the scent of the one it stood next too and she'd been really happy with it. As she knew Alice was having drinks in the alehouse, she had taken it there, also bringing some little pouches of sweet-smelling herbs and a special brew of cider for her friends.

Alice had taken the bouquet, but had looked nervous. When she had offered the cider and the herbs to the other women there, they had turned their backs. Alice had thanked her and said she would see her later in the week, then she had turned her back too. Assundra had tried not to cry, but sure enough the tears came, which only made everyone laugh at her as she ran out.

Now she was with Galvarin though, things were getting better.

She hoped Galvarin would understand the state she was in, but she knew he liked her to look nice when they went drinking with his friends. The dress, she noted with pleasure, wasn't as badly damaged as she'd feared, but it was covered in dirty water. Absent-mindedly she pulled the sleeve back down over her deeply tanned forearm. Galvarin had said he liked her with the same colour all over, so she didn't want her arms to brown further where the rest of her body could not. She'd chosen the pleated silk dress from her mother's collection because Galvarin hadn't seen it before. Floor length, it was higher cut than many of her dresses and robes, fastening, with the buckle her mother had given her that she always wore somewhere, on her right shoulder, but she'd felt like the delicate elegant touch was fitting today. The dress looked like it was all in one, but was actually three separate diagonal strips, the lower white, then purple, then blue, split across her hips then breasts, each segment held together by a strip of gold brocade. As with the arms, she worried that the right leg was uncovered whereas the left was, but that was the cut of the dress, she could do little about it. She'd chosen it because it was thin enough to bear in the heat of the Ostracian summer (she wore no undergarments, not when the dress covered her anyway) and had the lovely pleated white silk sleeves she'd now finished rolling back down her arms.

She sighed – it wouldn't matter how much things got better, not if she couldn't get Young Crafter off her back.

She'd make John suffer for this. He'd had his last chance. "I got in, Assundra, I found it! What you found all those years ago! It's in the well, I've left it for you," he had said to her yesterday. "Go before your shift starts, I'll be waiting for you outside the temple, we can talk then. It's important Assundra!"

Like a fool, she'd believed him. She thought he actually wanted to help her. They'd been close the few weeks before this, she thought like some of the others she'd won him over. Sighing, she guessed she was wrong.

When she'd raised the bucket from the well, eager to see what John had left her, Young Crafter had leapt out, pulling her in before she even realised she was surprised. It had only taken a few seconds and she was trapped in a bucket down a well.

"I'll be back for you my love," Young Crafter had said. She shuddered at the memory. "Tonight. We're meant to be, you and me, I can save you! You just have to stay hidden, until everything's ready my love! I know I've had to be hard on you these past few weeks, but you'll see! You'll see!" With that, less than a few seconds, he'd gone, before she could even raise herself to standing.

She forced herself to look down at the gaping hole where the bucket now stood. Slipping a hand into one of the folds in her gown she took out the knife she'd taken off a body last week. Flicking the blade from its casing she noted with approval that it was sharp. The sun glinted off the immaculately polished six inch blade and the four spiked knuckle dusters that flanked the handle, as in no more than three swift strokes she cut the thick rope holding the bucket.

She turned away before the bucket hit the bottom, where she heard it burst into splinters. She wouldn't be coming here again.

More than that, she wouldn't be leaving the temple where she and the Deathguard worked again, except to go home at the end of the day. She wouldn't give Young Crafter the chance to get her again, even though he'd never come here before.

The shaking wouldn't stop and she couldn't find the strength to push her legs to carry her back. It was only around the corner from here, on the western road. The old city square was about as far as she could get from the village where she and all the other Ostracians lived, where they'd moved to when they'd abandoned the old city. The square was bordered by the ruins of four of the most important buildings in Ostracian history. Streets wound off from the square at each corner. The old marble courthouse was ahead of her, missing some of its pillars and arches, a gaping hole in the walls revealing the decay inside. To her right was the Merchants' Guild, almost fully intact, save for the carpeting, curtains and suck like, which had all been taken. People had to have something to trade, after all.

On her left, nothing remained of the Great Temple other than a mass of rubble. Nothing was left to identify it other than knowledge that it had once stood there, there were no pillars, gargoyles or coloured stone, no stained glass, shining golden religious artefacts or indeed any indication of what building had once stood, just a pile of rubble so finely ground that it was almost gravel.

If the gods couldn't protect themselves then what chance did she stand? They hadn't even been able to preserve their names, Assundra had never known them, her father did not know and the Elders did not want anyone else to know. Assundra set her jaw as she looked at the rubble – she didn't really care what their names were, they had all deserted Ostracia when the outsiders had come.

In the distance behind her she saw the three spires, the tall blue stone towers, their huge domes topped with what seemed like bright red and blue jewels, each the size of a small boulder. It was just polished glass, of course, but it was still impressive. The spires dominated the skyline of the city. She'd never been past them, but she knew that beyond those towers was the maze of ruined palaces that had once belonged to the aristocracy and beyond them, only the sheer cliff drop to the bay. Elder Cairns didn't want anyone in that part of town any more and even Assundra obeyed that instruction now.

Assundra didn't think the spires, or the council chambers that stood on the opposite side of the square to the courthouse, had been touched since the day they had been sealed. They had once been seats of government power and artistic learning, but now they were empty shells – guardians of an empty city.

On the surface of the Council Chambers, there was no weathering, no damage at all. Nobody went near them to find out for sure. Assundra had tried, once, she remembered. She'd wanted to go everywhere as a child and nobody cared enough about her except her father and Alice West to stop her, but at harvest time even they were too busy.

So, every year until she they were ten, she and Simon had two weeks to explore the old city. She remembered approaching the council chambers, Assundra with her little hammer in hand. She remembered it taking them ages to walk across the city square, as if something was stopping them getting close.

It had been Assundra who had pulled the boards off the door with her little hammer. It had been Assundra who had been the first through the door, smelling the musty air that hadn't been disturbed in decades. They had explored, her and Simon, she remembered that.

She remembered what happened after that less clearly, as if she was watching her memories through a fog. She had found something, but she could not remember what it was, or where it was. She'd felt sick as soon as she had touched it and her head felt like it was made of lead. A low rumble had started at the base of her skull as if someone was screaming right behind her, but the sound was of such depth that it shook all the bones in her body. Her mouth had filled with the taste of nothing and it wouldn't go away, even when she spat the taste out, and she'd fallen, hitting her head on something hard.

When she'd awoken, she had been back in their cottage, sitting in the comfortable chair, the one her father normally sat in. She knew then that something serious had happened. Her taste had gone back to normal and the rumbling in her head was gone. Her little hammer sat on the table her father had made himself by the chair, on top of his book. She never did find out how her father found where she was in the sprawling mass of the old city, but it wasn't even nightfall by the time she awoke.

"You're alright," her father had said as she'd turned to look at him, expecting to have her hide tanned, at least and they'd never spoken about it again. They'd gone back, of course, a few weeks later, convinced the place was haunted and desperate to see a ghost. They'd searched all over again, but on no other visits had they found anything. Eventually Elder Cairns had found out what they were up to and had banned them from going and even though Simon and Assundra rarely listened to anyone, they knew better than to disobey an order from an Elder.

Assundra had wondered as a child what could have been so necessary to keep so tightly locked up and so important that the ghosts would want to keep her from even looking in. She didn't learn until many years later that there were, of course, no ghosts at all. The place had been artistically sealed.

She and Simon could have been killed. The two of them had been such a pair for trouble, she remembered…

"Oh, Sunny, how could you forget…"

She shook her head. Her childhood was a long time ago now. She was of age now, only last week, her birthday had been. That meant she'd been working for the Deathguard for five years. She hated the man. She knew it wasn't personal, he was like that with everyone, the man just wasn't cut out to be around people. The only ones he cowed his nature to were the Elders, to whom he was politeness, deference and helpfulness incarnate. To everyone else he was a dangerous, manipulative, careless and violent man who was crossed at the peril of the one crossing. Now she was indebted to him. The thought did not make her any more comfortable, although she did wish she'd seen the look on Young Crafter's face when he'd come face to face with Jessop in his rage.

A sharp twitter close by made her jump and she managed to catch herself on the raised lip of the well with her hands before she fell back onto the hard flagging. A small bird fluttered down from the top of the well pulley's housing, landing just feet from her, where it sat, hopping from left to right, looking at her. It chirped, once, its head bobbing around as if it were weighing her up.

"All is well."

The bird chirped again, almost as if in reply to the voice in Assundra's head, though she knew that couldn't be the case. It took instantly to the air, where she soon lost sight of it in the scorching and bright summer afternoon sun. Was she seeing things now, too? She knew the voices weren't real, but she hadn't seen a real bird in the old city for years, they kept to the Forest now, where they were safer.

The voice couldn't have been more wrong. All was most definitely not well.

She'd always liked coming here, to this well. Working for the Deathguard was hard, unpleasant work and the refreshing cool water had always made her feel better. She could also see all around in the city square, so there was no chance of a Crafter sneaking up on her, or so she'd thought. There were only four directions she could be approached from and the square was large, hundreds would have congregated here once. Nobody could have crept up on her, not without casting a shadow as big as one of the buildings themselves on what was basically a huge blank sundial, before they got to her, even if she didn't see them.

Then, a few weeks ago, the well had dried up. She hadn't stopped coming.

She would stop coming now, she thought, as she made for the western road, heading back to the temple, telling herself she was calm, telling herself she wasn't hurrying, that she was striding purposefully. She folded the knife back into its casing. She was glad Galvarin was going to see the state of her, what Young Crafter had done. She was glad her lover had agreed to meet her after work to walk her to the alehouse. She was glad Young Crafter was coming back. Assundra slipped the knife back into the fold of her robe. The little bollock hadn't been joking, like he'd said to the Deathguard. Young Crafter had been specific. This hadn't been about a quick fumble, or filthy proposition, which was normally what he was after in front of his friends – he had said he could 'save' her.

She set her jaw again. It was just going to have to be tough on Young Crafter – she didn't need saving. Galvarin had already done that.

It wasn't far to the temple and she found her steps taking her there without thinking about it. She took the road between the courthouse and the ruins of the Great Temple, turned left, away from the North Street that led to the trading sector, onto the winding back streets. Then right, left, then right again and she was there. The temple, much smaller than the Great Temple in the city square had been, was little more than a stone room, made out of the same light brown stone that wasn't quite sandstone that all of the buildings in the back streets of Ostracia were built from. The seemingly impossible dome that hung heavily above the simple structure had finally given way a few weeks previously and rubble lay strewn about the otherwise bare stone flooring. A small ramp to the left of the room led to the short tunnel between the old temple and the furnace room next door, the only point of access to the old crematorium.

The only furniture was the wooden cart on wheels, on which a body, her afternoon's work, lay covered with a sheet and the remains of an altar stood at the far end of the room, under which the Deathguard's filthy, stained mattress lay, blankets, stained with the gods knew what, askew. She sighed as she stepped inside – at least there'd been no new gnawed rat carcases in the corner for her to clear up today. Perhaps they were learning to keep away from the old city like the people had. The little basket of food she'd brought the Deathguard, that she brought every morning, with a selection of breads, cheese, olives and grapes, sometimes other fruits and seeds, was gone, she saw, he must have taken it with him wherever he went in the afternoons, although she remembered he hadn't had it with him when he'd pulled her from the well.

Sighing, she turned to look up out of the collapsed roof into the hot afternoon air. She didn't care what the Deathguard did with the food. He probably trapped the rats he liked to eat raw with it. Assundra could only take succour the man had never bothered to take a cottage in the new village, said he was fine where he was. He slept, ate and lived with the dead. Every day Assundra brought him some food and cider and every day the Deathguard told her to fuck off for her trouble. If she didn't bring them, he did worse.

She couldn't fight off the Deathguard like she fought off Young Crafter. When the rest of them had used carts to pull stones from the old city to construct the village, he'd simply carried them on his back. Assundra would back herself physically against most of the men in the village, except her father, but even Big Tom Franks wouldn't go near the Deathguard. Her father couldn't protect her from everything, but he had taught her how to fight. Perhaps, she thought sadly, he'd seen this coming, perhaps he'd known he was getting ill.

"Talking of ill," she sighed, pulling the back the sheet that covered the body.

She couldn't stop the shriek of alarm. The person under the sheet was John.

CHAPTER 2

From the roof of the Council Chambers, Simon watched Assundra meander back down the western road and breathed a sigh of relief. If the Deathguard had been much longer, he'd have had to…well, he wouldn't have been able to save her, not this time, but he would have to have done something.

Wincing as Elder Oldershaw withdrew the splint, the sharp piece of metal embedded under the Elder's fingernail, from his back, Simon waited as the world shimmered back into full view. Shrouding was an artistic skill he had no wish to learn. It was useful to hide with, but it put a fog on his eyes that he knew wouldn't shift for days. It wasn't even high artistry – it was simply a light barrier, allowing sight to pass through where it would have been stopped by their bodies and clothes. Or so the Elder said, anyway, Simon supposed he had to trust him.

It baffled him why Elder Oldershaw bothered with shrouding – he was an Elder, by definition he had enough artistic power to not need to bother, he could face any challenge head on and win.

Although right now he knew why. Elder Oldershaw hadn't wanted to be seen in the old city square because they weren't supposed to be here. They had scrambled to the roof of the Council Chambers when Elder Oldershaw had sensed Assundra coming. They stood there now, the Elder's white robes flapping around his ankles although there was hardly a breeze. Simon looked down at his own tattered linen shirt and sheepskin trousers. How long had he been wearing these same clothes for now? He couldn't remember.

"Your mind is not sufficiently clouded, Simon," the Elder rasped next to him in his clipped, measured tone. "I could sense far too much from you while we were linked. Try harder. Yes, try harder."

Simon scowled – it wasn't as if he was going to be in a situation where an artist had his splint implanted into his back very often! "Yes, Elder," was all he said, however.

"Interesting game by Young Crafter that," the Elder went on. "I wonder what his end goal was, if he even had one." Elder Oldershaw chuckled – Simon had grown to learn in the weeks he'd been tutored by the man that there was little Elder Oldershaw did that did not have a final goal in mind. "I see our esteemed colleague has the situation in hand, as ever."

"Only just," Simon replied, before he could stop himself. He reddened at once and looked at the floor.

To his surprise Oldershaw laughed. "Only just is still in time, Simon. Many a battle has been 'only just' won. At the last minute. Another one. Same sort of thing." The Elder sniffed, suddenly becoming serious. "It is the outcome that matters in the end, Simon, the victor tells the stories. Then he can say what he likes."

Frowning, Simon followed Oldershaw as he scrambled down the building to the ground. He didn't understand what Oldershaw meant – did he want Elder Cairns to tell the story? He thought that the whole point of what they were doing here was to prevent Cairns from being the victor.

"Now. Back to work, Simon," Oldershaw said curtly, interrupting his thoughts. "What had I told you before we were impeded?" Simon thought for a moment, but those thoughts were interrupted again. "You must school your expressions more carefully, Simon! It is not wise to let your enemy see you do not have the answer to hand."

"But you're not my enemy."

The corner of the Elder's mouth curved. "Am I not?" he said with a smirk, "I seem to remember a student of mine accusing me of subterfuge and disloyalty not too long ago!"

Simon's face reddened again. "That was before…"

"Yes," Oldershaw interrupted again. Simon was glad of it this time. "School your expression," he said firmly, extending his finger to make the point. "Unless you want your opponent to think you are giving something he has said careful thought, as a ruse. Yes. But understand this Simon, it is advisable to treat all as your opponent, even me. Who tells the stories?"

"The victor," he answered straight away.

Elder Oldershaw smiled. "Exactly. Approach every discussion, every action as a battle and emerge the victor and you will hold the story. Yes. Now, what had I told you before Assundra happened upon us?"

Simon looked up, holding Oldershaw's gaze. "To sense an artistic barrier before I reach it, to prevent capture."

"Capture, yes." Oldershaw sniffed again. Did the man have a cold? It was too hot for colds, surely? "Unfortunately to be aware of artistry at all times means to drain your power constantly. It is, however, worth it, as unfortunately you and Assundra found out all those years ago."

Simon flinched. He didn't want to think about that day. That was the day everything had changed, the day his future ceased to involve gardening and he became an Elders' apprentice. An unofficial Elders' apprentice, for nobody could be told. He wished it were only that simple, for now he was an unofficial Elders' apprentice to both Elder Cairns and Elder Oldershaw, with both insisting their counterpart not be told.

Simon had had no option but to accept both offers. To refuse an Elder was to invite pain, both from the Elders and from Simon's father, Max West. Max needed little excuse to use his fists and Simon wasn't about to give him another one.

So far it had been manageable – neither Elder had tried to tutor him at the same time, nor had they taught him anything that would give him away. In fact, they had barely taught him anything at all, but the main thing was that he remained undiscovered. Only recently, Elder Oldershaw had not only requested much more of his time, but was teaching him things far in advance of the rudimentary power expulsion techniques Cairns kept trying to force him to learn. Simon wondered what had changed Elder Oldershaw's mind and why there was this sudden rush.

Not that Simon cared – he just wanted to learn. He wanted to show them all, to show Assundra, what he could do if he was given the chance.

"It was painful," he replied eventually, hoping he wouldn't be scolded for his delay.

"Yes. Yes, it was!" Elder Oldershaw cried, almost triumphally, with a quick laugh. "I'd say you won't be doing that again, but that is precisely what I wish you to do. So. Come on."

Elder Oldershaw gestured grandly at the door to the Council Chambers. Simon swallowed, then wished he hadn't as his mouth went dry.

"Give me your thumb," he was instructed and Simon did so as Elder Oldershaw slipped the knife, no bigger than the thumb he was proffering, out of the leather pouch the Elder wore on his belt. "Same as before," was all the Elder said as he drew the sharp blade across the length of Simon's thumb.

There was no pain, almost no sensation at all as the blood welled up and began to coat his hand, soon covering the many other thin scars that now adorned his right hand.

"Now. As I told you." To Simon, the Elder's voice was already far away. As well as his vision being clouded with the fog of the shrouding, the rest of his senses were concentrated inside himself, the thing inside his body aware that there was an outlet now that the blood was flowing and that meant it could be used.

His mouth filled with the taste of nothing, but there was no excess power to spit, the outlet was in his thumb.

"Do not speak!" Elder Oldershaw warned, even as Simon heard words begging to be spoken, the thing inside his body pushing them out. Words he did not know or understand, nor would he ever.

"Now, send your senses from yourself." Elder Oldershaw's words had seemed foolish to him a few weeks ago, he remembered wondering how in the hells could his senses be sent out of himself, but the action came almost naturally to him now. His senses, those senses, followed the blood. That was why his senses of sight, smell and sound were dimmed – they had to be for the senses of the power inside him to find its counterpart, to sense power outside him.

He found it in no time. Around the council chambers was an artistic shield, not dense or powerful enough to prevent access, but enough to trigger a defence. Simon had to admit it was clever – there was a swell of power within the shield when it was breached, following which the artistry surrounding the building was focused and directed on the intruder in one swift burst.

"I see it," Simon said, although his voice sounded far away. An idea came to him – if all the power from the shield were focused on one intruder... "Surely if there were two..."

"Indeed, but it involves the sacrifice of a colleague," Elder Oldershaw replied sombrely. Simon at once saw what the Elder meant – whilst one person could indeed draw the attack of the shield, allowing another to enter the building unscathed, the one drawing the shield's attention would have to sacrifice his life. After which, the shield would reform, leaving the unscathed intruder trapped.

"What do you want me to do?"

"I want you to draw the shield while I enter."

Simon gasped in surprise and immediately regretted doing so as words escaped with his breath. A small spark shot from his thumb towards the door of the council chambers, where it scorched the wood. Simon clamped his mouth shut.

"Your mind is not sufficiently clouded and your will is not sufficiently strong!" Elder Oldershaw barked, but he did not sound angry, just frustrated. "Now concentrate, Simon, I want you to draw the shield. Not by touching it. Don't want you dead. Draw it with your power, bring it towards you. Imagine it is a wind, a breath you are sucking in, and draw the power."

Simon extended his arm and *felt* for the shield. All too soon it was upon him and he wasn't sucking the power of the shield, it was sucking him, pulling him bodily towards the council chambers, a deep ringing sounding in his ears.

"No!" he heard Elder Oldershaw shout in the distance and felt a stab in the back of his neck as the splint entered his flesh once again.

At once the shield ceased its attack and Simon fell back, landing hard on the steps. He realised he was panting. "What…" he started to say, but his breath failed on him before he could ask what had happened.

Elder Oldershaw, though, seemed to understand. "You cannot draw the shield in all at once, Simon. You must find a weak spot. Start from there. We will try again momentarily."

Simon let out a long breath as the senses he was used to took over from the senses of the power inside him. Try again? It was always the same with Oldershaw in the past few weeks – there was never any time for any respite, everything was urgent. If it was all so urgent then why had he not been instructing Simon in these skills for the months, even years, Elder Oldershaw had recruited him?

Cairns had approached him with almost the same speech as Elder Oldershaw had, almost the same appeal to his sense of Ostracian duty. Only Cairns had shown no interest in teaching Simon anything other than how to resist his power, how to stand back from it, to assess, watch and learn. Elder Oldershaw had tried to focus on what he could do, not what he couldn't. As a result, the lessons with Elder Oldershaw were much more fun, much more interesting than those with Cairns and Simon did much better. At least he thought he did, praise from Elder Oldershaw, from both Elders in fact, was rare.

"You cannot progress to manipulating artistry without first mastering the technique of separation," Simon remembered Cairns saying excitedly at their last meeting. Simon thought it stupid to get so excited over something so dull, surely the joy in artistry was the fantastic, the wonderful and the extraordinary, not the mundane, private techniques that nobody ever saw?

Within, without, in all places. That was the mantra that Cairns kept drumming into him. The technique of separation involved splitting oneself into three. Within, where the artistry begins; without, where the power is unleashed; and in all places, making sure what you create is contained. Each self watches the other.

With a snarl Simon realised the technique of separation would have prevented what had just happened – the self in all places would have seen the surge and drawn the selves that were within and without away from the danger. Elder Oldershaw never seemed concerned with such the technique, though – he had never mentioned it, in fact.

Simon had the feeling that Cairns was preparing him for one lesson and one lesson only and it wasn't one he cared to learn. He glanced up at Elder Oldershaw, who was studying the council chamber door with great concentration, his lips murmuring to himself. Cairns said Elder Oldershaw had no idea of the plan, but Simon wasn't so sure.

Then again, Simon didn't know much about the plan himself, only that he had to take their power. That was why the technique of separation was so important, or so Cairns said – it provided the barrier between him and the one he was taking power from that would prevent any retaliation. He could drain their artistry dry and expel it safely. Apparently this was the key to Cairns' escape plan, but Simon didn't see why they couldn't just mask the power with shields and shrouds, it would be simple enough, all Cairns would have to do is let the villagers learn artistry again.

With Elder Oldershaw keen to teach Simon everything he could, Simon was forced to shroud the cuts on his hands and Cairns hadn't spotted one cut yet so why couldn't any villager learn how to do that if they had power? The weakest ones, well, they wouldn't be likely to survive anyway, it would make no difference.

Simon also didn't understand why it had to be him, why Cairns couldn't take the villagers' power himself. It made him nervous – Cairns was a far more experienced, more powerful artist than he was, why did he want Simon to do it?

His father would tell him not to question the Elders and give him another beating, but thankfully his father knew about none of this. As far as Max West was concerned Simon was learning his gardening trade, as indeed he was, and nothing more. He was always out in the evening himself, dealing with some council business or another and Simon always made sure to be home before his father was.

"Are you ready? To try again?"

Simon looked up at Elder Oldershaw and sighed, nodding his agreement, too tired to speak.

"Threefold law," Oldershaw said and Simon creased his brow. "Why you're tired, threefold law. Can't expect to take something and not get it back – what you take will be visited upon you threefold, remember? Threefold law."

"But I thought…"

"There are ways to fight threefold law, but haven't taught you those yet." As ever, Elder Oldershaw had an uncanny idea what Simon was going to ask and answered before he had a chance to do so.

"Then how can I…"

"Will teach you them when you need them," Elder Oldershaw replied, cutting him off again. "Need to make sure you're on the right path, Simon."

The look Oldershaw gave Simon spoke volumes. The right path. Not the correct path, the right-hand path. It was why all Elders were splinted in their right hands, to remind them to follow the right-hand path of true high artistry and not slide down the left-hand path into sorcery.

When Simon had asked why Cairns was splinted in both hands, in that case, Elder Oldershaw had looked concerned and refused to answer, simply saying that, "nobody has a trouble-free past."

Did that mean Cairns knew of sorcery? The thought excited Simon. There was no threefold law with sorcery, necromancy or any of the other left-hand path disciplines that nobody would teach him. There were no rules, there was only your skill and what you could effect. As artistry ran naturally in Ostracian blood, it was limited in what it could achieve. The Elders claimed this made Ostracians pure, that it meant they were superior to outsiders who had to resort to sorcery and other methods because they had no natural skill.

Simon couldn't stop thinking that the outsiders had won.

Flexing his fingers, he was also forced to reflect that sorcery also required no blood, only the mind, which meant he would be able to do without the dull ache that was spreading through his thumb.

"I'm ready," he said impatiently, watching the sun begin to drop in the sky. He had to be back to join his family in the alehouse for the evening meal or his father would not be pleased. He wanted no other wounds to deal with today.

"Good! As before. Try again."

Simon jammed his nail into the seeping wound on his hand to get the blood flowing and began again. Glancing at Elder Oldershaw, he found the man's eyes focused on the building. This time he would try Cairns' technique of separation and hope Elder Oldershaw wouldn't notice.

No sooner had he started, feeling himself pull away from his body, within, without and in all places, than he felt a surge of power knock him from his feet once more.

Elder Oldershaw was quickly by his side, but did not make use of his splint this time, simply bringing Simon up to a sitting position.

"Another break. Then we can try again," the Elder said quietly., then grabbed Simon by the lapel. "Then you can tell me *where the hells you learnt to do that*!".

CHAPTER 3

John lay naked on the cart. Assundra couldn't decide which was worse, the grotesque marks on his neck or the angel lust lower down. It was clear now why he hadn't met her.

The light from the doorway was extinguished by a large shadow. "Was his heart," she heard the Deathguard say behind her and she couldn't stop herself flinching, cursing as she heard him laugh. "You've Guarded ones you know before, haven't you, bitch? Lots of good Ostracians died while you've managed to survive to Guard them, eh?"

Assundra didn't reply as Jessop as he lumbered past her into the room. She couldn't take her eyes off John's body. She knew from one look that this death had nothing to do with his heart. She guessed she wouldn't be making an official report to Elder Cairns of the marks around the neck, or the way his neck lolled at a horrible angle, as if it were boneless. The Deathguard said it was his heart that killed him, so she would ask no questions. He would be buried and forgotten, like the rest.

She'd seen John every day for the past five years. He'd worked for the Deathguard for even longer, his whole life, for all Assundra knew. John had always been able to laugh off the Deathguard's insults, his taunting and his attempts to humiliate anyone within range of his barbed tongue, but he'd also joined in when the Deathguard took his shots at Assundra.

Suddenly she wanted to be out of here, out of the old city. If John's last act in this world was to set her up for Young Crafter, then he would get the treatment he deserved.

Picking up the bottle of quicklime Assundra wearily doused the body lightly, not caring that there wasn't enough left to coat as the law dictated. She was sure it would be fine, John showed no signs of plague and anyway she didn't particularly care if it wasn't fine.

It was too hot for this work. The air itself seemed scorched. The Deathguard refused to work in the summer afternoons, he worked into the night, when it was cooler, but Assundra had plans this evening. In any case, even the heat was preferable to spending an evening in a cramped space with Deathguard Jessop.

She had hoped that the gaping hole in the roof would let air in to give some respite, but the attack of the sun's rays remained unrelentingly severe. Assundra was at least thankful that they weren't forced to use the furnace. She could only imagine what John and his predecessors would have had to go through, having to stoke the fires of a huge kiln, spitting out blistering embers at them when they were already being cooked by the sun. They wouldn't have had a choice back then, not with so many plague victims. That's why the temple was used to prepare the dead – the cremation kiln still sat in the next room to where she stood, practically worn out it had seen so much use. Since Elder Cairns had ordered there be no fires in Ostracia, the furnace been dead. Assundra had mentioned to the Deathguard many times that surely that meant they could move to a nice place, a better building to work in, but the answer she got was always the same – "the dead have been coming here as long as I've been alive, it's where they belong."

Assundra put the lid back on the pot and frowned. The stock of lime was dangerously low and without the furnace they could not turn and powder limestone. The Elders would need to be told and she did not want that task. Lime was the only strategy they had against the plague. It didn't make sense to Assundra – surely to stop the plague spreading they should burn the bodies? Not simply place them in the barrow with a thin covering of quicklime and soil?

She shrugged the thought off, sticking the jar back on the stone ledge with the other empty ones. It wasn't her problem. The workings of Ostracia were for the Elders to puzzle over and sort out, she knew better than to question their decisions.

"Time is passing, Sunny. Soon. Soon we will remember together."

"Shut up!" she shouted, immediately feeling foolish for shouting at thin air.

The Deathguard turned to look at her, his face twisted in amusement. "That how you deal with a departed colleague, is it? Or did he have something to say about it himself?"

She ignored him. The truth was, John had said something to her, he had sided with Young Crafter. She had told him of her visit to the council chambers, she had wanted to warn him, to make him stay away from there, telling him his stupid catalogue wasn't worth dying for, but he hadn't listened.

Turning the cart towards the door, she pocketed a brooch and a quill from where they lay on the cart. They never found much on the bodies, money was worthless in the village now and the other women were about a head shorter than Assundra at least so there was never point taking any dresses they had.

It was one of the things Galvarin said he liked about her – "the way I can't throw you about, you're not a little thing like them, elegant, you are. Big enough to put up a good fight!" he'd said, although he hadn't liked it when she'd teased him that she was taller than him in the fancy outsider shoes her mother had left her. She hadn't mentioned it since, nor worn the shoes.

There was one more thing John had that she wanted, but when she bent down to retrieve it, she realised it wasn't there. The catalogue! It had been his life's work, the meticulous recording of every building on every street of the old city. Yet it wasn't here.

She stepped back as the Deathguard threw the little wicker basket she brought his food in on to John's body. She caught it before it could fall off. "When you've done that you can fuck off home, leave the cart in the barrow, I'll fetch it later. I'm sick of the sight of you."

Assundra stood for a moment, confused – he never let her leave early. Was it some kind of trick? When the Deathguard started to slip off his tunic, clearly intending to lie down, she stopped thinking about it, hurrying from the temple, pushing the cart in front of her.

She stopped to think when she was outside. The sun made her squint. The Deathguard had told Young Crafter the time she'd be released from his service that night, or so he'd said, so why was he letting her go early? Had he told Young Crafter where to be, was he waiting for her at the barrow? Was the Deathguard being kind or being malicious? Assundra set her jaw – she'd just have to keep her eyes open. The weight of the knife pressed reassuringly at her thigh as she began to walk, slowly. Part of her hoped Young Crafter did show up at the barrow. On his own. She wouldn't have to wheel him anywhere, then.

"Sunny, how could you forget! Beware…"

Shaking her head, she ignored the voice. It was always the same, always telling her she had forgotten something, but what?

She was sure she was just run down. All this with the Crafters, sneaking out late at night to see Galvarin, too much drinking with Simon and tending to her father, who could no longer look after himself, it was all too much. She was just tired, exhausted in fact and she always heard the voice more when she was tired.

For years now the voice had been with Assundra. It was hard to remember when it started now. Sometimes she'd been glad of it – it had warned her when Young Crafter had approached her with the sack, for one thing. More often than not, though, the voice was a sad, spiteful feeling that she felt judged her for forgetting. How could she know what she had forgotten if it wouldn't tell her?

She'd never told anyone about it, even Simon and especially not Galvarin. If he was going to make her his then she wasn't about to give Galvarin anything to make him doubt her. She needed him.

He was already annoyed about her having to work with Jessop, but she didn't know why, he knew there was nothing she could do about it. Elder Cairns himself had requested that she become the Deathguard's apprentice so it wasn't like she had a choice. There was still such a backlog of bodies to get through, though far less than there had been five years ago when she'd started. There had been more than she could count piled up in the cellar of a once fine city house. For the first few months she'd been in the Deathguard's service John hadn't let her see the cellar, but then John had taken ill with a cold and Assundra got no such concerned thought from Jessop. There was no time for a let up in dealing with the bodies, they had to get through the backlog with more plague victims coming in every day, so she had been forced to go into the basement and drag them out herself.

Sometimes at night she was convinced she was trapped in that dark, dripping room, the mud from the floor, made wet with the gods knew what, the rats scurrying everywhere, the constant buzzing of hundreds of flies fizzing about her head, maggots bursting from the bodies where she touched them. When she woke the stench would stay with her for the rest of the day.

They still had to use the cellar. There were still flies, maggots and bodies, piled on top of each other. As they neared the bottom, the bodies were more and more decomposed, more and more…

Shuddering, Assundra began to push the cart along the thin streets, trying to stop herself thinking about it. She had to hope she got home without Young Crafter leaping out at her before she could rest and worry about what she would dream about.

The streets curved here on the west side almost with every building she passed and as she passed each one she expected Young Crafter to leap out at her. Assundra could feel her heart beating and was surprised it wasn't faster than it was, though she could also feel that she was tense, part of her would welcome a confrontation.

As long as it was just Young Crafter, she thought, what if there were more of them?

She was brought back to herself as the cart raced ahead of her, before she caught it. The old city was built on a large, gently inclining hill and the roads, or dust trails as they now were, that weaved between the buildings were all downhill or uphill depending on where you were going. The spires, the now-blind eyes of the city, were at the crest of that hill, the city square just below and the rest of the city spread out in a slowly meandering downhill sprawl from there. The only pattern to it came from knowing it, there was no logic to what was where – there was no trading district, no poor district – there were no districts at all. Only the city square was different.

All about her was ruination and decay. A loud crack made her jump and cry out, fumbling for the dagger in the fold of her dress, but as she saw the stone split, she relaxed. It was just a crumbling wall. The sound of another impact ahead of her made her jump again, but then her eyes widened as she realised she'd let the cart go. Running to where it had collided with some more fallen masonry she checked the wheels, finding to her relief that they weren't buckled or splintered.

John swayed on the cart when she set off again and when his arms flopped over the sides she had to stop and tuck them back in. She could understand that there wasn't enough stone to make a sarcophagus for everyone, not without a quarry and no time to cast any pottery, but she couldn't help think the dead deserved some dignity in their transport to the barrow.

She soon stopped that thought however, as John was heavier than she'd thought he'd be, she wouldn't want to be pushing around a sarcophagus as well. Or was this just another symptom of this weariness that was creeping over her? She'd pushed much bigger men than John down the winding streets on her little wooden cart, sometimes two at a time, but now she was panting after having barely got out of the door.

What was wrong with her? She would have to make sure she had more energy than this later, for Galvarin, although the cider usually helped with that. She didn't want to disappoint him and it had been nearly a week since they'd lain together. She wanted to make things right, after Simon watching them like that, wanted Galvarin to relax, so she'd just have to find a way of finding some energy. It was the least she could do, she thought, if he was going to save her.

Assundra smiled to herself – this would be the third time she'd gone drinking with Galvarin and his friends – that had to mean things were going well! It had been six months now, since he had kissed her for the first time. She'd argued that meant they'd been together since then, he'd said it was a couple of weeks later, when they'd first lain together in their glade, their place, where nobody could find them.

The sun went behind the only cloud Assundra could see in the sky as her stomach turned. Someone had found them, of course, last time. "Stupid little bollock," she whispered under her breath. Simon West sneaking up on her and Galvarin in the glade was something she wished she could forget forever. The beating Galvarin had given the boy, the only other person her age left in Ostracia, the only other child Assundra could remember there ever being, had been harsh, but then he shouldn't have been spying on them! Simon was avoiding her now, even when she tried to make a joke of it.

"At least you've seen me now," she'd said, popping over to where he was sitting in the alehouse the week before, "you wouldn't have got to otherwise!"

Galvarin's friends, who she hadn't realised had followed her, had laughed. "O' course he wouldn't have seen, little bollock like him, he ain't never going to see a woman, 'Sundra! Here, Simon, I hear your dad's brewing up a nice pig stock for the feast day, maybe he could busy himself with them 'til one of the widows goes blind or summat!"

Simon had stormed off as fast as the limp Galvarin's boot had caused would allow, giving her an angry look as if she'd caused his humiliation, but she couldn't control what other people said, could she? She'd tried to be nice, make a joke of it so he wouldn't feel embarrassed, but it was his own stupid fault, hiding there in the bushes watching them. Truth be told, she was glad it was him and not her.

Galvarin had told her to stay away from Simon after that. He'd said Simon was holding her back, that the people wouldn't truly accept her if she was hanging around with him all the time.

"He's weird, Assundra, don't you see that?"

"He's my friend!" she'd retorted. "I don't have that many, you know!"

"Look, do you want them to accept you or not?" he'd replied, losing his temper with her. She was always being stupid and making him lose his temper. "Don't you want to fit in? If you don't then why am I bothering?"

She'd told Simon to leave her alone after that. The excuse she'd used was that he'd ruined it for her, not just that night but every night, but he didn't seem to get it. Any crack from a twig snapping when they were in the glade and she couldn't relax.

She sighed. She knew it was for the best, Galvarin was right. Things had been different since she had started seeing Galvarin. She and Simon had always been close, she knew he was…keen on her, but she'd always been clear she didn't feel the same way. When Young Crafter and his friends came after her, Simon only got in the way. He'd taken some beatings for her that had allowed her to escape, but that just meant he was hurt instead of her, it didn't solve anything. When Galvarin had confronted them, mason's hammer in hand, they'd turned tail and ran, she remembered with a smile. Couldn't Simon see?

"Stupid little bollock," she said again, yanking the cart around a sharp bend she hadn't quite slowed down enough for, but she felt bad for saying it.

The fear spiked in her again as she got closer to the barrow. Would Young Crafter be waiting for her? She gulped down some air. There was nothing she could do but find out.

Gas escaped from John as she went over another bump, almost making her laugh, but something stopped her. It was too sad here, too decayed for laughter. The buildings here in the outer streets had all been dismantled, knocked down and left down, with what scraps of stone they needed carted away to make the cottages of the village in the valley below. She remembered being in the old city as a child, carting stones down on her little cart, as her father had let her construct her own small cottage, to see how it was done. There were stones of all shapes and sizes, all hues – sandstone, buff stone, strips of plaster and cement, harder, darker stone she didn't know the name of, it was all here, just lying around where there had once been homes.

At least it meant she could see better, there were fewer places for Young Crafter to hide. Even so, she kept looking about her, flicking her eyes from side to side. She wasn't going to get caught out again.

She was glad she was nearly there – her arms were aching. She knew it wasn't from pushing the trolley, it was because she was so tense. She would be glad of the release with Galvarin later tonight. She'd been so close so many times, surely they would get it right tonight?

Cursing, she stopped the cart again, holding it in place with her leg while she lifted John's arm, which had escaped again, back into the cart. The slope was steeper here, near the base, and Assundra was careful not to let the cart get away from her and go careering off like it had before. It wouldn't stop on this incline, as she had learned before. The body on that day had fallen from the cart and rolled halfway to the barrow on its own.

She couldn't remember who it had been now, she had buried so many.

Setting off again, she remembered that despite the decay, John had loved the old city. He would often stay up here overnight with the Deathguard, even though it was against the Elders' wishes, forever working on his catalogue of the old city, mapping each building and what was inside. She thought he'd decided to befriend her a few weeks ago when he had shown the catalogue to her. He said even his wife didn't know about it. The last time he showed her, it had been almost finished. He had been so excited that he'd only had a few more buildings to go.

"Just the city square, that's all. Then I'll be done!"

There had been such a look of excitement and friendship that she had smiled along with him. "Well you won't get into the council chambers, I can tell you that," she'd replied. She couldn't remember who they'd been working on now, but it was someone to be embalmed. They came and went for Assundra, she could recall little about those she disposed of.

"We will see about that, little Assundra Franks, we will see! I may just take a trip there tonight!"

She'd laughed at that – she always did at John's strange way of speaking. It was a shame he couldn't have been like that all the time. She'd asked him once, after a particularly difficult day, why could he talk to her like this, confide in her, show her his catalogue, something he'd told her he hadn't showed anyone else, and then treat her like he did when the Deathguard was around? Sometimes even when he wasn't.

John had looked at the floor. "You've got to understand, Assundra, I need Jessop. I need him to think I'm his man. He's the only reason I get to stay around here after dark, the Elders would never allow it otherwise. He watches, you know. Even when you think he's not around, he watches us, waiting for one of us to slip up, to give him an excuse. I think I'm safe now, but you can never tell with Jessop, can you?"

He'd smiled, but she hadn't smiled back. Not once had he apologised, nor made excuses for the things he said and did. She looked down at the naked corpse in her cart, oozing smells and swelling where the blood was settling. She was sorry the man was dead, but she wouldn't miss him. The good parts were too few and far between the other things. It was such a shame.

Remembering his neck, she put away the thoughts of John and the council chambers. She'd told him not to go.

Soon she had wound her way down the streets, each much like the next, in various stages of disrepair. She passed the mason's old workshop, a vast, sprawling building where four or more of them must have worked at a time. It made Galvarin's cottage workshop look tiny in comparison. She passed the armoury, a place she had loved as a child. The doors were locked now, the windows boarded, like the council chambers, but there was no artistry here, nothing to tell her to keep away. It was just Bryant, the swordsman, taking good care of his weaponry. The weaponry for the soldiers he didn't have.

She remembered the long swords, broad swords, short swords, hammers, axes and flails, some blunted or rusted by age, but all fascinating, all, to a small girl as she had been then, heavy and unwieldy. She still had a helmet at home somewhere. It was an old, battered thing that had surely seen glory in battle. She'd snuck away with it one afternoon and nobody had ever come looking for it. Her father had scalded her for stealing, but hadn't punished her. She hadn't taken anything else though, she thought the Elders might start to notice if she built up her own armoury in her father's cottage.

Although, she had a knife to go with it now. If Young Crafter ever learned her father was not in a fit state to protect her, perhaps an armoury in the cottage wasn't a bad idea.

As soon as she'd had the idea, she'd reached the burial plaza. She stopped at once, her body going rigid. She couldn't see anyone, but that didn't mean Young Crafter wasn't hiding somewhere.

The last resting place of the once wealthy and powerful stretched out across what she supposed was a plateau. She steered the cart off the stone flagging and onto the grass. All across the plateau were graves, in neat little rows, all topped with six feet slabs of marble. A long, straight path of shale and gravel led through them, along which she struggled with the cart until she reached the plaza itself, a simple monument of eight marble pillars on limestone, in two lines of four with the remains of a once finely sculpted pediment. The resting place of the best of the Ostracians. She walked slowly between the rows of pillars, head bowed, as she had seen the Elders do when carrying the urn of someone important, passing the inlaid gravestones of Elders past, of dignitaries and many more ruined slabs, with names and dates chiselled or broken off. The graves of the aristocracy, defiled in the revolution that followed the invasion. Assundra liked to think everyone was important, so when she buried the dead they got the same treatment as the rest. In her barrow Elder lay side by side with carpenter, farmer with scholar, alchemist with labourer.

There was a stillness here, a peace that made the stifling air easier to breathe. There was clear open sky, the ruins were behind her and the stillest of breezes made the leaves on the trees and the blades of grass dance, but only if you looked closely. If Elder Cairns had done one thing for his people, she thought, it was to move them out of that decaying old city.

The burial plaza was separated from the barrow by a sprawling and fragrant lavender, wormwood and rosemary hedge. A small dirt path led to the only opening in the hedge and the top of the mound was visible some twenty paces in the distance, rising just a few feet, the small hump of earth belying the cavernous depths under the surface. There was room to bury tens of thousands of Ostracians in there. With a sigh Assundra reflected that they already had.

Beyond the barrow, the plateau gave way to a sheer drop down the hillside to the cage, where prisoners were judged. Beyond that, she could see the western side of the village, past the copse that separated it from the old city. The village was built in a winding pattern, like a labyrinth, around the large village circle and the alehouse fortress, the oldest building in Ostracia, built even before the settlers arrived. The alehouse was thousands of years old and the Ostracians would have it that it could withstand any battle, any fire or flood damage and would be there until the end of time. It was the heart of the new Ostracia. The rest of the village spread out in its circular sprawl from that heart and from up on the barrow hill, Assundra thought that it seemed like the cottages were all crouched around that fortress, like children around a storyteller's knee.

The stench of the midden pits was already detectable on the air. The almost overpowering reek of excrement was one of the reasons she tried to spend as much time as she could away from the village. The other was the villagers.

"No," she told herself, she mustn't think like that, not now! Things were changing, things were improving, she just had to wait. She just had to wait for Galvarin to make her his then everything would be alright.

She headed off towards the barrow, still keeping her eyes alert to any movement around her, but there was none. She passed the large plot on her right where the ashes of most of the plague victims had been buried in the early days, before Elder Cairns had closed the furnaces. It was pockmarked, not unlike a ploughed field, but Assundra knew you wouldn't have to dig too deep to find the remains of an Ostracian in there. Nothing grew on the site, not even grass. John had once told her that even after a few weeks you couldn't tell what was ash and what was soil anyway, the poor souls laid to rest here had undoubtedly been dug up again and again to have their brethren added to the plot.

"There is no rest in Ostracia, even in death", he had said. Assundra had been around death long enough to know the reason there was no rest in death was not because of someone digging you up, but because death was nothing. She had been surprised at John – sometimes the villagers could be so old fashioned, believing those myths and tales about death-life, even persuading the Elders to issue a half-hearted order to stay away from Elspeth Wood, where the spectres had supposedly been seen again. Assundra thought it was all nonsense – John was dead, lying on the cart in front of her, he wasn't coming back.

It was the living she was concerned about. As she neared the mouth of the barrow, she felt for the presence of the knife despite feeling its weight against her leg. Should she take the torch that hung outside the entrance, she wondered? It would give greater light, but would leave her with no free hands if Young Crafter was in there. If she didn't, there were the pockets of darkness in between the hanging oil lamps where she knew she would wish she had a torch.

"Bollocks to it," she whispered without conviction, but the words gave her some courage. She wasn't going to let Young Crafter get to her. So he'd hidden for her once, he'd got her once, but in weeks of him trying to corner her she'd bested him every time. The little bollock was nothing to worry about. Was he?

"*We're meant to be, you and me, I can save you*!" she remembered him saying with a shudder. "Well," she thought, "let's see who needs saving when I tell Galvarin what you did!"

She wheeled the cart into the barrow quickly, not giving herself time to change her mind and the darkness closed in around her instantly, the dim oil lamps, dotted here and there among the sarcophagi offering less light than she'd hoped. The cart was moving slowly now, she realised, despite the beating of her heart and every instinct in her body trying to force her legs to either move more quickly or abandon the barrow altogether and run.

Chambers hewn into the earth and supported by timber beams led off from the main path she was on at regular intervals, but she knew them all by heart. Here, near the mouth of the barrow, were the oldest bodies, the plain sarcophagi badly worn and chipped, only the odd one still having some remnant of the elaborate painting they had used hundreds of years ago, all sitting in the same position in their little earthen niches that they'd been in for centuries. She pushed the cart on, moving through the ages of the Ostracian dead, her head darting this way and that at each intersection, her body tense, waiting for Young Crafter to jump out at her. Each time she breathed a sigh of relief. There was no sound, no movement, just her and the countless thousands of dead.

She passed The Missing, the empty holes where sarcophagi should have been and which the Deathguard had told her not to ask about. She passed the point where the sarcophagi ended and the wooden crates with gilt handles began and she turned instinctively left, avoiding where the newest bodies were laid to rest. She didn't want to dump John in a canvas sack and leave him, stacked up in the farthest rooms, with the others. The man had been horrible to her, but he'd also been nice, at a time when nobody else in the village would even greet her as she passed, in the days when if she went out and wasn't spat on it was a good day.

Her fears about Young Crafter subsided now, there was no way he'd think to come this way. Indeed, if he'd come in this far there was a good chance he'd never find his way out again, all the chambers and paths between them looked the same if you didn't know your way. The barrow was so large she assumed that by now she was somewhere underneath the old city again and for some reason this thought made her look up. The thick wooden beams across the roof of the barrow looked secure enough to her, but then what did she know. One day she was sure this place would topple in on itself, but it hadn't yet and there was no point worrying about it until it did.

Winding her way through another set of identical chambers, she came to the empty spaces. More Missing, but there were different, these weren't ordinary Ostracians, these were Crafters. She hadn't told the Deathguard about these, he hadn't been interested in the fact that almost a century's worth of bodies had gone missing, so why would he miss a few old Crafters?

With some effort, she turned John's body out of the cart and stuck his legs into a sack that should have already been occupied from one of the empty niches. "Goodbye, John Hommel," she said softly, as she pulled the dead weight of John's body upright, dragging the sack up his body with her, before letting it flop back into the cart. She sealed off the end with the cords and rolled him into the niche.

"Solomon Crafter," she read on the label stitched into the sack. Well, it would do. John wouldn't be disturbed here and he wasn't near the plague victims, piled on top of each other in the pits at the back of the barrow. The lime would hasten his decay, anyway, soon he'd just be a skeleton like the rest, if that was indeed what was in the sacks.

"You never got to complete your work, did you?" she said sadly as she turned away, but something made her stop in her tracks. Something about that wasn't right. Where was the catalogue? It hadn't been with his things, with his clothes and she knew John kept it in the old city, for some reason fearful of his wife finding it, so where had it gone? She began to walk slowly again. He said he was going to visit the council chambers. Now he was dead, clearly strangled, whatever the Deathguard said, and the catalogue was missing.

It wasn't her problem. It wasn't anything to do with her. John was dead, it didn't matter now, anyway.

She told herself this over and over, but she knew it wouldn't make any difference. She'd liked John's catalogue and it would make a nice addition to her collection. Perhaps she wouldn't speak to the Elder tonight after all, perhaps she could look for it. He must have left it somewhere in the Deathguard's temple or the furnace. She would find it for him, for the times he was the man he could and should have been.

She didn't worry at all about Young Crafter on the way out of the barrow and soon she was breathing the thick summer air again, but glad of it. She'd taken care to leave the cart at the entrance so the Deathguard wouldn't know she'd desecrated a Crafter grave, not that he'd have cared, but she didn't want him to have anything else he could hold over her head. It still puzzled her that Young Crafter hadn't been waiting in the barrow for her, she had been almost sure the Deathguard would have told him where to find her, off his time, to coin his own phrase.

John had always tried to laugh the Deathguard off as being "just like that", a joker, a loner who didn't know how to relate to people, but Assundra could see it in his manner and in his eyes, she knew Jessop meant every word he said. He might exaggerate, but he truly did hate the people of Ostracia. Assundra smiled to herself – really then, she thought, that meant he should like her, the descendant of an outsider, as the villagers seemed to think that she wasn't an Ostracian at all.

"All is well…"

Assundra looked up, ignoring the voice, and checked the position of the sun. She'd definitely be early to meet Galvarin, he wouldn't have finished in his workshop yet. For a moment she wondered if she should surprise him there and wait, perhaps even get him to close up early, she thought with a smile, but then her father was quite ill. If she was going to be out all evening in the alehouse then perhaps she should check on him now, make sure he had something to eat. He ate less and less these days, though he didn't seem to be losing weight. He always polished off his meat, she noticed. She'd got extra rations from Jolly the Aleman after her latest brew of cider had gone down a treat, and he'd gone through a month's supply of the cured rat in a week.

She smiled as she walked slowly down the path that led to the copse. These walks back to the village used to hold dread for Assundra – it meant that her torment would soon begin again, but then Galvarin had come along. She'd never even considered the mason like that, not until she'd started to find the gifts. Small things at first, a trinket or two – she remembered the turquoise he'd tried to mould into a bracelet most fondly, it had been the size of her thumb and inlaid in sandstone. The point of it had never been for it to become part of her fine jewellery collection, but to make her laugh and, of course, for her to know it was from him.

When she'd come home one day from a particularly hard day with the Deathguard and found her little herb garden, that she'd been neglecting for weeks, tended and weeded she had rushed over to thank him. She knew it was improper, she knew she was too young, but he had swept her up in his arms as soon as she'd walked through the door. There hadn't been any need for words, he had just kissed her, his lips soft but his arms strong around her and she'd known then that she would lay with him.

She hadn't known he would tell her he loved her just a few weeks later, or that she'd be introduced to his friends in the alehouse. She hadn't known she could be happy like she was now. He had saved her. Almost. If he would only make her his...but then she was working on that.

The darkness of the copse closed in about her as she left the old city behind and the fears about Young Crafter surfaced again. There were plenty of places to hide in woodland, but no, it was too close to Bryant's outpost here. There were ways Young Crafter could have got into the old city without Bryant seeing, but it wasn't advisable to stray off the paths in any of the Ostracian woodland. The undergrowth was so wild, the canopy so dense that straying off the paths the gardeners carefully laid out meant the traveller could get lost in seconds, could stray towards the infection barrier and they'd soon stray no more if they contracted the plague. The Elders kept a barrier around the village as best they could, but they couldn't protect all of Ostracia.

"You're early, Assundra!"

She smiled at Bryant, skipping past him as he made to come out of his little wooden guard post as he always did every night when she left the old city. "Can't stop," she called sweetly, "father needs me."

The look of disappointment on his face made her want to turn back, to share a few words with him – she hardly ever stopped these days and she knew it, but, well, since she had come of age, Bryant's conversation kept turning towards...things that belonged to Galvarin. That Bryant knew belonged to Galvarin. She didn't want to have to tell him again, she had enough trouble with Simon. She waved, turning happily towards the village circle as Bryant called a goodbye to her, shouting something about seeing her in the alehouse tonight, but she was no longer listening.

"Stupid outsider bitch, look what she did!"

Forcing herself to keep going, to not stop in her tracks, she walked quickly around the side of the first cottage she saw, but she'd seen enough. Young Crafter had been in the middle of a circle of people. She'd seen the nodding heads of the small crowd around him, small, but there were enough of them. She'd seen the way his nose had not just been broken, but crushed, clearly beyond setting back in place and in her mind she saw the blood on the Deathguard's hand.

It wasn't the baying crowd that scared her, nor what retribution Young Crafter would take, they were things she dealt with on a daily basis. What scared her was the Deathguard's hand. He had helped her, he had broken Young Crafter's nose, she could see it as clear as day. His face hadn't shown embarrassment, or pride at having helped her, it had sneered, revelling in what she thought had been excitement of what Young Crafter would do to her later.

She remembered the voice in her head telling her to beware.

If the Deathguard was looking out for her, that meant he had a use for her. Assundra ran home to her father's cottage, feeling sick.

CHAPTER 4

Cairns looked down at the mud stained and broken body lying in front of him. A single arrow to the heart had brought a quick death, but it was that arrow that held the Elder's gaze. It was huge – far bigger than an arrow needed to be, some five feet long, tipped with silver and with a shaft as thick as his wrist. The man wielding a bow that could loose such an arrow would need to be skilled and strong in equal measure – proving Cairns had chosen correctly.

That didn't make the dead fool's stupid decision any easier to stomach.

"Where was he found, Captain?" he asked the man standing half to attention in front of him. Captain Hoard's battered, tight leather cuirass, greaves and boots were as soiled as the dead man's linen. Whose boots were missing, Cairns noticed suppressing a sigh. It was ever thus with death in Ostracia these days – it had grown too familiar for those dealing with it or in it to retain any pride.

"In the chasm, Elder," Hoard replied in rough, heavily accented Ostracian.

"When?"

"Taken me a few days to get here unnoticed, that's for sure."

The body had been dumped on the rug just inside Cairns' front door, in front of the bookcase, which hinged on one side and hung open to reveal a dark passageway beyond. Elder Oldershaw had escorted Captain Hoard, who had travelled those days with the body, as he had reached the border of the village, to ensure they were not seen. His colleague and friend now stood back, knowing it was the leader of the Elder Council who should ask the questions.

Looking at the body, Cairns could see the Captain was once again honest – there was slight decaying around the features, the skin was pallid and even the pungent sodden earth the body was covered in after the sudden and brief rainstorm there had been not that morning could not hide the smell. More importantly, Cairns noted he had not been fed on. Well, that was the end of Carp's brother – there was nothing more to learn from the stupid dead fool. If he had succeeded in escaping, he would have ruined everything.

With a dismissive sigh, Cairns' mind turned to other topics. "I assume they still man the towers?" he asked, expecting nothing other than the same answer he got every month.

Captain Hoard nodded. "Took a bird up a few days ago, Elder and both towers are still manned, though not heavily. They change the guard every month, they are heavily armed and, they each have a sorceror."

The same answer. "The birds still pass the Maw undetected?"

Hoard nodded again. "We haven't had one shot down yet. It's my belief they don't know we can…"

"Yes, well that is just as well," Cairns hissed, cutting the man off before he could say too much. The reddening in the solder's face showed that he understood – for all Cairns' cottage was private, eyes and ears listened everywhere in Ostracia. Somehow people always found out things they should not, there seemed to be no end to his people's desire for punishment. Cairns had no wish to upset them further and if they knew that while they were slowly dying, while they were starved of the very artistry they needed to survive, Cairns allowed a select few to practice in secret, even though it was for their own good, it could cause unnecessary bad feeling.

It could cause further support to align itself to the Crafters.

The accursed family would care about sanctioned artistry far more than about a dead colleague. Cairns knew his enemies would waste no time in making powerful profit with those in the village who cared about artistry, who missed the old ways the Elders had banned. None of it would make any difference, of course, but it would make things harder and he was too close for any of this to get out now.

"Does Bryant know?" he asked idly, watching with some interest the look of amusement on Hoard's face before he brought it under control.

"Not likely," Hoard muttered, but ceased speaking when Oldershaw shot him a look.

"He knows nothing, Elder," Oldershaw replied for him. "Never does. Lets them slip through though. Doesn't he? Never know how, I suppose." Elder Oldershaw's fat, puffy face was deadly serious, his voice barely audible he whispered so low. If anything, Cairns thought, that showed the measure of the man – normally as big and loud in voice as he was in bulk, Elder Oldershaw was not a man to take at appearance – that brashness, that loud, booming personality, was not the measure of the man. Cairns had learned through trust that Oldershaw could be the most discreet of all those he could trust and had been grateful for it on more than one occasion. They had been friends for many years, longer than he allowed Oldershaw to realise.

As to Bryant, Cairns made a show of giving the matter some thought. "Keep it that way," he replied. "The man has discovered some notoriety recently with his third wolf kill. Those who knew Carp's brother was planning to run will know what has happened, once the funeral is held and those who do not will be worried about the plague once more, either way his death serves our purpose. For now. However," he added, turning to Hoard with some menace, "I do not want to hear this petty jealousy again! Captain Bryant does just as important a job as you do, Hoard and he holds my confidence in equal measure, do you understand?"

The man nodded, his face turned to the floor, eyes white. No taller than many of the women in the village, Captain Hoard was not a big man, he was dwarfed next to Oldershaw, but then he hadn't been chosen for his size. He had shown remarkable skill with Domination, controlling a simpler animal and seeing through their eyes, a natural ability that Elder Cairns shared and respected.

Along with Captain Coarse, the man strong enough to wield the bow, they lived in secret in one of the ruined outer settlements, beyond the chasm. It was their job to make sure no Ostracian was foolish enough to attempt escape. Any Ostracian seen leaving the Yawning Maw, the only way out of the Forest, risked alerting the outsiders to their continued presence. Another invasion, in their weakened state, would finish Ostracia.

It was another precaution he had been forced to impose where none should have been needed. It meant he had the confidence of two more people to worry about and the more who knew, the more likely his discovery was. Cairns refused the urge to grimace – it seemed like every day the villagers he was trying to save invented new and ever more complicated ways to prevent him from doing so.

Fortunately, buying the Captains' silence was easy, Cairns just had to make sure that revealing his confidence would harm them as much as Cairns and therefore his people. Ostensibly in return for the Captains' solitude, Cairns allowed them knowledge of blood magic.

That reminded Cairns. "Here are your supplies for the next month," he said, handing Hoard a small wooden case of powders. On seeing the box, Hoard's face dropped and for a moment Cairns thought he would question him, or request a feed, but the man's mouth clamped shut as he looked Cairns in the eye. "Unless there is another incident, I do not want to see you back here at the time we agreed, rather come when the moon is at its lowest, do you understand?"

The man nodded again and Cairns resisted the temptation to force him to speak, he was not a child after all and he had just lugged a body across miles of forest terrain whilst trying to remain unseen. He was perhaps allowed a little leeway in the realm of manners after such exertion. This time.

"How is Captain Coarse?"

Hoard's face was hard to read. "He pines for his wife. He's brought some of her things with him and when I'm on duty he sits there, sobbing, begging something to give her back."

"He is praying?" Oldershaw boomed, unable to keep his voice down at that. Praying was outlawed in Ostracian society – the gods had deserted them when the outsiders had invaded.

"Not praying, Elder, no, of course not, but, well, his mind's…"

"I understand, Hoard," Cairns interjected, holding an arm out to silence an infuriated Oldershaw, motioning him to find himself a cider. An invitation the man never turned down. "Keep an eye on him. Send me a message if you need to. You have done well tonight, but you must go while there is enough darkness to get you as far as Elspeth Wood."

"Elspeth Wood?"

"The gardeners will be chopping wood in the Forest at dawn tomorrow, Hoard, I do not want you or traces of you to be found. If you divert through Elspeth Wood you will leave no traces that anyone will find."

"I'm more worried there won't be any traces of me, Elder!"

Cairns laughed, the man might be afraid, but not so that he would disobey Cairns' instructions. Cairns found a result of the Drawing of another was that little scared you when little could harm you – but Hoard was by no means a skilled artist. The Drawing made him stronger, lighter and faster, but if it gave him artistic power Cairns made sure he didn't know how to use it. Hoard was only new to the Drawing, he would not be used to the feeling of invulnerability it gave, the power it released into the body. Unfortunately, there would be no time for him to get used to it either.

"Then go, send a message by bird if you need anything."

The man nodded a farewell to both Elders, infuriating Cairns further, then left through the passage. Cairns slid the bookcase back into place, turning to find Oldershaw in Cairns' own seat, the only seat in the room in truth, the three-legged chair he had made himself. There wasn't much room in the cottage, even though Cairns' dwelling was slightly larger than the rest, he had to have somewhere to store Ostracia's books, after all, but there had been no need to construct fine, large dwellings when they had moved from the Old Town. The small, square, adaptable cottages were all they needed. The homes were functional and comfortable and did not need hundreds of candles, fires and empty space using up materials they did not have.

He'd wanted to thatch the roofs, as the style had been when the Founding Families had first travelled from the West, but materials had been too short in supply, forcing instead the use of boards, lined with tar. Those boards were only about a foot above Cairns' head, but not a chink of light or breeze permeated through the small, slightly inclining rafters. The roofer really had been very good at his job.

It was a shame the carpenter and the mason did not possess the same dedication. In addition to the roughly hewn stonework, every time he consulted one of the books in the oaken cases that lined the back wall and corners of the room he ran the risk of the whole set toppling on top of him. He'd tried to nail the cases to the wall, but the hard, beige stone had bent or broken each piece of metal and he'd been forced to give up. Artistry could knock a wall down, but it wasn't delicate enough to knock a nail into one.

Aside from the rickety cases, only a series of hanging tapestries adorned the remaining walls, the floors carpeted with the finest, thick rugs that did not match the tapestries. Without fires, they needed the warmth from such things in the winter. The old aristocrats' perversity of power had certainly bought them some rewards, but those rewards had done them scant benefit. The ruling classes had all perished at the hands of the ones brave enough to wrest control from the powerful but cowardly. Now all Ostracia shared that wealth, as they ever should have.

Knowledge, now that was different. The books in Cairns' cottage were far from the only ones left in Ostracia, but these were books on history, on artistry and power. They remained with Cairns, for his people had no need of enhanced learning, the simpler their lives the better. If they were to forget artistry then it was better they knew nothing of it. Even so, there were always a few that reckoned themselves enough of an equal to an Elder that they felt able to break the law. The very fact they had to resort to attempted theft to discover that which they wished to know should have proved to them that the knowledge they sought was not meant for them. It never mattered how much he did for the villagers, they always wanted more.

He smiled as he poured himself a cup of cider half the measure of Oldershaw's and remembered the young Keeper, terrified in her first interview with the leader of the Elder Council, after her first theft. It was a shame she had been born a girl else a fine and powerful career might have awaited her on the outside, with her talents, when it was all over. As the outsiders would undoubtedly still possess their irrational hatred of artistry there were always ways to practice in secret, Cairns had proved that over the years. She had understood the books' true meanings far quicker than anyone he'd ever seen. She outshone Simon in every department. Only Simon had the power.

"…but *praying*, Cairns?" he realised his old friend was saying with a start. "Can we allow that? The man has lost his wife. Terrible. Yes, but that is a clear flouting of our laws, he must be punished!"

Cairns hoped he was not missing some vital part of the argument his friend had made earlier before he was listening. "I think we can excuse it in our colleague Coarse," he replied. "The powders affect us all in different ways, as does, I'm afraid, killing one of your own friends."

Oldershaw's eyes flicked to the body on the rug. "A shame. First one in quite a while."

Cairns propped himself up on one of the more sturdy bookcases, making sure it would take his weight before it did so. Oldershaw's eyes had shown no sign of a spark of interest at the mention of the powders. Good, that meant he was still in all likelihood in ignorance of the Captains' feeding. There were things he could not trust even his closest friend with.

"We should not tell Carp, I think," he said to Oldershaw. "That his brother died trying to escape, I mean. Let him think he had the plague."

Oldershaw coughed. "Yes. Meant to talk to you about that. Is that wise?" Cairns raised his eyebrows. "Telling people it was plague. Not had a death from the plague for two months now. The people, some of them, at least, consider that we've won, that we've beaten it."

"Yes," Cairns agreed, "but I think it preferable to have a one-off return of the plague, for one who strayed too close to the infection barrier, for a reason we must invent, oh, something like he wandered too close to the chasm in the fever of the early stages, the man was never one of Ostracia's high thinkers after all. I'll leave the details to you. Something to make sure we do not get a repeat of this."

It was now Oldershaw's turn to agree. "Too many already. I thought you were barmy when you set the Captains to their task. Can see now you were right. If we're to have any chance of catching the bastards unawares, they need to be bloody unaware!" Oldershaw laughed – a loud, grating boom that seemed incongruous in the middle of his whispered speech and made Cairns wince. "I remember Rime wasn't too keen on it either, was he? Thought I'd have to step in to prevent bloodshed between you both at one point!"

The cup almost cracked in Cairns' hand. He had the presence of mind to force a smile to his lips as the Elder babbled on, recounting the tale of how Cairns and Rime had held a heated argument about killing their own. *An argument Oldershaw should not remember!* If the Withholdings were breaking down as quickly as this, then it meant Cairns was already weaker than he was aware of. The well of artistry inside each man was not limitless, nor was it evident at any time how much was left, it was not as simple as feeling hungry. Yet his last Drawing had been three years ago, he shouldn't need to visit with Rime again for another two!

"I thought you were going to burst when he challenged you on the – what did he call it? – validity of the suppression of expression, that was it," Oldershaw was saying, in between sips, laughter playing through his words. "Said we should show the outsiders not only were we here, but we were here to stay, didn't he? Didn't agree with your idea of letting them think us dead." He laughed again, but it was a laugh shrouded in a cloud. "Can't say I agreed with him on much of that, I'm afraid."

Cairns grimaced. "Yet we know now why he was in disagreement with me."

It was Oldershaw's turn to simply nod at Cairns now. "Yes. Shame what happened to him."

A tingle shot through Cairns' back. Surely Oldershaw couldn't remember…

"An Elder working for the Crafters." Oldershaw shook his head. "Best not to dwell on such things. Better to remember how lucky you were to find out when you did."

Cairns almost breathed a sigh of relief before he collected himself – at least a few Withholdings on Oldershaw's memory had held. Rime was dead and buried, as far as the village was concerned and Cairns needed it to stay that way. It would not be long before it was not far from the truth, anyway.

"We were more than lucky, we were correct in our assumptions," Cairns replied forcefully. "Simon played his part in that, it was how we first discovered him as I recall."

The lies slipped off his tongue the story was so well rehearsed in his mind. In truth, it had been a happy accident finding that Rime was spying for the Crafters – it gave an opportunity to introduce Simon's powers to Oldershaw as a natural event.

"I had to work for weeks to stop you slaughtering them, I remember," Oldershaw said, more quietly this time, draining his cup and holding it out for a refill. "Old Crafter didn't want to budge an inch, denied everything the whole time, still does." Oldershaw frowned. "Funny thing is, I believed him."

Cairns was prepared for that one. "Who was to say it was Old Crafter? It could have been…"

"Oh come on man," Oldershaw scoffed, "who else could pull all those strings? No, it was the old bollock, it had to be. Still, showed him a lesson, eh? Heard virtually nothing from him since."

Which was true, Cairns reflected – Old Crafter had been suspiciously quiet since Cairns had taken Rime. It was also true that without Oldershaw's negotiations, there could have been no reconciliation between Cairns and the Crafters. Cairns had wanted them dead, all of them, to rid himself of their vile aristocratic superior air once and for all, but Oldershaw had been right, it would have led to what would have amounted to a civil war. Even with so few Ostracians left, a civil war would have taken many lives. Oldershaw had not considered the price of Ostracian life worth paying.

Elder Cairns sometimes wondered.

In his view, the lives of Crafters and those who supported them had not been worth saving, but the plague outbreak a few weeks later had taken so many lives that it had proved Oldershaw right. Ostracia could not afford to be at war with itself, there were too few of them left. It would not take much for them to vanish completely, which was why Cairns had to time everything just right…

"Shame about Rime though," Oldershaw said again, only more sadly, "plague doesn't care who it takes though, does it Cairns?"

"No, my friend it does not," Cairns managed to reply and followed his agreement with a large gulp of cider that burned his throat in a most pleasant manner. "I prefer to remember Rime when we accepted him as Elder, his excitement at being allowed to serve his people. He was an example to follow for them all, he was *their* Elder, lest we forget."

He was an example, it was true. It was why what he did was so disappointing.

"We all have to go sometime, some way, Elder. Only truth in life. We'll teach the outsiders that, you and me. Well, I'd best be off to the alehouse. Word is that bugger Young Crafter has been spreading some crap about the Franks girl breaking his nose, he's getting a mob together."

Cairns pursed his lips. "That is unfortunate."

Oldershaw seemed to share Cairns' concerns, for his face, too, was stern. "One of many unfortunate occurrences with that boy. Perhaps too many."

With that, without even a goodbye, Oldershaw pulled his huge bulk to his feet and, with a hefty shove to shutter-like door of Cairns' cottage, was gone. Cairns stared after him for some time. Oldershaw was another who had Cairns' confidence, some of it at least, yet the man's venom towards the outsiders was matched only by Max's. The two often shared a cup of cider describing in detail how they would deal with an outsider should one find their way into Ostracia. They had done so within earshot of Assundra.

Cairns sighed. Max and Elder Oldershaw. "Not tonight," he told himself, shaking the thoughts from his mind. He had time before he had to make that decision.

There were more pressing issues to deal with. For all he agreed with what Oldershaw said about Young Crafter, the man was an oaf, after all, Cairns got the distinct impression that Oldershaw had been speaking to himself and not Cairns.

Young Crafter was proving to be a bit of a puzzle and one Cairns could well do without. The man surely must have known he could never get away with imprisoning Assundra in such a way, Through the bird's eyes he had seen Assundra's escape at the hands of the Deathguard, indeed, it was Cairns, through the bird, who had informed the Deathguard of his impending role as saviour beforehand, a role the man had not looked favourably on. The Deathguard had laughed it off as a joke, a prank played on Assundra, but Cairns knew Young Crafter – he would only play a joke if there were others around to see it. There was a possibility he could have taken Erol Tyson and the rest of his disgusting troupe to take mirth at Assundra's plight that evening, followed by much worse, if Cairns knew the Crafter clan, but there had been something in Young Crafter's eyes that had disturbed Cairns.

He had seen knowledge there, an earnestness and serious manner that until now he would never have associated with the man. Young Crafter knew something. Which made him dangerous until Cairns knew what that something was.

Yet that was not the only curious thing.

"All is well," something had said. After Assundra had been taken from the well, after she had sat on the ground sobbing like a gelded lamb, something had…no. Cairns shook his head – nothing could have known he was there, nothing was powerful enough to send him a message like that. It must have been Assundra herself speaking. Perhaps that was how outsider minds worked – talking to themselves constantly, perhaps they could reassure themselves only by voicing their reassurance, but Cairns did not have time to think on it.

With the body to dispose of tonight, nor would he would have time to deal with the youngest of the Crafter clan, he would have to trust Oldershaw with that. If only someone would side with the girl, put their mindless prejudices aside, then he could get at Young Crafter and rid his village of the lout.

As it was, the Crafters were the one set of people he could not touch. Not because they had power, which they did, in abundance, but nothing compared to his, nothing compared to what Drawing from the living gave, but they had power of a different sort.

They were liked. They split Ostracian opinion, it is true, but they were the last of the Founding Families, their ranks very closed, their followers loyal to the death.

Many of their most loyal followers had died, in the plague, leaving few, but whilst that few would have been nothing when Ostracia was at its prime, now they were so few they had become an influence in their own right.

Old Crafter, he was the one to watch. He was the one pulling the strings, him and Mary Archer nee Crafter, who still harboured ill feeling towards the Elder about the death of her husband Jesmond. Erol Tyson was their muscle, the Tysons having served the Crafters for centuries, Patrick Crafter their sweet talker, Just Crafter the quiet one. Young Crafter was the misfit. He was a drunk and a lech, more than once receiving a beating from Max for putting his hands on Max's wife, Alice. Cairns had been alarmed at first – fearing he would have to punish Max, but strangely, no Crafter witnesses came forward. There was found to be no case to answer, on all three occasions.

Cairns had found that interesting in the extreme and had begun to try to cultivate the nauseating man, to try and learn what he could, a drunk was, after all, an easy man to manipulate, but Cairns had soon found out through several stomach-turning nights of being close to the foul man that there was nothing to learn, because Young Crafter knew nothing.

That did not mean that he would not be missed. Perhaps that was even what they were looking for and Cairns would not give it to them. He would give them no excuse. With any luck, whatever nonsense the Crafters were planning would have no time to be brought to fruition – Cairns was close now.

Oldershaw could handle Young Crafter. With a sad thought, Cairns collected Oldershaw's cup. This was perhaps the last time he would take cider with his old friend. If only Oldershaw had been more pliant, more placable about his nonsensical plots for revenge on the outsiders, he would have been a useful ally. As it was, the more intricate parts of Cairns' plan he had been forced to keep to himself. Oldershaw would not approve of the powders in the water or the acceleration of the plague, even though it was all patently necessary. For Ostracians to leave, to pass the infection barrier without the benefit of the power of Drawing, they had to shed their artistry from their blood. If it worked, he would have cured his people of the plague and set them free, to a new life on the outside.

He wondered, sadly, if Oldershaw would pass the barrier. Cairns, Hoard and Coarse were to stay behind to make sure any stragglers were dealt with, to make sure that the healthy Ostracians could leave quietly, one by one, so as not to attract attention. Not through the Yawning Maw. Not via the bay where the ships were moored.

There was another way. There always had been.

A rap at the door sent it swinging open, revealing the formidable shape of the Deathguard outside.

"What you brought me away from my work for?"

Cairns made no attempt to hide his disgust at the Deathguard's presence. The man didn't even wait to be invited before strolling in, parting both shutters and still having to squeeze past the door frame. Jessop was a grotesque, no wonder his mother had died giving birth to such a monster. Broadside went white whenever he spoke of it, the alchemists being the closest things Ostracia had to apothecaries for decades, his father had dealt with the birth and described it as sheer horror.

"Take a look," was all Cairns said in reply, pointing to the body lying sprawled where Captain Hoard had left it.

"Another one? Wonder who's killed more, eh, Cairns? You or the plague?"

The man laughed, a horrible, crackling sound. Cairns put the cups down, slowly. "I can be sure of your discretion, of course." He did not phrase it as a question. "I believe this one will be for the cellars, there is no need for the girl to see this."

"She's seen worse."

"But she will not see this." Cairns forced himself to remain calm. He needed to find out how Oldershaw had broken a full Withholding before he attempted another confrontation. Jessop liked to test himself against Cairns, ever since Cairns had requested the first favour from him, but there would be no examination tonight.

"Whatever you say, Elder. I got some news for you, anyway."

"Yes?"

"We got more Missing." Cairns' brow furrowed. This was not news he wanted. "Three of them, taken last night. No idea who took 'em, no idea how."

Cairns grimaced. "Thank you, Jessop." There were more every week. Why would anyone take a dead body? It was beyond Cairns. "I will ask Elder Oldershaw to look into it. And our other business?"

"Which business? The girl or John? Or had you forgotten about him?"

"It was John I meant," Cairns replied through gritted teeth. Gods, but it was hard not to hate this man.

"John was a good man, Elder," the Deathguard said with a sensitivity and gravity that surprised Cairns. "I liked him, we was friends. He was a good man."

"He was a spy. He was looking into things he had no place looking. It was nobody's fault, Jessop, but his own, I did not kill him."

"Not the point. He's dead and his throat looked to me very much like someone's hands had been round it. Someone whose hands were smaller than mine, I might add. Weren't me, like you said it were. Think you might have lied to me, Cairns."

Cairns stared at the Deathguard, hard. For all his way of speaking, for all his bulk implied the dopiness of the simple, Jessop had a keen mind for detail and he never forgot anything. It was why he made so few friends, people were never the sum of their parts for Jessop, they were simply what they did and, the way he saw things, what most people did was worthy of his scorn.

"I forget things…" Jessop went on, when Cairns didn't reply. "Things I don't reckon I should forget, but I always see after. When they're on my carts, I always see. If I'd done that his neck would have been snapped in two, but it weren't. It were just squeezed a bit. Enough, mind, but not like how I'd have done it. Weren't no mercy in what happened to him and I'd have been merciful, like I say, he was a good man. So who done it, Elder? I don't reckon you for the sort to strangle, from what I've seen you use them things in your fingers. Or other means."

"Quite." Cairns stood his ground, unable to move. He was used to Jessop's uncivil behaviour, he was even used to not being accorded the respect that an Elder deserved, but this outright disdain was new.

"The bodies, they tell me, see. They tell me a lot of things about what's going on in the village, enough for me to not need to bother coming down. I don't like coming down here, Elder, you know that!"

The man's voice broke at the end. Perhaps allowing the Deathguard to deal with John had been a mistake. "Did he find it?"

The big man heaved his shoulders into a shrug. "Don't know. Not with his things, if he did he's hid it somewhere, somewhere I don't know about."

"We need that artefact!" Cairns found himself yelling before he could collect himself. "Or rather, we need others not to have it."

"Never mind." Without warning, Jessop reached into his sack and with one fluid movement flung something at Cairns so hard he had to dodge out of the way, losing his footing. The Deathguard didn't laugh as Cairns' head hit the shelf of the bookcase, he didn't even flinch when the Elder sank to the floor. "Think you'll find that a good read."

"What..." Cairns managed as his vision went red.

"Don't worry yourself about Carp's brother, I'll see to him." The Deathguard picked the body up with one hand and slung it over his enormous shoulder. Cairns grimaced and closed his eyes, the red in his vision making it seem far too much like blood running down Jessop's face. Red blood, sugary, hot blood, pulsing. Cairns could almost feel the man's huge, juicy veins. The jugular would be inviting, rich, fresh and full...

"Oh and Cairns?" The Deathguard was feet from his face now, looming down over him, holding the body in place with only a few fingers. "About the other thing. The girl. If there's one thing I hate more than you Elders it's them bollocking Crafters. If it comes to it, I hope you know I'm your man. Id enjoy that."

Cairns bit at the air, but the Deathguard was gone, as if he'd never been there. The body was gone too, but the shutters stood fast. The Deathguard had sent Cairns one final message – he knew where the passage was.

Reaching quickly into the folds of his robe Cairns yanked out the pouch of powders Broadside had left him. Fumbling for the cord he swore, tearing the pouch open and pushed some of the yellow powder into his mouth.

"The last time..." he murmured as he slumped back against the bookcase and let the powders take effect. The sweet citrus taste filled his mouth as the powders dissolved on his tongue, but he didn't trust himself to open his eyes yet. He had to slow his breathing first, had to make sure he was calm, had to make sure the hunger had passed.

The alchemist had been commissioned to create the powders in secret, this hunger-diminishing brand was but one of many Cairns carried with him at all times. Nothing compared to a feed, nothing, but there was no way he could get to Rime, his stock, no way at all. The plans were in place, it would be far too dangerous to disrupt them now because he was too weak. This was what the yellow powder was for – to quell his urges until there was such time as they could be sated.

Slowly, Cairns opened his eyes. The cottage was as he left it when he closed them. Sighing with relief, Cairns forced himself to breathe slowly, in a more regulated way. He forced himself to get over it.

Then he started to think. The Deathguard was becoming increasingly unstable. To openly challenge an Elder like that was to ask for a death sentence. Cairns grimaced – he didn't like to think of anyone being so sure of their position that they felt they could speak to him with such disrespect, but the simple fact was that with John gone, Jessop was all Cairns had, he was the only option. He could hardly trust the Franks girl and nobody else knew the job. The Deathguard had him backed into a corner.

What concerned him more, was that he had felt a need to reassure Cairns of the fact that he was 'his man'. Cairns would expect nothing else! To offer his allegiance as a favour was the gravest insult of the many Jessop had given Cairns tonight and the man knew Cairns had to swallow each of them.

For now.

Too many concerns were cropping up, Cairns thought as he hauled himself to his feet, not trusting to put his arm on the bookcase to aid him. Too many things that could get in the way of the plan. Jessop knew nothing of what was to come, his threat was merely to insult and there was little chance of Cairns being abused in such a way in front of others as the man kept himself locked away in his church, no, Jessop's attitude was a concern, but not a threat. If they were all like Jessop, Cairns wouldn't mind – insolence could be punished cleanly and efficiently – but in the end, Jessop always did as the Elders' bid him to do. He was a liability, not a problem. His confidence didn't need to be bought, it was given willingly, out of duty, even if he hated that duty. He could be relied upon, which meant he could be saved.

Of more portent was the memory of Elder Oldershaw. The man could not have broken the withholdings Cairns had placed on the memories of all Ostracians intentionally, he would not have known there was anything to break and yet it had happened.

A Withholding was a simple way of controlling people. It was not artistry, not in the pure, blood sense that Ostracians once practised, the source of life that mixed with the blood in their veins and gave them life. If his people knew he was practising Withholdings, his position would be destroyed. They would try to destroy him, too. They would fail, but he had no wish to inflict pain on those he was charged to protect, no more than was necessary, so he could not risk them discovering his means.

For Withholdings were brought about through sorcery.

It was what he had discovered in the Transept Tower all those years ago, what those short-sighted Elders led by Hugo had wanted to make sure he never learned. Artistic sorcery.

The rebel Elders had perfected it in secret a century ago – a way to preserve the blood magic that raised Ostracians above their peers, to preserve their healthy crops, their superior products – to preserve their way of life – without having to resort to the stock. There were those who believed as he did even back then, that even though the stock had a perfect right to leave whenever they chose, to keep human beings as, as one esteemed Elder had described it, "milking fodder", was a barbaric practice.

They had been right. They had also found the solution, only for Lord North in his infinite lack of wisdom to suppress that solution, to seek out the rebel Elders and burn them, one by one, after what were, in all too true a sense of the word, witch hunts for those who would defy him. At least none of them gave up the location of the Transept Tower, even under fierce torture at the hands of Lord North's daughter, the last Gifted One recorded in Ostracian history. The secrets had been there for someone to find, the problem was that Elder Hugo had never allowed anyone to look.

If Oldershaw was remembering Elder Rime, then that meant one of two things – there was a sorceror in Ostracia who could see the signs of a Withholding and had broken it. That meant the sorceror was working with Oldershaw, without the man's knowledge. If not that, there was a purely artistic power strong enough to break the sorcery Cairns had weaved.

Neither seemed possible. Cairns would have detected the presence of another power that strong, just as the outsider sorcerors that roamed the camps outside the Yawning Maw could sense when an Ostracian approached – you simply had to look for the signs – no, there was another answer that Cairns could not see.

Cairns detested that.

With a sudden shock of memory, as if the world came back to him with a jolt, Cairns remembered the book. John's book. Picking it up from where the Deathguard had flung it, the small, battered leather-bound vellum volume felt light in his hands. Cairns was disappointed – for some reason he had expected such a thick book to weigh more, but he quickly laughed it off – the most important books Cairns had read in the Transept Tower had not been weighty tomes at all, but simple, handy little compendiums of the writer's knowledge, clearly and thoughtfully laid out.

Besides, the title written in fine old Ostracian handwriting on the front of what was clearly a journal had already gripped Cairns. This was John's catalogue! The Deathguard had found it after all!

The title was immaculately written in a bright pale blue, the likes of which had not been seen since the secrets of ink had been lost. Cairns himself had turned to writing in blood years ago, an act that he had discovered imbued writings on artistry with a terrific power, to the extent that they had to be kept under lock and key at all times, but this was a book of an entirely different sort of power – this was a book of knowledge.

Chuckling to himself, Cairns poured himself another cup of what he had to admit was a very fine drop of cider – the Franks girl did have her talents after all, even if the villagers did not accept them – and settled down to a read.

CHAPTER 5

"You've got such a knack for that," Alice said with a smile.

Assundra grinned back. "I have a good teacher!"

They chopped the herbs in silence for a while. They were in the back of the alehouse, a room Assundra had never been in before. Normally they met up to make their pouches, poultices and cooking aids at Alice's house, but to Assundra's surprise and relief, Alice had asked to meet here today. A pin prick of guilt jabbed into her stomach as she thought of poor Simon, but Galvarin had asked her not to speak to him any more after last night. She knew the duty of a wife was to obey her husband and she wanted to show Galvarin that when he made her his she would do just that.

Only she was putting off telling Simon. She knew how much he liked her. A quick glance at Alice told Assundra that she couldn't tell Simon's mother either. She dropped her eyes as Alice smiled back at her. Her son didn't deserve this, but it wasn't her fault. Why couldn't Simon learn she wasn't interested? If he stopped pursuing her, stopped mouthing off to everyone about how they were lovers when they were not, then she was sure Galvarin wouldn't have made an issue of it.

Suppressing a sigh, she added a pouch of spiced, dried rose petals to the basket with the others. It was almost full and they'd only been here an hour. The back room wasn't like the vast atrium of the alehouse itself, it was more or less like any normal cottage. It was a simple square room with whitewashed walls. In the centre was the long table they were working on, with the preparations for the evening meal half-started at the other end. The entire village ate in the alehouse now, apart from Assundra and her father, at the Elders' instructions. Dotted all around the back room were knives, spoons, pots and pans, and the only functioning fire in Ostracia.

"Fire's not been lit," Assundra said, as she noticed. "Won't they want to be cooking the meal soon?"

Alice grimaced. "They don't use normal fire now," she replied quietly, with distaste in her voice. "The Elders make their own, less smoke so they say."

Assundra's eyes widened. "Artistic fire? Can they do that?"

"Oh yes," Alice nodded, "they can set fire to anything, knock anything down, destroy anything they like, but can they do anything useful with it, that's what I want to know!"

Assundra clamped her lips shut, trying to suppress a giggle, but she couldn't. Catching Alice's eye, they burst into laughter, stopping only as Jolly, the Aleman came in to retrieve a plate. Shaking his head sadly at the girls, he walked straight out again without saying a word, which only made them laugh more.

"Well, I'd best get these out where they belong, I suppose." Alice took her apron off, throwing it on the table. Assundra found herself wishing, not for the first time, that Alice would wear something better than the blue hood-less wimple she had on again today. Although, she thought, looking down at her own simple brown tunica, she could level the same criticism at herself for once. Assundra knew Alice had some fine dresses, ones that showed just how good her figure was, ones that brought out the brilliant yellow in her hair and flashing, mischievous green in her eyes, but Assundra also knew that Max, Alice's husband, wouldn't like it.

Nodding to Assundra, Alice picked up the basket and followed Jolly. "Don't stop," she called on her way out, "can always do with plenty more!"

Assundra laughed to herself as she went back to preparing the herbs. Stealing a quick glance at the door to make sure she was alone she grinned – this was the perfect opportunity to make something for Galvarin! Whenever they laid together he brought along some powders he'd got from Broadside, to help her relax he said, though she noticed he never took any himself. She'd always thought it was a nice gesture, that it proved he cared about her pleasure too, so she wanted to do something in return.

Smiling, she took a pestle and mortar and ground some hawthorn berries, ginseng, maca and suma, scenting it with a little peppermint. The hot spring near the glade should be warm enough to steep it, she thought, tipping the ground mixture into an infuser and slipping the infuser into a fold in her dress. Alice wouldn't miss it, she was sure.

"Don't stop," Alice had said. Assundra put her hands on her hips – but what was she to make? They had enough rose pouches to last until winter and nobody had asked for any lavender pouches. They seemed to prefer the rose, even though the lavender pouches were better for keeping the smell of the midden pits at bay, or so Assundra thought. Their own cottage was always full of the smells of cider brewing so it didn't really affect her, although she kept a small bowl of moist lavender and nut oil next to her bed.

Thinking of moist mixtures, she decided to check on the ones in the pantry. It was always worth making sure they'd been shaken that day, else the scent sank into the oil without trace. Pushing through the pantry door, she was about to pluck the first jar from the shelf, when she saw with surprise that the door at the far end of the pantry, leading to the cellar, was open. That was careless of Jolly, she thought, as she moved to close it, but she stopped when she heard voices.

Assundra frowned – nobody had passed her and Alice for over an hour, what could anyone have been doing in the basement for that long? She edged closer, taking care to keep her footfalls light. She was surprised how clear the voices were, although they echoed in the curved stone of the cellar. They echoed because they were raised, she realised.

"There ain't gonna be no time, Max!" Max? Max West? What was he doing here?

"There'll have to be time! Else it'll all come down about our ears and I shouldn't want to be the one answering for that if it happens! The Elder'll have our faces for that."

The other man, who sounded older, scoffed. "There hasn't been a facing for years! Decades! He wouldn't dare anyway, worst we could expect is…"

"Dismemberment. Well, I have to tell you, Crafter, I don't muh fancy that either!" Assundra held the gasp in her throat, putting her hand to her mouth. Crafter? What was Max doing in the cellar with a Crafter?

"There ain't been one of them for ages neither!" the old man snarled back. Old Crafter, it had to be. Now she knew, the voice was unmistakable, even the man's voice sounded like it should have passed away years ago.

She heard Max swear and she pictured the two of them. Max was a squat, muscular, straw-haired man, still in his prime and as pure blood an Ostracian as you could find, his yellow hair and beard proved that. As long as you were topped by yellow or red, with blue, grey or green eyes, you had nothing to fear.

A wisp of her dark hair fell over her eyes. She didn't move it.

"You maybe as don't remember the last dismembering Crafter, but I do. I don't care to see another one, neither, not as long as I live, which I intend to be a long time! Seems like you have different plans for me though!"

Old Crafter was as old as anyone in Ostracia. He was a thin, wiry man who was grey all over, something he liked to play up as often as he could. His family knew different, though, as did Assundra; Old Crafter was a cunning, sly bastard who'd cut anyone down if they got in his way and that included Elders. Assundra didn't like the sound of what they were saying at all.

"There's still hundreds of us, Max, you don't need to worry!"

"And how many of them will come over with us?" The old man was quiet. Assundra couldn't see his expression, but she made a bet with herself that it wasn't a smile. "Come on, how many? Not many, that's how many! If we do this we've got to do it right!"

"We *are* doing it right, Max! Trust me! It's all sorted, we only need to wait for the Franks girl…"

"Assundra?"

The voices below her stopped abruptly and all she could hear were whispers.

"Careful, Sunny!"

She backed away from the cellar door when she heard the voice, unable to take her eyes from it, her head feeling like all the blood in her body had rushed to it, until it hit something hard.

She cried out and then heard a crash as the pots of moist potpourri fell. Groaning, she realised there was no point in hiding what she was doing now.

"Assundra are you alright?" Hands were suddenly fussing all over her and taking her hand away from her head she realised there was blood. Not much, but enough to make Alice start cooing over her. "Let's get that seen to, here, bend over."

Assundra winced as a sharp sting surrounded the wound on her head. A wisp of aloe scent filled the air, but was quickly replaced by a more pungent and acrid lemon and Assundra felt a compress pushed against her head. She felt her hands clench around something on the bench as the wound tightened and she closed her eyes, trying to think about something else. The only other thing she could think about was Max and Old Crafter. What were they doing in the cellar? She had to assume "the Franks girl" was her, but what were they waiting for her to do? Was it something to do with what Young Crafter wanted with her?

Shuddering, she put the possibility from her mind. Young Crafter was hardly secretive about what he wanted from her, Max and Old Crafter were hiding in a cellar, clearly terrified of being discovered, they wouldn't want Young Crafter drawing attention to them.

Away from them perhaps…*gods* would this never end? Why couldn't that family just leave her alone? She wasn't afraid now, she was just angry – gods help them when her father recovered.

Assundra heard a yelp behind her and the compress fell from her head. "What the hells are you doing?"

She span around to face Alice. "What do you mean?

Alice's face was white. Raising a trembling finger she pointed at the table. Turning back, Assundra gasped herself. Every herb and dried flower on the table had turned black, as if rotten. A smell of decay filled the room. Feeling something in her hand, Assundra opened her palm to reveal a sticky, flaky mass of what had once been a pouch of lavender.

"I didn't…" she started to say, turning back to Alice, but her friend was backing away from her in horror. "Alice! I didn't do anything, it wasn't me!"

"Well it wasn't me!" Alice's voice was quivering. "Get out of here, Assundra."

"But…"

"Now. And don't come back. I won't tell the Elders, but I don't want you near me again, do you hear?"

Assundra felt like she'd been slapped. "Alice, what are you talking about?"

"This ain't the first time, Assundra!" Alice virtually shouted at her. "Simon told me what happened in the old town all those years ago – I thought maybe you'd grown out of it, we all hoped you had, but clearly…"

"Grown out of it? Alice, what do you mean?"

"Keep away!" Alice backed off even further as Assundra took a step towards her. "Look at the table!" she screamed. "Sorceror! Now get out of here before I change my mind. Please!"

"What's going on here?"

Assundra ran as soon as she heard Max's voice. She heard Alice run to her husband. "Oh, Max, I was wrong! She is an outsider, look what she did! It's sorcery, Max!"

She let the door swing to behind her. She didn't remember getting home. She didn't notice if her father said anything to her as she ran up the stairs. Sorcery? She wouldn't know how to perform sorcery if she wanted to! As soon as she was in her room she let the tears fall.

*****

Some hours later Assundra caught sight of herself in the shard of metal just as it distorted her face into an ugly turnip shape, the petite nose she was quite proud of, given how everyone else in Ostracia had noses like tomatoes, stretched out as if it reached from cheek to cheek. She'd tied her hair up and in the brass it looked like the sprout at the top of her turnip head. It made her smile.

The little room at the back of the cottage wasn't much, but it was hers. There was a small cot in the corner of the bare stone room, her father not knowing how to plaster and nobody in the village being inclined to help the "outsider lover", as they called him. A large wardrobe housing her mother's things completed the meagre furnishings in the room apart from the small three-legged chair she sat on.

She had busied herself for half an hour or so trying to forget about Alice, worrying instead that she didn't really know how having her hair like that matched the dress she'd chosen, it would have been nice to make sure it didn't look too fancy, but they had no full brass anymore. In fact, she didn't have a mirror any more, just two halves of a cracked old hand-held bronze. Her father had thrown the others away.

"Every time I looked up from my bed there I was," he had said, "the loss of her all over my face. It was the worst part, seeing what you must've had to see when I was trying to be strong for you. It only made me worse. So they had to go."

Things were often as simple as that for her father. There had been no bronzes or brasses in their household since, she'd rescued the broken hand mirror from…well, she couldn't remember now, someone she'd buried. She kept the mirror in secret, with the other things she'd freed from the barrow, not wanting to press her father further about something as trivial as mirrors if it upset him. Her mother's death hadn't come as a shock exactly, death hadn't been a shock in Ostracia for many years, but Tom Franks was lost even now without her, she didn't need to look at his face to know that. Despite the long illness, when she went, she went, just like that, there had been no warning, no way to prepare, exactly as it had been for generations with her family. One child and then the mothers died soon after. Her mother had lasted four years, far longer than her ancestors.

Looking into the mirror again she tried to see what had upset Alice so much. There was nothing different. She didn't feel different, she didn't feel like she'd done anything, certainly not sorcery, that would take some sort of power, surely?

She swallowed hard. The voice would normally have interjected something by now, but it had been silent since she had…since Alice had accused her. Standing to let her dress settle, Assundra thought back to her decision. She couldn't have performed sorcery, she just didn't know how, so Alice must have got it wrong. Jolly must have come in and done something to the herbs while she was in the pantry, then fled when he saw what he'd done.

It couldn't have been her. Ostracians shunned sorcery, it was only the outsiders who used it. And she wasn't an outsider. Galvarin had said so.

Nor had her mother been, her father said. She had been born Ostracian, just like Assundra. Frowning, Assundra remembered that even though she was Ostracian, it was an outsider disease that had taken her mother.

At least it hadn't been the damned plague that killed her, she thought, although that might have been quicker. Assundra couldn't remember the death itself. She hadn't been allowed to be there, but at least she still had her mother's last words to her, cryptic as they were.

"Petticoats and brass. Do not fear them or their blood," she had said, but then her mind had been going by then, or so her father said. There were times when Assundra was sure her mother had said more and that it was important, but she could never hold on to the thoughts. She had been very small.

It always came back to the brasses. Assundra had seen grief in mirrors, like her father, but she had also seen her mother's face, smiling. Elder Cairns had dismissed all that as the illusions of a child's mind, that Nilha's death had been a "blessing seeing as how ill she had been". He was probably right but her father had never forgiven the Elder for telling a four year old child that it was a blessing her mother was dead. Assundra shook herself from the memory – her father was lucky to be alive after attacking the Elder like he had.

When she was still seeing the face smiling back at her when she was nine, she'd thought she was going mad, like her mother had before the end. She'd heard a voice in the wardrobe when she was hiding, too, but she knew neither wood nor mirrors held the dead. The ground did that and even then it held only what was left. If Cairns, with all of the Elders' knowledge, said that death-life wasn't real then it wasn't real.

Simon wouldn't accept that, of course. He kept going on about "ghost memories" and the rest of it. She'd tried to tell him that the fact they both were seeing memories of the past that made their heads hurt proved it had to be something to do with coming of age and nothing sinister, but something about them made her not want to consult the Elders about it as he had suggested. She had asked Galvarin, of course, and he had told her that Ostracians were special, that they carried more with them than just themselves, they carried the blood of Ostracia in their veins.

She had loved him at that moment – he had called her Ostracian, perhaps the first person ever in her life to do so. She'd felt part of the village then, part of him. She smiled – it wouldn't be long before she saw him now.

She had continued to see her mother's eyes for years, until she had smashed the mirror. She remembered crying for days afterwards, because her mother wasn't in any of the other mirrors. She had lost her forever.

She'd had to smash it though. One day when she had looked in to say good morning to her mother, she was greeted only with the slanting, shining red eyes of something…wrong. She'd thrown the shard of metal at the wall without thinking and it had cracked into pieces. Metal didn't crack like that, she knew, she hadn't thrown it that hard. She had just swept the bits up and thrown them in the corner, just as she had seen her father do with the others.

Turning from the brass she knelt before the wardrobe. It was so large she could almost lay down in it, and frequently had as a child. All of her mother's finest clothes hung inside and they were all beautiful to Assundra, if a little fancy for everyday wear. Running a hand on the board underneath the dresses, she found the small depression, so slight you would not know it was there unless you were looking for it, and pushed.

The compartment released with a click and it shot the board upwards with a clatter. Assundra quickly deposited the bronzes in the drawer with the rest of her finds. As large as the wardrobe, the drawer was almost full to bursting, she would have to find a new hiding place soon. There were rings and other trinkets, carvings of both stone and wood that had interested her, some drawings, small nicely painted clay urns, books…yes, Assundra thought, books. The loss of John's catalogue hurt her, she felt like it was a part of him that she had shared, she needed to find the book and get it back, for her collection. For her museum.

She'd read about the museums in one of the books that had come to her through her work. *Large buildings full of memories* was how the writer had described them and Assundra had thought that idea quite magical.

So she had created her own little museum in the drawer. It felt like Ostracian history was slipping away from them as the old town crumbled and it seemed to Assundra like only she and John seemed to care. His catalogue belonged in her museum, she had to find it.

But not today. Today was Galvarin's.

"Deathguard'll be wond'ring where you are!"

Her father's voice boomed around the cottage and she smiled – today was at least a good day for him and that had to make it at least partly good for her. Quickly pressing the board back into place, where it sat flush with the panelling as if it had never been loose, she strode through to the living area, pleased to see her father's eyes smile brightly at her as she walked in.

"Let him wait," she retorted, "there won't have been any deaths anyway." *In any case, I shan't be going*, she thought to herself. Elder Oldershaw had stopped her in the streets last night to tell her she would not been needed tonight, before she had even had a chance to ask Elder Cairns. The Elder had also told her that he'd had "a word" with Young Crafter for her, which had eased her mind, even though she knew it would only last a few days. Nevertheless, she was glad of a day out of the Deathguard's company and glad of a day with Galvarin.

"Come on, Assundra, you don't want to be late."

Her father coughed in the chair. He didn't seem to be losing any weight, at least. Tom Franks, like the Deathguard, intimidated through nothing more than his sheer size. He wasn't that tall, only a little taller than her, but then she was at least a head over the rest of the women in the village. No, it wasn't his height, but he was at least three times the Elder's bulk and Cairns wasn't a small man.

He dominated any space he was in, not that their living space was large. As with her room, the furnishings were sparse – a table, two more three-legged chairs – Assundra having to fetch hers if they ever had guests, which hadn't happened in years – an empty fireplace and a rocking chair that didn't rock, in which her father sat. Heavy cauldrons for washing in hung over the unused hearth, not that they had any soap any more – and a small smoke-fire in under the boards finished off the furnishings.

They did have carpets, tapestries and weavings, though. Assundra had put up an ornate, heavily embroidered, beautiful tapestry around where the washing bucket was. The window it had once hung in must have been huge; it reached all the way from the stone ceiling to the floor with much material to spare. Two more ornate tapestries gave them some privacy from each other and shut off the two little bedrooms that led off from the back of the kitchen from each other. There were no inside doors and the bedrooms were the only other rooms, apart from the 'cellar', which was really no more than a space in the foundations.

The living space was their main room. Their cottage wasn't that different from any other, besides the smoke fire, which the Elders would be very unhappy about should they discover it. Nobody else really cared, they didn't want the Franks family in the alehouse anyway.

"The finest living space for the finest people," Cairns had said. Built from the finest stone of the old town, malleable but heavy. Everyone else had the finest furniture, that hadn't been damaged or destroyed, sparsely furnishing their cottages that were all the same size because of the small amount of the finest stone that was available. The finest paintings, sketches, tapestries and weavings had finished off all the rooms and hid the bare stone walls. Cluttered walls surrounding nearly bare rooms.

Her father had got what was left. He had at least managed to secure enough stone to flag the floor. The outer cottages had resorted to baked mud floors.

She didn't care. She didn't need the finest furniture, or bed; she had the finest collection of clothes there was in Ostracia. Her mother's.

As she looked at her father she reflected, not for the first time, that he looked nothing like her. Where she was dark, in hair and eyes, something she hid whenever she could, he was light, his receding mane of red hair cropped short now to avoid looking foolish, but his green eyes were as young and fiercely bright as they ever were. Where his skin was as white now as in the fiercest winter, hers was now tan; the first flecks of the summer sun having bronzed her as if she were a material for dyeing.

His clothes, such as they were – tatty leather vest over a simple tunic – were not as bright, or as young as they ever were, but then the same could be said for most of the villagers, even Mary Archer who, until Assundra had opened her mother's wardrobe, was considered the best dressed of all Ostracians. She probably still was, but Assundra knew differently. Clothes were passed down in Ostracia; if you left aside the wool sheared from the few sheep they had left there were no means of tailoring any more and none left now who'd have the skill. With the plague, nothing had been wasted and now Ostracians had wardrobes the highest courts in the outside would have been envious of. And still some managed better than others.

In those wardrobes most of the finery stayed, gathering must and dust and it made Assundra sad to think of them. Yes, there was no call for fine ladies' dresses and fancy mens' robes and gowns for the day to day grind of Ostracia, but a bright dress gave a bright face and she was sick of seeing misery everywhere around her.

She hoped she wouldn't bulk out like her father said she was bound to after she passed into age. He said all the Franks' were "big-built" and Assundra had them to thank for her own figure. "Your hair 'n' your eyes, now they're your mother's," he used to tell her, "and your skinny waist 'n' all, I reckon that could only come from her side, but your shoulders, your arms an' your build, them's Frankses!" She'd never asked if the Franks women had the corsetry problems that she had; from her mother's clothes that didn't seem to be a trait than ran in that side of her ancestry. Assundra's development made work for her. She'd been forced to let out most of the bust and hips of her mother's more structured dresses more than once.

"Good child-bearing hips," Alice had described her lower half, always with the same curiously sad expression. Assundra wished she'd paid more attention to how Alice had hemmed the dresses and not run off now; there were still a few of them could do with being let out further before she could wear them and Assundra always seemed to end up with skewed hems.

If she wore them. They were all a little too revealing for the villagers. She was already tired of the men's eager glances when she was wearing nothing more than shifts and her father's shirts; if she survived a day without someone passing some comment on what they'd like to do to her rear end or her bust then she felt she'd done well.

That was all she was trying to do. Survive. She couldn't understand why they all had such a problem with that. When she was on her own with the Deathguard's work she was away from their eyes and words, it had turned out perfectly. She thought it would get better with so many of them burned and in the ground, but it had just got worse.

Sometimes she thought Cairns knew the villagers would act that way and was doing it just to get back at her for something she'd done. It was a memory she couldn't quite grasp, amongst all the others. She remembered shouting and loss, but of what she had no idea. Another ghost memory, as Simon called them, flitting across her mind. It probably didn't matter; it seemed to her like it was a long time ago anyway.

The deep blue coloured dress, pulled tightly over a white petticoat, the one emblazoned in raised brocade, a design she couldn't work out, probably some outsider thing, was a bit showy. In all senses of the word. It was a thick, soft natural fabric that despite its thickness didn't keep her too warm, even in these hot summer months, and no matter how often it was washed, it never wore out, nor lost any colour. The velvet shawl, an even deeper blue than the dress, would hide the brocade in case there were any villagers about.

A little twist of excitement turned itself in her stomach as she forced her smile down, feeling it thrashing against her, eager to get out, to show them how happy she was, despite them. The villagers could look all they wanted, say what they wanted, it was Galvarin, their favourite, that got to touch.

"I saw Oldershaw today, he came round for his usual."

Assundra knew he wasn't talking to get a response, he just wanted to talk, so she just looked up, smiled and raised her eyebrows. It made her eyes look big and inquisitive, even when she wasn't. She'd practised it for when she was with Cairns. "Elder Cairns!" she told herself, shaking her head.

"He said he'd never had a nicer brew than last months that I gave him. You did a right good job there, Assundra, a right good job!" Her father was beaming – he'd always wanted her to follow him into farming.

Despite herself she smiled back, for real, astonished, holding a carrot up in the air foolishly. "A right good job?" she exclaimed.

"Aye, a right good job! He said the tang at the back, past the apple, though he couldn't place it, gave it a real bang! He's had to come round for some Regular from stock to see him through, he's gone through it so fast!"

Assundra tried to cut the knife with the carrot for a few moments before she collected herself. She wasn't surprised her first try at brewing had yielded such a successful result, she'd had the idea of the cinnamon for a while, she couldn't believe nobody had thought of it before, it was so obvious, but why was she was so pleased? She hadn't thought she cared, she'd only done it to keep him happy.

She hadn't wanted to let him down. It would've been a disappointment too far; children were supposed to follow their parents into their trades, or select new ones long before they were of age so they could be trained, but Assundra had never really felt the itch in her soul to be anything. The villagers would have refused to take her on anyway. The offers she got from them had little to do with work. She'd been almost glad when Cairns had forced her into the service of the Deathguard, even though it meant her studies had to be postponed, she wasn't sure they were studies she wanted anyway and it meant she didn't have to disappoint him too much.

But farming was one thing; brewing was another. "It's important to have your first brew under your belt before you come of age," he had grunted one morning in what was his affectionate way, softly but firmly leading her down to his cellar for only the second time. The first time had been when she was a little girl, shortly after her mother had died. She'd gone down to cheer him up because she hadn't seen him for days and Alice West, who'd been looking after her, had told her it was because he was sad. She couldn't remember what had happened, or what she'd said, but she remembered almost being crushed by his bear hug of an embrace. He had come out of the cellar and sent Alice home immediately. He hadn't let her come back

"Why before I come of age?" she'd asked him, as he pushed her down the stone steps he'd crafted himself when he built the cottage, into the blackness.

"Because that's the way of things, Assundra," he had replied, slightly tersely. Assundra had bit her lip at that; it was only the night before he'd told her she asked too many questions. "And it's about time you learned anyway, whether you're coming of age or not."

There had been something about the edge to his voice that she'd found strange, but as he was clearly not keen on answering questions, she hadn't pushed it. They spent the afternoon trying things out, adding everything she could think of to the basic brews and she'd had a much better time than she would have thought before. Her father selected the best of them; an infusion of grape and cinnamon to the "Old Tom" brew. She'd preferred the peppermint and lavender but her father had said it'd poison anyone who drank as much as most of them did. She'd preferred that, too.

"We'll have to make up another batch," Tom said cheerfully. "Just like that, see," he added for good measure, folding his arms and looking wistfully into space. "Just like that and you've got your first loyal trade base! Now when I started only old Oldershaw would take my brews; they said I'd lost everything my Dad had worked for, but you, you've already got them eating out of your hand! Or your cups anyway!"

He roared with laughter at this and she found herself chuckling despite herself as she took a pouch of food she'd prepared earlier tied its string tight. Unhooking the floorboard under which the clay trough was housed, she quickly shoved the pot inside, replacing the board before too much of the smoke from the smouldering stones could escape.

It was "Old Tom" that had saved what little standing in the village Tom Franks had. Not that he would have starved, not in the new Ostracia, there was plenty of food for everyone, even if the meat was usually of suspicious origin these days, but carrying on his father's brewing was worth far too much to him for him to be able to take failure for too long. The villagers hadn't stayed away from his cider because they'd stopped liking the taste. It was because of the woman Tom had married. Her mother. Her father had closed his mind to this; even putting the villagers' absence of help when building their cottage down to their not knowing what to say or that they were too busy. It was usually Assundra though and not her father who had to suffer their dirty looks and snide comments she could only half-hear and even less understand, while her father dragged each block of their cottage from the old town himself and built their home. She'd helped as best she could, not telling her father what they were saying, something she stuck to even today. She'd filled the cracks of the whole of the last wall herself while her father had been off harvesting with the rest of them, helping them out even though they'd left him to fend for himself the whole time. They'd never stopped asking him for things when they wanted them, as if he owed them something.

She'd been so proud when she'd finished the wall; pleased she'd taken a load off her father's mind. It would never have got finished without the help she'd had. Only she couldn't remember who it was that had helped now. But she'd only been six or seven and she couldn't remember much from back then. People had come around to her father eventually, enough to ignore him at any rate, but Assundra could still hear their taunts of "outsider" and "traitor". They only ever said those things to her, never her father. Tom wouldn't understand, he wouldn't hear a word against Nilha Franks. So much so that he'd even tried to convince himself that the traders were staying away because they preferred old Mullard's brews!

Her head hit something hard and she opened her eyes to stare at the ceiling.

"Sunny! It's the boy!"

"Assundra!" Her father came rushing over, his face a picture of concern, but she could barely hear his voice. The other one, the one that made her head swim, was chattering something she couldn't hear properly, something she couldn't make out it was so soft and indistinct, as if it were coming from a long way away. She tried to focus on it, draw it out from inside her head; it was something she wanted to hear, a voice she desperately wanted to hear but every shake from her father shook the voice further away.

"Mullard..."

"What you on about? Gods, you just toppled over... have you been at my stock?" he said loudly, gripping her head slightly too tightly.

"Mullards... family..." she managed to gasp, but she couldn't speak, her breathing wouldn't work properly and she couldn't get the words out. And she really wanted to hear what the voices were trying to say...

The water her father threw over her face seemed to flood her ears, drowning out all traces of the voice. "What did you do that for?"

"You fainted!" he said firmly, grabbing her head with his hands. "I don't think you should work tonight..."

That brought her back to herself. "No, it's ok, I'm fine, really. I thought I remembered... Don't worry. I need the fresh air, it'll do me good."

"Well, I don't call that fresh air, it's not right for a girl if you ask me," he muttered, but he broke off, staring out towards the door.

"What is it?"

Her father's face had frozen like stone and she easily got herself out of his grasp. She stood, smoothing her dress out, hoping there wasn't too much dust on it, not that Galvarin would probably even notice. Tom still stared, crouching, looking at the door as if he were going to pounce and when she turned she saw why.

"That bloody boy's here."

It's the boy!

Simon West stood, looking through the open half of the door, perfectly still apart from his mouth, which was moving around in the way Assundra was only too familiar with, like it did while he thought of something to say.

He always looked at her in what she thought was the strangest way, but this time there was no concern, only puzzlement. "You alright?" he eventually managed to come out with. He never usually spoke in front of her father.

So he'd seen her faint – she just knew he'd be teasing her about that for months! "I'm fine," she replied quickly and rather more sternly than she had intended. Simon didn't seem to notice. He was shifting his attention between her father's poise and Assundra's cleavage, the corseted petticoat having chosen this moment to shift to an unfortunate position. It was always like this when she wore something nice; his never-still eyes flicking this way and that, up and down her body, hands clasped behind his stick-thin body, looking down at her while she thought of something non-provocative and non-insulting to say.

Which she nearly always failed to do.

She hoped it wasn't going to be one of his awkward days. There had been something about being around him that she just didn't like since the fire a few weeks ago, just after Feast Day. The ruddy tint to his otherwise mousy hair seemed redder, the fleck of silver in his blue eyes stronger. That hair of his might have stood a chance of looking good were it not for it's lack of washing, just like all of him really, but then he learned that from his father. Assundra couldn't understand why that family couldn't take care of itself properly – Alice was always well turned out after all.

Not wanting to meet his gaze, she dropped her eyes, which Alice would no doubt have said was "good and proper demurement," something she had often tried to teach Assundra to have, but the only result was that she was looking at Simon's tatty woollen shirt instead. It looked like it was made of straw. That wasn't his fault either, she knew Max didn't approve of grandeur or decoration. The man barely even acknowledged Assundra's existence, except to say that he didn't know why the Elders tolerated dirty outsider whores in their village. Simon had told her his father had said that, thinking it would make her laugh. Gods…

"I need to talk to you."

"Oh *gods*, Simon," she replied. He knew she was meeting Galvarin tonight!

"Get him out of here," her father said, so calmly that it startled her. Normally his reactions to Simon were considerably more violent. Now she looked properly, every part of her father's body seemed tense as he stared, unblinking at the door. "You'd better get out of here too, girl," he added in what was almost a growl.

"Father…"

"Quickly, now…"

"But father," she began, not wanting to go anywhere with Simon, who was now cheerfully holding open the door for her to pass through.

"I said now, Assundra!" Tom roared, standing up quickly and before she could think she was out of the door and walking swiftly towards the village circle with Simon at her side, knocking his hand away as he tried to take her arm, not looking back even when she heard the door slam so violently that she was sure the heavy oak must have cracked.

Her father wasn't better at all. He'd lied. If anything, he was getting worse.

* * * * *

She managed to get rid of Simon quickly, for once, but not before she'd agreed to meet him to talk tomorrow. What the hells he thought he needed to talk to her about, she didn't know, but she'd already been late enough to meet Galvarin.

He was waiting for her, in the middle of the glade as she blustered up to him. He was staring up at a bird in one of the tall trees that was squawking down at him. "Galvarin! Are you alright?"

"Where have you been?" he said harshly, spinning around.

She stopped, startled, the smile frozen on her face. "I'm sorry," she stammered, realising she was out of breath.

About a head taller than Assundra, the mason was an impressive sight. He was well built, you could tell he worked with stone, with hands almost as large in span as her stomach. Hours of labour at his wheels and benches had given him a physique that had earned him several admiring nicknames.

The stubbly growth on his chin gave age to a young face and if it weren't for his breadth, he would have been a typical Ostracian man; a shock of blonde hair that ran to his shoulders, but that, unlike Simon's, was perfectly groomed and tied back today with a golden clasp.

"I've waited for you for almost an hour!" he went on, his voice quietened to a hushed whisper, as if he had just realised people could have followed her, but the anger had not quieted in his eyes.

"I said, I'm sorry, but Simon…"

"Simon again!"

Her eyes widened – she shouldn't have mentioned him. "I didn't mean…"

"I told you to stay away from him, didn't I? I mean it, Assundra, I don't want you near him!" Assundra knew better to talk back and she bit the words back down. He was always less attentive and a bit too rough if he thought she was "going on", as he called it, so she just apologised again instead.

"Well, you're here now, though," he said eventually, his face softening as it usually did if she let him have his head and he held out his hand.

Even as she told herself she was going to stay back and make him come to her after he'd shouted, she found her hand in his and she was rushing forwards, a strong arm pulling her into an embrace. An embrace she needed more than anything. His mouth found hers quickly and Assundra stopped bothering to think about resisting.

CHAPTER 6

Galvarin lay next to her, his exposed chest rising and falling rapidly as he gulped in air, staring up at the sky with the simple smile he always had hanging on his face afterwards.

He hadn't taken no for an answer. He'd found her sobbing in the wardrobe. She didn't know how long she'd been there, so she couldn't tell him when he asked, so he'd made her eat some food, given her some of the powders he liked her to have then brought her here, to their glade, saying it wasn't healthy for her at the cottage.

Assundra had felt safe in his arms, so she'd let him do what he wanted. She hadn't thought she'd wanted to, but she found it took her mind off it too and she was safe here with Galvarin. She was always safe with Galvarin. Already the girl hiding in the wardrobe felt like someone else, someone she didn't know, respect or like. Someone who wasn't her.

The knife lay by his side. He'd never brought one before, yet for some reason he wouldn't let it out of his sight today. Assundra knew there had to be some consequences to what Max had been saying about her, but she hadn't expected Galvarin to take them seriously, indeed he'd assured her he did not. He'd been there when Elder Cairns had said there was no way she could perform sorcery, that you had to learn it, you couldn't just do it.

It didn't stop the villagers believing what Max was saying, though. Her father was gone, Alice thought she was a witch and Galvarin didn't want her to go anywhere near Simon. She had nobody left but the mason. Her heart fluttered when she wondered if he had meant it that way, if it meant he wanted her all to himself. Well, she'd find out today. As long as he didn't think she was a witch it wouldn't matter. Nobody was bringing any charges and they wouldn't as long as the Elder scoffed at the tales.

So why did he have the knife? Then, she wasn't one to talk, she took one wherever she went now.

She smiled as she looked at Galvarin. The wispy stubble on his chin, no longer than how he kept his hair, gave age to a face that was too young for the body it was attached to, years of working with stone stretching his muscles into hardened tools. It was his easy smile and his blue eyes that she gazed upon, however.

She wondered if the smile she forced looked real enough to cover up the fact she felt less than the same sense of satisfaction he clearly did. She didn't want to upset him. As he did nothing but stare up at the sky, she wondered if he'd actually even bothered to notice whether she was smiling or not. It was probably hard to focus when the feeling came over you, she couldn't really blame him. She just wished she could know that feeling then maybe she could share in his happiness more.

Running her tongue around her mouth, Assundra tried to work out and swallow the taste of the powders he had given her. He brought them with him every time, saying they would help her relax, make it better for her. She'd mentioned this to Alice who had agreed, said she used them with Max all the time, but they never seemed to make any difference to Assundra, they just left a bitter, citrus taste in her mouth and gave her a prickly tingle across her chest.

In truth, Assundra hadn't been able to concentrate since she'd got here. It was almost noon now, they'd been here for hours in their little glade and the sun shone down on them as if it approved. The glade was surrounded by large bramble bushes, almost impenetrable apart from the gap her father had shown her all those years ago when he had brought her here. There was just enough space to squeeze through the base between two of the bushes without cutting yourself and inside was the scent and sight of swaying heather, at first seeming improbable in the depths of the forest until the late morning sun swathed the glade in sunlight for a few hours. Assundra thought it rather like the valley beyond Halpse Hill – a strange anomaly, something that should not be but that served a purpose, for generations in her family, her father said.

Every noise from the trees made her eyes jump, unbidden, to seek out the beast. The red eyes. This was the first time she'd left the cottage since Simon had taken her home. Her father hadn't been back since. Elder Cairns had told her not to worry, but it had been days now. She looked over at Galvarin again – thank the gods she had him, she didn't know what she'd do without him.

Assundra wanted him to understand. Before he'd finished wasn't the best time, it never was, when the urge came over him it was as if he had to mount her, like it was all that was on his mind, but sometimes he let her talk afterwards, when he didn't want to sleep and he was wide awake now.

She had to make him understand, but it was so hard to find the words. Words had never been her friend, they were always jumbling about in her mouth and coming out wrong, but this had to be right. He had to understand that they had run out of time.

Her gaze shifted down to her own body and she threw an arm across her breasts as the sun toyed with her glowing skin. It wasn't to protect them, her skin never burned, but since Simon had happened across them here week she had been worried about others seeing. It wasn't so bad now the sun had bronzed her paler parts, her skin had browned everywhere nicely and not in bits, but whilst the sun could pleasure her skin, the pleasure of that skin was to be enjoyed by Galvarin alone. Shifting her body uncomfortably on the heather, she wondered if she would have to get used to this feeling of something not being finished. She was already getting used to the agonised screams for release from her body, and surely that couldn't go on forever? Next time. Maybe next time. She'd hoped it would help, today.

Now his breathing had stilled she knew she had run out of time herself. It was now or never.

"When I was a child," she said softly, gently placing the fingers of her free hand over those on his much larger hand, "my father used to bring me here. He said it was the only place of peace in Ostracia."

Galvarin didn't respond, but she could hear his breathing. A large, fierce looking blackbird watched them from the largest of the beech trees. There was always something watching you in Elspeth Wood, it was one of the reasons people didn't come up here. It was rarely even spoken of in the village; it didn't do to mention the Norths, it upset the Elders, but then everything seemed to upset the Elders.

"Yet he hates it, my father. He says the peace hurts now." Galvarin gave a grunt; this wasn't the type of conversation he'd be interested in. Well, she thought, he'd have to start getting interested. Even if he didn't like talking afterwards, she did, and she had something to say to him. Only she wasn't sure how to say it, so she had to work up to it, but for the first time she wasn't nervous to try.

"I suppose it's because of Elspeth." Galvarin's hand tensed underneath hers. "Oh, don't worry!" she said, rolling over to kiss him on the cheek, draping a leg over his, "I don't think Elder Cairns can hear us all the way out here!"

She rolled back, when he didn't respond, onto the soft, now flattened heather that coated the glade. Their glade. "I don't know why people don't talk about her; if she made a place as beautiful as this, she can't have been all bad."

The bird cocked its head and let out a sharp "caw" as it ruffled its wings, but its eyes never left Assundra. She met the gaze, not sure whether it was actually the bird or her lover that was paying more attention to what she was saying but she forced herself to go on, she wanted to share something with Galvarin, something more than just what his cock wanted.

"I remember when my father brought me up here after my mother died, I thought it wasn't real, that heather couldn't grow under trees. I thought he'd found it somewhere and dug it up, planting it here to try and cheer me up. Make me feel better. When he let go of my hand I remember running off and rolling over and over in the largest crop I could find."

She wriggled in the flattened foliage, the feeling of the crushed heather against her back soothing her. There was a faint scent of lavender to the air, but if it was here then it was hidden under the improbable heather, she couldn't see it anywhere.

"We came here every day for a week, until one day he just walked off, leaving me here." She smiled to herself as she remembered how the feeling of fear at being abandoned had slowly changed as the wood had seemed to coax her into staying, as if it were relaxing there with her while it watched over her. It had taken the role of protector, carer, in her heart until her father had returned. "It was every week after that. He never said where he went, but he had always returned sad. I always guessed it was something to do with my mother. He's never really let me talk about her. He gets upset enough without me going on about it."

She looked over to Galvarin, searching his face for a response, but he just lay there, tensed, not saying a word. She was beginning to enjoy this! Normally she was the one short of words. They had never been her friends; they jumbled up in her mouth and came out wrong or inadequate. Always had done, except with Galvarin. When he wouldn't talk, like this, afterwards, the first few times, she had lain beneath him, quiet and nervous, until he had been ready to go back, but recently she had started talking, even if it what she talked was nonsense. Even now, with this captive audience she doubted she'd been able to find the words to describe how it had felt that first time her father had brought her here. It was nice of Galvarin to let her try. Perhaps she was getting better at it after all and it definitely wouldn't be all nonsense today.

"People say there's things that watch you here. I like that. I know it upsets some people, but it makes me feel safer. Like there's someone watching over me." She smiled at the bird, letting her hand fall from her chest and enjoying the feeling of the sun on her skin again. Let the crow look. The words were flowing freely now; there was nothing to be afraid of. More importantly, it let Galvarin look at what he would be getting. It was definitely the time "It's like when I was small and out in the garden playing with father sitting and watching. I knew I shouldn't have been touching those plants, but I knew he was there and I knew he'd stop me if it got too dangerous, if I tried to eat them or something. It meant I could feel what they were like, so I'd know."

A frown crept over her forehead as she concentrated. "It's funny, I can remember that happening, but I can't remember a thing about what those plants looked like. Do you know what I mean?" Galvarin's face was stony, his eyes wide and he was still tense.

But she pressed on. "When you find something, when you learn what it's like and you learn the rules so that when you feel it again you're ready for it, to embrace it. That feeling. I know what it feels like now and I'm ready for it."

Suddenly she was afraid she shouldn't have said it as Galvarin took his hand from under hers to scratch his nose, but laying it to rest across himself where she couldn't reach it. He didn't say a word. Taking a gulp of air, she moved closer to him, curling her leg around him again and laying her hand on his chest. It was too late to go back now. After what happened in the old town square it was much too late.

The bird cawed more urgently as she forced herself to speak again, to make it clearer. "But it felt like that when I was here, too. I mean, it felt like if any of the bad things the Archer woman goes on about actually happened here, it felt like the wood, the trees and the lovely heather would be there to stop it before it got dangerous. It just...felt like it...like it would keep me safe. So I spent hours, days here, rolling around. We'd play here, there, everywhere, just running around and laughing, so simple."

In a sharp clap of feathers the bird shot up into the sky, startling her. We? "There was someone here with me...all those years ago...there was someone here, I'm sure of it..."

"Got to get back, Assundra." He snatched himself away from under her, shoving her to one side, his face white.

"Get back?" They never did it just *once*!

"Lots to do." His low, smooth voice was level, perfectly calm but he, like the bird, shot up from where he had been laying, his arms flailing, as if determined to keep moving.

"Lots to do...what do you mean? You're the mason, there's no houses being built, what have you got to do?"

He snatched his skins from the ground. "I don't know why you're making such a fuss, this is just a bit of fun. I told you that from the start."

"Told me that from the start? No you didn't!" Assundra sat up, looking up at Galvarin, who despite his pretence of calm avoided meeting her eyes.

"Well...it should have been obvious." Galvarin turned away from her, the sun casting a shadow from his shoulders between them. Her heart thumped, harder than it should, sending a jolt through her that landed in the pit of her stomach.

"I don't understand, I'm telling you I love you!" she cried, reaching out her hand to touch him, breaking the shadow between them. "I'm telling you I need you!"

"Don't' say that!"

She felt like he'd hit her in the gut. "Why? It's true!" she forced out, but it was like he wasn't even listening.

Was this some sort of game? Had she said too much? She knew he'd enjoyed it, he wouldn't have wanted to do it so often if he hadn't! They'd all be jealous, he'd be the envy of the village, surely that would inflate his stupid pride and she knew he liked that!

He jerked his leg away from her hand, pulling his skins on in a fury. "I'm sorry, Assundra, but it's just the way it has to be."

"I know you feel the same!" Assundra bit the tears back. "I need you, Galvarin, you know how much you've changed things for me, I thought that..."

"I'm happy to help," he said, slipping on his sandals and casting his eyes about for his shirt. "It's wrong, what they say about you, I thought that I could help you be more, I don't know, Ostracian. Through me, I guess."

"Through you? You think you're doing me a *favour*?"

He turned to face her. "Well I am, aren't I? Do you think I haven't noticed how some of them acted around you before? It's disgusting the things Young Crafter says, I feel like taking my hammer to his face every time he's anywhere near you, but I can't. What I can do is help you be accepted, involve you."

"And that's why you...that's why we're here?" Her voice felt small and ineffectual. She couldn't get any power behind it. She loved him, why didn't he understand?

He knelt next to her, his eyes drifting down to her breasts. "I know what you're trying to say, Assundra, but things are great as they are, why change them?"

So he didn't understand. She choked back the tears that she knew would just annoy him and strengthened her resolve to try again. "With my father gone, it's like the rules have changed, that's what I was trying to say – I want you to be the one to protect me, Galvarin, I love you!"

"I can't make you mine, Assundra, not now. Not yet," he added, seeing her eyes well up with tears.

A shred of hope trickled through her chest. "You don't want to stop, though?"

He laughed at her, his eyes kind again. "Of course not! I just can't make you mine, Assundra. Not now."

The trickle dried up. "Galvarin, I have to tell you something." She paused, waiting for him to get up and storm off, angry that she wasn't just listening, but he didn't. "The other night, in the town square, when Simon brought me back..."

Galvarin cursed, his expression covered in instant hate. "Not this again, we've been through this! You babbled on about it for the whole journey here, almost put me off!"

"But..."

"I told you to stay away from that little bollock, didn't I?" Galvarin roared down at her, spreading his arms wide. "Well, didn't I? And what do you do, just the opposite of what I told you, now you see why I can't make you mine? You don't know how to do what you're told, Assundra!"

Now it was Assundra's turn to feel her blood quicken with anger. "I didn't go to the old town to see Simon! He followed me, I can't stop him doing that! Anyway, it wasn't him who hurt me it was..."

"I don't want to hear any more about that, you hear? Nonsense about beasts and red eyes, there's nothing of the sort. It's your job, that's the problem. Surrounded by death every day, it ain't right for a girl like you, any girl for that matter, bound to get your fancies going."

"Fancies going?"

"Look, I didn't want to tell you this, but I came to see you when you were asleep. Snuck in your window while I thought your Dad was out, I didn't realise he'd gone, or I'd have come to see you. I saw the marks on your neck, Assundra."

She raised a hand to her neck instantly. "My neck?" she said stupidly, clamping her mouth shut straight away – Simon had told her so many times how annoying it was that she repeated what people said, but she couldn't stop.

Galvarin's face was grim. "I know what you said about the council chambers, but that's just not possible, Assundra. Maybe someone else grabbed you, maybe they didn't, but you've got to admit it's a bit funny if the only other bugger there was Simon and then you come home with bruises round your neck."

Her eyes widened. "No! He didn't..."

"Doesn't matter what we think, Assundra, the Elders are going to sort it out. I put in the charge myself. It's not right, Assundra, it's about time someone was punished for how they treat you."

Assundra felt like she was drunk. "Simon didn't do anything, he saved me!"

Galvarin sighed. "I know you don't want to admit it, but he's had his eyes on you for years, his hands, even, am I wrong? So," he continued when she couldn't answer, "you said he came up behind you at the well, when you saw the beast – that's where he drugged you."

"Drugged me?"

"Of course – that's why you saw what you saw! He drugged you, Assundra, or did something to you, then did the gods alone know what with you, but somehow you fought him off, he retaliated, then panicked when you passed out with his hands round your neck, he probably thought he'd killed you! He nearly as did, for all that."

"No!" she cried, "he wouldn't do that! Simon's…well, he's a bit different, but he'd never hurt me!"

"He's hurt you before!"

"Not like that!" Why was Galvarin saying this? He'd said he believed her, that he'd go back there with her and check, that he'd help her! He'd said that before…

"It's for the Elders to decide now, Assundra." Galvarin pulled on his skins. "Not for us. I'm sorry, but he's had this coming for years. Now, I've got to go, Assundra, and I want this to be the end of it, you hear? The other thing as well."

He had stopped shouting, but he finally looked at her as he spoke, seeing her clutching the shirt. She raised her eyes in hope at him, pleading with him but he ripped the shirt from her and turned his back again.

"Is it my father?" She was afraid, as if whatever fear was prompting that searching, manic look in his eyes was spreading to her, for she couldn't tell why she was afraid. She was afraid, but not upset. That wasn't normal. Or was it? She'd never had a relationship before. What was she afraid of?

She sat there unmoving but feeling like her mind was shaking whilst Galvarin dressed. What was happening? He still wanted her! His eyes strayed over her body as he jerked himself around looking for the pieces of clothing that had become detached in rather a similar hurry.

She clutched on to the possible explanation as it pushed further into her head. She didn't want to speak, not any more, but she didn't want him to go. "I'm not just saying this because he's gone, you know that don't you?"

"Your father!" Galvarin laughed out loud at her, and she felt like crawling back up inside herself. She desperately wished her dress were not six feet away. "By the gods, Assundra, you can be a stupid girl! Your father will come back, where could he have gone?"

Standing, she moved silently to where her dress lay against the tree, her back to him. "I don't know," she said quietly. Galvarin had told her not to talk about the council chambers any more, so she couldn't tell him.

"If I made you mine, you think that would be the end of it? You think that'd stop Young Crafter coming after you and the others fighting over you?"

"You're a coward!" He was right; he couldn't protect her. He didn't have the courage. And she could see now that was the only thing she really needed from him. She just didn't know what she'd done wrong.

"I am no coward!"

"What else do you call a man that runs scared?" she cried, rounding on him. "From his own friends!"

"I am no coward! I am one man, Assundra! I wouldn't stand a chance." His voice caught at the last words, but his manner told a different tale. He was scared, yes, but she could tell there was another reason for this spurning, for his being like this.

"You're one of the strongest men in the village, it's your will that's lacking! That or you're nervous they might actually please me!" He flinched at that, but she didn't care any more. "You won't protect me because you don't want to, don't dress it up like one of your stupid stone rings that nobody wants!"

She thought she saw a flash of genuine concern in his eyes for just a moment before it was gone, but she didn't care now. "You're trying to hurt me because you're upset, I understand that. I think we'd best call it a day now."

"Call it a day?" Assundra couldn't believe what she was hearing. Her head span and she lent back against the tree for support. "You're just going to leave me here?"

"You'll thank me for this one day. I swear to you that better things than me will come along. Better love. You don't want me to make you mine, Assundra, not really."

She was suddenly furious, finding the strength to pull herself away from the tree. "Better love? That wouldn't be hard, would it?"

Galvarin sighed. "I'm sorry. Believe what you want, it doesn't change anything." He turned to leave, his face showing more relief than sorrow, but he stopped as he reached the tree where they had carved their names together, after they had first been together months back. His head was bent as he looked at the marks on the base of the trunk, slight wisps of curly hair flicking against his pale neck. She hadn't noticed how red and blotchy his skin got afterwards until now.

"Forgotten something?" He would get no concern for his feelings from her, not now.

"Take these," he said, taking something from the fold of his trousers and flinging it behind him. "They're the powders I've been giving you, they'll help you feel better. Take them, Assundra and you'll feel better about all this soon, I promise."

"Galvarin?"

"Goodbye, Assundra."

"It's not that," she said, surprised by how hard her voice sounded. "You said you weren't afraid of my father. You should be now."

He didn't even turn his head. She didn't know if he'd even heard her.

Assundra stood for some time, her clothes in her hands, a ladybird making its way slowly across her chest. So that was that. She didn't understand, she'd done everything he'd asked!

Her arms felt light as she lifted them, slipping the petticoat over her head, the ladybird buzzing out of the hem in annoyance at being disturbed. There was a chill to the air. It had come on suddenly as it always did, the trees and bushes assuming a greyer hue in the fading light. Their glade didn't seem the same. Something had left, and before Galvarin. The bird had seen it. She didn't want to be here any more.

Choking back a tear she tried to tell herself she wasn't going to cry over Galvarin Jallel. Tears would solve nothing. He was nothing but a coward and yet he'd seemed so gentle, so loving. He had even told her once of how lucky he felt to lie with someone as beautiful as her and he had meant it, she had seen the truth in him when he said it, not like when Young Crafter and his mob all said it would be an honour, she could almost see their pricks getting hard in their eyes, but Galvarin had meant it. She was sure he had! They had driven him away. Well, she would drive them away!

He had held her hand as they had kissed before, telling her how lovely she looked and there had been warmth, real warmth in his words. That warmth had clearly left him with his seed, leaving him cold and afraid. Perhaps he hadn't meant it; perhaps he could be talked around.

If he couldn't, there would be nothing for her now, it was over. Any hope she had was gone. It had been her one route out, her one route to persuade the villagers she wasn't some outsider witch or criminal bent on destroying them all, her once chance to live. It was gone.

Normally she would rush home now, after they'd finished, but her legs wouldn't move, standing fast in case they wobbled.

After that first time, the glade had welcomed them, "come in, Assundra," it had said to her, calming her when she hadn't been sure. She had lain on the heather and the glade had shared her pleasure, even if that pleasure had not been as great she had expected, as great she'd heard the women talk of it. Now Elspeth Wood was empty. Changed to cold, just like Galvarin.

Assundra felt numb – she didn't know what to do. She wanted to run, but she didn't have the energy. She wanted to cry, but she was determined not to. She wanted to catch up to Galvarin and spin him around, say something right for a change and have him change his mind, whisk her up in his strong arms and tell her he didn't mean it, that he was joking.

But he had meant it. Which made her want to see his guts ripped out and devoured by the wolves.

As Assundra pulled at the things attached to her dress, bits of grass and hard-baked soil, a smile crept onto her face. She remembered how her father had thrown Bryant up against the alehouse wall with just one hand. All the swordsman had done was tell Assundra would develop into a woman fit to grace any man's side and ask to buy her a drink. The entire village had witnessed the results of even an innocent comment like Bryant's and Assundra saw now exactly why he had reacted so.

She could almost hear them whispering. "If Tom would do that for just words, imagine what he'd do if we did something worse!"

Well, they'd find out now. As soon as he came back.

If he came back. He had looked at Assundra differently recently, as if he were trying to forget something about her. Trying to talk to him about it did no good; Tom Franks was not a talker and she didn't know what to say anyway. Several times she had sat next to him at the hearth, resting her head on his knee, but he wouldn't so much as reply to her. It was as if he'd switched off for a while, his reassuring hand on her head letting her know he'd be back soon. It'd been the same after her mother had died, but the look in his eyes now was different. That, too, was cold. Was it her? It had to be! The two people in the village that she loved and she had turned them both cold with her warmth.

Her chest felt tight and she choked back the tears that would help nobody. She doubted this was even the end, Galvarin had raged at her many times before, he always came back when he wanted her again. He would want her again this time, too. Well, this time he wouldn't get it. She thought again of Bryant's frightened, teary face as her father had attacked him. Galvarin wasn't the only option she had. Bryant would protect her. It was that or…Simon.

Assundra shuddered. She knew Galvarin was wrong about Simon. There was no way he would have poisoned her or drugged her. He wouldn't know how, for starters. No, she knew what she had seen in the town square and it wasn't Simon. Simon had saved her from the thing that had killed John. She knew that as clearly as she had felt the hand around her throat, trying to snap it. She had felt the thing's frustration, the fight against something that held its fingers at bay. It had been fighting Simon.

Assundra shuddered again. Nothing could make her lay with Simon. Not even the protection he could offer her. He wouldn't help with the villagers, either, he would make it worse if anything, they hated him as much as they hated her. Could she lay with Bryant? She wrinkled her nose. It wouldn't be any worse than laying with Galvarin. She'd never particularly enjoyed the process anyway.

She had to do something. Maybe Galvarin would change his mind. She should at least try.

"Just wait a little, Sunny."

Nodding to herself, she scrambled through the gap in the bushes. She'd let Galvarin recover for a few days, let him get his seed back, then visit him. She could change his mind.

She'd always been able to change his mind.

CHAPTER 7

His body had quivered into a shiver as soon as he left his cottage, despite the heat. Cairns knew the ceremonial robes had their uses, keeping alive the traditions of Ostracia and the pride in the old ways, but even in the warmth of the summer afternoon there was a bite to the slightest breeze, the plain white cloth seemingly designed to hold the cold air and let all of his body warmth out.

Flicking his hand out, Cairns stilled the blood as it flowed from under the splints and words left him. The blood boiled and fused with the air, sending out a thin cloud of fragrance, something to try and get the stench of the midden pits in the village out of his nostrils. The smell was not that evident here in the Forest, but its remnants seemed to have lodged in Cairns' nose. Cairns had tried for years to find a solution, including scenting the midden pits themselves, but whilst artistry was useful for so many things, none of its effects were permanent.

They scaled the Forest surface as quickly as they could, Cairns following behind Max West and Artis Broadside. The terrain was tricky here, but nothing like in the deeper regions of the Great Forest. There were, nevertheless, a seemingly countless range of rock-filled banks, ravines and shifting earth to be negotiated. This part of the Forest was not tended by the gardeners.

Cairns watched Max closer than Broadside – the man hated the Forest. The vast, sprawling mass of trees, shrubs and untamed undergrowth unnerved most of the villagers, but Cairns had to have Max with him. The man had to be involved. Cairns had long since been forced to allow Max an exemption from his gardening duties as regards the Forest; ostensibly due to the lack of time and manpower available after the plague had struck, but in reality, like most of the villagers, Max was terrified of the darkness between the trees.

As Max trudged ahead of Broadside, not wanting to show any weakness, Cairns reflected not for the first time that the man could pass for a Crafter, which was not a compliment any Ostracian would cherish. Max was as ill-washed and yellow of untamed hair as were all of the last of the old Ostracian Founding Families. That hair also had a twig hanging in its mass that Cairns was sure he had seen there yesterday. Battered, torn leather pants and shirts were all he ever wore, the only concession to his always-immaculate wife's protestations for decency being the cloaks, one of which was permanently hung around his shoulders, today's being a vibrant purple that contrasted sharply with the dull brown of the leather. The unpleasant contrast was nothing out of the ordinary, however.

Broadside grunted as he shifted his bulk forward to stoop forwards on heavy feet. For all they were of a similar age, somewhere in their forties, Broadside was a different animal to Max altogether – if the alchemist was struggling to find meat like the rest of them he certainly didn't show it. He always wore dark, body-covering clothing to hide the sweat – today, a long coat of black velvet, which Cairns thought he must be stifling in. A good two heads taller than Cairns and just as bald, and a good three times as thick around the waist, the man was a walking battering ram and surprisingly nimble for one of his size. He had proved that by winning the annual melee last year. Cairns grimaced at the memory; who could call what was essentially a fight with fists and clubs a melee?

At last, Cairns saw something he recognised as the crested the latest of the rocky hills. There was no official marker, no way of telling it was there, but Cairns could sense the craftsmanship, the artistry used to create the opening and he called a half to Max and Broadside as they were about to walk past.

It wasn't exposed here, as the village circle would have been, but more importantly they would not be observed. This part of the Great Forest was rarely visited, indeed much of it was never visited. The canopy was so closely packed that even in the bright sun of a summer's afternoon, it was shady here, growing ever more gloomy and dank the further into the Forest one went. Small shafts of light radiated through the canopy, making the air itself seem dusty and the smell was of fetid wet soil, even though the ground was bone dry. There was simply too much here – the old pines and oaks stood firm while their younger, more adventurous descendants found trunk-wrenching ways to fold in and around their elder brethren, all the time chased up the bark by mosses who were, in turn, escaping the knee-high undergrowth of shrubs, ferns, fallen branches, years-old dead leaves, all on a rocky bed of sandy, dry soil.

Cairns felt an insect scurry up his leg, reach his inner thigh, then felt the tiny creature sink its jaws into his flesh. In the tiny instant where his blood made contact with its mouth, he felt the creature's surprise turn to consternation as it found its jaws could not let go of what was not an easy meal, as it had thought, but the sickly taste of death. As the luckless insect dropped from his leg, dead, where it was instantly tramped by hundreds of its counterparts, Cairns smiled. The movement round his legs intensified as the insects sensed the death of their comrade but it was unavoidable here if one stood still for more than a minute and they'd been here too long already now.

With a nod from Cairns, Max unhooked the leather satchel he wore across his shoulder and withdrew the handle. It was a small crank handle, grooved and cut at one end to make the key as thick as a finger for the lock and ornately carved with some sort of sea sirens on the handle. Cairns had always dismissed the designs as frivolous decoration, but he supposed that the more irrelevant an object such as this looked, the better.

Max inserted the key part of the handle into one of the four holes in the top of the tree stump. There was no click, no indication that the key fitted, no more evidence of success than if Max had stuck a twig into the hole. The only indication Cairns had that they had the right stump was when Max began to effortlessly turn the handle.

Slowly, very slowly, the tree stump lifted upwards, a low, sandpaper-like grating adding its voice to the rustling of the wind in the trees, eventually revealing deep-cut lines – the grooves of a huge screw. Broadside moved to Max's side and caught the stump just as it was about to topple to the floor. Together the two men lifted the gigantic screw from the earth and with some difficulty and much grunting, laid it to rest as gently as they could next to the hole that the undergrowth was already trying to conceal. The trickling sound of water joined the rustling from the undergrowth and the canopy.

"The powders, my good doctor," Cairns said quietly, the stillness of the place beginning to unnerve him. In the village there was always noise, his people were always around, nearly always demanding something of him, even though there were so few left now, but here it was too still, too quiet. The Forest did its work in secret, it was happening all around him, above him and underneath him and Cairns could not control it.

Cairns suddenly realised Broadside was hesitating. "Is there a problem?" he enquired.

Broadside coughed. "Are you sure about this, Elder?"

"There is no choice. You indicated your readiness, doctor, are the powders prepared?"

"It's just..."

"How many are going to die?"

Cairns turned to look at Max. "None are going to die. Isn't that right, my good doctor?"

The man took one or two quick breaths before answering. In the gloom, Cairns couldn't see, but he would lay a bet that the fat oaf was sweating. "It is quite possible that there will be no…that is, that we shall be lucky. We have never administered such a dose to the people before, it is impossible to tell."

Cairns' eyes narrowed – was the man covering his back or was he telling Cairns that he hadn't perfected the powders as he would have liked? It mattered not. There was no time for another course of action or another session of tedious preparation.

"We have to be quick," he snapped at Broadside, "are the powders ready or not?"

The man hesitated again. This was beginning to make Cairns angry – Broadside and Max had been silent for the entirety of the hour-long walk to this place and they were raising questions now? "Well?" he snapped.

"They are ready, Elder, they are, it's just that…well, we have been giving them only very small doses up until now and you must admit that the results have been mixed."

"It has been several months since there was a plague death, a real plague death," Cairns added carefully, "I would say that is enough time to judge how successful we have been! My good doctor, you have cured the plague! This is not something to hesitate about, it is something to embrace, a day in which to rejoice!"

"Yes, Elder, but…"

"It is far too late to interject with hesitations now, doctor. We have cured our people. This dose will not harm them, I am sure of that."

"But what will they be afterwards?"

It was Cairns' turn to hesitate. He had considered the same thing himself and had only been able to come up with the one answer, which he told them. "Free."

Broadside sighed and bent to pick up the ceramic pot he had carried almost reverentially since they had left through the passage at the back of Cairns' cottage, to make sure none of the villagers had seen.

"You remember the required dose?" Cairns asked, before realising there was no need to ask that question – the man would have gone over the precise dose countless times. Cairns could not still his desire to, nevertheless, make sure.

"Two parts per gallon, by my calculations, Elder."

"Good." Cairns watched curiously as Broadside withdrew a stone, no bigger than the average palm of a hand, from the pot.

Seeing Cairns' puzzlement, Broadside smiled. "I thought this safer, Elder – the stone will dissolve slowly into the source stream, reducing the likelihood of one source becoming more concentrated than another."

Cairns smiled – he should have thought of that himself. "Well done, Broadside," he said, for once, meaning it.

Gingerly, Cairns noticed, Broadside lowered the yellow powdery stone to the hole, never placing more than two fingers on it at one time, until he let it drop. It landed with a dull thud onto the underground stream bed and at once a puff of steam leapt from the hole, coupled with a loud fizz.

"Quick, get the bloody lid back on," the big man squealed and Cairns laughed, watching the two big men lug the piece of wood back onto its housing.

The laugh was cut off in his throat as Cairns thought that it was done, now. There was no turning back, no alternate plans, he was committed. His people would lose their artistry in just a matter of days, perhaps less time. Small doses of Broadside's solution had been placed into the water supply that fed the wells for the past decade. The powder had been perfected in that time, but the early versions had yielded…casualties of war.

The plague would have taken them anyway, Cairns thought to himself, he had long learned to not blame himself for their deaths, but the powders had hastened the process. They had been too strong – both Cairns and Broadside had been too keen. Removing the artistry in the blood all at once was akin to giving them the plague and it was not until Broadside had mixed samples of infected tissue with his powdered solution that the solution for Ostracia had become clear.

Elder Cairns had given his people, each and every one, the plague.

It had been so close to working. They had been so close, so near to success, but then they hadn't stopped dying. Cairns had realised too late that the legends had it wrong. Artistry ran in all Ostracian blood, it was true, but not to similar levels. Whilst some families thrived under their solution, others faded out of existence. Including the family Cairns needed most of all – the family he had foretold would yield the next Gifted One.

"It is done then," Broadside said stiffly.

Cairns had some sympathy for the man – he too felt the guilt and the shame associated with what they had done. He could not offer the alchemist the benefits of the clear sight he had been afforded on the matter that first time he had drunk from Elder Rime. The moment had been almost an epiphany – whilst the Gifted One's birth remained a problem, it was not insurmountable, the solutions were all there in the writings of the rebel Elders and with the village thinned to a few hundred, it would be much easier and quicker to escape the outsiders' clutches.

Ostracia was never to have continued after Cairns' plan was fulfilled. As it was, the strongest of them had survived. Cairns had to think that was for the best. He had to.

"Our work for the night is, unfortunately, not done, my good doctor," he said, scattering showers of insects from his feet as he moved closer to the two men. "We must bring the end to another of our experiments tonight."

Broadside looked tired, even going so far as to suppress a sigh. "Very well, Elder. He will need to be…"

"It is taken care of, I believe." Cairns turned to Max for confirmation and noted the man's curt nod. "Now go, there can be no mistakes."

"Bloody good day for it," Max said needlessly, looking warily over his shoulder as he spoke, as if the Forest was sending the wind out after them. A trip to the Forest was the same to Max as the idea of walking over hot coals.

"You're sure you want to do this tonight?" Broadside mumbled. "Only…"

Cairns turned sharply on him. "You indicated your readiness! Tonight, Doctor! It must be tonight! Do not make me regret placing my trust in you! You know what is at stake."

"Of course, Elder."

Without another word, the man scurried off at a pace Cairns had rarely seen from his great bulk. "I hope he remembers to go back on the correct path," Max murmured, echoing Cairns' own thoughts. Most of the village circle was exposed; the whole area had been cleared of trees and was simply a large expanse of the greenest of grasses, immaculately maintained by Max and his gardeners. With the old town on one side and the Forest surrounding them on all others, the wind was often snatched out of the air by the trees, but here in the open the wind seemed to collect in circles and attack from all sides, following them as he moved.

Broadside would find it impossible to reach his workshop without being seen unless he used the passages. All the cottages in Ostracia doubled as places of what could only loosely be termed trades. Galvarin's workshop, Broadside's laboratory, many other such places of business were all open to the street through the large wooden doors that formed part of each cottage's back wall. Broadside's experiments had even taken the place of street theatre once all the actors had died.

Only there was no trade for the trades to ply. They made only what the village needed – the carpenters repaired houses and dealt in any necessary woodcraft, the mason shaped stone, the gardeners tended to the hungry spread of the Forest that threatened to engulf them, all as the village required. The cobblers paved the streets while someone else caught their meat. Everything worked perfectly in its imperfect incarnation.

Yet they should be so much more. Without artistry, without that which Cairns had been forced to starve his people of, they were no better than outsiders. It was how it had to be if they were to survive – if they were to leave this place – they had to be no more than outsiders, they had to live among them and give away no signs as to their birth. They had to suppress the hunger, the need. It was all necessary. *But Ostracians should be so much more!*

"Come Max, we have work to do." The man just nodded. Cairns doubted he would speak again until they were back on the paths he tended with his own hands.

Cairns didn't understand the fears about the Forest – it was dark and oppressive, perhaps even dangerous, certainly at night, but for purely practical reasons. In the deeper forest, towards the chasm and the Yawning Maw, a wrong footing could send you tumbling down a ravine full of rocks so sharp they would tear your limbs from your body as you fell, but here there was only the dark. For some of his villagers, that seemed to be enough.

The stories of the sightings of death-life on the Forest border with Elspeth Wood had raised their heads again, despite the Withholding Cairns had placed upon them. Strange, misty shapes forming, eyes watching from the trees; the usual nonsense purveyed by those of weak minds. It was no surprise to Cairns that the lead protagonists of these unfounded myths were Young Crafter and the Archer woman, who had been for some time rivals for the role of alehouse 'sage'.

It was another worry for Cairns that the Withholding had failed; things were moving much more quickly than he had anticipated now Simon and Assundra had come of age, more quickly than he had planned.

Too many things were out of his control. Simon's power was growing at a rate Cairns himself was astonished by. Cairns had found himself asking the question if he had done the right thing by inducing such a one as Simon amongst them, in persuading Alice and Max to allow him to alter their son's birth, but the writings had been quite specific – a Gifted One would provide the solution to Ostracia's plight. The rebel Elders had needed a Gifted One to fulfil their plans, which meant Cairns needed one now. Only now, just as then, the Gifted One was proving difficult to contain.

Simon's memories were virtually intact, something which Cairns had not reckoned upon. There was nothing in the writings to suggest that sorcery would have no effect on the most artistically gifted, after all Cairns had successfully placed Withholdings on his own memories, the ones that were of no useful purpose to him, without incident, yet they had all but failed on Simon. "Ghost memories" the boy called them. It was easier to let the boy think he was losing his mind than to invent an elaborate explanation, so that was what Cairns had done.

If Simon were to take the villagers' power, it might be as well the boy was insane. It would make his life easier afterwards. Cairns put a hand to his face where, despite what the others could see, he could feel the torn, withered flesh. Cairns wasn't powerful enough to Draw just artistry, he needed blood, it would mean their deaths, but Simon…well, there was a chance.

In a short time, he and Max had reached the crossroads, the paths that led back to the village, to Elspeth Wood and the one they were to take, to Halpse Hill.

Sensing movement by his side, he turned to see Max wrench a sapling from the earth in one quick movement, a look of peace finally on the man's face. "A hand span," the man said, almost in awe, "a hand span grown in just one day."

Cairns pursed his lips. "Then it is accelerating again. Organise another sweep of the village tomorrow, Max, we need not stoke any fear."

Max's expression turned serious. "If this continues Elder…"

Cairns nodded, placing a hand on Max's arm. "We will be gone before it happens, Max. The Forest will not claim us."

Max raised an eyebrow and pocketed the sapling, breaking its stem in two before he did so. "It only took a few weeks to claim Septar and that were at a growth slower than this," the man said almost reverentially. "The old trees stretched to take the foundations, then the saplings rooted in the cracks, the buildings were rubble. In just weeks, Elder."

"I know Max," Cairns said in the most soothing voice he could muster, "but those were untended settlements. Ostracia houses hundreds of people. The Forest will not weed us out as easily as they took Septar, Nemar and the others. Besides, our gardeners are ready for it, are they not?"

Cairns sucked in the clear late afternoon air, marvelling as he always did at the beauty of the village he had created. A haven in the middle of a storm of misery, somewhere they could feel safe. No Forest, however it was created, was going to encroach on his creation.

"Ain't no natural growth, Elder. No Forest I know, even this one has ever grown like this. It's since they came. Them in the darkness." Cairns eyed Max suspiciously. "It's not right, that Forest, Elder, something's leaking into it that shouldn't be! Sooner we leave this place the better."

Cairns winced as that clear late afternoon air bit suddenly into his lungs. He wondered if that was what Ostracians had come to – terrified of their own nature. Artistry was nothing to fear, it was part of them, part of their land!

Gods, he needed a powder. Which meant he had to get rid of Max for a while. No. He'd just have to manage as best he could and hope there wasn't a struggle.

"There is nothing in the Forest but the darkness created by the close canopy, Max," Cairns said, trying to keep the annoyance from his voice. "There are no spectres, nothing unnatural and the Forest itself certainly does not possess artistry. Artistry comes from blood, from that which can bleed and the trees do not bleed."

"It does for now."

Cairns shot a sharp look at Max, but the man's head was once more turned to the floor, any dissention apparently passed, if it had even been dissention. All he had spoken was little but fact after all.

"Come, we have much to do," he said and set off, Max following behind as he always did. Elder Cairns normally detested that – Ostracians were equal, there was no need for Max to walk some paces behind, but today he was glad of it. If the man was going to prattle a lot of childish nonsense about the Forest intentionally swallowing up Ostracia then Cairns saw no need to listen.

The path up to Halpse Hill was comparatively clear and wide, as it weaved through the borders of the Forest, but even so few trod this route. The light was dimmed here, but the ruffling of the laurel and apple trees against their taller pine, oak and ash brothers contrasted deeply with the grating stillness of the Great Forest. Unlike the spare calm of Elspeth Wood, in its young, century-old ordered planting of pine and evergreen and its delicate picturesque running streams, this was where the Forest began to grow wild, always seeming to Cairns to be alive, for all its absence of wildlife. There was the odd beetle, a few lizards scurrying up the bark, but the birds and animals, even the insects that had tried to make Cairns their evening meal kept to the Great Forest.

The hill was not far from the village, a mile at the most, and they were soon nearing the climb. It wasn't really a hill at all, merely a rise leading to an outcrop, but the climb was fairly steep. Cairns pushed his legs on, beginning to pant already, ignoring the easy-breathed whistling of his companion behind. His weakness disgusted him. He could hear Elder Hugo jeering at him now from the grave. Laughing at him. That would never change, Cairns had made peace with that. It was the past and the past held no power.

As the ground inclined, the rocks grew more plentiful, a reminder that they were moving back towards the Great Forest, with its series of heavy outcrops, ravines, uneven ground and dense undergrowth. A wind rose and turned the rustle of the canopy into what seemed like a shaking warning, but Cairns had no such fancies as to be put off by a breeze. There was no path up to the top of the outcrop and Cairns was forced to expend more effort reaching the top, stretching from boulder to boulder, using the hanging trees as support, though they felt brittle in his hands. He cursed himself again – there would be no rest, even after tonight, this was all just the beginning.

Eventually the incline ceased and they were at the top. Cairns grimaced when he saw they were not alone.

"Tom, you bollock help us!" Max cried, rushing past Cairns with large strides and hauling himself up to the plateau, before lowering a hand to Cairns, making him scowl again.

Cairns forced himself to thank Max as he forced himself to get his breath back, ignoring the stream of obscenities that poured forth from Max in Tom's direction. The farmer didn't even turn, keeping his back to them. It was as if he were not even listening, he just stood, staring over the outcrop. Cairns had never seen the valley of flowers at close hand, only ever from this vantage point. There was no way down the sharp, overhanging precipice at the edge of which Tom stood, the bright circle of the sun ahead defying one to look anywhere but at the magnificence below. The only way to the valley itself was through the Great Forest and the route had never been found. Cairns himself had tried many times, even scouting with a bird beforehand, but somehow, when he was in the Forest, the climbs, the outcrops, the ravines, the valleys, the dense undergrowth up to the waist in parts, the slime, the mud and the pungent smell of soil deterred him each time before he could make enough progress.

The valley beyond Halpse Hill was an astonishing feat of nature. In a clearing, some thirty feet below them, was a sea of colour – of purple bells, white hearts, yellow sunbursts, pink spiky balls, bright blue hearts, with thin red fingers pushing through between them. The gardeners did not tend here, this was pure, this was simple, this was what his people should be – vibrant, independent and free, their magic intertwining as the beauty of the flowers below, leaving no space uncovered, nowhere for the eye to look but at their beauty and pride, a power in itself. A pleasant aroma of spring, despite the depths of summer, rose from the valley, giving the air a sweet taste. If Cairns looked closely he could see the insects buzzing around, as the outsiders should buzz around the wonder of Ostracian artistry.

A pang wrenched Cairns' slowly beating heart – none would buzz around Ostracian artistry again. He had ended that. Suddenly sick, Cairns stopped himself speaking before he could start. *It is all necessary. All of it.*

Whilst the mass of colour could well take the breath away, but Cairns had not before heard of it taking the ears away. Eventually Max gave up shouting at Tom, turning away and muttering curses to himself. Cairns noted that not once during the volley of abuse had Max stepped closer to Tom Franks.

"Tom, it is time," Cairns said, showing a hand to Max to encourage his silence. As ever, his gesture was obeyed. "Events have forced us to move faster than we would have liked, that business with the wolf and Assundra…"

"Did you put my daughter in danger, Cairns?"

The voice was soft, but there was an edge to it. Tom Franks had never referred to the Elder by his proper title in private, nor in public and now the lack of respect brought another volley of abuse from Max.

"I did not, Tom," Cairns replied, matching the tone of his voice with Tom's and once again motioning Max to silence. It was necessary to bring Max to this meeting to ensure his cooperation, but Cairns deeply wished it were otherwise. The man was such a boor. "It was a lone, dying wolf, it presented no danger to your daughter. Bryant dealt with the beast in minutes, he is even now dining out on the experience, or drinking out at the least!"

Cairns laughed, but the laugh was not returned.

"I hope you don't bring the wolves down on us with your noise, Cairns."

Cairns pursed his lips. "And I hope for the same thing for you, Tom! Lest you forget there is only one of us here who can communicate with the beasts!"

Tom turned to face them at that and Cairns saw the full force of the changes that were upon him. No wonder he had not rushed from his cottage to help his daughter as Cairns had expected! The man's nose had been stretched across his face, hair was sprouting up to nearly his eyeballs, but it was those eyes that drew pause from Cairns. The pupils had swallowed up the iris and spread to almost the corners of the eyeball, leaving a huge black oval surrounded by a thin line of white in each socket.

"Do you know," Tom said with a sneer, "that wolves don't see colour? I didn't know that. I look at that valley below and I know what it should look like, I know what it looked like when I brought Nilha here to make her mine. I remember the colours, the shapes. Now all I see is a grey mass. All I can smell is rank soil. All I can hear is blood, your blood pumping in your veins, Cairns, and I want to tear it out of you."

Cairns curled his fists into his palms, ignoring the pain as the splints pierced his skin. He knew full well what Tom meant – the pull of blood, the throbbing veins of the weak, ready for him to gorge upon, they were made for it, all of them, fodder to be chosen, hunted and fed on, their delicious, sweet, hot sickly blood made to flow down the throat...

He said words, ignoring the smile that played across Tom's face. Ignoring the man's long teeth.

"I thought you might know. Disgusts you, doesn't it?"

Cairns suppressed a chuckle – it did anything but. "Yes," he lied, forcing the splints further into his palms and he spoke more words inside himself. Slowly, the hunger dropped, as his blood surged back to his heart. His head began to feel heavy and thick and his mouth filled with the taste of nothing. Out of the corner of his eye he saw Max spit, confused.

"I don't care if it begins tonight or not," Tom went on. "It doesn't affect me. I'll do what I do when you tell me to do it, I don't want any part of your plans."

"You want your daughter to be free, do you not?"

"What you're doing to her..."

"Is necessary for the survival of our race!" Cairns found himself crying, releasing the splints from his hands and enjoying the slow trickle of blood that followed. "We cannot just leave, there has to be some hope of a pure Ostracian line!"

Max snorted at this, but stopped himself speaking when Cairns rounded on him. "There is no other, Max!"

"Every time I see Galvarin Jallel I think about what it would look like for you if I tore his throat out in the middle of the village circle," Tom said calmly, almost wistfully.

"Your daughter is lucky to be alive, Tom," Cairns said, forcing his voice to be calm once more, feeling some of the pressure leave his head. "For her crimes I could easily have had her executed, but I showed mercy, at your request."

"Been paying for it ever since."

"That is why we are in the positions we are in! Because we have sacrificed what we love for our people! Max has sacrificed his child in no less a fashion than you have, Tom, do not forget that. You would think it would present the two of you with some common ground! Yet you squabble and bicker, and challenge me when you know what is at stake, when you know what we *must* do to save our people!"

Both men were silent and Cairns realised his voice had risen to a hoarse scream. He was losing control more and more. It had been too long since he last Drew, he would have to pay a visit to the Transept Tower, to his stock, to his Rime, soon or find someone else. There was a ready made replacement in Young Crafter after his antics in the past few days, but Cairns could just not bring himself to feed on a Crafter.

As if reading his mind, Tom spoke again. "What about Young Crafter? I hear he was trying to round up a mob last night. My daughter came home very upset. I hear Young Crafter…"

"Elder Oldershaw has spoken to Young Crafter," Cairns interrupted quickly. "There will be no more…"

"He's not planning to put his hands on my daughter, Cairns," Tom replied, interrupting in turn, "he's planning to kidnap her."

Cairns frowned. "Why would he do that?"

"I'm telling you to find out."

Pursing his lips, Cairns took a step forward, but stopped as Tom immediately squared up. "Look, Tom, I have given you my word that nothing will happen to Assundra as long as you cooperate, haven't I? And has anything happened to her?"

"She's scared out of her…"

"Has anything happened to her?"

Tom was silent for a moment. "No," he ended up agreeing, as Cairns knew he would have to.

"Galvarin, Bryant and the rest are keeping an eye on her, don't worry, Tom." Cairns tried to keep his voice calm, aware of something inside him desperately wanting to strike Tom Franks. The man was wrong, Cairns' whole body sensed it. Then an idea came to him that was so brilliantly simple he wondered why he hadn't thought of it before. "Max, will you do me a favour?"

"Of course, Elder," the man replied quickly.

Elder Cairns smiled. "Will you get one of your men to tell Young Crafter that Assundra has been asked by your wife to gather some herbs in the Forest tonight?"

Tom turned slowly to Cairns, his mouth twisted into a horrible sneer.

"Elder, I don't think…"

"Just do it, Max." The gardener gave a curt nod. It was so simple! With Tom's final dose being given tonight, Young Crafter and his clan would stand no chance! As it slowly purged the remaining human from Tom's blood, the wolf would take over and if it looked like Young Crafter and his friends were torn apart by wolves, Old Crafter would have no grounds for complaint!

Elder Cairns smiled – he had just rid himself of two problems at once!

"That'll do for now, Cairns," Tom snarled, "but what about Simon and Galvarin? What happens to them afterwards?"

"They're nothing to do with you, either of 'em!" Max spat at Tom, "so just leave it be. You have your instructions, the only reason we're here is to give 'em to you, so why don't you be a good dog and do as you're told?"

A loud howl, a deep, long, echoing call sounded from below the outcrop, somewhere close. Max yelped before he could collect himself and Tom smiled, showing those teeth again. Cairns reflected that Broadside really had done a marvellous job.

If all went to plan, after tonight, artistry would begin to cease to flow in their blood for good. If his plan did not work, it would be the end of Ostracia.

They would all die.

The young would be first, with the others following possibly a mere few hours later.

Another wolf call sounded in the distance. Tom stood, his eyes directed right at Cairns, not moving a muscle, seeming to not even breathe. As a third howl sounded, the Forest became a cacophony of wolves. Slowly, as if he were raising his hands in supplication, Tom leaned back and *howled*!

At once, the sounds from the Forest ceased, but Tom's call went on, his fists clenching and unclenching, his body throwing itself backwards in obvious torment, and still the call sounded, only ceasing when the man had no more breath to propel it and he sank to his knees, sobbing.

Cairns walked close to Tom and leant down to put a hand on the farmer's head. "You know you are the one I trust, you know what to do," he whispered, so Max could not hear. "Do not make me regret placing that trust in you. For your daughter's sake."

He had watched Bryant baying to the crowd about how he'd scared all the wolves off. He had seen their jubilation, their pride in such a simple act. He smiled. It was all going to go to plan. It had to. It would work!

"Max, let's go."

Cairns drew his hand away as Tom began to laugh. A sharp, high-pitched, whining laugh that was only just human. Max was already halfway down the slope leading down from the outcrop before Cairns had reached the top.

Tom's raised voice stopped him.

"I'll do what you ask, Cairns!" he roared and as Cairns turned, he saw the man crouching, arms outspread, hands curled. "I'll do everything you ask, for her!" Tom howled again, but the sound was cut off abruptly by a sharp crack as the man's jawbone tore itself in two.

As the screams flew on the wind through the Forest around Halpse Hill, Cairns slid down the slop as quickly as he could.

"After this is done, Cairns! After this is done I'm coming for youuuuuu!"

Max was nowhere to be seen when Cairns descended the slope. It had been unwise bringing him here after all, he did not need Max to lose his nerve tonight of all nights! As the broken screams began again, Cairns felt for a powder and let the pinch dissolve on his tongue.

This will be the last time he told himself. And it would –after tonight he would have no need of them any more.

Cairns just hoped that Broadside had kept the antidote for Tom. Assundra's worst nightmares, both of them, were about to come true, she would need her father after all this was over.

The screams were all around him as the powders took, his vision cleared, his ears pricked and he heard the screams for what they were, the torment of an inferior animal. Cairns broke into a run, hoping to beat Max back to the village, his mind racing too, about how he would save them, how he would set them free, how they would sing his name to their children, their Ostracian children born in outsider towns, right under their noses.

And when he thought about how Young Crafter and his cronies would sleep in the Forest when they heard Tom's howls he laughed.

CHAPTER 8

The streets of the old town were thickly dark, without even shadow. The sound of her breath catching in her throat, the girlish whimpers that accompanied each resultant sharp intake of that breath, would have given away her position every step of the way, had there been anyone to hear.

Her father had disappeared. Which was impossible! She'd followed him all the way to the barrow, making sure to keep her distance, but he had broken into a run when she'd fallen at the barrow. She'd got scared. She didn't know why. It was always dark when she laid her charges to rest in the barrow, in amongst the coffins and tombs, she did not fear them then, so why after nightfall?

After her father had bolted, Assundra had wasted no time in getting to the old city square. She'd managed to keep her father just in sight, just catching his heels each time he dashed around a corner, but she never caught him.

He'd been disappearing every so often and he'd be out all night. It wasn't regular, there was no pattern to when he'd be gone, but when she'd asked about it her father had told her she was dreaming, that he hadn't gone anywhere.

So she'd decided to follow him, although he had left so quietly and so quickly that she'd barely had time to pull a shawl about her before she set out after him.

Galvarin had said it was a bad idea. "I forbid it, Assundra!" was all he would say when she had what he called the cheek to ask him for a reason. Part of her wanted to say to the hells with Galvarin, she could go where she liked and do what she liked, there were no restrictions on her time or behaviour, not yet, not until he made her his, but then a larger part of her told her to not rock the boat, not to anger him. If she wanted him to make her his then she would have to please him, like she did when she laid with him.

Yet the smaller, rebellious part of her had won out, and now her brain was screaming at her heart to turn back. She felt as if her skin were being pulled away, pulled backwards, as if her body were trying to snatch her away from the old city itself before she could do any harm.

"Too late now," she told her body quietly, trying to keep the panting that had replaced her breathing as inaudible as she could, having already found that there was no way to stop it, no matter how many deep breaths she forced herself to take.

The city square was bathed in moonlight and everything was still. Where could her father have gone? He would have entered the city square from the North Street, only a few seconds before her, yet the square was empty. There was no sign anyone had been here in days, let a long a few seconds before her.

She kept thinking about John.

"Just the city square, that's all. Then I'll be done," John had said.

Well, she thought, he was done now, dumped in the barrow, in a Crafter's recess. Assundra had wondered since that night if she had done the right thing and had contemplated moving John to a nicer plot, in her darker moments considering that the plague pit was a nicer plot than a Crafter's, but something about moving him now didn't seem right.

The Deathguard would laugh at her for that – she could almost hear him now – "wheel him down the street arse-bare naked in a cart, stick him in a hole to rot and you're worried about offending his honour?"

John had been killed here, without honour. Her breathing quickened again – what if that happened to her father? What if the Deathguard had been waiting for her father? What if that was why she couldn't see or hear him?

But if that was the case, where were they?

She forced her legs into action, fearing she'd stay there all night where she felt she was hidden if she did not. She'd been watching for long enough, there wasn't anything to fear. She would just have to search until she found him.

The four buildings of the old square. Assundra wondered where she should start.

The church was a pile of rubble, she would have heard if her father had gone in there.

"No."

Shaking her head, she ignored the voice. Why was it always stronger here, when she was in the old town? "Because of the well, you stupid girl," she told herself, avoiding looking at the place she had been held prisoner. It was always worse when she was around where bad things had happened to her.

Assundra slowly, quietly, moved past the skeleton of the church, turning her head in to look, avoiding the well. She felt as if it were looking at her. Her spine prickled and she knew then that she was going to look.

"It has no power, Sunny."

Her head was suddenly fuzzy. The mouth of the well was suddenly yawning up at her, its black, intimidating darkness all she could see, but surely she hadn't moved? A cry escaped her lips as she heard something crack against the bucket far below. She put her hands out just in time, as the mouth of the well threatened to swallow her and they found the wall. Another cry coughed itself from her mouth before she could stop it and the echo from the depths of the well sounded back a scream of its own, turning to laughter as it faded. Forcing her feet, which were off the ground, into the side of the well, she hauled herself back from the mouth of the well, slumping backwards to the ground, exactly where she had been tossed a few days before when the Deathguard had saved her.

She was unable to breathe and her head swam. How the hells had she got to the well? She was right next to it. Her mouth fell open – she had no memory of moving from the church to the well, what was happening? Her heart started to beat faster again and her breath finally forced itself out of her, though drawing it back in was painful.

Assundra looked at the well hard. The little housing for the pulley cracked, making her jump. The pulley… the pulley that held the rope.

The rope she'd cut.

The rope that was now hanging intact, thick and strong.

The pulley housing cracked again, louder this time and a scream forced itself out of her again, seeming quite small and useless against the echo, but it would not stop. She kept on screaming as the pulley started to turn, pulling the rope up as it tightened. Her scream turned to a hoarse bite in the back of her throat as the pulley span faster, the handle turning on its own, pulling the rope, pulling the bucket up, faster, squealing and cracking as it did until with a clatter the bucket shot from the well, crashing into the pulley housing.

Assundra had nothing left to scream with and her breath wouldn't come. She couldn't move her legs to get away, she couldn't do anything, only watch as the well housing cracked again, even louder this time, but differently, the crack turning to a split as the housing followed the empty bucket down the well with a horrible splintering, tearing sound and the world started to spin. She felt the stone on her hands before she felt her head hit…

…the church wall.

All was quiet. Just as quiet as it had been before she'd found herself at the well. The well which was now fifty feet away from her, across the city square.

Spinning, she forced the urge to be sick down, not that she'd eaten anything all day for her to be sick with. The well was intact, its housing intact. The end of the rope swung gently, frayed where she'd cut it a few days ago. Slowly, she walked towards the well.

She couldn't hear her own footfalls on the stone flagging. She couldn't hear anything. The torn rope didn't still in its movement, swaying from side to side, as if it were pointing down into the well. The city square seemed larger than it had been before. Was she getting any nearer? It was still so far away, surely the city square wasn't that large? She glanced quickly at her feet to make sure she was moving and the stone flagging passed as she took the step. She was definitely moving.

As she looked up she screamed again. She was right on top of the well, once more teetering on the lip, her head tipping. She scrabbled out with her hands, trying to catch hold of the side of the well, but she was overbalanced – but how the hells had she got there? She had been at least twenty feet away, what was happening?

She tried to catch her balance with her feet again, but this time they couldn't find any purchase. Her head wouldn't balance right on her shoulders, she couldn't tell where it and her body was, only that the well mouth loomed up in front of her, eager to swallow her back, take her back to its depths where she should never have escaped from.

Then the well blinked at her.

Her breath froze in her throat. Somehow she balanced on her stomach on the edge of the well. There was still no sound. There was only the well and, now, the eyes. Blinking red eyes. They were the eyes she'd seen in the brass, the eyes they talked about in Elspeth Wood, they were here, they were with her.

She tried to pull herself back, but she couldn't move, nor could she look away as the eyes focused on her, narrowing, almost as if they were smiling, then something lunged, from the depths of the well, the eyes bobbing as powerful limbs drew it upwards, bounding up the well and Assundra saw the flash of red in its throat as its mouth opened wide, gods, it was close, but she couldn't move, she couldn't do anything! It was almost on her, faster now, pulling itself up the well towards her, its mouth a bare red maw amidst the blackness, she could make out nothing else, hear nothing at all, she could just see the mouth and those eyes, those hatred-filled eyes, burning into her, almost on her…

"Assundra!"

She was jerked back, something catching her before she hit the ground and she kicked out, closing her eyes. She screamed, throwing punches, tearing at the thing that held her with her nails and she heard it scream and curse her…

Heard it scream?

She felt herself pushed back hard against a wall and she opened her eyes. Her mouth filled with the taste of…nothing…a complete absence of taste, as if there were a numbness coating her tongue and she spat, instinctively.

"What was that for, you mad bitch?"

Simon West stood about ten feet away from her, three large red deep welts torn across his face.

"Simon?" she called out softly. Was it him? Was this just another trick her mind was playing on her?

"Of course it's me, you bollock, what the hells is going on? I heard you screaming..."

"The well..."

She stared past Simon to where the well was. It was just like a few minutes before. The rope softly swaying, pointing into the blackness. Assundra didn't move, pressing herself against the wall.

"Someone's cut the rope," Simon said, turning towards the well."

"Don't go!" she wanted to shout, but she didn't. She didn't say anything, she didn't do anything. She let him walk. She let him walk across to the well, let him put his head over the side. She wanted it to get him. Not her. It could have Simon.

"Yeah, someone's cut it right through," he called to her, fingering the frayed ends of the rope.

It wouldn't be long now, she thought. It would be running up the well, underneath his nose, where he couldn't see it, then it would get him, not her, then she could run. Get away from this place. This wasn't a place to come after dark, her body had been right, she should have run when she'd had the chance. Now she'd woken something up and she'd seen hunger in its eyes. Just a bit longer, just a bit more, then it would have Simon, then she could go...

She watched Simon turn his head to the well, his hand still holding the rope. For a minute he stopped, standing still, staring into the well. Assundra held her breath, but couldn't turn away – this would be it. He'd seen it and it had seen Simon. She'd be able to get away soon, when it got him.

"Can't see the bucket," he called. She blinked. "Must have fallen to the bottom. Shame, that. Carp's brother's dead, just heard it tonight. With Carp's hand bad, he was the last carpenter we had, won't be able to make another bucket."

Simon pushed himself away from the well and walked towards her. She didn't understand.

"Look, Assundra, what's going on?" he said, nearing her.

She shrank back to the wall. "Don't come any closer!" she cried. If the thing in the well hadn't got Simon, then...well, something had come out of the well and grabbed her and now Simon had cuts on his face... what was it the voice had said, "it's the boy?"

"What did you do to me?" she managed to gasp. She was pressed right against the remains of the church wall, Simon a few feet away. Whichever way she chose to run he'd catch up with her.

He was frowning at her. "I didn't do anything to you except save your life, you ungrateful bitch! What were you doing bent over the well anyway, trying to kill yourself?"

Assundra felt for the fold in her dress and pulled out the knife. She watched Simon's eyes flick towards the blade, confused. Well, he wouldn't be confused in a moment. Assundra was sick of being attacked, sick of people forcing themselves on her, or trying to. She'd send them a message. She'd send them a message with Simon and if Young Crafter didn't get that message she'd send him one personally.

"Was it you who cut the rope?" Simon asked, his mouth curling into a smile. "I knew you hadn't lost all your fight, I thought you'd gone all soft since Galvarin…"

He stopped mid-sentence as she lunged at him, but she knew all too soon that she'd miscalculated. He didn't even need to step back, the swing she took didn't get anywhere near him and she overbalanced, falling to the flagging, the knife spinning out of her hand.

Her arms were pulled behind her instantly and she started to scream again, tears filling her eyes, and she kicked back, driving her heel into his shin and now it was him screaming and he let her go. She ran for where she could see the knife, scooping it up and turning around, blade poised, waiting for him to attack.

He just stood there, rubbing his shin, a confused look on his face. "What's wrong with you?" he cried, but now he wasn't angry. His voice sounded hurt. "What have I done? I only came up here to see if you were alright!"

"I saw you in the well!" she cried, pointing with the knife. "What did you do to your eyes?"

"My eyes?"

"Yes, your eyes!" she screamed, the world seeming to vibrate with her anger. Why were people so *stupid* that they couldn't understand her? "They were all red! In *there*!"

The look of hurt vanished from Simon's face. "You saw red eyes? In the well?"

"You know I did, I saw you!"

"It wasn't me, Assundra. I pulled you from the well, you were toppling over the side, you were going to fall, I pulled you back."

"I don't believe you!"

Simon laughed. "Assundra, how the hells would I run up the side of a well? Answer me that!"

She didn't say anything. The knife wouldn't stay still in her hand. She tried to keep the point in line with his face, but it kept moving about, wavering. Something had tried to attack her. Something had tried to take her, and then Simon had been there. It had to have been him in the well. She wasn't wrong about this, not again.

"This isn't the first time, is it? The first time you've seen them, I mean."

"Shut up!"

"Red eyes?" he went on, taking a step towards her.

"Stay back or I'll cut you!" she screamed, but Simon didn't stop.

"Sunny, it's the boy! It's the boy!"

"I knew it! You said I was imagining it, but I'm not, am I? They're coming back for you too aren't they?"

"Coming back?" She pulled her shawl tighter about herself, before becoming conscious that the act pushed her chest together. She looked away in disgust as Simon licked his lips.

"Ghost memories!" he said, focusing on her face again. "Things you can't remember remembering? Cairns says…"

"*Elder* Cairns!" she chided in a whisper, out of habit, but she began backing away from him slowly.

"*Cairns* says it's just ancestral Ostracian memories, or something, things all Ostracians get when they come of age, but I think he's lying."

"Lying? What are you talking about? How in the hells do you know all this Simon, or are you just making it up?"

Oh gods, he wasn't trying to make some sort of connection with her again, was he? She could tell from his wide eyes and that smile, the one that said 'I'm just like you, see, there's no reason for us not to be together'. His mother had told him the best way to get to know Assundra was to show her that they had things in common. Simon, being Simon, had told her she'd said it.

"I told you last week," he said impatiently. "I've remembered things too. Heard things."

"Heard things?" Assundra shook her head – she wasn't going to have that conversation again. "I haven't heard anything."

"I don't believe you," he said, his face proud as if it should matter to her what he thought.

"Nobody asked you if you did." She kept backing away, but he was following now.

"This is important! It has to be!" She sped up. "Look," he went on, matching her pace "I think we should talk about this properly, I'm trying to help you, I don't know what from, but I think something's wrong, something to do with last week…"

"Elder Cairns told you not to talk about it," she said quickly, swatting his hand away again.

"I need to talk about it! Please, Assundra, something's happening to me, and I think the same thing might be happening to you!" She clenched her teeth as his voice developed the whine she'd grown too familiar with. It was how he got before he got angry. "I've heard…"

"It's called growing up, Simon! Just get used to it and *keep your hands away from me*!" She didn't know why, but he was scaring her again. There was a faint taste of nothing in the air.

"What have I done to make you so angry with me?" he screamed at her. "Ever since you've been with that bollock Galvarin you've shut me out! Me, my mum, everyone! What's the matter with you? We've all tried to help you…"

"Help me with what?" she cried back, waving the knife at him, making him step back. That made her feel good. "The last time Young Crafter tried to get me the only help you gave me was to get beaten up!"

"Assundra look, you have a life outside of Galvarin! That's all I'm saying!"

"Life outside of Galvarin?" she laughed, but felt tears spring in her eyes as she did so. "What life? A life of being chased, grabbed and used by Young Crafter? Galvarin is the only one who can make that stop!"

"What makes you think things are going to be different after…"

"Because to touch another man's wife means a charge of death! They'd never dare!" Assundra became aware she was panting again, but she couldn't stop. Her head started to feel light again.

Simon was quiet at that. "I could do that for you, protect you. You know I could, if that's what it's about. I could make you mine, I could…"

"No, Simon!" she yelled. "We've been through this before, I just couldn't! Please don't ask again! Now please ,leave me alone, I've got to find my father!"

"He's not here, Assundra."

"Not here? What do you mean? I followed him here, he has to be!"

Simon snarled. Assundra gritted her teeth – so this was the part where he got angry. "Look, Assundra, you need to understand a few things about the village. Things aren't what they seem, all you need to do is wait a few days and I'll have proof!" He took a step closer. She took a step back. "You're not listening to me! I'm telling you I've heard things about…"

"I don't care what you've heard!" she shouted, feeling a stab of pain from her throat. She wanted to get away from him now! It was another stupid attempt to get her to go somewhere, like that story about finding one of the hidden tunnels the other week. She'd gone deep into the Forest with him, tying a string to see where they were, to find nothing other than a tree stump. He'd spent an hour trying to tell her the tunnel was under the stump, that all they had to do was lift it up, but they hadn't been able to lift it because tree stumps don't lift up. There was nothing there.

"What's wrong with you?" he shouted back. "I'm trying to help you!"

"Help me? Help me with what? I don't need any help! I've got to go!"

"It's not normal to faint like you did the other day, Assundra!"

She was only a few steps away from the council chambers now. She forced herself to slow down. Simon didn't stop.

"Can you remember your mother?" he sneered at her, and she recoiled from his breath, it hit her in the face like a gust of wind and the stench…no, not a stench…there was nothing, just a taste of…nothing…

"Talk to the rest of the villagers, they remember her alright." His voice was sugar now, taunting her, just like the others did.

"What are you talking about?" This was too strange; Simon never made fun of her mother like the rest of them did! His eyes, usually watery, were bright and clear, boring into her own like pokers. She wouldn't look away, the backs of her eyes couldn't be burning; it was just her imagination.

"Get *off* me!" she screamed shoving him back and she slashed out with the knife.

Simon brought his arm up and pointed a finger at her as she was pointing the knife. He flicked the finger at her and the knife seemed to boil with heat, scorching her hand and she dropped it, yelping.

"What the hells…" she said, but Simon was just looking at his finger in awe, a curious smile on his face, and she knew she had to run. Turning, she ran, not caring where she was going, hearing his footfalls behind her. Why wouldn't he just let her be?

Simon was behind her calling her name, something urgent about his voice, but she couldn't stop her legs running, only when it was too late realising she'd run the wrong way. The steps of the council chambers loomed ahead of her and she couldn't stop her legs. They ran up the steps, two at a time, until she was beating on the door, turning the handle but getting nowhere.

"Sunny, no!"

Something grabbed her around the throat, lifting her off the ground, turning her away from the door. It held her there in mid-air as a green haze, like a mist, slowly wrapped itself around her, the grip on her throat getting tighter. Simon had reached the bottom of the steps and was shouting something at her but she couldn't hear. She caught sight of the well in the distance, strangely illuminated by the green haze floating around her eyes and a creature sat there, perched on the well side, its red eyes smiling at her, shoulders rising and falling as if it were laughing, for just a moment, before it leapt back into the blackness of the well.

She looked down desperately at Simon, begging him to help her, but she could say nothing, the grip around her throat was too tight and getting tighter, the haze starting to cloud her vision. Everything was getting darker, the world stuttering before her eyes.

Then the world stopped. The green haze froze, ceasing its shimmering. Her eyes stopped moving and she heard words spoken. Dark words, words she didn't understand but that at the same time she knew, that spoke to something inside her and there was a crash behind her. The green haze turned to white and then the world was moving again, but too quickly, the ground was rising too quickly to meet her and she felt it hid her head and before she felt nothing more, she thought she heard the voice inside her head screaming.

CHAPTER 9

Elder Cairns paced towards the Franks' cottage wearing an expression that seemed to terrify those in his way. For the moment he didn't care. The evening was cooler than most had been recently, but it hadn't cooled Cairns' blood.

"Elder! Thank the…" Alice paused as Cairns glared at her, daring her to mention the gods. "Thank you for coming."

"Where is she?" he barked at Alice, something inside him enjoying watching her flinch.

"Inside. Elder, she's badly, she's…"

"I thought you considered her a sorceror now, Alice? I am surprised you are concerned with how she is feeling. I can diagnose her condition without your help, thank you."

Brushing quickly past the woman, ignoring her sobs, Cairns strode into the living quarters of the cottage. A shambles. Tom had certainly done some damage here before he had been subdued. Finding nobody in the living quarters, he brushed a large tapestry aside.

"Elder!" Broadside tried to stand up from the bed too quickly and almost stumbled. Cairns narrowed his eyes as the alchemist's face reddened. "I was just…"

"Of course, Broadside, thank you," Cairns replied without sugaring his voice. He was too angry to deal with the bloated man's protestations of innocence. His hands had been anywhere but where they would have done Assundra some good. "Leave us now."

"I have noticed…"

"Leave us. If you wish to be useful, find Elder Oldershaw and bring him here."

His fellow council member changed from red to white and he quickly left the cottage, taking great care not to brush against Cairns on his way past, which, considering his bulk, was quite a feat. Cairns watched the man's back as he left, feeling the snarl on his face.

Slowly, he uncurled his fingernails from where he'd embedded them into his hands and spat, just to make sure. His head was too cloudy for this, he couldn't trust himself.

Yet again the people he was trying to save had done their best to hinder him. The whole village would be talking about how Simon and Assundra were found near the council chambers now. They were already talking about Assundra's supposed sorcery, idiocy though that was.

Cairns pursed his lips – he supposed that was better than them talking about the plague or the lack of meat or one of the other things he could not change. It would not be long before the Crafters weighed in on the issue – not in public, not raising a charge, but by wagging their vile tongues behind closed doors.

Tom's reaction to Simon bringing Assundra home in the state she was in had not helped. They would be talking about that too. Fortunately, Cairns had been able to make sure the Deathguard dealt with Tom promptly, before anyone could see how the illness had progressed. The man even walked on all fours now.

Cairns gently placed a hand on the welt on Assundra's neck and sent some blood into the wound. Closing his eyes, he spoke words and quickly followed his blood around Assundra's body, checking for any other damage she might have suffered. Luckily, there was none and Cairns withdrew, allowing Assundra's body to deal with the invading blood.

He looked down at Assundra with sympathy. With Tom gone, Cairns knew she would be even more vulnerable, but he could not allow her to leave, not yet, not until he'd kept his promise to the Keeper.

So much had gone wrong in such a short space of time! Assundra and Simon had trespassed where they shouldn't, Tom had succumbed to the illness far quicker than Broadside had anticipated and, most importantly, Max had failed to get Young Crafter and his followers into the Forest. The odious oaf had even had the temerity to smile a greeting to Cairns as he had rushed from his cottage a few moments ago.

Was Max, too, something for Cairns to worry about? He had been instructed to make sure Young Crafter was in the Forest overnight. Cairns did not appreciate failure but worse than that, Max hadn't even bothered to report that failure to Cairns. Well, he would be reporting as soon as he found Max later tonight.

He felt his blood boil again – both Max and Broadside were getting to comfortable, too sloppy. They knew they were safe. Well, Cairns could rectify that – something would have to be done to show his council that they were not untouchable. Cairns might need them, but this intolerable behaviour could not be tolerated. Cairns had not created positions of power so that his council could lord it over the other villagers, so they could do what they liked – the role of the council as a whole was to serve the villagers, nothing more and to do that the council members had to serve Cairns. A lesson would have to be taught, but it was a lesson Cairns did not have time to deliver!

None of that addressed the fact that it would not take long for the Crafters to capitalise on all of the fact that in just one short evening so much had gone wrong. The villagers might not know what was at stake, which was for their own good, but any mistake weakened his authority and if he was in the Crafters' position he would be making as much out of these small failures as he could.

Cairns detested not knowing what the Crafter's reactions would be – he couldn't counter what he didn't know! It would be so much simpler if he could rid his village of their presence, but no Withholding could cover the murder of such an amount of people. He and Broadside had tried to localise a plague infection to their houses once, but to no avail. They always survived.

There was once chance, though.

A stirring from Assundra brought Cairns back from his murderous thoughts. A large red welt was seared into her skin around her throat. The same as John, Cairns thought. Only John was dead, as she should be. She was lucky Simon had been with her – it would have taken a massive surge of power to defeat the protections on the council chamber without the correct artistic key, power even Cairns did not possess.

With a sudden thought, Cairns realised he should have covered the girl's dignity. Making sure he was not observed from the door, he lifted Assundra's dress back up over her shoulders, recovering her breasts. What Broadside had thought to find to examine medically there Cairns knew not. Did the man think he could escape punishment for such an assault?

Angrily, Cairns realised that he probably could. Broadside knew far too much to risk humiliating the man in public – he was part of Cairns' trusted circle now and it was too soon to consider removing the alchemist from that position, that would have to wait until after he began to set his people free.

"How is she, Elder?"

Cairns' heart bounced in his chest as he span to face Simon. There was a large burn down the side of the boy's cheek which for just a moment reminded Cairns of his own disfigured face. Thanks to the glamour, Simon, nor anyone else, would see Cairns' molten features and he forced a smile, feeling the scarring on his face pull tight, but knowing Simon would see only what Cairns wanted him to see.

"She will be fine, Simon, you did well."

Simon was quiet, just staring at Assundra with a strange expression on his face. Cairns had noticed Simon did that a lot.

"She said she saw a beast," the boy went on, "a beast with red eyes, coming out of the well. Then she accused me of being the beast, accused me of attacking her, Elder!"

Red eyes? *"Take your blood out of the box!"*

Simon didn't look up from Assundra once. Had he heard too? Cairns shook his head clear. He was too tired for this, clearly. "Assundra is confused, Simon. With everything that has happened recently I would try not to blame her."

"I don't blame her!" Simon retorted angrily, but still didn't take his eyes from Assundra. "How much longer are you going to let Young Crafter do this to her?"

Cairns resisted the urge to tell the boy to mind who he was talking to. Simon was the one person Cairns could not afford to alienate at this stage – he would need the boy's power in the coming weeks.

"You know as well as I do, Simon," he replied as calmly as he could, "that there is nothing I can do until someone brings a charge against Young Crafter that I can prove. Until then, his people will simply lie for him and I believe the situation will get worse for Assundra. You must be patient."

"I've been patient enough!" Finally Simon turned to look Cairns in the eye. "She's seeing beasts in wells, Elder, she's terrified of walking down the street! I can't protect her because that bollock Galvarin has told her not to be seen with me! Tom can't do it because he's lost his mind, so it's up to you, Elder! You want my help, you help her, that's the deal."

Cairns narrowed his eyes at Simon. "I do believe we already have a deal. Are you suggesting that we break that arrangement?"

Simon hesitated. "No, of course not," he replied, more quietly. "But I don't think it's too much to ask for a favour."

"Of course not, Simon," Cairns cooed, smiling. "Ultimatums between friends do not get us anywhere, they just create resentment. I have already given you my word on several occasions, as I have given to her father, that no lasting harm will befall Assundra."

"I don't want any harm to come to her at all, never mind lasting harm!" Simon looked back at Assundra, his eyes wide. "She's all I care about, Elder. If something happens to her then I don't care what happens to the rest of them."

"Can none of you see?" Cairns cried before he could stop himself. "I am doing everything I can to protect Assundra, do you think it a coincidence that every time Young Crafter has attacked her, someone has been there to stop it?"

Simon looked up, an expression of dumb non-understanding on his face. It made Cairns even angrier.

"Nothing will happen to her, Simon, you have my word. Is that good enough?"

"Of course, Elder," Simon replied, but Cairns knew a learned response when he saw one. Simon didn't believe it was enough at all, he was just saying what he thought Cairns wanted to hear. They all thought he couldn't spot when they were doing that, but they were all wrong.

"I'd protect her myself, but I couldn't even scratch him last time," he went on. "I don't see the point of having all this power you say I have if I can't use it."

Cairns frowned – what did the boy think he had done tonight against the council chambers barrier other than use his power? Simon was powerful, but he was no artist when it came to learning or understanding. It was all show with him, all posturing and extravagance, none of the subtlety a true Gifted One should have. An idea came to him even as he thought. Simon's lack of learning meant giving him access to his full potential was dangerous – he would be spitting artistry all over Ostracia once the power started to build up in him, but there was an easy way to release it,

"Simon, I have an idea, but I will need to discuss it with my council," he lied. He simply didn't have time right now. "There is a way to control your power. It will make it more difficult for you to live on the outside after all this is over, however."

Simon looked up, interested. "What is it?"

"Not here," Cairns replied, eager to be rid of the boy. There were more important things to deal with, but if he could send Simon away happy perhaps he would be quiet for a few days. "I will summon you once the council have approved."

"Thank you, Elder!"

"It will perhaps be advantageous to have someone else looking out for Assundra, it does take up more of my time than the rest of you seem to realise." That, at least, was true.

Simon nodded and thanked the Elder again. "I just want to help, Elder."

"Then leave me to help Assundra, Simon. As I said, I will summon you when I need you."

At last getting the message, Simon turned and with a ridiculous bow left the cottage. Tonight had proved something to Cairns at least, something that he had been waiting for – the power was no longer building in Simon, it was built. Splinting him would give that power somewhere to vent itself to, somewhere to escape and once Simon learned how to control that escape, he could be trusted with performing the actual artistry he was constantly pressurising Cairns to teach him.

It had to have been a lucky break tonight, defeating the protection around the council chambers. It would have taken hours of practice and more than that, a perfection of the technique of separation that Cairns had never seen Simon show any signs of developing.

Turning back to Assundra, Cairns once more places his hand on her neck and sent a little blood into her system. Almost as soon as he'd tried to follow the blood, the finger placed to her neck began to burn and Cairns at once pulled away from the girl. Raising his finger he saw that the tip was completely black, the splint molten and misshapen.

Cairns backed away from Assundra. So it was true…

"Elder!"

Oldershaw bundled into the room, knocking into the wardrobe as he did so. Cairns quickly folded his finger to his palm before it could be seen. Sighing inwardly he saw the man had clearly been in the alehouse all night. What worried him was that he saw Oldershaw was trying to hide it. A simple shrouding, surely he didn't expect it to work on the head of the Elder Council?

"I just heard! Is Simon alright?"

The man's breath almost made Cairns recoil as he drew close. "He is fine, Oldershaw. That is not why I asked Broadside to fetch you."

Oldershaw visibly relaxed. "Oh, that is a relief. Relief indeed. Was worried…"

"I asked you here to inform you that we have a problem. Deathguard Jessop has informed me that more bodies have been taken from the barrow. I would like you to look into it. Quietly, for now."

Elder Oldershaw blinked. "But, Elder…"

"Your expedition will have to wait." Cairns moved closer to Oldershaw, hoping to give the impression of disclosing something of great importance. "I have noticed that Old Crafter has not been seen much about the village," he lied. "I am concerned that he is taking the bodies for…purposes that we have forbidden."

Oldershaw's eyes widened. "That is not the case! Can assure you. Would have noticed."

"I hope so, Elder, I really do. Nevertheless, I want you to post a watch on the barrow, someone you trust. Whilst they watch I want you to see if you can detect any sign of Drawing in the village.

"You mean…but Elder, that will leave me unconscious for days!"

Cairns raised his eyebrows. "I will be here, Oldershaw, I don't see what could happen to the village in only a few days. You would have been gone for close to that long on your expedition anyway."

Oldershaw blinked again. Something about the man was making Cairns suspicious, but he couldn't think why. "Focus on the last few days," he said carefully, "recent power."

"Anything older than a week would be gone anyway. Used up."

Cairns nodded. "Quite so." He put an arm around Oldershaw's shoulders and led him towards the door. "It is probably nothing more then a precaution but it is one I fear we must take."

"Very well, Elder," Oldershaw sighed. "I shall begin at once."

"One more thing," Cairns said quickly, "was Max in the alehouse?"

Oldershaw blinked again. Cairns kept the smile on his face – it would do to let the old man see that no shroud could get past his senses. "Um…no, Elder, I did not. Haven't seen him for days."

Cairns nodded. "Thank you, Oldershaw."

His counterpart left, clearly dispirited. Well, it could not be helped – Cairns had to know if the Crafters were Drawing – if they were Drawing from the dead, he would have something. Old Crafter was too cunning to leave any evidence Cairns could use in a charge, but a simple public test would force the man to either show the greater artistic force any Drawing, even from the dead, would provide, or to hide his power, suffering a public defeat. The first option would allow Cairns to prove the Crafters had been practicing artistry, a forbidden act. The second would give the Crafters' supporters cause to pause once they saw their patriarch defeated.

Both would buy him time. In a way, Cairns thought, he hoped Oldershaw did find something. It would give him the chance to rid himself of the Crafters before he needed to involve Tom Franks.

As he made to leave the cottage, Cairns paused and turned to watch the peacefully sleeping Assundra. His finger throbbed where he held it in his palm. She would have to be isolated. Yes, he would have to speak to Galvarin tonight. Assundra could no longer be trusted.

Not if she was a sorceror.

Cairns allowed the grimace to return as he left the room. Looking back, he tried to fathom why he felt he'd left something behind, why he felt lighter. No, there was nothing. It was just some ridiculous feeling leaving the girl like that, probably. Cairns knew she would recover. In many ways it was even convenient she would sleep for a while, it put off having to deal with her questions about her father.

Cursing at himself this time, he finally left the cottage. Alice didn't bother to say anything to him this time as he passed, but he felt his mood darkening further from just being in the village. He needed a powder, just one. Just one more time.

CHAPTER 10

Simon put a hand to his cheek and winced. Why had the stupid bitch struck him again? He'd only wanted to make sure she was alright. It had been two days since she'd woken up, a week since what had happened in the old town and she was already pretending it had not, in fact, happened, like she always did.

It infuriated him. Why couldn't Assundra ever deal with things as they were? She was forever putting things to the back of her mind, ignoring what things really meant, always refusing to deal with the realities of a situation.

Then this morning she had the cheek to ask him to help her look for her father! He'd clearly been in a hurry, he'd even told her so, but she hadn't bothered to ask him what he was in a hurry for. She'd just stuck her head out of the door and asked him. She clearly hadn't washed in days and certainly hadn't been out of the cottage.

More importantly, she didn't seem to have any comprehension that to ask him for help after she'd treated him like that was completely unacceptable. The blank look of non-comprehension she'd given him when he'd said no had felt good at the time, but now, for some stupid reason he was regretting it, wishing he'd said he'd help her.

Simon kicked out at a stump as he passed. This part of the Forest was all ash trees and head-high undergrowth of ferns, which here and there hid the prickly surprise of thick brambles beneath their greenery, Thankfully, he could stick to the paths tended by the gardeners to get to Nemar. Simon didn't fancy having to hack through all that vegetation – it would have taken him hours, or even days. Simon sighed – the gardeners really did have the best job in Ostracia, but he wouldn't get to experience that now.

Why Elder Oldershaw had wanted to meet deep in the Forest Simon had no idea. He hadn't seen the Elder since that day in the old city square. Simon hadn't been able to hide the fact that Elder Cairns had taught him the technique of separation and Oldershaw had got quite angry. A beating would be nothing new to Simon, but he knew Oldershaw couldn't admit in public that he too had been teaching him, so there would be no charge of slight that Simon could answer.

Gloomily, Simon thought that Elder Oldershaw had probably brought him out here to administer a punishment of his own, away from prying eyes.

Although the Elder himself hadn't been seen for a few days, not since the plague house had been sealed. The Elders had put up some sort of shield, a shield that Simon knew, as soon as he saw it, was no more than a colour shield to fool the stupid villagers into thinking they could enter with safety.

The family were dead, of course. Well, Simon thought, that's what you got for keeping yourselves to yourselves, nobody came looking for you until it was too late. The Sandfires had been dead for a few days by the time the Elders had got to them, emerging a few minutes after entering with black looks on their faces. They had declared the plague contained, blaming unofficial practices of artistry for attracting it to the Sandfires.

The stupid people had nodded sagely in agreement. Simon knew it was rubbish, as did most of them. They weren't about to speak up though – someone in authority had spoken and that was good enough for them, it meant they could stop thinking about it and get back to their gossiping over cider. Gods, why was Cairns so keen to save them? The Elder was trying so hard to be secretive but Simon didn't see why he needed to bother – as far as he could tell, if the Elders told the people something they knew to be demonstrably false they'd still believe it because it meant the decision wouldn't have to rest with them. In other words, if Cairns told them they had to leave, they would, there was no need to bother with all this subterfuge.

It wasn't his job to do it for them. They could all be surprised by it because they were too stupid to ask the right questions. He couldn't wait to see the look in their eyes when he and Cairns took their artistry from them and sent them out like scared rabbits into the big world of wolves.

Then Elder Oldershaw had reminded Simon that he was just as secretive as Cairns when he'd sent Simon a message to meet him by the ruins of Nemar. Simon hadn't believed Erol Tyson when he'd delivered the message.

"It ain't a trick," Erol had said. "Look, he gave me the message to give you, your choice whether you accept it or not, you little worm."

Simon didn't have a choice, he had to find out if the message was really from Elder Oldershaw. He knew Erol and Young Crafter wouldn't waste their time with him, but he had been worried they would try something with Assundra with him out of the way. He had tried to warn her when he'd gone to make sure she was alright, but she had just stared at him and asked what he could have done to stop them anyway.

Simon couldn't find Elder Cairns to warn him they might be planning something either, the Elder would have wanted to know where he was doing and Simon didn't want to upset the Elder after he'd offered to help. So she would have to fend for herself for once.

With a snarl Simon thought that Assundra would probably run to Galvarin if she needed someone. She always ran to Galvarin.

A twig spiked into his cheek, right where it was sore and Simon swore. He knew the hidden paths in the Forest well, he had been exploring on his own for years, but the vegetation changed every day. Angrily he pulled the twig from its branch and flung it aside.

He was almost there.

"Simon," a voice said softly behind him. Spinning round, he saw Elder Oldershaw wearing a grave expression. "Sorry to bring you here like this. No other choice. Time has run out, I'm afraid, got to teach you things I wasn't going to."

Simon frowned. "What do you mean, Elder?"

Oldershaw motioned for Simon to follow him. "I have something to show you. Not far from here." The Elder must have seen the look on Simon's face. "I know you think you know the Forest, Simon, but you don't know it all. For instance, have you found the Transept Tower? Or the old manor site?"

"There are no such places," he replied at once. "My father has shown me everything there is to see in Ostracia, right up to the infection barrier."

The Elder's face creased into his familiar smile, but it was an expression that didn't sit well there today. "Your father has indeed shown you all he knows. That is not everything there is to know. Do you remember the lesson I gave you in the barn?"

Simon's eyes lit up. "Glamour!"

"Yes," Elder Oldershaw nodded, "glamour." He chuckled. "I remember you had some difficulty revealing a bucket. Well, what about this?"

They came to a halt at a part of the Forest that looked identical to the rest – all undergrowth, rocks and thinly spaced, large trees. The air was wet and the ground heavy on the feet, but Simon didn't mind any of that. There weren't any people around, that was the main thing.

"Now, what do you see?" the Elder asked, spreading his arms out ahead of them. Simon turned to where the Elder was indicating and looked, as he had been taught to.

There was no need for the technique of separation when looking for that which was hidden – glamour was simply an advanced shroud, but a much stronger application. It could change one's appearance for life, anything from hair colour to perceptions of size. It could be used to trick someone into thinking a rotten apple was sweet and juicy, something the traders had got into a lot of trouble for back in Marchman's day.

There was no artistic technique for detecting glamour, only using the eyes to tell what shouldn't be there. In the barn, Elder Oldershaw had changed the bucket into an extra wheel on a cart. Simon hadn't spotted there was an extra wheel and so had not spotted the bucket.

Here, all he could see was the Forest. Tree after tree after tree…wait…what was that?

Simon checked. Yes! The deformed tree! There were two of them, one on his left and one behind them, that they passed a few steps ago! Simon had spotted the first tree without even looking – he could tell when an ash tree had the wilt. Yet here on his right was an identical tree, with the same disease. The leaves looked scorched and had gone yellow, its canopy sparse, as if it had been shredded, the bark of the tree itself cracking and splitting. Fungus was growing in the wounds.

Turning back to confirm, Simon gasped. The other tree with wilt, the entire section of Forest behind him, even, had vanished – replaced by a small glade.

"Well done," Elder Oldershaw said gently behind him, placing a hand on his shoulder. Simon flinched, expecting a splint to be pushed into his neck, but after a few pats the hand disappeared.

Simon flexed his shoulders to try and relax them. "What is this place?" he asked quickly.

Elder Oldershaw smiled again, but Simon could tell this time that it was genuine. "This is the shrine of Lamia!" he said in a hushed tone, spreading his arms like Simon had seen Cairns do on countless occasions.

Simon was distinctly unimpressed. The 'shrine', as Elder Oldershaw had called it, appeared to be a broken statue. Only the plinth and lower half remained standing. Some distance away half of the smashed head lay amongst the ruins of one of only three buildings Simon could make out from the ankle-high remnants of what had once been walls. The features of the half of the head looked like they'd been burned, sloping grotesquely down the face. Whoever this Lamia was, they couldn't have loved her much.

"Was she a god?" he asked, feeling as if he should say something, but not really caring.

Mentioning gods drew the grimace from Elder Oldershaw that Simon knew it would. "Not a god. She was an idea. She was the first of us, Simon."

"Us?"

"What we once were." Looking at the Elder, Simon saw something in the old man he had never seen before. For just a moment all the haughty self-confidence, the proud, controlled superiority, vanished from his face and Simon saw only a distant sadness, before it all returned with a blink. "What we will be again! Now, let me tell you about Lamia."

Simon half-listened while Oldershaw told him the tale. Apparently, long ago, after the settlers had moved to Ostracia from the West, Lamia had been the first of the blood artists. "She came out of the West to show us how to conquer the land around us, to master it and become its servant, rather then till and plough and beg for its mercy every year as we had done," he said. "With what she showed us, we became the Ostracia you have heard of from our lore. We became the magnificent peoples we were before the outsiders took it from us with their jealousy.

"They saw what was coming, of course. Once we had mastered the land and its intricacies, once, long after Lamia's departure from us, many centuries after, we had mastered ourselves, the outsiders knew there was only one alternative."

"Lamia died?" Simon interjected, surprised. So she was human after all.

Elder Oldershaw just grunted. "Nobody knows, as you know our lore from that time is limited. We only have fragments, accounts pieced together from folklore and, of course, we have the shrine."

"So why was Nemar built around the shrine? That doesn't make sense, surely there were other places…"

"Where better to keep the shrine safe than in the bosom of our people? No, to leave it unguarded would have been shameful."

Simon's brow creased. "But it has been left unguarded."

Elder Oldershaw was quiet for a long time before he answered, then said only, "yes."

Deciding that the Elder needed to be left to this peculiar reverie of a broken piece of stone, Simon edged away to get a better look at it. A pair of legs, covered in part by a swirling robe, carved to look cheap. Sniffing, thinking that there was little here that impressed him, he moved instead to the head. The deformed, melted features interested him much more. From what he had seen of statues and busts in the old town, part of their purpose was to show their subject in their most favourable light – great military people were shown looking fierce, great thinkers thoughtful, and so on.

Lamia was shown deformed. Simon looked back to Elder Oldershaw, who seemed to have collected himself. Why was he so concerned with a deformed woman? And why had she been depicted so? She had been important enough to erect a statue to, yet not important enough to try and hide her disfigurement from the world.

Suddenly, Simon realised he was interested after all. "Why the…"

"She suffered for what she taught us," the Elder replied, simply. "You remember little of what you are taught, do you, Simon?"

Simon prepared himself for a volley or a lecture, but neither came. The Elder simply sounded disappointed. He looked back at the statue and tried to think. What could cause a disfigurement like that?

Looking back up, he saw Oldershaw shaking his head. "The Threefold Law."

Simon gasped and looked back down, feeling stupid. Of course! "What she did was visited back upon her threefold," he exclaimed.

Oldershaw sighed. "As the first, she had no warning that it would happen, no way to alter it after it had happened. Afterwards, she began to see it as her gift." Seeing Simon's incredulous expression, Oldershaw tutted. "What better way to teach someone of the dangers of what you are teaching them than to see that danger quite literally written on the face of your tutor?"

"But..."

Simon stopped, mid-sentence, with a yelp. For a second, no more, Oldershaw's face literally melted before his eyes, the lids drooping, the mouth half-sealing and dropping down, the skin blistering and peeling. Just as with the statue it was if it had been horrifically burned, but only for a second, then it was gone.

"So you see, Simon," the Elder said, "lots to learn. Lots to do. Think you understand now."

All trace of whatever it was that had affected him gone, the Elder clasped his hands behind his back. "Yes, Elder," was all Simon could say. He wanted to know much more, now, but he knew from the Elder's gait and expression that he had missed his chance. Just like he knew he always did.

"Now, to your lesson." The Elder's voice was back to its clipped, haughty style. Gods, why was he so stupid, why couldn't he have listened at the time? "Pay attention! This is important. Today, I'm going to teach you about dismemberment."

Simon's focus snapped right back at that. "Dismemberment? But...why?"

"Never mind that now. You'll find out. For now, simply turn around."

When he hesitated, Oldershaw motioned with his fingers, ushering Simon to look around and when he did so he almost fell back.

Behind him, standing with one paw on the head of Lamia was a large wolf, fangs bared, blood-red saliva dripping from its jaws, Simon leapt back in alarm, but slumped straight against the statue.

"Don't worry, Simon. Won't hurt you," Oldershaw said quietly, moving to stand by his side. Now he looked properly, Simon saw that the wolf wasn't moving, although he could see its muscles straining. Oldershaw had the animal Bound. "Now, the first move is to?"

"Separate," Simon replied quickly. He had been practising all week and had worn himself out most evenings doing so. He was determined to get it right first time just once in front of the Elder. Slowly, carefully, making sure not to rush, but also making sure not to listen to the wolf's snarls, nor look at the clearly fresh blood-red saliva in its mouth.

He still couldn't do it without thinking about it, as Oldershaw had said he should, but quickly, Simon was within, without and in all places.

"Good, well done," Oldershaw commented and Simon wondered if it was the first time he had heard the words. "Now, to dismember. Can be done much more quickly with a splint. Seconds, in fact, but not always possible. If you can Bind the subject, then use the technique, it's much neater, much more...artistic."

Simon nodded. Anyone could stick a splint in a neck and get lucky, but artistry of the mind took much more finesse. Slowly, he pushed against the wolf, as he had learned to do with the shield around the council chamber, but this time met no resistance, only the warmth of the creature's blood. He didn't even wince as Oldershaw sliced the blade down his finger, he was used to it now.

As he flicked the blood from his thumb, he sensed his mouth fill with the taste of nothing. Simon listened as Elder Oldershaw talked him through how to use the blood itself to change the droplets. He knew he could heat the blood and surrounding air to create a ball of flame, or cool it to create ice. "To enter a body from a distance, you must allow the blood to travel to its target. There are more efficient ways than what I am to show you – a few droplets in a subject's drink for instance will make sure the blood is in their system before they know how to stop it.

"Here, however, you must transport the blood yourself. Ride it on the wind, Simon."

It was all so simple. Simon blew on the cut on his finger and smiled as words escaped his mouth and a few of the droplets changed, capturing the breeze. Simon found he could control the tiny air-fuelled pocket and pushed it around at his will, watching himself laugh as he did so.

"Concentrate, Simon," Oldershaw reminded and Simon once more set to pushing the pocket of blood towards the increasingly frustrated and angry wolf. "Wait for the right moment. The blood needs to be inside the wolf."

Simon didn't wait. As the wolf opened its mouth to bare its fangs yet one more time, Simon pushed the air pocket of blood hard. He coughed as he did so but words came with the cough and all too soon Simon realised he'd released too much power. The blood swelled in the wolf's mouth and its snarl turned to a howl.

"Simon, pull back! Never just within! Remember the technique!"

Quickly, Simon focused on his third self, the presence that was watching his physical form and drew back from the blood. Just in time, For just a brief moment, the world flashed white. The wolf's head burst apart without a sound, shattering into fragments of bone, skin and gristle. Elder Oldershaw cursed as blood spattered onto his robes and started ranting something about taking care and being too hasty, but Simon wasn't listening.

There was a buzzing in his ears, like a swarm of tiny bees. He snapped back to himself, ending the separation. At least he had managed to control that, he though miserably. Then he stopped. Something was wrong.

Something was wrong with the technique. He wasn't separated any more, there shouldn't have been any leftover traces of its effects, yet in the back of his mind he could see two eyes, flashing a clear, bright playful blue.

"Never mind," he heard Elder Oldershaw say next to him. "I do believe our little experiment has had the desired effect."

Simon didn't care about the wolf. All he could focus on were the eyes but he could see now that they were not part of him. They were looking through him, through his eyes and into him at the same time. As he tried to focus on them a warm feeling spread throughout his body, a comfortable feeling. A strong, powerful feeling. A caring feeling.

"Yes," Oldershaw said quietly, "I believe it has worked just fine."

CHAPTER 11

Captain Hoard raised his bow quickly enough, but Cairns was quicker, flicking his fingers out, releasing the blood from under the splints. Everything slowed as the words left Cairns, not words from his mouth, but words that willed the blood to do his bidding.

Hoard dropped the bow where it fell with a clatter onto the roof of the building he stood on.

"Elder!" Hoard cried, as Coarse burst from the building, his eyes clearly half-bleary from sleep, fumbling for an arrow for his huge bow. "I didn't realise it was you, I'm sorry!"

"You raise a bow to an Elder?" Cairns roared, turning his fingers to Captain Coarse, who dropped his own bow instantly, terror on his face. Cairns liked that.

"I'm sorry," Hoard called again, but there was no panic in his voice. It was why the younger, smaller man was in charge. He knew Cairns would not seriously harm them, that he needed them. At least the man wasn't simply nodding this time. "It won't happen again, Elder. We expected you to come quickly, but not that quickly."

"I was delayed, I had to bury the bird."

That did seem to rattle Hoard. "Yes, I couldn't...that is, I wasn't careful enough, Elder. It's heart..."

"I know what happened," Cairns interjected impatiently, "you think I don't know a slippage when I see one?"

It was how Cairns had known something was seriously wrong, the bird itself had been agitated. He had not been surprised when it had dropped out of the sky even as he had followed it through the Forest – the poor creature's heart must have given out. When dominating a creature, one had to make sure to monitor the condition of the creature you travelled with, it was a lesson he had learned long ago, as he had watched his friend become lost to a bluebottle. Rolf had accidentally steered the creature into a candle flame, burning one of its wings and, in his sympathy, had dropped his guard. The bluebottle's nature had reasserted itself, flying off with Rolf's brain, the parts that mattered anyway. Hugo had killed the man on the spot, the only act of mercy Cairns had ever seen the man administer, but the lesson was equally apt in reverse – dominate a creature too ferociously, push its nature down too far and it was lost and no man, no matter how skilled, could control both his own internal organs and those of another.

Cairns' own heart beat a slow, steady rhythm in his chest, as it always did, despite his panting, despite the pace he had been forced to keep up, pushing himself through the Forest. The Forest sloped gradually downhill from Ostracia towards the plains beyond the Yawning Maw, or settlements Cairns supposed he should now refer to them as, but it was not a steady slope. It was not steady terrain – it was as if the mountains had thrown a cloak off and left it where it lay crumpled and uneven on the ground.

"I'm waiting for someone to tell me why I am here," he asked, not lowering his hand, although the muscles in his shoulder screamed at him. The powders had got him this far but they were beginning to wear out, it was a long way to the outer settlements.

It was Coarse who spoke up, eventually. "It's an outsider, Elder."

The blood spilled from his finger without warning and Cairns was forced to force it into nothing before it surged toward Coarse. Even so, the man stepped back. An outsider? Here? No, no it was too soon, he wasn't ready, they couldn't be here now!

"How?" Cairns managed to squeeze out in a whisper. Coarse answered almost before he finished speaking.

"Something's attracted him. He's not armed, we know that much," he said with a smile. "He's not exactly tough from what we can se…"

"What attracted him?"

Seeing Cairns' annoyance, the smile faded from Coarse's face. "We don't know. That is, we heard something a while back."

"Something…not right." Hoarse added, scrambling down from the roof to stand next to Coarse. "Anyone in the Forest, Elder?"

Cairns pursed his lips. Damn Oldershaw to the hells! "Nothing of importance." Something else was bothering him. "If he is not armed, if he is not a guard, then what is he doing here?"

Hoard shrugged. Cairns narrowed his eyes. "We were waiting for you to ask him that, Elder."

If he wasn't a guard he might not be missed. Although it was just possible that they had sent someone in disguise. Or had Cairns' plan worked too well – did they think Ostracia dead?

"Did he come through the Maw?"

"That's the other thing, Elder," Coarse said before Hoard could open his mouth, "he says he doesn't remember how he got here."

"Then I had better speak to him." Cairns strode towards the Captains, who parted to let him through. The inside of the building behind them was dark, with only a few small candles on brackets providing a flickering light and also the pungent smell of badly made wax, mixed with the clear evidence that whoever the man was he had soiled himself. A table and two chairs were the only furniture Cairns could see.

Flicking his fingers out in front of him, he formed the blood into a ball of light and sent it into the eaves, where it cast a dim light across the room, which Cairns could now see was carpeted in dry leaves, the wall having collapsed in one corner. On a chair in the middle of the room sat a man about the same age as Cairns should be, with long greying hair, matted with blood from the grotesquely swollen and broken lips and face. His jaw hung slack, but Cairns did not think it was broken. Other than the dark eyes, which flitted this way and that, giving an alert lie to the slackness of the face, the man could pass for Ostracian. Taller than most, perhaps, but otherwise very similar. He'd been stripped to the waist and dark blood was matted into his chest hair.

"Who are you?" he asked softly, meeting only a rasped chuckle in return.

"He gave up talking a while ago, Elder," Hoard broke in from the doorway. "He called himself Canton Dark."

The name meant nothing to Cairns. It didn't really matter, he realised quickly – the man was hardly going to receive a formal burial. Cairns took hold of one of the two simple three-legged chairs in the room from next to the table and brought it closer to his captive. The smell of his faeces was drowning out the scent of blood, for now. Cairns didn't position the chair too close.

"Why are you here, Canton Dark?" There was no answer again. This time Cairns addressed the Captains. "How long until daybreak?"

"Just over two hours, Elder," they replied, in unison. Cairns cursed under his breath – he had to be back in the village before Oldershaw's expedition returned, if it returned. He would have to speed this up. It was just a shame artistry could not help a man talk if he didn't want to.

It could persuade, though.

"We could dominate him, Elder," Hoard said, stopping Cairns just as he was about to speak. "You know, send him out, make him act as if everything's ok, get him to wherever he lives then leave him to die there."

Cairns was incredulous. "And you know what his voice mannerisms are, do you? The way in which he walks? How do you plan to release him back to the outsiders, through the Maw? If his story is true and he does not know how he got here, then he could have entered Ostracia unseen, what effect do you imagine sending him out through the Maw would have? One more thing," Cairns added, enjoying the look of embarrassment on Hoard's face, "how would you make sure he was dead? Or do you intend to send the outsiders an animated corpse?"

Turning to leave Hoard to his misery, he noticed that Canton Dark was smiling. "I'm to die here then?" he asked in a stuttered, hoarse gasp, his jaw remaining stationery. If it wasn't broken, it was damaged beyond quick repair, beyond Cairns' healing skills at least.

"Yes," he replied simply, "but I have never killed anyone I have not known personally so perhaps we can speak for a few moments." Cairns smiled. "The speed of your death depends on this conversation, so that at least is in your control."

The man swore and the smile faded from Cairns' face. Not once during any of the beatings he had received at the hands of Elder Hugo all those years ago had he lost his temper or cursed his tormentor. Even when his kneecap had been shattered, necessitating repair by one of the other Elders, he had taken the punishment silently, acknowledging the position of the one in authority. He had realised early on that to have control over what happened to your person, you needed to have the power for yourself, yet all these people, this Canton Dark, the Captains, all of those under his charge, they all looked to others to protect them, whining and moaning when the powers that be, those with the power that they either shirked away from having or were too lazy to seize, acted in interests other than their own.

Yet power also came with responsibility. Elder Hugo had abused his position, had taken enjoyment in his actions. Elder Cairns did what he did for his people, he did not enjoy it. Kings sent armies into battle to die for the country's interests, Cairns had no army, he had to work closer to home. He wouldn't be remembered as a hero, he sought no place in the history books – if he did this right, his people would fade into the background, into nothing and he would not be remembered at all.

So Cairns calmed himself and reinserted the smile on his face, whether he felt it inside or not. The Captains, at least, were due an apt reminder of the correct way to wield power, for they had made a poor job of it so far with Canton Dark. Questioning a man who could barely speak was not a good starting point.

"My Captains tell me you do not remember how you got here. As a starting point, would you care to share how you came to be in Ostracia?"

The man's eyes widened in horror. "Ostracia?"

"Of course," Cairns replied, confused. "You do not know where you are?"

The man's breathing had become dangerously short. "Caraizan jail! I thought! I was drunk and…well, I'd had a row with the wife, our son had…I'm in Ostracia? No!"

Canton started struggling fiercely against his bonds, shaking the chair violently. Cairns motioned to the Captains and the moved behind Canton and held the chair in place by his shoulders.

"How did you get here?" Cairns repeated.

"I don't know! I swear!" the man screamed, terror plain in his eyes. Cairns gritted his teeth – so he had been right. They still feared Ostracians on the outside. All it would take would be one guard with a bow, with this fear, and the bloodbath would begin. It confirmed to Cairns he was doing the right thing. Ostracia could never rejoin the world.

"Was it through the Maw? Perhaps you stumbled through in the night." Cairns ventured gently, worried that the man's heart would give out if he had any more shocks.

Mentioning the Maw had the opposite effect Cairns had intended – far from providing the man with a plausible explanation, it seemed he had provided further horrors. The man's breathing was violent now, his eyes wild and gibberish sprang from his foaming mouth. His violent movements had opened the wounds on his face again and the blood ran fresh.

Warm, hot blood. Red, dripping, pulsing blood, fresh blood. Cairns could no longer speak. He licked his lips. Looking up, he saw the same fight happening in his two colleagues, but his eyes flicked back to the trickle of red soon enough.

"You…you have to tell me…" Cairns tried to say, but it was no good. The man was just screaming now, begging, pleading too, but mostly shrieking in horror and Cairns could take it no more.

Leaping from his seat he grabbed Canton by his collar, roughly yanking his head to the side, hearing something snap and sank his teeth into the vein at the throat. The blood spilled, filling his mouth, dripping down his chin and he let more out when he laughed with joy, but only briefly, before clenching his teeth around the man's neck again. Canton's body convulsed in his hands as the vein throbbed in his mouth. Cairns' mind span and he forced himself to stop, falling back, panting, smiling, laughing to the filthy floor.

Looking up, he saw Coarse pull back the wrist and slide to the floor as Cairns had. Hoard had ripped the man's jaw open and was feeding directly off the tongue. The man bound to the chair wasn't moving. Cairns frowned. Had he passed out? The blood on his neck had slowed to a trickle.

"Hoarse!" Cairns cried. The man didn't move, continuing to…oh gods, he was chewing on the man's tongue! "Hoarse, leave him, what are you doing?"

The Captain looked up, blood oozing down his chin. "There's still power…"

"*We never feed on the dead!*" Coarse shrieked. To Cairns' horror, Hoarse just grinned, bending to put his mouth on the man's wounds again.

Cairns could take no more of it. "Hoarse, get away from him now!"

Hoarse sprang from the body and for a moment Cairns thought he was going to attack. His eyes were wild, staring, but gradually the look faded into satisfaction and he, too, slid to the floor.

The man had been feeding on a dead body! To feed on the dead was beyond the pale, beyond reproach. It bordered on sorcery! Was that what he had been doing out here?

That made up Cairns' mind. It was not their fault, it was his, he had not had time to make them aware of the risks of Drawing. Hoard had thought to feed until all of his hunger was gone, but that was not how it worked. To feed on the dead was obscene, a violation of their humanity, if he couldn't see that then he couldn't live on the outside.

Cairns took his eyes from the torn corpse. All the man had to do was talk. Cairns would have spared him this, but gods did it feel good! There was no rush, no artistic Draw as there was with Rime, the man was an artless outsider after all, but Cairns understood now what the writings in the Elder Council spoke of. He understood why they'd had to feed every week. Without the artistry of an Ostracian's blood, it was just life force and Canton's life force had already been weak.

Blood was caked untidily and gaudily on the Captains' faces, but Cairns felt no hunger now, his need was satisfied. Now the blood just looked cheap, like a wasted effort. "Clean yourselves up," he found himself saying, "you look like animals."

As they turned their heads in confusion, Cairns realised he must look the same. He licked his lips and found surprisingly little blood there, certainly nothing compared to how it was caked over Coarse's face.

Canton Dark had told him something, at least. Something that troubled Cairns. Outsider blood would not sate him when he was on the outside. Canton had been his first outsider. Until now, he had fed only on Ostracians, something forbidden even in the old times, but it was for his people, it was to save them, Cairns felt no guilt. Each feeding had lasted at least five years, often a lot longer, but Cairns could already feel that the effects of this feed were different.

Pulling himself to his feet he found that he felt strong, where he had felt weak before coming here. The Captains had a refreshed look in their eyes and Cairns wondered if his old eyes showed the same satisfaction.

"I'll give him to the wolves," Hoard said distastefully and proceeded to pick the body up with one hand, slinging it over his shoulder.

"Well that's better than wolf, I'll wager, Elder?"

Cairns looked at the man in confusion until he remembered that Coarse knew nothing of Rime. He had told the Captains, when he had shown them about Drawing, that his strength came from animals, that his long life and resistance to the plague were down to this. He had told them that he couldn't allow the villagers to Draw as it would interfere with his plans. He had told them how Ostracians, if they were to flee their prison, would have to be artless, not reliant on stock and able to blend in with the outsiders, which was true.

He had also told the Captains that he had an antidote to the need, to the hunger, that he had powders which would replace the hunger until eventually it would be gone, then Cairns and the Captains could leave Ostracia quietly themselves. It had been true at the time, but Cairns could see now it could not happen.

Coarse and Hoard would have to be dealt with. After the last Ostracian had left, he and Simon would have to give the Captains their final rest and Cairns would make it quick for them, they had been valuable servants. It was a shame, but it was necessary – it was all necessary, his people needed him and he needed this strength, he needed to be strong for his peoples' needs.

"Still don't know how he got in here, though."

Cairns looked at Coarse. He was right, of course. It was troubling – a man wandering into the Forest at will. "How did you spot him?" he asked Coarse.

Coarse nodded to the door. "Was Hoard who spotted him." Cairns nodded – he was beginning to see that it was Hoard who handled most things around the outpost. "Had a bird up, saw someone being chased by a wolf." Coarse uttered a wry chuckle. "He thanked us at first, thanked us for saving his life."

Elder Cairns didn't laugh. "He would have died one way or the other as soon as he set foot on our soil," he replied. "I want you and Hoard to keep a keen watch on the Maw and beyond, if you can, over the next few days," he said earnestly, drawing himself to his feet and happily noticing Coarse do the same. "I want to hear about anything that is unusual. Any sign of armament, any sign of agitation amongst the people, you know the sort of thing.

Coarse nodded. "Could do with Bryant here then, watching the ground while we…"

"No," Cairns replied quickly. The swordsman had no knowledge of domination, it would not do well if his stories reached the village. Coarse was not aware of this, of course. "I have need of him in the village. I'm afraid you will have to manage the best you can. Keep an eye out over the Forest as well, make sure the wolves are hungry."

"Hungry?" Coarse asked, confused.

"As if they haven't had a man or two to eat," Cairns replied pointedly. Coarse's eyes opened wide as he nodded. It made Cairns smile – if he had a village made of men like Coarse he would have no problems. For all his faults and the gods help him if Oldershaw came out here after he found out about Coarse's praying, he was a loyal man who knew when someone was working for his good.

"I must get back to the village. I will be lucky to get there before noon as it is. Make sure you tell Hoard of my plans and send a bird the instant you see anything. The first will be sent out in hopefully no less than a week." Cairns felt his heart swell with pride at the thought. A week! Just one week and his people would start to be free! "Make sure the tunnel exits are clear."

Coarse nodded and saluted, his blood-drenched smile and wide eyes creating a strange picture. Cairns turned his back on it and set out for the Forest.

An outsider in Ostracia. To his knowledge, the first since the invasion. Cairns gritted his teeth and quickened his pace. How the hells had the man entered Ostracia without passing through the Maw? If he had, in fact, done so. If the outsiders had sent him…

Cairns broke into a run. There was never enough time! Simon had to be readied at once.

CHAPTER 12

The candle flickered inside the cramped space. She knew she should put it out, but she couldn't bring herself to be in complete darkness in the cupboard where she'd been hiding since the old town. Things were slithering and scurrying about in her room already, thinking her gone. Part of her didn't want to see the creatures, but every time she saw the shadow of a rat, no matter how big, running across in front of the candle she felt reassured. Rats weren't risen corpses, they weren't spectres and they didn't have red eyes.

They weren't Crafters either. They were cleverer than that bunch of in-bred simpletons.

Pulling the blanket about her to try and quell her shivers, she opened the catalogue. There was something in here, the voice in her head kept telling her to read it.

Someone had left it for her. She'd found it by her bed when she'd woken up. She'd stayed there for a day, barely able to move, just looking at it, panicking in case someone came when she couldn't defend herself. She'd kept seeing a green haze around her body, faintly coating her skin, but as soon as she'd got out of bed that had vanished.

Nobody had come. Nobody had visited her. Nobody had come to take her. Not even her father, she hadn't seen him since she'd followed him into the old town. Nobody.

Nobody except Simon and she didn't want to see him. She'd hidden here, in the cupboard, when he kept coming back. She knew how to stay quiet, how to stay still, she'd learned that from when her mother had been ill, it was the only way to learn anything because nobody told her anything. He hadn't found her. Only today, she'd had to slap him to make him go away. She'd only wanted his help and he'd said no, so why should he pretend he cared how she was?

He'd been at the old town. She didn't know why, she didn't care why, but if he hadn't been, she wouldn't have gone near the council chambers and it wouldn't have happened. It wouldn't have seen her.

She shook her head. These hallucinations were starting to be too much for her. Like the voice she kept hearing, they couldn't be real, the red eyes couldn't be real. The beast had vanished when Simon had found her in the city square. No, it hadn't vanished, it had never been there.

It had to be all part of this madness that was descending on her. Galvarin was probably right to get rid of her, she thought glumly as she turned the pages in the catalogue. Hearing voices in her head, seeing things. She couldn't shake the fear that she was getting what her mother had. Nilha had said crazy things before she had died. Perhaps she saw things too, Assundra didn't know.

Assundra shook her head – she didn't want to know. She had to stay awake, stay alert she had to help her father and there was only one way to do that – the catalogue. She only had a little to go, she had to finish it. Already she'd learned that what John had said to her was true. He hadn't been working with Young Crafter.

She sighed in despair – she hadn't even checked the bucket, in the dark, to see if there was anything there and now she'd cut the rope on the pulley whatever John had left her was probably at the bottom of the well smashed to smithereens.

"No self-pity," she whispered to herself.

"Trees give way to saplings!"

Assundra smiled. She no longer even flinched when the voice in her head spoke to her. She knew now it was helping her. Trees give way to saplings. "A tree bears fruit that leads to its children," she thought aloud. "Or perhaps, if you break a branch another will soon grow?"

There was no reply, there never was. Assundra knew what the voice meant, though. What was in the bucket had been lost, but she had something else. Something she'd found by her bed, something left there for her, by whom she didn't know.

She had John's catalogue.

As she didn't want to go outside, or let anyone else know she had it, she'd decided to shut herself in the wardrobe and read it. It was safer than being out there, where she the red eyes were waiting to get her, that the beast was waiting to step out from any shadow and was responsible for any loud noise. She knew it wasn't but it didn't stop her thinking it.

So she was distracting herself with the catalogue. She'd wanted to read it anyway, and here in the wardrobe it was quiet and she could hide from anyone who wanted to come and see her.

The catalogue haphazardly organised, this must have been only a draft, but she remembered the system John had used, he'd shown it to her. There was a knack to it, he had said and she smiled at the memory – there was no knack if you knew the old city like she did, it was simply a matter of following the streets in the book.

She walked around them in her mind, walked the streets and turned the pages until she found the city square. She wanted to start reading as soon as possible. It would help, it would take her mind off it, she knew it would. It had to.

The square at night is a complex and puzzling place. When the temple stood, it would have dominated the landscape – the sheer amount of rubble alone is a clear sign of a once magnificent structure. It certainly would have been a breathtaking sight.

I feel forced to confess that I find myself troubled by this place, reluctant to proceed past the temple, even eager to run to its grounds and walk the city square no more. I put this down to the fact that my endeavours for the past decade will cease after tonight. My catalogue will be complete, my wife may become known to me again and I can cease this ghastly pretence of friendship. I feared I could never make amends to Assundra, but…

The rest of the page was charred. But what? Flicking the page, she saw that the writing was present on the other side of the page – but how could that be? How could paper only burn on one side? Perhaps she would find whatever John had meant elsewhere in the book. It was referenced throughout, each page having a number and every so often John would write little circles with the number in, but flicking through it didn't seem that there had been enough time for John to complete, let alone reference the city square. Assundra's curiosity about what he had found took over from what he could have done to make it up to her. It didn't matter now, he was dead. She had already known he hadn't meant what he said, but he'd still said it. She couldn't think of anything he could have done to make that right.

The well in the centre of the city square has stood here for many centuries, indeed the city square was built around it and formed part of the first settlement here, away from the alehouse fortress in what is now the village. The reason for the depth of the well has been lost, but by the length of rope on the pulley, it must be hundreds of feet to the bottom. It raises the question – how did the peoples of those times construct such a thing? Unless it were built from the ground up it would appear to be an impossible thing, yet exist it does and it fills me with foreboding. Sounds emanate from deep within the well, as if something were scrabbling to get out. Tonight I made sure that the rope was fully wound and the bucket secured at the top before I proceeded. It may sound foolish, but there is a reason I have left this place until last.

In my travels through Ostracia at night, for the purposes of this catalogue, I have seen through the flickering light of my trusty lantern many wondrous and also troubling things. The spires, the once-proud seats of our rulers, are empty and full of sadness, their rusted cannons pointing inwards. Our smithies, weavers and taverns are simply derelict rooms. Even the houses are shells, the life that once dwelt within them long since dead.

Amongst the decay there are strange fractures – swathes of the city that we raiders, for that is surely what we are, have not touched. The whore houses in the east have been left as they were when they were vacated, with their wild, flowing gaudy tapestries of such scenes as would make my wife's hair fall out, beds half-made and left half-used. It appears nobody wanted anything from these dens. In one house just south of these I found a chamber in the basement resplendent with shackles and other torture devices. My first thought was that this must have been the residence of some evil and notorious fiend, and yet on closer inspection, the devices were in many cases blunted, or scaled down replicas of the real devices. They had clearly been designed for what one can only assume was the purpose of pleasure. I spent many hours making a detailed study on each item, which can be found on page…

Yet for all theses discoveries, for all this time, I have stayed away from this place, from this well, from this city square. It is now time to venture forth for my last entry.

Ruined temple, East of Well

As described above, there is little left of what must once have been a magnificent structure, yet I begin tonight's entry here out of necessity as much as anything else. I feel a need to be here, I feel something is watching me and that I am safe here, as long as I am within the temple walls. I cannot explain why, perhaps a lingering memory from childhood I have suppressed, perhaps I simply do not want to acknowledge the superstitions in my own mind.

There it nothing more to tell about the temple. Without sifting through the debris it is hard to progress beyond the entrance and walking around brings one only into contact with more of the standing shell, the protective case inside which the priceless contents have been smashed.

It is with a heavy heart I move on to my final three entries.

Courthouse, South of Well

Its exterior shattered, the old courthouse is a reminder of the old Ostracia – the system of law broken down, those in charge fallen,, their treasures looted. The gaping hole in the side of the building seems like a wound, a shot in the boughs of a once fine vessel of the law. Parts of my family are descended from learned law men, although only my grandfather, a merchant and failure in the family's eyes, survived the invasion, indeed bringing the destruction on the place himself. A dark day in our history. The stumps of fine marble pillars make the courthouse seem like a patient with freshly amputated limbs. The courthouse is a sad place.

The first thing that strikes one about the courthouse is that there are no courts. All of the panelling has been removed, taken to make either furniture or roofing, the gardeners ever continuing with their inane fear of the Forest and its wood – we have a ready made source of material on our doorsteps and we choose not to cultivate this source – the outsiders may have made fools of us but I wonder what we were before their arrival.

Being only one story tall, the building is notable for its high ceilings, the rooms echoing with a cavernous thunder with each of my footfalls, tempered only by the raucous scurrying of the hundreds of rats that infest this building from one end to the other. This is the work of

Deathguard Jessop. He feeds them, throwing in the fine, fresh food brought to him by Assundra every day. There, the rats feast until the Deathguard selects the best of them for his evening meal. The once fine mosaic floor here is so covered in their droppings that I do not wish to investigate further. Whatever treasures this place hide, though as one of the first places to be sacked after the rebellion I doubt there are many, are to be unrecorded here, I regret. The army of rats masses behind me, thinking me Jessop. I must leave.

Merchant's Guild, East of Well

Throughout the cataloguing of this once magnificent city, locks and bolts have presented no problem to me. Without giving away my methods, let us say I ended up inside the Merchant's Guilld and was happy to be so. Until later.

Some buildings are locked for a reason and this should have remained so. Upon entry I found myself in a pleasant enough entrance hall, still carpeted but covered in many years' worth of dust and grime. The winding staircase to the next storey had fallen in halfway up, leaving a tidy pile of white debris behind the oval on the carpet where the indentations of a heavy desk could still be seen. I took the route to my left, eager to see the hall where I had understood, from the many other documents I have witnessed in the old city, that the main business of this establishment took place.

I was not, at first, disappointed. The hall was vast, reaching to both the storeys of the building, with a gallery of mock marble, with arches cut in the rail to match the doorways of the sumptuous, almost palatial surroundings I found myself in. I was charmed by them, imagining in my mind the hordes of people bidding or cheering on other bidders in the frenzy that must have taken place in this large, marble-floored room. Little did I know what horrors were to await me on that gallery.

This was my first experience of an Ostracian public building that had adornments still attached and I was most excited by these. There were a series of huge tapestries hanging from the walls, each much taller than a man and depicting scenes from Ostracian pre-history, that is to say from the times of our founding fathers. Old Ostracian buildings, the likes of which are lost to us now, with their thatched roofs, men wearing thick, formal clothing that in the climate of this place would leave them a sodden mess, colourful times from our past and our history which I was both proud of and pleased to see.

It was then I noticed something on the farthest tapestry. Something I had not expected. The scene was a small one, in the relief of the main picture. It showed an underground cave or chamber, with four characters holding burning torches. Something about this section of the tapestry was so detailed, so vibrant, but more than that, I noticed at once that one of the characters was not Ostracian. Rather, she was like Assundra in appearance – dark yet fair – not outsider and not Ostracian. I had to have a closer look, but the relief was too high up to see properly from the ground floor. I had to reach the gallery.

Retracing my steps at a hurry, I passed through the main chamber, past the now useless main staircase and through to the back offices, hoping to find a servants' entrance or some other way up to the next storey. At length, amid fears about how much longer my lantern would last, I by chance forced open the locked door to a set of stairs I now wish I'd left uncovered.

Those stairs were dark. Plain stone, cut simply, winding solidly as if around a pillar. All was quiet as I reached the top and I realised I would have to traverse the length of the entire building to get to the gallery, knowing nothing about the security of the flooring beneath me. Expecting to fall to a painful conclusion with every step, I nevertheless forged on, some hunger driving me forward. Something about that section of tapestry that reminded me of something else, of something I had read. After some time, I reached the main hall and hurried across the landing to the balconies, not noticing the draped finery and luxurious furniture as I passed it, none of it seemed important, though I know I should have catalogued it here.

With a sense of elation and excitement I reached the door to the balconies and pushed hard, expecting it to give resistance like the other doors in this place had given me, but this door welcomed me in, asked to be opened. In some darker moments this evening I found myself wondering if it even opened itself before my hand reached the handle. Nonetheless, I stumbled forward, losing my balance and fell, towards a gap in the arches.

I did not fall to the hall below. To have had to retrace my steps at that point would have been cruel to my nerves, but perhaps less so than the sight of what stopped me. For in the alcove I fell into and, as I was later to discover, in all the alcoves, was the skeleton of, I presumed, an Ostracian.

Its jaw hung slack, dead, empty eyes stared back at me and I am ashamed to say I screamed. It was at that moment I became aware that I was not alone in this place. At my cry, I distinctly heard several sharp intakes of breath. Startled, I regained my feet, casting the torch about, looking for any signs of my discovery, but the gallery was silent and still. Slowly I began to walk around, my eyes unable to keep themselves from looking down to the long-dead corpses that were my companions, lying in each and every alcove, rags clinging to their gnawed bones, some with unsheathed, rusted weapons beside them. I cried out again as upon one inspection a rat poked its nose out of the skull of one of the unfortunates as if to chastise me from disturbing its sleep.

At my cry, once again, I heard the sharp intakes of breath, as if I had startled something, but they were louder this time. Aware of my panic building, I considered leaving, but my resolve had become strong, or so I thought, after my many years searching the darker and remote places of Ostracia and I pressed on, ignoring the skeletons now. As I reached the tapestry that was the cause of all these horrors being shown to my eyes, my fear turned once more to excitement.

There were the dark eyes of the dark-haired girl, mesmerising in their detail and on the level of the balconies perfectly level with my own eyes. As I stared, in awe and pride at the craftsmanship, my lantern light failed and I was plunged into darkness.

Only the eyes did not stop staring. Their dark depths spread to reveal a bright red that haunts my thoughts even now, even after what I was to see after I left this place, those eyes are things I never wish to see again. I felt something brush my shoulder in the dark, unable to take my eyes from the red demons staring back at me and then another, thing, touched my other shoulder. "Go," something whispered to me. "Go…leave…go…" they spoke, for there were many and then I was swamped, my ears full of their urges to flee, my skin crawling with their touch and I turned tail and ran. Bones went flying from their owners under my feet and I began to hear the whispers shriek, terrifying, blood-chilling screeches of anguish and I knew they were coming after me. By some miracle I made it to the doors which I swear to my gods were already closing by the time I reached them. I screamed something, something profane, something appropriate to the sheer frightfulness of that room and flung myself at the doors, landing on the hallway outside, sprawling to my knees, the sound of the heavy doors closing behind me ending their screams, their pleadings, whatever they had been.

The lantern flickered back on.

I stared at it for some moments before I came to realise what the words on the tapestry had meant, for they had read…

Assundra almost cried out in frustration as the page tailed off into a burnt cinder once more, this time enveloping all of the vellum, plus a few leaves that followed it. What had John seen? What did the inscription say? John had said the girl was like her in appearance – what did that mean? Was it one of her ancestors? Or a visiting outsider? Did it hold some clues as to her ancestry on the outside?

Hidden red eyes. They were everywhere. She'd been right to stay in her wardrobe, with her museum safely underneath her where no beast could get at it.

Simon had said the eyes were just manifestations of hidden ghost memories, but how could they be? John wasn't coming of age, he was well past thirty, how could he be having the ghost memories? No, Assundra knew she had seen those eyes, no matter what anyone said, she had seen that beast, that *thing* in the well and John had seen something similar, in the very next building to where she saw it.

That made it real! That meant she wasn't going mad! Who was to say that beast was not using the sewers or water systems to travel from building to building in the old city unseen? It was probably some horrific pet of the Deathguard, something he had conjured up from the hells, which is why he needed all the rats to feed it.

She began to come to a conclusion. This book was telling her part of the story. It was leaving the rest out for her to find herself. Had John released this monster? Was the clue to its imprisonment hidden in that tapestry? John had mentioned Assundra so often now, but how was she relevant? Could it explain why she was drawn to the place? Why she could see the beast at the well but Simon could not?

The Merchant's Guild was still there. The answer was in that tapestry, she could go and have a look, perhaps even cut the tapestry, put it with the rest of her finds in the drawer to study when this was all over…

"Sunny, no!"

She heard the page tear before she was aware how stiffly she had begun to hold the book.

"Be safe, Sunny."

"Shut up!" she replied, before she could think. Instantly she held her breath, expecting footsteps to come surging into her room and arms to be pulling her from her hiding place but there was nothing. She waited a bit longer, not trusting herself, not trusting anything now.

"Be safe!"

There were no footsteps. No arms grabbed her. Gods she wished the voice would stop! It disturbed her sleep, it followed her everywhere she went and it was beginning to scare her. Why was she hearing this voice? Simon had said something about it too. He had heard something but even he had been wary when she had explained.

Was it something to do with the beast? With the red eyes?

She would never know. She couldn't leave here. Here she was safe.

Shifting to make herself more comfortable she brushed away a tear. There was a mystery in the old city square, but it was not one for her. Not now, anyway. She had to stay alive, she had to follow Cairns' instructions. She could at least finish his catalogue, she thought. If nothing else it stopped her mind from asking her eyes to search for hidden red glowing counterparts in the darkness.

Council Chambers, North of Well

I hung back from approaching the Council Chambers for some time. Crossing the square past the well on one more occasion was not good for my nerves and I was forced to take pause and consider what I had seen in the Merchant's Guild.

The well has changed. I neither heard, nor saw any soul tracking my movements in the city square, nor did I hear anything above the sounds of the rats and my own exclamations of fear, but nevertheless, something has altered the well. The bucket has been lowered, the rope extended to its fullest length.

All is silent in the city square now. It is as if the rats have hidden themselves, the air is still and close and I confess to feeling afraid. I crept along as far away from the well as I could, yet never taking my eyes from it. I was, however, determined. There was but one more building to visit and my catalogue would be complete! My lifetime's work done with, I could at last rest.

I heard a sound. A sound, from the Council Chambers! I stopped in my tracks, not wanting to take my eyes from the well, yet I could now distinctly hear murmurs from within the Chambers. I had to look. The door stood open. In my attentions to the well I had not even noticed the door. The hairs on my body stood on end – had someone been watching me? I had hardly been discreet, blundering about the city square like a buffoon.

The opportunity was too good to resist. If I hadn't been discreet with my movements before, I was now – they wouldn't see me from the windows, they were black with grime – and I crept towards the door. Once inside, I could smell the must and decline of a long-sealed building. The chambers opened onto a long corridor, with doors leading off at each side. All were closed. The voices were stronger here and I dared not risk opening the doors for fear of finding the source of those voices.

Creeping down the corridor, I noted the absence of decorations of any kind and not, as with the most of the buildings I had catalogued, due to them having been removed, rather there was no sign of the building ever having had any. The walls were bare, the doors plain wood, the floors uncarpeted. It was then I saw it.

A jewel. A bright green jewel, glinting in the light from my lantern, which I had foolishly forgotten to extinguish but was now glad I had not. The jewel had been placed in a crevice of the wall, where it met the floor. It would have been impossible to see without the lantern, I had found it utterly by chance. As I bent to pick it up, I heard the scream.

Feeling as if I were tearing my head on a spike, I glanced through the crack in the door that was opposite me and there I saw the greatest horror I have ever witnessed. May the gods forgive me, Assundra…

Assundra stared at the page. Once more, there was burning to the page, but it was clearly written upon on the reverse. That was three times – three times he had mentioned her by name and three times what he had written had been burned – had he changed his mind about what to write? What could burn one side of a sheet of vellum but not another?

She was too excited to think about it now, she had to finish. There was but one page more, perhaps John would explain himself.

I fled. To my shame, I fled when they saw me. I do not think they saw who I was, but they know someone was watching. I will not complete my catalogue tonight. I fear I may never complete it, I may never recover my nerves enough to go back to that place. To see the beast, to see them with it…these are men I respected! Men I have served and for what? To support such devilry?

I stumbled as I ran, across the city square, in my desperation to get away, and I looked once more at the well. The bucket was once more up, but not fixed in place, simply swaying on its rope. Blood trickled slowly from one edge of the bucket. Once again I had heard no mechanism, heard nobody behind me operating the pulley. It is clear to me now what has happened, why out of all the buildings the temple was destroyed, reduced to a shell.

The city square is infested with demons. Something came out of that well tonight, something I hope never to meet. For I shall not be returning to this place. Jessop will understand, I have cultivated a relationship of sorts with the maniac, I believe he will release me from my obligation. I wish to return to my wife, to forget these happenings and forget this catalogue.

I want to forget what I saw them do to Tom Franks in that room. They spoke of 'cure', but what I saw was simply torture. No, not torture. I cannot describe it. My pen shakes as I write, I am forced to blot to stop the tears running the ink. What I saw was not torture. It was something else. Something…worse.

Jessop has returned, I hear steps in the temple next door. This will be my final entry. One day, perhaps, my nerves will have recovered enough to go back. Perhaps it is little more than too many late nights, too much darkness when I should have been asleep with my wife. Oh, Lydia, forgive me!

Assundra closed the book firmly. Bloodstains had marked the final page. This was where John had died. They were quite literally his last words. After he had written that Jessop had returned. He must have been in the old furnace room when the man he thought was his friend came home.

Her heart was racing. Not at the thought, any longer, of the tapestry, not at the thought of the thing waiting for her in the well, not at the thought that it might have been John who released that beast, but at the thought of her father.

A cure! They had mentioned a cure!

Was the answer hidden in the Council Chambers? Was that where her father had gone? Even if it were, how could she get in? How did John get in? Did the beast leave the way open? The last time she tried to gain access to the chambers something… had grabbed her. Something strong enough to lift her off the ground with one hand.

Deep in the distance, Assundra heard a wolf howl.

If she could save her father then everything would be alright. He would protect her, they would find a way to survive, just the two of them, just as they had done before Galvarin had come along. It was her fault her father had got worse. She had neglected him, left him slumped sick in his chair while she went to enjoy herself with the mason. This was her fault.

She felt sick every time she thought about it, as if someone were running their hands down the insides of her stomach.

If the answer was in the council chambers then she had to find it, but she couldn't go back there on her own. Not with the…thing there. Not with the Deathguard there and certainly not in broad daylight.

She needed help.

"No, Sunny! Sunny be safe!"

She'd heard the commotions in the village. It was the day of the play today, she'd been looking forward to it for months. Galvarin would be there. Maybe he'd help her. Maybe if she…

"Sunny, no! You know you have to be safe!"

Assundra clamped her jaw shut. She couldn't be safe. Not with the Crafters out there, not with her father gone and getting worse and not with a demon, as John had described it, infesting her mind.

She put her eye to the crack in the cupboard door. It was quiet outside, not even the rats were stirring. Licking her fingers, she put the candle out and pushed the door open. It was dark in her bedroom, but she didn't linger long there. She put a hand up to her eyes as the light bursting from the open front door hit them. Every part of her wanted to run back to the cupboard, where nobody would find her. But she couldn't. She had to help her father.

She, the girl who saw beasts with red eyes around every corner, she who heard the voice in her head. She who had hidden in a cupboard for days. She who never seemed to need to eat any more, despite the burning hunger inside her. She who since she had awoken a few days ago had not slept and was not tired.

She who was terrified.

Before she closed the cupboard door she pulled out a dress at random, not caring which one it was, before shrugging off the filthy one she was wearing. Her body odour hit her immediately and stopped her in her tracks.

Galvarin would just have to help her. She knew how she could persuade him, it had been a while now, his blood would be up, it always was and she knew he knew she could calm it.

But he wouldn't want her to if she smelt and looked like this. Cautiously, quietly, she closed the front door. If she was going to sate Galvarin she needed to appeal to him first.

She scanned the room quickly, though it was in quite a dishevelled state. Her father had left in quite a hurry, or at least that was how she told herself she left, the truth of the matter was just too violently repulsive. There had to be some water she could wash in here somewhere, there was always water. She couldn't go out into the village in this state.

There. By the long-since useless hearth in the kitchen – the bucket they used to wash their cutlery, pots and pans and things. Scum floated on the top of the water. Assundra swallowed. Was there nothing else? The bath stood empty in the corner, that would be no use. The well was out in the village. Suddenly, as if waking up, she became aware of the state she was in. *Gods*, how could she have let herself get like this?

She looked down at the dress in her hand, the one she'd pulled out of the wardrobe without looking. Her best orange dress. Her mother's best orange dress. There was no way she was going to sully her mother's memory by allowing herself to wear one of her best dresses in this state!

Leaning down and touching a finger to the dank, cold water, she swallowed hard. The other thing she would have to do in the dress would be in a good cause. It would be for her father. Her mother would approve of that. Blinking hard, she saw a bright green imprint, an after-image, flash across her eyelids.

"Ouch!" she yelped, yanking her finger back from the water. It was boiling hot! How could water suddenly boil like that?

"This is madness!"

"Yes," she replied sadly to the voice that couldn't be there, "I do believe this is madness."

CHAPTER 13

"Outsiders? Here?"

Cairns allowed the outrage to mount amongst his council for a few seconds.

It was only an hour after midday and still the sun withered behind the clouds like a coward. The Council Chambers were gloomy. Like the Transept Tower everything was covered in dust, which paraded itself through what light did shine through the filthy and in some places broken windows. Cairns glanced at the sky in distaste; he'd had his fill of cowardice today.

The large table in the centre of the room had many chairs around it in various states of repair, but all were of the finest quality. A lavish heavy curtain hung covering the door and a chandelier of musty candles hung from the ceiling. Lining the room were a series of workbenches, all for different purposes, including the one where Cairns had clamped Simon's hand to stop him snatching it away.

Simon had whimpered like a gelded lamb. Truth be told, there had been an alarming spill of blood, far more than he had expected, enough to make Cairns glad he had fed the night before and could maintain control, but one thing he would have expected was the will of one on the verge of manhood to compose himself through such trivial concerns. Instead the boy had shown none of the aptitude for the Eldership he claimed he so keenly wanted, even possessing what he had been blessed with. If it had been a real contest for the Eldership, Cairns would have taken the Keeper of the Transept Tower over the new Gifted One, but it was not to be. It had to be Simon. It was well that the façade of the boy's training was almost done with.

The boy's mother had spent an age scrubbing the wide spatters of blood from the once fine mosaic in the Chambers' back rooms. He couldn't tell if the woman shook from the effort of the scrubbing or from the weak sobs that had been wracking her since she had burst in on them. Something about Alice crying had weakened his resolve. He hadn't even punished her for bursting in uninvited!

"Elder?"

Feet were shuffling and they walked Cairns' mind back to where it should have been.

"Unfortunately yes," he called out finally, spreading his hands wide as he sensed someone prepare to speak. "We have much to discuss, my friends."

Max grunted. The gardener stood apart from the rest, as he had done since the procedure on what he thought was his son had begun. He was wearing a red cloak today, Cairns noted, that contrasted horribly with the yellow of his hair and the stained brown of his clothes. The man was constantly fidgeting – Max hated being indoors and even now he was stood looking out of one of the windows. Cairns thought he would have to reward the man for not putting up a fight about his plans for the boy and not for the first time. Trust, though, was a different thing. It wasn't the trust Cairns had in Max that would be put to the test before the end, rather it was the trust Max had for Cairns.

Leaning on the table around which Galvarin Jallel and Broadside, the rest of his Council with Oldershaw still absent were preparing to sit, he began. "As you know, we have a problem." Broadside sat down without ceremony or permission, the old wooden chair creaking under the man's weight. Cairns turned his gaze onto the alchemist. "We may have to move things forward faster than we had anticipated."

"Faster?" The light voice, almost a boy's, came from Galvarin, the mason. "You've just given Simon a bloody splint! How much faster do you expect the bloody boy to develop?"

Cairns flexed his own, all splinted, fingers. The boy had made far too much of the pain; Cairns barely felt it any more when one had to be replaced. The thin, sharpened strips of stone were hammered in just underneath the fingernails until the spike was about to break through the base of the nail. There it stayed; keeping the blood flowing, allowing the owner far greater control of his power. Their use had been banned under Elder Hugo. His mentor had cost them so much time; time that the plague had made more than full use of.

"Calm yourself, Galvarin," Cairns replied, reserving an easy smile for the mason who had, at least, performed his own tasks without complaint and without creating problems, although it still puzzled Cairns why Galvarin's tasks had not been enough to keep a permanent smile on his face. "Your feelings about Simon are well known, but I assure you it was more than necessary to acquiesce to at least one of Simon's demands."

"But to give him such power! He's wild enough as it is..."

"My son is not wild. And last time I checked we don't defy the decisions of the Elders." Max didn't raise his voice, low and booming though it naturally was, nor did he turn an inch from his position at the window and yet Galvarin was cowed instantly. It was well it was what was between Galvarin's legs that Cairns needed and not his bravery.

"You are right of course, Max," Cairns said, making sure his voice was as low as the gardener's, "your son is not wild. But what is within him is."

"So why did you let him go?" Galvarin asked, incredulous. "I put the charge in, as you asked, he was here, so why didn't we arrest him?"

Max snorted. "Not public enough. We just bring him in like that, Old Crafter will smell a rat."

Cairns murmured an agreement. This wasn't what they were here to discuss, however and he was getting impatient. "Simon will be taken care of Galvarin, do not worry, you have done well. There is a more important matter to discuss, however. My friends, we have very little time. An outsider was, indeed, found inside our borders only last night and, unfortunately, died under questioning. It appears our plans have worked a little too well, perhaps they consider us a little too dead."

Broadside shifted his bulk on the chair. "That is good is it not, Elder?" the man asked, trying to make it sound like he was not questioning Cairns. "We are all on schedule, I think, perhaps the sooner this is over the better."

"Cold feet, doctor?" Max sneered. "How do you propose to get the villagers out before the outsiders attack? Round them up and take a swipe at their sorcerors head on?"

"Well of course not," Broadside virtually coughed. "There's no evidence they will attack, I mean, is there, Elder?"

"We're in more danger from Simon running around showing everyone his artistry!"

"Well, I could prepare some powders, if the council wished," Broadside replied, his hands patting down his fine all in one tunic, kept as tight as it could be kept around the waist by a lavish leather belt, "something to, ah, calm the boy's natural urges?"

"It's half the council that's the problem, not my son. Begging the Elder's pardon." Broadside stiffened as the gardener spoke. Cairns had found the energy of their feud a useful tool for over the years. When one was played off the other in competition, their rivalry brought out the best in them, producing a much greater result than there would otherwise have been, but it was a feud that was becoming harder and harder to control.

"As you say, Max and no, my good doctor, I do not believe we need to tame Simon to that extent. Indeed, in addition to the news you have just heard, I believe Galvarin has filed a charge against your son, Max, which, coupled with the untamed nature of his artistry, is exactly the distraction we will need over the coming days. Simon is, however, lest you forget, the tool that leads to our salvation."

"I've heard of the charge," Max said through teeth that were almost chewing each other. Cairns held up a hand to stop him.

"Nothing will come of it, Max, you have my word, but procedures must be followed. It will get him away from the villagers while the splint heals into his hand."

Galvarin groaned, moving to lean his head on a bare muscled arm. Did the man never wear a shirt that fitted him? His doubloons and white open shirt were horribly matched, but designed to clearly hide his skinny legs in comparison to his broad chest. Cairns found himself recalling for a moment a vivid picture of the couple in the glade as the mason was on Assundra, the thought sending a shiver of excitement through him before he collected himself. The mysteries of women were not for Elders, he had only been present in the bird to make sure Assundra got her powders.

"You're planning to proceed without Oldershaw?" he realised Broadside had said.

"Yes, my friend."

Cairns watched Broadside closely, noticing Max throw a smirk at the weighty alchemist, whose sweat had begun to bead upon his thick brow. Broadside pretended to scratch his head, to hide his wiping of the sweat away. "This is most irregular," he came out with eventually, to which Max laughed out loud.

"I hope you're not saying you agree with his little trips?"

The chair creaked ominously Broadside sat back with a thump, his face like a shredded beetroot where the sun had caught it in streaks. "Begging the Elders' pardon, but of course I don't, but it isn't a trip that he's gone on now, is it?"

"Thank you Broadside," Cairns acknowledged. "Elder Oldershaw is looking into the Missing. Apparently our grave robber has put his head above the parapet again, as it were."

Max and Galvarin stared into the distance, uninterested at the news, but Broadside was agog. "*More* Missing? Who can be taking them? Surely we would know, bodies are hardly things one can conceal easily!"

Cairns shrugged. "It puzzles me as well, my friend, but as I say, I have passed the matter on to Elder Oldershaw, he has more time for these trivial concerns than I do."

"I hardly think the disappearance of bodies from the barrow a trivial concern, Elder!" Broadside began, but Cairns cut him off.

"Nevertheless, we have more important things to discuss."

He waited a while before speaking again, allowing everyone time to think. It was a fractious council at best. Max had never got over the defeat to Broadside in last year's melee, but then he had wasted too much time trying to best Tom Franks, ignoring the alchemist's stealthy advance from behind. Tom had found it so amusing he had ceded to Broadside in mock defeat. Even so, even with laughter, with him not at him for once, ringing around his ears, the farmer had still been shut out of the celebrations. Cairns believed that had been the last straw for Tom. They had shared a cup of cider at the Elder's insistence that night and a very productive cup of cider it had proved to be.

"The pressing matter tonight is the outsiders," he went on, "Where one has been, we have to assume others will follow, even if this man did indeed blunder into our realm by accident. If more do come, they will not come straight away. They will want to assess what has happened to their man and how to proceed. Remember the last time they invaded they brought forty thousand men. There are nowhere near this number in the settlements outside the Maw, there can't be."

"That just means they have a few days to summon reinforcements! What can we do in a few days? We were planning to have months for the evacuations, not days!" Galvarin cradled his head in both hands now. Something was wrong with the mason and Cairns could not think what – he had been given the most pleasant of tasks and had done it well.

"We have to proceed as planned, for now," Cairns replied, to them all. "No unusual activity has been detected outside the Maw as yet. I have people watching the Forest, we will have time to prepare should the worst happen. The man was not a guard, not a man with military training, it may be assumed by his people that he has wandered off in search of spoils, or simply left the settlements for good."

"Perhaps he was looking for spoils," Max commented. "That means more could come."

"Indeed, Max. These are the thoughts I formulated on the way back through the Forest to speak with you all. However, there is no way to be sure."

"What would you have us do?" Max turned, finally, to the Elder and met his gaze with a steely flash of blue.

"Your task, Max, continues as it did before. I would not wish it's timing upon you sooner rather than later if I were you."

"Can I go then?"

Cairns stiffened his lip. "Perhaps you would care to offer your report before you are dismissed?"

Max faltered. As he always did. Cairns hadn't even needed to call any of his reserves to the back of his throat in readiness; the man was so afraid of artistry the mere scent of the taste of nothing it left on the land turned him into a craven.

"I've been doing as you asked," he said, his strong voice booming in the stone cottage. "As far as I'm seeing they do a lot of talking but none of that talk is about actually doing anything."

"No new recruits?"

Max shook his head and Cairns instinctively flinched, worried that bugs might fly off the man's unkempt mop as he did so. "Not this time, though Mary's putting herself about the village more."

"What a disgusting thought," Broadside interjected, cutting his broad laugh off when nobody joined in.

"Look, all I'm saying," Max went on, folding his arms over his puffed-out chest, "is that I don't think they're up to anything. Yet."

"Please explain, Max," Cairns asked gently, motioning Max to sit in the spare chair but the man didn't move. Cairns pursed his already stiffened lips. The artistry was there inside him, just waiting to bring Max down a peg or two. Just *there*...

"All Alice will say is that Mary Archer keeps saying she's got these sack fulls of people who are with her, but none of these people are appearing out of thin air at any of the meetings. It's always the same folk; Mary, the wife, Crafter and the rest of his clan, the Tysons and Bill Barnarby."

Galvarin snorted. "There's only ten of them! And some of them old men."

Cairns rounded on the short-sighted fool. "Where there is a Crafter there are dozens of his *subjects* to support him!" he hissed through gritted teeth. "The hells know I've tried to master the old fool and his brood, but my *good colleague* does not share the depth of my concerns." He forced himself to stay in his chair, though his body screamed at him to get up and pace the room, despite the complete lack of purpose that would serve.

"Well, I may have some news there," Galvarin said, for the first time not raising his voice to a whine.

"What is it?" Cairns snapped, annoyed at the smug grin adorning the mason's supposedly handsome face.

"Oldershaw's party..." Cairns gave him a look. "I mean *Elder* Oldershaw's party, of course Elder, sorry, the party he's taking out tonight, there's only four of them."

"He couldn't persuade any other bugger to go with him, that's why!"

"I know that, Max, but do you know who the four are?"

A look flickered across Max's face. "Of course I bloody don't, you fool, otherwise I'd..."

"They are the Elder, Captain Bryant, Carp, who's one of yours I think, Max, and *Crafter's son*!"

Cairns widened his eyes. What was Oldershaw doing with a Crafter? Images of Elder Rime flashed unbidden into his mind, the moaning, the begging, when the man could still speak. The blood. He had been betrayed once before...

"One of the older ones," Galvarin continued. "He's just called Crafter I think, I don't have much to do with them."

Max snarled at the barb, clearly pointed at him. He and Young Crafter were often seen about the village together, but then Young Crafter was another one of Max's, as Galvarin put it. "Patrick Crafter?" Cairns ventured, trying to picture the undesirable wretch he no doubt was.

"No, not him," Galvarin said, his eyes squinting together with the effort of thinking. "I'm sure this one's just called Crafter."

"He's right," Max interjected, "Just Crafter, we call him, if it's him you mean. Though he's anything but, of course, just like the rest of 'em. Never a more useless bollock's been put on this earth than Just Crafter. Least that's what you think when you first meet him. Not later."

"Just so, Max," Cairns smiled, in an effort to sooth himself as much as the others – what the hells was Oldershaw doing inviting a Crafter on his expedition? "However I notice that two of those on the expedition are, as Galvarin puts it, yours. Perhaps you could explain that."

"Nothing to do with me, Elder."

Max met Cairns' gaze again. The man was anything but cowed. "You have five people working for you do you not?" Max nodded. "Then surely losing two would be a blow to your productivity."

The man almost blustered a reply, but checked himself. Broadside and Galvarin sat as still as stone. "There's always more work than we've got men!"

"Perhaps they'll find what they're looking for this time," Galvarin interjected.

Max laughed again, but there was no mirth in his voice now. "That's as likely as sparrows nesting in my groin! Everyone who goes on Oldershaw's little trips comes back either hurt or worse, won't be no different this time."

"Only this time," Galvarin said, more angrily this time, clearly growing in confidence the more he talked, "someone got hurt before they even left."

Cairns eyed the mason suspiciously. "What do you mean?"

"Frank." Cairns noticed Max flinch out of the corner of his eye. Frank was another of Max's men. "He's dead."

"Dead?"

Broadside's shock contrasted sharply with Max's forced calm. "I have heard nothing of this, why is that?"

"Crafter's got his body," Galvarin replied. "Don't ask me why, I've got no idea. All I know is he was supposed to be going on the expedition with Elder Oldershaw, then all of a sudden he shows up dead. Old Crafter was mumbling something about a terrible accident with his son, this Just Crafter, and Old Crafter's ordered that son to take Frank's place. All a bit fishy if you ask me, why would Crafter keep a body…"

Cairns let the man drone on. That explained much – Oldershaw would have had no option but to accept Old Crafter's suggestion for a replacement, or risk giving a public insult by rejecting the offer.

"What do we do if they do succeed?"

Cairns fixed his gaze on Max. "Why Max, you just said yourself, there isn't much chance of that."

"That was before I knew the Crafters were involved."

Cairns pursed his lips again; he had been thinking on exactly the same lines. "Crafters being involved does not create a guarantee of success or mean there is anything that we do not know of. It could be simple posturing."

Max leant heavily on the table with his hands. "Look, maybe they won't find it, but there must be something in it for Crafter to risk one of his sons! The old bollock wouldn't normally let any of them near a pair of shears, let alone allow them to go on a little jolly where at least one person ends up dead every time!"

There was silence for a moment after Max spoke. Cairns knew they were waiting for him and it was always worth making someone wait a little longer than they wished.

Notwithstanding that, Cairns had to think about his answer. Oldershaw shared with Cairns the desire for freedom, but the man's zealous pursuit of revenge and his constant hunt for this mythical weapon could spell disaster for Cairns' plans for the villagers to emerge free and unknown into the outside; the only way they would stand a chance of survival.

Cairns could feel it too, of course, just as Oldershaw could. He could sense the power, vast, beyond any Cairns had ever experienced. But Cairns knew where it was and he had the key. He was also determined it would stay hidden, no purpose could be served by taking revenge on the outsiders, they would simply regroup and come back with an even bigger force. No, his way was the only way.

"The greatest secret to our success!" Oldershaw called it. If that were so, then success was nothing other than the vanity of the Norths and the doom they helped impose upon the people they had undertaken a duty to protect. They had destroyed Ostracia, condemning them to a life of imprisonment, hardship and disease for nothing other than an insane lust to hold on to the very power that had brought Ostracians to their knees.

"We have no control over Elder Oldershaw's expedition," Cairns said eventually. "We must focus on what we do have control of. We must proceed as planned, outsider or not, Oldershaw or not. We have no choice."

"And the Crafters?"

Cairns turned to Galvarin, finally having something to smile about. "Well, let us hope they find some reason to speak up. It will save us a very messy problem once people start to go missing with no bodies and our purpose becomes clear." The others' pursed lips showed their understanding. It had been agreed at the last council meeting – they couldn't allow Crafters to leave Ostracia.

"There's just one thing, Elder," Broadside interjected, "you still haven't told us how you plan to remove our people from Ostracia without passing through the Maw."

There were murmurs of agreement from Galvarin and Max. "All in good time," Cairns replied, "there is actually more than one way."

There was only the one way, of course and Cairns would have to make sure of it tonight. Any problems with the tunnels and all of their options were lost.

"Broadside, your report."

The alchemist leaned back in his chair proudly, seemingly oblivious to the sound of splintering wood that made Galvarin wince along with Cairns. "By now the powders will be in all of the wells and springs around the village. The underground stream serves them all. We do not have that long, Elder."

"We have long enough, Cairns replied. He hoped it was true. "You have prepared the schedule of who will need to be evacuated first?"

Broadside nodded. "Yes, Elder," he added quickly, seeing the look on Cairns' face. "Based on those with the least artistic ability, I believe the first to leave should be Carp, he has virtually no detectable artistic presence in his blood."

"Timely as well, considering what happened with his brother," Galvarin said, his voice half-murmured by his hand.

Broadside ignored the mason. "I have left those close to us until later. That is the four of us here, Captains Bryant, Hoard and Coarse, Jolly the aleman who I believe would be too keenly missed, the Deathguard and Simon, naturally." Max grunted at that. "You would have been third out if we were allowing council members to leave with the rest, Max."

"Alright," Cairns said loudly, seeing Max about to turn on a very self-satisfied Broadside. "And for those…" Cairns searched for the word, "staying behind?"

The smile left Broadside's face. "The Crafters, Mary Archer and the Tysons. Yes. Tom has the list, Elder. He knows what to do and when to do it."

"Good," Cairns replied. It would buy them some time. When the Crafters were dealt with, finally dealt with, then Cairns could attend to the list of his own. The Captains would not be leaving, nor would the Deathguard. Simon…well, that was up to Simon. Assundra was the key. She had to survive. "And of Tom himself?"

"He awaits only the right conditions," Broadside replied, the self-satisfied smile back on his face. "I believe he has made contact with the wolves and is now recognised as their pack leader. He will do as we bid as long as we guarantee Assundra's safety."

"Safety?" Max shouted suddenly, making Broadside jump. Cairns pursed his lips. "What about our safety? He killed a man, Broadside, one he had no business killing! It was a message, he sent us a message, he'll no more do as he's bid than Old Crafter will. Tom Franks is just an animal now."

"Calm yourself, Max," Cairns soothed. "We all know why Tom delivered us that message. We promised him Young Crafter and we did not deliver." Max was quiet at that. Cairns decided to ram the message home. "Had my orders been followed, Assundra's safety would not have been severely jeopardised as it was."

Galvarin groaned at the mention of the girl's name. "And as to that, Galvarin," Cairns addressed the mason, "I take it Assundra has been given what she needs?"

Broadside collapsed into laughter at this and Cairns pursed his lips, realising his crass mistake, before being forced to grin along with the guffawing buffoon. Galvarin did not look too pleased.

"Yes," chimed in Broadside in a booming acknowledgement, "well done, old boy! Knew you could do it!"

Max laughed with Broadside this time. Cairns noted with happiness that for once the gardener declined to make any comments about the girl's heritage.

Galvarin didn't so much as smile. "I've given her the powders every time, like you asked," he said quietly, "although I'm still not sure to what end."

Broadside shrugged amidst a chuckle. "They inhibit the inhibitors," he said proudly. "She will retain the natural artistry that she has, in whatever half outsider form it has taken in her and she will pass it on to her children. Being an outsider, she won't have to shield herself from them like we all will." Broadside sniffed. "She will be the mother of our new race."

"Must be a relief that it's almost over," Max said, showing genuine sympathy for Galvarin, "having to touch that outsider skin, knowing she could kill you at any moment and she wouldn't even know anything about it, wouldn't wish that on my worst enemy."

Cairns pursed his lips again. The gardener would just not let this go – the girl did not have sorcery, it was impossible! Yet Max would not accept Cairns' word, had claimed he had seen it, which was clearly impossible. Thankfully, Max knew he could not bring charges for Assundra to answer, reducing his credibility amongst the villagers greatly, but the allegations did little to help.

The decision on what to do with his council members had not yet been taken. Cairns had known for some time that Max's opinions of outsiders would be sure to draw unwanted attention to himself and shortly afterwards his fellow Ostracians in the outside sooner rather than later and that could not be allowed to happen.

Galvarin groaned before he spoke. "Do you need to be told again, Max? Elder Cairns has explained this, she can't be doing sorcery without it being taught to her, it doesn't work like that, it doesn't leak out like artistry, like your son's does."

"What did you say about my boy?"

"When does she leave?" Galvarin asked, ignoring Max. Cairns raised a hand and Max backed off again, turning back to the window, spitting curses and shooting the occasional glance full of poison at Galvarin.

Cairns kept his face neutral – Galvarin had known Cairns would stop Max, but it would have been different elsewhere – the last thing Cairns needed was his council members brawling in the street. Why couldn't they just do as they were told and accept it?

"As soon as possible," Cairns answered. "You'll understand that I cannot give you the details of her departure. You will, however, be given details of where she is to go, once you yourself depart."

His eyes brightened at this. "Thank you, Elder."

"You understand that she's going to be the most missed of all?" Max chimed in, suddenly no longer laughing, but leaning back as if he'd said something of world-shattering importance.

Cairns shot a look at Max. "Of course I realise that, Max. The situation is hardly helped by your constant reminders to the village of how she is different and this latest rumour has made things very difficult for us!" The gardener's gaze dropped at once. These little periods of defiance from the man were getting to be quite tiresome. Cairns hadn't intended to mention the man's rumour mongering but he would not have his authority or knowledge challenged. "That is why, when the time comes, I have decided Young Crafter will be blamed for her disappearance."

Cairns smiled as a look of surprised happiness came over Galvarin and Broadside's faces.

"What of Tom?" It was Galvarin's turn to interrupt now. "People won't believe he just sat back and let Young Crafter…"

Galvarin tailed off. Cairns could swear he saw a tear in the man's eye before he blinked it away – he would never understand the mason. Did he care about the girl or not? "Tom has been ill, as far as everyone is aware, for a long time, Galvarin, he will not be missed. Young Crafter's assertion, of course, will be that it is Tom who is to blame and that is why he has gone missing. The trial will drag on for days, giving you, Max," he pointed, "and you, my good doctor, time to begin the evacuation in earnest."

"Where you going to put hundreds of Ostracians in the outside then?"

Cairns pursed his lips – Max was just full of questions tonight. "When we undertook this project," he said softly, "we all understood the risks. Not everyone would survive, not all would gain their freedom, but Ostracians would be free. Some will be found. With luck on our side, Simon will prevent most from being discovered. Your son, Max, will save them. They will then go their separate ways where they will. We can only try, Max, the alternative is the plague. It will come for us all eventually."

Max nodded but the look on his face spelt disgust. Cairns had some sympathy for the man – he felt that what Cairns had done had taken his child away from him, that Simon was somehow no longer the spoil of his loins. Cairns couldn't tell him the truth, the man wouldn't understand.

"Is Simon prepared?"

"Almost, Broadside," Cairns replied, "The knowledge he needs to take our powers is within his grasp, though he does not realise this yet." He sighed. "There really is such little time that I think that will have to do. Thank you all…"

With a final grunt, Max threw the heavy curtain aside, tearing several runners from the rail as he did so, and left, his cloak billowing out behind him foolishly.

A wink from Broadside showed his understanding as Cairns shot another, more pointed look at the alchemist. "Well, I think I'll line my throat before the meal if there's nothing else, Elder? I do believe we have the luxury of rat pie in the alehouse."

Cairns gave a genuine smile. There were always rats. "We needs must make do, my friend. At least there remains some of Assundra's excellent cider to wash it down with."

"Aye, for you maybe!" the man laughed. "It's not called Elders' Reserve for nothing! It's a shame, of course, she'd have made a fine brewer. But needs must, I suppose." Cairns smiled again. He knew Broadside was thinking of the girl with anything but sympathy. That's if his cock was letting him do any thinking at all and it rarely seemed to where the female form was concerned. "*Special* Elders' Reserve, Jolly's calling it now there's only a few barrels left. I don't suppose I can tell him you've put today's share aside for a friend in need?"

"Ah, I think not!" Cairns replied and the big man left, his laughter echoing down the street. Galvarin followed after, his expression the most curious mixture of dejection and hope.

The door clicked to almost without a sound. Cairns sighed; one could not mould men to one's choosing, one simply had to make the best use of what was given. It was people like Galvarin he was fighting to save and at least the mason understood that, unlike the rest of them.

He forced his creaking bones out of the chair. They were stiffer after the run back, but he felt good after feeding. A good meal, a proper meal, and a few drinks should lubricate him before he summoned Simon again. He fished around in the folds of his robe and dipped his hand into the little store of powders he kept there. This would be the last time, he thought as he licked the finger.

Cairns took a last look around the Council Chambers then he too stepped through the door, making sure to replace the enchantments on the building. He almost walked straight into the Deathguard.

"Ann's dead," he said simply, with a sniff. "Plague took her, she's in the cellar."

Cairns cursed, much to the amusement of the Deathguard. How could things be unravelling when he had planned them so carefully? He only needed a few more days! "Thank you for the information, Jessop. I'm sure you do not need my skills to enable you to deal with her body." He made to leave, then turned back with an afterthought. "And how is out guest?"

"I've got him chained up," the man said, quickly putting a hand out to stop Cairns getting past. "Only there was a little accident."

Cairns' stopped, his eyes narrowing. "What sort of accident?"

"I sent Sam over to give him some food, some nice rat I'd been saving for myself, but unfortunately Tom took a liking to the arm Sam was giving him the food with."

Cairns felt his stomach crease, wanting to double up as his lungs emptied in a sigh. "Is he…"

"I had to get rid of Sam, of course," the Deathguard said. "Another one, eh, Cairns? With that Ann and that other family of plague victims I've got waiting in my cellar, it's not been a good week for you, has it?"

The man's sneer brought a counterpart to Elder Cairns' face.

"Very well," Cairns said slowly, "I will have a few words with Tom. "I think," Cairns added with a quick smile, "that in future you had better feed Tom yourself, don't you?"

Elder Cairns enjoyed the Deathguard's grimace.

CHAPTER 14

Assundra struck out at the wall in frustration. She'd waited for hours for Galvarin in his workshop, she'd practised what to say, run through what she was going to do, even though the thoughts disgusted her, and all he had done when he had got back was to throw her out!

He hadn't said one word to her, even after she'd refused to leave. He'd let her speak, let her get it out. He'd let her beg him. He'd let her...

She shook her head to clear it, the noises of the busy village immediately assaulting her senses again. She wouldn't think about what she'd done.

Assundra didn't understand. Why was he still ignoring her? Afterwards, she'd tried to talk to him, but he'd just picked up his hammer and got on with his work. He wouldn't even look at her. Even when someone coming in to drop off some goods for trade had, almost absent-mindedly, called her an "outsider witch", which at least made a change from 'bitch', he hadn't so much as looked up from his tools.

She leaned against a cottage across the village circle from the mason's yard, watching, telling herself she was hoping that it was just that he didn't want to be disturbed at work, that after he'd finished for the day they could steal off to their glade and he would tell her he'd been thinking of how to help her all afternoon and had come up with a plan.

"Madness!"

Twitching, she wondered why she felt safer here. Or was it that she felt safe? The hustle of people around her, even the insults they threw at her, drowned out the voice in her head telling her to leave, to run. She felt safer here because she could think clearly here.

She'd never seen the beast here and, for all his horrific brazen acts, Young Crafter had never tried to take her in the middle of so many people.

With half an ear she listened to the play rehearsals going on across the other side of the village circle. She shouldn't be here. She should be doing something to help her father! Last time she saw him, he had been half-asleep, half-awake, his breathing ragged, his speech as if it were scraping across stones and the hair…

Assundra wouldn't allow herself to think about the hair.

The bright orange of her favourite dress might not have been the most practical of choices she thought, it didn't exactly blend in with the surroundings, but she couldn't stay in the cupboard for ever. The catalogue had only served to make her fears worse and with nobody to talk to they'd grown inside her, until they had taken over.

"You have nothing to fear, Sunny."

Assundra frowned. The voice wasn't right. She had Young Crafter to fear. She had the fact that she'd lost Galvarin and her one chance at being accepted in the village to fear. She had the fear of what would happen if her father didn't come back. She had the prospect of someone finding out she'd overheard Max and Old Crafter's conversation to fear, although as long as she didn't tell anyone, anyone at all, they couldn't find out she'd heard, surely, could they?

She had the fear of what would happen if someone found out that what Alice said about her was true. Water didn't just boil on its own.

She tried to avoid the fears, they made her heart race, made her mouth dry and they stopped her thinking clearly. She had felt safe in her wardrobe, but she couldn't stay there forever. She felt safe in the glade with Galvarin, but then he'd ruined that. Now she felt safe here, where people could see, where nobody would bother her.

Where she was near him. Near the only thing she knew could protect her, she just had to make him want to.

More than trying not to notice the fear, though, she tried to avoid noticing that Max West was staring at her and had been for a while now. Across from him, near the actors, Mary Archer was watching Max whilst she barked instructions.

"You! Always standing around when there's things to be done! Come on, you can help dress Alice! Come *on*! Max, your wife has been working very hard on this project, you wouldn't want to let you down, would you? Of course you wouldn't. Not after she's worked so hard."

Mary Archer, known as the Archer woman for her unerring ability to strike at the centre of her chosen gossip prey, bumbled off to find her next target and Assundra breathed again, watching the woman's ridiculous frills and bustles bobbing with her as she trotted around, fussing over anyone who wasn't doing the tasks she had no doubt appointed for them. The woman didn't even have the figure for that corset; it looked like she was wearing a Feast Day Pudding. Her hair was no less bouncy; a mop of unruly red curls, bursting out from under a hat that looked like a small dinner plate with bits of lace added. Assundra hated hats; all they did in this heat was seal in the sweat on your forehead, giving you spots. She hated more the fact that Mary Archer didn't have a spot to try and hide.

At times she wondered it they hated her as much as they made out. When she was alone in the orchard she'd planted with her own hands, or out with her father in the fields watching him work, or even when she was burying the dead, she'd often sit and wonder what it would be like to be like Alice. To be wanted but accepted and respected as well. Most of the time, she wasn't sure she wanted that; it seemed to mean you had to agree with what everyone else said even if you didn't agree. She hoped that was why they treated her like they did.

A lump in her throat made her turn away from Galvarin again. He knew she was there. Instead, she pulled back around the side of the cottage and leaned out to look at the actors where she couldn't be seen. A little stage, part of which seemed to be made from some of the alehouse's tables, was surrounded by torches. The simple, curtained wooden platform was at the back of the village circle and some people, ferociously corralled by the Archer woman, were laying out benches in an oval around them.

Assundra frowned – why were they setting out so many benches? There were clearly not that many people left in the village. If they were putting them out for the dead they hadn't put out nearly enough.

Alice looked fantastic, she thought, as someone fiddled with her dress. Max and someone else had been harangued into hanging the thick red velvet curtain which was to stand in front of the stunning, though aged tableau of the old city square, correct to the last detail, including the intact, huge church on the west side and…the well. For a moment she held her breath, unable to take her eyes from the painting, expecting the beast to rise from it and attack them all at any moment.

"Right, people! People! One more time, there isn't long now," Mary Archer called, clapping her hands together. Not only did the actors and stage hands stop as the shrill, tinny instrument that was her voice called out, but so did everyone around the village circle. Assundra heard a few people curse. Looking across, she saw Galvarin pause in his work. For a moment their eyes caught and she smiled, rolling her eyes towards the Archer woman, and he smiled.

A wave of hope rolled over her and she realised she had stopped breathing, but all too soon the smile dropped and he went back to work. Perhaps she was right – perhaps after he had finished work he would listen and she could explain! She gulped back and fought the urge to run over to him and thank him for the smile, thank him for the gift of hope he'd just given her, but she knew it would just annoy him. No, she had to wait for him to be ready, that was all!

In the meantime she had to wait. As Mary had drawn the attention of the entire village to the play, she thought she might as well watch now. There were three of them – Alice and two others, two men, but she couldn't tell who they were. One was a tall figure dressed in fine, bordering on gaudy, robes of office that spoke first.

"Alas!
Our plan has come to nought!
Alas!
Time is short, it seems
They plot, they plan, they scheme against us,
They betray us, curse us, they all desert us,
Twain but the end remains!
Death visits plainly with us in sight!"

Alice's turn came next, her sleek, smooth blonde hair catching even the slightest shard of light and shining across the village circle. Assundra was pleased she'd won the role ahead of Mary Archer, though she saw the gossip's hand in the simple blue wimple of a dress Alice wore that did little to show off the figure she was famed for.

"Alas!
All plans have come to nought!
Our leaders sit alone in court,
Whilst all around our souls are bought
And sold like leaden harps of woe,
Alas!
Their end shall bury us!"

Much clapping followed the speech from the men dotted around the village circle, making Alice giggle when Assundra was sure she was supposed to be looking serious and in dread. The third figure, who looked a lot like Jolly the aleman, turned, his Elders' robes too large for him and flapping around in the evening breeze.

"Alas!
Their plans have come to nought!
Our time runs out, we are betrayed,
The knot of time it frays and snaps,
The compass points have pointed last,
But Ostracians do not take flight!
Ostracians do not take fright!
Ostracians fight!"

"What's happening?"

Assundra almost screamed as the boy appeared next to her as if from nowhere. "Simon, you bollock! Don't do that!" she hissed, driving her elbow back into his stomach. She didn't bother asking him how he'd got there without her seeing or hearing. She didn't want to know; those sorts of things were only too common with Simon these days. She kept telling him he'd lose his limbs for it, but he didn't listen.

"What's got into you?"

"What's got into me?" She looked up fearfully towards Galvarin's workshop, but she couldn't see from this angle. She breathed a sigh of relief – that meant Galvarin couldn't see her with Simon either. "How many times?" She couldn't find the words to go on and looking at his confused face just made her angrier, so she shut up.

"I don't get you sometimes. Is my mother doing well?"

"No," she replied tetchily, "she's messing it all up, look, she's laughing all over the place!"

Simon laughed too. "Good! That'll show the Elder!"

"Don't be such a bollock!"

"It's only a bloody play!" he said moodily. "And what sort of language is that anyway, it's not very ladylike is it?"

"I'm no bloody lady."

"I'm sure Galvarin would agree with you," he snorted, so she gave him another, much harder, dig with her elbow and looked away as tears stung her eyes. He must have seen as he was quiet after that.

She tried to focus back on the play and ignore Simon, who was fidgeting awkwardly next to her. Why couldn't he tell when someone didn't want to talk to him?

They were rehearsing what happened after the invaders had left now. The real battle. Helpless, scared and fighting for themselves. That's how her father always described the Elders, not the people. His father had told him from *his* father's own account and he had been the son of Marchman, who had fought the Norths himself years before and who had been slaughtered in Lord North's trials.

The Ostracians had turned on their nobility after the invasion. After the stock had begun to die, there had been only thievery, killing and despair. It was true, the Elders had restored order after the outsiders had left, *after* Ostracia was sealed in its plague-ridden prison, but the way the Franks family told it they instilled that control with nothing more than yet more killing and threats; nothing better than what the Norths and the rest of the aristocracy had done before.

Large sections of Ostracian society had wanted to travel beyond the borders, to take revenge on the outsiders, but the Elders had held them back. Assundra's father said this had given the outsiders time to let their plague take hold. No Ostracian could get near the Yawning Maw after that, the plague took them too quickly.

Assundra deeply doubted that the play would show things that way but you could ban all the books and plays and refuse to teach people to read all you wanted, the truth remained in the families.

Her attention was brought back to the play as the Lord North character, who had withdrawn, cowed in the far corner of the stage, which was painted up to look like one of the spires, began wailing. Was this after Elspeth and Kryman, Lord North's children, had been murdered? She knew the invaders had been unable to enter Stracathri, as the Norths called their spire, but the Gifted One and her brother had borne their father's warning no heed and had strutted out to meet the invaders themselves. Their bodies had never been found, but as her father told it, they had taken hundreds of outsiders in minutes. Assundra stopped herself shivering; that sort of power scared her. She didn't even like the melees.

Whoever the actor was, he was trying to portray Lord North losing his mind, which she had often heard the Elders say is what had happened, but her father would have none of it.

"Never more bollocks spoken", he said. "If there's one thing my family know from Marchman's time, it's that the Norths always, always knew what they were bloody doing. Losing his mind my arse, they all planned it, all of 'em."

Whenever she asked him what the point of that plan was, how they could have possibly planned to die, he always just looked at her sadly. She didn't think her father knew and she didn't press. Tom Franks didn't like to be pressed, especially these days.

She glanced over her shoulder at the sullen Simon, whose eyes were fixed firmly on her breasts. She stopped herself shuddering as she found herself contemplating him touching her. There was no way she could do it. He troubled her.

"It's Young Crafter, isn't it?" he whispered into her ear eventually.

Assundra sighed. "Young Crafter?"

"Why you won't talk to me, why you're scared! It's not Galvarin at all, is it, it's him!"

"Simon what are you talking about? It's nothing to do with you!"

"You said I couldn't protect you like Galvarin can. Well, I can now! I'll show you!"

"Show me?" Assundra span to face him. "How can you show me, Simon? All that will happen is he'll beat you down just like last time! Then you'll get in trouble again, just like last time! And nothing will have changed for me, *just like last time*! Why can't you accept what you are!"

"I don't care about trouble!" he retorted, far too loudly, and she shushed him. "I don't care!" he repeated, but he'd lowered his voice. "I don't care what any of them think! And I've told you, I've changed!"

"Well why don't you tell Young Crafter that?"

"I will! I'll tell all of them they're stupid for following that bloody Elder wherever he goes like they're his pet dogs."

Simon was really starting to annoy her now. "Pet Dogs? What are you talking about?"

"The Elder!" he exclaimed, spittle flying from his mouth. It was disgusting. "They follow him like dogs, doing everything he says without even thinking about what they're doing."

"Who'd keep bloody dogs as pets? They never do what they're told, I should know, they've been after me enough times. You're being stupid; the Elders haven't got anything to do with it!"

"They don't stop them though, do they? You'll learn."

"I'll learn? What's that supposed to mean?"

"You'll just learn, that's all! And wolves aren't dogs, anyway."

"And you're a fine one to talk!"

Simon turned onto his side to look at her. "What the hells do you mean?"

Before she realised what she was doing, she turned too, leaving her face inches away from his and her leg nowhere to go but to touch his. Abruptly, she turned back away from the stupid boy. "Well you follow the Elder don't you? You're his apprentice."

"Shut up," was all he replied.

She hated it when he got like this and he was nearly always like this these days. Everything seemed to annoy him. He'd never have the guts to actually say anything to anyone, he knew he'd never get away with it. He'd come of age, but he wasn't man enough to deal with Young Crafter yet. He was more like a girl than a man – he only had a few wisps of fluff on his upper lip and other than that he barely had a hair on his body, to say nothing of how scrawny he was.

"There's no proof of what Barth wrote in his play all those years ago, either," he went on, apparently oblivious to her being desperate for him to leave. "Everything from back then was burnt, I reckon Cairns has made this all up."

"*Elder* Cairns!" Assundra hissed back at Simon. "And the play survived, didn't it? So some things must have!"

"So why aren't we allowed to see them then?" he hissed confidently.

Assundra let out an exasperated sigh. "The Elders do all that! You couldn't read them if he showed them to you anyway."

"Don't you care about…"

"No! Now leave me alone!"

Simon shuffled his feet behind her again, but he didn't move. Assundra pursed her lips. She didn't want to draw attention to herself by leaving. Truth be told, she didn't want to leave. She had nowhere else to go. She worried that if she moved now she wouldn't be safe any more. There were villagers all around her, Max was still…no, she noticed, Max wasn't there any more. She let a little tension leave her body now she knew he wasn't staring at her any more, but she still didn't want to move. If she didn't move, everything would be alright.

"They haven't even shown Lord North's bit," she heard Simon moan behind her.

"What bit?" she replied irritably, wondering why she was replying.

She turned to see Simon quickly raising a hand to his head, shaking it as if he'd received a blow. "Nothing."

"Did you take the script? Have you been stealing again?" she hissed, slapping him on the back of the head. "From your own mother! If your father catches you it'll mean another beating!"

"I don't care! I've had so many they don't hurt anyway."

Assundra didn't say anything; he wouldn't have wanted to remember that Galvarin had made him cry when he'd dealt out his own justice.

"And for your information," he went on, "I didn't steal anything! As you so caringly pointed out, I wouldn't have been able to read it anyway! I heard my mother reading it out loud and there was a whole bit in there about Lord North and how he tried to help us. It said it was all a big gamble that he lost, but that he was betrayed and it wasn't his fault."

Assundra looked at him. Was he telling the truth? It would fit in with what her father said. Had the Norths just run out of time? "That's a lot for a little scene in a play to say," she ventured carefully.

"Well…well, I heard it somewhere anyway."

"Right." He'd tensed up. "Stay there, Assundra. I'll show you what I can do."

Before she could turn around, she saw Simon striding towards the alehouse.

She called out for him to stop, but a voice rang booming across the village circle. The man playing Lord North had a voice that she'd never forget. It was Young Crafter.

"Betrayed by all, it falls so thus,
Mired in a selfish tourney of lust,
For power not love, the angels cuss,
To damn us."

She saw Simon stop as he heard the voice. He turned on his heel and marched towards the stage. "Simon no!" she called out, but he didn't hear. Or didn't want to.

Alice's voice cut through the air.

"Our hands are blood, our souls are crushed,
Our bodies held, our spirits set free,
To damnation they ride.
Our city in ruins as it stands intact,
The disease that festers is cured and thrives,
T'wards damnation we stride."

"You bollock!" Simon screamed and Young Crafter turned, but his garb stopped him from moving quickly enough. Simon's fist crunched straight into his face, but Simon had overreached. He fell flat on his face on the stage. Laughter sounded from all around and Assundra felt her face flush. She looked away from Simon as Young Crafter's friends picked him up from the floor with sneers on their faces.

When she did she saw Galvarin standing back in his yard, arms folded, looking at her. She held his gaze as Jolly's deep voice boomed out. Assundra was thankful that they drowned out the sounds of Simon's yelps as the blows hit him.

"Nothing lasts forever. They were warned.
Nothing remains. They were warned.
Nothing is left but the sentence imposed,
Nothing is left as the fear stands alone,
They were warned.

It's gone now. They were warned.
Their Tower, their refuge, their stronghold, their power.
They were warned.
In the care of the Elders they should have resided,
Instead of the claws of outsiders invited,
Their punishment a surety as certain as death.
I here warn.

Ostracia returns, there will be a new dawn.
They are warned."

Assundra's mouth filled with the taste of nothing and she saw Young Crafter suddenly fly back, crying out in pain. Simon was on his knees, his hands held behind his back by Erol Tyson and Patrick Crafter. His face was covered in blood and he was grinning.

"Run, Sunny. Run, now!"

"Run?" she said stupidly to herself, she never got a reply, but this time the voice surprised her.

"Run for the Elder!"

Assundra found her legs moving before she could think about it. Cottages passed by her vision – she didn't want to run across the village circle so she ran down the alleys between the cottages. She wasn't safe here now. She had to go to the Elder, she was safe there. Elders were always safe.

In no time at all she was at Elder Cairns' cottage, bursting through the door.

"Elder!" she gasped, but was stopped right in her tracks. The room was in tatters. Books were strewn about the floor, pages torn from their bindings. Candles were tipped from their holders, covering the ancient and expensive tapestries in molten wax.

Max and Elder Oldershaw were standing, frozen like children caught doing something wrong, Max with his hands in Elder Cairns' desk. For a moment the three of them stood there, just looking at each other. Just as she thought she should run, her mouth filled with the taste of nothing and she had to spit.

She couldn't move. Max walked towards her with a snarling grin on his face. "Well look at this! No need for your fancy book reading leading her to the council chambers after all!"

Elder Oldershaw had left the book for her? Assundra's heart lifted – that must mean he was going to help her!

"No need for your imbecilic idea of kidnapping Galvarin to force her hand, either!" Elder Oldershaw grunted in reply to Max, making her frown. Why would they want to kidnap Galvarin?

"That would have worked!" Max shouted...shouted...back at the Elder. The man didn't know! She hadn't had a chance to tell anyone what she'd heard in the cellar! She opened her mouth to tell Elder Oldershaw Max was working with the Crafters, the he couldn't trust the gardener, that he didn't realise what was going on, that he had to let her go, then he could help her, find her father and make everything alright, but she couldn't move her lips to speak.

"Seen too much now," she realised Elder Oldershaw was saying. "Have to put a stop to that. Changes the plans for her afterwards."

Max leered a grin at her and picked up a heavy book from the floor and lifted it above his head. "I can sort that out, don't you worry." As he swung the book down, her hand went instinctively to the fold in her dress, but she was too late.

"Oh Sunny...you're not safe...I'm coming. I'm coming now."

CHAPTER 15

The cage was about the length of a man lying down by half his height. The thin but sturdy rods of wood were bound together firmly with cord. The ground where he sat was covered in fresh human faeces.

Simon felt the vomit surge up to his mouth again as the smell found a new breath to ride in on. At least he could see the faeces – the straw to his right smelled like it was hiding all sorts of other bodily fluids under its soggy, brown mass, it had certainly had his own urine added to it since last night. He wondered if the straw had ever been changed, but the thought just made him angry.

Closing his eyes, Simon breathed slowly, the way she'd shown him how to. Breathing from deep down, from deep inside, spreading the calm throughout himself. The anger was not good. Not since the shrine.

The eyes flickered in the back of his mind. His heart fluttered at the same time.

The shrine had changed everything for him. Sometimes he found himself sweating for no reason, wondering if they had changed for the better.

"Simon," a voice called from nearby. Simon sprang to his feet, ready to try and give Bryant a bloody nose again, but forgot the height of the cage. His head smacked into the bars above, the bruise left by Young Crafter's fist feeling like it stretched across his entire skull.

A figure approached the cage in the fading light. The Captain had easily parried his blow earlier, when he'd dragged Simon to the cage, but then Simon had been off balance and hadn't used any of his…special skills. He found the best way to summon them was to suck the power out of his stomach, almost a retching motion, but it sucked something to the back of his throat, something that had power when he spat it out, when he used it.

Once more the eyes flickered, flashing blue lightning and the power he'd sucked up was gone in an instant.

"Simon," the voice said again, calmly, and the figure crouched beside the cage, allowing the light to show his face.

"Elder!" Simon said in surprise. "What are you doing here? I thought…"

"That you wouldn't see me until the trial, yes, that is what would be proper. I have tried to instruct you on such matters before, but it appears you have no comprehension of *just how serious this is*!"

Simon felt his heel dig into the dirt, or whatever it was. The eyes blazed in the back of his mind. The eyes that watched him, always. That knew what he was thinking. That helped him.

"Do you have nothing to say?" Cairns was whispering, but with the force with which he delivered the whispers, he may as well have been screaming. "Simon, if I am to help you, I need to know that what I have told you remains secure!"

"You let Bryant drag me off in front of everyone!" Simon found himself saying. "He kept yanking at my arm, I thought he'd tear out my…"

"Do not show that splint!" Cairns hissed as Simon raised his arm. The Elder looked about him, to see if anyone had seen, Simon presumed. He folded his hand back into a fist. "Knowledge of that splint would not go well for you at this trial, Simon! You know I cannot reveal your apprenticeship yet, it would jeopardise everything."

Simon scowled and didn't bother to hide it. "Your secrets are safe with me," he murmured.

"They had better be, Simon! Or did you think I would leave our future to the chance of your mouth?"

The eyes blazed and Simon spat again, getting rid of what he had called, without even realising it. Looking up, he saw Elder Cairns looking at the spittle thoughtfully. "Then again," the Elder said quietly, "we do not want to be too hasty. I am sorry, Simon, it is just that this trial has come as something of an inconvenience. I do not blame you for attacking Young Crafter at all – how could anyone? – but an idea has just occurred to me."

"But the trial…"

"I am not going to allow you to become a figure for their humiliation, Simon. There will be a trial, yes, for show, nothing more. Justice must be seen to be done, I cannot just rule in your absence, it would make it much more difficult for me the next time there was an actual crime before me."

Simon snorted, but didn't say anything. The Elder was probably right, he usually was. He winced as the eyes in the back of his mind shot a stab of pain through his head.

"Are you alright?" Cairns asked with sudden concern. "Was Captain Bryant over-zealous in his duties?"

"Yes! He beat me round the head with the hilt of his sword when I had the cheek to fight back!" was what he wanted to say.

"No," Simon lied, "nothing like that." He knew if he made a complaint about the rough treatment there'd be more than one witness to Simon attempting to thump Bryant before it had begun, which would lead to another charge. Something crept up inside his gut, its tendril-like fingers reaching up and making him bow his head.

The Elder drew his lips in as he always did. It made his face look too small when he did so and that face was too symmetrical anyway, Simon had always thought there was something not quite right about it.

"As long as you are undamaged, I believe I still have a way out of this that will benefit both of us. The plan should not need to change."

Undamaged? Is that all Elder Cairns thought he was, a tool of some sort? Simon was sick of this – the presumption, the expectation without Cairns ever giving anything back! He knew he could tear the Elder's nerves out of his neck if he could get close enough.

"You still plan to kill me then?" he said.

Elder Cairns smiled. "Of course! It will be a good spectacle for them."

Simon grunted a reply. Cairns was laughing. He was always laughing. One day he'd wipe that grin off Cairns' face, he was sure he would.

"If anything," the Elder continued, "the extra charges you seem to have incurred upon your person will aid our cause, the Crafters will be easier to convince if Young Crafter is playing into our hands. Well done, Simon. The diversion should help convince our fellow villagers that the appropriate punishment for your crimes is death, for a persistent offender. With Elder Oldershaw otherwise engaged, I will receive no challenge and will offer to carry out the sentence myself, due to the dangerous nature of the powers you have been developing in secret.

"The admittance of your powers will allow Young Crafter and the rest to maintain face as to why they could barely damage you, despite their assault and will satisfy them that justice has been done."

"What then?"

Cairns shrugged. "Then I will hide you in the tunnels beneath Ostracia, until you are needed. You have helped to distinctly turn this to our advantage, Simon."

The eyes flashed and Simon spat again. "What about Assundra?" he said at length, ignoring the fact that he had attacked Young Crafter out of rage, not as part of some grand plan. For some reason she hadn't been able to stop him. Simon assumed that she must have seen the advantage in attacking Young Crafter that Cairns was talking about. The only other explanation was that he was so angry that he somehow defied her, but she had shown him that to defy her was foolish and impossible, so that couldn't be.

Cairns was looking at him sternly. "Assundra has my personal attention to her safety, Simon. I thought we had discussed this."

"It's not just Young Crafter, after what I saw her do the other night I'm not worried about him, but what if she can't control it?" The eyes in the back of his mind glowered, but distantly. Simon had learned to tell when the presence in his mind was angry, but she seemed fine. He didn't know why he was sure it was a female presence, but he was. Something about the curve of the eyes.

"There is nothing to control, Simon," Elder Cairns was saying. "Has she exhibited any other signs of…similar behaviour?"

"Not since," Simon replied, dropping his eyes. The memory of it was troubling and he seized at the only other explanation he had been thinking about. "Elder, was she drugged? I know the spell on the Council Chambers was what held her in the air, but she was mumbling something about beasts and red eyes, mad stuff."

"Yes," Cairns replied thoughtfully, "I was wondering that too, however when I examined her I could sense nothing on her breath nor in her body that would indicate the use of powders. The darkness can often do strange things to the mind, my young friend."

The Elder smiled again and Simon forced himself to smile back, the eyes in the back of his mind flashing amusement as he did so. Somehow he knew the eyes were there to help him, to guide him. To show him what must be done.

To show him when he was being lied to.

"I must go," Cairns said quickly and Simon heard footsteps approaching from behind the ridge under which his cage sat. "I will see you at the trial Simon and do not worry. Just trust me."

With that, the Elder was gone, scampering down the bank with surprising agility for a man his age just as Captain Bryant rounded the corner with…oh gods…his father.

"You stupid little bollock!" his father roared, even startling Bryant he was screaming so loudly. "What have you done this time?"

"I haven't done…"

"Don't give me that, you wouldn't be here if you hadn't done anything! I am so sick of you. You want to get yourself faced that's your business! You want to count your luckies that you're in that cage or else I'd be beating your hide so hard you could make armour out of it!"

Simon took his eyes from his father in disgust. He didn't even bother to hide it these days, one beating was the same as another and besides, she'd shown him a way to make it hurt less. "If you're so sick of me then why are you here?"

"You impudent little bollock! Me and your mum have given you the best years of our lives and this is how you repay us?"

"Yes, it clearly is, isn't it?"

His father slammed his fists down on the roof of the cage. "I've always known there was something wrong about you. Not even had a woman yet, have you?" Simon dropped his eyes before he realised what he was doing. "Didn't think so! Do you know what I was doing by the time I was your age?"

"I don't care," he replied. She made him spit.

"No, I bet you don't," his father laughed back at him. "I bet you don't want to hear about anyone who's a success. Why do you think that outsider bitch chose the mason over you? A mason, Simon? You're useless, no wonder you have to force yourself on women. I hope you get what's coming to you. You disgust me."

"Thank you for your support, father, it means such a great deal to me." She made him spit again, but only just in time. Her eyes were blazing.

"I've told your mother not to come," Max went on, ignoring him like he always did. Bryant laughed alongside him. "I've told her not to bother with you again, you're on your own, you hear me? Attacking a girl! And getting *caught*! You're no son of mine."

Max turned and stalked off, muttering to himself. "There goes my father for the last time," Simon said softly, looking up at Bryant, "we can only hope. Now why don't you piss off with him?"

Bryant's smile faded quickly and he jammed his face against the bars. "Look, you little bollock, I heard what you did! If it had been up to me, I'd have taken this cage and thrown it into the Forest, let the wolves have you!"

"I know, Bryant," Simon said softly, "I know you would. Because you wouldn't have the courage to do it yourself."

"Courage? Little Simon West talks to me about courage?" Bryant laughed. "Oh, they're going to take you apart down there, you maggot! And if they don't, believe me I'll come back and make sure they finish the job! At least Assundra will be safe from you prowling around after her, trying to leech onto her like a…well, like a leech!"

Bryant seemed pleased with his little speech, even though it did little except make Simon laugh. Bryant stalked off down the hill after Simon's father, back towards the village.

They'd be here soon, he could hear them. Elder Cairns would have rejoined them by now and ready to preside over this farce. Simon rattled the bars of his cage even though he knew it would do little good. It would take the work of a moment to either burn the wood or crack it, but every time he tried to call power the eyes in the back of his mind cut the supply off, forcing him to spit the artistry out before it could be formed. In any case, this was all part of the plan.

The plateau just beneath the barrow had become the place where most of the judgements were carried out. Simon had seen enough judgements now to know what was awaiting him – he would be held in the cage, what villagers were interested would gather around and then Elder Cairns would begin asking questions, of him and of the one making the charge.

Galvarin bloody Jallel.

Simon spat again. The mason would pay for what he'd done! Not because of the charge, Elder Cairns had told him about that, but because of how Galvarin had turned Assundra against him. The mason had come to find Simon, shortly after kicking two of Simon's teeth out, to say that he wasn't through with Simon, that he had something special lined up. Simon had wanted to tear the skin from his flesh, to watch while the mason's eyes had boiled in their sockets.

He had done nothing.

As the first few villagers crested the steps to the plateau, he allowed himself one final scowl, before spittle landed in his eyes.

He spat himself, again, then covered his face with his hands as more spittle rained down on him from all sides.

"Coward!"

"Rapist!"

"Always knew there was something wrong about you!"

Simon waited until the flow of spit stopped before lowering his arms. There was a much bigger crowd than he had expected. At least a hundred people had surrounded the cage in a circle, all quiet now as Elder Cairns raised his arms out wide.

"A charge has been levelled against Simon West, son of Max and Alice. He is of age and of no fixed trade." Murmurs followed the Elder's words and Simon got the distinct impression that the Elder was milking the pause for effect. The eyes in the back of his mind narrowed. "Would the leveller of the charge please step forward."

Galvarin must have been behind him, for Cairns was looking straight past where Simon was crouched. Simon thought that it was as well for the mason that he couldn't be seen, or he could find his tongue torn to shreds. Simon spat again.

"Galvarin Jallel, son of Samuel and Tania, you are of age and you are chief mason to Ostracia," Elder Cairns called in what Simon assumed was Galvarin's direction. He must have had some sign of assent as he moved on. "What is the nature of your charge against Simon West?"

"I charge," Simon heard Galvarin call out from behind him, "that Simon West did follow, drug and then in some form assault Assundra Franks, daughter of Tom and Nilha, who is of age and apprentice to the Deathguard."

"In some form?"

"I was not present for the assault, Elder."

Murmurs rose among the crowd. Simon smiled – he didn't think this was going to take very long. "If you are not present then how can you raise the charge, Galvarin?"

Galvarin coughed. "I am raising it on behalf of Assundra Franks, who confided to me the nature of her assault, Elder."

More murmurs followed this, higher-pitched this time. Simon guessed that this confirmed the rumours the women had heard from Mary Archer, who was the starting point for most rumours. He tried to keep the scowl from his face – he had seen with his own eyes that the rumours about Assundra's sorcery were true.

"Why doesn't she raise it herself?" Simon heard his father growl from somewhere in the crowd. Simon was surprised – he hadn't expected his father to show up.

"Will Assundra Franks step forward," Cairns called out, silencing the crowd. Simon smiled again – there was no answer, nor would there be. "In the absence of Assundra Franks, with Galvarin Jallell please justify his charge."

Simon listened, his mood growing ever darker, as Galvarin outlined what he was supposed to have done.

It was all lies. Lies Elder Cairns had invented. Lies Simon had agreed to.

"Do you deny the allegations made by Galvarin Jallel, Simon?"

It took some time for Simon to realise Elder Cairns was talking to him. He set his face as hard as he could and made ready to lie himself. "No."

The crowd murmured its disapproval and Simon laughed at them.

"There is a secondary charge," a crusty, withered voice called from somewhere in the crowd. Simon scanned the faces but could see nobody. It didn't matter – everyone in the village knew Old Crafter's voice when they heard it. "The unprovoked and vicious attack on my son, Young Crafter must not go unpunished!"

Elder Cairns raised his hands once more to quell the clamour of agreement that met Old Crafter's words. Simon frowned – Cairns was right, the Crafters really did have a surprising amount of support. Simon tried to read Cairns' expression, but there was nothing to be read, only that half-smile he always wore, posed on the brink of laughter.

"The charges will be heard together," Cairns' called to the crowd. "As the charge against Assundra is the more serious, the sentencing for this charge will be sufficient. As there seems to be little doubt about the second charge, I do not see a need to discuss it."

"My son deserves satisfaction!"

There was another cry of support, but it seemed to contain far fewer numbers than before. Cairns audibly sighed. "There is no provision in Ostracian law for satisfaction! The charge has been heard and it is now my job to provide sentence! I find Simon West guilty of both charges!"

A murmur from the crowd signalled its assent to the verdict. Simon caught the words "beating" and "severe" floating on the breeze. Old Crafter's disgruntled shouts were drowned out quickly.

Simon pursed his lips – so this was his moment to 'die'.

Cairns started to speak but was again silenced by the crowd – this time by startled groans. Looking up, Simon saw someone pushing his way through the crowd to the front.

"There has been another!" someone cried, then bursting through the crowd came the portly bulk of Elder Oldershaw. Simon couldn't stop himself inhaling audibly. Thankfully, even though it was his trial, nobody was paying him the slightest bit of attention. Except her.

"There has been another plague death!" Oldershaw announced, speaking directly to Elder Cairns, who had a look on his face that Simon was glad that for once he had not caused.

"Elder, they are asking for you, you'd better go."

Cairns didn't move. "We have finished here, Elder, I was just about to pass sentence."

"He is guilty?"

"He is," Cairns replied, frowning.

"Then the sentence is clear – a beating, to be administered by Captain Bryant. Max, will you…"

"I object!" Old Crafter cried, pushing his way through the crowd too.

"Your objection is noted and forgotten, Crafter," Oldershaw replied. "The sentence will be carried out as laid down by the Elders' lore. Max, will you accompany Captain Bryant?"

Simon stared in horror as a wide, toothless grin spread over his father's face. "With pleasure, Elder." He looked up to Cairns, but the Elder was standing open-mouthed.

"Cairns!" Simon hissed, but Cairns was looking at Oldershaw with just as much astonishment as Simon himself was feeling. With a shiver, Simon realised Cairns was no longer in control of this situation.

"Elder Cairns, will you accompany me please? The situation is urgent, we must prevent further spread of the plague."

The eyes in the back of Simon's mind flashed with amusement but Simon himself felt nothing of the sort. What was Elder Oldershaw up to? To the crowd, to Elder Cairns even, Oldershaw was simply concerned for the welfare of the village, wanting to prevent further spread of the plague, but from the way Oldershaw shot a look at Simon he knew it was about something else. This was Simon's punishment. This was how Oldershaw was going to repay Simon for taking lessons from Elder Cairns and not informing him.

He couldn't help be unaware of the disaster his desire for petty revenge could have on the village! Elder Cairns had told Simon many lies, but one truth was that his plans were essential to the village's survival, even Simon, who hated Cairns, could see that.

Cairns himself stiffly nodded to Oldershaw, through a smile that Simon needed no artistry to inform him was not real.

She made Simon spit. He hadn't even been aware any artistry had been called upon. He found he was furious. This apprenticeship was over. The eyes flashed again, wide open, searing blue into the corners of his own vision. This time Simon did not spit.

The crowd was dispersing now. Laughter echoed in his ears all around him as they passed the cage, spitting again. He could feel the power there, at the back of his throat, but the eyes in the back of his mind warned him into ignoring it. For now.

She would tell him when he was ready.

Simon was dimly aware of an exchange of words between the Elders as he was being dragged away before his father caught up with them. "Told you you'd get what you deserved you useless bollock! Take him to our place,"

"No, Max," Bryant replied, shifting his grip under Simon's armpit, giving Simon a dead arm.

"What did you just say to me?"

Simon had heard that phrase many times before, normally as a precursor to his ears ringing from another blow to the head. "Elder's orders, we're to take him to Elspeth Wood."

"What the bloody hell for?"

Bryant chuckled. "Did you hear me say it were Elder's orders, Max? Now you going to give me a hand, or what?"

As a member of the Elder Council, Simon knew his father outranked Captain Bryant, but there was no way he was going to countermand an Elder's order. With a grunt, his father took the slack from under Simon's other armpit and he was lifted from the ground.

Max grunted again. "Sod this," he heard his father say and felt himself fall to the floor again as his father let go.

"Bloody hell, Max!" Bryant exclaimed and let go of his side too. Simon tasted dirt in his mouth, which was preferable to what he had tasted when he had been thrown in the cage. The power was just *there*…and this time the eyes didn't stop, they just blazed, encouraging him – telling him it was alright, that now it was time!

"This'll make him easier to carry," he heard his father say, but all too late as a weight crashed down on the back of his neck. Something dribbled from his mouth and Simon tasted dirt one more time before everything went black.

CHAPTER 16

Assundra pulled against the shackles once more, sobbing, hoping the brick had somehow come loose since the last time she pulled at it. Slumping back when the brick held fast, she cried out loud in frustration.

Just like when she'd been in the well, there was nobody to hear and screaming only made the sticky wet bump on her head hurt more.

Two small candles provided some illumination to the gloom in the basement, but not much. There wasn't much to see anyway – a couple of large desks and a pile of chairs in one corner, a large grating in the floor and the wall lined with shackles were all there was. Here and there it looked like the walls had been daubed in ink, but she couldn't make out what anything said. In the ceiling at the far end was the trapdoor through which she'd been bundled hours earlier.

She didn't even know where she was. The Crafters had got her in here through some tunnel or other. Max had knocked her out with the spine of a large book, but she'd come round quicker than they'd expected. For a moment, in the struggle in the low tunnel, she'd thought she'd be able to get away, she'd got free of their arms in their surprise at her coming round, but all too quickly they'd grabbed her again and this time held her firm.

It seemed like the whole clan were here, wherever here was, but she couldn't be sure. Young Crafter was there, she knew that, and the rest of them had all been there waiting for her. As she'd come out of one trapdoor and quickly down another, they'd given her a slow hand clap, jeering at her. The look on Erol Tyson's face made her feel sick. It was the presence of Old Crafter and Mary Archer that Assundra didn't understand – surely they couldn't want to witness what Erol Tyson and Young Crafter wanted to do to her?

"Let me out" she screamed, pulling at the chain again, but to no avail. "Where are you now?" she screamed at the voice that was usually in her head. "Where are you now?"

"I'm right here, Assundra," a thickly rich, female voice replied from the shadows. "I've been here all the time. It's been interesting watching you struggle."

Assundra pulled at the chain again, though she did not know why. She just had to do something. "What do you want with me?"

Mary just walked towards her, half-shrouded in shadow and her face hidden in blackness, but Assundra knew it was her. Only one woman in Ostracia was that tall and that round. "I don't want anything to do with you, my dear girl, you can rest assured of that."

Perhaps it was the gloom, or the musty smell that filled the air, but somehow Mary didn't seem the same here as she did in the village. The village gossip, busybody and know-it-all rolled into one, she was usually so bubbly, bustling this way and that, bossing people about. Here she seemed, even though she was nothing but a dark shadow, dignified, almost refined and Assundra was sure the Archer woman had a stronger accent before.

Assundra felt the knife press against her leg where it was hidden in the fold of her dress. So they hadn't searched her at least. It was useless to her while her hands were tied like this though. She would be safer if she could get to her knife!

"No words, outsider? You were ever the sly, quiet one. We have been watching you for some time, as I am sure you are aware. This process could have been made much more painless for you had your father chosen to cooperate with us but unfortunately he has allied himself with the Elder Council…"

Mary stopped as Assundra burst out laughing. Once she'd started she couldn't stop. It felt like a relief and a pain at the same time. "My father? Allied with the Elder Council? You must be off your nut."

"Watch your tone, young lady." Mary stepped forward again. Nothing more, just stepped forward. "There is still some prospect in what is to come for you should you cooperate with us now. That inconvenience on our part could easily be avoided."

"What are you talking about? My father would never ally himself with an Elder, I'll tell you that. I know him…"

"Do you, Assundra? I wonder if you do, really."

Assundra laughed again. "Better than you, clearly." Something inside her stirred, some defiance. So she wasn't safe. She wasn't ever going to be safe, not here, but she could fight. Her father always fought and he'd shown her how. That was how she would become safe again.

Mary paused. In the gloom Assundra couldn't tell if she was fuming or smiling. "Did you know that your father has been accepting powders from our good alchemist for a good many months now?" Assundra was silent. She wasn't supposed to mention her father's illness. "I see you do. Do you know the purpose of these powders, Assundra?"

"They…" she started to say, but checked herself, clamming her mouth shut.

"They do what? Cure him?" Mary put on a sing-song voice and did a little mocking dance. Assundra would normally have found the idea of the rotund woman dancing hilarious, but somehow, here in the basement, there was little that was funny about Mary Archer. "Oh Assundra, you have much to learn about how our little world of Ostracia around us works."

"Why don't you tell me then."

"Well aren't you the ice maiden!" Assundra smiled; she could tell by Mary's voice that she was starting to get to her. "I see you have developed a skill for reading. Something our other prodigy never managed to do. However I do believe that for all his faults, Tom Franks has been a better father to you than Max has to Simon."

"What's Simon got to do with this?" She had a sudden shock. "Did he know about this? Has he helped you bring me here?"

Mary laughed. "Now you wish to engage with me, do you? Well, I shall be gracious and tell you that no, he did not help us. That he knows of, that is." Mary flung something at her feet that fell with a heavy thud. "You have been reading John's reason for being."

"Reason for being?"

"Oh really, dear girl! The catalogue!" Mary sighed. "You outsiders have always been so slow to understand the importance of things, did you think it was merely a hobby for him?"

Assundra said nothing – that was exactly what she had thought. "Is that why I'm here? Look, I don't know where I got this from, so if someone stole it…"

"Cairns didn't give this to you? We assumed…" Mary faltered for a few seconds but quickly regained herself. "It is of no importance."

"What do you want with me?" Assundra repeated, feeling herself get angry and she pulled at the chain again.

"The chain is not going to come away from the wall, Assundra," Mary cooed at her, infuriating Assundra further. "I can also assure you, should you be worried, that Young Crafter and Erol Tyson will not be allowed to indulge their lustrous interests in you whilst you are our guests. That is not why you are here."

"Let them just try," she spat back, but inside her heart leapt and sank at the same time. What did they want with her if it wasn't…*that*? That was always what they wanted!

"They will, after we have finished with you, but not while you are under my roof."

"Your roof?" Assundra replied, determined to keep the anger boiling inside her – it stopped the fear. "You've brought me to your house?"

Mary laughed, that high, superior laugh and it grated through Assundra's nerves. "This is the basement of the Council Chambers, Assundra. The Elders do not know it even exists. We built this chamber whilst the Elder was busy demolishing our fine city to turn us into the yokels we are today. Through the passages that link this chamber to others in our possession we were able to prevent much of Ostracia's…specialist…knowledge from falling into the wrong hands, both then and now."

"Specialist knowledge?"

"You are a bit of a parrot, are you not?"

"Parrot?"

Mary sighed again. "It is an exotic bird, they used to be plentiful around Ostracia. They were famous for an annoying habit of being able to imitate their superiors."

Assundra was incredulous. Was the Archer woman looking down her nose at her? The town gossip, the butt of most of the jokes? The one woman all the men agreed they wouldn't bed if the plague took all the rest of them?

"It is an interesting analogy, now I come to think of it," Assundra realised the woman was going on, "Ostracians as parrots, imitating their betters, repeating slogans for tricks – yes, that is exactly how they behave with the Elders! Cairns particularly…"

"I don't care what you think about anything, aren't you bored of the sound of your own voice yet?"

Mary froze. "Of course you wouldn't identify with the parrots, would you," she said as if her voice held venom. "No, you would be more akin to an interloping magpie, tempted by the shiny things you could see in the next land. Neither welcome nor wanted."

"Was that an outsider joke?" Assundra asked in her own sing-song voice.

Mary's hand cracked across her cheek with a slap, the movement in her dress so ferocious that the wind it caused nearly blew out the candles. The woman stood over her for a moment while Assundra panted with shock, as if she were checking for something. Seeming satisfied, she moved back again.

Assundra felt the familiar curling in her stomach. No! She was not going to fall apart in front of this woman! She had to keep the anger going, to stop the fear. Oh gods, but it was creeping up on her, she could feel it. She wasn't safe!

"Do you know who I am, Assundra?" Without waiting for Assundra to answer, she went on. "I am the first daughter of the Crafter family. Do you know what that makes me?"

Assundra looked up. "An in-bred, mad bitch?" she ventured, raising her chin again hoping Mary would strike her once more. She'd had stronger beatings by accident from her father, it didn't hurt, but it kept the anger flowing. She needed the anger. She needed something! She wasn't *safe*!

Mary just ignored her. "It makes me the only viable vessel for the birthing of an heir. Young Crafter, Just and Patrick have tried, but to no avail. It seems we are not compatible."

"Oh *gods*…"

"You think it despicable?" Mary snorted. "After what your father did to my husband, I was not left with much choice. The Archers were long since distilled from Crafter stock, the correct blood ran through their veins, blood from the founding families, but then your father had to go and kill him before he could perform his duty."

Assundra remembered the scandal. Jesmond Archer had been a guard under Bryant's command and resentfully so. A few years after Bryant had been made Captain, Jesmond was killed chasing after her father, who had been exposing himself after drinking in the alehouse. It had been good-natured enough, some villagers were cheering the chase on when her father had tripped Jesmond and he had landed face-first on a scythe lying against the alehouse wall. The Elders had judged that breaking his neck had been a kindness, given how there had been nothing left of his face. Mary disagreed. The way she saw it, her father had left Mary a widow, just past the age when she could gain another man. Assundra remembered that her father had not been seen for months after Jesmond had died. He had gone somewhere then, as well.

"My father didn't mean…"

"It matters not what is meant, girl, only what is! The end result was that your father killed my husband and left the Crafter family without a natural heir."

"I'm here, Sunny."

Assundra tensed. Mary shifted, noticing something. "What is it, girl? Are you worried that I will try to substitute your womb for mine?" Mary laughed, that snooty, self-obsessed chortle that was so new to Assundra and yet already so annoying. "I would not have one of my brothers foster a child in your womb if you could guarantee the riches of Arcadia!"

"Arcadia?"

Mary sighed again. "Perhaps not even a magpie. Some sort of ferret."

"Wait!" Assundra shouted as Mary made for the stairs. "What do you want with me?"

"You will find the answer to that question soon enough," Mary called back without breaking stride. "For now I must leave you. I have a revolution to organise."

"What do you want with me? Please, you have to let me go, I have to help Simon!"

"I don't care what you need or want, Assundra," Mary said disinterestedly, without breaking stride, "and Simon will be just fine without you, In case you were wondering, which I note you weren't until now, despite having had ample opportunity to be asked, Simon has been charged with attacking our youngest. It will come to nothing, of course, we will see to that, but he will be in a cage, Assundra, a filthy, faeces-stained cage, because of you. That is what your kind brings to Ostracians, though isn't it?"

Picking a broom from the floor, she tapped twice on a trapdoor above her head then stepped back as it swung open and a ladder was dropped through. Assundra felt sick. Simon had been charged! Because of her.

With some effort the Archer woman clambered up the ladder that looked to Assundra like it would topple at any moment. "Bring her," Mary barked at someone once she'd reached the top and another shape began to descend the ladder.

Her skin felt like it turned to ice as she saw that it was Young Crafter. He wore a horrible toothy grin on his face as he stalked towards her, his shirt hanging loose where she'd torn off the toggles in the struggle. Wispy blonde hair showed through underneath and Assundra looked away in disgust. "Come now, my love," Young Crafter cooed at her, "don't you want to know what plans we have for you?"

"Just bring her!" she heard Mary shout from above.

Assundra looked back at Young Crafter in defiance, expecting to find him annoyed that his games had been interrupted, but there was only that grin. "You'd better be ready this time," she said as darkly as she could muster, "I'm ready for you now."

"You've been ready for me for years, my little treat," he replied, bending close to her. "I tried to help you, you know. Tried to make this easier, but you wouldn't have any of it. Well, it's your own lookout now."

As he reached for the pin to release the shackles, she spat in his face. Feeling the pin come loose she made to bring her hands down on Young Crafter's skull, but he was too quick and her arms too slow from being held upright for so long. She heard the bone in her face crunch as Young Crafter's fist made contact and she fell back against the wall. Grabbing her wrists, he hauled her up and dragged her across the floor to the ladder.

"A little help please, Erol," he called out cheerfully and Assundra saw another smiling head appear at the top of the hatch. Suddenly fearful she started kicking out, but Young Crafter had her wrists held firmly.

"Here," Erol shouted, throwing down a length of small rope. With a skill that Assundra could only assume was practice, Young Crafter tied her hands together, all the time smiling.

She swore at them, but they just kept smiling. Starting to panic, she started to beg with them, but this only made them laugh. Erol threw down another length of cord and Young Crafter tied her legs. Before she could tell what was happening, Erol had climbed halfway down the ladder and had grabbed her wrists. Young Crafter picked her up by her behind and followed Erol up the ladder, hauling her as he went.

With every rung the knife banged uselessly against her leg. She strained with her hands, let herself go dead weight, tried to unbalance so he would fall – she tried everything she could think of, but he simply hauled her up as if she were no more than a light sack.

Eventually, with a final yank, he pulled her with him up through the trapdoor and she screamed. Everything was blurred with the tears, but she could make out that she was in a large room, lined with workbenches. There were people everywhere, standing around in groups just talking. Some were wearing robes Assundra did not recognise, like Elders' robes, but red.

A table had been arranged on one of the workbenches so that it ran to the floor like a ramp. At the top and bottom were strong iron hooks. The table was so stained with blood that it looked like it was sodden right through.

"Please!" she begged, but the men holding her just laughed again. She kicked out and struggled all she could, but Erol and Young Crafter seemed like they were impervious to pain. One good kick landed right in Young Crafter's nose as he tried to pick up her feet, but the grin never once left his face, he barely even flinched.

They carried her bodily to the table and laid her against it. A few of the people standing by the upended table pressed their hands pressed down on her stomach to hold her there while Erol and Young Crafter tied her hands and feet. They didn't even break their conversation to do so.

"It's a bit of a stretch," she heard someone behind her say. Assundra yelped as her arms were pulled up far too high above her head, stretching her chest. She heard Mary whispering something to whoever had spoken, but she couldn't make out what. "Well, she wont' be on it for long," the man replied, causing much laughter.

"Who's there?" she called out, but was met with yet more laughter, from all around the room, it seemed like there were dozens of them here! "What are you doing? What do you want with me?"

Only the grotesquely fixed grins from Erol and Young Crafter and the laughter behind her met her words.

All at once the laughter and the sounds of conversation stilled. "Ready, is she?" she heard a gruff, rushed voice call out behind her and then Elder Oldershaw walked into view. Her hopes lifted for just a moment as she thought an Elder would stop this, they couldn't let this go on, but then she remembered it was Elder Oldershaw who she had seen going through Elder Cairns' things.

"She's a bit small for the rack, Elder," Mary said, "but I don't think she'll be strained too much."

Elder Oldershaw peered closer at her and she tried to turn her head away as the cider-soaked breath washed over her, but strong hands forced it back where it was. Seeming satisfied, the Elder nodded. "Yes. They'll still seal up well enough. Don't have to be perfect after all. If it doesn't stop flowing, take her down," he said, with force, to Patrick Crafter.

To Assundra's surprise, Patrick bowed, something she'd only ever seen him do in mockery, but he seemed genuine.

"Sunny, be strong. You're safe. Trust me, you're safe."

Assundra coughed out a laugh at the voice. Safe? She was anything but safe, but strangely, now the worst had happened she felt calmer than she had done for months. There was nothing she could do now. Setting her jaw, she resolved that anything coming towards her mouth would be bitten off.

"I'm sorry, Assundra," the Elder said. "Can't be done another way. Meant it when I said I'd protect you, really did, but not from this."

"Galvarin will find you," she replied, but was dismayed by how raspy her voice sounded. She was stretched too far on the rack to catch her breath and talk at the same time.

She wasn't sure if it was her voice or what she said that made Elder Oldershaw laugh. "For once you are right! I do imagine he will. Won't work, of course." He moved away from her suddenly. "Wish I had more time to explain to you, really do, but my esteemed colleague has caught us on the hop."

She gasped a reply, but words were beyond her.

"I hope you don't find out the extent to which Elder Cairns has lied to you my dear," Mary interjected. "I know what it is like to lose one you love, let alone two and for that I feel regret. Happily, you won't be in a position to feel any of what I have had to suffer since your father killed my husband."

Her voice cracked at the end and Assundra smiled. She smiled again when Mary made to strike her but was held back by Elder Oldershaw.

"She's right, Assundra," he said quickly. "You will be spared knowing what Cairns has done to you. Won't lie to you, this is going to hurt. But it's worth it. We need an outsider, you see, Ostracians just don't work in the same way. Artistry in the blood I shouldn't wonder, makes what we have to do too difficult. Cairns knew this, it's why he kept you alive."

"It's all lies!"

Elder Oldershaw seemed to be wearing a permanent frown. "There really is no other way."

Assundra gasped again and forced herself to speak. "Are you trying to convince me," she panted, "or yourself?"

High pitched footsteps moved towards her and Mary's smug, fat face came into view. Assundra made to spit again, but Mary slapped a backhand across the very point where Young Crafter's fist had crashed into her cheek.

Another yelp from Assundra sounded loud, too loud in the quiet of the room and she closed her mouth. The sound of sobbing was deafening to her.

"My friends, shall we begin?" Mary said cheerfully, raising her arms like Cairns did when he was making a speech. For the first time Assundra saw the large, golden, curved knife in Mary's hand.

CHAPTER 17

The world had flashed white again and he had heard the buzzing in his ears. The eyes had blazed in the back of his mind. He hadn't been able to help it, whatever it was. Had he?

Simon sat, panting, on the stump of a long since departed tree, taking in gulps of soft air that for once were fragranced with greenery and not the midden pits. It didn't smell of anything, his mouth was full of the taste of nothing. With a shaking hand he tried to force the last crumbs of a slice of stale butter bread and eggplant past his ruined mouth. Grimacing he tasted the fresh blood that the chewing had produced with his tongue, letting the blood-soaked rag containing two of his teeth fall to the dirt.

He didn't know what had happened. He didn't know how it had happened, or if he had done it. He only knew what She told him.

It was getting close to being too dark to see anyway. Even so, he couldn't take his eyes off it.

Biting the end of the strip he'd torn off his shirt he tugged, wincing as it pulled tight around his shredded forearm. He had stopped the bleeding, but as soon as he'd let go of the arm the shreds of skin in between the deep cuts had split apart again. His father had shown him that the large, flat mushroom that grew on the birch trees were good for wounds so he'd cut some into strips, tied them around his arm and had now made a bandage out of his shirt to hold it on. It seemed to be working but the wounds were pretty deep.

His father had shown him many things with plants, many ways in which they could help and heal. He also caused the injuries Simon needed to heal.

Simon was surprised that Captain Bryant still hadn't returned with more men. He did remember the swordsman fleeing, yelping like a frightened calf, his eyes full of terror, shrieking as he had tripped on the uneven ground. It had made Simon smile. Hadn't it? Or was that Her smiling?

Taking his feet from where they rested, Simon tried to avoid looking at his father's face. Max West lay at the feet of the remains of the statue of Lamia, his lifeless eyes wide open, staring in shock up at where the statue's head should have been.

Simon knew too much power had been used. Had it been him? He had found himself panting on the floor, a useless wreck, his father's bloody fingers clawing their way through his arm. If Bryant had not run, Simon would have been an easy target for the man's blade, which Simon was sure had been the true reason for their visit here all along – why else take him so far from the village?

The eyes in his mind were closed now, little more than a dim remembrance of a presence, but he knew She would return. She had to, She had to explain what had happened – had he done this to his father? And if he had, why was he not sorry?

Year after year he had suffered at the hands of his father, beating after beating, scalding after scalding. Nothing he had done had ever been good enough. Well, as it turned out, nothing Max had ever done was good enough for Simon, either, something his father had never considered.

"You won't be considering it now either, will you, you bastard?" he asked the lifeless form at his feet, but Simon ended up turning away. He couldn't look at the face. There was no hostility in it now, only surprise. Surprise and fear. Which was what his mother would feel when she found out. Alice wouldn't see she was saved from him too.

"You see what you've brought on us?" he screamed, the eyes in the back of his mind flashing open as he did so. "You caused this, not me! Bryant will go running back telling everyone I murdered you, but you killed yourself! I had no choice!"

Simon kicked the knife away from his father's hand, wincing as his muscles cried out to him for rest. He didn't deserve the rest. He had failed. All he had been trying to do was protect Assundra and now what would happen to her? Without him there, the gods knew what they'd do.

"Bloody Assundra Franks," he whispered to himself and sat back down on the stump as his head started to spin. Why did she never see what was best for her? Simon knew he could have protected her, given her everything she could ever have wanted, even taken her out of Ostracia, through the tunnels Cairns had shown him, once he'd found a way to break the Elder's artistic block, once he'd learnt enough from them, but they'd all put paid to that now.

Even after he'd found her with the stone shaper he still knew he was the one to protect her. The eyes had shown him different. They said Assundra was just using him, but he couldn't believe it.

He couldn't go back, though. Even with his splint, even with Her helping him he was no match for an Elder, not yet. The eyes in the back of his mind flickered and closed.

He had power, he knew that. She had shown him that. Or had She? Had he seen it for himself? Simon wasn't sure any more, things were popping into his head from nowhere, memories he'd never had before, feelings he couldn't account for and knowledge of artistry he'd never learned. She had told him she needed his artistry to survive and as a reward She'd show him things and help him to feel things. She had been right; She had made him feel things he'd never experienced before, as long as he didn't think about Assundra. But he couldn't stop thinking about Assundra. She didn't like that. Sometimes She hurt him for it, but now, when he tried to remember, it didn't seem clear how She had done so.

It didn't matter how much She disliked it, he had to put it right, he had to make sure Assundra was safe.

Simon sighed; he hoped She'd come back, or wake up, or just return in some way, soon. He needed Her.

It was time to make a move from here before Bryant got back. There was nothing more to learn from this place, Simon had explored it thoroughly last time he was here and besides the entrance to the tunnels, under the stump he sat on, it was just a typical Forested ruin.

Which way to go, though? All the Forest looked the same, especially in the dark. Tall, thin trees with only the occasional thicker, older oak were packed so closely together that off the path barely two people could pass between any two trees. They rose to a canopy that in daylight threatened to block out the sun, but in nightfall was lost itself to the blackness. No stars could be seen in the Forest; it was just you, the trees and the earth.

Taking up the almost blunted bone vegetable knife he had taken from the kitchen at home and placed, with the food and the other items he had thought he might need several weeks before, several weeks too early, and hidden by this very spot, he got up to continue, grimacing as he did, the dried blood from his battered mouth cracking on his chin.

The weather was changing, though it wasn't exactly cold but the evening air had a bite to it, and sleeping rough in only half a woollen shirt and breeches would not be ideal. What would She think the best thing to do was? She was still there, in his mind, but not wholly present, her attentions were elsewhere. Simon didn't like it when she wasn't with him; he got fidgety, started sweating, hot and then cold, although She always came back before it got too bad.

His surroundings gave no clue as to what to do next. The ruins were fragments of stone formations, inlaid into the turf at the side of the path. He knew because he'd fallen over them, but if you looked hard enough, paths were still there. The trees could gobble their surroundings but remnants of the paths always remained. Man always left his mark on the land, his father had said.

The power built inside him as he thought of his father, like it always did when he got angry. He could feel it now, insistently pushing for a release. Perhaps it was the artistry that had helped him to remember, to break the hold on whatever had taken his memories from him before. If they were his. If they were real.

"Look, I'm here!" he shouted to nothing, forcing his vision to see the sleeping eyes at the back of his mind. "I'm here, I'm waiting, what do you want me to do?"

He kicked out with his boot and yelped as it made contact with his father's body. Max moaned and turned his head.

The eyes in the back of his mind opened wide and there was a blistering flash of white light that became all he could see.

Reeling, he tried to keep his legs still until his balance and sight returned. He was standing in the same place, in the square ruin, but something wasn't right. Everything was greyer. It was also deep in the midst of night, where he was sure it had been early evening a moment ago. The body had gone, but it was the statue that took his attention.

It was fully formed, the head somehow rebuilt, its pure white marble features totally unblemished, the beauty of its subject beyond compare. Simon frowned – hadn't the face he had seen on the broken head been disfigured? Melted?

Shaking his head, he thought he must have been mistaken. This woman was beautiful. Her arms were spread wide, reminding Simon of how Elder Cairns used to address people when at his most pompous.

"It's very good, isn't it?"

Simon span round, this world taking a moment to catch up with him, but saw only torches, attached to trees by iron brackets. He turned back and yelped as he found himself just inches from the statue, crept down from its perch in total silence, its eyes icy and dead.

"Yes, the eyes were the only flaw." The voice did not come from the statue's lips, they were just stone, they couldn't utter anything. No, the voice belonged to someone else. She was back!

"What… what's happening?" he asked softly.

"It looks like marble does it not? Yet it is something wholly more appropriate, something I'm sure your Elders know nothing about. I made it from the bones of the dead, just like the original sculptors did," the voice said cheerfully. Simon was nearly surprised the revelation did not upset him. "There were some buried in the forest."

Simon looked around again, the voice seeming to come out of the soundless world directly to his own brain. "We bury our dead in the barrow, not out here," he replied.

"Well, someone put some dead here," She said cheerfully, the voice flitting about his head as if the speaker were dancing around a maypole.

"Where are you?" he ventured; and immediately felt like a fool for asking such a childish question. The snort he got in reply affirmed his early failure. He revised his question. "I thought you needed me to survive, that you couldn't exist without my artistry? How could you dig bodies up if you weren't with me?"

Swivelling back around he was confronted not with the cold, lifeless eyes of the statue but with the stunning deep blue eyes of the women he knew was the most beautiful woman that there could be. Far from being icy, these eyes warmed Simon's heart. He knew these eyes, these perfect, beautiful blue eyes. They were Her eyes. They were also the only parts of the woman he could see. She was a little shorter than Simon, a scarlet robe pulled tightly about Her person, defying him to gauge the shape of Her body, Her face was shrouded somehow in darkness, but a darkness that shimmered as did Her entire being. Yet within the hood those lightning eyes were clear and piercing.

"You were with me," She said simply, but as She spoke, the world sprang into life. He heard birdsong, the crackling of the torches and the slight breeze through the trees. Weight came to his body with a jolt and his legs tried to pull him into the ground, causing him to sink to one knee in front of her. The woman either didn't notice or didn't care. "Impressed?"

"Birdsong at dusk?" The immediate flash, like lightning, in Her eyes burned into the back of Simon's mind. He suddenly knew She could silence anything that displeased Her. It would take Her no effort at all. She was magnificent!

"Perceptive. That's a reflection of why you were chosen, I suppose," the woman said, staring straight through Simon's own eyes into what lay beyond. "Though your education has been sadly lacking."

The words stung Simon's mind into action. "That's Cairns' fault!" he cried. A smile formed on Her lips, Her face gradually becoming more visible. The smile sucked Simon's anger away from the moment he saw it.

"Good! I see that you and I shall get on well!" The eyes were as much in him as looking upon him.

Struggling to find his voice, Simon looked at Her feeling a kind of calm fear. She looked down from her hood at him with her deep blue eyes, beautiful, hypnotic eyes and now there was that smile that warmed where the rest of her chilled. Simon found himself panting and, embarrassed, tore his gaze from Hers as he tried to compose himself. She had been with him for – how long was it now? It seemed like She had always been with him – and he couldn't even talk to Her properly! He didn't even know Her name. The dawn was now rising over the building and rising rather more quickly than usual. Time was passing.

"Why don't' I remember digging up bodies with you then?" he said eventually, aware his pulse was far too fast and his blood far too hot.

"You do, you just choose not to." The woman was once more by his shoulder, whispering into his ear. He could feel Her breath on his neck. "I do not Withhold memories, Simon, not like the Elders have done to you."

"Withhold?"

Her voice was grave. "Sorcery, Simon. Primitive, but effective. The Elders have used Withholdings since they stole control of Ostracia from those deserving of it. My brother has been watching them. They set about twisting your pliant minds to their own ends, playing with your memories as if they were toys. You are not a toy are you, Simon?"

"Who are you?" he almost snapped as She laughed at him again. "I mean, what goddess are you?" An awed, cowed feeling came over him as a thought popped into his head. "Are you Lamia?"

The entire world seemed to burst into laughter. It echoed all around him, making Simon's head shake. "I am no goddess! I am just Elspeth." The voice was behind him now and in his ears, not his head.

Simon once again turned and found he had no breath. The shrouded figure had become a slim, beautiful woman of around twenty-five. Her head was still covered by the scarlet hood, from which wisps of curling, blonde hair reached down to her shoulders, but it was her pale face that stunned him. It was a face he had seen in his dreams. Small, perfect features, set upon pure white skin, those large, round eyes giving the face light. That scarlet robe was now pulled back behind her body, revealing a shadowy dress of pure white, shimmering strangely as did the rest of her. It was a dress made of no cloth, just as she was made of no flesh. It seemed to be part of her when she moved, moulded exactly to her figure. That figure, though slighter than Assundra's, was no less womanly. Assundra would seem like nothing if she stood next to this woman.

Raising two immaculately carved, slender hands from her sides of to her hips she spoke in a voice that seemed to Simon to be glowing, if sound could glow. Gods, even his thoughts were muddled! "You know who I am now."

As she walked, no, glided, in a slow arc about him, he realised he did indeed know who she was. Tales had been told of her, always in hushed tones. The Elders had forbidden reference to her, yet none of them dared rename her wood. She was the most powerful of all Ostracians. She was…"Elspeth North," he replied, surprised at how loud his voice sounded in this dream world. "The Gifted One."

"A title your people bestowed upon me," she returned, with a little of the force of personality she had been famed for, for whilst they were forbidden to speak of the Gifted One, all in Ostracia knew her story. "The writers of your legends have much to answer for."

"Our legends? Surely you are…or were one of us?"

"No," she laughed, seeming to Simon like the birdsong itself. "My father was Lord North. I never knew my mother. It was what set me apart from the rest of my family. I was only half part of it, not like my brothers, whose mothers were around to poison my father's mind against me and the rest of our people. But when it came to it Simon, I sided with them, not our people, so no, I was not one of you. Partly one perhaps, yet I died because of that part."

"I'm glad you're here," he blurted out, feeling himself turn red instantly.

"I am not anywhere, Simon, it is you who have come to see me." She looked at him kindly, that smile encouraging him to speak. "Don't you know who I am? Who I am to you?"

"Elspeth. The one who…you've been helping me." He found himself pulling his fingers around themselves, twiddling strange shapes in front of him. He felt slightly sick, wanting to run from and run to this woman at the same time.

"I am here to help you, that's why I have returned. In fact, I hope we can help each other."

"Anything…"

"Sh, Simon," she said, resting a hand on his own, stopping his breath. Damn this; he was acting like a smitten girl! "It is the meeting of two powers, it causes a frisson in the mind, it confuses you. It will pass."

He wanted to tell her it was more, so much more than that; that when she touched him it was the purest, most perfect feeling he had ever felt, but he couldn't. When he'd told Assundra how he felt, he'd got so scared he'd blurted it out in front of everyone and they'd laughed at him. Assundra had laughed at him. He didn't want Elspeth to laugh at him. All he wanted was her body in his arms, but she'd never want that.

"The meeting of two powers," she said again, as if to reinforce it. "I didn't realise until you finally tapped into them how strong yours were, Simon. That is why I did not come before." Her voice carried along the air like music, perfectly intoned, none of the coarse, lax speech that he heard all the time in the village.

"You speak…"

"Within, without, in all spaces," she whispered, and Simon found himself performing the technique. Suddenly there were three Simons, three Elspeths and he could see them all, feel them all. "Yourself is more than your body, your artistry is more than your splint, your power is more than your own. The Gifted Ones take power from themselves, from beyond themselves and from their targets."

"I don't understand."

She smiled that beautiful smile again. "Simon, everything we do together is amplified. We are the same, you and I."

The eyes in the back of his mind were blazing blue and the power blinded his own vision, causing all three images to blur into one. This was pure artistry, the new ways, the ways they had lost. "It's beautiful," he began, but she silenced him with a warning mental slap that shook his brain and then he began to hear the words that were not words. They were channels, focusing the mind on what it was trying to do, pouring and targeting the artistry through the blood.

"You have mastered the technique well," she said, "he has taught you something, at least." Simon fell to the floor panting as something released him, the eyes in his mind closing. He rubbed at his own, convinced they were bleeding they stung so much.

"Now, you have questions." She spoke kindly, stroking a perfectly formed hand through his hair, but his head throbbed as though there were a hand clasping his brain and squeezing.

"Can you show me something else?" he blurted, desperate to see more of her power, to feel her inside his head again.

"No," she replied softly, "using artistry takes up much energy and we as yet have no means of reviving you should you use too much."

He remembered. After the fight with his father, it felt as if his blood had burned. Every breath had been an effort.

"When you are fully empowered, you will be able to do far more to your enemies. Like *this*."

The world seeming to slow and an image leapt into Simon's mind. Thousands of men were spread before him, even some women, all dressed in light armour, all roaring at him, their expressions fierce, their weapons sharp. He was gliding through them, turning in mid-air, words leaving his mouth, until his hand struck one of them in the centre of the chest, with barely any force. The man burst in front of his eyes, raining blood and bone in all directions. Only the head remained intact and fell.

The image was gone as soon as it had come and the pain returned to Simon's head. Through the haze of the searing, stinging discomfort, he knew one thing.

He wanted that…

"That is one side of artistry. There are two sides, remember."

"I know," he mumbled, picturing the look on Cairns' face as his chest burst asunder.

"Do not lie, Simon, why would you know?"

"It's written. Oldershaw told me, the right and left hand paths. Cairns has often said the darker side to artistry is too hard to resist, that's why Lord North…" He looked up in horror, an apology ready on his lips, his stupid, unthinking lips, but she was already talking.

"The writers of your histories have a lot to answer for. They made demons out of those of us who dedicated our lives to perfecting artistry, striving to improve ourselves rather than just getting by trading pointless goods for pointless pieces of metal. In order to perfect ourselves, we had to have power. That power had to come from somewhere, Simon. A true artist takes power, as I said, from themselves, from beyond themselves and from their targets. Or from others."

A thought suddenly struck Simon. "Where are we? This isn't where we were, I know that, but this feels like no dream. You are real, I am real here, so where are we?"

Looking into his thoughts with the sky darkening behind her, Elspeth said, "We are in your mind, Simon".

"But…"

"Outside your mind, where your body has slumped, is the shrine of Lamia. It is not, as your fool Elder believes, the power of a goddess that is held there, such an idea is foolish. It is rather a focal point, a store of earthly artistic power, not blood artistry, the artistry of the land. It serves to allow the bridging of life and death-life.

"It allows you and I to be here," she said, smiling now. "I'm glad you agreed to help me, Simon, we're almost there. Only one more thing need be done."

Simon did not reply, preferring to simply stare back into her eyes. She didn't make him nervous, like Assundra did. Somehow he knew that because she was strong, because she could tear a man's eyes from his head without so much as touching him, that he was safe with Elspeth.

"Do you know what you are?" she asked suddenly.

"What I am?" Simon felt his brow furrow in confusion. "The Elder said..."

"Elders are rarely of consequence, Simon, your first lesson should be this. Yet in this case they are right. You are the one born with power. The Gifted One of your line. Elders have played no part in this, for all they think it is their destiny, or some such nonsense. They do not concern me. There is one particular Elder I am concerned with, however."

"Cairns?" Simon offered eagerly. He had seen how her eyes had flared at Cairns during his trial.

"My father, Lord North," she said, seeming to ignore him, "along with the head of the Elder Council then, Elder Costrange, presided over what we called Stracathri, the most perfect place of power ever devised. The Elders had chiefs of their own among their ranks, but it was generally recognised that my father was our peoples' artistic leader and therefore theirs, even though he was not of their number.

"Elders! Nothing but fools." Her voice was more disappointed than angry, her eyes cast to the floor. "Petty little amateurs, working at their inane little theories behind my father's back! Thinking he didn't know! The sum total of their achievements a pathetic tome they called The Knowledge. A record of their futile and primitive works. It, like the Elders themselves, was nothing of consequence; their artistry undid more than it created but it did contain the only research ever conducted into the outsiders' primitive, pathetic sorcery. It was entrusted to my brother, Carstan, in good faith but he betrayed them and, in turn, us. The people sided with Elders working outside of my father's control, so my father abandoned them…and his children."

Simon found himself placing a hand on her shoulder. Despite the shimmering of her form, she felt real. Something swelled in his throat, stopping his breath, as she reached up and clasped his hand. "You see I know how you feel, Simon. I have experienced the same as you, for I suffered at the hands of my father as you suffered at the hands of yours."

Images flowed into Simon's mind again and a sickness invaded his stomach. The image of his father's eyes stared up at him from where he left him, the wound in his neck from where Simon had jabbed the splint into him dripping a tiny amount of blood.

"Do not grieve for him, Simon," Elspeth said, "he is not worth your discomfort. My father was a great man, he was our leader, but I too made him pay for my suffering at his hands."

Simon looked into Elspeth's eyes. He did not see sadness there, but a determined, unbreakable will. It was what he wanted. The eyes in the back of his mind flicked open and she was looking at him from both sides. The sickness faded away, replaced by tingling warmth and a knowledge that he had done the right thing, that he had no choice. That he had done it for Elspeth and that made it right.

"Yet the death of my father counted for nothing," she went on, the eyes in his mind closing again as his sickness subsided. Her voice was like honey to Simon. "Our people believed the Elders' lies. My father's hand was tied by the rebel Elders' vile stronghold, their Transept Tower. That place is sorcery, artistry and the old ways all combined into one cannibalistic, perverse centre of power. Even now, your Elders believe it will save them but something so primitive will never endow them with the power they seek."

She looked up at him, her brilliant blue eyes full of sadness. "Only you can take that power."

"The power Oldershaw is looking for?"

Elspeth nodded. "My brother Carstan was guilty of the same crimes as your Elders are now. Crimes that meant he failed his people. He was a vain man, jealous of our younger brother, Kryman. It was always Kryman who had the women fawning around him, praised by the people for his acts of charity across the land and beyond and I could tell you a thing or two about the truth of that. No, Carstan did not get on with the family. He despised me for my mother and my brother for his popularity, yet it was Carstan who had the most talent for the arts, for all them naming me 'Gifted One'.

"Carstan murdered Elder Costrange in a fit of rage," she said, without the slightest trace of emotion. "He felt that the power should have been harnessed to repel the invaders. It would have meant the deaths of thousands, including most Ostracians, excepting the most gifted, to do it and my father refused. I'm afraid I agreed with Carstan."

Elspeth's face grew sad once more. "For all his power over his people, my father was not a powerful artist, even with…the advantages we had back then. It took seconds to beat him. There wasn't even any satisfaction in it, only a faint sense of anti-climax."

Simon put a hand to her arm – he knew exactly what she meant. Decades of beatings had been put to rest tonight with his father and yet the act itself had been so sudden, so final, that it was as if nothing had been put to rest at all. Elspeth shook herself once more, her blond curls swinging just once, then falling still. "Well, there wasn't a choice after the only two people who really understood the power were dead and we didn't have time to learn the outsiders' primitive little sorceries enough to repel them ourselves."

"Lord North was dead before the invasion?" Simon exclaimed, astonished. He had assumed Elspeth had been talking about something that happened after the battle had been won.

Elspeth nodded. "After he killed him, Carstan took on Costrange's countenance – an act that requires great wells of artistry, great power and something which was forbidden in even those times. It completely deceived Kryman, who was somehow convinced that Costrange had found the answer to repelling the outsiders without having to cause so much death. I had resigned myself to the battle at that moment, having found that I had destroyed the only thing that could have saved us all. My father. It was he who commanded the power and with his death, the power of Stracathri, that which was held deep in the bowels of our spire, left us. My brother, realising what we had done, fled and watched as the outsiders burned the defenceless tower with my family inside. Only Kryman and I escaped, after sealing the chambers, of course. We then faced our own end."

"I thought…"

"The Tower itself might not have burned, but the rest of them did." Simon shuddered. So the writings were half right; it was a North who condemned his people, but not Lord North. Or the Elders who chose to remain loyal. He knew Cairns had lied!

"We were much stronger than the people, Simon, we had Stracathri behind us, or so they thought. The rebels, buoyed by the power from their abomination, murdered the Ostracians loyal to us by hand, those who could have saved them, who knew how to find Stracathri again, then Kryman and I found that it was our father who had the last laugh on us.

"We never found out who helped the outsiders defeat us." She laughed at his surprise. "Simon, my brothers and I were the most powerful artists this land has seen, the armies couldn't have stood against us! My father's intransigence may have riled the outsiders, but they had help. We would have slaughtered them otherwise."

Finally Simon understood. "You suspect the Elders?"

She nodded. "Well, the rebel Elders, though they all knew who the rebels were. They are all guilty in my eyes."

"But why? Why would they?"

"They were stupid. They thought to trade a century of imprisonment for power." Her face set hard. "The outsiders had other ideas."

Simon frowned. "I don't think Cairns knows…"

"Simon, you are the Gifted One! Your power may even exceed mine. Your duty is to us, to Stracathri, you deserve this power, it is your birthright! All Cairns has done is lie to you your whole life. He has lied and Withheld knowledge from you, using you as if you were his puppet! You know how much you hate him, how much he deserves your hate!"

He was different to the saps in the village. The Elder had told him he was superior, now he knew it to be true. She wouldn't lie to him.

"So you're here for me?" he dared.

Elspeth smiled at him from under her hood. Her power intoxicated him. She had shown him that she could dispose of him in an instant, should she choose to do so, and yet he'd never been more attracted to anyone in his life. Even Assundra.

Even as he thought of the farm girl Elspeth's smile faded, replaced by a scowl. "You waste your thoughts on such as her, when there is so much at stake?"

"She needs my help! I left her there to Cairns and if what you're saying is true then how can I let her rot there?

"You saved her!" she said softy, but her anger turning to praise simply infuriated him further.

"No. We've got to go back."

The eyes in his mind flickered open. "Of course we do, Simon," she said, smiling. So she did understand after all. His heart fluttered; was she jealous? "But first I think you must understand why my brother and I are here, now."

"Your brother?" Simon looked about him, but could see nobody.

Elspeth laughed. "Not here in your mind, Simon! He is not a Gifted One, such connections are not possible for others." She stroked his cheek. "A century of power connects us, Simon. There are none in history who have shared the bond we do."

Simon's breaths started to come in spurts.

"Though he is a very powerful artist indeed, nonetheless, more so in our current form."

"Why is Carstan here?"

She laughed again, her face glowing slightly as her head lifted back, her pale, shimmering skin shining with the sun. "Not Carstan, he is dead. In a very final sense," she added firmly, when she saw his raised eyebrow. "My brother Kryman and I are not what you would call dead, exactly. We are death-life. Cursed by our father to return here to finish what he started after we finished him.

"My father was convinced it was an Elder who persuaded Marchman to do as he did. They wanted the invasion! What else could turn the people against us? We gave the people everything they could ever want, they needed no other rulers, they were happy! Even the stock were happy under our rule and believe me, that had not always been so. No, they wanted control of Ostracia for themselves and did not care how they got it!" Elspeth turned her back on him, her face once more hidden behind her hood. "I wonder just how many of them reckoned on the price they'd have to pay to get that control, if they even cared."

Simon remembered the story of Marchman. One of Tom Franks' ancestors, so it wasn't surprising his descendant was an oafish fool. Marchman had been the one who had started the trouble with the outsiders. Elspeth was there, so Simon presumed she knew better than their paltry records and writings. Marchman had been an Elders' apprentice, but had developed far too fast for the Elders to be able to control him, so he had deserted them.

Marchman was the first to use artistry to alter his trade ware. Artistic alteration within Ostracia was allowed, even encouraged, but by an agreement with outsider leaders, Lord North had decreed that all trade ware be artistry-free. Outsiders had begun to order Marchman's cider in droves before Lord North found out, but by then most of the city was using artistry to enhance their wares and it was too late to call a halt. That didn't stop Elspeth's father. When Marchman's final, misguided and badly made artistic brew had caused the death a rich foreign trader, the son of an important man, Lord North had put Marchman to death in the Trials. The witch hunts of all those practising artistry outside of the influence and permission of the Elders.

Things had already gone too far, though. The outsiders had demanded reparations. They had demanded the return of their stock. They had demanded that Ostracia cease to trade. They hadn't even given Lord North time to reply to their demands.

"What do you plan to do?" Simon asked finally as the shimmering spectre of Elspeth North turned slowly back to face him.

"We are going to claim back that power, Simon."

Simon smiled. "Cairns won't even notice, he's bent on some foolhardy attempt to free the villagers through a tunnel," he replied instantly, laughing.

"The Elders will never have what they need to complete that task, Simon, because they will never have you! This Cairns, though it matters little to me what his name is, will not even have his life shortly."

Now that got Simon's interest. "So we can save Assundra from him?" he exclaimed, before biting his lip and waiting for the mental slap that accompanied all such thoughts of the farm girl.

"Yes," Elspeth replied, walking softly towards him and raising a hand to his cheek. "We need her unharmed."

"What do you mean need her?" he asked, but the world flashed white again before he could say any more and he sank to his knees, his eyes feeling as if they were on fire and his cheek aflame. "Elspeth!" he called out, but received no reply. He raised a hand to his cheek and screamed as charred flesh fell away from his face. Waves of pain flew across his cheek and his breath stopped in his throat. He coughed something up, in the gloom he could not see what, nor did he want to.

"Elspeth!" he called again as more and more flesh fell away, and he could feel his brain beginning to burn.

He felt shapes swimming around him and suddenly there were three of him again; himself, the self that watched him, but the third was flailing around in despair, with nothing to focus on. Slowly, the eyes in the back of his mind opened, blazing their cool, blue light onto his mind and the power froze. He felt his eyes cross as the three images tried to blur into one, the right one, but they wouldn't, they just stayed there, three images overlaid onto each other, each in front of the other.

"Focus on your face, Simon."

He felt his power self jerk away towards where his cheek smouldered and he was forced to see his own scarred image. With horror, he realised the scars were almost identical to the ones on Cairns' face! He heard the words that were not words before he realised he was saying them, if, indeed, he was, and then the skin was all he could see.

"Think of sewing."

As the words that were not words grew stronger, the eyes in his mind blazing further, his mouth emptied of all taste and his senses went numb. The artistry built in his throat and he spat.

"No! Do not waste it!" a voice was saying. *"Concentrate! Knit the skin! Think of sewing!"*

Simon could only see the burn. The artistry was building again, but this time he held it back, where it burned against his throat. His whole head felt like it would burst aflame, but he could do nothing. He dredged a memory of his mother sewing his shirts from somewhere, seeing the needle flick in and out of the material, was that what the voice meant? He pictured the needle piercing his own skin, dragging the thread through and sealing the tiny holes where the lumps of flesh had fallen away, but each pinprick felt like it was jabbing every inch of skin on his body. He couldn't hold it any more, the artistry was too much, it was all burning too much, and he spat again.

"Gifted One my bollock," he heard someone say, a man, it wasn't Elspeth, where was she? All he could see were the three images as they began to fall apart, splitting back into their three separate parts and he was aware of himself falling.

"Help him!" someone shouted urgently, but everything to Simon was just a blur. He didn't even have the strength to move his head away when he felt a pressure like a hot iron on his already shattered and burned face. It was just like after he had burned the barn; he couldn't move, couldn't think, he couldn't even see. He couldn't do anything. Was this artistic exhaustion? For the second time in no more than a few weeks, Simon was sure he was going to die.

Then, suddenly, it was over.

Blinking, he saw he was back in the ruins, all traces of Elspeth's world gone, though he saw her shimmering form crouching next to the stump that unscrewed. Simon felt his heart tear as he saw how unconcerned she looked.

"This one's about as much use as you were before I took you in hand, sis," someone said from behind him. Simon span around. "You sure this is the right time?"

Another shimmering figure stood behind him, much paler than Elspeth, to the point of being opaque, wearing, if it could be called that, a shimmering scarlet tunic and hose. Simon recognized them as dress clothes, though he had never worn any in his life. What held his gaze were the eyes. Bright, scarlet eyes, matching his outfit. They seemed to burn…

"Of course it's the right time, we wouldn't be here otherwise!" Simon heard Elspeth say impatiently behind him.

"You don't need to worry about saying thank you for healing your face, by the way my boy, all in a day's work! Though I am left to question," the figure said, stretching a pair of thick, colourless lips into a lop-sided grin, "why my sister's taste spirals ever downwards with each man?"

"Who are…"

"Kryman North, my dear Gifted One!" the spectre replied before Simon could finish, before falling into a ridiculous parody of a bow. "And on second thoughts, I would like you to thank me for healing your face, much as a good disfigurement might have improved such an article as yours, I'm feeling rather unloved at the moment." His face hardened when Simon didn't reply. "Say thank you," he said, but the intimidatory effect was entirely lost on Simon due to the high-pitched voice that delivered it. The man squeaked like Assundra!

Just as he was raising his smile and preparing to retort, he felt Elspeth by his side. "Say thank you, Simon," she whispered, concerned. The eyes in his mind flashed fully open again. "*Say thank you, now.*"

"Thank you, Kryman," he said, and he felt the presence in his mind relax. What was Elspeth so afraid of? It was they who were the Gifted Ones, not Kryman! She had said as much herself. He raised a hand to his face and found nothing but smooth skin. Smooth, *new* skin.

"How did you…"

"Smooth as a baby's bum, isn't it?" Kryman said, cutting him off again. "Though you're not much older than a baby really, are you, what are you, twelve?"

"I'm sixteen!"

"Sixteen!" the spectre shouted in mock astonishment. "Well, that does make you one of the oldies, doesn't it? Certainly *elder* than I thought, look sister, are we going to go and see about this Transept Tower or not? Time's pressing on, you know, the girl doesn't have long left!"

The spectre stopped speaking suddenly and Simon saw Elspeth flash him a look. "We are leaving now."

"What did he mean?" Simon asked her, but she wouldn't turn to face him.

"Haven't you told that lad yet, sis? Oh, but that's really too bad, you shouldn't be so afraid of the competition, it's not fitting, as father would have said. If you'd only chosen that nice emissary from Archaea you'd have been out of all this mess. Gods, even the one from Azoia would have been preferable to being cursed, surely! He might have eaten bits of you, but at least you'd be rid of all this. Though I hear the Azoians favour the death-life approach to burial as a matter of course, perhaps it was that emissary who gave father the idea…"

"Shut up, Kryman," was all Elspeth replied.

"What girl?" Simon said, ignoring Elspeth's brother. The man was clearly a posturing fool, for all he had helped with his face and Simon wasn't yet convinced he hadn't done that himself, but this was more important. "Do you mean Assundra? What did he mean doesn't have long left?"

"Asks a lot of questions, doesn't he sis? I take it he hasn't worked out how to find out any answers in life for himself? Or has mummy Elspeth nursed him through life's trials thus far?"

Elspeth carried on ignoring her brother and Simon realised it didn't matter what anyone else was saying as long as they were there together. She smiled. "If we do not release Ostracia from all of its Withholding in four days Assundra will die," she said simply, her smile not moving an inch. "They will all die for nothing."

"What do you mean?"

"Oh, it's simple, boy, rather like you," Kryman butted in, "you see as this Assundra is utterly artless, completely without any artistry in her dirty little outsider blood, the Withholdings my father placed on Stracathri will not tolerate her presence. Which is the fascinating paradox, you see, because my dearest brother has rendered the power useless without having an outsider with us. You see our quandary?"

"Assundra is not an outsider!" Simon yelled, shooting a worried glance at Elspeth as soon as the words left his mouth.

"Of course not, dear boy, of course not, but her blood is. Utterly artless, as I said. Which means it carries the ancestral knowledge of the outsiders, her branch of the outsiders anyway and we'll need that if we're going to get out of this."

A thought struck Simon. "Why do you care?"

"Death-life cannot live in life for long, Simon," Elspeth replied, taking his attention away from Kryman's mocking smile. "What happened to your face was my fault, but it was necessary for you to see; this is what happens when death-life and life mix."

"It turns into death for the life."

As Kryman turned away, chortling at his own humour, Simon tried to take Elspeth's hands before he remembered. "So I can't touch you? At all?"

"Not yet," she smiled sweetly. "But if you want to save your friend you must do as my brother and I say. You are not yet ready for this on your own, do you understand?"

He was. He knew he was, but more than anything he wanted to be beside this girl, this Elspeth, this woman who treated him like a man. Even Assundra refused to treat him like more than a child. Elspeth was different. And she had such power…

"What do we need to do?"

"First of all, we must deal with the Elders. They must have no part to play in this, they are an abomination, a travesty! It is our place to rule, Simon, people like me and you, not theirs. Power and authority run naturally in blood, they are not stolen."

Simon thought for a moment – how did that tie in with having stock? Surely that power was stolen? But no, Simon thought, Elspeth had said that the stock, in her time, gave themselves willingly to the Ostracians and, indeed, according to the Elders' lore, the Ostracians had never been more powerful than in those times.

Something else nagged more at his thoughts. "What about the villagers?" Elspeth's spectre gave the image of raising an eyebrow. "Cairns is planning on getting them out, like I said, if he's not there…"

Kryman snorted behind them, but a look from Elspeth silenced him. "Simon," she said, "that is taken care of. Everything has been planned."

The eyes twinkled at the back of his mind. She was right. Elspeth had everything under control, of course she did. This woman deserved to rule! Simon smiled. "Then let's go and get Cairns!" he said, ignoring Kryman's laughter.

"No, Simon," said softly, raising her face as close to his as they could allow and even then Simon felt sparks of heat begin to scorch his lips, "let's go and save Ostracia!"

Snapping her fingers at Kryman, she began to stalk back toward the village and Simon made to follow her.

"Boy," Kryman was suddenly in front of him, blocking his path, though he hadn't seen the spectre move. "I know not how you have deceived my sister, though she has always had a soft spot for the little vulnerable men, something I've tried to beat out of her in many ways, but clearly not hard enough, you don't fool me."

Kryman North was really beginning to try Simon's patience. He felt the artistry at the back of his throat, begging to be spat into the spectre's face. "What are you talking about?"

"You are about as much a Gifted One as is I am! You're powerful, yes, in a childlike way, but you are nothing compared to my sister. Yet she seems convinced otherwise. Know this – the first mistake you make will be your last! Now follow my sister like a good boy."

Simon spat, sending the full force of artistry into Kryman's face, but the spectre simply laughed.

"My point exactly!" he laughed. "Now get down the path before I undo the work I've just done on your face!"

Simon made to follow Kryman with a scowl. His foot struck something hard and he looked down. It was the fragment of Lamia's head, scarred, melted and broken. Raising a hand to his still tender cheek, Simon frowned and followed them into the Forest.

CHAPTER 18

Somehow, Cairns managed to force some cider between his clenched teeth and swallowed. The apple stung his throat, but the drink warmed him. Cairns knew already that it would not warm his mood.

The plague death had been a false alarm. There had been a death alright, but there had been no plague symptoms. According to Elder Oldershaw, he had only heard second hand from Jolly's wife, who'd found the body when she happened to be calling round. Cairns supposed he had to believe him, but he was finding it difficult. Oldershaw had claimed he needed Cairns to create a suitable shield against the plague, but the shield was just colour a colourful glamour for the benefit of the villagers watching, it did nothing. It was true that Cairns was the greater expert in plague matters, but if so why had Oldershaw not simply told Cairns as much when they were alone, rather than telling what he must have known was an easily seen-through lie?

The old man was certainly doing a good job of celebrating in relief with the rest of the village – he was on his third cider and they had hardly been there long. Such excesses alarmed and upset Cairns. The man was in a position of importance, how could he allow himself to be seen to be like the rest of them? They had to set an example.

Cairns subdued a snarl – was that what Oldershaw had been doing? Giving Cairns an example of what he could do?

Oldershaw was sitting on the next table, the alehouse having three long tables left after the construction of the village took the rest, each seating about twenty. Almost the entire village had come to share in the Elder's celebrations, but truth be told, there was little else to do, with the harvest having been gathered. Cairns wondered if Oldershaw could see that, or if he was too in his cups already to realise.

He'd never realise how much more difficult he had made things for Cairns! At least Max could be trusted to carry out the punishment satisfactorily, though he doubted whether Simon would see it like that.

Cairns had been sitting alone at the table opposite for an hour now, waiting for Oldershaw to have the decency to speak to him personally, but his colleague hadn't so much as glanced in his direction.

The alehouse, the only one of the old buildings Ostracians still used, was more than large enough to accommodate the whole village should that ever be required. It had been converted into a defensive fortress before the invasion, housing the women and children of the rich and powerful and a good deal of the stock, those that there had been time to save. The alehouse had stood firm through fire, sword and battering ram. It made the people feel safe.

It was also where the Ostracians, in their rage and frenzy, had slaughtered the rich and powerful.

The bloodstains of the aristocracy could still be seen on the raised floorboards that hid the hundreds of scurrying rodents, Jolly's food stock, from view. As long as enough food was stuffed below the floorboards they didn't make an appearance above those boards and everyone had grown used to the movement beneath their feet. Those that couldn't find enough food and came up to forage became food themselves. Cairns often marvelled at how such a food chain had developed so quickly.

The alehouse had its own well and deep midden pit as well as the now flooded tunnel that gave access to the Forest. The two walls of stone were filled with hard clay between them, making the outer wall at least two feet thick. The wooden galleries of the first and second floors had long since either burned, rotted or simply been used for other purposes, so several ladders of varying lengths, tied to the wall by suspiciously frayed twine, led up to the rooms and lookout points above in what was now a cavernous central atrium, at least thirty feet in height, dominated by the stone bar constructed in a large square in the centre, around which Jolly the aleman and his assistant, Alice West, were pouring generous measures of Cider Shorts.

Several nervous glances went out periodically, some from the crowd, but mainly from Jolly, towards the door. If Tom caught them in here drinking Cider Shorts – cider infused with malt and sugared wine, making a thick sludge far stronger than ordinary cider and brewed by Jolly in his own basement – without Tom knowing, then it would break the farmer's heart, a heart which had gone into making the village the best cider he could. And if the farmer's heart were broken, Cairns imagined the villagers were rightly assuming, that would lead to several broken people.

Cairns had sympathy for the farmer's point of view as the thick brown slime tasted like it had come out of the midden and went to the head quicker than a dizzying blow. He was sticking with what was apparently the last, reserved, "only for the Elders, this" barrel of Assundra's Old Tom Infusion. It was a fine brew and he admired Jolly for trying to mix it with water to make it last, hoping that an Elder wouldn't notice. In fact, he doubted whether Oldershaw would notice. The man had been plied with drink constantly since they had returned to the village.

Downing the rest of his cider, Cairns stood quickly, drawing curious looks from those sitting on the tables near him. This insult really was too much. If Oldershaw wanted to stake some sort of claim for power, then he could do it without Cairns being present to act as some kind of dumb victim. Cairns had more important things to do.

Apart from a few curious glances, nobody paid Cairns much heed as he left the alehouse. They were all too engrossed in Oldershaw's tales. Nothing about what Oldershaw had found troubled Cairns – it was not, as he had assumed the weapon, the power that the Norths had constructed and as long as Oldershaw had not found that, then nothing the man had found could have been that important.

It was the slight that angered Cairns. He had allowed the old fool his head during Simon's trial, allowing that ridiculous punishment to go unchallenged when the only evidence to put before the people had been dangerous evidence. Oldershaw had let the secret of the trick loose and once Ostracians had calmed down from the excitement of today and started to think about what Oldershaw had said meant, they would come to the same conclusions he would in their position.

That the Elders were up to something in the Council Chambers.

It would only take a short while before people started snooping around after that, out of nothing more than perfectly harmless curiosity, but what Oldershaw had failed to include in his recounting of Simon's supposed crime was that anyone who tried to break the lock on the Council Chambers should be dead, as John was.

Cairns sighed as he neared the village circle, across which his cottage lay, which was where he was heading. There was no time for a Withholding, he would have to suppress this in another fashion. Looking around him, he sought signs of Broadside. Neither Max nor Bryant were back yet, for neither had been in the alehouse and it would take a pack of wolves to keep them away from a gathering like that. Cairns knew he could not very well go in and retrieve Alice to find her husband, not after leaving so abruptly. Out of the corner of his eye he saw motion near the mason's cottage.

"*Galvarin will do*," he told himself. Setting off to the masonry Cairns congratulated himself on his choice – the man would be feeling neglected after the morning's events, it would do well to boost his confidence with a visit.

"Elder!" the man cried with surprise, straightening.

Cairns smiled a greeting in reply. "Working, Galvarin? I would have thought you would take the opportunity to rest with the rest of them."

The mason stared at the Elder in shock for a few moments before replying. "Elder, what happened? I thought you'd be fuming, after what Oldershaw did with Simon!"

"*Elder* Oldershaw," Cairns admonished, but with a smile. "I won't deny it has put a dent in our plans, but not an insurmountable one. We will simply have to find another way of keeping Simon out of the way until the evacuation."

Galvarin looked angrily at the alehouse. "I hope it's as simple as that. I've had people asking me all day whether I think the punishment was hard enough. I've had to tell them 'of course, it was all I wanted'. Why did he interfere? Did you buy that he needed you for the shield?"

"No," Cairns replied quickly, reminding himself that as far as Galvarin was aware, the colour shield was an essential part of prevention against plague. "Elder Oldershaw is more than capable of creating a shield on his own and assessing the voracity or otherwise of a plague claim, no, there was definitely another reason."

Galvarin shifted. "Let's hope he was drunk."

Cairns nodded – it had been what he had assumed. "The alternative is more…complicated."

"The alternative involves a reaction from Simon I wouldn't wonder," the mason replied quietly.

"That was out of my hands. There are a few things that escape me even as head of the Elder Council. I do not know what Elder Oldershaw's intentions were but I do know that…" he broke off as he realised Galvarin was staring past him with a confused look.

"Elder…" the man said and Cairns span on the spot. Captain Bryant was running madly across the village circle, panic-laden gasps of terror accompanying his every breath. His sword was not in his scabbard and half of his battle armour was torn off. Cairns wanted to move, to push his feet into motion to stop the Captain before he got to the alehouse, but he knew it was already too late. The swordsman crashed headlong into the door of the alehouse and barrelled straight through.

The sounds of the crowd inside stilled at once.

"Galvarin, where is Broadside?" Cairns asked, hoping his voice wasn't shaking.

He heard Galvarin gulp behind him. "I don't know, Elder. Elder, what…"

"Go to the Council Chambers," Cairns replied quickly, "the artistry will not stop you entering. Go there now and wait for me, do you understand? Admit no-one! On your way, tell the Deathguard that it is time to fulfil a promise."

With a confused nod, the man fled in the direction of the old city. Cairns turned back to the alehouse. The silence was oppressive. The taste of nothing crept to him on the air, making him sniff deeply. A massive discharge of power! Not here, not in the village, from somewhere in the Forest…Simon!

Cairns could recognise the unrefined power anywhere, it was like a child striking a hammer blow where a deft stroke would do. Swallowing hard, he softly closed the door of Galvarin's cottage and, less decidedly than he would have liked, began to head for the alehouse. As he did so, Oldershaw and Bryant burst from the door, followed by a good number of the villagers. Spotting Cairns almost straight away, they rushed towards him. Cairns quickened his pace to meet them in the centre of the village circle.

"Elder!" Oldershaw cried. "Have you heard?"

Cairns scowled – how in the hells could he have heard as Bryant had only just got back? "I have not, Elder," he replied, trying to keep the anger from his voice. "What is it that I should hear?"

People hung back on the village circle, looking about them nervously. Oldershaw, Bryant, Samton Shorte and Carp came to stand just behind the Elder.

Forcing himself not to stare at the squat, puck-faced man smoothing his receding long blonde hair back over a reddened scalp, Cairns kept his gaze on Oldershaw. "What is it?" he repeated, with more force this time. His hand flinched.

"Max is dead," Bryant cried and Cairns turned his gaze slowly to him, looking for the lie. The man was close to being deranged, his eyes wild, never still, his hands shaking. Cairns' hand clenched further – there was no lie here. "He's dead, Elder! Simon killed him, his own father! His own dad, killed him right there, killed him dead! He's dead, Elder!"

"Alright, Bryant," Cairns replied soothingly, putting an arm on the swordsman's shoulder, struggling to keep his grip light. *Why were they always trying to hinder him?* He let a splint slightly pierce the Captain's skin, making sure it was out of Oldershaw's eyeline. Bryant's shaking stopped. "You saw this happen?"

Bryant nodded, too vigorously and too often. The man was in no fit state to help Cairns now, nor would he be again. *Another lost to their interfering stupidity!*

"Stuck his finger in his neck and killed him! Right there in front of me! I barely got away with my own life," he added quickly, his eyes shifting. So, he had run. "He just killed him, Elder!"

"Calm down, Bryant! Did you see Max die?" More frantic nodding. "Alright, calm down – now, did you see Simon after Max fell, was he wounded? Did he pass out, or was he still standing?"

Oldershaw's eyes flickered at this – Cairns should have known the old fool would not have asked the right questions. As always, his counterpart would have got caught up in the emotional drama of everything, making rash decisions, not thinking things through to their conclusion. It was his emotional sentencing that had led to this. *Why could they never just sit back and let him do what was necessary?*

If he was still standing that meant Simon's power was tapped and controlled. If, however, he had fallen, it meant it had been an undirected attack. Cairns might even be able to get away with calling it an accident and removing the splint as a punishment.

"I didn't see, Elder," Bryant replied. Cairns pursed his lips. "He just killed him!"

Cairns nodded, taking his hand from Bryant's shoulder. The man immediately started shaking again, each breath coming with an audible sob of shock. "Take him to his cottage, Carp," Cairns directed, making sure it was loud enough for the crowd to hear. "I'll send Broadside along presently with something to help him sleep."

Turning to Oldershaw, Cairns tried to read the man's eyes. "Do you think this is the wisest place to discuss this?" he hissed, placing an arm around his colleague's shoulder to lead him away from Carp, who was making no attempt to move. Cairns felt something stir in his mind. Another gardener…

Oldershaw stopped firmly, not letting Cairns draw him away. Cairns turned to look at the old man in surprise. "Look," Oldershaw said firmly, raising a finger and jabbing it in Cairns' chest. "it was your decision to give Simon that splint! I told you no good would come of this!"

Cairns started at Oldershaw in astonishment. What the hells was he playing at? "The decision of the Elder Council is the decision of us all, Elder," he replied firmly and just as loudly as Oldershaw had spoken. "We stand and fall by the decisions together, do we not?"

Cairns saw movement out of the corner of his eye coming from the old city. It had to be the Deathguard, Smiling, Cairns couldn't help but feel relief as the shape made a beeline for the village circle.

He realised Oldershaw had not responded. "Elder, I will ask you again, do you not think we should we should retire to a more private location…"

"Such as where, pray, Elder?"

Cairns' muscles tensed as he heard the speaker. The shape had neared the village circle now and Cairns turned to meet it. Cursing himself, he realised that whilst the shape was big, it was still too delicate for the Deathguard. Mary Archer stood but feet from him, as Cairns had never seen her.

The blue was fierce in her eyes, the black of her dress sleek and glossy. There was a ghostly fetch to her pallor and a grace about her movements that Cairns was sure hadn't been there before. He had been staring at her for some moments before he saw her knowing smile.

Cairns bit a part of his tongue and spat the blood into the air, towards Mary. It fizzed into nothing as soon as it got close to her. Cairns openly snarled, not caring who could see. It didn't matter now.

Mary Archer had been Drawing.

Elder Oldershaw stepped back, as did Carp. Bryant was looking about him in confusion, his breathing short, uncontrolled, panicked. Cairns realised he was circled.

"Such as where?" Mary repeated, speaking as loudly as Oldershaw had spoken. Cairns withdrew his fingers from the palm of his hand and realised he was barely breathing. He let the blood flow. "Do you not think that such a discussion should involve your people? Were you planning to tell them at all that you had introduced a splint to one of their number?"

Cairns did not reply. Turning, he saw people dripping out of the alehouse and forming a loose ring about the circumference of the village circle. Oldershaw had moved back to join them and he saw Carp being handed a club. *Oh by the gods, what did they think a club was going to do?*

"Simon is my apprentice," he somehow managed to find the words to say as more people joined the ring around him. Flicking his eyes to the entrance to the old city he saw no sign of the Deathguard. "The decisions taken regarding his apprenticeship are for me to take and no other. As head of the Elder Council it is my responsibility. They were consulted and I speak with their voice."

"And yet," Mary cried back, her large frame supporting a cavernous voice, "Max West lies dead as a result."

"Well how do you know that, Mary?" Cairns countered at once, pleased when he saw her flinch. "You were not in the alehouse when Captain Bryant returned and you were not here on the village circle with me when Elder Oldershaw informed me of this sad occurrence, so how did you know that?"

To his surprise, rather than the fear of revelation that he expected to see on her face, she showed nothing more than an expression of satisfaction. "I believe it is time to inform our fellow Ostracians that Simon was not the only apprentice Elder they had." Murmurs rose from the crowd, which interested Cairns. Looking across, he could see that around Carp and Samte a small group had gathered. Further to the right of the half-ring, some of the crowd still had cider mugs in their hands and confused expressions on his face. So, it wasn't all of them…

"I did not sanction another apprentice," Cairns shouted, throwing his arms wide. "As such I charge Elder Oldershaw…"

"Charge me?" the man bellowed, the force of his force belying his years. "After the negligence you have shown these great peoples?"

Cairns heard footsteps behind him. Seeing the satisfied expression on Oldershaw's face he could not help but turn. Young Crafter stood behind him, his expression unusually serious. Turning back, he saw Patrick Crafter and Just Crafter appear from behind cottages on his left. Erol Tyson and his father came from the right. *Where the hells was the Deathguard?*

Elder Oldershaw turned to address the people gathered around the village circle, bringing Cairns' attention back to him. "This man has lied to you for years!" he roared, spreading his arms wide. "I have the proof I have been seeking! With the help of the Crafters I have found the proof!"

Cairns felt the fury begin to descend. He heard Mary laugh softly behind him but did not give her the satisfaction of turning to her. If they had all Drawn…he would stand no chance. He would have to take them one by one. He was still Chief Elder. He could charge them all without fear.

"See how he says nothing in reply!"

"There is nothing to reply to! If you have an accusation then *charge me*!" Cairns roared back at Oldershaw, but the old man just smiled.

"This is not a charge," he chuckled, "these are just facts, things which your charges rarely are, Elder. The first of these facts is that whilst you have denied these people their birthright, their artistry, on pain of death no less, you have been allowing others to practice in secret. Do you deny it?"

Cairns grimaced, but did not reply. Why didn't they just get on with it? *Why were they always getting in his way?*

"You dismembered my father for that," a voice shot from the crowd. Cairns looked, but could not see who it was from. There were murmurings from others.

"Yes my friends, there have been many such instances! Elder Cairns has been pursuing a vendetta against his own people's nature for the sake of what?"

"To eradicate the plague!" Cairns screamed, to a reaction of silence.

"The plague still exists, does it not? You have failed. As I knew you would all those years ago when you embarked down this path against my judgement and advice." More murmurs from the crowd. More joining Carp and Samte. "We tried to stop you peacefully years ago," Oldershaw carried on, "but unfortunately we did not plan for your cruelty."

Cairns felt like his brain jolted. "It was you!" he cried, before he realised he was doing it. Oldershaw smiled and Cairns felt sick.

"You punished the wrong Elder," he said quietly, so only Cairns could hear. His face twisted into a sneer. For a moment Cairns couldn't move or speak. He wasn't aware if he was remembering to breathe. Oldershaw was the traitor, not Rime! All he had done to the man, all he had taken…*oh gods*…it was the wrong man! What had he done?

Oldershaw turned his back on Cairns and went on. "The solution to our predicament has been clear for some time. We have to leave this place! It is infested with the outsiders' sorcery, this plague, we cannot escape it! It closes in on us every year and yet we cower and accept its fate like mice! Are we not

Ostracian? Did not forty thousand men invade us a century ago and only ten thousand return?"

The murmurs grew to a loud assent from the crowd. Cairns' attention snapped back from disgust at himself to focus on the crowd. What were they doing? Cairns tasted nothing. It filled his mouth and nose and he had to spit.

"Cowering out of the sight of outsiders, this is not the Ostracian way! Had it stopped the plague, I would have continued to offer Elder Cairns my support, believe me my friends! But it is I who have been among you, heard your tales, seen the loss you have had to suffer, not he! It is I who will lead you to a new life, a life not of skulking in the shadows in fear, but a life of success and triumph!"

Cairns ground his teeth. "Elder Oldershaw," he roared, moving towards his colleague.

"If we fight the outsiders again," Oldershaw continued, "we will win again! This plague has cursed us to lose what is rightfully ours, the power of Ostracia can no longer be called upon by us all, but there are other ways to win a war and I have found one!"

No! Cairns could take no more. This had to end – the man was not going to bring that to this fight! He alone had the solution to the salvation of his people, why could nobody just accept that?

He moved closer. "Elder Oldershaw I charge you with treason!" There were gasps behind him. Cairns saw red behind his eyes as he closed on his colleague. Flexing his fingers, all of them, he flicked blood out before him and smiled as he saw the old fool's eyes widen in terror. "As leader of the Elder Council I charge you and find you *guilty*!" The words left the back of his throat in an eager surge and the blood held before his gaze turned to fire in the air. Cairns flicked more blood and sent the flaming ball surging toward Cairns. Cairns smiled.

"I don't think so, Elder."

For a mere second, there was a shimmering in the air between Oldershaw and the ball of flame. In that second the ball vanished, falling to the earth in harmless droplets of blood once more.

"Sorcery!" he exclaimed, turning to the one who had spoken to him.

Mary smiled. "It is time for this to end, Elder. It is time," she cried, raising her voice, "for those with the right to rule to take it back!"

Cairns had had enough. As the Deathguard roared the signal of his arrival from the trees, distracting Mary for just a second, Cairns leapt at the woman, plunging his fingers into her neck. She cushioned him as they fell, Cairns turning her head so the vomit spilled harmlessly onto the village circle.

"Mary, I charge you…" Cairns grunted at her, aware of movement rushing towards him from behind. "Never mind. Goodbye!" Words left him and he felt the vein in her neck burst first, underneath his fingers. As the blood poured over his sleeve, Cairns allowed more words to leave him and found the nerve, severing it from the rest of her body.

Hands were on him before he could prepare himself and they held his arms back by the wrists. "It is over, Elder," Oldershaw pleaded, coming close. "We do not want any bloodshed!"

Cairns saw Carp and several of the others with weapons run towards the Deathguard. People were pouring out of the alehouse now, keen to see what the commotion was and Cairns saw Broadside among them, adjusting himself, Alice West following shortly behind. Broadside called to Bryant and in no time at all there were two sides to the crowd.

The sound of axe on wood cracked across the village circle as the Deathguard swung into action. Broadside had found a club from somewhere and held it aloft, a might war cry coming from the broad man's big lungs.

"No," Oldershaw pleaded, turning from Cairns. "This is not what we want, please, if you would just listen…"

Cairns took his opportunity and flicked blood from his right hand up onto his wrist. As the words left his mouth he braced himself for the pain but when it came it was far greater than he had imagined. The flesh on his wrist burned instantly, blistering and sizzling, making Cairns sure the scent of burning flesh would have permeated his nostrils were his mouth not filled with the taste of nothing.

Whoever was gripping his wrist had screamed, letting him go and Cairns instantly swung himself round, driving the now free splints into the nearest body he could find. Screams filled the air again and Cairns found a leg free but then a clubbing blow to the skull dazed him and he fell back, hands grabbing him once more. More pain followed throughout his body in bursts as hands and feet drove themselves into him time and again.

If he couldn't save them, then let them remain unsaved!

He tried to flick blood, but the world was moving too slowly, not catching up with his eyes and the words would not come. As he blacked out, Cairns swore he heard a low, guttural howl pierce the village circle.

CHAPTER 19

Simon swore, ducking sharply, only just avoiding the garden fork that was swung at his head, cursing again as he stumbled, losing his balance. Hearing Samte roar again, Simon dropped to the ground, rolling to one side, but not quickly enough – the fork caught the edge of his shirt, pinning him to the turf.

"Got you now, Elder's pet!" Samte growled, but Simon wasn't wasting any time replying, grabbing hold of the fork and wrapping his arm around it. Samte yanked at it and it came free, but the fork had given Simon the angle to kick out, his foot connecting hard with Samte's weight-bearing leg. The man grunted as he fell forwards and Simon tore the fork from his grasp.

"That's it, Gifted One, show them what you're made of!" he heard Kryman calling from not too far away. Simon realised Samte was begging, pleading for his life, not just for him but for his wife.

Simon swore again. "I'm no Elder's pet!" he screamed angrily driving the fork down until it crunched through flesh, holding firm in the turf beneath. He turned quickly away as Samte's pleadings turned to screams. With his hand pinned Samte wouldn't be going anywhere for a while.

Gasping for breath, he saw the village circle resembled what remained of a battlefield. The battle brewing between the hundreds of villagers had petered out into nothing after the villagers had fled at the sight of the Norths. The spectres walking into the village circle had been too much for them.

Simon didn't know what to do. Elspeth was nowhere to be seen and the eyes in the back of his mind were closed tight, as if they were concentrating hard on something. Something inside Simon pinched at the realisation she wasn't concentrating on him.

Simon was shocked at how easily Cairns was losing. The man, who had always seemed to have the village in the palm of just one hand, never mind two, was slumped, unconscious in the centre of the circle, with only Broadside, Bryant and…something Simon didn't want to think about…flanking him.

On the far side, the Deathguard was struggling against Oldershaw, Just Crafter and Jolly near the entrance to the path to the Old Town, Simon himself was near the path to the Forest and Kryman was tormenting five villagers against one of the cottages backing onto the village circle. He couldn't see his mother or Assundra anywhere, though he had heard someone ushering the women into the alehouse.

Bodies were everywhere, at least two dozen, maybe more, most laying on the route Kryman had taken through the village circle and around the Deathguard's feet. Simon didn't know who were Cairns' men and who were Oldershaw's. He could guess that the bodies circling the Deathguard, which Simon noted with a smirk included Patrick Crafter, were Oldershaw's men. As Elspeth and Kryman had strode before him into the village, Simon had seen Oldershaw, Just Crafter and Jolly take weapons to deal with the Deathguard, who, until he had halted against Oldershaw's attack, cleaving a path through the village with a smile on his face, to Elder Cairns' side.

The big man was wielding a huge axe, the like of which Simon had never seen before. It almost glowed with a blue light. Oldershaw was raining artistic attack after attack, but the weapon seemed to absorb every one, cracking a static charge out from its pommel to the earth as the attack was dispersed. Simon narrowed his eyes. Did Just Crafter just send out an artistic attack?

He shook his head – the man couldn't have.

Simon didn't understand Oldershaw's strategy. All it was doing was giving Cairns time to recover while the…thing…picked off Oldershaw's followers! Old Crafter, Young Crafter and Erol Tyson had backed off now, clearly as disturbed by what was in front of Cairns as Simon was. He tried to avoid looking at it. It sent a chill through him. Something about it was wrong. It wasn't a man and it wasn't an animal. It used its teeth where Broadside and Bryant were using weapons. Elder Cairns lying helpless and that…thing…were things he didn't need to see.

Simon slumped to his knees as the nerves in his wrecked arm squeezed together. It felt as if something were clawing its way out.

Whose side was Simon on? What side had Samte been on? Simon had to assume that he was now on the opposite side, not that Kryman seemed to be discriminating in who he killed.

Every instinct told him he was for anything that was against Cairns, but Oldershaw hadn't spoken a word to him since the shrine, how could he be trusted? Cairns also couldn't be trusted, but Simon knew the plan Cairns was working to – and surely it was a good one?

He needed to find Elspeth, she'd tell him what side they should be on. Gods, it sounded so juvenile, picking sides! Simon gritted his teeth – why could those in power never work together?

They'd got separated when they'd burst from the Forest. Kryman had announced their presence by burning a villager . They had fought. Someone had torn the bandage on Simon's arm loose and it was bleeding again.

On the far side of the village circle, near the entrance to the old city, the Deathguard was fending off Elder Oldershaw and some Crafters with ever-decreasing success, although Simon noted with a smile that Patrick Crafter's body lay in two pieces at the Deathguard's feet. Along with many others. He couldn't hold off an Elder, though, not for long.

Kryman had left a trail of his own bodies on his way to where he stood, to the left of the village circle, five terrified villagers pinned by his presence against a cottage wall. Kryman looked like he was playing tag with them, only they had nowhere to run.

A low howl echoed through the village again. Simon heard more people scream behind him, almost perfectly in time with a loud cry of pain, not aggression as the Deathguard fell, but not before he'd put his weapon through Just Crafter, the man who had dealt the final blow with…nothing.

Simon frowned. He flicked his eyes back to the battle with Cairns, avoiding looking at the thing fighting with the Elder's protectors. Young Crafter was one of the ones holding back, waving his arms and dodging as if he were dancing. Did the Crafters have artistry?

Simon's mouth opened as he looked out across the village circle – each fight was being dominated by one man using artistry! One man on the side of the Crafters! Along with Young Crafter, there was Old Crafter, Erol Tyson and Jolly – what in the hells was going on?

"Samte," Simon cried angrily, turning back to the prone man who was trying to pull the fork out of the ground with his free hand, to little success. "Time for you to tell me a few things."

The man screamed but nobody helped him. Eventually, Simon learned that his mother had fled and was safe in the alehouse along with the other women. He'd also learned that nobody had seen Assundra all day. That meant he had to find her. Didn't it?

"Elspeth!" Simon called, but received no reply. Thinking it best to keep on the move, as Samte's screams would no doubt have attracted attention he didn't want, he dodged around the side of the nearest cottage, avoiding two brawling men rolling around in the dirt as he did so. "Elspeth!"

"Leave her, Gifted One, why don't you have some fun?" As he rounded the next cottage, his stomach contracted as he saw just how Kryman was toying with his captives. They were all screaming, their flesh burning if they got too close to Kryman. Jerram Drake, one of the few elderly Ostracians, easily in his sixties, was trying to roll on the ground to put out the fire that was consuming his leg. Grace Hart's face had peeled on one side. Simon put a hand to his own face, remembering what had happened in the Forest.

Simon scowled and felt the anger boil at the back of his throat. Out of habit he spat, instantly wishing he hadn't wasted the power. Striking the wall of the cottage with his palm in frustration, he turned, all too late seeing one of the men he'd just passed in the dirt lunging at him with a club.

Unable to dodge in time, Simon threw his arms up to protect his face and the club struck hard against his makeshift bandage. Crying out and cursing again, Simon turned tail, running from whoever had attacked him, he hadn't even seen who it was, darting this way and that between the cottages.

Whoever he was he wasn't far behind. Several times Simon heard the man grunt as he swung the club, then the thud as it landed harmlessly in the dirt. Simon dodged between cottages, doubling back, never keeping to a straight line, but he couldn't shake his attacker. Turning around the next cottage, Simon knew his only chance was the crowd, he had to lose the man in amongst the people.

"Got you!"

Simon threw his hands up just in time as the club swung at his face, his attacker having doubled back without Simon noticing. This time the blow knocked him from his feet. The pain in his arm turned to a dead numbness and he felt blood rushing from the wound. Rolling, Simon made to dodge another club attack but instead, the man kicked him in the gut, winding him and almost making him retch.

Gasping for air, he groped around for his attacker. "Here comes number three!" he heard as if from a distance. No, not like this! Feeling power building at the back of his throat again, Simon spat, speaking words as he did so, wishing he knew what they were, wishing he knew how to control them. There was a sizzling in the air and he heard the man grunt in surprise, then fall onto his backside heavily.

Not stopping to see what he had done, Simon pulled himself to his knees, crawling away, around the side of the next cottage. He hauled himself up the wall until he was standing, then stole a look over his shoulder. Carp, who Simon could now see was his attacker, lay still on the ground, but his broad chest rose and fell smoothly.

At least he hadn't killed again.

Swallowing hard, Simon quickly scanned the surrounding streets. There was nobody else near. Gasping, he fell back to his knees and turned again, so he could look out over the village circle.

He didn't pull the makeshift bandage off the arm to see the damage. Blood was dripping steadily from the wound. It was impossible to lift it, or flex his finger. Simon swore again – why did it have to be his splinted hand? Even if he had power he wouldn't be able to use it properly now, not that he wanted to after what had happened with his father.

Resisting the urge to call out to Elspeth again, fearing it would bring another attack, Simon tried the door of the cottage he leant against. He had lost his bearings completely now, he didn't know what side of the village circle he was on, let alone whose cottage this was.

It was dark inside. Something covered the windows, though he couldn't see what. A thin sliver of light from the other side of the room was the only illumination and that didn't illuminate much. Simon took a few tentative steps into the room, as the eyes in the back of his mind snapped open.

It was the low growl he heard first. Spinning, Simon lost his footing again, falling hard, unable to stop his fall with his ruined arm. He cried out despite himself, but stopped as the growl sounded again, closer this time.

Simon felt heat, close by, a presence, something. The growl was constant now, coming in short, quick breaths like…like laughter. Reaching out with his good arm, Simon found the wall and slowly picked himself up to his feet again using the wall for support.

No sooner had he got to his feet than the low howl bellowed from whatever was in front of him. He heard large, padded feet move backwards away from him, but could see nothing. The howl sounded again, stronger this time, followed by a growl that was more like a roar and Simon heard those large feet moving quickly, running, towards him.

Alarmed, he threw up his hands, pleading with the eyes in the back of his mind to do something, but he knew he had no power, there was nothing to draw on, she could do nothing to help him.

There was a huge crash and light streamed into the cottage. Simon looked up just in time to see the rear end of a huge animal bounding through the now destroyed thick wooden door. Splinters rained down from the support beam and there was a metallic clang as the hinges hit the stone floor.

"Gods," Simon exclaimed, looking about him – this was Assundra's cottage!

Simon heard screams from outside. Two more, smaller hairy shapes sped past what had once been a door and he froze as a third stopped. Turning its large, grey head towards him Simon found himself staring into the eyes of a wolf. Saliva dripped from its bloody fangs as it curled its mouth up into what Simon could only describe as a smile as it turned to walk slowly towards him.

It had taken no more than a few steps when a shimmering shape stepped between it and the door. With a yelp the wolf was raised bodily from the floor and through the shimmering spectre Simon saw it begin to burn, snapping its teeth at what held it before its jaw burned away.

"There," Elspeth said softly, dropping the steaming carcass and turning to face him with a smile. "Oh, Simon," she said, rushing forwards, her smile fading, "your arm!"

"It's nothing," he started to say, but she was already reaching for his arm. "No!" he said, pulling away. The look on his face as he shouted pained him, but when his eyes strayed to the bones of the wolf, her expression softened.

"Then you'll have to heal it yourself, won't you," Elspeth said brightly. "Look at me, Simon."

Simon didn't need telling twice to look at her. Her mouth curved into a smile as he realised he was staring, open-mouthed. Elspeth was beautiful, even shimmering as she was. Simon wanted to drop his eyes to the floor, but he couldn't, her eyes held him fast, both the eyes of the spectre and the eyes in the back of his mind, which were blazing bright blue. The eyes seemed to go through his body, searching him and he felt a tingling in his gut, which seemed to spread out into the rest of his body with a heartbeat.

"Now," she said softly, before allowing her lips to curl into a broad grin.

Simon was confused for a moment, but then he felt it – somehow he had power again. "I don't know how," he began.

"I will show you. Call the power, Simon."

He did as she asked at once, anxious to keep the smile on her face. He willed the power to the back of his throat. His eyes widened as he coughed, the power anxious to escape, but Simon felt his throat contract as he did so and something held it in.

"Now, focus, Simon." He heard the voice as much in his head as with his ears. "Do you remember Lamia's shrine? Within, without, in all spaces. The technique is the same, though the method is different."

Simon tried to remember. *"The power lies within you, you must draw upon it then shape it."* This he had done already – the power bubbled at the back of his throat, making him want to swallow and spit at the same time. *"Focus on what you want to achieve, see it, see yourself do it."* Frowning, Simon remembered this was the part he found tricky.

"You are trying to heal," he heard Elspeth murmur gently beside him, "so what is without is your own arm. It may sound strange, but it is the same technique."

He could feel the blood flowing around his arm. A lot of it was dead, having been exposed to the air for too long, but Simon could make out just enough of the live blood still flowing from the wound underneath. As soon as he found it, he was flowing with it, fighting against the tide.

"Do not follow it, Simon," Elspeth warned, "you must stay focused. Remember artistry is of three parts, not just two."

"Your power lies within you, your focus outside you, yet the world is in all spaces. You must be vigilant."

Simon heard himself gasp, but all he could see was the blood. It was a torrent, forcing him back, pushing him away. He panicked and tried to force himself against the tide. He heard Elspeth bark a warning at him, but knew it was too late and came back to himself with a jolt. He looked up at Elspeth. "I'm sorry."

Her lips were pursed. "Try again, Simon."

Swallowing, he lowered his head to his arm, feeling the eyes in the back of his mind watching him closer this time. "*Within, without, in all spaces.*" He found the blood easily this time, but stayed above it. In his mind he pictured himself hovering over his arm. Without warning, he felt power leave his throat and suddenly he was aware of where he was. All he could see or hear was the blood, but somehow he was aware of the room he was in, the fresher air coming from the door, Elspeth's presence near him, the fact that something dangerous had recently been here and he should not stay. He could sense it all and felt himself smile.

"Good," Elspeth said and he was aware of her moving a step closer. "Now let us start small. Try to find the tear that is causing the greatest loss of blood. We are going to close it."

Simon knew where it was already without sensing it artistically – it was the lower of the two cuts. The membrane was beginning to show through, as if it were being squeezed out.

"Find it with your artistic senses," she commanded. Simon did as he was bid. It was the same technique, she was right. It was just like finding the sinews that held together the arm he had shattered in the shrine. He could see, no, not see – he could *feel* how the swelling was causing the problem.

"Now."

Concentrating, he found the swollen area. Words left his mouth and Simon felt the build up of power in the back of his throat release. It was as if everything was happening more quickly – the blood was flowing faster, the skin knitting together more quickly. As the swelling decreased, Simon was instantly aware of what to do next, of where on the arm he should heal next.

"Good," he heard Elspeth say, but he was too busy to listen. Now the swelling had subsided, the bleeding fell away and Simon was able to force the blood to heal the rest, all the time watching, sensing what was around him. Simon was within, without and in all spaces.

*****

"Simon!"

He came to with a start, realising it had grown darker outside. Panicking, he lifted himself up off his back to his elbows – wait, how had he got to the floor?

"Has our precious Gifted One awakened?" he heard a nasal, high-pitched voice say. "I'm so glad, after all a little healing must have taken it out of his vast powers."

Simon scowled, looking up at Kryman to retort, but the eyes in the back of his mind snapped open, blazing fiercely in a warning. He closed his mouth.

"Wise move, boy," Kryman said quietly, his red eyes bright.

Elspeth sighed. "Is the Elder secure?"

Kryman turned his attention from Simon at once and nodded. "He is with the other one, I believe out little pet Elder had some questions for him." Simon frowned. Pet Elder? "I suggest we see him soon, sis," Kryman went on, "before…"

"Yes," Elspeth cut in. "And the people?"

Kryman smiled. "Forty dead, quite a lot actually, but then I did lose my temper at the end there, I wasn't expecting…well, what we got."

"Where is it now?"

"I have no idea," Kryman replied, his smile fading. "Nothing could touch him, sis. Only thing was, it was like he was looking for something, or someone. He was running for the city before I could catch up, then I got waylaid by, well, you. I got the big one, though," he added, the smile returning, "he was quite a challenge, I almost…"

"Thank you Kryman," Elspeth replied, cutting in again. "I think it best if you keep an eye on the Elders, we'll join you shortly."

"Anything you say, sis, anything you say." Kryman laughed as he glided through the ruined door.

"Forty dead?" Simon found himself saying. He expected the pain, but the eyes in the back of his mind were closed tight.

"This wasn't my choice, Simon," Elspeth replied, "nor was it my fight. You have seen what we can do," she said, looking down at her hands with a curious expression on her face, "but that holds little in the way of persuasion. Kryman's ineffective slaughter has shown us that."

"Forty people!" Simon repeated, then a thought made his skin prickle in fear. "Where is Assundra?"

"We do not know. All we know is that the beast that came from this cottage was looking for someone, it could have been her."

"Tom Franks?"

Elspeth nodded. "When he showed up with the wolves, the villagers scattered – he probably saved countless lives."

"It's like you don't care about them," he said, wondering if he did himself. Forty of his people were dead in one afternoon. They had buried that number in a week before, at the worst heights of the plague, but Simon had been younger then. Surely their deaths should mean more to him now?

"Come," Elspeth said, smiling, "we have an Elder to question. We can mourn the dead when this is over, in the meantime we have a problem that I think you can help with."

Turning, she glided from the cottage after her brother. Simon stood for a few minutes, not wanting to leave. He looked down at his arm – it was completely healed, but yet again he felt drained of power, as if he had nothing left. He tried to call some to the back of his throat, but there was none. Frowning, Simon slowly followed Elspeth from the cottage.

He didn't look at the bodies as he followed her across the village circle. He didn't want to recognise them.

He didn't want to be reminded of his father.

CHAPTER 20

"Sunny! Sunny, you must move!"

Assundra sobbed and the sound echoed around her. She felt weak, even bringing herself up to her elbows on the damp stone seemed impossible.

She was right back where she had been when Young Crafter had last grabbed her. "I told you to stay down here," he'd screamed at her, after it was all over, fury in his eyes. "I tried to help you, tried to stop this, but you wouldn't listen would you, you stupid outsider bitch!"

They'd tied another rope to the well, to replace the one she'd cut, but as there was no bucket, they'd simply tied the other end around her waist and lowered her down. The top of the well was just a pinprick of light above her now, far above her head, far too far to climb.

"You must move!"

Assundra ignored the voice, instead curling her hands around her knees. She wasn't safe. After what they'd done she didn't think she'd be safe ever again.

Mary Archer had been the one to cut her, slicing the knife through her with a calm, pleased smile on her face. She'd looked down at Assundra as if she were doing her a favour. Assundra had pleaded with them, begged them, even while that bright knife, shimmering in the candlelight like a jewel, had been pulled through her flesh. It had felt hot and cold at the same time as it had made deep, jagged cuts in her arms and legs. Then they had…

"Sunny, no!"

She retched again and screamed – how could they? Gods, how could they? Assundra had watched them do it, there had been nowhere to turn her head to. Everywhere she looked there had been another person with that hunger in their eyes, another gilt cup pushing past countless others and if she closed her eyes now she could hear them, their slow, wrong breathing, which was somehow worse than anything else.

Her mouth had filled with the taste of nothing, but more so than it ever had around Simon or the Elders – it was as if her tongue had swollen to fill her mouth, drying up, so that when she retched it had stuck in her throat. She remembered losing the strength to struggle. She remembered feeling the blood dripping down her arms and legs, but they caught it in their little cups before it could drop to the floor. Then they had…

"Sunny, you must move now*!"*

She remembered Mary stroking her cheek softly, her hands stained with Assundra's own blood. "There, there," she'd said, almost caringly, licking up some stray drops of Assundra's blood from her lips, "it's done now. Now let's get you healed, we'll have to be back for more after our work is done."

Mary and someone else had done something to the wounds on her arms and legs then, making them numb. Her stomach had felt like it would burst, like it was a burning ball of flame, spewing burning bile past a throat that felt like dust.

How long she'd been there she couldn't say. It didn't seem like long, yet at the same time it seemed like the longest time. She was so tired. After Young Crafter had screamed at her with tears in his eyes, he'd struck her about the face and lowered her in to the well. Young Crafter confused her. He hadn't come near her. Young Crafter had been the only one who hadn't...

"It's past, Sunny. Try and move."

The voice was talking to her a lot today, she thought, almost absent-mindedly. It hadn't helped her though, had it? She made no attempt to move. Her eyes closed.

"Over here! Over here!"

They were running, the two of them. The heather was thick and they ran in circles, trying to catch each other. Assundra thrust at the heather with her arms, flinging it out of the way as she ran.

"Catch me if you can!"

The squeal of a rat near her ear brought the blackness back as her eyes snapped open. She realised she was leaning on an arm quite happily, the other stretched out in front of her, fingers smarting as if she'd swiped at something. The squeal and the fading patter of swiftly moving feet confirmed it.

"See! You can move, Sunny!"

The ball of pain in her chest licked a fiery tongue up to her throat to strangle the giggle forming in her throat. The voice never spoke for long, only in these short, unhelpful bursts. This time it was right, she found she could move, but it took a lot of effort. She slumped on the ground again, aware of hitting her head before it began to feel all light. She thought to herself that her skull should bump, not squelch as bright sunshine flooded her mind.

"I could do it Sunny, I know I could!"

"What could you do?" she remembered saying, entranced by her friend's ever-moving eyes, always searching for something new to focus on, but try as she might Assundra could not recall the face that came with the straight, perfect blonde hair.

"The books, cloth-ears!"

"Books?"

"Yes Sunny, books! The ones in Cairns' cottage. I know I could read them if I could just get them!"

"Get them? It's too dangerous!"

"Oh, Sunny," her friend had exclaimed at her in exasperation. She never understood Assundra's fear of rule-breaking, but then her friend broke the rules so often it probably came naturally to her.

Assundra remembered a hand brushing across her cheek, only as gently as the breeze touching as it passed, and yet the reaction in her body was as if a fire had been lit inside her.

Only now, back in the blackness, there was a fire that felt like it was branding something onto her insides. She coughed something up that she couldn't see in the gloom. Something dripped down her chin.

"I just need to rest," she said, but the voice in her head didn't reply. It never did. It never listened, only told.

Somehow she found the strength to sit upright, holding a hand to the wall. Looking up, she saw only blackness. A circle of lighter darkness hung somewhere above, but she couldn't judge the distance. She knew from last time in the well that even if she had the energy, the well was too wide and too long to climb. Feeling down to her stomach, she found that the rope was still attached to her waist.

"You can't move while tied."

Why was the voice saying that? Surely she could climb up the rope?

"They're waiting up there."

Assundra shuddered, beginning to pant in panic. The voice was right, but try as she might, every time she put her hands to the rope the joints in her fingers felt like they were fused solid. She couldn't grip the ends of the knot tightly enough to pull, to release herself. Slowly, painfully, she reached down into the fold of her dress and managed to wrap a few fingers around her knife.

The knife that had been in her dress the whole time. Fat lot of good it had done her, but perhaps it would now. Some faint glint of light shone off the blade into her eyes and seemed to stay there.

"Help me, Sunny!"

Pale hands, always with some design or other drawn on with crushed berries, were in hers. Her friend had been trying for hours to tell her about what she had overheard outside Elder Cairns' window. They'd been talking about sorcery, about the old times.

"They had to use symbols, you see, not words, otherwise all their servants would've run round casting spells on them," she had said, her eyes wide with fascination. "That's why they were secret, too, because of that, so that's why I've got to try them all out, to see what does what!"

Assundra had not had the heart to tell her that most servants would not have been able to read if the sorcery had been written down. So they'd spent a few weeks coming up with their own symbols for things they could do. Her friend had said it had to be a secret, so they kept it in their box of secrets in Assundra's wardrobe. Nobody would find it there, they knew.

"Try this one!" her friend had said, and Assundra had laughed. It was the symbol she had made up while bored with the Deathguard a week before. "Remember the rules!" she said, very firmly, "no words, just close your eyes and think very hard!"

Assundra had closed her eyes as she had been told, squeezing her friend's hands tighter. They had burst out giggling almost immediately, but her friend had soon regained her seriousness and told Assundra to do the same. She never wanted to disappoint her friend, so she'd calmed herself down and done as she was bid.

Focusing on the symbol, Assundra tried to force what it stood for to happen. She couldn't stop herself smiling the whole time, but hopefully Bethlinda would have her eyes shut so she wouldn't notice.

Assundra's eyes snapped back open to the gloom.

"Oh Sunny, how could you forget?"

The knife clattered to the stone of the tunnel floor beside her. She made no move to pick it up. What was happening? Was this real? She could remember the straight blonde hair, the pale skin, the hands, but nothing else. She'd remembered a name, but what was it?

Were these the ghost memories Simon had been talking about? Assundra found she was breathing too quickly and tried to slow herself down, but she couldn't. Until now she'd only had these sort of waking dreams about her mother. About the deathbed, the strange things she'd said about trees and saplings. They felt real, like they were happening at the time.

Like the beast. Like the red eyes. Like what had happened with Simon in the old city square.

"They're as real as you make them, Sunny."

"Oh gods, Simon! I'm sorry!" she said out loud and made to stand up, only remembering the knife at the last minute. As she stood she remembered the rope, but somehow she'd managed to cut it already and it fell away from her as she pulled herself to her feet. Tucking the knife back into the fold of her dress, she felt for the sides of the tunnel.

The tunnel was wide, wider than her arm span. Why couldn't she slow her breathing? Her head felt light and she slumped back against the tunnel wall, turning in the other direction.

Her panted breath stuck in her throat. Red eyes stared out of the depths of the tunnel at her. It was so dark she couldn't see the sides of the tunnel, but the slanting, fierce eyes were blazing in the distance, bobbing up and down as the beast strode toward her. Assundra stood, transfixed to the spot. The knife was in her hands again.

"It won't help, Sunny! Run!"

"All you want me to do is run," she snapped angrily at the voice, but as ever, there was no reply. Her body didn't want to listen to her mind, though. It wasn't safe. It didn't want to be here any more.

The feeling stole up on her as if it crept up her spine, then unfurled and folded its tendrils through her mind. The voice was right. She wasn't safe! She had to run.

The beast roared and hot air burst against her back as she turned, stumbling blindly down the tunnel away from the beast.

Heavy, padded feet sounded behind her and she heard panting, fierce breaths that she wasn't sure were coming from her or the beast behind her. There was scratching of claws on stone as whatever was behind her sped up. She did too, feeling for the tunnel walls with her arms, the brickwork scratching her arms they scraped past.

Another bellow from the beast behind her told her that she couldn't slow down. She didn't know where she was headed, she couldn't see anything. Something snapped at her legs and she yelped, hurrying her pace further.

If her father were here he would run the beast off! He would keep her safe! She had to find him. She had to help him! She had to…

Something hit her hard in the forehead and she was briefly aware of falling back, the beast triumphally bearing down on her, but she was soon unaware.

"What did you do?"

Bethlinda was staring at her, her bright green eyes wide in fear. Assundra's grin was frozen on her face. She hadn't done anything!

"What did you *do*?" Beth repeated and suddenly Assundra realised her friend wasn't angry with her, or scared, as she'd first thought. She was astonished. Looking down, in between their hands, which were still clasped, she saw they were filled with a fleshy, blood-filled, still pumping heart.

"What was your symbol for?" Beth asked, gripping her hands tightly again.

Assundra couldn't find any words. She wanted to tell Beth, she wanted to tell her everything, about how the symbol wasn't something she had come up with off the top of her head, like she'd told her friend originally. She wanted to tell her that it was something she'd seen on her mother's things since childhood. That it was something that was printed, along with many other symbols, on the petticoat that hung in the wardrobe that she wore when she wore the fancy dresses.

The heart jolted in their hands, making both of the girls jump. One last intense, pulsing thrust before it was still. Blood started to leak out of the vessels. Then it started to pour.

She'd pulled her hands away from Bethlinda's and they'd dropped the heart, where it had squelched sickeningly on the hard summer grass.

They had run quietly back to the village, vowing never to go back where they had been again. It was somewhere in the Forest Assundra couldn't recall now. An open space. A statue. The details were vague.

They'd passed a stream. "We have to wash our hands," she'd yelped breathlessly at Bethlinda, grabbing hold of her wrists. She dropped her friend's hands at once. They had been clean, but were slick with moisture. As if they'd been licked clean. "What happened, Beth?"

"Nothing," was the only reply she'd got. Beth had run on ahead back to the village and Assundra hadn't been able to catch up. She'd also forgotten to wash the blood off her own hands. The villagers had seen Bethlinda run, straight to Elder Cairns' cottage, then seen her following, her hands covered in blood.

It was when she had been beaten raw, beaten by Crafters and Elders until her father had come to rescue her. It was when her father had almost struck Elder Cairns. It was the last time her father was truly…himself. It was when she realised the villagers would never stop hating her, the jeers on their faces with every fist or belt that struck her had shown her that. It was when she ceased to care about them.

It was when Bethlinda, her friend, her lover, had disappeared.

"You'll see me again soon, Sunny. Soon."

She opened her eyes back to the tunnel. Everything was quiet around her. Assundra felt wetness slide down her face in trickles. When she raised a hand to her temple she cried out in agony, swiftly taking the hand away again, but not before she'd felt cracked, bruised skin leak more blood. It filled her left eye, but as she couldn't see anything anyway she didn't think it would matter.

Feeling around her with her arms, she couldn't find a wall. After some exploration, she realised she was at a crossroads of sorts. The tunnel split into two ahead of her, left and right, and straight behind her, the way she must have come. Wherever she looked there was no sign of the beast.

She sank to her knees again. She had no idea which way to go and she wasn't sure she could stand again in any case. At least she wasn't where the Crafters could get her. They wouldn't be able to…do that again, not unless they came down after her and then the beast…where was the beast? She swung her head around but the world was having none of that and the floor rose to meet her back, hard.

She was in the village circle, nobody around them. There was never anyone around them. She was angry. "I've no idea who you're talking about, Simon!"

The boy wouldn't stop grabbing at her arm. He was always like this these days, ever since...well, since recently. He'd hadn't been like it before whatever it was, anyway.

"All I'm saying is, there used to be three of us! I'm sure there did!"

Assundra had sighed. "Look, Simon, there's only ever been the two of us our age, alright? I can't remember anyone else. It's just a dream of yours or something. Forget about it, there's only ever been us two."

She swatted his arms away again. "There were three of us! I'm sure, Sunny!"

"Nobody ever calls me that," she'd snapped, "and if you bring it up again, there won't even be the two of us, do you understand? I never want to hear your stupid ideas again!"

"Sunny?"

Something sounded like it was close to her head. Assundra couldn't move. Her right eye had filled with blood too now. Her arms no longer felt heavy, they didn't feel anything at all. Everything felt numb.

"Sunny!"

Something was definitely by her head. It was right behind her! She wasn't safe! The instinct to flee was quickly quelled by the pain. Nothing would work.

"Sunny!"

"Sunny!"

Hands clasped her head, firmly at first, then when she cried out, they softened. A face came down level with hers. A large blue stone, about the size of a thumb, attached to the girl's forehead by a thin ribbon, began to shine a light, instantly illuminating a pale face. Long, straight blonde hair fell halfway down a slim body. In the strange blue light, the girl's eyes were almost opaque, but there were flickers of flecks of their true emerald green.

"Oh, Sunny, why couldn't you remember?" Bethlinda Mullard said. The girl leaned forward and kissed her lightly on the lips. Beth licked the blood that Assundra's lips left and swallowed, her eyes glinting. Assundra couldn't say anything in reply.

Beth fished another shining blue stone, as unremarkable and yet as beautiful as the one attached to her head, from her delicate, simple dress and placed it against Assundra's forehead. A warm feeling drifted over her, a comfortable feeling. A safe feeling.

"You'll be safe with me now. I won't let them hurt you any more."

They were the last words Assundra heard.

CHAPTER 21

Cairns felt the cold before he felt his muscles stiffen. He couldn't turn his head to see who it was, nor open his mouth to ask. He couldn't scream. No…no, he wouldn't scream!

"You're not the man you were, are you?"

A great stench of nothing, the stain artistry left on the land, but greater than he had ever experienced, filled his nostrils and the half-open slit that was his mouth as she spoke. There was no breath from the voice, even though he could feel her next to his ear, but something turned the goose bumps to blisters. His arms and legs felt far too heavy for him to lift.

"It's disgusting!" a young, deep voice was saying, somewhere to his right. Cairns flicked his eyes across instinctively, but he knew who it was. Simon had been prattling on about his face since Cairns had woken up tied to the chair. Clearly the Glamour had finally worn away.

"His face is the least of our concerns, Simon," the voice laden with silk and ice said in his ear again. "I am more interested in how easily our little pet was tamed."

"But he's so…"

"Oh sis, can we please dispense with this childish procession of ineffectual mockery?" So one of them was a brother. Cairns could swear he could hear the voice in his ear hiss in anger. There was little he could do with the information now, but if she possessed anything like the intelligence he could sense she did, she knew that any information was worth having.

"It's a Glamour, dear boy," the voice of whoever the brother was continued, "a simple matter of an illusion, the gods know we all do it every day! A little lie here, an over-emphasis of one element of the truth over another there, it's the stuff of infantile schooling!"

There was real anger behind the brother's light-hearted chuckle. Cairns could sense malice too, but it was the temper that interested him. One with a temper could be controlled, manipulated.

Cairns inhaled sharply, breathing in a lungful of more nothing as he felt hands push through his back without breaking the skin and begin to fondle his insides. As he was about to retch, hands caressed the spasm and pushed it aside.

"Typical, artless Elder," the icy voice spoke, blistering his ear. "You didn't even see me coming. You didn't know I was here! And now look at you!"

Cairns called the artistry to the back of his throat, but it wouldn't come. His entire body was frozen, his limbs made a hundred times heavier, rendering them useless and his tongue felt like it had swollen to fill his entire mouth. He was incapable of reply even if he could open his mouth and if he did, he felt that his tongue would simply carry on growing in the space it would create until it choked him.

"I can't see your thoughts," the voice continued in a more interested tone. "This is strange, your petty little Withholdings have no effect on me, before you try, and yet I cannot break those you have placed upon yourself."

Before you try? Whoever this was, she did not know Withholdings could not be performed without blood and sacrifice. Or could they? He felt the soles of his feet try to curl in on themselves as they always did when his curiosity was aroused; only one family had mastered the art of Withholding using nothing more than artistry, but the records of that were lost…unless this was what Oldershaw had found!

He couldn't find out like this. Without his splints he was as helpless as an untrained child. An untrained, but *powerful* child. Only there was no power to call on. The rebellion had exhausted him.

"How confusing for you it must be! To be treated as one of your subjects!" Her voice glistened like an iced jewel. Cairns knew the voice, though he had never heard it. "Not fitting for one such as you, an *Elder*! Your perverse human sacrifice you call a heart wouldn't care for that, I'd wager. Lowering the tone of the Elders!"

A chuckle followed the woman's words, but from the back of the room; a room that had become warmer and colder at the same time. Cairns felt three of them. One, the woman, was cold. Another hot. The last one was Simon!

"How could I not see his face? Gods, what an ugly, twisted bastard!"

What had they done? Cairns struggled to lift a hand to his face, but they were held fast. What had they done?

The hands left his body, leaving him even colder than before. "I remember," the woman's voice continued, "when we first learned of your plans. Not yours, of course, your path had been set in motion long before your birth, you had no part in them, no, I mean the plans of you elders. To coin a phrase. We took three of your number that night and my, did it take a long time to get them to talk. But talk they did, Elder. Do you want to know what they said?"

He felt a lick of power at the back of his throat as the wells of artistry replenished inside him, but still he could neither move nor speak. His eyes, burning from the need to blink, registered a shape stepping coolly in front of him and he tried to focus. "Not so powerful now!" the figure crowed.

"None of the rebels ever were, Simon, for all they thought they had an answer to us. They draw their power from an abomination and when one draws one's power from an abomination one can be nothing other than just that, can one, Elder?"

Cairns tried to ignore the hands pushing right through him, for naturally they were not truly doing so. How she was doing it was curious, how she was causing no pain, even more so. This was no Domination, nor did it feel like a healing, the one branch of artistry Cairns had never mastered. It had to another form of mental projection.

"Answer her!" Simon shouted, driving a fist into Cairns' cheek, which did not move.

A few trickles of blood from the cut his tooth had made in his cheek ran down his throat. He would have smiled had be been able. The artistry began to gorge.

"Thank you, Simon," the woman's voice said tersely, "but I think you'll find it is I who prevents the Elder from speaking."

Cairns tried to force his eyes into a smile, but he couldn't see Simon. He couldn't see any of them. The blood had at least given him what he needed to focus. A few more trickles fell down his throat. Blood from pain was always better than anything a splint or stock could provide. Not for the first time Cairns fed on himself.

"Tell him what you found, sis."

The artistry flared in the back of Cairns' throat; now he could focus, he knew that this third voice, the voice of this brother, was one he had heard before! But where? It was a man's voice, but only just, the pitch was high and the inflections nasal…where had he heard it before? His memory raced, avoiding the places it was not supposed to go as it always did, trying to find the memory of the owner of the voice…

"What I found from the Elders? They told me a story, my brother. A tale of treachery where there should have been loyal love, of rebellion where there should have been fealty and of a sad, misguided adherence to ways the Ostracian race had long since outgrown."

"*Our* race," the second spectre hissed and then Cairns knew who he was, or who he had been. And he knew where he had heard the voice before. *"Take your blood out of the box!"*

"Be quiet," the woman's voice answered, before he felt a wave of cold as she traced what felt like a nail sharply down the centre of his spine. "Now, Elder, what do you think that betrayal I spoke of could have been?"

"Their abomination," Simon replied almost instantly, folding his arms in pride.

Cairns felt the artistry chill in his throat for just a moment before it continued to build. The man whose voice he knew stepped slowly around Cairns' side until he could be seen. The blood-red smile on his lips looked ridiculous, even as it shimmered. Shimmered. Cairns knew what they were.

Only it was impossible! Death-life and life could not co-exist at the same time, the consequences would lead to devastation! They could not be here!

The woman laughed and tickled the base of his spine, sending him into spasm for a moment. He knew who the man was now, unless it was a very good imitation. He needed no clue other than the eyes. Red eyes. Only one Ostracian in history had red eyes. This was Kryman North.

Which meant she was the Gifted One. No wonder she thought the Transept Tower to be an abomination; its power had been the only thing strong enough to stand against Stracathri and give Ostracians this second chance of life. Their so-called advancements had failed against the simplest of attacks, unable to repel something as simple as a fire.

Something chilled Cairns' thoughts as she chilled his insides. Why had Kryman North helped Cairns all those years ago? Or, what was worse, had he helped him at all?

"Abomination it is, Simon," he realised she was saying. "How many good men died while your kind made that heart, Elder? Is that recorded in your lore?"

A shape glided round to the periphery of his vision on his right. The hand didn't leave his insides.

"I don't think he's listening to us, Simon," Elspeth said cheerfully. Cairns called the meagre artistry up. It wasn't enough.

"Maybe I should make him listen!"

Simon hit him again, in the same place, and the blood flowed, passing over his tongue like hot, nourishing broth, collecting where the artistry held it, boiling, in his throat. He felt his anger rise through him, sending the seething artistry into a fury and he felt the first of the burns against the back of his throat.

Cairns spat.

He had just enough time to allow his eyes to feast on Simon's shocked expression as the stupid boy fell back against the cottage wall, his face covered in Cairns' blood, before his head felt like it had burst in pain. Two hands now, as hot as fire, were pushing their way into his brain.

"Take it out of the box! Take it out!"

The hands were gone at a shout from Elspeth. As the mess of colour in front of his eyes blurred into recognisable shapes, he made out a shaking Simon, slumped against the wall, his staring, terrified eyes looking right at Cairns.

"Wonder why he screamed like that?" Kryman said, crouching beside Elspeth, who was tending to Simon with surprising care. If the lore were to be believed, Elspeth rarely showed tenderness toward anything. The Gifted One had been well liked by the Ostracians of her time, but solely for the simple reason that those who did not well like her found themselves in Stracathri's deep vaults. He had heard some fool, probably the Archer woman, say once that the animals that crowded the lake shore were drawn there by the tortured spirits of those Elspeth had taken to the vaults. Idle, thoughtless nonsense.

In contrast to her brother's shimmering lack of clarity, Elspeth's form was immaculate, only the faint shimmer when she moved and a greying of the skin telling of what she was. What shouldn't be. When she was still, she would pass for life, not the shade she in fact was. The small features of her face were perfect; slightly shadowed by what Cairns supposed was the illusion of a heavy red cloak she presented the image of wearing. Red was the family colour. It covered the blood they spilt.

"Make sure the Elder is awake," she snapped at her brother. *The Red Devil* the lore named him.

Cairns found himself calmed as he watched Elspeth heal the singed skin on Simon's face. It barely seemed to cost her any artistic effort at all, perhaps the stories of her almost limitless power were true. Even so, he had nothing to fear from shades, particularly shades of Norths. All they could to was kill him and that wouldn't stop him for long.

"Of course, sis," Kryman replied, his voice sugared, throwing Cairns a wink. He strode over to the pot of mulled cider and dredged a cup through its contents. What was he doing? Surely he knew…

"Have you gone mad?" Elspeth said, at once at Kryman's side, without seeming to have moved, knocking the cup out of his hands. The look of her shifted, becoming something entirely different. The illusion her looks created faded and she became to sight what the Norths really were; a lineage of arrogant, cruel people who revelled in the repression of and power of their subjects. There was little that was pure about the blood of the Norths, for all it was Ostracian.

Stracathri had known, at the end. The three men Elspeth assumed she had broken had seen to that.

"Perhaps I have gone mad, sis, I could have sworn, for instance, that you just assaulted me and that would not be a sensible thing to do now, would it?"

"Can't you smell it?" she exclaimed, pointing to the pot. "I said make sure he was awake, not for you to nurse him!"

With some more bickering, water was thrown in Cairns' face instead of the powder-enhanced cider. The stinging ceased at once as his eyes soaked up the liquid greedily. Cairns thought he saw Kryman smile.

"And we were going to be so nice to you, Elder," Kryman was saying, walking several inches above the floor. "Such a shame that you've made my sister angry, I've seen her when she gets protective before, you know, though she's usually only protective of herself. It's not a pretty sight whatever she's protecting." He leaned in to whisper and Cairns realised that where the breath from Elspeth's voice burned with cold, Kryman's produced not the slightest waft… "I'd do as she says if I were you."

"He'll be alright," Elspeth said, getting up from the recovering and seemingly very angry Simon and throwing the illusion of her hood back to reveal a shimmering mass of blonde hair.

Kryman simply scoffed. "I'm so glad he's alright, sis! For a moment there I was truly worried that a simple childish ball of artistic phlegm would have done some serious damage to an adult Ostracian!"

Elspeth ignored the sarcasm, floating forwards through her brother until she stood, bowed, almost nose to nose with Cairns. She was truly a beautiful woman, but then the Elders knew little of the ways of women. Beauty always seemed to Cairns to hold little other prospect than danger.

"My brother is right about one thing," she said, the droplets of water on Cairns' face turning to ice as what had to be an illusion of breath hit, "it's not going to be a pretty sight. Though we should really get to know each other before we have that sort of fun. How about this? You answer one of my questions I'll answer one of yours, what do you think?" Her voice hummed at him, giving rise to the temptation to feel that she was soothing his nerves, but Cairns felt the icy cut as his artistry was impeded.

"You've gone soft in your old age, sis." Kryman sounded almost disappointed. The lore recorded that it was Kryman who had been the disappointment to his father, but then fraternisation with the commoners' wives, something Kryman had been famous for, had never been something Lord North had been keen on.

"I am not myself though, Kryman, am I? I'm just a shadow. The Elder is no doubt confused as to how that came about as well. I am sure his lore dictates that life and death-life cannot exist together in the same space. But then that exemplifies what none of their sort ever understood about Stracathri; it really doesn't matter what should. Laws are things the powerless follow."

"We all follow rules, sis. Except our dear brother."

"Yes," Elspeth replied, touching a shimmering finger lightly to Cairns' face and solidifying the remaining water droplets to ice, "and look where that got him. Now, my dear Elder, I'd like you to tell me a few things."

He felt his skin pull away with the ice as she picked it off, piece by piece, never taking her eyes from his. He couldn't avoid her gaze and his eyes were starting to stream. He busied himself with trying to find some small speck of lingering artistry he could use.

"He doesn't seem to be too keen on chatting to us, sis." Kryman spoke in a nasally, aristocratic whine, far removed from Elspeth's melodic, almost harmonic tones. "Want me to prompt him?"

"No, not yet," she purred, "we have plenty of time for that And it would be nice to have some fun whilst we have the time."

"Elders were always like this, I recall," Kryman said, ignoring her, "always the ones with the words until words were actually needed."

It was just as well he couldn't move or he would have fallen to the floor in agony. Or worse, tried to run. Elspeth had begun to blow onto his face, icy blasts of cold searing right into the wounds the strips of skin had left. She was very careful, he noticed, to touch none of his blood, but surely artistry would have no effect on death-life?

"There, there," he heard Elspeth say, "all you have to do is agree to talk to us and I'll make the pain go away."

Cairns desperately wanted to grit his teeth, or sink them into Elspeth's face, but his mouth remained half-open, there was nothing he could do. His eyes felt like the stalks were going to burst through his pupils now Kryman's water had been turned to ice. He had thought, at first, that the Red Devil had done him a favour.

"You see Simon," she said, perfectly calm, never taking her eyes from Cairns, "death-life does not react too well with living flesh, as you saw in the Forest. A mutual distaste from one regarding the other, as my father once described it." At least the pain was producing some tears for his drying out eyes. Her face had blurred to him, and he felt his mind begin the whirl that always came before the darkness. But as always he did not fall. His mind jerked back as he heard Elspeth giggle.

"Only with Stracathri beginning to leak, Ostracia is covered in artistry. The air's practically thick with it, not that any of you would notice now the Elders have taken your power from you. It would feel like nothing more than a hot summer's day, but it means you can see us and hear us. The little Elder wouldn't understand that, though. To him, power comes from life. Others' lives. Isn't that true, Elder?"

He heard a moan, like the braying of a cow, accompany his breath. He could talk again! But she hadn't even touched him to remove the curse…

He felt heat as Kryman drew near. "You know, I really was planning on meeting that fine looking young lady of yours, Elder. I'm quite disappointed she's not here, I'd heard she was something rather special. Is she special to you?"

"Oh, she's special, brother, make no mistake about it. The good Elder here, the watcher over his people, he's been taking care of her to make sure she's special." Cairns was glad he could no longer see Elspeth's eyes, but he could picture the hatred they'd show, hatred for all Elders, for those who dared to question the Norths' ancient right to rule. He'd see the cowardice of arrogance. "Tell me Elder, how can you do it? How do you justify enslaving an entire race of people for your own ends?"

Enslave? He was saving them! He tried to speak but a groan was all he heard coming from his mouth. In any case, he wouldn't expect a North to understand.

"Oh, sis, haven't you learned? They're all the same, they all think they're doing what's right! They don't have the ability to stand against Stracathri, so what do they do? Build their own tower, only they have to use the old ways to do it. Then, when it's built, they think it's given them a purpose, some reason to go on, something *important*. It's pathetic."

"The inadequate seeking parity usually is, brother. Now, let's see what Elders are really made of."

She gripped the icicles on the base of his eyelids and pulled. His eyes immediately filled with tears and he strained his arms, pushing against what felt like weights that held them to his side, but they wouldn't budge. He told himself he wouldn't scream even as the plaintive wail surged from his lungs. Cairns felt his eyeball split with a curious alleviation of the pain as the vision on his right turned to red and then nothing. The blood soothed the wound, but he couldn't move his head to allow any of it to drop into his mouth. With another girlish giggle Elspeth blew the wound closed and the moment was lost, the blood freezing.

Cairns heard himself whimper. Stupid, panicked little breaths, why was his body doing that? What was the purpose? They would kill him soon, their mistake would be made, he only had to wait. His mind was clear, so why was his body reacting so?

The icy blast of Elspeth's breath had left the wounds on his face smarting more than what had once been an eye. The bloodstained, partly frozen, fading vision in his remaining eye saw Simon leering at him.

The creature that had been Elspeth North must have had the boy in her thrall for too long for him to resist. Cairns had been outplayed, he hadn't seen this coming and it hurt. Simon wasn't the sort that revelled in pain. Nor did he wish to study it for the sake of learning, as the Keeper had; the boy ran from it. Any real confrontation, and there were many, caused by his surly mutterings, and Simon always ran.

That had been before Cairns had given him the splint. They had all advised him against it. All except Max, who, as usual, had not even thought of questioning the decision. Cairns had thought that a sign of his loyalty, but now he wasn't so sure. He had sent Max to his death.

"Now you know how it feels, Cairns!" Simon hissed at him, the effort of speaking clearly leaving him exhausted, as he slumped back against the wall.

"He's fading a little there, sis."

"Oh, but I haven't finished yet! Let's see…" He felt Elspeth's hands, or the energy coils that made up the image of her hands, on him again and prepared himself for the icy burning, for the needles shooting into his body, but they didn't come. Cairns heard the words her power pushed forth, but he didn't understand them. He couldn't prevent an exclamation of astonishment leave his mouth – how long had it been since he hadn't understood artistic words? Forty, fifty years?

What she was intoning had to be far in advance of anything he had mastered and there was not much he had not mastered.

Cairns shrieked as he felt pain all over his body, the likes of which he had never felt. Every inch of skin, every vein, muscle, every organ shredded with agony, and he screamed again, not hard enough, not loud enough, if could never be loud enough, as she played with the nerve endings, like she was blowing on a dandelion. Cairns willed himself to pass out, shutting himself down, but she simply brought him back, and the pain filled him once more, but as soon as it did so, it ended, and a cooling air spread instantly through his body and pain left as the cool spread, as if she were running her tongue all over his insides.

"I think that's enough," Elspeth said cheerfully as her hands left him.

"I think he wants more, sis, look at him, he's practically in tears. Do all men cry when you use your hands on them?"

"Shut up, Kryman." Cairns panted. It was close now. "Cairns, I do believe that was your first experience of a woman's healing! It's really quite a feeling, isn't it," she chuckled, "but then I'm sure you're sticking to the Elders' old rule of knowing nothing of the ways of women. Well, at least I've given you a taste of what can be yours if you agree to help us."

Cairns rolled his eye downwards to meet Elspeth's with some effort, wincing as it cracked, a jagged line of red spreading across his vision, and spat.

He was pleased at her rage.

"For the entirety of my father's life", she said, spreading her arms, "he was forced to guard himself against the plotting and scheming of traitors like you in the base of our tower. The base, mark you, where you belonged! How many of you made it out of the dungeons into my father's research teams? Four. Out of four hundred! You may have had numbers, but we had the power, the power was with us, where it belonged!"

"Didn't save you," Cairns pushed through his immobile mouth.

"You dare question me? We had the answer, your little traitors gave me that much before they died! If you Elders had followed your instructions it would all have finished before the outsiders even got there!"

"Are you alright, sis? Only I was rather under the impression that we were here to deal with him, not lecture him on how great you and Dad were."

"I told you to shut up."

Something in Cairns tried to prick up his ears, but he'd had enough. He wanted it to end. Kryman didn't want something said, he could tell that, but he didn't care what it was now. Elspeth's temper was clearly as great as her power, he was surprised one so gifted had such a puerile weakness. He was fading too fast, too much of his body was being damaged, but with her temper she could be goaded into finishing it quicker than she'd like.

Then he could begin again.

This damned shortness of time; he would have given his right arm to know what would have been 'finished' by Lord North! But then he'd already given an eye.

"Save us all," she said, pacing behind him. "Your precious Elders were trying to save Ostracia when it didn't need saving! They've always had a lust for power, it's handed down to them in their little schools and blasted folklore."

"Elders bad, us good, yes, I know, sis. But what exactly are you expecting to do about it?"

"I'll show you."

The light from the window exploded in Cairns' eyes, burning through his vision as he stared, unable to close his eyelids to shut out the blinding image. He let the scream leave his mouth, he was beyond caring what he looked like to them now, he didn't need the respect of preening posers who weren't even of Ostracian blood.

As his eye burned in his skull he took his spirit into himself and focused his energies on locating the stream, there was nothing else for it. He just hoped it wouldn't take as long as last time for the coma to break.

"No!" he heard Elspeth exclaim, but she was soon drowned out by the enveloping rush of blood. He couldn't see it, all he could see was the blinding light and he didn't want to look at that. He would have to let his blood guide him this time. The artistry flowed through an Ostracian's veins in a similar pattern to blood, but there was a source, a point that produced it. Cairns had discovered the stream by chance, resulting in a three-month coma, which had told him it was dangerous to tap directly into it. He had only done it the once, but it was Cairns' only chance against such power. Down into his veins he went, urged on by his own body's defence systems. His heart pumped faster, pushing his consciousness through with the blood, eager to get to the source.

He was dimly aware of Elspeth screaming at him from somewhere that seemed very far away. Without his protection, his eye burned with the light, but he could afford no distractions.

There! It was small, barely formed, like a child's first artistic attempt, but the stream had produced some artistry nonetheless. He grabbed it furiously and did the only thing it was meant to do, what a child would have done; he spat the artistry at Elspeth's face.

There was a scream and the light burned through his eyes with it as Cairns fell heavily to the floor, his limbs bursting into pain and for the first time in his life he wished he were dead. He heard himself screaming as he writhed on the lavish carpet, trying in vain to find a position that didn't send him insane with the pain, but there was none.

"Clever!" It was Kryman's voice, very close to his ear. He felt a pressure in his mind. "Now it's time to thank me."

Cairns' mind was suddenly clear, the pain something for his body to worry about, not something the higher being should be troubled with. Just as things should be. Except he couldn't see. His eyes saw nothing and yet the curious after images of the light that had burned his sight to nothing danced on.

Someone screamed his name and there were no hands on him any more. Sounds came and went as he allowed the dead weight of his body to go slack.

Then a voice spoke to his mind.

"You were nothing but a slave! Such a pity, you could have been a valuable ally to the cause, but your hatred of what is a fine family got in your way." *It was Oldershaw!* How was the old fool in Cairns' head? Where had he got the power?

"Assundra!" Elder Oldershaw seemed not to have heard. Had Cairns even spoken?

"It took years of searching, but I've done it, Cairns! I found it! Right under our noses!" the voice laughed. "All the time, right there! You slaves to the Transept Tower never saw it. Did you think I did not know? Where else could your power have come from? Well, it will not help you now."

Something pressed on his head, as if it were being stamped on. Cairns felt nothing. If Oldershaw had found the weapon…

"It is us who are the slaves!" he heard himself say, the simple pleasure of being able to form words sending a trickle of recognition to his higher being. "We had only ever tried to serve, to help. It is your masters who damned us. We have ever only wanted to protect our people!"

But there was nobody to hear; Cairns spoke too late. He doubted he would have convinced them anyway; Norths were ever obstinate fools, too self-absorbed to see beyond their own ends. The black was coming now, accelerating at his mind in annoyance at having been kept at bay for so long. He had never felt so drained, and the coming oblivion had never appeared so good. As the darkness overcame him and the life left his body, that body sent out the call.

CHAPTER 22

"All they do is complain!"

Elder Oldershaw slumped into the ornately carved chair, letting out a yelp as the hard wood met his back. Simon started to chuckle, but stopped himself short when he saw Kryman was doing the same. The shade didn't seem to notice, but then as far as Simon could tell Kryman was never concerned with anything but himself.

A swift knock at the door to the council chambers brought Carp's head around the door. *Captain* Carp, Simon supposed he should call him now.

"There's one more, Elder," Carp gruffly mumbled.

Simon saw the Elder nod. "Send him in," he said quickly, waving a hand to dismiss Carp. "Simon, I'm not sure you should be here for this, perhaps you should..."

"I'm staying." Simon wasn't going anywhere. Elspeth was elsewhere, trying to track down what had once been Tom Franks, and Simon wasn't going to face her return and questions about what had occurred with the answer 'I wasn't there'.

"Very well, but I warn you..." Oldershaw was cut off in mid-sentence again as the door was kicked open, slamming back on its hinges. Galvarin was brought into the room struggling, Carp and Patrick Crafter holding him.

Simon snarled – Patrick and Old Crafter had been put in charge of the reopened jails, which by now were little more than rotten cellars under the council chambers, where they now stood. In truth, half of the council chambers were beyond use, only this main large room was really usable.

Simon pulled his aching finger into his palm – it was here that Cairns had forced him to take the splint. The means by which his father had been killed. Simon knew it was Cairns who was really to blame. He'd had no choice. Cairns had given Simon the splint, Cairns had sent Max along with Simon to the Forest, Cairns had brought about every situation that had led to Simon killing his father.

It was Cairns who was responsible. Looking up, as Galvarin was brought to his knees before the Elder, Simon saw Kryman leering at him. Simon met the gaze. It was Kryman who had cost Simon his chance to get revenge on Cairns for what the Elder had made him do. Kryman had killed Cairns with the same leer on his face that he had now.

Well, Simon thought, he'd just have to take his revenge out on Kryman instead.

"Galvarin, what is it?" Oldershaw said, through the hand that was plastered to his face. "You have already been found guilty and sentenced to a mind cleansing, what is there to discuss?"

"Assundra Franks!"

"What of her?" Simon had to give Oldershaw credit, the old man hadn't even paused in breath at the mention of the girl's name. Pursing his lips, Simon cursed Galvarin under his breath – he was hoping everyone would forget about Assundra.

"Where is she?" Galvarin shouted back. "Look at me!"

The Elder didn't move. He didn't take his hand from his face, nor did he reply.

"I think our dear Elder is beginning to lose a bit of his nerve, my young friend," Kryman interjected. Galvarin was keeping his eyes firmly fixed on Oldershaw, Simon noted. The mason swallowed hard as Kryman moved closer. Clearly he wasn't keen on acknowledging the existence of the shade.

"I want to know where Assundra is,"

"No, Galvarin you don't," Oldershaw groaned in reply, "you want to know if we know where she is. You wish to discover if we have any plans for her, you wish to know if we know everything you know about her."

"No, I want to know…"

"Whether your efforts were in vain or whether Cairns succeeded in his aims. You wish to know whether we have discovered your little secret plot. The thing is, Galvarin, there is no need." At this, Oldershaw leaned forwards, slowly, until he was inches from Galvarin. "There is no need, because the mind cleansing will offer us the perfect opportunity to learn anything we wish from you without the tedious process of questioning and deciphering truth from lies. Take him away, Carp."

With a dismissive wave of the hand, Oldershaw sank back, his hand once more covering his face.

Simon ignored the protests from Galvarin. Something about Elder Oldershaw wasn't right. Had the fight taken more out of him than he was letting on? Frowning, Simon tried to remember seeing Oldershaw in the fight, but could not.

"We will find out what he knows from the mind cleansing. Yes."

Kryman scoffed openly. "Well yes I rather gathered that from when you said it before, but do you not think we have rather more pressing concerns?"

"No, I do not think we do, Kryman, not until your sister catches that *thing*."

"That thing, as you call it, is the very reason we have more pressing concerns to be dealing with! *Contingencies* my good Elder! Exactly what do you think my sister is going to do with it?"

Oldershaw sighed. "Well I imagine, Kryman, that she will dispose of it as she sees fit."

This time Kryman opened his mouth and laughed long and loud. "Dispose of it? You can't dispose of things like that, they have to be tamed first! Tamed and cured, how do you think she is going to do that when nothing I could throw at it would even scratch it?"

"She's better than you," Simon said matter-of-factly.

Kryman span round and was toe to toe with him instantly. "Better than me, is she? We shall see…"

Simon leapt back as the healing skin on his face began to blister, calling artistry to the back of his throat, but the instant he did so the eyes in the back of his mind snapped open, choking the power back.

"Stop!"

Simon gasped – Elspeth was back! "See!" he cried, "I told you she wouldn't need long to deal with it!"

Kryman snorted. "She has caught nothing, you little fool, you called her back with your childish little attempts at calling power. Just as I was about to show you what real power was, too!"

For all his words, Kryman backed off. Oldershaw, Simon noted, hadn't moved once during the whole exchange.

"Do I take it you haven't caught the beast?" the Elder said quietly.

Simon flicked his eyes to Elspeth, expecting anger from her as he was feeling himself – how dare the Elder speak to her like that!

"As my brother has just told you, Elder, Simon called me back," Elspeth replied, surprising Simon by how calm she was.

"How did I…" Simon started to say.

"Linked to her, dear boy!" Kryman almost roared. "Really, sis, do we have to keep explaining every little thing to this little pet of yours? It's how she's here, Simon, it's how we're both here! She's linked to you, I'm linked to her, we're all one big happy family, isn't it wonderful?"

Elspeth ignored Kryman and glided across to Simon. "The eyes you can see in the back of your mind are the key to my existence, Simon. They are the second stage. I only need…"

"There are other things to attend do before then," Oldershaw cried, suddenly animated. "Come, we have much to do! The mind cleansings will leave me weakened for a time and there are things I must know first. I said come!"

Simon held his breath. His eyes had to be playing tricks on him. Otherwise, he had just seen Elder Oldershaw click his fingers at the spectres before striding from the room.

"Come on, Simon," Elspeth said, smiling sweetly at him. Kryman was already following the Elder out of the door.

"I don't understand," he said quietly to Elspeth, making to hold her back by her robe before he remembered the robe was not there. "The way he spoke to you, how can you allow that? He's an Elder! You said to Cairns..."

"Cairns was very different, Simon," Elspeth said with some force. "Until..." she paused, frowning, appearing to struggle with something. Ahead, Oldershaw turned sharply on his heel and stood, staring at her. Simon's mouth filled with a taste, but not the taste of nothing, not the taste artistry left on the land. This taste had an unpleasant tang to it, a smell not unlike mould and Simon spat.

"What is it?"

"Nothing," Elspeth replied quickly, motioning to Simon to follow her as she glided towards where the Elder stood waiting, a fierce expression on his head.

"You said until..."

This time Elspeth visibly winced. "Be quiet Simon!" she hissed. "I cannot say any more!" Her voice cracked like she was in pain, but only for a moment, then she collected herself. "Come on," she said again.

Simon understood and asked no more. All the same he made to keep on his guard – something was not right here. Did Oldershaw have some hold over Elspeth? Even Kryman was keeping quiet, keeping out of it, which Simon had already come to realise was completely out of character, so what was going on?

Now she had recovered, both she and Kryman wore strange contended smiles. Simon felt his own expression crease into a frown. Something was not right here.

"Elder! Elder!" Bryant rushed out from behind a building, his rusty sword shaking in his hand. Simon gasped – he had seen Bryant die! "Elder, I'm sorry, but I have to do this!" Bryant screamed, his voice cracking.

Oldershaw raised a hand to stop Kryman advancing. "Captain Bryant, it is good to see you, we all thought..."

"Don't try any of that!" Bryant cried, his voice even more shrill than before, waving the sword madly at the Elder. One knock would send it out of the man's hands. Unfortunately there was nobody around. "Yeah you get back Devil! I know what you are!"

"I've been called the devil before," Kryman hissed in reply, "once. Once and once only, though I do hear the title has stuck. The Red Devil. Do you know why I received the title? It's an interesting story, really." A look from the corner of Kryman's eye told him that the bragging, arrogant, obnoxious shade was buying him time. Using Oldershaw as a shield, Simon began to creep around the side of the nearest building.

"It was just after my first kill. Oh don't panic, boy," Kryman shouted, seeing Bryant's horrified expression, "My first hunting kill, not human! A boar, as far as I recall, one of the last before they died out. When my father's party arrived, after I sounded for the kill, they found my face covered in blood, dripping out of my mouth, in my ears, everywhere. They all thought I'd wrestled the boar to the ground myself and torn out its throat with my teeth."

Elspeth laughed, a beautiful, chirpy birdsong-style sound that soothed Simon's tense nerves, then they were lost to sight to him as he slipped around the side of the building. The eyes in his mind stayed alert. "He'd shot the boar with a crossbow," he heard Elspeth say.

"Sis is right, of course," Kryman said, scowling at being interrupted in full flow. "I'd tripped and fallen into the wound face first. Nothing more."

"I don't care about that" he heard Bryant screaming. Quickly, Simon slipped between the next two houses and stopped himself short as he stood staring straight at Bryant's back. From here he could see the blood caked down Bryant's left leg from the wound on his back. How was the man still standing?

"Bryant, I assure you we mean you no harm," the Elder's voice bellowed out, any attempt at reassurance lost at once with the sheer volume of his voice. "If you would just lay down your sword, we can talk about how we can resolve our differences. Elder Cairns is gone, there is no need for you to remain loyal to his memory."

"Memory?" Bryant laughed, a strange, high-pitched, almost insane chuckle. "I am not loyal to his memory, Elder, I am against your currency! Or whatever the word is!" Simon readied himself. "Cairns warned all of us about you! You will lead us straight to them! Why have you brought us back here? There is no reason! You'll alert them! You'll bring them back! You'll…"

The eyes in Simon's mind flashed. At once he leapt from his hiding place, his shoulder crashing into the wound on Bryant's back. The Captain screamed, falling heavily to the ground, but he held onto his sword. With a shrug of the elbow he threw Simon off him. Simon tasted the dirt and span about, raising his splint finger, but it was too late, Bryant had stepped back and was bringing the sword down.

A shape bundled Bryant to the ground and the air was filled with the taste of burning flesh. He turned away, having learned by now that it was better not to look at what death life did to the living.

"Leave him alive!" Oldershaw barked and Simon was surprised to see Kryman leap straight back as soon as he heard the words, turning to Oldershaw with a snarl.

"I see no reason to do that, Elder!" the spectre hissed, turning to Bryant again, but, almost as if he were being pulled back, he was stopped again.

There was quiet all around, except for the sounds of Bryant's whimpering. Elspeth glided past him and Simon turned to wipe the dirt from his face. He'd failed in front of her again. Every fight he had, he lost. If she wasn't disgusted with him before, she would be now, he just knew it.

"You are weak, Elder!" Kryman cried out, advancing on the old man, but once again he was stopped in his tracks, as if something prevented him from reaching his target. Simon frowned again – it was clear now that whatever was influencing Kryman and Elspeth was coming from Oldershaw, but how could one old man control two of the most powerful artists Ostracia had ever seen?

"He will recover," Elspeth said beside him, "the burns are only superficial, apart from his hand. He will not wield a sword again. I think we can safely leave him here, he will pose no threat."

"Why are we wasting time?" Kryman cried. "Unless you have both forgotten, we still have the not insignificant problem of a man out there none of us can fight, not to mention that we have still not begun to try and find the crystal…"

Kryman stiffened suddenly, his form ceasing to shimmer, becoming instead a static, indistinct, almost transparent statue. Looking at Oldershaw, Simon saw the old man's hand raise, a finger pointing at Kryman.

"For a long time I have known you would come." Oldershaw pulled his other hand from his side and beckoned with a finger. Elspeth, as if she was being pulled at the waist, glided across to stand next to her brother. She too had ceased to shimmer, although without it she simply seemed human. "I've been waiting for something, a sign, anything that your father's plans were not in vain."

"Little that my father did was in vain, old fool," Elspeth said…no, not said…somehow the voice came from her, but not from her mouth…

"Then I found the secret!" Oldershaw went on, ignoring her. "I know how to make sure Stracathri's power does not fall into the wrong hands! Cairns could not be allowed to have it!"

"Well he's not likely to get it now, is he?" Simon called back, standing. Oldershaw didn't have any free fingers, he couldn't control Simon too. The eyes in the back of his mind flashed a warning, but Simon paced forward slowly.

"He would share it with the people! They wouldn't understand, couldn't understand what to do with it, it would be wasted! We can show them how it must be used and shaped by those who have the right ability and knowledge, to return Ostracia to glory! To get our revenge!"

"Traitor! Cairns was right about you!" Bryant knocked Simon to the floor as he barged past him, sword in his hand once more and raised to attack, but the old man was too quick for him, his decrepitude shown to be as much of an act as Cairns had confided to Simon he had always suspected it to be. As Bryant reached him, Oldershaw reached around with a single hand, and with a cry in a language Simon didn't understand, broke Bryant's neck with just a flick of a finger.

"Not as slow as you've made out, Elder?" Simon asked, his blood heated. Bryant had been a fool, but there had been no need to kill him! "There was no need for that, you could have knocked him out. Or was that part of your revenge too?"

Oldershaw just smiled at him. Simon could see Oldershaw for the first time now. He could see him within and without and he felt the surge come through the pit of his stomach, eagerly groping its way up through him, just waiting to be spat, right in Oldershaw's face…

The eyes in his mind flicked instantly, blazing a blue light onto the artistry that was trying to force its way out, sending it, seething, back down to where it had come from inside him. "Calm yourself," he heard Elspeth say soothingly, but Oldershaw's smug grin made him snarl.

"Who else have you told of this?" he heard Elspeth say, but there was a humming clouding the words, as if a lullaby was being sung in his head.

Oldershaw looked at Simon in disgust again. "All I have told are dead, as Simon knows. He killed one of them himself! His own father!"

Elspeth turned on him, the eyes in the back of his mind probing him, forcing the anger inside Simon down once more.

"Max West was a loyal servant, he would have given her life to the cause…"

"I thought you just said he did?" Kryman interjected, laughing.

"I saw the whole thing, my good Elder," Elspeth's voice said, "and let me assure you that Simon had no choice but to do what he did. It was a fitting answer for the years of abuse given to one he should have served."

"He already had a master, he had his instructions!"

"As do you!" The voice was all around them, reminding Simon of the dream in the Forest, but Oldershaw just smiled.

The thought of his father was preying on his mind once more. Simon had seen people die his whole life. It had never moved him; it was something that had been happening since before he was born and would happen after he himself had passed on. Whether through plague, accident or what Tom Franks did to Jesmond Archer, people had always died around him. He'd seen dead bodies many times, even seen them burned when he sneaked off to watch Assundra at her work in the old town. Why was this different? Elspeth was right, he had been left with no choice and he hadn't even liked the man, so why this crushing squeeze in the base of his stomach?

"We need to go left from here," Oldershaw said, "there is much to do and as you now I need your cooperation." As soon as he lowered his fingers, the spectres seemed to come to life, their bodies beginning to shimmer again, Kryman's almost seeming to flicker in and out of existence.

"I have had enough of this!" Kryman cried. Simon couldn't tell if he was furious, or embarrassed, or both. It made Simon smile. "As it seems none of you are going to deal with the problem at hand I shall have to myself!"

Simon couldn't resist it. "Seems like Elder Oldershaw should be the one to deal with any problems, he seems to have taken control of you easily enough."

Elspeth turned to him in annoyance and Simon cursed himself at one. He was so stupid! Oldershaw didn't just have control of Kryman, he had control of her too, why did he let his mouth say such stupid things?

Kryman, however, had turned on Simon with little more than contempt. "He bears the mark of being in our service. He has drawn power from Stracathri and none but our true servants could do that. Unfortunately, that means that in our current state, thanks to our esteemed father, Stracathri considers Oldershaw its master."

"Which makes me your master! Your father left clues," Oldershaw said reverently. "In the end, it was he who helped me bring the ideas together."

Elspeth didn't seem impressed. "The parchment?"

Oldershaw nodded eagerly. "Yes! It was fascinating! As if I were speaking to your father himself. A most wonderful application of artistry, wonderful!"

"How could he have spoken to you?" Simon laughed, eager to seize on the man's mistake. He had to show Elspeth he wasn't as stupid as he'd made himself seem! "He's dead, you old fool! He couldn't have spoken! You probably made it all up in your cups!"

"Is that so, Simon? Well if it is so impossible, perhaps you could explain why we are here talking to the two spectres we see before us? Or perhaps we are both drunk!"

Simon scowled. Elspeth hadn't intervened again.

"He's right of course," he heard the nasally whine sneer at him. "It's such a shame Cairns chose such a stupid boy."

"Be quiet Kryman! I have warned you before!"

Once again, Kryman was silent when Elspeth spoke, but this time Simon was left feeling as if he wanted to drive his fist through the spectre's face. "In any case," Oldershaw went on, laughing at him, just like everyone laughed at him, "your father confirmed to me what I have always thought, my dear; that Ostracia, even the Ostracians, should not be our main concern. It is the *name*, the reputation of Ostracia that should be sung on high again! This necessary sacrifice of the past century has allowed the world to forget about us and about artistry. We have them in our pockets now!"

Simon was incredulous. "You plan to attack the outsiders? With a few hundred villagers and one sword? Are you mad?"

"Mad? No madman could have achieved what my ancestors and I have achieved! For generations we have worked in the linkage chambers underneath the soil. Such a simple matter," Oldershaw said, turning to stride past them with a sneering look at Simon as he passed, "to create an artistic illusion of being drunk. For hours, I was left alone to 'sleep it off', giving me time to complete my work!"

"You are mad," Simon retorted, taking a few steps closer, but stopping when the eyes in his mind flared. "If not, how come it took you and your ancestors so long to find a solution?"

"The records were burned! When the Ostracian name is returned to greatness, to the position it belongs, they will realise the folly in making an enemy of my line!"

"And you say you're not mad? I can practically see you foaming at the mouth!"

Kryman burst out laughing behind him. For just a moment, it made Simon smile, before he remembered who the spectre was. "By the gods! A good line from the boy! Perhaps he's not a useless article after all, sis, perhaps he can be trained to be our new house fool!"

"I had to rediscover so much that had been lost!" Oldershaw's eyes had glazed over, but Elspeth seemed strangely reluctant to stop the Elder's prattling, simply looking at him in a strangely curious manner, as though she were trying to puzzle something out. "All I had was the knowledge passed down by mouth from my ancestors. When Stracathri called Elder Alders back his wife hid herself and her child in the linkage chamber until the outsiders had gone. With tears in her eyes, so the tale went, the mother had left the baby with her sister, for she could never return to Ostracia herself, not with her husband being one of the traitors. Elders were forbidden from taking wives. Mary's sister had raised the babe as her own."

"Alders!" Elspeth hissed. "He was always trouble."

Oldershaw laughed. "But not as much trouble as Barth and the rest! He got away with everything while your eyes were diverted onto the Transept Tower. It is not the only other place of power in Ostracia."

"Not the only place?" Simon echoed, before realising he was doing what Elspeth hated, mimicking Assundra's annoying habit of repeating the last thing anyone said. "You'd best tell us where the others are!"

Oldershaw ignored him. "When the boy was nine, the sister, Margery, began to bring the child to its mother for lessons, swearing him to secrecy. The child never knew of its ancestry until the end, but the simple act of seeing her son gave Mary more joy than she had ever had, after nine years spent below ground. She had taught him everything. All that her husband had known.

"Then the true curse of the outsiders began to strike Ostracia. The plague. For appearances, Alders' son, Brian, had been presented as a year younger than he was. So when he reached his sixteenth year, he was thought of as fifteen, too young by a year to learn to shield himself from straying too close to the infection barrier.

"His insides were torn apart by the outsiders' primitive sorcery. By chance, he had been one half of an illicit affair with a married woman, who bore a son, though she did not know who the father was, Brian or her husband. That did not matter to our order, however, there was no time to wait any longer. Sure enough, that child lived and passed into adulthood in the normal way and exhibited signs of great artistry. That child was me. Margery, clinging on to life by her very fingernails, took me to Mary's old hideaway, the linkage chamber between Stracathri and the Transept Tower. Mary had long been dead, bricked into the walls, but her journals remained, along with Brian's own work."

"What a lovely story," Kryman said sarcastically, "can we get on now please?"

Again, Oldershaw paid no heed. It was as if he was in a trance, held by Elspeth's eyes. Was she doing this? Drawing the story from him? "I bricked Margery up in the oubliette next to her sister. I spent years trying to find the hidden ways into Stracathri from there, but I found nothing." Suddenly, Oldershaw snapped back to himself, his eyes recovering their life once more. "That is why I had to sacrifice our people to the cause, Simon! I had to find a way in! I had to know the truth!"

"Now you want the power. Very noble, very honourable, I'm sure. This Margery woman would be proud!"

Oldershaw scowled. "Not for me, Red Devil!" he shouted. "For Ostracia! For the memory of what we once were and can be again!"

"With what?" Simon shouted, stepping slightly away from Kryman, who had come to stand next to him. "How can we be great with no children and no future? Even if we cancel the Withholdings we would die out in a matter of a few years! For all your protestations, I know what Cairns told me and I know he wasn't lying! The lack of artistry in the people is the one thing keeping them alive, it's what the plague feeds on!"

"The boy is right a second time!" Kryman exclaimed with mock shock. "However, I do seem to remember asking *what the hell we were going to do about Assundra's father*!"

"Yes," Elspeth said, her voice stern, "and then there is the question of Assundra herself. She is crucial to this."

"It is being taken care of. Follow me," Oldershaw barked and Simon saw Elspeth bristle. This wasn't a woman who took to following orders gladly, but nonetheless she obeyed, as did Kryman.

Soon, Simon was completely lost. They had rounded corner after corner, passed through alleys between buildings until he thought Oldershaw was trying to make sure they didn't know where they were, before they stopped outside a nondescript, half-ruined stone house that didn't look any different from the others on the street.

"In here," Oldershaw barked, pulling open a decrepit wooden door that looked as if it were going to fall off its hinges at any moment. Wrestling it aside, where it ground to a halt against the stone flagging, Oldershaw disappeared into the blackness beyond the door. Following behind, Simon almost tripped and fell down the steep set of stairs. What was this place? The staircase was too long for it to be a mere cellar, this led right underneath the foundations of the building and further.

As it turned out, the staircase, though long, wasn't as long as it had first appeared and soon gave way into a short stone tunnel that led to a tall, circular open tower. Simon understood – this had to be the oubliette Oldershaw had spoken of! He had to admit that it was stunning. It gave off the impression of being lit with artistry; the soft orange phosphorescence to the walls soothing Simon's mood.

"Stones from Stracathri!" he heard Elspeth exclaim, almost in awe as she and Kryman glided through from the passage behind him.

"An escape route," Oldershaw replied, not even close to being out of breath, despite the hectic pace since they had left Bryant lying in the street. "From the very old times, before artistry took its grip on Ostracia. These stones date back far further than those that built the Tower."

The oubliette had to be no bigger than twelve feet across and had but the one entrance, other than the hole above their heads. Simon could sense artistry here.

"Well, now we are here, I shan't linger, if you don't mind," Kryman sneered, causing Oldershaw to turn. "Stones from Stracathri, dear Elder, I do believe they will be masking your control over us! So I shall take this opportunity to do what we should all be doing and that is find a way to deal with the one thing that could stop us!"

With that, Kryman was gone. Simon instantly chided himself for stepping back in alarm, then jumping when he hit the brick wall. Cursing, he turned to Elspeth to see if she'd seen, but she seemed distracted by oubliette. Oldershaw just stood, clenching and unclenching his fists. This had clearly not been part of his plan. Simon couldn't tell if he was pleased Kryman had got one over on Oldershaw or not. All he knew was he hated both of them.

"This has been perverted to Elders' power," Elspeth said softly. "This is where you draw your strength from." It wasn't directed to Oldershaw as a question, just a statement of fact.

"Amongst others," Oldershaw replied, watching her carefully. Simon smiled – clearly he had no control over the spectres in this place. So why had he brought them here? It was clearly a mistake.

"Though it is nothing compared to the strength at Cairns' disposal."

"You didn't seem to have any trouble with him!" Simon said quickly, eager to make sure Elspeth knew he knew how strong she was. How impressive she was.

"True artistry will always triumph over perversion, Simon."

Elspeth held Oldershaw's gaze at that and for a moment he thought she was going to strike, but they just stood looking at each other for longer than Simon was comfortable with.

"Patience is a virtue, Simon," Oldershaw said, pompously, seeming to sense the tension in him. "I imagine Elder Cairns has not bothered to instil this particular virtue into you, but I would caution you to examine his current position! My ancestors and I waited many years for our chance to return Ostracia to its rightful glory. Elder Cairns, no doubt, thought his plan to accelerate things, to pass by natural processes, would bypass the necessary time, as your youthful impetuosity does now! Do not fall the same way as the rest, boy!"

"What do you mean accelerated things?" Simon shouted in retort, ashamed at not having understood much of what Oldershaw had said. "And you don't need to call him Elder Cairns any more! He's dead, he's no different to the rest of us now!"

"He never was, Simon," he heard Elspeth's slick voice hum by his ear. "Elders are nothing but servants, it is well to remember that."

Simon watched Oldershaw's surprised and foolish blinking with a smile. The man thought he had found allies, but they didn't need Elders. Simon had never needed Elders. Cairns had given him the splint, but Elspeth had shown him that he didn't need that. It was all just primitive Elder foolishness. When you had real artistry, real power, you didn't need those puerile devices.

"Open the door, Elspeth, please," Oldershaw asked, politely enough, but Simon knew an instruction when he heard one.

To his surprise, Elspeth just smiled. "Very well, Elder. Though I do believe you have some pressing business outside."

Turning his head sharply, as if to listen, Oldershaw scowled. "They do nothing but complain!" he cried, gathering up his robe and starting off back towards the stairs, turning back to Elspeth almost as an afterthought. "I can trust you to do what is necessary here?"

Elspeth smiled sweetly. The eyes in Simon's mind flashed with malevolence. "Of course, Elder," she said, her voice matching her smile. "You know I can no more go against my father's wishes than you can now."

Snarling, Oldershaw turned to leave and Elspeth turned to Simon. "Now," she said softly, moving so close to Simon that he thought his breath was going to choke him. By the gods, she was magnificent!

A soft hiss alerted Simon to the fact that several bricks were sliding out of the wall, seemingly on their own, and laying themselves neatly to rest in a pile beside the opening they left.

"What's through there?" Simon whispered, marvelling at the technique – there was no taste of nothing, no stain of artistry upon the land – this was the purest power he had ever sensed! He wanted this!

"Why don't you go through and see!" Elspeth giggled playfully, giving him a little shove in the back.

Laughing, Simon eagerly made for the opening, but was stopped in his tracks by another spectre. It was a girl. Simon gasped as he realised he knew her! Tall, thin and elegant, her thin blonde hair was tied back into a ponytail with a blue ribbon and a bright blue gemstone, as bright as Elspeth's eyes, was tied with a band around her forehead. It almost shone! As quickly as he opened his mouth to speak, to alert Elspeth, the girl was gone, as if she'd never been there.

"Simon, get up!" he heard Elspeth shout and he realised he had fallen to the floor.

There was a flash of light ahead of him and he looked up to see Elspeth and the girl, the one he knew he had once known but could not remember, were wrestling with what seemed to be a solid sheet of light, but with sparks flying from each side as it crackled. The smell and taste of nothing took over his senses.

Neither of them seemed to be winning. Simon stood, ready to help, but the eyes in his mind blazed even as he called the artistry and readied his splint.

"The experiment!" the girl hissed in anger. "You were the one to betray us!"

With a final scream of effort, Elspeth's arms surrounded the girl and her entire spectral being fizzed with energy. The girl's eyes didn't leave Simon once.

"I knew you were a bad choice ever since Elder Cairns told me of you!" she hissed into one of his ears, though she was nowhere near him. He did, however, know the voice.

"Bethlinda!"

As she began to burn, the girl laughed. "This is the Elders' place! You will find nothing here!"

"The only Elder left is helping us!" Simon cried triumphally.

The girl smiled a cruel, mad smile. "Oh there are several more Elders here, can't you feel them? They're *in me*!"

With a final burst of light that struck Simon dead in the chest, sending him crumpling to the floor, the girl vanished, her laughter echoing on the air for a moment before that, too was gone.

As quickly as it had come, the pain in his chest softened and left him. His veins and nerves filled with a sense of utter ecstasy that until now he would have thought impossible to feel. He looked up through eyes nearly sightless through pleasure and saw Elspeth.

He knew in that instant that he loved her, as without another word, she placed her lips, which were not human lips but something else, pulsing in coils, upon Simon's. Her cool, soothing lips were all he wanted to think of even as his lips and face began to burn at her touch, as Simon, for the first time in his life, felt contentment. He passed into dreams.

CHAPTER 23

Assundra awoke with a start and screamed. "Where is it? It was behind me!"

At once soothing arms were around her and she felt soft round breasts pressed into her back. "It's gone, Sunny, it can't come here. Trust me."

Assundra remembered!

Not like in the tunnel, not in drips and drabs. Not like before, when the returning memories had made her feel faint, or worried. This time, as the memories rushed through her mind, somehow slotting into place, as if a veil was lifting from a cloudy, murky depth. As if she was opening her eyes. She felt her mouth curve into a smile.

Whispers were telling her everything was ok as legs encircled her body from behind to join the arms lightly holding her. Bethlinda had brought her here, wherever this was, had lain her down here and then had lain with her, taking Assundra's fears and pain away as much with her body as the strange crystal.

"Oh Sunny, how could you forget?"

Assundra flinched. She couldn't hear the voice any more. She doubted whether she would again. That had been a memory, a fleeting moment, one thing among many that Bethlinda had sent to her, but she was sure those words would haunt her forever. No matter how many times Bethlinda assured her it wasn't her fault, how she couldn't help it, how it didn't matter now they were together again, Assundra couldn't get the words out of her head and she heard herself apologise again.

At once the arms pulled tighter around her naked body. "Sunny!" Beth exclaimed in what Assundra now remembered was her usual bright, excited voice, teetering on hysteria but somehow still warm. "You don't need to apologise to me! You've been through so much, I told you, you don't need to worry, you're safe with me now. I won't let them hurt you!"

Assundra absent-mindedly dropped a hand to stroke Bethlinda's leg and leant back. "Three years, Beth," she said quietly. "I don't know how I could have…"

"Sunny!" The reprimand was quick, fierce and made Assundra laugh.

"I'm just saying, Beth, I don't know how I could have forgotten something…someone so wonderful."

It was a long, slow kiss and it left Assundra trembling. Bethlinda smiled and stood. As soon as Bethlinda's arms left her, Assundra remembered the dream and started shivering.

Only it hadn't been a dream. The body, half-rotten to a skeleton, had been real. Just sitting there, in a chair in the corner where the circle of the large room she had first awoken in met the inlay of the passageway.

For a moment Assundra had panicked, thinking the body was Bethlinda. Thinking the voice was her ghost, reprimanding Assundra for leaving her on the day she had disappeared. For many minutes she'd screamed, confused by the pulsing blue light that was only getting stronger, until Beth had run from the bedroom where they now were, ripped the stone from her forehead and taken a hysterical Assundra into her arms for the first time in three years.

It was only then she had seen the tattered robes that littered the floor around the body. White robes. The grey, crusty shell that had once been a person looked like it would crumble to dust the instant it was touched. Even in such a state, Assundra could tell from the twisted jaw-line that the death had not been a peaceful one. The empty eye sockets seemed to still have a kind of life, staring at Assundra. What had happened here to create such a death mask? She had seen dead bodies before, plague-ridden, putrid bodies, but never a skeleton. The blackness of the corpse's eye sockets were imprinted on Assundra's mind, pleading with her with their nothingness, the slack, broken-jawed bone of the mouth open, trying to tell her something.

The tall, slim girl took it all away. Watching her slip the simple green robe back over her body, Assundra watched the blue crystal pulse brightly, fixed in a pendant suspended on a band of gold clasped tightly around the girl's head, lost behind the silky strips of blond. If anything her eyes were even more fiercely bright, eagerly lapping up whatever was before them.

"Oh, Sunny," Beth laughed as she caught Assundra gazing, "haven't you seen enough?"

Assundra's mouth curled upwards as she slowly shook her head, making Beth laugh again. She just wished she felt the feelings she was portraying rather than the sickening, sinking feeling in the pit of her stomach.

Bethlinda smiled in a calm, measured way. "Sunny!" she said in a slightly admonishing tone, but Assundra could see the smile in her eyes. Though she was no older than Assundra was she had a captivating grace and tone, the manner of an older woman. Moving towards her, Bethlinda locked her arms around Assundra's shaking body and as she laid her head in Bethlinda's neck, planting wet kisses onto the wonderfully warm, smooth skin, Assundra thought that she had smelt the scent of her before, in the valley of flowers beyond Halpse Hill, the place where Assundra found her peace.

It was many minutes before either could break the other's clasp.

As Bethlinda finally pulled away, murmuring something about relieving herself, Assundra was once more alone and once again the half-putrid body in what Bethlinda called the chamber floated before her eyes, taunting her. Quickly slipping her petticoat back on, feeling as if she were being watched, she scouted about for her dress. She could not see it. Flitting this way and that, she tried to find something in the room to occupy herself with until Beth returned.

There was a bed in the corner, intricately carved out of a light, stained wood that brought a faint scent of the Forest into the room. A huge, thick bright red rug, adorned by a stitched yellow sunburst carpeted the floor next to it and candles of all colours and sizes burned, held in golden brackets shaped like gargoyles on the windowless blue stone walls, illuminating battique sketches, which Bethlinda had said were made by her own hand. Drapes depicting scenes from the outside world, things Bethlinda had always been interested in like guards and battles, brightly clad and mysterious magicians and sorcerors, covered much of those stone walls and there were two or three ornate, gilt-edged wooden chests, one of which supported a bright brass mirror that leant against the wall.

Assundra was sure most of it had not been made in Ostracia. She moved over to the brass to take a closer look and gasped. How had she not noticed them before? "Oh gods!" she whispered to herself. Two long, jagged cuts ran down the length of her upper arms, past her elbows and to her wrists. They were thick, red and puffy, though completely sealed. Assundra just stood, looking at herself.

How the hells could Beth be attracted to her like that?

She turned from the mirror to see Beth standing in the door, making her jump. She instantly pulled her arms up to her, looking down to the floor, but that just made her see the equally large, red sealed wounds on each of her legs. She began to panic, not wanting Beth to see, even though she already had. She was hideous!

"Sunny," Beth said severely, grabbing Assundra's arms and pulling them down to her sides. "Look at me." Assundra didn't want to. *Gods*, how could they have done this to her? "Sunny, listen," Beth said, but Assundra couldn't.

"Beth, don't look at me!" she cried, trying to pull away, but she couldn't. She didn't want Beth to see her, she didn't want anyone to see her ever again, she would just stay here, alone in this room, that was the only way she'd be safe!

"Sunny!" Beth cried, shaking her. "These scars do not make you hideous!" She looked Assundra straight in the eyes. "They make you beautiful! They show your strength, your pride and your bravery! They show that no matter how much you've been through you're still the wonderful person I remember from all those years ago! You're amazing Sunny, well, you amaze me at any rate!"

"Why did they do it, Beth?" Assundra sobbed.

Beth turned Assundra firmly around, making her face the brass. "Look, Sunny," she said, pushing Assundra closer. "Look."

The scars were gone. Assundra gasped. "Beth…"

"It was Lady North's," Bethlinda whispered in her ear. "It came from a place I don't know the name of, somewhere on the outside, I would imagine, it doesn't look Ostracian, does it?"

Assundra didn't speak. She didn't know what to say. Her scars were gone! The wounds…it was as if they'd never been there! She felt her mouth fill with the taste of nothing and a trickle of fear crept up her spine. "Beth…"

"It's ok, Sunny. The mirror amplifies healing. It works with the Gozon Stone to regenerate what is broken."

"You healed me?"

Beth laughed. "The mirror and the stone did. I just gave them a prod in the right direction."

Assundra simply smiled in bewilderment. It had been so long, so much had happened since they had last seen each other and yet Bethlinda still seemed to have the same permanent smile Assundra now remembered carved perfectly onto her face. Beth pulled her arms away from Assundra, leaving her staring at her body in bewilderment. She ran a hand down her arm and felt only smooth, undamaged skin.

"Beth, you're…"

"Shush now," Beth whispered and a cup of something hot was passed into her hands. "It's just some dried leaves in hot water, I found loads of them in the storeroom. They're really quite nice, it makes the water taste a little bit like mint."

"Hot water?" Assundra exclaimed, her eyes wide. "But how do you heat it? You can't light a fire, Beth, what if Elder Cairns found out?"

Bethlinda laughed. "It's a hot stream, Sunny, it flows through the lower passages." Assundra frowned – hadn't they come through the lower passages? She didn't recall seeing any streams or hearing any water.

"Beth, it was your voice I heard, wasn't it?" Assundra said, afraid of how comfortable the silence was between them. "I thought…I'm sorry, but I thought the voice I heard had to be dead."

"Voice?" Beth seemed confused. "Oh, I suppose you would have heard it like voices, yes. I forget how other people see the arts differently.

"The arts?"

"Yes, I've really got quite good!" Beth's eyes flared with excitement, the way they had always used to when she talked of artistry.

"I can see that! Beth, thank you so much! I don't know..."

"I said shush about that, Sunny. I would do anything for you." For a moment they sat looking at each other silently, smiling.

"So you've been learning?" Assundra said eventually. "Like you always wanted!"

Beth nodded excitedly. "Elder Cairns has been helping me, there's a mountain of books here, Sunny, and to think I only ever wanted the one!"

"Elder Cairns knows you're here?" Assundra was shocked; how could he not have told her! He knew – he was the only other one who knew – what Beth had meant to her!

Beth saw the look on her face. "Don't blame him, Sunny, he was doing it for the best! After all, you couldn't remember me, it was kinder to allow you to forget with the others."

She didn't seem upset, that same calm she had always had when an injustice upset Assundra. To Beth, that was just the way things were when they went wrong, and there was always a reason for the best. It had always infuriated Assundra, but now she found she had missed it – it made the anger fade away. She had missed it so much.

"But he took you away!" she heard herself moan like a little girl and she was instantly cross with herself for doing so.

"You remember? Yes, he did. Oh, of course, you were watching, weren't you?" Beth giggled; a sound that to Assundra was more pleasant than a chorus of chirping birds. "It was necessary, Sunny, this place needed someone to take care of it and Elder Cairns would have been followed eventually."

"So he imprisoned you?"

"Imprisoned? No! I came her perfectly willingly!"

"Willingly?"

"Yes, of course! There was so much to learn, too much to prepare for! It was an honour, and I've learned so much, Sunny, it was the best thing that ever happened to me!"

Assundra believed her; it had always been impossible for Beth to lie convincingly. When she fell out of a tree Assundra had warned her not to climb, Beth had denied it had hurt at all, whilst she was crying and holding it for dear life. But that didn't make what she said any easier to take. "What about me?"

As if she had realised what she had said, Beth pulled Assundra in close to her. Assundra only just had enough balance left to stop the drink spilling all over the rug. "Sunny, if you only knew... it's all been for you, all of it. I knew it wasn't forever and I knew you wouldn't remember, though I hoped you would."

"You knew?"

"Yes, Elder Cairns told me. And Sunny, what would have happened if I had stayed? People would have found out and…well, you know what they would have done."

"Yes." Assundra knew only too well. They had been terrified of being found out, even though they had been too young to really know why. "I don't understand though! Why didn't Elder Cairns bring me here too! He must have known…"

Beth shook her head. "You had to stay in the village, Assundra, you would have been…different if you'd come here."

"Different?"

This time Beth nodded. "This place changes people, Sunny. In a good way, don't worry," she added, seeing Assundra's concern. "You had things you had to find out, things you had to see. You had to change in a different way."

"But I haven't seen anything!"

"Oh, Sunny, you have! You found the catalogue, you saw what Simon can do, you helped him, even if you don't know it. You saw what happened to your father. You know now how serious this is, how we have no choice."

Her father! "Oh, Beth, my father!" Assundra started, trying to leap to her feet, but Bethlinda's surprisingly strong arms held her fast. How could she have forgotten her father again? The knot in her stomach burned to chastise her, and she let it, her shame engulfing her. "I've got to help him! And I've wasted so much time, where is he? Beth, do you know?"

"Sh, calm down," Beth said, rushing back to her side and squeezing her tightly. Assundra didn't let go, despite the searing pain in her stomach. "I know about your father, Sunny, it's horrible. I'm so sorry."

"I always forget everything!" Assundra moaned. "I have to help him!"

"You can't go out there, Sunny, you know that," Beth said gently, but firmly. "You know what they'll do. You know what they did."

Assundra froze. "You know?"

"I know. It's why you're here, it's why you came to me, Sunny, there was nothing out there for you any more. I knew it was time to bring you here."

"Oh, Beth! I couldn't even remember, I'm so sorry!"

"Your memories will return, the withholding is beginning to be broken. Oh, I've missed you so much!"

Assundra wanted to say she had missed her friend too, but she could not. She hadn't even remembered her until now. But now she knew of her again, her joy matched Bethlinda's as they embraced once more. Beth was right, she couldn't help her father, not from here. Not yet. Maybe Beth could bring him here too, but they would have to find him first and Assundra didn't want to send Beth away from her to find him yet.

She wondered if Bethlinda could do what she said and protect Assundra from the Crafters. From whatever the thing with the red eyes was. If she could couple how Bethlinda made her feel safe with her father's physical protection then she would be safe. If she could just make everything alright…

But there was something Assundra didn't understand. "Why are you here then? Why didn't you need to see these things? And how do you know about them? Beth, what's happening? Why is Cairns doing this to us?"

"*Elder* Cairns, Sunny," Beth admonished tenderly. "And he is doing this to save us! That's what the Elders have been working towards for years, trying to find a way to free us from this place. We can't stay here now."

"Can't stay?"

"Ostracia has become nothing more than death to us, Sunny, after what the outsiders did. You know about the plague?" Assundra nodded – she knew only too well, she'd seen the results of it. "Well, the plague attacks the artistry in our blood. It attacks what makes us different to the outsiders. There is no cure, no way to escape it, so Elder Cairns did the only thing he could and prevented the use of artistry so the plague couldn't spread."

Assundra frowned. "But he practises artistry! Him and Elder Oldershaw, I've seen them! And Simon, what about him, why hasn't he got the plague then?"

"Simon is…something different, Sunny. His power comes from another place. Our power, Ostracians' power, comes from our blood, there is no other way to tap into it. The plague attacks the blood once it is exposed."

"Once it is exposed? Why?"

Beth laughed. "I don't know, Sunny, I only know what Elder Cairns told me! This place protects the Elders, but it cannot do so forever. It is starting to become affected itself. It is dying."

"Beth," Assundra said, suddenly remembering, "what if Elder Oldershaw found what he was looking for? We have to warn Elder Cairns before something happens, Beth they're planning something awful…"

Beth squeezed Assundra to her so hard she had to stop talking. "It's too late, Sunny. It's up to us now. I didn't get to you in time."

"In time?" A sob on her shoulder made Assundra clasp Beth to her as she was being held herself. "Beth, what's wrong? What's happened?"

The question brought a louder sob from Bethlinda, but it was cut off, Beth pulling back from her. Assundra saw the stone was glowing. The tears seemed to dry on Bethlinda's face and her breathing returned to normal. Assundra frowned.

"Don't worry, Sunny," Beth said, all traces of the sobbing gone. "The Gozon Stone heals. It's what healed you, another one anyway, a smaller one. They take the pain and hurt away."

"How?"

Beth laughed again and Assundra couldn't help the corners of her mouth curling as she watched it. "You were always so curious! I don't know how, Sunny, I only know it does. It's from the outside, but I don't know where."

"The outside?" Assundra was always interested in the outside. "Can I have a look?" Assundra reached out a hand to the stone and was surprised when Beth shrank back from her, a look of horror on her face.

"I can't take it off!" she cried, making Assundra flinch. "Sorry, Sunny, but it's still doing its work, I can't take it off now. It's healing me as we speak, you can't see it because it's inside, but no, Sunny, I'm afraid you can't have a look."

Assundra frowned again. "Did Elder Cairns give this to you?"

"Yes, but why does that matter?"

"Look, Beth, we have to find him and warn him! Whether it's in time or not, we have to tell him about Elder Oldershaw and the Crafters!"

"Oh Sunny, I mean it's too late. He's gone."

"Gone?"

Beth could only nod and Assundra finally understood. "Elder Cairns is dead?" Beth just nodded again. Assundra didn't know what to feel. She'd never liked Elder Cairns, but she'd been counting on him helping her father. Helping all of them. "What do we do now?"

"We carry on, Sunny. We have to figure out what to do for ourselves. We have to help them though, Sunny! We can't just stay here, Oldershaw will find us eventually."

"Elder Oldershaw," Assundra corrected absent-mindedly.

"Not any more," Beth retorted with more aggression that Assundra could ever remember seeing in her. "He no longer merits the title. Warning people wasn't in the plan, Sunny and we have to follow Elder Cairns' plan."

"Plan?"

"Yes, Sunny, we have to help them! Elder Cairns put me here for a reason, to learn and I know I can do it! I'm ready, Sunny, but we don't have much time! I'm afraid I'm going to have to ask you to…"

Assundra didn't understand. "But why bring you here?"

Bethlinda smiled again at Assundra, but more playfully. Assundra remembered that this was how the conversations used to go when she was a child. Assundra would listen, wide-eyed, whilst Bethlinda told Assundra how things in the world really were. Assundra had never realised how much she had missed her all these years.

No. She hadn't missed her. Her best friend, the person who meant most to her in the world besides her father, had been taken away and she had just forgotten her.

"He brought me here because this place needs a guardian. A Keeper. This is the Transept Tower," she said grandly, spreading her arms. Assundra got the impression it was meant to mean something to her, but it did not. As she remembered always doing when they were younger, she just nodded as if she understood. "It used to lead to the tunnels throughout Ostracia. To the Elders' Council, the Town Hall, the linkage chambers and Stracathri."

"So why…"

"The tunnels are all in disrepair, as you saw. They collapsed after Stracathri was destroyed."

"Destroyed? I thought you said…"

"That's what's so fascinating, Sunny! There's no mention of Stracathri anywhere after the outsiders set it on fire. There is no way that amount of power could have been destroyed altogether. It would have… rebuilt itself."

"Rebuilt itself?"

"Yes, Sun. This tower you sit in now has been destroyed as well, the earth compacted in upon it long ago." Standing, Bethlinda moved to the mirror, checking her hair. "Yet at the same time it did not!" It was hard not to find Bethlinda's enthusiasm infectious.

"Try this," Bethlinda said, holding up a blue shaded dress, almost exactly the same design as her favourite top at home. "You always used to like blue. Come on, try it on!" her friend exclaimed with a nervous smile and a glint in her eye that Assundra couldn't place. "Oh, we're going to have to cut it off, wait a minute…"

Standing, suddenly acutely aware that much of her body had been on show the whole time, she dropped the dress over her shoulders and allowed Bethlinda to deftly and swiftly hem the dress to the right height with a needle she'd plucked from somewhere. Assundra adjusted her bosom in the dress – yet another dress that needed letting out at the top.

Bethlinda's eyes never left Assundra's body. Assundra felt like her mind was paralysed by the memories. She didn't want the dress on, she wanted Bethlinda to see her, she wanted to see the look in her eyes that she had only seen on the men in the village.

She wanted Bethlinda. She'd never wanted Galvarin like this.

"Do you remember when we first knew?" Bethlinda said, the look Assundra desperately wanted to see pouring out of her. "We'd seen Broadside and Alice West behind the alehouse one night when we'd snuck out. We thought we'd try and copy what they were doing. As much as we could, anyway."

She remembered. Soon after that, she hadn't had her friend any more and hadn't thought about her since. But now she remembered everything, how it had felt, how she wanted it to feel again but never had the chance. How it had never felt with Galvarin.

Her look of wonder at her friend must have spoken volumes, for Bethlinda was suddenly standing, her lips on Assundra's. She wanted to feel Bethlinda's hands on her much more than that dress, to do what Galvarin's hands had done, only she knew Beth would do it better. Before the thought had finished, Beth let out a tiny, almost embarrassed giggle and they clumsily broke their kiss, but Assundra didn't mind. She didn't mind when Beth's hand moved slowly to softly touch the curve of her breast. She didn't mind when her friend's other hand took hold of her waist and pulled her close so their lips could meet again. Nor did she mind when, feverishly, Beth pulled her down onto the bed. And when, later, as they lay naked and breathless together once more, Beth told Assundra she loved her, she didn't mind at all. She had never felt so right.

* * * * *

Bethlinda let the dress fall over her slim, graceful form, the green splitting into many shades in the now dim candlelight, half of the stalks of wax having blown out through the night. If it had been night, Assundra wasn't sure. "Here," she said softly, pressing another hot cup of the herbal mixture into Assundra's hand. The golden light shone off Beth's hair, making it seem like it was glowing, contrasting against the pink and cream perfection of her skin, reddened slightly in places. She turned back to Assundra, who was more than slightly aware of the childish grin besetting her face, yet, to Assundra's surprise, it was now Bethlinda who had become bashful. She wouldn't meet Assundra's gaze, the red tint to her face more than just the results of pleasure, although there was more than a trace of a smile on her lips as well. Assundra both wanted to hide her own, entirely ungraceful, form and show it to Beth at the same time, as her friend, no, her lover, sprang back onto the bed, her hand encircling Assundra's waist, where it seemed to belong.

"Not going to get dressed then?"

"Maybe in a while." Assundra knew they were skirting around it. All of it. From the way Bethlinda moved her hands it was clear her passion had not been sated fully, but Assundra did not have the time. "Then again, perhaps you're right," she said, stealing a kiss from a disappointed Bethlinda before finding her petticoat and new dress.

"Time for the talk then?"

Good, Assundra thought, at least she knows why. And she did feel more comfortable with the smooth material covering her. She hoped with a sort of panic that it had been as special for Bethlinda as it had been for her. She knew what it was for it not to be special. She'd known Galvarin. She now knew he was nothing compared to this.

"I'm sorry Beth but it's my father, I have to…"

"Help him, I know, Sunny. You know I'll help you if I can, but I think you're supposed to ask what's going on, Sunny! You seemed to get quite a fright in the chamber, I was worried about you, do you remember much?"

Assundra was glad, she couldn't stop thinking about it all anyway. "I don't know." Bethlinda guided her down and they sat on the large bed, there being no chairs in the room. "Oh, Beth, I'm sorry, I can't stop thinking about it" she blurted out and the shaking returned, making her spill the drink all over the downed quilt they sat on. "Oh gods! Sorry, is it rare?"

"Don't worry," Beth soothed, through her laughter, "there are hundreds of them in the store. This placed used to be full of people, you know." Despite what she said, Beth took the drink that Assundra was throwing all over the bed from her and held her hand. "It's normal, Sunny, believe me."

Assundra shook her head. "No, Beth you don't understand, I've seen bodies before, hundreds of them, it's what I do. I'm the Deathguard's assistant," she added, seeing Bethlinda's confusion.

"Elder Cairns has you dealing with the dead? Sunny! What about the things we used to talk about? What about...you know, the books, leaning? What about those things you used to do…"

Assundra pulled her hands from Beth's quickly. "I don't talk about that," she said, knowing she sounded angry but not able to help herself. She *never* talked about that!"

"Of course," Beth soothed. "So Sunny, if you've seen hundreds of bodies before…"

"I know, Beth, why has this one upset me so much!" Assundra let Beth clasp her hands again as a tear started to tall. She choked it back – she'd cried enough today. "It was like it was watching me, trying to tell me something."

She looked up to a smile. Bethlinda's eyes never left her, despite how she must look. There was brick dust along with twigs and mud covering her, mostly in her matted and tangled hair, which was protruding from her head in angles it should not. In a complete contrast, Beth's skin was smooth, pale but healthy, her hair brushed so it shone, the blond strands falling perfectly straight from a central parting, snaking past her shoulders.

"Everyone sees death differently, Sunny. Some deaths are harder than others, they leave traces on the land. You know, how some rooms just make you sad after someone has died there. Some deaths also leave traces on people. Some people see things, some hear things."

"Hear things?"

"Yes, voices, thoughts, footsteps following them, that sort of thing. Some people only hear or see things in dreams, others all the time, it depends Sunny."

"Depends?"

"On the death. I can tell you one thing though, the man out there died of natural causes. It may sound gruesome but I need someone to study, Sunny. Besides, I have nowhere to put it, I can't just tip it into the pits, I just can't…"

Beth was getting quite distressed and Assundra shook her hands. "Beth, it's ok, really. I don't know why it affected me so much, I'm sorry. It's certainly not your fault!"

Beth's head dropped. "But it is," she said softly.

Nudging her, Assundra forced Beth to look up again. "Beth, like you said, you couldn't move it…"

"I wanted you to see it," Beth said quickly, her eyes filling with tears. "I'm sorry Sunny, I know I lied, I don't know why I did, but you had to see it!"

"Had to see it?" Assundra was confused.

"Yes, I was told."

"Told? By who?"

"It doesn't matter!" Beth almost shouted at her she was getting so agitated. The blue stone tied to her forehead was glowing faintly. "You had to see it Sunny, there's something you have to do!"

"What do you mean?"

"Look at your petticoat."

"My petticoat?" That was the last thing she had expected Bethlinda to say.

"The symbols, Sunny. They're outsider symbols. Do they remind you of anything?"

Assundra looked at the symbols woven into the cloth. She had always worn the petticoat, her mother had said it was important, but she had never said why. *"Petticoats and brass."*

"Think about the symbols, Sunny," Bethlinda prompted. "Think about where you've seen them before."

Assundra tried, but she could not think of anything, her mind was blank. "I don't remember, Beth, I don't think…"

"No words, just close your eyes and think very hard."

The memory came back with what sounded like a rush of wind to Assundra's ears – the symbols she and Beth had used all those years ago! "Sorcery!"

Bethlinda nodded. "There's something only you can do, Sunny, something that could help us all!" Suddenly the worried look on Bethlinda's face was replaced by an easy smile. "Didn't I always say you were special?"

Assundra barely heard the words. Sorcery! The thing she was always trying so hard to hide, to ignore, why was that important? "What do I have to do?" she asked softly, not wanting to hear the answer.

"It's quite simple really," Beth replied quickly. "Elder Cairns would have shown you himself only with what has happened..." Beth's face fell. "He won't be showing us anything any more and now I can't feel his energy..."

Assundra's eyes widened. "What do you mean, his energy?"

"This place, the Transept Tower, is made up partly of the energy of Elders. Their artistry runs through it and it runs through them – only I can't detect Elder Cairns' energy anywhere. It's how I know...it's up to us now."

Assundra frowned. "When I was in the...when they...Mary said they were going to take back what was theirs. Beth, Elder Oldershaw was there..."

Bethlinda scowled and Assundra jumped slightly at the anger, seeming to bristle off her in sparks. "Primitives!" she cried. "Taking blood enhances artistry, Sunny, it gives you power if you know the correct way to draw it, as well as prolonging life and mind. It would have made them strong, even in the primitive way they took it from you." The anger turned to sadness again. "Even primitive, together they would have been too strong for Elder Cairns."

"Too strong?"

Bethlinda ignored her, the sadness changing at once back to the determined, pleasant stubbornness Assundra remembered from all those years ago. Assundra remembered this – Bethlinda's emotions always seemed to change with every moment that passed. "Which is why we have to do his work for him."

Assundra was still nervous. "But sorcery, Beth? I don't even know if I can do it, most of the time it happens by accident. Wanting it to happen seems to stop it happening." She thought of the flowers on the table, about how Alice, her friend of many years, had disowned her at once, how the villagers had wanted her faced, some of them anyway. Beth had always accepted her, encouraged her, although it had got them into a lot of trouble. Beth, Assundra remembered, had always taken the blame.

"You're thinking about the villagers aren't you? About Alice?"

Assundra gaped in surprise. "How did you know?"

"There'll be more things like that," Beth replied in a kindly tone, "I saw, Sunny. I felt you change the flowers, now that the power is returning those of us with skills will be able to use them more and more to sense things like that. It's why we don't have time."

"Power? Returning from where?"

"You must have seen it? Simon didn't get his skills from nowhere!"

Was that why Simon could do what he could do? Was he absorbing this power that was returning? "But why him? Why don't I have it?" *Why couldn't anybody but him have it?*

"Artistry runs in our veins, it always has, but there will always be some for whom it runs stronger." She'd not heard Beth speak like this before, it was as if it were Elder Cairns talking. "With Elder Cairns...well, now, with no withholdings keeping the power at bay, Simon will be quite dangerous."

Assundra thought that he had been dangerous enough before. Besides, she hadn't told Beth about the boy's obsession with her; she didn't know how Beth would react. "What are withholdings?" Assundra asked instead, pleased when she saw her eyes light up. Beth always did love artistry.

"Oh, of course," Beth said, blinking, "you won't know! The Elders sometimes keep things from you, keep you from remembering things that might not do you any good."

"Any good?"

"Yes, you know, like, artistry, in case it brought the outsiders back to finish us off."

"The Elders use artistry on us?"

"Only to help you," Beth insisted, seemingly puzzled Assundra was bothered by this.

Assundra herself was shocked at her friend's casual attitude. "How can making us forget help us?" Beth flinched as Assundra shouted at her. She didn't mean to, but she couldn't stop, she was incensed at what she was hearing. She trusted Elder Cairns, she had to trust him, but hearing that the Elders deliberately withheld knowledge from people's minds did not endear her to the man. He had kept her from Bethlinda!

"Think about it, Sun. If you had remembered me, you would have come looking for me, probably found me and the village would have discovered this place."

"So?"

"So, Sunny, if they had discovered this place then they would have discovered the things that are kept here and if that had happened Elder Cairns would not have been able to help us."

"Help us?"

"He is trying to save us, Sunny!" Beth got to her feet and began pacing. "If we stay here we'll die, all of us. Without the withholdings, without being able to stop us using artistry we wouldn't have been able to prepare in secret. They'd have come back."

"Come back?"

"It's why it's all worth it! All of it! I knew that once we were all out, once we were all safe, I'd see you again! We could go anywhere, do anything, we could be together, that was always my goal, Sunny, it's why it's so important to me!"

Something about Bethlinda's manner was upsetting her, but she couldn't put her finger on what. She said the only thing she could think of. "I don't understand."

"I'm not explaining very well, am I! Am I pushing you too soon? Here," she said, passing the cup back to Assundra, "drink your drink, it'll do you good. You need to rest."

"Well whose fault is that?" And they giggled, just like they had all those years ago.

"Drink your drink!" Beth scalded her playfully. Beth was older by a few months, and she'd always used her elder status as the excuse for acting like the one in control. In truth, Assundra had always been glad to follow her, sharing in her adventures, her dreams and her fears. Now she needed to follow her friend's advice again, but the drink Bethlinda had given her was making her feel strange.

She stroked hand absent-mindedly along the soft blanket, which was much smoother than the wool it was clearly woven from. She imagined that despite not being real, it was exactly how an animal pelt would feel. The only animals Assundra had ever touched were Herder Young's sheep and the various ducks and birds that used to congregate around the village square, before they were eaten to extinction. She had seen a rodent once, out in Elspeth Wood, but it had run away before she could catch it. She remembered the little high-pitched squeaking noise it had made when it spied her before darting off amongst the trees.

"I think that's enough now," Beth said softly, taking the drink from Assundra's hands just as she was about to take another mouth full.

"Enough?" Assundra managed to say, but only just, she was now beginning to feel very woozy indeed.

"Sunny, I'm sorry, but we really have no time. The tea should calm your nerves when you see it again. I'm sorry."

Assundra was aware of Beth grabbing her hand pressing something cold, hard and sharp into it, before the world span around her as she was pulled to her feet. To her surprise her legs felt secure beneath her, but her eyes would not obey her instructions, seeming to pull in different directions, blurring her vision and making her swoon.

"Beth, what's happening?"

"I'm so sorry, Sunny, I had to do as he said, I always have to do as Elders say it's part of being the Keeper. I don't have a choice!"

The movement stopped suddenly and Assundra felt herself being lowered slowly to the floor. She turned her head sharply as a hiss of wind blew into her ear.

"Welcome!"

The voice came not to her mind, but on a hiss of wind, barely as loud as a whisper. "Beth? Beth is that you?" she called out, in a panic.

"It's not me, Sunny. I'm sorry. I'll do everything I can to help you. Just...just don't trust your eyes!"

"Come to play with us have you little girl?"

"Who are you?" she called out, but there was only laughter – or was it just wind whistling through wood? – in reply.

As her vision steadied, Assundra looked about her, focusing her eyes directly onto the putrid, decaying body she had seen before. "Beth?" she cried out, but still there was no reply. Why had Bethlinda brought her here? And why wasn't she looking away?

"Look into my eyes, little girl! Let me tell you a story..."

The eyes bored into her until she seemed to enter them, they were all she could see. The voice was no whisper any longer, but a man's loud, mocking laughter. She closed her eyes and she felt something leave her. Something that she always tried to keep inside.

Abruptly, the laughter stopped and she could hear nothing.

"Beth!" she tried to call, but her throat made no sound. The body in the chair had gone and the chamber seemed to have become a lot brighter. Looking up, she saw scores of candles hanging on elaborate, ornate brackets around the circular room, in the centre of which Beth lay. Assundra dashed over to her, shaking he by the shoulder, but there was no response. Bethlinda seemed to have fallen into what looked like a disturbed sleep, the stone tied to her forehead pulsing faintly.

What was she supposed to do now? She knew she'd done something. Something had escaped her, something sorceric, she had felt it. Bethlinda had said there was something she had to see, something to do with the body. Had it been the body that had spoken to her?

Assundra knew without checking that too much had changed, this wasn't real. There was no sound, no sense of travel to her movements, no air brushing against her cheek as she walked. These waking dreams were becoming only too familiar to her now.

"Welcome," a voice said to her left. Assundra turned slowly, feeling no fear. If it was a dream, she knew nothing could hurt her. "That is correct," the robed figure said in reply to her thoughts, "you are safe here because you are not anywhere."

"Elder Rime," she said matter-of-factly as the man began to smile in that way Elders did, that knowing, mysterious smile when they'd said something of no substance as Rime just had. "So the body is you?"

This time the smile was genuine. "In a sense. In another sense I am not Elder Rime, but as his vessel was chosen to be your vehicle, it makes sense to use me."

"Why am I here?"

The smile was fixed on Elder Rime's face now. "There is something you must see. Something they want you to see."

"They?"

"The Elders. The hearts of the Elders." Smiling the Elder wrinkled his top lip and raised a finger to stroke his moustache. "Curious!" he exclaimed. "What a strange thing to have on one's face! Why don't you take a look around," he said suddenly to her, before vanishing completely, leaving the void of sound once more.

Pausing only to make sure Bethlinda was in a comfortable position Assundra did just that. Slowly she span, taking in the room, looking into the darker corners, ignoring the vaulted ceiling and drain for now, and it wasn't long before she saw the faint glint, just behind the candle bracket nearest to the entrance to the bedroom.

She moved closer, as she did so able to see that what it was a small, finely detailed, gold-painted carving that was reflecting the flickering flames.

She ran her finger along the grooves, trying to memorise them. She stood, moving her hand in the air, tracing the symbol to make sure her mind had got it right.

"At least the paint's impressive," she told the wall in an inaudible voice. The village had tried many types of painting after Arn had taken the secrets with him to his grave, glue, gum from trees, everything they could think of. Mixing the dye with plaster had created a new line of work for the plasterers, but people soon grew tired of the green, red and yellow walls and once a wall had been plastered it was more work than was wanted to remove it again.

"Well done," she heard the voice say as the world blurred until she was once more facing the rotting corpse sitting in the much darker chamber. Looking down she saw her knife in her hand.

"Now let's see what you can do, little girl!"

For just a moment Assundra saw faintly glowing red eyes, deep within the empty sockets of what she now knew was Elder Rime's corpse, but as soon as she blinked they were gone.

Turning quickly, she saw Bethlinda on the floor, exactly where Assundra had left her in...well, had it been a dream?

"The quicker you follow, the quicker you're back! What are you waiting for?"

The voice wasn't Elder Rime. This was something else. She raised the knife. One of the few remaining pieces of untarnished skin was on Elder Rime's right cheek. There would just be enough room, she thought, with a sigh.

It wasn't difficult to cut the symbol into the man's dead flesh and she was soon finished.

"Such a delicate touch!" the voice chuckled at her. At once Assundra raised her hand and touched he palm to the cheek, which somehow had spilled blood, even though there could have been none to spill.

With laughter echoing in her ears, Assundra felt something leave her once more and this time the world blurred into something very different.

CHAPTER 24

Was the sun dimming? Was it? Had they put the curtain there again?

"Why is the curtain there? I said no more curtains!"

"Of course, sire, no more curtains."

None of them made any movements to pull the curtain back so he could see out. There couldn't be a curtain there. They wouldn't dare disobey the King, it had to be his eyes. They were failing just like the rest of him. He was aware of hands moving under his bedclothes, soft, feminine hands that would once have aroused what he was assured was the finest manhood in Arcadia, but which now simply plucked out the pot from under his backside without so much as a twitch from his genitals.

Was this what natural death was? Was this what he had begged, bribed and, eventually, enslaved the best apothecaries in the land to keep him alive for? "Have the apothecaries killed," he said absent-mindedly, not even bothering to listen to the Castellan's response. He didn't need to, what he said happened, he was the King. He was still the King.

Wasn't he?

He was sure he was. He should have been at any rate, which meant he must be. Nobody would depose the King of Arcadia, there hadn't been a usurping of the throne in the history of the kingdom, it would be unheard of, so he must still be King, he was still alive after all. For all that life brought him. Confined to a bed, fed some slop three times a day by a funnel, shitting in a pan, constantly surrounded by the people he loathed, the people he'd wanted to preserve his life, there being no heir.

He would have to name his successor. Something told King Daseae that he would need to do that soon. If his eyes were going, he'd want to make sure that they put the right person in front of him when he did so, else they could all lie and say he'd pointed to the Castellan, or, worse, his son, Prince Gadae. Did he have a son? He was sure he had a son.

"Where is my son?" he cried, or attempted to, but the noise that came out of his dry, cracked mouth was a feeble croak. The stronger the voice, the more authority it carried, that was what his father had told him. He'd died a proper death, Daseae thought – wounded on the battlefield on one of the many occasions he'd been forced to counter an Archaean rebellion. King Pho the Laodicean had killed himself before the enemy could capture him. Daseae had been twelve and had been prouder of his father in that moment than he had ever been.

The fat Castellan coughed. He was a horrible man, he wouldn't make King. Daseae had already decided he would not allow it. The man wheezed whenever he came into the King's bedchamber, he clearly wasn't fit enough to lead the Arcadian army or even to give something as simple as a show of strength when one was required, and it often was of a King.

Karlner, now there was a loyal Castellan. He had been a good adviser, a good friend, but the apothecaries had not been able to save him. He'd only been forty-something and that was two decades ago now. Since then there'd been a new Castellan and Daseae hadn't even bothered to learn his name. It didn't matter. He'd seen how Karlner had died, he'd seen the same signs on himself. He was sure he'd only stayed alive so long because of his willpower.

"Where is my son?" he called out again, pleased that his voice was stronger this time.

He was aware of the Castellan stepping forward, but could make out none of the man's features. "He is not here, sire, I'm afraid you banished him ten years ago and nobody has seen him since."

"Banished? My own son? You are a raving lunatic! Guards! Execute the Castellan!"

The Castellan, whatever his name was, bowed. "Of course, sire, I am sorry I offended you. I will go happily to my death once I have seen to my duties here.

The King grunted. He supposed that was acceptable and in any case, the grunt brought on a coughing fit so severe he was unable to think of anything for a few minutes. The soft, feminine arm was near him again, this time wiping the thick, foul wetness that tasted of decay from his lips.

Daseae turned to the window again. He was only sixty-five! Twice as old as his father had been, it is true. Did that mean Gadae would live twice as long as he did? "My son will be over one hundred years old," he said absent-mindedly.

"Of course, sire," the Castellan replied.

"You say that a lot these days, but you won't be saying it tomorrow without your head!"

"Of course, sire."

The man was a fool, Daseae had known that even when he had appointed him Castellan, but the other man, the one he couldn't quite remember now, he'd had too many ties to the monks. He didn't want monks near the palace, Karlner had made sure to tell Daseae that, right after he had apologised to the King for leaving his post of office before the suited time.

The memory brought some calm to Daseae. He wondered if he would know the man he spent countless hours strategising and planning with in his new life, in his new body, if the gods allowed his reincarnation. They may demand he sit with them on the highest thrones, it was tradition for Kings after all, but Daseae had been deserted by the gods long ago, he did not think his request to them for reincarnation would be denied. He had to make sure it was done. He had to make sure they wouldn't come back.

It was there, just outside the window.

Daseae looked away. It couldn't be. There was nothing there but the courtyard of the palace some three stories below, the blue sky overhead and the occasional bird. There was nothing else.

He saw the Castellan murmuring to someone whose shape he did not recognise, but he could not speak to demand this stranger identify himself. He could not speak at all. The words were stuck in his throat and he was suddenly aware that his breath was as well. He couldn't force it out! No, he wasn't ready! He hadn't named his successor! Daseae turned his head this way and that, but when he faced the window it was there again, larger this time, calling to him. He felt the sickness, felt the pull, felt it dragging him in and this time he couldn't escape, couldn't get away, and it was getting close, the dark hole, Yawning Maw, it was coming for him.

He wrenched his head away from the window and heard something crack loudly. There were hands holding him down. His neck felt soft, he couldn't move it, could only look at the Castellan. Why were they all helping the maw? They should be bearing him from this place, somewhere safe, in one of the vaults he'd had built under the castle. Why were they leaving him here? All he could see now was the Castellan's dark green robes and the door. Then it was there, too. The keyhole rose out of the door, towards him, creeping slowly to his bed but Daseae couldn't fight now. There was no breath left, his head felt like it had exploded on his body and the Maw was here. It knew it was time. It had stalked him for all these years and now here it was. It was all he could see, all he could feel, and suddenly he didn't want reincarnation any more. He begged silently and wordlessly with his gods, but it was too late, the Maw had him now.

"There are some things that must be dealt with. I choose you! I believe you already know all about Lamia…I grant your wish!"

"No!" the King cried, with his last breath. "By the gods, no!"

*****

The Castellan watched the Scythian envoy vomit through the tower's only window. The admonishing cry from down below would have made him laugh was he not forcing his own meal back down where it belonged.

"Cover him!" he managed to say, feigning a cough as he tasted the vomit at the back of his throat. "Cover him!" he shouted at his personal guard again. The man just stared at him with an expression of dumb shock on his face, as if he didn't know he was there. The man was new, was this the standard the court produced these days? It was as well the man was nothing more than a focal point for the public, Loris was in no need of protection from others. "Are you a simpleton? I said cover the King!"

Gods, the eyes…

The girls pulled the sheet up above the King's dead face before the guard could move, their hands trembling in panic. Castellan Loris waved them from the tiny room at the top of the tower and they left gladly. They would have to be sent back to Archaea as soon as possible before they talked. There was no way to safely dispose of them, but they were simple girls, enough money should see their mouths did not meet with the unfortunate accident of spilling too much information and when they were back in Archaea, who would listen? The very idea that a couple of Archaean whores would be allowed to tend to the King of Arcadia, the Saviour of the World, in his dying moments was ludicrous, just as Loris had wanted it to be.

"At last you are dead," he said quietly to the body of the King, covered by a once white sheet, stained by weeks' worth of the foul-smelling bile the King had been coughing up. "I have been waiting so long. Many years, sire, for you to die."

"His eyes…what happened to his eyes?"

Loris turned to the man who thought he was his master. It would be the work of moments to push him from the tower, claim he attacked the King, the shock of which killed their precious monarch. Only that wasn't the plan. The monks would not be happy, they wanted their envoy to report back to the Royal Dahae, to say they were on schedule, to say that Arcadia was weak, ripe for infiltration. Which, of course, it would not be.

"We do not know what happens to their eyes," he replied, coating his voice in a calm syrup. "It has happened to them all, surely you have heard the accounts?"

The envoy stiffened. "There have been no such demonic abominations in Scythia! *Oeto-syr!* To suggest such a thing would not please the Royal Dahae, my Lord Castellan!"

The man's eyes bulged with terror that he tried to pass off as fury. A head taller than Loris, Ariapithes was a broad man, though the menace of his bulk was tempered somewhat by the bright yellow silk shirt and trousers he wore, elegantly embroidered with green woollen stars and moons, and the tall turquoise conical cap which he never seemed to remove. The man looked like a court jester, although the shining pure gold buckle he wore on a large horse-hide belt, on which hung two gilded daggers and the huge recurve bow slung about his shoulders showed Ariapithes was anything but a figure of fun. His red-blonde beard was unkempt and tatty and wisps of similarly uncared-for hair were now escaping from under the turquoise cap. The green eyes stared wildly at Loris. He had been shamed by his illness, Loris knew he would have to be careful not to give the man any reason to create a fight.

He needed the Scythians. For now.

"Your man, why does he stare at me so?"

The Castellan turned to the guard, whose name he had already forgotten and cuffed the man round the back of the head, making him let out a girlish whimper. "The standards of men they send me these days…" he found himself saying. To his relief, Ariapithes nodded in understanding. He had noted the Scythian was never accompanied by a bodyguard.

"All we know," Loris went on, "is that death does not allow those who were present at the…event, shall we call it, to rest easy in death. The blackness that spreads is always the same, as are the tales of this Yawning Maw, which, thank the gods I have never seen for myself. Our blessed departed King, Daseae, sent forth painters to the deathbeds of some of these unfortunates, none of whom knew of each other, to record of their fantasies and without fail they each brought back the same painting. It was as if each painter had stood in front of the same object and painted it from his own perspective."

Ariapithes looked at him, unmoving, his breathing fast and short. It was a nonsense, of course, for the man to claim no such aberrations afflicted the dead amongst his people – the Scythian philosopher roaming the streets had even described it in detail the King would rather his people had not known about. Not that what the King wanted mattered now.

"I wish to see these paintings!"

Loris bowed, leading the way from the room, snapping his fingers at the guard to follow. Appearances must be maintained. He took one last look at the dead King. His death would not be announced for a few days, not until the Prince could be brought from Scythia, at which point Ariapithes would be sent back with word of the King's sudden death, thinking their ward, Prince Gadae would be open to grant his saviours in Scythia many boons for their kind treatment.

They would find Gadae in no such mood.

As he closed and locked the door, Loris reflected on Daseae's life. He was glad the King had passed of natural causes. He was the last that they knew of, the last survivor of the event, the tragedy that had occurred as they had boarded up the Yawning Maw. His predecessor, Karlner, had advised against such a move, but the King had been insistent. To this day Loris did not know what caused the tragedy but he did know that all fifty of the men who had travelled to the Ostracian border that day with their King had suffered the results of it for the rest of their short lives.

Loris had expected the King to die shortly after Karlner, not hang around for another twenty years, although keeping the King bedridden and focused on his ailments had allowed Loris to run the Kingdom properly.

Loris, pausing only to lock the whores in their room, overtook Ariapithes as he strode towards the turret steps – the man was clearly keen to get out of the tower. The two bedrooms were the sole feature of the fifty-foot tower, on the eastern wall of the palace. They had moved the King there at his request, he had said the noise of the main palace had offended the problems with his ears, that he could hear people whispering all day long, despite being in an empty room.

Symptoms of the madness, Loris thought as he led the way down the steep spiral stairs. The King had no business being in charge of the gods' own empire, any more than an Eastern Arcadian had any business rising to the rank of Castellan. Now both were gone, Arcadia was open to be ruled by those who deserved to rule. The people needed a figurehead, a monarch, but they also needed a monarch who was aware that the subtleties of leadership required firm and subtle hands behind the scenes, men who need not be tainted with the frailties of being seen to act according to a set of archaic rules. Loris smiled – it would not be long now.

They reached the courtyard in just a few minutes and their solitude was instantly broken. There were people everywhere – merchants, servants, soldiers, all going about their business. The two armed guards at the base of the stairs stood to attention as Loris and Ariapithes passed. The castle was split into three – the outer circle, where they were now, formed the outside walls of the castle, surrounded by a huge moat. Here was where the markets and courts were held, where the philosophers held their own form of court and where the less secure of the rich paid a high price to the King to hold residence. The second circle was where the barracks and meeting halls of the King were housed, as well as the castle gardens. The third circle was the vast palace, almost a castle in its own right, the pride of Arcadia and the seat of the King. There were always statesmen, dignitaries of some kind or other residing there and an army of servants to take care of them. Loris had made sure to know them all by face and name and, more importantly, to make sure all of them knew him.

The royal banners flew high on their masts on all four towers that sat just inside the outer circle walls. The flag was clear-sky blue, with white forward and reversed epsilons, signifying the fifth King, side by side on the centre of a black star of vergina. Loris was suddenly struck with the dark thought that King Gadae, the sixth King of Arcadia, would be the sixth King. His symbol would by stigma. It was not an auspicious start.

"Where are these paintings kept?" he realised after a short while Ariapithes had asked. Loris felt a twinge of anger that the man seemed to be struggling to keep his pace down to Loris' standard speed rather than trying to keep up. He suppressed a belch and put a hand to his ever-increasing belly – this fine living did not agree with him.

"They are in the King's private vaults, only he has the key."

"Then how are we to get in, my friend?"

The Castellan returned Ariapithes' toothy grin. The man had clearly forgotten the horrors of the King's death and Loris felt it better to keep things that way.

"You will be privileged to see many treasures of the Arcadian empire, as we pass through the vaults," Loris said proudly, "very few of those outside our borders are lucky enough to witness such grandeur."

Ariapithes smiled again. "My friend we have much in the way of finery in our wonderful empire. We do not fear our people and hide away our glories, our Royal Houses are open all day and full to the brim with the many gifts of golden trinkets, fine tapestries and other such wonders that I believe in this part of the world you have never seen, but I shall be pleased to view your small collection."

Loris kept the smile on his face as he scowled inside. That was the Scythians' problem, of course – they were too wealthy. Their only threat had been the Ostracians and that had not been a threat worth allying with, even if it would have provided strength against the Scythian Empire. That had been the view of the people and the King. Loris had always thought differently. On the holy days, Arcadian priests sacrificed animals to the blood of their King. There were rumours of cannibalism in Azoia and even Scythia and yet there were no attempts to raise an army of the world to conquer these places. What were a few human sacrifices to the Ostracians if they had brought the empire, the people as a whole, greater prosperity and power?

The Castellan had been too young, then, for his voice to have had any influence and in any case, the voices of the brothers in his movement lay silent either in graves or in the dungeons, he would not have made a difference even as Castellan. But now…

"We near the palace," Loris observed and his friend seemed to understand, beginning a rambling, loud monologue about how wonderful it was to be able to see the seat of the marvellous Arcadian Empire, how even a few short years ago this would not have been possible and to be allowed to be in the presence of the Saviour of the World, how magnificent…

Loris buttressed his ears against the assault of the foreigner's words, waving a greeting to the guards that let them through first the portcullis, then the long, narrow tunnel, through which there were murder holes placed every few feet in the ceiling, of course, until they reached the huge fountain of the gods, the centrepiece of the courtyard of the palace of Arcadia.

"Such a shame," Ariapithes commented loudly as they walked past the guards, "that you have allowed such a magnificent piece as this to be defaced."

Loris was unable to stop himself scowling this time – he was getting sick of the foreigners jibes about his gods. The twenty-foot high, four-tier fountain was the greatest attraction they had. People came from all over Arcadia to worship at the feet of Chronos, Gaia, Hemera and Aether, the four remaining statues rising up from the base which was itself five feet from the ground, and gladly offered the required funds to the King to do so. The two gods of whom no more than feet remained, had not been lost, they were the King's gods. Ariapithes would soon see them as they passed into the vault.

The palace main entrance was up some fifty marble steps, directly opposite the tunnel. It spread back into the third circle from there, the entrance being the only feature besides the fountain – the King and the gods needed no bedfellows.

"Mention nothing of our purpose to any servant here," Loris reminded, but the Scythian just smiled. If it were supposed to be a winning smile then Loris reflected it needed work. To him it was the smile of a man who knew too much.

"What of him?" was his only reply, jerking his head to the guard who strolled behind.

The guard, Loris noticed, who seemed to have developed the strangest mincing walk since the King's death. "He is responsible only to me. If he talks, the court will silence him themselves. It is part of their agreement with the Castellan's office."

As they rounded the corner, Loris was forced to reflect that the palace took his breath away every time he saw it. The entrance hall was taller than any hay barn, with two gilded marble staircases curving up to the gallery above, off which the private chambers of the King stretched the length of the palace. The guest quarters were all on the ground floor and were sumptuous enough, but no foreigners were permitted entrance to the King's private chambers.

They were not there for a tour of the grandeur of the living space, however. Guiding Ariapithes away from the staircase, towards which his eyes had turned, greedily, Loris made headed to the left of the entrance, passing another set of guards standing stiffly to attention as he did so. The corridor beyond was just as ornately decorated as the entrance hall, curving around the palace as it wove it's way towards the servants' quarters. The occasional bust or statue broke the line of pillars and frescoes that Loris didn't have time to properly make Ariapithes aware of the significance of.

"You are taking me to see the servants?" Ariapithes asked, in confusion and Loris laughed.

"In a manner of speaking, yes," he replied, slowing to a halt before a pair of great double wooden doors, as tall as four men, each with a spiralling gilded trim, the left with a smaller door built into it for easier access. Loris ignored both, turning instead to the statues that stood immediately to the right of the door.

"Axiocerus and Cadmilus," Loris said proudly. "The Cabeiri."

Ariapithes' eyes widened. "From Phrygia?"

Loris smiled. "Yes. We believe some of them still exist, but after Phrygia was brought under the Arcadian banner, we tore their temples down."

"Your religion," Ariapithes shook his head, "you have so many gods! Atar and Agni would brook none of these rivals!"

Loris laughed – from previous discussions with Ariapithes he knew the man to have a religious conviction equal to his own – that if perceptions of belief kept the people happy or, at the least, controlled them, then there was no harm.

"These underground gods serve us no purpose."

"Ah, underground! Those below, servants! I understand!" Ariapithes broke off into a fit of laughter.

"That is not the only function these gods provide us with," Loris whispered and, after making sure they could not be overseen, placed his hand delicately between the buttocks of Cadmilus. With a click, the side of the plinth on which the battered statue stood swung aside, revealing a dark well, torches hanging on brackets illuminating the steps that formed the 'ladder' cut into the well's face. "It is not deep," Loris reassured Ariapithes, "and below I believe you will find the answers you wish for. Come, quickly."

Loris guided the Scythian and his increasingly troubling guard down the well, then followed himself, swinging panel shut after him. A few short minutes later and they were half-crouching, half-walking through the tunnel, carved into the earth, that led to the vaults. Another lever at the end of the short passage opened into the back of a once-precious sarcophagus, the front of which had been hinged to provide a makeshift door.

That door led to a vast underground cavern, the remains of the old palace before the first King of Arcadia, having united the kingdoms of Athens, Thrace, Sparta and Phrygia, amongst others, under his banners, erected this magnificent structure. The air here was dusty, the only light from the crackling torches on the walls, some of which had burnt out. For all the beauty of the palace proper above, for all its grandeur took his breath away, this place gave his breath back to him with gusto – there was history here and history held power, if one knew how to wield it.

It was why Loris did not aspire to be King – far better to pull the strings of your leaders than be subject to their accountability – and this room held more than one secret to ensure the strings remained firmly around his fingers.

That was not what they were here for today.

"This place is a tomb," Ariapithes sneered, confirming to Loris the man's innate lack of cultural appreciation. A few nights ago Loris had offered the Scythian a night of exquisite music and dance, a feast and the chance to converse with the greatest actors, philosophers and historians that Arcadia could muster under one roof. Claiming pressing state business, the man had declined, only to be found by Loris' spies drinking and whoring his way through the slums.

"Tombs hold the dead," Loris finally managed to reply, "this place holds much more than that. Come."

The paintings were not far away. Keeping to the wall, the centre of the room shrouded in darkness, Loris heard the Scythian's steps halt. "What is *that*?" Ariapithes uttered in a hushed, reverent tone.

Loris knew the Scythian was talking about the statue. "Lamia," he replied with some disgust and without turning. The half-serpent, half-woman, draped in snakes, with the most alluring beauty any man could dream of, her faithful dog, her hell hound, laying by her feet. Thousands used to worship Lamia. She led to… "A myth," Loris added quickly before his mind could get carried away and start remembering.

"She is beautiful!"

Loris stopped at that and turned. "She has the lower body of a serpent."

"But those eyes…"

"She devoured children. Drank their blood." This appeared to refocus Ariapithes' mind. "She is not one to revere, mythical or otherwise, we have seen too much of such works to allow their worship and reverence!"

Ariapithes stood up at once, that curious, almost impassive half-smile on his face once more. Loris instantly regretted having spoken in such a manner. He had no doubt he would be reminded of that before the Scythian departed for his homeland, but he did notice that his companion paid the statue no further heed. Loris did not look once. He knew too well the allure of those eyes. The same allure he had heard his father speak of when the Ostracians had walked the streets of Arcadia all those years ago.

It was an allure he wanted no part of.

"Here," he said quickly, trying to shake of the brusque mood he had suddenly begun to feel the pressure of and pulled aside a large tapestry which was, unlike the rest of the room, bathed in light, with large torches positioned either side. There were five paintings.

"Oh my…"

Ariapithes reeled off a much longer list of gods than he had hitherto admitted allegiance to. Loris got the feeling that he was in fact naming any god he knew. The man's eyes were manic and wide once more and for a moment Loris feared he would vomit again, but eventually he grew quiet.

The paintings all showed the same thing. They all showed the death mask of the portrait's subject, the twisted, shrieking contortions of agonising deaths, but that was not what turned the stomach.

Loris turned to motion the guard to help Ariapithes, perhaps fetch his servant, but the man was not paying them any attention. He was staring straight at the base of the statue, at Lamia's dog, mouthing the word "no" over and over again in a high voice, too high. Then he just collapsed.

Loris could only understand. This place was the only thing that caused Loris, a man who was famed for the strength of his stomach, a stomach that would be needed with what was to befall the Arcadian Kingdom, to shudder. He never once stole a glance at the paintings after he had pulled the tapestry back. It was the eyes.

They all had Lamia's eyes.

All the subjects, in all the faces of death, just like in the death mask of King Daseae, fifth King of all Arcadia and Saviour of the World, were stained by Lamia.

It was all starting again…

CHAPTER 25

The tunnel Assundra was in was only big enough for her to crouch as she moved slowly along, her face hot where the flame of the torch she'd found at the start of the passage burned too close. She hadn't wanted to leave Beth and now the pain that seemed to be ever-present in her stomach these days was masked by a sinking feeling of sickness that Assundra had let her down.

Just like she let her father down. Big Tom Franks, the man who never needed any help, for once, had needed her. So why had he run away from her? Why had he run when he needed her help? The answer was obvious. He didn't think she could help him. He didn't think she could do anything.

The voice – the new voice, not the voice that helped her, not the voice she now knew was Bethlinda – had told her the same thing.

"You can't help anybody yet!" it had screamed at her in a frenzy when she'd come to. *"Not until you see! You have to see! Did you see?"*

The body of Elder Rime had begun to turn slowly to dust right before her eyes the moment she opened them. "Follow the trail!" the voice had said to her, laughing at her, screaming at her, so loud it hurt, every time she went near Bethlinda, and eventually she'd followed it, through the open, rotting doors into the passageways beyond.

"There are things you have to see!" the voice had insisted, hissing in her ear. *"Things they want you to see! I'd keep them from you, you are not what will save us, not by a long way, but they want you to see! So go and see!"*

So she'd gone. She had no idea where. The voice screamed at her if she went the wrong way, or at least that's what she assumed that's why it screamed. It stopped if she changed direction through the maze of passages. The small tunnels were dim, but not dark, the soft light glowing from the bricks enough to stop her losing her footing.

The voice was like a persistent, petulant child. A child, or Simon. The same aggression, self-fascination and pleasure in power that she had seen grow in Simon. Once she had felt safe with him, with his clumsy advances, his presence, but no longer. Not because of what he would do to her. Because of what he would do around her. And without Elder Cairns to keep him in check…

It wasn't Simon who scared her the most, though. She knew it was real now. The monster, the thing with the red eyes, the thing that had stalked her all her life, the thing in the well in the city square. Lamia was real. What was at her feet was real. The beast. The thing that looked just like…

Assundra shook her head. Being away from Bethlinda made her feel unsafe again. Made her think stupid things. In these dark, twisting tunnels, the thing with the red eyes could be waiting around any corner and she wouldn't see it until it was too late.

She pushed the thought away. She couldn't turn back. She had only one option ahead of her if she wanted to stop the hissing voice driving her insane – to do what it said, go and see whatever it was the voice's masters wanted her to see. Then she could go back to Bethlinda and *then* they could find her father. Stop him before…before Lamia…

"Thinking, not walking, little girl? First you must see! Then you can think!"

Slowly, she edged along the tunnel, the backs of her knees starting to ache. What had she just been thinking about? She couldn't remember. Something about her father.

"No thinking!"

She coughed, desperate to pull more air into her lungs. The scream sounded in her head again and she changed direction abruptly, without thinking. This passage was much narrower. The air was stuffy here, even though there was a slight breeze tickling her hair. A soft, sticky substance leeched onto the walls was trying to glue itself to her arms. She could just about manage to turn around if she had to, but she didn't want to try.

"Bloody tunnel," she moaned, catching her arm on the only piece of sharp, hard stone without any sticky substances growing on it there had been for hundreds of feet. As she rounded the next bend, the ground began to slope again. There had been a gradual drop since the chamber – surely there couldn't be much further down she could go?

This time, though, the air changed as she descended, seeming thicker than it had. Reaching out her free hand she felt at the wall. It was damp. The splash of water under her feet breaking the silence confirmed it. This tunnel had been flooded, and recently. If she strained her ears she could hear a distant tap of water on water. But there was no way back. She couldn't face the screaming voice in her head again.

"Trap or no trap I've got no choice," she told herself, "and there can't be much more." Though what she expected to find when the tunnel ended she was not so sure.

Realising she had not moved since she'd heard the water, she moved on, running her hand down the wall, its sticky lining moving slimily under her fingers. Without warning the wall ended beneath her fingers, leaving her hand groping at thin air. The dim light ahead of her showed Assundra it was not just a bend in the passage, but the first offshoot passageway leading off the main tunnel she had found since leaving the chamber.

Without hesitating, Assundra moved into the gap, which bent sharply to the left. The faint, blue, soft glow from each and every brick, dimly illuminated a thick wooden door at the end of the short passage.

Grabbing the thick rusty iron handle that was set into the centre of the door, she pulled and with the pained groan of hinges not used in many years, it swung open, puffs of dust falling from the door edges making her cough.

The bricks shone much more brightly in this room, a darker shade of blue than the other passages. More importantly, she could stand here! Assundra felt taller than she ever had, stretching her hands up as far as her arms would allow and swearing as they met contact with stone far earlier than she would have liked. So she just knelt down and stretched until she could feel the muscles pull, a glorious feeling, like jumping out of a box, like she had done when she was hiding from Beth when they were small. Leaping up, she made sure to drop her arms before jumping as high as she could.

Something stopped her laughing abruptly, but she didn't know what. Something at the back of her mind. She guessed there wasn't a lot to laugh about.

Certainly not in this room. It looked like it had once been someone's bedroom from what little she could see – the room was covered in cobwebs, clinging grimly to any corner or overhang so it was hard to see properly. At least the spiders weren't dying out. Which meant that the insects were thriving too. As if to prove the point, she looked down to see several beetles making themselves known to her shoes.

Assundra took a few tentative steps into the room. Yes, definitely a bedroom. There was the biggest bed Assundra had ever seen in the middle of the chamber against the far wall. It seemed to invite her in. It had been so long since she had slept properly; she doubted whether she had managed more than a few hours downstairs in Bethlinda's little room. Or had it been days?

She was about to move towards the inviting bed for a closer look when the mattress moved. Hundreds of little movements, rippling under the sheets. The room was infested! Her legs twitched, wanting to turn and run, but she made herself stand her ground and look for something useful. Bugs didn't worry her; all they did was squirm and patter around over you until they discovered you were too big to eat. She had come home to her father one day as a child with her entire arm covered in beetles after she had found an infestation in Elspeth Wood. Her father had panicked, and she remembered laughing as he slapped at her arm to get them off. They had left of their own accord eventually.

Looking around the room, she realised how bare it was. The huge bed dimmed the senses somewhat to the sparseness of the other furnishings. The room reminded her of her own, back in her little cottage, just a dressing table, a bed and a chair, only here there were two wardrobes rather than just one and each was three times the size of her own. Assundra found herself wondering how much greater a museum she could have hidden in a wardrobe that size. A small table each side of the bed and a large cobweb-covered bronze mirror on the wall completed the furnishings. A bronze mirror! Very beautiful, but entirely unpractical, Assundra found herself thinking – you'd spend half your time polishing it.

What took her attention the most, however, was a small badly made table in the corner created by the two wardrobes past the bed. The crudely made and ugly, obviously Ostracian, furnishing was offset by the most magnificent chair Assundra had ever seen. "Another relic of Lady North?" she wondered to herself. The pink material did not move as the mattress of the bed did. It was covered in no cobwebs. Assundra immediately set off across the room, scattering swathes of the thousands of complaining and agitated beetles as she did so.

As she sat down, the chair seemed to close in around her, cutting her off from the infested room beyond and she didn't hear the beetles any more. It was as if the chair had no wooden frame, as if it was all feathers and padding, folding itself over her like a blanket.

"What did you see?"

She span around and the round, shining emerald, playful eyes of Bethlinda Mullard met her gaze, a smile upon her lips in the same vein. "Beth!"

"Sunny, what did you see? I tried to be there, to help you, but I couldn't see anything. Something stopped me."

"Are you alright?"

Beth nodded her head, but did not smile. "What did you see?"

"It's ok Beth, I wasn't in any danger," Assundra replied, making sure she smiled, making sure Beth was reassured. "I don't really understand what I saw, it was something on the outside I think. Something to do with a King dying."

"A King?" Beth's face shrugged into puzzlement. "King Daseae?"

Assundra nodded. "That's what they called him. I was a guard, or… no, I wasn't the guard. I couldn't move, or feel anything, but I could see through his eyes." Assundra remembered with a start. "Beth, I think they saw me…"

Now it was Bethlinda's turn to smile. "It doesn't matter, Sunny, if it was Daseae's death that was a long time ago." The smile faded. "Things have got a lot worse on the outside now."

"Worse?"

Beth smiled again. "Yes, Sunny, worse and before you ask I know, I don't know. I feel like something told me while I was...while you were...but I don't know who. It wasn't the Transept Tower, it wasn't the old Elders. Did you know Elder Cairns always watched them just as they watch us?" Assundra found herself shaking her head. "The forces surrounding us are the weakest they've ever been, Sunny, but it won't stay that way for long." Beth moved forward. "That's why it has to be now. That's why I must know what you saw!"

Assundra told her then exactly what she'd seen, about how Ariapithes had been terrified of whatever it was Loris had shown him, about how all she had seen was the red eyes, just like she'd seen in the tunnels where Bethlinda had found her.

About the beast at Lamia's feet.

"It's not your father, Sunny," Beth said, but still she did not smile. "Your father is...what he is. The beast is something else. Something we must be careful of, but as soon as we leave here we won't have to worry about it any more."

"But Beth, don't you see? That's three of us! Me, John and these people on the outside, they've all seen this red-eyed...thing! It's real! Beth, it means I'm not going mad!" Beth was just staring at her, her mouth twitching as if she were trying not to laugh. Assundra was suddenly angry. "What are you laughing at?"

"Oh, Sun," Beth laughed in reply, "you looked so impossibly cute slumped there! I just had to tell you. I bet the boys in the village all fight over you!"

Assundra put a smile on her face, forcing down sinking sickness that made her want to cry out. *"Yes, they do, and they will do worse, and to you too, you beautiful girl!"* Beth couldn't know, not yet. They would spare Beth no less than Assundra.

"Yes, actually!" she said instead, "but they don't make me feel like you do." Something in Bethlinda's manner had made her think that she knew that it hadn't been Assundra's first time, but neither of them had spoken of it. Assundra sat looking for a moment, wishing she had never realised what she had to protect her friend from. "How are you here?" she said softly, suddenly worried that someone would hear them. "They told me to leave you, I'm sorry Beth, I had to, the voices were so loud!"

"I know, that's why we have to leave now. I left the passage open for you, they can't find you in here, but I couldn't stay awake, the Gozon Stone needed to heal me. I thought you'd wait for me!"

"There wasn't time," and there wasn't now, Assundra thought, cursing her weakness for allowing so much time to go to waste! She listened quietly for a moment, but could hear nothing. "Beth, you're right! They've gone!"

"Not yet," Beth said sternly, pushing Assundra back into the chair as she tried to get up. "You haven't eaten in days, have you? You look so weak."

"I'm fine…"

"Sunny, it's not normal for a stomach to growl so when you're lying with someone! At least, I don't think it is." Assundra swore now that she would protect Beth, protect that innocence. None of the men were going to take that from her love! "Eat this."

Beth gave her a thick hunk of stale bread that she had brought with her in a pouch and before Assundra knew what she was doing, she had snatched the food and begun cramming it into her mouth, resenting every chew fir the time it took delaying the food from entering her belly.

"Beth, what happened to you?" she said between mouthfuls. "From how you were sleeping it looked like…did something hurt you?"

"Only a little. Don't be angry, Sunny," Beth cried as she saw the expression change on Assundra's face, "they're not the Elders they were any more, their minds have gone mad with the plague. That's why I'm here, normally I am forced to obey an Elder's every word, but Rime no longer merits the title, just like Oldershaw. The Transept Tower has rejected him."

"It doesn't matter if he's an Elder or not!"

"I have to do as the Elders say, it's part…"

"Bollocks to the Elders, Beth! Look at what they do to you, it's not right!"

For a moment she thought Beth might cry, and Assundra's own throat tightened at once. "Would you complain if you were hurt trying to bring your father here? To save him?" Beth said eventually. "It's no different, Sunny." Assundra pulled Beth into her arms, murmuring her apologies and thinking she deserved to hurt herself for being so selfish. Whatever she thought of her friend being taken away, this was Beth's choice, her calling.

Assundra wanted to tell her that there was no hope to save the village, that she had no interest in saving the village after what they'd done to her, that she just wanted to hide away, here with Beth, but Beth's eyes were too full of hope. In any case, Assundra had to find her father.

"Beth, how do you hope to save the village? There are only two of us, what can we do that decades-worth of Elders couldn't?"

Bethlinda looked up from her hands full of excitement. "Sunny, they've just been waiting for you! Well, you and Simon. With his power and your sorcery, it will be the work of moments to free them all!"

"Here! Search here!"

The voice was half-lost on a lisp of air, as if it were straining, fighting against a bond that were holding it back.

"What is it?" Beth must have seen something on her face.

"There's something here, I heard the voice again."

Bethlinda blinked. "How can you have…what did it say?"

Assundra was taken aback at the force of Beth's voice. "That there was something here. I think it means something we have to find, Beth, help me look…"

"There's no time, we have to leave."

Assundra was puzzled. "But the voice said to look here, you took me to Elder Rime's body to hear what it had to say, didn't you? Why don't you…"

"I was wrong! I'm sorry, but Elder Rime is not himself! I did what I had to do, it was a direct instruction from the Tower, I had no choice but to obey, but now I do!" She pulled Assundra to her feet and clasped her arms hard. "Sunny, this Tower is infected with plague! It's driving the Elders' essences mad, there are no instructions now, it's up to us and I think we should leave! Now! Before they instruct us to do something equally as insane as they are!"

The whispering started again. Quietly at first, but growing louder with every second. Assundra couldn't make out any words, just sounds, but before long she didn't want to make out any sounds – it was just a cacophony of noise that hurt her ears. She cried out in pain but couldn't hear herself as she sank to her knees.

"I'm sorry!"

The voices were all speaking at once, dozens of them, shouting at her, laughing at her, as they had in the corridor when she'd tried to go back, but it was so much worse this time. Assundra screamed and put her hands to her ears, but they shut nothing out.

"I'm sorry! We'll stay, we'll search! I'm sorry!"

At Beth's words the voices stopped. Beth fell to her knees beside Assundra with a whimper, the Gozon Stone shining a bright light. For just a moment, in the pale shadow it cast, Assundra saw a face lined with cuts, bruises and mangled beyond all recognition, but only for a moment.

"I'm sorry," Beth was whimpering.

"Beth?" she ventured, putting a hand out. Her own voice sounded too loud, making her ears ring.

"Sunny, I'm sorry…" Beth repeated, panting, and Assundra noticed that Beth's voice didn't hurt her ears at all. She wondered why. "We have to look, I'm sorry." Bethlinda began to sob. "We have to look…"

Bethlinda tailed off, sadly, as she began to search. Slowly, trying not to disturb cobwebs as much as possible and trying to keep her eye on Bethlinda. She couldn't help smiling when Beth let out little yelps of disgust at the life flowing around her feet.

Assundra tried to put forward an air of unconcerned mirth but she was filled with a sense of dread. Bethlinda's mournfully apologetic mood had passed in an instant and Assundra was moved to wonder just how much of an effect on her this healing Gozon Stone had. Beth's moods had always been changeable but in the years since Assundra had seen her it seemed to have got much worse.

One thing Bethlinda didn't seem to feel was uneasy. She was always sure of herself, something Assundra felt not a glimmer of at this moment. Something had led them to this room, it had not been an accident.

A scream from Bethlinda made Assundra spin around, her heart in her mouth, but it was just thousands upon thousands of nesting termites spilling out from one of the big wardrobes. Beth quickly slammed the door on the nest and turned to Assundra, laughing. She moved straight on to the second wardrobe and Assundra saw it at once.

"Beth, wait," she called out and rushed over to the wardrobe, her feet crunching on the hundreds of scurrying insects, now panicked out of their minds. "Look, there," she pointed, but the confusion on Beth's face showed she couldn't see. Grinning, Assundra pulled at the board. "It's too high up, Beth, just like the one at home," she said quickly as the board came away in her hand. Assundra had wondered what she could do with such a hiding place for her museum, but it seemed someone had already had the same idea as her.

"A hiding place!" Beth exclaimed, making Assundra smile again.

Peering inside, Assundra could see in the dim blue light from the stones that there wasn't much inside, indeed the hiding space was a lot smaller than Assundra would have thought. There were only a few things inside – some very old, very worn pages torn from a book and a long object wrapped in a filthy cloth.

"What's that?"

Assundra pulled the cloth out of the recess quickly and pulled it carefully apart, revealing a long, thin knife. It was crafted from what she could see had once been a bright silver, almost blue-silver, metal, the surface of one side of the blade carved with symbols she didn't understand and nor did Beth when she asked, just shaking her head in wonder. It was not beautiful in the same way as the knife strapped safely to her thigh, certainly as it was missing a hilt, but it was beautiful in its simplicity. "Look, there's a scabbard to go with it."

"Just as well, there's no handle!" The blade was simply that, a sharp blade. No hilt, no hand guard, just the blade.

"Do you know what this is, Sunny?" Assundra didn't bother shaking her head, she knew from experience that Beth wasn't really waiting for a response. "It's a withholding dagger!"

"A withholding dagger?"

Beth smiled. "Yes, Sunny, a withholding dagger!" The girls laughed briefly, before Bethlinda's sense of wonder at the blade returned. "It is for use against death-life! That could be…" Beth tailed off, a look of almost triumph in her eyes.

"Death…"

"Don't do it, Sunny!" Beth cried, slapping her playfully on the arm as they both laughed again. "It will take death-life out of existence. We should take it with us, but I think there's something else."

Assundra cringed at the sight of the myriad of bugs that scurried up the flapping sleeves of Bethlinda's loose dress. Assundra could see moving shapes all across Beth's body, underneath the fabric. They weren't dangerous, but she didn't want Bethlinda to be alarmed.

"Look, there's writing…"

Bethlinda handed the aged, worn paper carefully to Assundra. The symbols written on the page were not Ostracian. Looking across to Bethlinda, she saw the same playful smile she was growing used to once more. "You know full well I can't read it and you can, Beth!" she chided in jest, handing it back and returning the smile, Assundra waited for Bethlinda to speak.

"Well, Sunny, it is a letter. It is written in one of the older, outsider languages, which I do not know the name of. I'll read you what I can."

"My friend, whomever you might be,

I received notice today that the time for my passing is nigh. Oh, my name is Elder Barth. The time in which I write this, save that it is near that of my end, is not relevant.

You are now occupying the room that I used to call my sanctuary. There are things that will have preserved it for you, yet it will not be the same room that I once inhabited. I long ago abandoned attempting to discover the secrets of the Transept Tower; it has properties directly linked to the abomination of Stracathri. These abominations lie far beyond the reach of my power to tackle or question and my will has ceased to offer sufficient effort to try.

Yet I digress, a feature perhaps of my impending end that my mind wanders into places it is not supposed to go.

You are here because it has been written you come here. The ones who withhold would not allow you to be here if that were not the case. Of your quest there is little I can do to help you, as I do not as yet have any knowledge of what it is that your quest is for. Yet I can impart one grain of knowledge to you that will aid you on your journey.

Artistry is not a negative force. It can, and will, be wielded in such a fashion, but so can a sword or a spoon. Even the darker side can be used for good purposes. The world was wrong to write artistry off as dangerous. You can make it see the folly of its ways if you so choose. Or, you can destroy it forever.

The weapon you will have found is blessed with a particular power that I hope to all of our people's adopted gods are never relevant to you, it will never need sharpening. Once when I was a boy, I cut down a tree with it. I got into a lot of trouble for that, I can tell you, what with orange trees being so rare. I'd leave it here if I were you, but it serves to show that the sword is never without its scabbard. Your choices are crucial for the future of us all. Well, not me, I shall not benefit or otherwise as I shall soon rest for good, but I have found that the only choice worth making in life is which of the two you are: sword or scabbard.

This is the choice I leave you with. I go now to my rest.

Elder Barth

PS If there are Norths involved, don't trust the buggers an inch.

Assundra found herself seated on the floor, not caring about the carpet of insects that now busied itself about her as well as Beth. "Sword or scabbard," she found herself repeating under her breath. "Petticoats and brass. Trees give way to saplings." She found herself getting angry. "What does it all mean, Beth? What saplings, what swords? What brass?"

She looked up to find Beth keeping a level, unblinking gaze upon her. "Why would an Elder write in an outsider tongue? It doesn't make sense. He wouldn't."

"Wouldn't?"

"An Elder wouldn't write in an outsider tongue. I don't believe it, Sunny."

"Don't believe it?"

"No. I think it's a fake." Beth screwed up the paper and threw it back into the small chest that had been hidden under the bed.

"What are you doing?"

"Sunny, it's not genuine, trust me!"

Beth spoke softly and Assundra realised her heart was racing. *"Your choices are crucial for the future of us all,"* it had said. Written in a letter in the tongue of the outsiders. The only reason for that was if an outsider was to be the one to read it. Assundra flicked an adventurous beetle off her arm, turning her head away from the sight of it.

"Sunny, what is it?"

"Nothing," she said quickly. This was hers, hers and her father's and she didn't want it. She'd never see the outside anyway, so this outsider power, this choice, whatever it was, could go to the gods! The only choice she was going to make was to help her father and then stay far away from the lot of them with Beth. "We've lingered here too long. You were right, Beth, we should have left straight away."

Assundra stood, holding out an arm until her friend grasped it, levering herself up with its assistance. Picking up the long withholding knife, she sheathed the blade in the sheepskin scabbard, pulling the little clasp over the top to hold it inside, throwing the scabbard's holster over her shoulder. She wasn't going to leave this here. Why would Elder Barth, if it had been him, left the blade if it wasn't meant to be taken?

"Wait, Sunny," Beth whispered, gently turning her back to face her friend and kissing her softly, their tongues meeting for but a moment before Beth pulled back, kissing her cheek instead and leaning in to whisper softly again. "I'm with you." Bethlinda took Assundra's hands in hers. "It will be our life."

They stood for a few moments, time stopping with them to watch as they smiled upon each other.

"It will be alright, we still have time. I will help him, I promise. When this is over, it will be so much easier, but I have to…"

“I know.” Assundra interrupted. She didn’t feel sad. Her father would just have to wait a little longer. Beth would help her, but she was bound by the instructions she’d been given. They would be in time. They had to be. She would not be the scabbard any more, hiding away, waiting for a blade to be thrust into her. Her father needed the sword.

Leading Bethlinda, Assundra strode out of the room. “Sun, wait a moment!” Assundra turned to look at her friend. “How the hell am I going to get all these bugs out of my clothes?”

Assundra smiled. “You’ll have to take them off, Beth!”

CHAPTER 26

Simon lay still, panting, his body covered in burns. Even breathing was difficult, he could feel the skin cracking as his chest rose and fell. Something he didn't want to think about was dripping from his face.

There was no pain. There hadn't been any pain during what had been the most amazing moments of his life, just the ecstasy of Elspeth's eyes, her lips and her body. Her whole body. Simon beamed at the memory – not that he'd seen her body, as such, but he'd...sensed it. He'd known it.

Then she had vanished. Just smiled and vanished, the eyes in his mind gone as well. He hadn't minded that she had laughed. Nothing else mattered, other than what had just happened. The most beautiful experience of his life.

"You have damned all of us."

Simon heard, rather than felt the flesh on his neck split as he turned his head. A small, blue figure stood next to him. He laughed – he wasn't surprised he was hallucinating. Something that felt that good, something so amazing, was bound to have an effect on his mind. He found himself wondering with a smile if he was dead. Elspeth had said life and death-life could never mix, yet they had just mixed as much as any two people could, so surely that would have killed him?

It made sense. It would be why he couldn't feel anything, why he couldn't move. He was dead and this blue thing was some heavenly creature here to help him move on. He made up his mind at that moment to try and come back as death-life, to be with his Elspeth when it wouldn't cost him his life.

The blue figure shimmered slightly, almost as Elspeth and Kryman did, but not quite. This small thing shimmered in colour, from top to toe, slowly, very slowly, but shimmering from white to blue all the same. Looking at her now she was still, Simon could see she was a young girl, no older than about ten.

"You are the Gifted One?" she said with disdain, with knowledge and tone far beyond her years. Simon supposed angels would be like that.

"I am," he replied, his tongue sticking to the roof of his mouth. He tasted blood. That made him frown – why would he taste blood if he were dead? "Am I dead?" he asked, but this time unsure of what the answer would be.

"I think not, but much may have changed since my time away. This could be a new type of death. Death inside, perhaps, while the shell lives on."

"What?" Simon could barely be bothered to listen – memories of how Elspeth had felt around him kept pushing themselves to the front of his mind. He did not dare look down to see what had happened to his manhood. If his body was this burned, this cracked and dry from being near her then what had been inside her…

"Do you have any idea what you have done?" the blue girl asked him. She was not angry. Simon knew that tone from his mother. It was disappointment.

Simon didn't if he'd disappointed this blue thing. "Yes, I do," he replied cheerfully, though the cracking to his voice did not help him sound happy. "I've done…"

"I do not need to hear any details," she said matter-of-factly. Her voice sounded to Simon like it wasn't hers, as if something was using this child's body to speak to him. "You have brought back to this world something that should have remained dead. You have brought back the woman who killed me. More importantly, you have brought back the last piece in the puzzle that could destroy our race."

"Our race?" Simon laughed. "I don't remember too many of our race having blue skin!"

The blue thing didn't laugh, get angry or even change expression. "

"There was a girl once," she replied. "This girl was but ten or eleven years old, I forget now. Long flaxen-coloured hair that had never been cut, so long it had to be tied in a long plait down her back so it wouldn't get in the way. She wasn't a special girl, just a farm-hand's daughter, helping her father live through the death of his wife, the mother she had never known."

If the girl she spoke of with a smile had not had flaxen-coloured hair, Simon would have said the story was of Assundra.

"The child was happy; content with its meagre existence, but there were those who begrudged her. Not for her, or the simple existence she led, but for something her brother had done."

Was this Elspeth the nymph was speaking of? She had been persecuted by the villagers for her birth, but no, she was no farm-hand's daughter, unless the villagers could be counted as a farmer's sheep. The blue child had that way of talking that made him wonder.

"Her brother had seen some things he should not have, heard things that were not for his ears. When the Norths came for her brother, she followed, despite her father's warnings. He was he brother, after all. But she was a young girl she had no skills in subterfuge and deceit.

"And so she was caught. And she was subjected to the same treatment as her brother."

"What treatment?" he croaked. His voice was beginning to leave him and his mouth was so dry. If he was not dead he needed to do something about that. "Can I have some water please?"

She ignored him. "We were bound into iron maidens first. Then our captors slowly removed limbs, flayed skin and burned us with foot-long, red-hot needles as amused them. That was how my brother and I died."

Simon couldn't speak. Was this girl death-life? Like Elspeth?

"I see you are shocked. I am glad; I should be worried if you were not."

This time Simon found words. "Aren't you angry? How can you be so calm after what they did to you? I'd tear their hearts out if it had been me!"

The blue child shrugged. "Over time sorrows give way to hope, responsibility and a calling. They cursed me." At this the child's eyes dropped for the first time. She looked so forlorn, he reached out a hand to touch her, to hold her, tell her that he would have found whoever had done this to her and made them pay, but he knew she was lying. It was a good act, but she had to be lying. She said Elspeth had done this to her.

"I don't believe you…" he began, but a snort from the blue child cut him off.

"It was Lord North who gave me my calling, after his daughter had given me and my brother our deaths. Then he had my parents killed."

"That may be true," Simon coughed through his dying throat, "but Elspeth would never have done that to you. You can't know it was her, you were too young to remember properly."

"Can't know?" Her voice was fierce; her manner that of one who could kill, yet tears, unmistakable this time, fell from her shimmering eyes. "Can't know? You think I do not know the woman who placed red hot irons into the eyes and ears of me and my brother?"

"Shut your mouth!" Simon knew she was lying! She had to be; his Elspeth would never do something so inhuman. More tricks and lies, but they didn't fool him any more, the Elders had tried that too often, he knew the signs. People always tried to turn you with stories about the ones you loved.

"Yes, Simon! Your *mistress* did that to me and my brother! I have failed…" her voice tailed off.

Simon felt nothing. The girl should cry, he thought, for telling such lies. What kind of father was Lord North to let rumours like this be told about his own daughter? If he were alive today, he would pay.

"If I did not believe you were confused because of what her father did to you, if he indeed did do those things, I would kill you for saying that about her," he said calmly. Where was Elspeth? He needed to go. Now. Only he still couldn't move and his burns were starting to hurt.

"Yes," she said, her voice once again the sad tones of a child, "I do believe you would."

"I would. Nobody insults those I care about." He saw her about to mock him again, but he didn't want to have to hurt the dwarf-child, or nymph, or whatever the blue thing was, so he kept on. "Can you help me? If not, then please go."

"Help you? Why? So you can damn us all once more?"

"When were you damned?"

"Look at me!"

"You said that was a blessing a moment ago!"

"You are a fool." He bit back hard on his tongue to stop the artistry out of habit, but there was none there. His face hurt when he moved it now.

"Is it starting to hurt?" the child cooed. "It will get worse. She will not return, she has what she needed from you."

"And what is that?" His voice was nothing more than a croak now. His throat was on fire, making him pant to take in breath, to try and cool it, but nothing did.

"She has taken your Gift. That will return," she added casually, starting to walk about his head. "but your innocence will not."

Simon tried to laugh, to tell the child he didn't want his innocence anyway, that he was glad it was gone, but ended up just whimpering in pain. Gods, this hurt!

"I see it is useless, she has clouded your mind. She knows all that you are doing. She smells your thoughts. She will never leave you now, not now she has you, but you will never have her again."

Simon didn't care. He didn't want Elspeth to leave. Ever. The anger calmed within him in the same instant that it began, the feeling of calm purpose returning. As if calmed by another.

The eyes in the back of his mind snapped back and snapped open. The blue figure jumped back in alarm at exactly the same time.

"Kylerian," Elspeth said, from somewhere Simon couldn't see. Her voice sounded wonderful to his fading hearing, his ears filling with a loud ringing, growing ever more shrill and painful.

"You cannot be here!" the girl shouted. "You can't be! Carstan said you couldn't be!" She had lost all pretence of being older than her years now. Something in the girl had changed.

Hands were placed on his head before Simon could think anything else and instantly all of his pain was gone. Something flowed through him, something hot, strong and determined, through every vein, every muscle, every sinew, tendon and bone. It did not feel pleasant – it was as if someone were scraping him clean, inside out. His skin bristled and he cried out, but as soon as he did it was over.

"What happened?" he cried, pulling himself to his feet instantly, spinning around and coming face to face with Elspeth. "Oh by the gods," he exclaimed.

"She can't be here, she *can't* be!" Kylerian cried. "Carstan promised, he said…"

"He said much, Kylerian," Elspeth replied, her voice smooth, deep for a woman and now with none of the harmonic double tones of death-life. It was nothing but sweet to Simon. "He said much to you, none of which was true. Simon, I did not torture and kill this girl."

"I know," he replied instantly, moving towards her and pulling her to him so hard she gasped. Her lips felt like soft perfection on his, her tongue like power licking at his, her body hot against his. She felt perfect. She was perfect.

"Simon," she gasped, pulling away from him, "there is no time! We have to…"

"Not until you tell me how!" he cried, laughing. "How are you…Elspeth, you're human! You're really human!"

He moved to kiss her again, but Elspeth pushed him back. "Not now, Simon, there is too much to do!" she snapped, pulling his arm away from her waist.

"It's you!" Kylerian cried, between sobs. "You were the third trigger! You think she cared about you? She needed you!"

"Be quiet, nymph!" Elspeth screeched. Simon had never seen her so angry, nor so ragged.

"Why do you keep calling her nymph?" he asked, wondering why he was so concerned with how Elspeth had become human, when he should just be glad she was.

"She's blue, Simon, what do you think she was cursed as? It's not only spectres one can be cursed to return as, there are nymphs, shades, you can even reanimate the flesh! The things you people have forgotten…"

Elspeth turned away exasperatedly, muttering to herself. "But…" Simon started, but Kylerian screamed in anguish before he could finish.

"The first trigger was Elder Oldershaw taking you to Lamia's shrine, the second was spilling blood there – when you killed your father, do you remember that, Simon? Did you think she didn't plan that? The third was to lie with the Gifted One and take his power – she's wrapped you round her little finger at every turn!"

Simon didn't want to listen to this. "That's nonsense, Elspeth didn't plan for me to kill my father, she tried to stop me!"

"Really?" Kylerian laughed. "She's managed to stop you performing artistry many times before without much effort, what makes you think she couldn't have stopped you if she'd wished this time?"

Simon opened his mouth to reply but couldn't think of anything to say. Elspeth rounded on them both again. "At this very moment Elder Oldershaw is manning the cannons to attack the ships in the bay."

"What?" Simon suddenly understood the need for urgency. "We have to stop him!"

"She won't," Kylerian moaned, crying now and stamping her feet. "It's all over! Carstan was wrong, he was wrong!"

"He was not wrong, nymph, he was lying! Why do you people need to be told everything three times!" Tearing off her crimson shawl, Elspeth pulled her hair about in her hands, an expression of joy on her face. "It feels just like it did that day," she murmured. "Just before everything crashed down around me. Just after I found out what my brother had done."

"No, it's you that's lying!" Kylerian whined in reply. "Carstan promised! He said if I did as you wanted I'd be helping, I'd save everyone!"

"Carstan lied, how many times? It was my father who cursed you in any case, do you not remember? Now, do what you were created to do."

Simon frowned. "Don't be so hard on her," he said gently, "she's only…"

"*Never* correct me again!" Elspeth cried, fury in her eyes. Simon took a step back. "I healed you because I felt sorry for you, by rights I should have let you die!"

Simon's brain juddered in his skull. "What are you talking about?"

"Two Gifted Ones? Do you really think that could work? You fulfilled a purpose, Simon, now when this is over perhaps there will be time for us, but do you really think this is the time for sentiment and childish emotion? Our world is dying around us, your Elder is about to take us into a battle we cannot win and my brother is the gods knows where with a creature that should never have been brought into existence! And you want me to be *gentle*?"

Simon felt anger growing to match hers. "That girl was only ten when she was murdered, she says by you, do you not think it likely that if she thinks that, she is perhaps a little afraid of you? Yes, I want you to be gentle with her, your family did this to her after all!"

For a moment he thought Elspeth was going to strike him, but she held back. "My family did nothing! My family were never even concerned with my existence! My family sold me like a trinket to secure their own futures! My father may have been Lord North, but the Norths were never my family!"

Simon frowned. "But your brothers…"

"Were nothing to me! They had been poisoned to me by their mothers, the harpies my father kept around after he knocked them up, they were nothing to me! Kryman will have it that it was he who showed the true power of the North lineage, but do you think I showed them everything I could do? I showed them nothing! I just brought you back from the brink of death in mere seconds without even a drain on my power, what do you think I could do to hurt a man in just as much time? I constructed a wood in a day! I can do *anything* Simon, anything except stop your damned Elder bringing ruination to our people, for that I need you and I need this child and I do not need your questions and complaints!

"Now," she cried, turning to a cowering Kylerian again, "you claim my brother promised you that everything would be alright? Just let me hurt you and he and my father would offer you a chance to save your people, is that right?" The girl just nodded. Simon wanted to stop Elspeth, to make her let the girl be, but he did nothing. He said nothing.

"It was Carstan who did this to you. He had a habit of disguising himself as other people – me, my brother and Elder Costrange were his favourites. Only my father somehow managed to prevent him from taking his likeness, though of course, we only have my father's word for that. It could have been Carstan at any time.

"In any case," Elspeth went on, Simon feeling ever more sorry for the ghost of the harangued little girl, "you were created for one purpose, please discharge your duties now, then you will have peace."

Kylerian looked miserable. However, she closed her eyes and spread her arms. There was no blood, Simon heard the artistry in her release no words, but he felt it. The air was thicker and something inside him shifted at the presence of magic of an older kind. It was as if his blood was licking at it, wanting whatever it was that was being used.

The nymph began to slowly dissolve before his eyes, she turned her head to him. Simon's heart almost broke as the little girl's features faded away. While there was no sound, Simon could swear he could hear the very air scream.

"That was horrible," he said, giving a reproachful look to Elspeth. "What has your family done?"

Elspeth rounded on Simon again, but this time there was no anger. "What we had to do, Simon," she replied softly, moving slowly towards him. It was strange, he thought, to see her walking, not gliding. He found himself wondering very hard what her legs looked like and looked up to see her approaching close to him with a smile.

Whatever the nymph had done was finished now – the air returned to normal and Simon's blood calmed, though his heart was still thumping like a fist in his chest. "What happened?" he asked. He never seemed to know anything. Everything seemed to be happening around him, why was he being kept in the dark? With Elder Cairns at least he knew he was being deceived, but he got no such idea from Elspeth – every instinct told him she was telling him the truth, that she was the first person ever to tell him the truth, but yet she held things back.

"I'm sorry you had to hear everything I said to Kylerian," Elspeth replied, "but she was not the little girl she portrayed any longer. You must have seen that? She was nothing more than another device of my father's, to try and drive a wedge between us, to try and turn those who are close to me against me, I could not let my father know how important you are to me, Simon."

She raised a hand to his cheek and Simon felt something stir in his stomach. "How could your father…"

"If my brother and I are here, Simon, I would not wager against my father having a presence here too. He would have been more than capable of cursing himself to death-life as he cursed us. If we are to stop him and Elder Oldershaw we need to stick together, Simon, but he must have no idea of this! There isn't much longer to go now."

"We should stop Elder Oldershaw now," he cried, "before he launches the cannons! Shouldn't we?"

Elspeth just stood, looking at him with a strange mix of sympathy and kindness. "If we stop him now, what are we to do with him while I do what must be done?"

"I don't know, seeing as you won't tell me what must be done!" Simon was growing sick of this – everyone treating him like he was a child, nobody telling him the whole truth! "What must we do, Elspeth? What could be so important that it's worth risking another invasion? If Cairns was right about anything it was that we are no match for the outsiders any more, we don't want to give them an excuse!"

"Simon," she cooed, raising a hand to his arm in an attempt to calm him, but he felt his blood heat again. He felt suddenly hungry, a deep yearning inside him. "You can feel it, can't you?" Elspeth hissed excitedly. "Burning inside you? It's alright, I can too."

"What is it?" he asked, just managing to get the worse out without spilling artistry alongside them.

"Kylerian was the final part of the puzzle. She was an outsider, Simon, that's why she seemed so different to my brother and I. In order to seal the power away, to give it time to build safely, we had to use sorcery, which meant we needed outsider blood."

Simon's eyes widened. "Assundra is an outsider!" he exclaimed.

"Yes she is," Elspeth answered quickly, "that is why my father cursed Kylerian, my brother and I. We are fail-safes, Simon, back-ups. In case the Elders did exactly what they have done and figured it out." Elspeth smiled, her eyes sparkling. "They may have figured it out, but they will never have the power now! Can you feel it, Simon? Doesn't it feel exquisite inside you?"

Simon didn't answer. He didn't trust his mouth to open. Power was building inside him to a frenzy. He felt heat from his hand and looked down to find it singed.

Seeing his gaze, Elspeth took his hand. "We're going to have to stop that," she said, frowning in concentration. With a swift movement she took hold of the splint embedded in his nail between two of her fingers. Simon felt more heat, felt something surge from his hand.

"Elspeth, wait!" he warned, trying to push her away before the artistry left him, he couldn't stop it, it needed somewhere to go, there was so much inside him – too much – he had to let it out! With a cry of anguish, he saw Elspeth's finger begin to burn as well but then the splint was gone, melted in the fierce heat between them, heat that was then directed right at his finger. The wounds were sealed in an instant with the heat and at once the power stopped flowing from him. Elspeth snatched her hand away and sucked it to her mouth.

She drew the finger slowly in and out of her mouth, her tongue licking around the tip. Simon gasped out loud as blood surged to his manhood. Withdrawing the finger completely, Simon saw that it was healed. How could that be? In just a few seconds…

The realisation of her power only increased his lust and he pulled Elspeth to him, groaning as she pressed against him. He kissed her hard, but she pulled away.

"You have done so well so far," she panted, "I cannot tell you what it is I must do, but you must trust me for only a little longer, then I will tell you everything. When my brother returns I will have need of you once more, Simon. Will you help me?"

Simon began to understand. "So you wanted him to think you were…that you had no need of me?"

"Yes," she smiled.

"But you do?"

She leaned in and kissed him softly, her body pressing up against his hard manhood. She giggled, pulling away and thrust her hand inside his skins, caressing his manhood. "I think we have a need for each other at this moment," she whispered into his ear.

As her hand squeezed and her tongue licked at his neck, Simon told her he loved her. "I'll do anything you want," he murmured, surprised to find that he meant every word.

CHAPTER 27

"Beth," Assundra began before stopping, She needed to think for a moment. They continued in the mean time to feel their way along the passageway, their arms outstretched, feeling with their feet. This passage was even smaller than those Assundra had walked through before, and pitch dark. Dank water came over the soles of her shoes. Bethlinda's arm was locked around her waist so they wouldn't lose each other in the darkness.

She needed something to keep her mind from thinking about whatever these cryptic outsider phrases meant. She'd already decided to be the sword, not the scabbard. That one at least was taken care of. But what of the petticoats and brass, or trees giving way to saplings?

She shook her head, she needed something else to think about and as it happened, something else was bothering her. "Beth, there's something I need to know."

"Of course, just ask Sunny, you don't need to ask to ask."

Assundra chuckled. "How are we going to save them?"

It was Beth's turn to chuckle. "I was wondering when you'd get around to asking! I should be flattered I suppose, you just took it for granted that I knew! It's the power, Sunny. The power will save us."

"Power?" Assundra replied, confused. "But I thought Elder Cairns wanted to take away the power?"

"Yes, from the people. We need to take it from the Towers, from the land, as well."

"But someone with that much power, surely the outsiders will sense them..."

"With that much power, with all of the artistry of Ostracia, that person will be able to hide it," Beth replied simply. "They would be able to control it."

"One person? Who?"

"It was to be Elder Cairns," Bethlinda replied. Assundra couldn't help but be moved by the sadness in her voice. "Now…I'm not sure. I know Simon is to take the peoples' power. I don't know how or when. As to Stracathri's weapon…"

"Weapon?"

"The power," Beth explained. "The power was always the weapon. The only weapon anyone ever needed. Lord North took that power with him and hid it. Others wanted to fight with it, to use it."

Assundra was quiet for a moment. "What would you do with it?" she asked softly.

Bethlinda didn't reply. Assundra found herself alone with her thoughts once more, only these thoughts seemed dead to her. Vast power, saving the villagers, messages from the Elders of the past, none of it mattered to her. All she cared about was never seeing anyone in the village again and somehow saving her father's life from whatever this illness was before it was too late.

That, and being with Bethlinda. The rest of it could all go to the hells. Only everyone seemed to need her to make it happen. Elder Cairns and Bethlinda needed her because she was some sort of key. The dead Elders seemed to think she had to make a choice. The visions, from all over the place, kept pushing her towards sorcery, the one place she definitely knew she didn't want to go. Mary and the Crafters had needed her for…

"Why me?" she blurted out before she could speak.

"Sunny, we've been over this," Beth replied softly, squeezing her arm around Assundra's waist. "You're the only one of your kind.

"But…"

"The Transept Tower is dying. Others are figuring out that the secret to the power lies in Stracathri. Others are figuring out that it is you, Sunny, who holds the key to that place. The Crafters wanted other things from you."

Assundra shuddered. What more could those people do to her? It clouded everything she thought about and even in the moments when she thought she was clear of the thoughts, some part of it came back to stab her mind.

"Stracathri is more than stone and artistry. The Transept Tower is held together by the heart, the essence of dead Elders, but Stracathri has a personality. It has a morality."

Assundra furrowed her brow, feeling stupid for not understanding. "A morality? But surely it was built by so many different people, how can they have one character, or morality?"

"Yes, but they were bred from all sorts of artists, Sunny. Sorcerors, mages, alchemists, Elders, wise men – all their gifts, and they're all part of artistry, came from the artistry in their veins. Stracathri acts as a focus for that, the Transept Tower for the Elders' power. We don't have as much power any more as a people," Beth said sadly, "but the Tower has lost none of its own."

"So there's a lot left over?"

"Something like that." Beth's voice was distant, almost awestruck, as it always was when she spoke of these things. It worried Assundra; she had only ever seen artistry used for harm.

It scared her.

"So they're alive? The towers?"

"They are, yes, it but at the same time they're not – they have no natural lifespan, no imagination, but they do have instincts. At the same time, they only exist to perform what they were constructed to do. To do as they're told, in a way.

"Nobody, even the Elders of the Transept Tower, ever figured out how to break half of the artistry protecting and flowing through Stracathri, or the instructions withholding its nature, its behaviour – and the rebel Elders were true masters."

"But I thought Marchman was the first master?"

"No, he wasn't the first, he was just the first normal Ostracian to use the power of all of the arts together."

"The first commoner, you mean?" Assundra's blood heated at the thought, though she was not sure why.

"Yes, if you want to put it like that. It's always been in Ostracians' veins, it's what sets us apart, but most never know how to develop it, not because they can't learn, but because they don't want to. They occupy their minds with other things. More still are afraid of it."

A faint sound of splashing echoed behind them in the darkness. Assundra ignored it, eager to hear her friend speak. Beth was always happy when she was telling Assundra how things were.

"I'm afraid of it too," she said softly, squeezing Beth's hand to let her know that didn't mean she was afraid of her.

"But why?" Beth exclaimed nonetheless. "You shouldn't be afraid of it Sunny, you should embrace it! It's a wonderful feeling!"

"It got you locked up!" *And taken away from me*, she added silently. The sounds of their own splashing through the water was growing louder and Assundra realised it was up to their shins.

"Yes, it was after I read the book that I let my secret out. You see, I could actually read the books, Sun! I knew what they meant. I even did a little spell."

"A spell?"

Chuckling, Bethlinda grasped Assundra's arm with her other hand, although strangely not causing pain, the damp of the tunnels seeming to have numbed the feeling around the large wound. "Yes, my girl, a spell! I knew nothing of the terrible power I had unleashed!" Beth said in the deepest, most pompous voice she could muster.

The girls picked up their pace a little as they laughed. "That's very like him, you know. I can't imagine Elder Cairns being too happy with that."

"Elder Cairns? Dear me, I can't be very good at voices then. I was doing Elder Oldershaw."

"Elder Oldershaw? But…"

"Yes, I know you thought that. No, it was Elder Oldershaw who taught me at first."

Elder Oldershaw? Just how big a part had he played in all this?

"Just as well really, I never knew what I wanted to do anyway. Well, I did, but they'd never have let me do it."

"What? Be an artist?"

"Yes, of course. Travel Ostracia, such as it is, making things happen with just my mind and the energy around me. I wonder what they would actually have done."

I know exactly what they would do, Assundra thought, *and I don't want you doing something that dangerous!* Bethlinda deserved her innocence; it was another thing Assundra had to protect. She mustn't learn what her beloved villagers had turned into.

The tunnel branched out three ways, at least Assundra thought it was three from her groping around in the now only semi-dark. Too busy talking, Assundra realised they had not checked any of the wall in between that place and where they were now for any more drops or passages or, as Assundra had become convinced were there, cupboards with weapons for defence of the tunnels.

"Shall we go back and check…"

She was interrupted by a splash somewhere ahead that sent sound-wave reverberations crashing all about the tunnel.

"No, Sun, lets not."

"What is it?"

Several quieter splashes followed, some distance apart. Something was running towards them. There was at least half a second between each splash.

"That thing is something big."

"Come on," and without waiting for another word, Beth pulled Assundra into a sprint down the middle tunnel. "I'd best lead the way. I can't feel the Tower now, we must be going the right way."

"What is it?" Assundra gasped again as the water flailing around them almost drowned out the sound behind them. She didn't stop to check.

"You remember those bugs in the room?" Assundra shuddered at the memory. Something was still stirring underneath the clothes on her arm. But the image was tempered somewhat by the rather more pleasant memory of Bethlinda disrobing to remove them from her person. "I think that there were so many that some things may have got very large indeed feeding on them."

"Oh gods…"

Assundra didn't speak again, but allowed herself to be dragged along. The pace they were setting didn't leave her much time to ask any more questions between gulping breaths for air, anyway.

Bethlinda's hand was jerked away from hers in an instant. She heard a cry before the ground vanished beneath her own feet. Water closed all about her, shutting out all sound, sucking her down. She choked as it flooded her lungs, but the choking just made it worse – almost at once her lungs started to hurt, feeling like they were bursting against the inside of her chest. She tried to struggle, but there seemed to be water everywhere, on all sides and no matter how far she tried to push herself up, there seemed no end to it.

She felt herself swallow water as her mouth tried to breathe. Her throat felt full and it was in her nose, it was everywhere, she couldn't breathe and now she couldn't move. Her arms stopped working and she tried to be sick, but that just brought more water into her body. Her head began to throb, pushing her swollen eyes out too far past her skull.

The sound of crashing water rushed to her ears as a hand gripped hers and lifted her up, another slotting itself under her arms, hauling her head clear of the water in one move. "Sun!"

Assundra coughed, vomited then coughed again, mouthful after mouthful of water hurling itself out of her. Hands were pressed under her rib cage and they pulled at her, hard, making her throw up again. Then she felt cold stone under her face, her eyes opened and sweet, beautiful air was pulled into her lungs in watery, jagged breaths.

Bethlinda let out a yelp as the splashes stopped back at the curve of the tunnel. Two oversized, bright red eyes gleamed out of the darkness at them. The creature's heavy, panting, growled breaths echoed around the tunnel, making it sound like the beast was all around them. Assundra wanted to scream, but couldn't stop coughing. At once the blue crystal was placed on her forehead. Warmth spread through her, soothing her aching limbs. The rest of the water in her lungs dribbled out of the corner of her mouth, spilling down her chin.

She couldn't take her eyes off the monster. Why was it stalking her? Why was it looking at her with such hungry eyes, what did it want? John, man scared by little other than the Deathguard, had returned from the city square a broken man after his encounter with the beast, but he had got away as had Assundra, until now. The wall behind what Assundra had to assume was an over-flown well was solid stone. There was nowhere for them to go.

At least it was hanging back. Did it not like water? Why would such a creature not like water? Assundra could tell it wasn't an animal, it wasn't a man, it was something else. Something she never wanted to know anything more about other than it was far away. It was dabbing at the water with a foot, or a paw, or hoof, or whatever it was the creature had, Assundra couldn't see. The creature let out a cry in frustration, a shriek that echoed around the stone tunnels, repeating over and over. Assundra pulled her hands to her ears as they started to vibrate inside with the echo of the shrieking.

"It's too late, it's coming – into the water, Sun!"

Assundra tried to protest, but no words could be pushed from her throat – it was all she could do to breathe.

"Trust me!"

Feeling herself being grabbed once more, she was once more in the water, being grabbed and pulled not, this time, by the murky water but by Bethlinda. Down Beth swam, pulling Assundra with her, the thing behind them letting out a cry that became a low, rumbling growl, under the water. It did not make the sound any less horrendous.

Still they went down. The large piece of rock in front of them had an opening, she could see that now, the blue light shining like a beacon, telling them where to go, but it was so far down and she had such little air left in her lungs, still aching from before, that she knew she wasn't going to make it. Her limbs were turning to lead even as Bethlinda pulled her through, under the jagged end of the rock, and then she felt her legs slacken and the blue light became a blur.

Assundra was dimly aware they were rising once more, as they lifted their hands and Beth pushed her legs, dragging the almost dead weight Assundra through the water. First their outstretched, clasped hands broke the surface, then their heads.

Dipping back into the water more than once, they eventually found a bank of sheer stone and Beth pushed Assundra up against it. Assundra tried desperately to get her breath. Her body had no strength left. Something was pressed into her back and she felt the warm feeling spread through her again.

"I'm sorry, Sunny, but we have to keep moving! The stone will heal you, I promise, you'll feel better. Sunny, I'm so sorry."

Assundra's breath wouldn't come, her throat was stuck, retching itself to get the water out but the water was slowly dribbling out of her mouth again, much more this time. The urge to vomit fought with the urge to breathe and her eyes were burning from whatever had been in the dank depths, streaming tears down her cheek. All at once her breath returned, her limbs regained life and, instantly, pain. Bethlinda did not release the pressure of the crystal pushed into her back. Her neck felt limp and her vision only of the inside of her open eyelid, where the water ran, unchecked, there being nothing to stop it.

Arms stronger than they should have been pushed up to her armpits and she felt herself rise, the contractions in her neck shorter now, not as painful. She felt like she perhaps didn't need to breathe after all, not if it hurt so much. There was a loud sound through the water swimming in her ears and hands were pushed her behind hard, shoving her up and over the ledge and onto the side.

It was colder out of the water and now she could close her eyes, if only Beth would let her be, but she kept manhandling Assundra, folding her arms before rolling her over, pushing at her chest, planting the sharp stone into uncomfortable places. She thought perhaps she would at last be allowed to sleep when Beth rolled her on to her side, but a finger was jammed down her throat, and the last, violent contraction forced a torrent of water out of her mouth and her lungs coughed, seeming to bring her ears back to life with them.

"Sunny!" a voice screamed, as water ran out of her ears. The name reverberated around her skull, and she had to vomit again. "I almost killed you!" the voiced sobbed, so Assundra grabbed the hand that was holding her tightly, pushing the crystal against her. The warm feelings were spreading now. Her breathing became gradually easier, but the dead weight of her limbs was not dissipating at all.

"No, Beth, you saved my life." But only sobs met her words. Beth kissed her softly on the cheek, then on the lips, they locked eyes for just a moment, communicating things no words could say. Assundra hadn't been scared. For once, she hadn't been scared. She had known Bethlinda would save her. Hadn't she?

"Where is it?" she pushed from her lungs, spewing water with each word.

"I don't think it followed. Sun, I'm sorry. I'm so sorry. I promised you'd be safe with me, I'm sorry."

Bethlinda seemed dejected. As the warmth of the stone pressed into her spread finally to her limbs, she raised a hand to hold Beth's. "You told me to stop apologising for forgetting you," she panted. "I'll make you a deal – you stop apologising for saving my life and I'll stop apologising for that."

Only sobs met her words, but something else was playing on Assundra's mind. "Beth, how did it find us? How did it get down here?"

"The flood," Bethlinda replied quickly, "it must have collapsed some of the tunnels, they all link together, remember. I didn't think any of the Transept Tower tunnels would still be flooded, but if that was, I have no idea what the state of the rest of the tunnels in Ostracia are like. We must find out."

Assundra felt a prick of panic strike every spot of her skin at once. "Find out? Why? I don't want to go back into any tunnels!"

"We have to," Beth whispered, her face close. "We have to get our people out of Ostracia. The plan was to use the tunnels. If we can't…"

Assundra waited but Beth was quiet. "If we can't then what?" she ventured.

Bethlinda sighed. "Then I don't know what we do, Sunny. There's nobody here to ask." Assundra clasped Bethlinda's hand, but to her surprise Beth pulled it away and pushed herself to her knees. "We have to keep moving."

"But it's not following," Assundra complained – she needed more time! Whilst the stone had spread the warming healing to her limbs and body, her head was thumping and her lungs ached. "Beth, can't we rest a moment?"

"There's no time, Sunny, I'm sorry," Beth half-shouted, half-sobbed. "We have to go, there's so much to do, if only you knew!"

"Then tell me!" Assundra exclaimed, hauling herself to a sitting position and immediately choking back on some water that had been lurking in her chest. "Beth, you say there are things I have to do, but what? What are they? What does Elder Rime, or the Elders' essences, or whatever, want me to do? Beth, what is going on?"

Beth just turned her back and didn't answer for a long time. All of a sudden she raised her hands and Assundra saw drops of blood falling from each. She must have hurt herself pulling Assundra out of the water! Assundra swore at herself – she hadn't even asked how Beth was! Even as Assundra was leaping up to see how she was, Beth cried out and two jets of bright light shot out from her wrists in balls, hanging gently in the air for a few moments before bursting, the light so bright that it made Assundra bring her hands up in front of her eyes.

In just a few moments it had dimmed, but the partly ruined cavern, which Assundra could now see they were in, was bathed in a sweet, soft light. "Beth…" Assundra exclaimed and Beth turned with a smile of delight on her face.

"I did it!" she exclaimed, "what do you think, Sunny!"

Assundra flinched inside again but forced a smile. In truth any artistry frightened her, but she didn't want Bethlinda to see that. She didn't want Beth to know something she was so proud of scared Assundra to the very bones. Or that Assundra didn't want to be anywhere near it.

"You're amazing, Beth," she ventured, keeping the smile and was pleased when Beth laughed, clearly very happy. She'd got away with it.

Now there was light, Assundra could see they were no longer in a man-made stone tunnel, but a cavern. It didn't even look like it had been hewn into the rock, this was a natural formation, with huge stalactites and stalagmites of what, in the soft light Beth had created, looked like sandstone but clearly could not have been. There was noticeable moisture in the air and the stone above her head looked wet, as if it had been soaked recently – this cavern had clearly been underwater until recently. The yellowy tint the light gave the stone gave the feel of a sunset to what Assundra was sure would otherwise have been a dank cavern.

"Come on," Beth cried excitedly, dashing off to what, other than the water, seemed the only exit to the cavern – a small opening about half Assundra's height, partly hidden behind a thick broken stalagmite.

Once again, Assundra was worried about Bethlinda's mood swing. All thoughts of the red eyed beast behind them, presumably even now trying to think of a way to best its clear distaste for water and somehow follow them, seemed to have left Bethlinda without a trace. The childlike excitement at exploring, however, was charming, Assundra had to admit, and not a little infectious, but Assundra could not forget about the beast with the red eyes. Stalking her. Following her.

Now it was she who had to follow Beth, who had already slid through the opening in the cavern wall with a chuckle. Assundra pulled herself to her feet and was about to check herself over when a scream from the other side of the opening made her forget her worries about her fragile body. Leaping forward, she crouched, scrambling through the opening, clumps of the wet stone dropping onto her back as she brushed past, pushing through to the other side, where she straightened up as soon as she could, bumping straight into Bethlinda, who was bent over, not two paces from the entrance.

It seemed it was Beth's turn to vent her stomach contents. The sound reverberated off the stone, making it sound like there were a whole host of retching people. It made Assundra's own stomach gurgle threateningly, though she doubted there was anything left now the searing ball of flame, licking pain this way and that inside her, had done its work.

Somehow the Keeper managed to maintain her grace even when throwing up, simply matter-of-factly allowing her body to do as it wished, holding her surprisingly still silky hair back with one hand, leaning on a pile of blue stone rubble with the other.

It was obvious what had caused Beth to be ill. They were in a small stone room, made of the same blue stone as the Transept Tower, only here the phosphorescence was brighter. Assundra recognised it as a cellar from the musty, underground tint to the air, which had been strangely lacking in the tunnels she had been in up to now. She also recognised the thick, bitter taste of the long-dead.

Assundra supposed that other than Elder Rime, these were the first bodies Bethlinda had seen in this state. Whilst this was nothing compared to the Deathguard's storage basement, the bodies here, piled like rubbish, one on top of each other, were so rotten it was sickening. Assundra had seen many times this amount of bodies during the plague, had interred people she had seen up and about a few days earlier, this was nothing new to her, but even so she was touched by the lack of care shown for the dead here. Barrows or fires were the proper place for the dead, not dank caverns.

Assundra knew there was nothing she could say, it was just a disgusting sight, so she just laid an arm on Beth's shoulders and tried to breathe through her nose. She was feeling no ill effects now, save the tightness in her chest and lungs, but that would pass. She felt a little weak, but more than that she felt ashamed. If Beth could look good, even when throwing up, why couldn't she? The stone on Beth's head glowed brightly, showing that the stone was healing her, so she must be in some pain somewhere. Assundra was glad of the stone – she hated to think of Beth in pain.

Absent-mindedly Assundra turned back to the bodies. They had not remained untouched by the years, but the elegant clothing, somehow perfectly preserved over the years, interested Assundra. Some were dressed in the simple white robes of the Elders, others in far greater finery. Looking closer, Assundra saw something odd. Leaving Bethlinda to her coughing, Assundra moved closer. Looking at what had clearly once been a woman she could tell why. Their skulls showed no sign of the terror of death, the fear of what was to come or the pain of passing as so many of the bodies she saw did – the mouths were closed, serene. Almost happy.

"It's disgusting," Beth part-choked, part-gurgled.

"I know. We can't do anything for them though…"

"I don't want to do anything for them, they did this to themselves."

Assundra turned to look curiously at Bethlinda who had in those few seconds somehow completely recovered, her face not even showing the signs of the sickness she had just endured. The Gozon Stone shimmered dully on her forehead. "They did this to themselves?"

"Yes, Sunny, they did this to themselves!" Assundra was annoyed with herself for repeating her friend, but at least it had made her smile. "These are the Elders of Stracathri. Good riddance to them all."

"Who are the others?"

"Norths," Bethlinda spat, presumably getting the last of the spittle out of her mouth. "This is the final resting place of the Norths and their servants."

Assundra found herself staring at the bodies with none of the revulsion she had previously felt. Norths! The ruling family of Ostracia for many generations, here, dead, at her feet! With less ceremony than even poor John had been given. "Which one is Lord North do you think?" she asked, turning to her friend, pleased she could at last share in some of the excitement, but Beth seemed more confused than excited, her eyes scanning the bodies in turn.

"He's not here!"

"Not here?"

Beth didn't answer her this time and Assundra shuffled her feet, waiting for her to find the man as she poked around, moving one body, strangely not all stiff as the ones in the village had been, trying to find the right one. Assundra didn't like it here, it made her feet itch. Bethlinda knew so much more about these things, Assundra felt like she was in the way.

"Look," Beth cried, pointing to some of the bodies, "that's Elspeth and Kryman…and that's Lady North!"

Beth bounded over to the far side of the tomb, which was what this place now was if it had ever been anything else, whilst Assundra took a closer look at what had been Kryman and Elspeth. The one Beth had called Kryman was dressed in a ridiculous bright scarlet tunic with equally gaudy leggings. The outfit of a nobleman, Assundra supposed; several of the other men were wearing similar attire, although they had gone for more conservative and traditional colourings. The Gifted One, Elspeth North, had been wearing a once beautiful white dress with a red cloak when she had died.

"Strange," she found herself saying aloud and Beth turned and raised her eyebrows in question. "I thought Elspeth and Kryman died fighting the outsiders, so how are they here?"

Beth blinked, then simply shrugged her shoulders. Assundra closed her mouth. Of course Beth wouldn't be interested in that. Galvarin had been right – she was surrounded by too much death, she was too curious about it. Assundra sighed – she had hoped to be able to talk more freely with Bethlinda.

Now Beth had kicked some of the bodies away, she could see a small wooden altar was at the end of the room, four bodies at its feet looking as if they were trying to crawl up its sides. The room couldn't have been more than twenty square feet and the only entrance seemed to be the one leading back to the cave.

"What are you doing?" Assundra softly asked Beth, who was crouching over the dead body of the strongest artist ever to have lived. Beth didn't seem to hear her, stroking a hand lightly along the withered body with a fascination Assundra didn't like one bit. "What are you doing?" she repeated, more sternly than she intended it to sound. Bethlinda stood up instantly and moved over to her, kissing her full on the lips. It was so unexpected that she pulled back at first.

"You know, I really think I'm getting the hang of this dramatic entrance thing."

Assundra pulled herself away from Bethlinda violently and screamed. Red eyes! "Beth!" she screamed, but Bethlinda was already rounding on the beast, fire somehow in her hands, her face darkened with fury. With a cry she launched the fiery fist at the beast, but with nothing more than a sidestep it caught Beth's arm, twisting it behind her back, before flinging her across the chamber. Beth screamed in pain as she hit the altar hard.

Assundra screamed again as the red eyes turned to her, but the scream caught in her throat. This wasn't the monster! The red eyes were the same, uncannily the same, but they were the eyes of a man, or what had once been a man. Men didn't shimmer. Men didn't glide above the ground.

"Your eyes…" Assundra blurted out, backing away, but the shimmering figure just laughed, his thin lips curling unpleasantly into a parody of a smile. Was this what had been chasing her?

"Now that's just not the way to treat guests! And after I come all the way down here just to see you! Not that it's the first time I've seen you of course,

I wouldn't want you to think that, I've been watching you for a long time. We've grown quite familiar you and I haven't we my dear?"

"Who are you?" Beth hissed, her expression filled with venom Assundra had never seen her show, but she couldn't take her eyes from the shimmering man. Was this what had been chasing her? Was this the thing that had haunted her all these years?

It never took its eyes from Assundra, though it spoke to Bethlinda. "My dear, can you not work it out? I am Kryman North! I seem to be surprising people quite a lot recently by telling them that, but really, are you that surprised? Did you really think my father would have left the future of our people to the likes of you? Elderling servants?" Chuckling, Assundra saw his corpse catch his eye. "Hmm, stranger than I thought, seeing myself dead. Still, I look happy, must be happy. Are you happy?"

Assundra recoiled as Kryman stepped closer to her.

"Don't let him touch you, Sunny!" Beth cried, but there was no need, Assundra had no intention of letting the leering, shimmering thing near her.

"What are you?" she managed to say, but her voice was shaking.

"He's a spectre. And he can't be here…"

"Now, now, lets not start on all that, I haven't come here to engage in the old philosophies and you knew I was here anyway, you've seen my sister already, haven't you my dear?"

"Seen your sister?"

Kryman laughed, a nasally, high pitched, annoying whine. Assundra felt anger begin to take over her fear. This thing wasn't anything to be scared of! He was just the same as all the men in the village – all mouth. He was just another Young Crafter. Assundra gulped as she realised Young Crafter had been part of what happened to her. He had hurt her after all.

"What are you doing here then?" Beth was snapping back at Kryman. "I presume you have your sister's permission?" It was true, Beth didn't seem to be surprised he was here at all…

"Elspeth? Oh, she doesn't know I'm here. She's probably guessed by now, but she doesn't know. I'm sure she sends her regards, though." Kryman stood staring at them for some moments. "Well, you would appear to be the Keeper, though what you are doing here I shall have to ask you later, but will you not introduce me formally to this, may I say, far more beautiful young lady?"

Her mind was too full of thoughts – was this really Kryman North? And Elspeth, the Gifted One, she was here too? What did that mean for Elder Cairns' plans? Stopping short, she remembered she had no idea what Elder Cairns' plans were. All this could be part of it! She knew he was planning to save the people, to take them out through the tunnels, but how? How was Beth planning to continue his work? There was so much she realised she hadn't asked – what were they doing here?

"I'm Assundra," was all she said in the end. She couldn't help but gasp after she spoke, fearing she'd given something away.

"I know that, my girl, I was simply after a little formality to jolly this little session along, but then I've probably seen enough of you by now, admittedly from the mildly annoying distance of death, to not need formalities. You did seem to enjoy your times in the woods with that young mason, didn't you?"

Assundra felt herself reddening, instantly looking over to Beth. To Assundra's horror, Beth was looking at the floor. She wanted to speak, to reassure Beth that Galvarin was nothing compared to her, but she couldn't think of the words to say.

"So you are what all the fuss is about!" Kryman was carrying on. Neither of them said a word. Kryman sighed. "More thrilling conversationalists; Ostracians really have lost the art of entertaining. The question you will answer is what are you lovely ladies doing in my Tower?"

"*Your* Tower? I hardly think so!"

"The weapon, is it?" Kryman ignored Bethlinda entirely, his sickly smile directed solely toward Assundra. It almost made her shiver. "We're about at that stage of things now, aren't we?"

"Things? How do you know…"

"Be quiet, Sunny!" Beth snapped, her voice harder than Assundra had ever heard it.

"I'm sure our special little girl here knows what she should say and what she shouldn't, doesn't she? Why are you involving yourself, Keeper? Perhaps I should ask why you are bringing her here now rather than waiting fort he power to be released, why you are neglecting your duties without permission? Or do you have permission?"

Beth cut in before Assundra could defend her. "She needs my help. She is an old friend, of course I agreed! Why are you here? Why is death-life here?"

Death-life? Was this what Bethlinda had been talking about in Elder Barth's chambers, what she wouldn't explain? Elder Barth had said he hoped they wouldn't have to use the blade they'd found, was this what it was to be used against?

Assundra felt a pressure inside her head and raised a hand to her temple. *"Sunny use it! Use the knife!"*

Assundra whipped her hand around to pull the blade from the scabbard, but it was gone.

"Looking for this?" Kryman asked in mock innocence, holding the scabbard by the strap, taking great care not to let the blade touch him. "You know why I am here, Keeper" the spectre replied, turning to Bethlinda. With a flick of his wrist the scabbard and blade were gone. Bethlinda's shoulder slumped.

"It's never that easy, Keeper. Now, what was I saying? Ah yes, why I'm here. Well, I'm sure you both know why I'm here or…have you not told the outsider that part? Tsch, so many secrets, so much she has to learn…"

"She is here to help her father! Nothing more!" Beth shouted back, but Assundra had seen Kryman's eyes scanning her body. She couldn't stop the anger building now.

"You should be thankful my father isn't here, he wouldn't let you talk to us like this!" she cried, furious with herself for letting her voice shake.

"Oh, I know your father quite well, we've become quite firm friends."

"You've seen my father?"

"You lie!" Beth cried, her voice growing harder and even shriller.

"I speak the truth, I left him not ten minutes ago. Seemed to be in a bad way. Really starting to show a new side to himself."

"He is in a bad way, that's why we have to help him, do you know where he is now? You have seen him?" Assundra felt the blood pump through her body more quickly – her father was still alive!

"Be quiet, Sunny!"

"But Beth, he's seen my father!" Nobody was going to change her mind; her father had to come first, even if that meant trusting this thing that had been stalking her for years.

"Don't listen to him! You don't understand, he's the one who killed Elder Cairns!"

"Well that's gone and spoilt it!" Kryman seemed genuinely annoyed she knew what he was talking about. "I had an entire play of words set out for telling you about that. Artistic link, I suppose?"

"I am the Keeper, I know what happened."

"Told you he wants to help, did he?"

"I told you, I knew myself, I haven't seen Elder Cairns for months."

"Now who lies!" Kryman laughed a sweet, sickly laugh. Assundra was filled with doubts. Nothing was going to make her doubt the woman she loved, but he said he knew something about her father! Beth had brought her this far, she could take them to the end, but what was that end? "You look a bit pale," the spectre said softly, mock concern on his face, "have I hit too close to home?"

"She's been ill!" Assundra shouted, stepping forward in front of Beth, despite her protests. She wouldn't even be here without her friend. "Your disgusting tomb is enough to make anyone sick!"

"Hard words for a pretty lady…"

"What do you care anyway? You'll never have her!"

"What?" Assundra tried to turn to look at Bethlinda, confused.

"Have her? That would be rather difficult given my situation, don't you think?" He laughed again. More and more, Assundra was reminded of the Crafters – men constantly blabbering on, full of their own importance, covering their malice with sarcasm. Another doubt bubbled its way to the surface of her thoughts – her father would hate a man such as this. If it was Kryman North, though, if he really was as powerful as the stories said…could he help her father? Could he cure him?

"So let me just set out the history for our young outsider friend here," Kryman said, full of condescending pride.

Assundra wanted to scream that she wasn't an outsider, that she was sick of people saying she was, that she was as Ostracian as her father was, but the knot in her stomach stopped her. She said nothing.

"Here's what happened," Kryman went on. "Step one, Elder Costrange, puppet and moron that he was, splits the Elder Council, forcing the rebel Elders to build the Transept Tower, am I right?" Beth was silent. "Actually, it doesn't matter what you say, Keeper I know I am right, I was there. Of course, the only problem with that was, Elder Costrange had died many years before. The Elder Costrange who split the Elder Council, who ensured none of you were prepared to deal with the invasion and certainly not the plague that he knew full well was to come afterwards, was none other than my brother, Carstan."

"You lie!" Beth shouted, but something about her manner wasn't sure. "In any case, the rebel Elders had no choice but to split – the Council were nothing more than your puppets!"

"Yes, they were," Kryman agreed, "but there was a reason for that – you see, Assundra, my father knew about my brother's actions but could not bring himself to dispose of his first born son, not when his opinion of his other heirs was so low. No, my father had another plan, his grand weapon, but we managed to put a stop to that."

Beth was silent, her mouth set as if her teeth were clenched in fury. "What weapon?" Assundra ventured, sick of the hints, sick of the pronouncements. "It seems to me that everyone has these grand plans to save us, but I haven't yet heard any specific plans as to how anyone is going to do it!"

Seemingly surprised at her outburst, Kryman was silent for a moment, but only for a moment. "Well done, Assundra," he said mockingly, "but of course, the plan I speak of was really very simple. Wait for the invasion then use the weapon."

"What weapon?" Assundra shouted again.

Kryman laughed. "That is what the rebel Elders failed to comprehend, my dear, there was no weapon! The weapon was artistry itself, the weapon was the power chambers beneath Stracathri, the weapon was the Transept Tower. The weapon, my dear, was the Ostracian people!"

Beth gasped. "That's horrible…" she exclaimed, disgust on her face.

"Will someone tell me what the hells it is you're talking about?" Assundra tried to force the anger down but was too late. She felt the sorcery leave her body, but nothing seemed to happen. Looking up, she saw that neither

Kryman nor Bethlinda seemed to have noticed anything. Assundra breathed a sigh of relief. She had to learn to control this!

"With Stracathri, the Transept Tower and the Ostracian blood artists all linked, Sunny, they would have made an army of Gifted Ones."

"My sister would not allow it, of course," Kryman said, the first traces of his mood shifting entering his tone. "I could never prove it was her and not Carstan who tipped the outsiders off."

"She wouldn't…"

"Keeper, you do not know my sister! She loved her people, yes, but she has never countenanced a rival. Simon had better watch out for that once the third trigger is pulled," he said with a chuckle, but was quickly serious again. "She knew nothing of the outsider plans for a plague, you see. She thought she could handle them on her own, but she reckoned without their sorcerors."

"You always underestimated sorcery," Bethlinda accused, but there was only sadness in her voice, no anger.

"Yes, well, that is past. Isn't it?" Assundra shrank back again as now both Bethlinda and Kryman turned to her.

Assundra's mouth filled with the taste of nothing, without warning, making her spit. At once Kryman turned his head, as if listening, suddenly looking genuinely worried. There was a faint crash somewhere above their heads.

"What did you do?" he hissed at Assundra, the first sign of a genuine emotion on his shimmering face. Fear.

"Oh, Sunny…" Bethlinda's face was full of disappointment.

"What? What have I done?" She started to panic. Fear and disappointment. *Gods*, what had she done? What had she let out?

"Sorcery was the last piece of the puzzle they needed! What did you do?"

"She cannot control it," Beth replied plaintively for her, "she has not been taught."

Kryman let out a frustrated laugh. "Well isn't that marvellous! I've been sitting here enjoying this lovely diversion with you and all the time she's unwittingly giving them the final damn piece! We have no time, Keeper, you have to trust me! Whether you want us to have it or not, you do not want Elspeth to have this power!"

The next crash was louder and the earth seemed to shake slightly. Long trails of dust fell from the ceiling.

"We have to stop that." Kryman was growing agitated. "Let's go the way I came in." Kryman walked over to the wall, seeming to select his spot carefully. "Oh, by the way," he added, turning back to Bethlinda with a sneer, "Elder Cairns is not dead. Your artistic link is perhaps not as mutually inclusive as you might think!" Turning quickly, Kryman glided through the wall. Assundra was shocked to see Bethlinda leap to her feet and run right after him, not sparing Assundra even a look, straight through the wall.

"Beth! Wait!" Assundra flung herself at the space in the wall where they had passed, passing through what was clearly an illusion. "Beth!" she cried again, tears in her eyes, "I didn't mean to! I'm sorry!"

She ran off down the tunnel, down which she could hear the Bethlinda's footsteps. She ran having no idea at all what she was running towards. She didn't care. She only knew she was running after Bethlinda.

CHAPTER 28

He was small. The world seemed huge, too large. Too many things were out of his reach. Even the puny wooden structure that held him in, barely four paces wide, was too tall for him to climb, too strong for his chubby little arms to break. He tried to call some power, but there was nothing there save the pocket of air that now forced itself from his throat.

"Boy! Don't be rude! No!" A woman leered over the cage, eyes wild with fury, scaring him. He recognised the face and he tried to call her by name, but all he could produce was a meaningless drawl. All that brought was the need to shout, and a cry came from his lips unbidden, wetness staining his vision. "Not now, flower!" And the lady was walking away, his outstretched arms remaining empty. He tried to say he was sorry, that he only wanted to make her smile, that he liked it when she smiled, but instead provided an imbecilic gurgle.

She was talking to a man on the other side of the room. Pulling himself to his shaky feet by the bars of the cage, he pushed his head to a gap so he could see. The man was wearing a white robe, from neck to toe, and he seemed familiar too but not in the same way as the woman. "Not now," she was saying, to the man this time, but he didn't seem to understand. Why was he angry? He let out another cry without meaning to as the man grabbed the lady's head and shoved his lips onto hers.

The man left soon afterwards but he had already become transfixed in the meantime by a wooden painted brick with symbols upon each side. Was it some kind of artistic artefact? Again, he tried to call some power, just a simple identification exploration, but it only resulted in him picking the brick up and bashing it repeatedly against the soft, blanketed floor of his prison.

"Come on, flower," the lady said; lifting him bodily from the cage with seemingly no effort. "I'm sorry, I'm sorry, flower." The wetness was in her eyes now and he reached out with his hand to brush it away. "No, flower, not my eye," she said, a smile coming to her lips as she removed his finger. He felt itchy, nervous, and began to fling his arms and leg around, to try and get rid of the feeling. "Sh," she said softly, "Mummy's here now, flower."

Mummy? His mother?

Then there was blackness. Voices sounded around his head; a head that felt too big on a giant, ungainly, bony, broken body.

"Is he awake?"

"No, he's just feverin'."

"What the hells has happened to his face?"

"I don't know, but I know those things had something to do with it. Who'd have thought Mary Archer was telling the truth about something for once? I don't know how Elder Oldershaw can trust them."

"He trusted Crafters, is it really any surprise he trusts demons?"

The man grunted agreement. "His face does look bloody awful though. Look, some of these are old scars, they aren't open wounds…"

"Never mind that, I shouldn't have brought it up, what if he can hear us? What'll we *do*?"

There was a pause. "Take him to my place, and go and get Broadside."

The voice was familiar; high-pitched and old. It was Jolly, the keeper of the alehouse. Cairns tried to speak, but again the words would not come, but not because his mouth didn't know how to form them; because his mouth wouldn't work at all. He was lying on a hard floor, that was all he could tell.

"I'll let you thank me later," the dead thing had said before… before it had all happened.

The memories of the pain brought back the agony itself, and Cairns' mind closed once more.

And he was back in the cage, which seemed slightly smaller this time. He stood, without the aid of the bars, looking towards the door. There was something wrong, but he didn't know what. His behind was dry, his stomach was full and he wasn't hurt, but he could tell there was something not right.

He was lifted bodily from behind and he gave a squeal of delight as he was turned, his whole body excited that he was going to get to see the lady who called him 'flower'; the lady who inexplicably made him smile by doing nothing other than being there.

"Now, boy, it is time to begin your lessons." It was not his Mummy. It was the man in the white robe. This man didn't make him want to smile, he made him want to run away. The sounds he could not control came from his mouth, even though he knew that it was the worst thing he could do. The man's lined face creased further into a frown and his lips moved in a way that made him squirm in the man's arms even more. Then the sounds stopped, his mouth sealed by something that wasn't there. The feelings inside him pushed the sounds from his body up to his mouth, but he couldn't let them out. His mouth was almost full, the sounds filling it, pushing their way into his nostrils and filling them too. He was going to burst! He kicked out with his legs as he felt the redness come to his face, couldn't the man see? His Mummy would have seen. She wouldn't have hurt him to begin with.

Then the man's frown furrowed into concern and his lips moved again. The scream leapt from him until he could breathe again, and then was silent, his body seeming to shrink back into itself, understanding what the man wanted.

"Good," the man said, sealing him into a badly made wooden high chair he hadn't seen before. He felt a splinter dig into his leg and opened his mouth to scream again, to alert someone to what had happened, but the man snarled. He shut his mouth, turning his head to his left, looking towards the door, but a hand grabbed it, jerking it back to face the man again. This time he didn't try to cry out.

"She's not coming back, you hear?" the man was shouting, "she's never coming back! You're mine now!"

And then Cairns saw the familiar blackness of his mind. There were no voices, no surroundings, he felt like he was floating. What had made him think of his mother? And why had she gone away? Cairns realised he had never known. He had known the man in the robe had been responsible but he had never known what happened. Was she dead? He had no way of knowing. Ostracia's dead in those days had been burned; the only traces being memories of them.

He would never know now. The only man who could tell him, the man in the robe, the man who had taken him in as an orphan, was definitely dead, Cairns knew that for sure. He had killed him.

More importantly, *he had withheld those memories*!

When those first few tests on the withholding process had been completed, when he had been needlessly and inconveniently distracted by his mother's birthday, he had withheld the memories of her from himself. He had spent too long in fruitless mourning when things needed to be done and it had been so many years since she had left him that he had decided to rid himself of the problem at its source. There was nothing that could break a withholding on oneself until that person removed it themselves.

Kryman! "I'll let you thank me later," the spectre had said. With no effort at all Kryman had removed a self-withholding – that meant he had power far in advance of that which Cairns could command! With the power of Stracathri backing them they were too strong for him. Too strong for now. When it was over, when the power was his, then he would indeed thank Kryman properly, over a number of years.

Cairns wondered why he was not unconscious, deliberately putting his mother's smiling face from his mind. Not out of his mind, he no longer wanted to forget her, but it was not for now, he had to concentrate on his duty. His own concerns could wait. What had his mind been playing at? He could see no connection whatever between his mother's disappearance and what it was his duty to do, now, for the village.

Somewhere outside his mind, his body was dropped heavily to the floor. He hadn't even been aware of being carried. It was another hard floor, this one cold. Good, that was another sensation returning! When Broadside administered the correct dose, as Cairns had instructed, he would recover quickly.

Then he had to think about why Kryman had spared his life.

The jolt had brought the surroundings back to him and he heard the voices once more. "Well, where is he?"

"Can't find him, Jolly."

"Bloody hell…well, what are we going to do now?"

"I don't know, it was your idea to bring him here!"

"No-one saw you, did they?"

"No, they're all up in the old city, not a soul around – would have thought Oldershaw would have set watch."

"*Elder* Oldershaw!" the second voice said.

"He's no Elder to me! Not any more, not if he's with them, not after what he did to Cairns."

"But still…" The man was afraid. And he should be – Cairns needed Broadside! And soon. He needed the powders! There was no time to have another life taken to help him, he couldn't have swallowed the blood anyway, that would have to wait. He would have to use alchemic artistry. It was a subtle blend that he and Broadside had worked out in the man's youth. The alchemist would not remember now, of course, the withholding saw to that, but it had been valuable work nonetheless.

The voices were speaking more quietly and Cairns tried to send his ears out to listen, but the agony burst at once, his mind falling back into the blackness.

He was being picked up again; but this time he could tell it was a man. His skin burned where the man's hands gripped him roughly, pulling him from the big wooden chair.

"Coochie coochie coo!"

His wide eyes were staring into the glowing scarlet eyes of Kryman North. The spectre laughed at him as he realised he was no longer small, but a full-grown man, held fast in the air by the spectre's grip. Kryman began to squeeze and Cairns could hear, no feel his bones crack and splinter into his flesh as the giant spectre pushed his hands together through Cairns' body, crushing his heart as if it were paper.

"Well, are you going to say thank you?"

Elder Cairns screamed.

The blackness was waiting for him, concealing Kryman's laughing face, which he knew would still be there, waiting for him to be weak enough to allow him to appear again. Whatever the spectre had done, and not knowing what it was drove more spikes of irritation into his mind, was undoing his ability to bypass sleep. He had forgotten how troublesome and mind-numbing he found these night visions and for the first time he could recall he yearned for a return to the sleepless recovery he had grown accustomed to.

"It's getting worse, tell them to hurry up!" They were still there! Why had they done nothing?

"There's nowhere left to look!"

"What about the sheds round the back?"

"You've got the only key, Jolly."

"Well, come on then, he'll have us roasting for the next feast if we don't hurry."

Cairns was thinking how practical an idea that would be when the wave of pain smashed itself at his body. He was sinking into the blackness before he was even aware of it, but Kryman didn't appear, there was only the pain. He had nothing left to stop it; his power recovered quickly, especially with the powders, but fighting people as strong as the Norths had taken his reserves back down to empty. There was no stream to tap now. Normally, as the artistic exhaustion hit, Cairns could use his skills to create a mental and physical reef of energy, like protective stones for the wave to break against, but this one just smashed against his frail form full on.

And he was a child.

It was after Jon had been brought to live with him. He knew that because the house was empty. His mother's things were gone, along with his mother. The house was quiet, but still he didn't feel safe. The man, his uncle, would be back soon, but Cairns just sat here, with the one dress of his mother's he had left in his hands. He was eight years old and he knew, now, that his mother would not be walking through the door but he didn't know what had happened. He hadn't wanted to know what happened, not before now, not before his uncle's mind had begun to turn to drivel.

He curled the dress around in his fingers as the door latch rattled, and the young Cairns lost his confidence, at once thrusting the dress back under the loose floorboard where he had hidden it. When someone died in Ostracia it was the custom to give their belongings away, as he, himself, had been given to the Elders' Council. She had hidden the dress for him, the dress she had worn when giving birth to him, showing him where the floorboard was regularly when he had been very young, imprinting its location into his mind. At eight, he knew now that his mother had hidden the dress for him because she had known she would be leaving him.

"Where are you, boy?"

"In here, sir," he answered at once – even the slightest delay would prompt the back of his uncle's substantial hand. There was no point in lying either, his master would be able to tell. Cairns would be in trouble for even being in this room, let alone for the red puffing under his eyes that seemed to be determined to give him away. His uncle despised tears.

"What in the name of the gods are you doing in there? Again!" his tutor roared, slamming his bulk into the door, which cracked into the wall behind, the top hinge giving out under the pressure, leaving the buckled wreck unusable. *That was his mother's door!*

"Nothing, sir," the young Cairns replied, his defiance returning, looking his mother's brother directly in the eye.

"I will ask you one more time, boy." There was no shouting now, what happened next would be methodical, slow, sure, just like it always was.

"I wasn't doing anything."

Cairns fell to the floor under the force of the backhanded blow, his head reeling, making the room spin about him, refusing to whimper.

"Control it!" his uncle screamed, before his boot made full and free contact with Cairns' behind, sending him rolling across the floor. "Find where the problem is and solve it! Go into yourself!"

His uncle had been trying to teach him the control for months, how to heal himself, how to push back the fear and the pain. After weeks of beatings, Cairns had but once done so, raising a rare smile to the snide features of his tutor as he had stood straight up after being knocked down by a broom handle. He tried to remember how he had done it, what he had found in himself that allowed the control. He could reach inside himself easily enough, but it all seemed like a jumble of red, pulsing shapes, he couldn't make any of it out. Cairns was trying to tell his younger self where to look, how to look; that you had to find the flow of artistry and attach yourself to it, allow the power to lead you where you wanted it to take you, but the boy was only a child and didn't understand.

"Too slow!" The second kick knocked something into place; there it was! The unmistakeable flow from the source, rushing towards the throat to be let out, the child's way of using artistry for defence. Cairns was drawing back from the boy now, a powdery taste on his lips, as he watched the child stand, no trace of pain, nor fear, on his face, whilst his uncle, clapping, delivered words of praise that left the boy entirely unmoved.

"Where the hells have you been?" the voice that wasn't Jolly shouted.

"Shut your mouth," was the only reply Broadside gave. Cairns felt his mouth forced open, a thick, ungainly finger shoved into his mouth and his tongue pushed down. Liquid poured down his throat. He wanted to gag, but nothing in his body would move. The liquid filled his mouth and nose for a few moments, but soon there was no more. He felt his mouth unceremoniously slammed shut and fierce murmurings begin, voices all around his head.

One murmured the same thing time and again. *"I have her! Elder, I have her, what should I do? Where are you? What's happening? I can feel…"*

The Keeper! Cairns searched for her voice amongst the others again, but it was gone.

"I'll let you thank me later," he heard a voice call clearly amongst the whispers.

The blackness hit his mind like a fist and this time stayed there. Cairns bristled with anger – had Kryman spared his life only to humiliate him like this? To have him suffer the ignominy of powerlessness?

Nothing throbbed through his blood as it should, nothing secured his knowledge of himself, what he could do. Elder Cairns became aware of a hunger. A deep-rooted cry for succour, not like his need for powders, nor like his desperate, familiar need to save his people, not even a hunger for the replenishing power of blood – this was a hunger for the very ingredient to make him the man to do all of those things.

Cairns hungered for power and he hungered for it because he could sense it. Something had shifted in the old city, something had been released and Cairns could feel its un-tethered tentacles thrashing around, searching for something to attach itself to, something to feed off as it would feed off it, something to share in power. It was huge – a well of artistry larger than any Cairns had seen, but then it had had a century of dormancy to build, to grow, to develop and it had done so.

Now it had been awoken and it was only waiting for someone to come and claim it.

Elder Cairns opened his eyes.

CHAPTER 29

Her hands were clawing at him, tearing small lumps of flesh from the backs of his shoulders in their frenzy. Simon felt the lust grow as his hands met the welcoming curves of Elspeth's breasts for the first time. He could hardly breathe, stupid little breaths coming too short, his body shaking, the ache down below almost bursting. Gods, this was far superior to any feeling he had once felt around the farmer's daughter. This was a real woman! The pain of the fingers of one of her hands in the wounds she had created only made him want to go harder into her, to numb the pain through pleasure.

"I need a rest," Simon gasped with a chuckle and was mildly surprised when Elspeth pushed him away from her at once, tossing him aside him like a sack. "What did you do that for?"

"Do you know the names of the stars?" she said coldly, standing, the dying light glistening off her naked body, her perfect body, through the cracks in the walls.

"What?" he said, unable to think clearly, increasingly feeling anything but an urge to rest rise in him as he watched her.

"The stars move around us, just like the sun does, and each of them has a name."

"Stars don't move, they're always in the same place every night. And you can't even see them tonight, never mind if we were outside!" Simon's manoeuvred himself into a flat position, enjoying the cooling air on his hot skin.

"You don't even know what you've lost, what we've all lost." Elspeth spoke softly, her back to Simon. Her hair moved in the breeze, the dying light both taking and enhancing its colour. Her whole body seemed to glow.

"We've lost our power, I know that, but we'll get it back, you and me. Together."

"Power?" Elspeth snorted. "It is far more than that which we have lost. When my father did what he did all those years ago, regardless of the curse it left on his family and the other unfortunates, he did so for a good reason, he truly did. But all he has achieved is the death of our culture."

"You can thank the Elders for that," Simon grunted, "they make sure everyone knows their place, and that they never stray from it."

"That is not their crime, Simon. Everything does have its place, even those stars, they follow the same path every day, uncomplaining and unnerved, simply doing their job. That is the secret of the order of their lives, it is why they never suffer torment or pain, their order of things is complete in its unmoving steadfastness. No, it is something more than that which we have lost but you are right, the Elders are to blame."

"Well, are you going to tell me what it is?"

"Patience, for one thing." Now it was Simon's turn to snort. "Patience and concern. From what I've seen of Ostracia today, all pursuit of knowledge is regarded with suspicion rather than joy. All actions dependent on the reward those actions will gain, nothing for the sheer development of the individual. After we did so much to encourage them!"

"I'm telling you, it's the Elders! Pursuit of knowledge, as you call it, is forbidden, most of us have never read a book."

"Knowledge is not only taken from books, it comes from observation, from talk, from curiosity. From not waiting to be told everything from beginning to end. From a desire to unravel the mysteries of life oneself. From heart, desire and courage, not a desire to remain a spoon-fed child forever."

Simon laughed exasperatedly. "Then you are in favour of the Crafters and what they have done?"

Elspeth turned, her face set hard. "Yes, Simon, I do. It does not make them any the less wrong in what they did, but that is why our family always guided our people, steered them clear of the pitfalls and dangers of the gaining of knowledge. Remember, Simon, in my father's time, there were thousands of Ostracians with more artistic power than even your Elders can wield now – most Ostracians were blood artists after all – yet it was the most peaceful time in Ostracia's history. With knowledge comes security, with security comes a lack of need for material gain for one's actions, but that can only be gained by having the desire for that security and to take control of oneself and be the best one can be.

"Now you do not even know the names of the stars." Elspeth turned away from him again, picking her dress up from the floor. Simon was saddened as she draped it over herself, for all she still looked beautiful in the jewelled, fine silk dress, she was no longer naked. "Yet, it is more than that still," she continued sadly. Simon wasn't sure she even knew what she was talking about now, a strange, distant look had come over her. "Ostracians have their purpose, however banal their simple lives have become, their sole purpose is to keep going, to stay alive until now, which they have done. In that respect the Elders have succeeded."

"Succeeded?" Simon shouted incredulously.

"Yes," his Elspeth snapped, "succeeded. Where they failed is in committing a far more serious crime – they have robbed Ostracia itself of its purpose! In saving our people, they have destroyed them. The stars circle as normal, safe in the knowledge that their purpose is fulfilled, but Ostracians eat, shit, sleep and die. Nothing more. Their purpose should have to further humanity, to study and learn how to open the doors of the mind and of their own power, to grow and evolve as a race, but now their only purpose is not to die, whilst all the time living only a life of a spoon-fed child."

"What are you talking about?" Simon finally asked, getting to his feet himself. Feeling self-conscious as Elspeth's eyes scanned down his naked body, her lips curling into something Simon could not decide was a smile or a mocking grin, he reached for his own stained, dirty clothes and dressed. When dressed, able to smell the clothes and seeing himself next to Elspeth's immaculately dressed figure, he felt more self-conscious still.

"I think you're wrong," he went on. "The Elders tell us what our purpose is; blacksmith, mason or gardener, or whatever, there's nobody left who remembers anything else, remembers how to be free! They all live to follow the Elders' instructions because there's no other option, to disobey gets you locked up!" He didn't understand why they were talking about this – if they weren't going to lie together any more, then surely they should be doing something to stop Elder Oldershaw's insane plan to attack the outsiders, not sit here debating life. He could help if only she'd tell him what she was doing.

His resolve softened when he saw the sadness etched onto her gentle features. "Then the Elders must never get the power."

"I thought we'd already established that! What is this really about?"

Elspeth sighed softly. "All that you needed to stop the plague, to heal the rifts in our society, to mend our people and defy what the outsiders had done to us was all around you. For a century my brother and I have watched you accept more and more control from your Elders, retreat further and further into yourselves, using the excuse of the pain of the invasion, of the deaths. We have watched you relinquish your minds and your bodies to those controlling you to the extent where now, you don't even have any idea of what your strengths of mind and body are.

"Listen…" he began, putting his hand out to her, but Elspeth shrugged him off.

"When I was six, my father took me to learn the names of those stars you dismiss the importance of so quickly. It took me three days, without sleep, sealed in a room with the eldest Elder, only water and dry bread to keep me going. But I did it."

Simon scowled. "Your father should have been taught a lesson."

"That's my point," Elspeth replied with sharpness, "it's what you don't seem to understand. It was me that was being taught the lesson, and I was glad to learn it! My father had me stand beside him at the feast the night I finished, naming the constellations and the stars you could see through the open stones in the roof of the Summer Hall. There were so many people there, learned men from across the kingdoms and freeholds of the outside, men from where my mother had been from. They had all seemed so proud."

"Outsiders. They may have seemed proud but they were probably plotting our imprisonment even then."

"Not the learned men, they were no more than pawns in their leaders' games."

"What is it you're saying?" Simon snapped, growing weary of the nostalgia.

"I'm saying it's a shame we've lost all that. That's all. It's a shame we lost it and now it's too late to get it back. I'm wondering, Simon, why we are bothering to save our people when our people have already been destroyed."

"It was the outsiders who destroyed it! Not us!"

"You're snapping again, Simon, you should really control that temper."

"Please, look, I'm sorry we don't all meet up to your high North standards, but surely that doesn't mean our race isn't worth saving!"

"I think maybe you should all deal with it yourself this time. It's time you learned something, the gods know the Norths have tried to show you enough times!"

"Die, scum of Lamia!"

The man was upon him before Simon had even heard him approach. Instinctively Simon drew power to his throat and spat it, an undirected, unformed artistic attack, but enough to knock the man backwards, just as he was about to bring his longsword down.

"Simon, stay down!" Elspeth said, quite calmly, walking to stand between the man and Simon. Almost casually, he saw her tear a nail down her palm, letting the blood flow. The instant she flicked her hand forward, the man's head exploded, blood pouring from burst eye sockets, slack-jawed mouth and nostrils. He slumped, dead, his sword making more of a sound as it struck the floor than his body did.

"What the…" Simon began, before realising he was winded and coughed for breath.

"The fool has started too early," Elspeth hissed. "Look at the man, Simon what does his body tell you."

Simon wanted to say that it told him how powerful and magnificent Elspeth was, but he could tell from her stern manner that wasn't what she wanted to hear, so he looked at the blood-soaked corpse, the red stains spreading everywhere under the shining amour…armour! "He's an outsider!" he cried.

Elspeth grunted. "So you haven't totally lost your analytical skills. You are right, of course, his insignia is that of the Caraizan people, those who patrol our borders. I'm sure you did not know that, as you will not have sought out the knowledge, simply accepting what you were told that all outsiders were the same, but the Caraizans were perhaps the most reasonable of all the outsiders. They provided us with much of our stock willingly, they understood. Or at least they used to."

Simon was incredulous. "Elspeth, there are outsiders here! We have to warn people!"

"No, Simon, we do not. It is not our concern."

"What? How can it not be our concern, these are our people! We are the Gifted Ones, we have to help them!"

"No," Elspeth repeated. Though it did look like she was making to leave as she retrieved her shawl. "My brother will be here soon, they are not far away. We have to somewhere to go."

"We can't just leave them to…"

"Simon," she snapped, moving to stand right in front of him, her nose pressing against his. "I told you I would have need of you and you accepted that, are you now saying that you will not help me? If you will not help me then I have no need of you, is that something you want?"

"No," he said before he even thought about it. "But Elspeth, if the outsiders are coming…"

"We have to stop them. We will not stop them by alerting Elder Oldershaw to the folly of his actions! With any luck, he and his followers will be wiped out. It will save us the job."

"Elspeth, what are we doing? What is the plan?"

"I cannot tell you," she replied, but she kissed him lightly. Simon felt stirrings from his manhood again. "A century has been building towards this. An entire century of planning, of watching, of making sure everything is right and ready. The state of our people is something we will have to attend to afterwards, if we can. I hope we can, Simon, I really do, but there is no point in fighting the invaders, in alerting the people, if we do not have the means of saving them."

"What means?" Simon was growing more and more furious, why wouldn't she trust him? She had just lain with him, didn't that mean she liked him?

"Simon, we have no time. My brother is now waiting for us - be quiet and follow me."

"Elspeth, why won't you trust me!" he pleaded, pulling her back as she turned to leave.

"Do you ever stop whining? By the gods – if it wasn't how *mean* the little villagers were being to you, it was how *mean* Assundra was being to you." She rounded on him now, the bright blue of her eyes blazing in the moonlight; this was the Elspeth from the Forest and it made him take a step back. "And now I'm being *mean* to you! Grow up, Simon! I do not need a child to help me, I need a man!"

"How dare you! After all we've…"

"I am the Gifted One, I dare what I like! It is you who should watch his tongue, *boy*!"

He felt the pressure in his throat, his blood turning to steam in his veins. "Shut up! Don't make me do this."

"Do what, *my love*? You would do well to do nothing other than as you are told. It's been a while since my brother and I had a little pet to play with, I think he'd enjoy having a new toy."

What was happening? Why was she being like this? She had been so tender, so attentive in their lovemaking, she had told him she loved him back, so why was she being so different now? "Mmph…" was all Simon could manage; the artistry was stuck in his throat; a leering smile all over Elspeth's beautiful face. They were all the same! All the same!

"You can't even spit a little ball of boy's power at me!" she crowed, walking closer to him, until he could feel her breath on his cheeks. And now he was afraid. "You should be afraid of me, that is a perfectly understandable feeling considering what I could do to you, but surely the idea of being my brother's pet does not scare you?"

He swallowed the ball down, hard, where it burned in his throat. "What could he do to me? He is nothing."

"He could kill you in an instant."

"Ha!"

"He could scald the flesh from your body without a moment's thought."

"That is not true!"

"Oh, but it is!" Elspeth was suddenly on him and he fell back hard, crying out as his spine jerked on the impact; and she stayed on him, pinning him down. Surely she was not this strong! He tried to lift his arms, but they were held fast. Yet it was her eyes that surprised him more. They shone, as had the eyes of the dark Elspeth that had been in his mind when he had first left the village.

"You are not trying, Simon! I have no time to nursemaid you through this! You have to grow up *now*! It would take my brother but a moment for him to burn the life away from you." Elspeth's eyes, then her entire figure turned a darker shade. "Like this!"

Simon arched his back as Elspeth's hands blazed into the skin of his shoulders. His nostrils were met with the smell of burnt fabric. "No!" Something was happening inside. He did not want to be burned! He did not want this, so he had to stop it. The urge to do just that was like a small ball in the pit of his stomach. With a single thought, Simon lashed his mind to the ball and brought it up until it lodged in his throat. He coughed the magic out of his body, where it hit Elspeth in the chest. To his surprise, the Gifted One flew back through the air. The pressure left his insides in an instant and she got up, laughing.

Pulling himself to his feet, he called more power, poised to let it out again.

She rushed to him before he was ready and was on him again, pulling at his head, yanking it towards her. Simon braced himself for pain, but instead felt her soft lips on him hard. "You see the power you have," she half-whispered, half-kissed. "That's what I've been waiting for, my love. I had to force it out of you, there's no time left. I'm sorry. No," she said quickly as he made to swallow the power back down, "you need it, do not get rid of it. Hold it there, have it ready at all times. You will learn how to use it naturally."

"But I can't control it," he whispered back, planting his own kisses on her neck, hoping they hid the trembling fear that was coursing through his hands.

"You are not like the others, Simon, you do not need to be spoon-fed instructions on how to do everything. You are a Gifted One! Do not hold back from that gift, let it loose as you did just then, let it ride with your emotions, become part of you and you will learn how to master it, I promise! Now, we must go, Kryman is waiting for us."

She pulled back from him. "Do you trust me?" she asked simply, her smile causing tiny dimples to appear at the corners of her mouth.

"With my life," he replied instantly. She smiled and laughed, pulling him away from the place he would remember forever, from the events he would remember forever. He just hoped they would not be their last. She wanted him to use the power, to hold it ready – she did not know that he had hardly used any to send her crashing across the room. He could have killed her, like he had already killed his father.

This power was nothing to want, nothing to be proud of. It scared him. It scared him because it brought death.

Elspeth turned to him and smiled as they emerged into the light of the setting sun. "When this is over," she said, with fire in her eyes, "the power you have now is going to seem like child's play! We are going to have it all, Simon!"

As she pulled him along, laughing, Simon felt sick.

CHAPTER 30

How could the man have been so stupid?

"What are the forces?"

"We have no idea," Broadside replied, his voice shaking for the first time in Cairns' memory. "There have only been a few. The thing…the North has taken care of them all so far."

Elder Cairns cursed. "Has he fired the cannons yet?"

"No, thankfully, he seems preoccupied."

Cairns frowned. "With what? It was your assertion, Broadside, that this urge to take revenge had consumed Elder Oldershaw, that he was rushing into a confrontation?"

"He is, but…"

"But what?" Cairns roared, acutely aware of the fact that his impact was impacted itself greatly by the fact he was not strong enough to stand. Artistry would not help with that, not with the cocktail of powders running through his system, diverting his reserves to where they were needed. It would be some time before he could effect artistry again. Cairns felt wrong without it. He felt less.

Broadside still shifted uncomfortably in front of him. Cairns had been propped on the bed of Broadside's cottage, his head lolling uncomfortably against the brick wall. The cottage was much like the rest of them, only all along the walls were thin cabinets Broadside had presumably appropriated from the Council Chambers, each filled with various alchemic equipment – phials, alembics, retorts, even a few mini-fires with brackets attached. There were jars of herbs and liquids too, some of which Cairns guessed was giving the room the faint, but definitely detectable, stench it had.

"I can't tell you any more than something seems to have caught his attention, he hasn't been seen for a number of hours. The North and the boy, too."

Cairns scowled – what a disappointment Simon had turned out to be. There could be no redemption for such betrayal. Simon would pay for it with his life. "You know where they are at least I take it?"

Broadside shuffled again. Cairns was growing increasingly impatient with the fat oaf – what had he been doing the whole time Cairns had been unconscious? None of them not Broadside, not Jolly, not one of them had achieved anything! They didn't even know where Galvarin was! Eventually the fat man shuffled closer, offending Cairns' senses further with both his stinking body odour and the arrogance of assuming he could have Cairns' confidence.

"They were last seen in Stracathri, Elder," the man whispered, with a wink that made Cairns want to rip the man's eyelid off.

"Stracathri? Have you lost your mind?"

Broadside was not offended, merely shaking his head before *interrupting* Cairns as he was about to speak! "Elder, we were wrong! Stracathri was not lost, it was under our noses the whole time!" Cairns was speechless. Did Broadside really have the nerve to be telling Cairns to his face that he was wrong? "There is an oubliette, Elder, in the west of the old city, none of us knew it was there! It's Stracathri, Elder, it has to be!"

"It has to be," Cairns repeated slowly. Broadside blinked. "Have you seen this oubliette then, Broadside?"

The man blinked again. "No, Elder, I…"

"Someone else saw it and told you about it?"

"He…that is, my man saw them go in – the Elder, Simon and the two spectres, it must mean…"

"It means there is something there, yes. It does not mean that something is Stracathri!" Indeed, Cairns thought, it meant something far worse. It was more than likely where the weapon was located! "Who is watching them now?"

Another blink. Cairns felt a surge of pain through his arms, but pain meant life! "Well, that is…"

"Is nobody watching them, Broadside?"

"Look, Elder, I don't think you understand what has been happening here! I only had one man to send and he came back here to tell us the news, tell us what he'd found, there was nobody else to send! You have nobody left, Elder! Everyone has gone over to Oldershaw after they saw…after what happened," he quickly corrected himself. "Elder, they have *spectres* with them! You told them spectres did not exist, that alone has given Oldershaw leverage over anything you would say!"

Cairns smiled at Broadside. "You are still loyal to me, are you not?"

Without hesitation the man replied. "Of course I am Elder! What a question." Broadside smiled too. That sealed it for Cairns.

He raised a hand, flexing the fingers experimentally. "Broadside, do you know the secret of artistry?"

"No, Elder," the man said in a hushed voice, his eyes wide.

Cairns stretched his other arm. "Do you know the secrets of the Elders?"

"No, Elder!" the man said with even more excitement. "I hope that I have shown enough desire to learn!"

Now he flexed his arms at the elbows. The pain shot through his upper arms, making him wince, but he kept moving them. He could almost feel it now! "Come close," he said softly, raising his eyes to meet Broadside's eager, boggling gaze as the fat man did as he was bid. "Do you want to know how I have amassed so much power, Broadside?"

The man nodded feverishly. "Elder, all my life I have wanted to follow in your footsteps, to learn the secrets of the world! I have made advances beyond many in alchemy, yes, but that is nothing compared to artistry! My father always wanted me to become an Elder. Anything you need from me, Elder, you have it!"

Cairns smiled with genuine amusement. "Have you been consoling Max's wife, Broadside?"

The man's eyes boggled even further if that were possible, but not for long. Cairns grabbed the man's head and with an ecstasy of expectation from the gnawing hunger in his belly, sank his teeth into Broadside's neck. The man screamed, louder than Cairns had anticipated, but that scream soon turned to a gurgling rattle. The blood flowed deep into Cairns' mouth, almost too much to swallow. His body almost laughed in manic delight at the surge of strength that began to pour from Broadside into Cairns.

Two men burst into the cottage, rusty axes at hand, but Cairns simply shot them a look and they stopped where they stood. Their arrival had diverted his attention, though and Cairns realised all too late that Broadside was dead. He took his teeth and tongue from the man's neck and tried to pull back but it was too late – Broadside's bulk was falling, pinning him to the wall. He found his face thrust into soft, ample breasts as Broadside's entire bulk came to rest on him, pressing on his ribcage.

"Get him off me!" he managed to croak, his lungs feeling like they were going to be pushed through his back, every breath soaked in the stench of the fat man's odour and blood, the latter being a pleasant aperitif to the air. As he was about to use the last of his breath to order the men again, Broadside's fat, dead carcass was pulled off him and dropped to the floor with a loud thud.

The two men looked at him with a mixture of fear and indecision. Cairns mind was racing, working ten times faster than normal – he had never drawn from someone whilst on a full dose of powders! The effect was intoxicating, but nothing like alcohol or herbs – this heightened his senses rather than dulled them, this pulled at his nerve endings, twitched at his muscles and licked its way through his gut.

Nothing had ever felt this good! Not even Canton Dark, but then he had been shared with the Captains, this had been a big man, all for him! A childlike glee, the sort he'd seen in Assundra and Bethlinda growing up, made him want to move about quickly on his feet, run somewhere, dance somewhere, just move, but he would have to be patient. Walking gently would be an achievement today, especially with how his extremities seemed to be pulsing with vibrations of pure pleasure.

Slowly he flexed his arms again, pleased that this time there was no pain. A laugh spurted from his lips as he swung his legs from the bed. The two men jumped back. Baring his blood-soaked teeth, he snarled, sending the armed men running from the room yelping like kicked dogs. Gods, this felt good!

"Oh alchemist, I've been commissioning you to create the perfect powders for so long I'd forgotten what the perfect powder is!" he chuckled. What was the point of resisting now? What was the point of pushing every urge in him down for the sake of his people now? What was the point of enduring the pain every time a person with a well of artistry walked past? What was the point of slowly pursuing an endless course of denial and sacrifice now it had all been torn away?

They had turned on him so easily! Everything he'd done for almost a century had been to help them, to save them from their prison and from themselves and yet all they saw was an autocrat, a bully, someone to blame their own failings on, someone to hang the coat tails of their misfortune on when they'd happily yanked the coat from his hands in the first place. It wasn't the Elders, or the Norths, or anyone in a position of power who had caused the outsider wrath, it had been Marchman! Their champion!

They had caused this themselves and now they had turned on him in favour of a man who promised them cheap revenge, a quick solution to a problem dating back through the ages – a solution that would lead to their deaths.

Well, it would not lead to his.

There was still the way out, even if he couldn't get his people through it now. There would be no point, if outsiders were here already, even in small numbers, more would follow before Simon could render their artistry null and void. Cairns chuckled – the boy, unwittingly, had done the one thing that could lead to his survival in defying Cairns. If Simon's Gift was used to drain all of the artistry in Ostracia, if it hadn't killed him, which Cairns was almost sure it wouldn't have, given the Gifted Ones' potential for power retention, then the sorcerors would have when they found him. And they would have found him. While the others escaped, they would have found him.

There was a chance, now, that Simon could get far enough away to master the art of concealment, to mask his powers behind a façade, a glamour, similar to that which Cairns himself had used for decades to prevent others seeing how ruined his face had become. He would have the power to do so, with or without Stracathri's power and Cairns meant to make sure Simon was not the one rewarded with that prize.

It was his. It had been his since he rose to the head of the Elder Council. It had been his since he had rid Ostracia of the cowardice of the other Elders, as it was clear he would have to do again.

"If they thought you strong, Oldershaw," he murmured under his breath, "wait until they see what I can do when not encumbered by withholdings and glamours! Let's see what they think of me now I'm free from them!"

He could already feel his power tenfold greater than it had been before the rebellion! Most of his splints had been ripped out, for the second time in his life – there would be no reinserting in those fingers if he wished to keep the feeling – but even so, the trickles of blood from the three or four remaining crackled with power. Cairns could almost swear he could hear the tiny droplets fizzing as they fell.

There was a permanent taste of nothing filling his mouth, making it feel dry and swollen, but then that could also be from the beating. Gingerly, he raised a hand and ran it over the many contours of his distorted face. A wry smile came to his lips – it wasn't as bad as he remembered. The left side drooped and oozed, yes, but the right side was almost untouched. A simple glamour, with this level of power, would have hidden it forever from all but the most in tune with their Gift, but Cairns couldn't see the point.

Nobody was going to judge him any longer. Not Elder Hugo for his weakness, not his uncle for his slowness, not Tom Franks for his steadfastness and certainly not Elder Oldershaw for his inaction. Hugo and his uncle were dead. Tom and Elder Oldershaw soon would be.

Thinking of Tom Franks made him pause. He wondered how the Keeper and Assundra were getting along. "I have her," the Keeper had said. Smiling, he realised he was glad Assundra was alive. Amongst all the lies, the manipulation and the despair around him, Assundra was the only villager whose eyes he had looked into and seen an honest distrust and fear. She never hid it, she never pretended it wasn't there, or that he was her friend. The simple care she showed her father and the strength and patience she showed with Simon's childish advances were an example to the rest of them and she wasn't even Ostracian!

Was she? The villagers might have had the power, Ostracian blood, but Cairns would spit sooner than call most of these cowardly, easily swayed sheep the title of Ostracian. Assundra, the outsider bitch as they called her, showed more Ostracian spirit, strength of will and desire for knowledge that only the Keeper would rival. The rest sought the simple things – power, sex, individual survival at the expense of anything.

Cairns wondered why he'd bothered trying to help them for so long. The bitterness crept up his gut like a tendril tickling his intestines. A century of his life given up to help them! For what? Everything he had planned, everything he had tried to do, for their benefit, had come down around his ears. Brought down not by unfortunate circumstance or twisted sneer of fate, but by their own hands.

Their hands, which had finally, after so many years of useless endeavour, built something that would last. Their own destruction. Well, let them live with their creation.

A chirp from outside his window made him twist his neck too quickly, causing a nauseating click. The window fell upwards in his vision as for a moment he was disoriented, the trapped nerve in his neck throbbing with pain before it settled down, as if it had never been damaged. He had sunk to his knees but found himself laughing. So the power drain left him human after all!

For now.

Regaining that privilege would come later. He would have to find a new means of artistically drawing rather than just gorging on power as he had just done with Broadside. The alchemist's power would augment his own, for how long depended on how much he used, but it would not steady his lifespan as an artistic Drawing did. There was time. Rather, there would be time. Cairns sighed happily – for the first time in a century, there would be time.

Only first he had to make sure nobody else got Stracathri's power. None of the villagers could handle it, it would tear them apart, only Cairns, Simon, Elder Oldershaw and Bethlinda could wield such a force. Bethlinda would defer to Cairns without question, there would be no problem with her, but Simon or Elder Oldershaw…

Cairns slowly paced to the window, moving his neck around to try and loosen the stiffness after the pinched nerve. "Here, birdy birdy," he found himself saying softly. No, Simon would not be able to handle the power. Elder Oldershaw would just use it for destruction. The man was nothing but pure hate, Cairns could see that now. How could he have been so blind as to not see it? He had thought Oldershaw a useful but drunk, blind old fool, keeping him around because he was grateful for exposing Elder Rime…

Cairns frowned and stopped. That had been a mistake. Yet the man had never pleaded his innocence. Perhaps they had both been in it together…

No, time to pull yourself together!

Cairns huffed a breath, concerned a little that his chest felt tight as he did so. Without meaning to he coughed a Domination at the songbird, by some fluke managing to hit just the right spot, with the right intensity and at the right time! The bird flew off with a jolt, part of Cairns' consciousness going with it, soaring above the jungle, moving more swiftly than he ever had – but he could feel none of these sensations, only see them.

Soon, the bird would be with the Captains. Then, he would have some fun with Elder Oldershaw.

Elder Cairns tipped back his head and laughed as the terrified bird sped on.

CHAPTER 31

The skeletons were scattered all around the gallery. Assundra held her breath, listening. Even Kryman, for once, was quiet. He had been for a while, listening quite intently while Assundra explained about John's journal.

She hadn't wanted to come here, not after what John had written about the place, but Kryman had insisted. In fact, he had threatened Bethlinda if Assundra had not accompanied them and if she had not told her tale. Kryman had laughed, saying it gave him a perfect hold over the key to the game, whatever that meant. Assundra was too preoccupied with keeping Bethlinda safe and not doing anything else to alienate her. They hadn't shared a word since leaving the tunnels. A few times Assundra had caught Beth looking at her with utter distaste, but she always looked away quickly. Assundra felt sick – surely Kryman couldn't have ruined it all with one mention of Galvarin?

She had to talk to Bethlinda! She wanted to get rid of this *thing* threatening them, while pretending to be their friend – but Kryman said he could help her father! Assundra didn't know what to do. Gulping, she took a step into the room, Beth and Kryman behind and flanking her.

"Be careful," a sharp female voice warned and Assundra turned quickly to look at Beth, but her lips were still. She turned her eyes away as soon as she looked around. Assundra felt like crying – what had she done wrong?

"Sis!" Kryman exclaimed, with what Assundra hoped was mock excitement, else it was far too over the top. "Sorry we're a little late, I found an extra one. Most interesting, I think you'll like this…"

"Shut up, Kryman," the woman snapped. Assundra didn't turn away from Beth, mouthing her a question, asking her what was wrong, but Beth was staring past Assundra, her mouth open in awe. Her eyes sparkled. Assundra remembered when her eyes had sparkled like that when they'd…

Assundra span round quickly, suddenly furious and was shocked to find a woman standing not more than a few paces from her. She could tell instantly there was something strange about her. She hadn't heard the woman approach, she either had the footfall so light as to be unnoticeable or…no, it was more than that – there was something strange about the woman's presence…almost as if she had none! She had beauty, Assundra could see that, she had a figure even Alice West would have been jealous of, but she was lacking…something.

"Assundra Franks, it is a pleasure to meet you," the woman said, in a tone so vague Assundra couldn't tell if it was a pleasure or not. She said nothing in reply. "And who is your friend?"

"Sis, this is…"

"I asked Assundra, Kryman," the woman quickly fired back. When speaking to her brother Assundra felt something from the woman – almost hatred, but not quite. Her expression, though, never changed, like…like it wasn't real. It was like she wasn't real!

"This is Bethlinda Mullard," Assundra said eventually, when it became clear that nobody else was going to speak before she did.

"Keeper of the Transept Tower, sister. I think perhaps caution…"

"Kryman, I shall not warn you again!" The woman smiled. "Welcome, Assundra. I am Elspeth North, the Gifted One. It really is good to meet you, at last. We've been watching you for many years."

"I know," she found herself replying before she thought, quickly biting her lip.

"I do not think you do," Elspeth replied without a change in her expression, "but you will. I promise you, you will." For a moment Elspeth stood looking at Assundra, smiling, but curious. Unblinking. Assundra stared back, but then remembered Bethlinda and turned her eyes to the floor. "Bethlinda Mullard," Elspeth said softly, "ah yes, I remember her too. A powerful artist!"

"Thank you," Beth stuttered behind her. Assundra felt her face flush. She could hear the smile in Bethlinda's voice. "I can't believe I'm talking to the Gifted One! This incredible, but how…"

"There will be time for that later," Elspeth chuckled back at Bethlinda. Assundra wanted to punch her. "For now, I'm afraid we have a problem."

"A problem, sis?" Kryman growled. "Why are we just hearing of this now, after all this ridiculous preamble?"

"The problem, dear brother, is that someone has been here before us!" Assundra flicked her eyes up to look at Elspeth. Whenever she talked to her brother a fury came over her. Assundra recognised it, she had seen it in her father when he talked to the Elders. It made her wonder if Elspeth had a temper similar to her father's. If she was as strong as the legends said, Assundra did not want to find out.

"I know they have," Kryman sneered back at his sister, "I was just hearing about it from our friend here, who you seem to have taken such a shine to. Strange, I thought your shine was reserved for the new Gifted One, as you call him, where is he, by the way?"

Elspeth's smile broadened. He is here, dear brother!"

"Simon's here?" Assundra could tell Bethlinda's smile was gone as soon as she spoke. She could almost feel crackles of power flicker out of Bethlinda into her back. Her mouth filled with the taste of nothing.

Elspeth's smile didn't move. "Don't try that," she said calmly, with a wave of her hand. At once the taste came back to Assundra's mouth and she heard a little whimper from Bethlinda. Assundra shot a look at Elspeth, but once again, the Gifted One's smile was fixed.

"So he's perfected a shield, has he?" Kryman said, sounding for once genuinely impressed. "Interesting. I suppose that has entrenched your opinion of his supposed gift, has it?"

"I am not discussing this again, Kryman," Elspeth replied, turning her eyes back to Assundra. "I believe other matters are pressing themselves on our attention."

"Such as why in the hells you haven't got rid of this bitch yet!"

A yelp from Bethlinda made Assundra spin around. "Simon, get off her!" she shouted, but even as she moved to rip the boy's arm away, Bethlinda, with nothing more than a touch to Simon's stomach, sent him flying six feet back against the wall. Assundra's mouth went numb from the taste of nothing again.

Kryman burst out laughing behind them. Bethlinda just looked annoyed, as if she'd swatted a fly. "Leave her alone!" Assundra cried, stepping between Simon and Bethlinda.

"Sunny, it's alright," Bethlinda said irritably, but she stroked a hand down Assundra's arm. It was a touch that felt better to Assundra than anything had all day and she turned with a smile, only to find Bethlinda watching Elspeth, whose lips were pursed. Assundra's smile ebbed.

"Assundra," Elspeth said quickly, the harsh tone back in her voice, "in John's writings, was there any mention of the skeletons?"

Assundra nodded. She glanced at Beth, who was still focusing her gaze on Elspeth. She found herself hating the Gifted One. "He said they were coming after him. He heard them scream."

"As I thought," Elspeth nodded. "He's here, brother."

"What?" Kryman's chuckling stopped in an instant. "Carstan is here? How?"

"It is where our father finally found a use for him. It raises a number of questions, does it not?"

Kryman didn't reply. Assundra looked from one to the other, then to Bethlinda. All wore an expression of concern. Assundra just didn't understand. "What questions? Why are we here?" The questions started pouring into her mind as anger took hold of her. "What does what John saw have to do with the skeletons? Why the hells did you need to kill Elder Cairns? How are you here and what the hells do you want with me?"

For a moment Assundra thought Elspeth was going to strike her. Beth must have seen the same thing because she made to move between them, as Assundra had with her and Simon, who was still slumped in the corner, groaning.

At once, Elspeth raised a hand. "I will explain," she said quickly. Kryman grunted behind her. "I truly am sorry you've had to be kept in the dark, Assundra. As I said, we have watched you for many years, my brother and I, but only to protect you."

"Protect me?" That only enraged Assundra further. "How has what you've done protected me? I've been terrified of the red eyes for as long as I can remember! How has that helped?"

"The red eyes?" Elspeth frowned.

"Yes, red eyes, just like his," Assundra snapped back, pointing at Kryman. "I know it was him watching me! Him waiting for me in the tunnels, him in the well, chasing John and then me!"

"In a well?" Kryman laughed in response. "Do you really think I'd lower myself to such depths as to skulk in a well?" He laughed again.

"Shut up, brother," Elspeth snapped back impatiently. "Assundra I don't know what you're talking about, but I assure you, you would not have seen us watching you. It wasn't until Simon activated the shrine of Lamia that we were able to physically penetrate your world."

"The shrine! Of course, that's how you…" Bethlinda tailed off as Elspeth smiled at her.

"Indeed, Keeper. Perhaps you would care to explain the presence of such a beast in the old city?"

"Explain?" Assundra echoed, looking up at Beth, but Beth's gaze was locked firmly on Elspeth now. Assundra felt a surge of relief as she saw anger flash through Bethlinda's eyes as she looked at Elspeth, not the sparkle of excited interest there had been before.

"Very well, then I shall explain for you." Elspeth turned back to Assundra with another of those smiles. Assundra had to admit, Elspeth was a beautiful woman, but there was something…unreal about her beauty. Something wrong.

"I want to know what I'm doing here!" Assundra cried, feeling more confident. Simon was clearly no match for Bethlinda and Elspeth seemed to have Kryman's malevolence in hand. Assundra was beginning to feel safer. "I know you can't have brought me here to talk, yet we've been standing here like washer women ever since I got here! I want to know what you want with me, right now!"

Elspeth's smiled didn't waver. "You want to know why? Because of your family, Assundra. You must have heard the tale. Callara was the first, do you know about her?

"Callara?" Assundra echoed. She remembered her mother drumming her ancestors into her. Callara, Callia, Ellendra, Nilha, Assundra, she could reel them off and their tales at will, she had heard of them so often, but what did her ancestors have to do with this?

"She was the outsider. The temptress. It was she who lured Marchman's married son, Fallian, into her bed, just days before he was killed. She bore his son on the night the outsiders came. Fallian's own wife, Sarah, delivered her husband's misstress's baby on the very night the sorcerors were poisoning our stock.

"We had people watching, of course. That was a room absent of love, for the birth of a child that wasn't wanted by any but her mother. And Callara passed away with the new-born baby in her arms, with the bairn uttering not a sound."

A picture flashed into Assundra's mind, blotting out what she could see; an image of her father all those years ago, locked into a room with his wife, wanting to touch her, hold her, but being forced to remember this tale as she recounted it over and over until he could remember every word, just so he could tell his daughter at the right time. They hadn't known she could see, that she could hear. They hadn't known the person holding her hand could see, either, they weren't supposed to be there. This was her mother's message to her, this was her tale. The image snapped out of her eyes, leaving her head feeling like she'd been hit, as Elspeth carried on.

"It was Sarah's whim to leave the babe there, in the arms of the woman who had taken her husband from her before death had taken its revenge, but the child had such an aspect, such a quiet way about it that she couldn't do it. For the next few days she cared for the babe, but each time she looked at it she saw nothing but her husband's betrayal and she knew she couldn't raise the child as her own.

"The little girl, still not named, was taken greedily by the worst family possible. The Crafters." Assundra's distaste mirrored that in Elspeth's voice. "The Crafters had plans for the child. The youngest brother of the head of the family was to wed her when she came of age."

"Why?" she interrupted. "Why would the Crafters want their son to marry an outsider? They're always going on about how much they hate them!" How much they hate *me*, she thought. Images of them all in the room came flooding back. The words, the leers, the grunts, the *drinking*...

"This was long ago, Assundra. Many of the old families survived the invasion, before they were slaughtered, Crafters weren't accepted, not like they are now. People saw them for what they were back then. They had to take what wives they could get and by then they were running out of their own family."

Just like now. Assundra swallowed hard. The image of Young Crafter just wouldn't go away. She took Beth's arm.

"But they'd heard something else. Something about outsider blood, I don't know what, but mostly they wanted to raise themselves up."

"Outsider blood?"

"They named the baby Callia," Elspeth went on, ignoring Assundra, "after her first word. Callia grew up amid horrors we can only guess at but which you, Assundra I fear have experienced."

Assundra's eyes widened. "They have done this before?"

"Of course," Elspeth replied casually. "They have always fed on outsiders, we all did. It was nothing new. Only they never saw the need to reward their stock, to treat them like human beings. There were a few like that."

"Can we get on, sis?"

Elspeth shot a look at her brother, but ignored him. Assundra felt numb. "So you saw what they did to me?" she ventured slowly.

"We saw everything," the woman smiled in reply.

"You saw everything? Why didn't you stop them?" Beth hissed, that strange, dark anger Assundra had seen in the tunnels with Kryman returning. Assundra didn't like it one bit, it wasn't her Beth, she had never been like that.

"Why didn't you? I believe you were watching as well?"

Assundra turned her head to Bethlinda, who avoided her eyes. "Beth I know you couldn't stop them…"

"Of course she could have, just as we could have," Elspeth replied with a chuckle. Assundra opened her mouth but nothing would come out. "Only we needed the Crafters to think they had won, we needed Elder Cairns weakening and we needed the village out of our way, as you can see it is. We also needed you to learn, Assundra. I'm sorry you had to go through that, but I'm afraid it was necessary."

"Sorry?" Assundra yelled. "Do you have any idea…"

"No, of course I don't, nor will I ever, I'm far too powerful to succumb to that, but so are you."

"Far too powerful?" Was the woman insane? "How can you talk about what happened to me as if it were a good thing?"

"Sunny, calm down…"

"Calm down?" Assundra yanked her arm away from Beth's. "What in the hells is wrong with you people? They *drank my blood!* Laughing while they did it! I thought I was going to die there, how can any of that have been a good thing?"

Silence followed her outburst and Assundra realised she had been screaming. Bethlinda and Elspeth were looking down, steadfastly at

Assundra's feet, their eyes wide. Following their gaze, Assundra saw snakes, dozens of them, curling around her feet. They fanned out around her feet in a circle, hissing and spitting at anyone near and Beth and Elspeth took a step back.

"What's going on?" Assundra asked, her heart racing. She hated snakes! "Beth get me out of here!" she cried, holding out her hands and at once, Beth stepped closer, narrowly avoiding the mouth of a lunging snake and pulled Assundra free of the circle.

There was a loud sigh behind them. "I'll deal with this then, shall I?" Kryman glided forward, circling slowly around the snakes, smiling that sneering smile that told the world he thought of nothing in it as anything more than a game. He reached down to the snakes with a hand and began to laugh as one by one they burned the instant their flesh made contact with…whatever Kryman was made of. The stench of burning flesh filled the air and Assundra's stomach turned over, but this time with hunger. Gods, how long had it been since she had some meat?

"You see?" Elspeth said softly behind her. "That is called a summoning. It is sorcery, Assundra and it is what the Crafters awoke in you. What your family has always had, since the lineage of artistry and sorcery met in Marchman's son and Callara. Your ancestors have used it ever since. After Callia fell in love with a married man named Peter Rost, she used her sorcery to influence and induce a suicide in the man's wife, before seducing him. The couple bonded in secret, with the blessing of the Elders who knew all to well about the Crafters; they didn't want that family elevated anywhere beyond their lowly status. Soon enough, Callia became pregnant and gave birth to Ellendra a day short of her nineteenth birthday. As with Callara the birth was difficult. Callia was young and healthy, stronger than Callara had been, but still it proved too much for her. She died a year to the day the child was born, but not before she had passed on her mother's gift."

Assundra couldn't breathe. Her head wouldn't stay still, spinning around her like a child's top. Her stomach contracted suddenly, bringing a burning pain, but she forced herself not to cry out. How could a few words bring her pain?

"Go…"

"Now who in the hells was that?" Kryman said, his red eyes blazing.

"Go…leave…go…" It had started out as one, but now there were many. *"Leave…go!"* The voices swarmed around them, growing more insistent. Assundra shrieked as it felt like something passed into one ear and out of the other, and she didn't stop screaming. Beth was sobbing and fell to her knees.

"Do it!" Kryman was screaming, but she could barely hear him above the rush of pleading whispers, like a wind through her skull. "Do it!" he screamed again, louder this time.

"Do what?" she screamed back, but he just kept saying it.

"Do what you were born to do," Elspeth joined in, her voice piercing, not lost in the wind.

"Do it now!" Kryman screamed, getting louder.

"I don't know what you're talking about!"

"Remember, Assundra! Remember your mother!" Elspeth's voice was soft, gentle in the rushing madness of the voices.

"Go…leave…go! Go no!"

"Do it, girl, what is the matter with you!"

"Assundra, think hard, remember what your mother told you, what she learned from Ellendra, remember! You have to Assundra, it's the only way to make it stop!"

There was a roar from the far side of the room. "Sunny, please!" Beth cried. "Do what they say!"

"I don't know what they mean!" she cried in reply, but her words were lost as the rushing wind became a gale in her ears. She screamed, but could not hear the scream, as two huge, red eyes appeared, bursting through the wall in a shower of masonry, the head bobbing up and down as if carried along by a body on all fours.

"Assundra, do it now!" Kryman bellowed, somehow audible over the gale.

"Go! Leave! Leave!"

"There is no time, Assundra, let it go, let it out, as you did with the snakes, let your ancestry do what it was meant to do!" Elspeth put a hand on her arm and Assundra screamed again. "You must do this Assundra!"

"Do it *now*!"

"Sunny, please! Please, just do it!"

Assundra felt her head slam back as if someone had struck her with a fierce uppercut. The beast with the red eyes began to run towards her, veering off to follow the balcony around. It would be on them in seconds! Why weren't the Norths doing anything? Why wasn't anyone doing anything? Why were they all just screaming at her? She wanted to run but she couldn't move. Kryman and Elspeth's voices merged into the ghosts in the gale until she could hear nothing but the roar of the wind, see nothing but the huge, angry red eyes on the otherwise black shape, bounding towards her, almost upon her. She screamed but nothing happened, the beast leapt towards her and she put her hands up, something leaving her mouth with the scream.

Everything stopped.

The beast hung in mid-air inches from her face, its eyes burning with hatred. She couldn't see a mouth but she knew it was there. She tried to move away, but she couldn't. There was no movement, no wind, no presence of any feeling whatsoever.

She couldn't move her eyes. She couldn't move anything. The red eyes blazed, alive somehow in the stillness, huge, too big for the body that carried them. Something flickered across the right eye. It seemed to grow in front of

Assundra's face and she tried to shrink back, but nothing moved, nothing breathed, nothing lived here now, except what was in the beast's eyes. Assundra saw symbols flash across the beast's eye. Symbols that were all wrong, all repellent to her. Repellent!

She almost felt them pass through her own, unmoving, unblinking, unfeeling eyes into her brain. They lodged there, making her want to shake her head, to shake them out, but she couldn't. They were wrong, these symbols, too wrong, too repellent, too much, nobody could ask this of her, her father wouldn't ask this of her! She didn't breathe, she couldn't and she knew she wouldn't until whatever was pouring into her mind was done with her.

Then, they stopped. They symbols burned themselves into her brain, invaders torching the landscape of her thoughts, but then in the beast's eyes she saw a faint image. Tiny, almost lost among the repellent memories she didn't want, a hazy, flickering image of her mother and father at their wedding; two people in love, but then the image seemed to tear, to split in two. Her father changed into nothing more than a beast, clawing at the tear, trying to get through. Assundra saw her mother fade slightly, but not entirely. A shade of her tiny image remained, reaching out a hand across the tear to stroke the beast's fur across the tear in the picture, love clear in her eyes, but the beast turned away. The beast calmed and her mother turned to stare out of the beast's eyes at Assundra.

Her eyes were so sad! Assundra watched in sorrow, her heart breaking, as her father turned and padded away from her mother, whose hand remained outstretched, pleading, with a sorrow of his own, a sorrow Assundra could see was needless. He didn't know that Nilha loved her!

Something left Assundra and she could move. She couldn't take any more, she had to make this right! She reached out a hand right into the beast's eye, but even as she touched her mother the image rippled and faded like a reflection in water.

Everything started moving too quickly. The best's mouth closed in around Assundra's face and she fell back, feeling teeth begin to puncture her cheeks, the pressure of her bones being crushed in the thing's massive jaws and the wetness as the tongue licked at her, but her hand was still on the beast's eye. With a final, desperate lunge she pushed her hand through, feeling the jaws release from her face instantly, and the thing screamed a silent, air-changing scream. She felt her hand grip around something soft, wrapping her legs around the beast's neck as it tried to pull away from her.

Something was moving her, something was making her do this, all she wanted to do was run, but she felt her legs tighten, forcing the beast to the floor, gripping harder, wincing with revulsion as whatever was inside her hand squished, making the beast scream its silent scream again.

Her mind burned again and she saw the symbols rally and gather, abandoning their raping of the landscape of her brain. One by one they rushed from her, pouring down her throat and out of her mouth. The beast swelled and changed under the weight of the symbols that flowed out of her. She felt herself lifted off the floor as the beast reared onto two legs, its body thinning, its face shortening. Bone and flesh tightened around Assundra's wrist, but she didn't let go.

With a piercing shriek, the thing's scream bled into the real world. The thing fell, falling heavily, its rib cage rising and falling, slowly, then slower, before it came to rest. The blackness left its form, peeling away like ashes, revealing a naked, pale, withered and wasted human body.

Assundra didn't scream. She didn't do anything at all, other than calmly pull her hand out of the man's skull, the brittle bone cracking, allowing her hand back through.

"Sunny!" she heard a tearful voice cry, before there was silence. An utter silence as there had never been. They all stood behind her, completely still.

"I did it," she said, turning slowly, feeling blood and…something else…drip off her hand.

None of them had time to move before a noise so great it made Bethlinda and Kryman fall to their knees in pain poured into the room as the gale of voices screamed. Assundra stood still, allowing her hair to blow across her face, staring into the eyes of Elspeth North. Bethlinda and Kryman screamed and writhed in pain as the gale picked up the skeletons and began tossing them around. Assundra was aware of a thigh bone coming right for her head, but that didn't matter now. She saw Elspeth wave her hand and the bone disintegrated.

The gallery began to shake, all around them was chaos, the gale growing ever stronger, but Assundra and Elspeth stood still.

"Time for you to see what we can do," Elspeth said, her voice somehow penetrating the howling gale. The Gifted One lifted her arms high, scratching her nails down both palms hard, until blood flowed. Assundra was aware of one last symbol almost limp its way down to her mouth and say itself. A green haze, exactly as she had been caught in outside the Council Chambers, enveloped her as Elspeth began to glow, light pouring from her hands.

In seconds, the room was quiet. Skeletons fell to the floor as the gale ceased. Bones fell and splintered, hitting with such force that in places they crashed through the gallery floor, smashing against the stone flagging below. Bones rained onto the haze surrounding Assundra and turned at once to dust.

Assundra held Elspeth's gaze as gradually everything became still once more.

Bethlinda was unconscious. Kryman leapt to his feet at once, smoothing his shimmering form down and laughing.

Neither Assundra nor Elspeth said anything. Assundra became aware she could move the green haze as she moved. Slowly, holding Elspeth's gaze, she moved over to Bethlinda, making sure to brush the haze surrounding her against Kryman's shimmering, wrong, body as she did, pleased when he winced in surprised pain. Keeping her eyes set on the Gifted One, she knelt as she reached Beth's prone body, extending the green haze around her too. Reaching a hand down, she gently rolled Beth's head around. She could see out of the corner of her eye that the Gozon Stone was glowing brighter than Assundra had ever seen. A splinter of bone pushed itself out of Bethlinda's cheek and fell with a small clatter, the only sound in the room.

"She's going to be alright," she said to Elspeth, refusing to add "*which is just as well for you.*" From the way Elspeth pursed her lips, Assundra could tell the message got through in any case.

"You killed my brother," Elspeth murmured.

"Yes," Assundra replied, keeping her voice steady, "I did."

For a while none of them spoke. Assundra felt the confidence spread through her like a warming drink. It was as if something in her mind had been unlocked. She knew what she was now. She knew what she could do. She knew they couldn't hurt her any more. They had never been able to hurt any of them – not Callara, not Callia, nor Ellendra or Nilha. Now they wouldn't hurt Assundra Franks either. The gift had been passed on. The ball of burning pain in her stomach was gone. The shivering tightness in her chest was gone. She was the outsider. She was different.

And she was glad of it!

Inevitably, it was Kryman who broke the silence. "Sis, I don't want to worry you…"

"Shut up, Kryman," Elspeth said quietly. "I didn't expect you to survive, outsider. That is unfortunate for you. Simon, come here," she commanded, holding out a hand. Assundra felt a giggle escape her lips. Did the woman think she was some kind of queen? Holding her hand out waiting for Simon to wait on her?

"I do believe that is what I was trying to tell you, sis," Kryman sneered, "only it does seem like Simon has either been dashed to smithereens, or and I hasten to add I think this more likely, although not preferable, he has turned tail and run like the coward he is."

Elspeth's eyes widened and she span around. Assundra followed her gaze to the door against which Simon had fell after Bethlinda's attack. He was gone.

"Better get after him, don't you think, sis? I can take care of things here." Assundra turned back to Kryman and watched the evil sneer spread across his face. "In fact, I'm going to rather enjoy avenging my brother!"

CHAPTER 32

Cairns didn't bother with his teeth this time as he killed his fifth man of the day, simply sticking his splints into the man's neck, twisting, severing and shredding his nervous system with no more than a thought. As the unfortunate outsider dropped, Cairns took stock. There was fierce fighting in between him and Stracathri. There had been fierce fighting in the city square too, but that had been just men. Once they'd seen what they were up against, the outsider soldiers there had simply stood aside and let him through.

Here, was a different story. There were a lot more of them, for one thing and for another, the fighting was punctuated with attacks on whomever Tom Franks, or whatever remained of the farmer inside the monstrosity Cairns and Broadside had created, wanted to attack. Lines of attack had formed in front of Stracathri – a terrified hotchpotch of Ostracians made a semi-circle protecting the tower, in front of whom stood two rows of outsider soldiers, each looking identical to the next in the shining silver helmets and painted leathers, one facing the tower, back-to-back to the row pressing onto them – the row facing the second line of Ostracians, who had managed to successfully trap them in a pincer.

Only the second line of Ostracians was half caught up in fighting with and half against, Tom and his wolves. They were quick, fit and worked as one unit – Cairns had to admit he was impressed, in just a few short weeks Tom had drilled them into a fighting force to rival men, although much of that force was separating one man off from the rest for Tom to deal with.

Which was what was happening to one unfortunate now. Tom had certainly found his preferred source of meat, Cairns thought as he tried to think of a route into the tower. He could kill them all, of course, but it would leave him weak. He didn't know if the Norths were in there with Oldershaw or not. He needed more information. He needed a better way in.

"Die! Die, you disgusting excuse…"

Cairns flicked at the man's presence with a splint finger without looking round. He heard the body fall to the floor somewhere behind him, it didn't matter where. Not a very artful way to kill someone, but sometimes a ball of fire to the face was as good as any. He didn't have the power to waste on anything fancy, in any case.

Cairns frowned as he leant against a wall, not caring that several of the Ostracians had seen him now, they weren't foolish enough to attack without the Norths or Elder Oldershaw to lead the charge. The Captains should have been here by now, though and he needed a distraction.

"Elder, don't attack!"

Cairns stopped his hand even as he was about to flick, spitting the artistry out of his mouth instead. "Galvarin!" he exclaimed, turning.

"Barely," the mason grunted in reply and Cairns soon saw why. His left arm was gone, the stump a few inches below the shoulder tied tight with a heavily stained rag. His right arm was hanging limp at his side, broken at the elbow. Several of his teeth were missing and he was standing crouched, as if protecting the ribs on his right side. His clothes were ragged and torn, his hair matted in blood.

"Galvarin, what…"

"Tom found me," Galvarin replied simply. "He wouldn't listen. The wolves, they just stood watching. Not even salivating. Just watching."

Cairns pursed his lips. "Tom was told not to touch any of the Council," he replied, aware even as he was saying it that the words were useless.

"Can you do anything? Please?"

Cairns stared at the mason. He wasn't sure if he wanted to do anything. He could expend energy healing Galvarin, but was there time? Did he have the inclination? Frowning, Cairns decided to heal one injury. The man had served him well on the Elder Council, but his task had been quite a pleasurable one, bringing its own rewards, could he really be praised for that? He had bedded Assundra Franks, could that really be considered a sacrifice? However, he had followed instructions when instructed without question. He had also fetched the Deathguard, who had nearly managed to take Elder Oldershaw's head off, before several artists had taken the big man down. He deserved some credit for that.

Reaching out his hand, Cairns paused – which wound to heal? Smiling at Galvarin, who was ready to drop on his feet, he decided to be generous. Flicking some blood to the front of a splint, he placed it directly into the swollen skin above Galvarin's right elbow. The bone was shattered, Tom had done a very good job of trying to make sure Galvarin could never work again, but it was fixable. Galvarin winced, but to his credit did not cry out as Cairns forced the shards of bone first to a ground dust, then added some of

Galvarin's own blood to mix it into a bone pulp. He drew himself out of the wound carefully and yanked his splint from the arm.

"It will take time to gel into bone," he said as he saw Galvarin's puzzled look at his slack arm, "but it will heal quicker than bone. Now, let's see about that blood..."

All it took to staunch the flow of blood was heat. Flicking a few drops of blood into his hand, he created a small covering of flame. "This," he warned, "will hurt." This time Galvarin screamed, but only for a second. That was all it took. "That will be ugly, but will serve you as well as any poultice."

"Elder, my ribs..."

"Will take up too much of my energy, Galvarin. Be grateful for what you have." Cairns looked the man directly in the eye. "Of course, if you were to do something for me..."

Galvarin blinked. "What is there to do? Elder, it's over! I don't know how you managed to escape them, but a lot of things have changed."

Cairns was losing patience. "Of course they have, Galvarin, Elder Oldershaw has destroyed our people, that will result in a lot of change!"

"No, Elder, you don't understand." Galvarin's eyes were wide. Cairns decided he would do the mason the favour of listening to him. "The woman, Elspeth North...she's human!"

"What?" Cairns laughed. "Her form is well structured to be sure, but she is no more human than...." Cairns stopped himself. He was going to say "*than I am*".

Galvarin was shaking his head fiercely. "No, Elder, she is human! Something happened! She went into the back entrance of Stracathri with Simon...whatever she was, and came out human!"

Cairns didn't believe it. The mason had to have been hallucinating from the pain of his injuries. "Elspeth North is dead," he said quietly, "there is no way for her to have returned to human form. Death-life and life do not mix, there would have been such a disturbance that it would have levelled the city! Trust me, she is not human."

"But she looked..."

"Just like us?" Cairns paused. He had to admit that was interesting – if she had perfected such a pure death-life form, to the extent she did not even shimmer, that was considerable evidence of her power. Or was it... a thought struck him. "She must be feeding off Simon's power!" he said excitedly. "That gives me a chance... thank you Galvarin, you have done well!"

Cairns made to leave, but Galvarin called him back. "Elder, what shall I do?"

He looked back at Galvarin, whose eyes were wide, unknowing. The man was scared. For years Cairns had cared for Galvarin. For years he had involved him in his decisions. Without Cairns the man would be lost, they would all be lost. There would be no way out for them, no way to escape the soldiers. Galvarin was lucky he had lasted this long and he almost hadn't.

Cairns looked Galvarin in the eyes. "That's up to you."

Turning, he left the mason mouthing silent, confused words. He saw several of the Ostracians look over to him in hope while they fended off the outsider attacks. He saw their looks of hope cloud over into fear and disbelief as he walked away from Stracathri. There was no entrance to the main tower from the back entrance, in the winding back streets, Cairns knew that, but there had to be a way around. Cairns looked up. The three spires all rose to the same height, he could easily climb one of the unoccupied towers, but after nearly a century were they still stable?

There was also the question of whether, when he got there, he would be able to summon the power required to leap the considerable distance between the towers. No, there would have to be another way.

It would have to be the tunnels.

He set off at a jog through the back streets, ignoring the pleas for him to come back. Out of the corner of his eye he saw one of the Ostracians, he couldn't see who, trying to run after him, presumably to stop him, get cut down by an outsider blade. Flicking a fireball out behind him, he didn't turn to see who it had hit. It would hopefully buy some of the Ostracians some time whatever the outcome. As the screams started, he rounded the corner to the narrow side streets.

Cairns didn't even look where he was going, he knew this route from the air. Many times he had flown birds down this route to make sure they were abandoned, but clearly Elder Oldershaw had been able to evade his scouts. Cairns scowled – in truth, he had never bothered to watch the old man too closely. His search for the weapon had been as pathetic as it was futile, Cairns hadn't thought him a threat. It had been his only mistake and it had nearly cost Cairns his life.

There would be no mistakes now. There would be no plans for anything to go wrong. He was going to take what he deserved and he was going to destroy anything that got in his way. If Elspeth North was indeed human then it only made her vulnerable. The way he felt right now, with the powders and the power flowing through him in tandem, nothing could stop him. Nothing would stop him!

The open space of the city square came upon him almost like a jolt, even though he was prepared for it. The tight, winding corners of the back streets bled straight into the city square but Cairns did not pause. He made for the Council Chambers without breaking stride, lowering the artistic shield…that wasn't there!

He coughed the artistry to the side as he finally slowed his pace. He could sense something was wrong as soon as he entered. This place had seen an artistic Drawing, performed on a scale Cairns' mind boggled at. He could taste the remnants of the pain and despair on the droplets of blood mixed with the air. Outsider blood!

What could have caused this? Was this how Elder Oldershaw and the Crafters had got their power?

The answer came to him almost as soon as he had asked himself it. The old alchemic workshop was dimly lit by only a few candles. There was no sound other than a faint scrabbling and panting from an old man, who was bent over in the corner of the room, desperately licking at spots of what Cairns could tell by the residual smell was dried blood, on the floor.

"Crafter!" he exclaimed, making the man who was almost as old as Cairns himself start.

"Elder! Elder, I was wrong!"

"I know," Cairns replied simply, advancing slowly on Old Crafter.

"I didn't think…didn't think he'd go so far! I just wanted our birthright! I didn't want to destroy our people!"

"I know," Cairns said again.

"Elder, I'm sorry! I'm so sorry!"

"I know," he said, more softly this time, "I understand." He reached Old Crafter and took his hand to pull him to his feet. The man smiled at Cairns for a few seconds, his tongue licking in hunger, before surprise, then concern, then pain flew across his face in less than a second as his hand burned through to the bone.

"You said you understood!" he screamed as the fire spread to his clothes, then the rest of his flesh.

Cairns raised a quick barrier between himself and the fire. "I do understand, Crafter, we have danced this dance many times before. This is not for me. This is for Assundra."

He let the steaming carcass of Old Crafter drop, still burning, flesh breaking off in lumps as he hit the floor.

Cairns spat, but this time in pure disgust. The table, propped up against the workbench, was stained with blood in places. The straps were sodden with a mixture of blood and saliva – clearly Old Crafter had been scrabbling around for a replenishing dose. Cairns scoffed. The Crafters and Elder Oldershaw may have bested him, with the aid of the manifestations of two of the Norths, but if Old Crafter was any guide, they had completely failed to grasp the fact that the power of a Drawing was finite. These were no opposition! And yet they had won.

Had it been the surprise? Or sheer numbers? No… he couldn't think like this, it was done. It had to have been the Norths. Only an alliance of perfidious aristocratic has-beens would be so arrogant as to be ignorant of the drain Drawn power brought about. The Norths always had others do their work for them. Elspeth, of course, would have been immune to drains, her power would have been so vast, but Cairns doubted the rest of them even properly used the power at their disposal.

Yet they had bested him! Nobody had ever bested him – not Elder Hugo, not his uncle, not even those who had taken his mother!

"Come on, flower!"

Cairns shook his head, cursing. As soon as he had dealt with Oldershaw he would have to work on putting the withholdings back on these memories Kryman North had awoken.

"You can thank me later."

Scowling, Cairns turned and headed for the trap door. Thank him? He would be more likely to end Kryman's necromantic existence if he saw the spectre again and what was in the cellar was just the thing he needed to do it.

* * * * *

When he was out of this, he thought as he dashed underneath a falling brick that promptly vanished, he thought he would find a woman to share out his days with. Cairns had so far somehow managed to pass through the shrinking walls, falling masonry and blackouts the Tower was throwing at him. Just like the passages under the Transept Tower, the passages leading to the closed-off parts of Stracathri were seemingly endless, each identical to the last, just squat, slim blue-stoned walls, shining with power. The journey was taking too long, he was giving Elder Oldershaw too much time to prepare. Someone from the cordon around the front entrance would surely have relayed the knowledge of Cairns' presence to the old fool by now.

"Patience, boy!" both his mother and Elder Hugo had told him. Well, he had been patient just about enough. Patience and solitude. Learning and planning, had been his life. He had never lain with a woman, never tasted the sweet sensation of another's seduction. His life had been about servitude and self-denial, fighting for what was best for his people, for what was right, at the expense of himself.

No more.

Cairns threw his head back as he reached yet another dead end, putting his hands out to search for the glamour hiding the passageway, and was caught by the reflection in an unusually shiny, old candle bracket. Finding a woman to accept the grotesquery that was the face he lived with would take more effort than simply making a decision to have one. He could just have to erect a glamour, but without Drawing when he was on the outside, that be too much of a constant drain on his concentration, even with Stracathri's power. Perhaps there was some form of outsider artistry or craft somewhere that could heal his disfigurements.

Just to be with people, to talk, to laugh as an equal! He had spent so long cramped up in tunnels, passages and rooms of old books that he had two lifetimes to live. With Stracathri's power, he could probably live a greater number than that.

Yes, he would look for some foreign art, or whatever primitive system they used now. It was about time he was allowed to relax.

As his hands passed through a gap in the stones, Cairns swiftly edged himself through. Truly, this part of Stracathri was a strange place. It was as if the century of solitude had driven it mad, as if it had been alone so long now it wanted nobody within its walls. Cairns couldn't believe it had always been like this. Something stirred inside his withholding-free mind, something about walking down endless dimly-lit passages like this one with his uncle, asking endless questions, back when his uncle had been just that, not his guardian and not his teacher. The hundred years of festering and ruination, true of Ostracia as much as Stracathri, was true of what had happened to all of them.

For the outsiders it had all made sense, imprisoning them, giving their plague time to do its work. , to reduce the village to the manageable size it was now. This number of people would barely be noticed in the outside if they went their separate ways, especially ones as artistically weak as those left. Why had Lord North allowed any of it? Why hadn't he used the great power at his disposal? He had to find out what the man had wanted before he left and with Stracathri's power there would be nothing to stop him discovering the secret.

Cairns sighed happily as he passed out of the last of the dim stone tunnels and into much more plush, though dusty and decaying surroundings. The entrance hall was dim, even with the phosphorescent stone. A carpet of thick wool shielded his slow, careful steps forward. He remembered this place!

"You'll be master of this some day, flower! Make a better job of it than we have."

Cairns shook his head. The memory had passed his mind like a dream – he and his mother, standing right where he was now, at the base of the double-ended staircase leading to the upper levels. Her kind, encouraging smile, the arm around his shoulders, something he hadn't felt for a century.

"You!"

Cairns span around. Elder Oldershaw stood in the frame of the door to the study. Instinctively Cairns called power to his throat, ready to use, but quickly spat it out. Oldershaw didn't look ready for a fight. In fact, he looked broken. He was weeping bitterly, clutching a thick, red-bound book in his hands so tightly the knuckles were white.

"You did this! You did all of this!"

Cairns allowed a trickle of blood to flow down out of his middle, splinted finger, just in case. "What are you talking about, Oldershaw?"

Oldershaw laughed, a manic, tear-filled, shrill burst of sound that almost made Cairns take a step back. "You've hidden amongst us for so long! I did as you instructed! I did as you commanded! My entire family has worked to your ends! And it's all been a *game*?"

Cairns stood his ground as Oldershaw advanced. "What are you talking about?" he asked again.

Spittle fell from Oldershaw's mouth, catching in his beard. "You know what I am talking about!" the man cried, his voice catching and breaking. "You did this! What I don't understand is why? You wanted to make peace with them?"

Cairns hardened his stance, allowing another of his splinted fingers to drip blood. "Attacking the outsiders has led to the death of our people! All I have done is work to save our people, end their imprisonment…"

"By destroying us as a people! All of this time you had the solution! All of this time you had the means to destroy our enemies, even before the plague, before the invasion even – and you did nothing!" Oldershaw waved the book in his hands at Cairns and took more steps forward. "You said it would be fun! You think the death of our people is *fun*?"

Cairns finally took a step back. Oldershaw's eyes were wide, staring, unblinking, flickering this way and that at Cairns. Something had driven the man mad… "Oldershaw I have no idea…"

"I know you don't!" the old man cried in reply, spit hitting Cairns in the face. "You withheld it! *Withheld* it! Necromancing your own blood! You are a disgrace!" Oldershaw was screaming now. "I have served a disgrace! My life is a disgrace!"

The force of the blast struck Cairns directly in the chest, sending him reeling back. "Stay back, Elder, this one's mine!"

Hoard rushed forward, catching Oldershaw straight in the chest. They fell to the floor, rolling over each other, Hoard snapping at Oldershaw's neck. Hoard screamed as Oldershaw's knee made contact with his groin and with that Cairns knew the man was dead. With a fierce cry Oldershaw drove a splinted finger right into Hoard's eye. The Captain screamed for just a moment then both of his eyeballs burst, blood pouring from the sockets and dribbling from the dead man's mouth.

"Slaves of Lamia? Have you no shame?" Oldershaw cried, pushing Hoard's lifeless body off him.

Strong hands pulled Cairns to his feet. "Elder, leave this to me," Coarse whispered, attempting to move past Cairns, but with a push, Cairns sent him backwards.

"No," he replied as Oldershaw turned to run at him, "I am tired of this."

Flicking blood and calling power to his throat, he turned to spit the power at the blood but even as he did a fireball exploded around Oldershaw's head. Cairns threw his arms up, staggering back against the fierce heat. In only a few heartbeats the fires were gone, consumed by Oldershaw's flesh. His colleague's headless body, skin and bone from the shoulders up burned to nothing in the flames, fell against Cairns, the man's hot blood, thick with artistry and half-congealed in the heat, staining his white robes.

Cairns shrugged the body to the floor, looking up. "Feed, if you want," he said tersely to Captain Coarse. "I want none of it."

"Nor me," Coarse replied, his voice husky. "Where the hells did that come from?"

It had come from the tower. As soon as Oldershaw had attacked him, Stracathri's defences had been brought in full force against him. Such power, such strength of pure artistry that it could be directed from nothing but stone, turned a spike of excitement in Cairns' stomach. That power would soon be his!

"I don't know," he said to Coarse. The man was nothing but the most basic of blood artists, he didn't need to know the truth. "Keep a watch," he said, kicking Oldershaw's body over so he could pick up the book, its red covers streaked with already drying blood.

The question remained, of course – why had Stracathri's defences been activated? What had Oldershaw done here? Indicating to Coarse to stay where he was, Cairns moved into the study. He wanted to look at whatever this book was in privacy.

The study was large and cluttered – books had been pulled off bookcases onto the floor, papers were strewn on the desk, drawers open and in disarray. Oldershaw had been searching for something here for a long time. The air was filled with the scent of the burned wax of massive, dripping candles, hanging as if they had been burning for years in their brass brackets on the walls, heavily laden with tapestries, still as bright now as if they had been hung yesterday.

The book was what interested Cairns. It was old, he could see that, as he prised the pages open through the drying blood. At least the writing was in Ostracian, he thought as he moved around to sit at the desk to read.

It wasn't long before Cairns worked out that it was a diary and not one with many entries. Flicking blood, he spoke words and tried to find where Oldershaw had been reading. It was not difficult. The last entry was covered in traces of Oldershaw.

Time runs out, alas. It is such a shame. The game was just about to get interesting! Both Marchman and I were so close. I had allowed him as much rope as I could, it had even begun to get interesting, but I'm afraid I had already grown bored. A new game has begun to interest me, one with a prize that will be of my own making!

I know I should wait. I should see this out, I should make sure Ostracia survives the next phase of the game I have instigated, but the lure is too strong. I never dreamed I would find the key to eternal life! Lamia held the truth all along, as her followers always claimed! They must be dealt with. Here and elsewhere. I will leave instructions. That meddling King will suffice.

I have decided not to allow the use of the weapon. Not yet. Finding the secret has spoiled the game somewhat. I will lock it away, perhaps see if I can discover the secret again. That will be part of the game.

I wonder if I can win before the century passes? I know thousands of my people are about to die, but by the gods this is exciting! I wonder, even, if I shall be reading this at some point in the future?

I must be quick, I can hear my son at the door. I believe he is ready to kill me. It is about time, he has been prevaricating for months now, although if he had just gone ahead and done it I suppose I would not have thought of this new game.

Life begets life, the parent feeds the child so he may grow.

My father always used to tell me that. It will always be a regret of mine that I did not feed off him in revenge for trying to teach me such nonsense. I will be forgetting him soon. And mother. My children, wives, everything. Even my art. Everything I have worked for.

I have chosen my new identity, the life I will be reborn into. There is a young initiate of Elder Costrange's, he will be most suitable. Cairns, I believe his name is. His mother will have to be dealt with, of course, I will leave instructions for that too, although one of our drone Elders will suffice for this.

Ah. My defences are breached, it is time. I must lock this diary and this life away and begin on the scraps for the diversion. I wonder if some poor sap will be fool enough to follow the trail…

"No!" The bright purple words seemed to grow out of the page and dance before his eyes and his breath caught in his throat.

Cairns retched. A heaving, tearing gnaw from burst inside him. The purple writing just stared up at him, unblinking. As what Cairns knew to be the last contraction of pain hit him, stinging his eyes, he straightened,

"You can thank me later," he heard the voice say again, only this time he saw Kryman's face leering towards him. Plunging the knife into his chest. He saw the days of silence, of blackness before the child finally gave in. He saw the horror in his mother's eyes as the man came to take her away. He saw his uncle's tearful, caring concern turn to understanding and then hatred. He saw the life of Cairns stolen away by a man desperate to escape death, a man who thought of people as nothing more than his playthings, toys to manipulate.

That was why Stracathri defended him. That was why there were Withholdings on his memories. That was why he saw the images of Kryman. That was why he saw the power as the prize.

That was because he saw himself. He saw Lord North.

CHAPTER 33

"You still haven't left, sis," Kryman hissed, standing in between Assundra and Elspeth. He tried to back in towards her as Elspeth advanced, but the green haze, the shield, whatever it was Assundra had erected around herself, seemed to cause Kryman pain whenever he came near.

"Let me past, brother."

"No." Kryman had stopped making jokes, Assundra noticed. Elspeth wouldn't be leaving, Assundra could tell. "You need to find the boy, sis," Kryman went on, clearly attempting to mimic his usual syrupy, mocking tone, but it seemed like an effort. He also seemed to be shimmering more than usual. "Without Simon, you can't do anything here, so why not just leave?"

Elspeth smiled that sweet, innocent-looking smile that Assundra now knew was part of the glamour of her beauty. Not artistic glamour, not fooling of the eyes, but glamour nonetheless. It was a glamour of lies that hid Elspeth's malice and contempt for others. "You are fading, Kryman. It seems we have lost this little game, can you not feel it?"

"Game?" Assundra cried, outraged. "Is that all you people think we are, a game?"

"Yes," Elspeth replied in a perfectly steady voice, "of course. What none of you, your Elders, nor our father seemed to understand was that there was never any way out of this. The outsiders were always going to invade, sooner or later, my father was always going to betray us in some way, he was never going to let the weapon be used. Everything is fixed. The only game he left us with was for the prize." Elspeth's smile turned into a sneer. "You aren't even going to last long enough to try and claim it, brother!"

Assundra saw Kryman bristle and could almost swear she heard him growl. "Assundra, you see that hole? Pick up your friend and go through and wait for me there."

"Wait for you?" Assundra was incredulous. "If we're going anywhere it's out of here, why would I…"

"Assundra, trust me. You do not want to see what my sister is going to do with this power, there is a way out, but it is through that hole, what do you think my brother was guarding?"

Assundra didn't know what to do. She turned her gaze from Kryman, who was tensed, ready to pounce, to Elspeth, who seemed to somehow lounge while standing, playing with the ends of her hair. It all seemed to amuse her and that made Assundra angry. "I'm staying right here," she said, patting Bethlinda on the cheek slightly, hoping she would wake. Assundra was confident the Norths could do nothing to harm her, not any more, but she didn't know how to attack them. She didn't know how to stop them. Beth could tell her.

"Do you want to see your father again?"

"My father?" She snapped her head back around to Kryman.

"He is outside, fighting the outsiders that have invaded. He doesn't have long left. I told you I would help him and I can, but I won't unless you *do as I say*!"

Elspeth laughed. "Her father? By the gods, such trivial concerns! If it's not someone's family or their wealth or some pathetic idea of standing in society it's something else, when will you people learn to see the big picture? None of you matter, none of you! In a century, who has been recorded in history? The Jallells? The Broadsides? The Wests, even? None of them. Your father, Assundra, will die just like everyone else, whether it be tomorrow or next week or in a hundred years. Only us, only the Norths will go on! *That* is the game! *We* are the game!"

Kryman splurted out a snarl. "You sound more and more like him by the day, do you know that?"

At last something changed in Elspeth's expression. "I am nothing like our father, Kryman! Gods knows I tried to help these people, to prevent what was happening, but I was being just as much a fool as them! Nothing any of us can do can change the inevitable! We took outsiders and *fed on them*! How long did we think we could get away with that? We were lucky the outsiders did nothing more they did! What my father knew, what I now know, is that after a century the outsiders' sorcery will not have dwindled as our artistry has! Their numbers will not have succumbed to sorceric plague as ours have! Their will has not been driven into the dirt by a realisation of their own lack of power and influence as ours have! Our defeat is complete, there remains only salvage!"

"And that salvage is yours, right, sis?"

"Are you any different brother?" Elspeth screamed. Kryman was silent. "I thought not! I know your thoughts, I know why you are here, my father did not curse you! You necromanced yourself into this form, did you think me ignorant of this?"

Kryman was silent again. Assundra was growing weary. "What does any of this matter?" she said, intending to sound weary but it seemed to come out as a threat. "How is any of this helping?"

"At last," a voice boomed from outside the balcony doors, "someone has said something that isn't a complete waste of time!"

Elspeth and Kryman both span to look at the door straight away. Bethlinda's eyes flickered open, but before Assundra could exclaim or ask her how she was, Beth put her finger to her lips.

"Be quiet, Sunny. It is time. It will all be over soon." Assundra gaped – how was Bethlinda still able to talk inside her head?

Elder Cairns pushed slowly through the ruined doors, dragging Simon by the ear behind him, his other hand hanging limp at his side. "Cairns!" Assundra couldn't help herself exclaiming, as it turned out, in perfect harmony with Elspeth.

"Assundra, it is good to see you still alive," the Elder said quietly, with a smile that dripped blood down his chin. With a sickening wrench to her stomach she saw the wound on Simon's neck. "And so powerful! I take it you haven't instructed her where her power is drawn from, Kryman?" Cairns laughed.

"Drawn from?"

Cairns ignored her. "Is she alive?" he said, nodding at Bethlinda. Assundra nodded her own reply. "Good. As for you, my children…"

"We are *not* your children, Elder!" Elspeth roared in reply. "We do not pander to your people's misguided reverence for your kind, you are nothing!" She took a few steps towards Cairns, the blood still flowing from her hands.

"Have you tasted him yet?" Cairns smirked, pulling Simon up, making him whimper. Elspeth stopped in her tracks. "I've never tasted a Gifted One before, it's slightly disappointing. Leaves a bitter taste."

"Didn't expect to see you so soon," Kryman said with distaste. "Do you have something to say to me?"

"You mean something like 'thank you', Kryman? No, no I don't think so. Although murdering me was a fairly good attempt at silencing me and it did force my hand."

"Only he seems to have failed again," Elspeth spat.

"Oh, daughter, he wasn't trying to kill me this time! He was trying to torture me, weren't you Kryman? Or was it me, was it this Cairns creature that was your target?"

Elspeth turned to her brother, puzzled. "Oh sis," the spectre laughed in reply, but now his shimmering form was blurring at the edges with every laugh. Something was wrong here, Assundra knew it. Gently, she lifted Bethlinda to a seated position, making sure the shield held around her. Out of the corner of her eye, she saw Kryman's hand, shimmering in and out of existence, wave her toward the opening the beast had left. Beth saw it too and nodded agreement.

"Why are you laughing, Kryman?" Elspeth had turned her back on Cairns. All traces of her smirking smile had vanished. "What have you done?"

"Me? I have done nothing!" Kryman laughed. "If you had let me kill our father when I had wanted to we could have prevented this!" His voice was suddenly stern again. "All of this!"

"I should thank you, daughter," Cairns sneered, "rather than Kryman. Although he held the dagger that bled me to my new life, your snivelling delays, your ignorant sentimentalism allowed me the time I needed to prepare my new vessel!"

"What the hells are you talking about?" Fire leapt from Elspeth's fingers to the floor. Assundra knew it was time to move.

She tried to encourage Beth to her feet, to pull her towards the opening while they were all distracted, but she put out a staying hand. *"Wait!"* Assundra heard in her head.

"Did you think I was just going to let myself die? Did you really think it would be that easy to win the game?" Cairns chuckled. "My dear, do you not recognise me? I am your father!"

"No!" Beth whispered, clutching Assundra's arm tightly, her eyes wide.

"That is a lie!" Elspeth said confidently, swinging her hair back, that smile playing on her lips again. Assundra had sensed it. Elspeth was too alluring, too appealing, it wasn't real. None of this had been real, it had been lies from the start. Their whole lives had been lies.

"I assure you daughter, it is no lie. I have finally come to my senses and remembered who I am! This creature, this Cairns, resisted me for a long time. I hadn't anticipated how the merging of his personality and mine would affect my resolve and drive, but one thing has been constant – this has been interesting! Far more interesting than any of the pathetic challenges of leading our sheep through life. Oh my dear, I know how you must feel," Cairns said in mock concern to Bethlinda, "but in truth, I was still an Elder! Cairns and I, together, were an Elder, you have nothing to reproach yourself for."

"Our people!" Bethlinda squeaked, in a voice so soft Assundra thought she was sobbing. The Gozon Stone was glowing brightly.

"Your people were nothing but pawns in his game," Kryman coughed. Coughed? Assundra looked up to Kryman, this time pulling Bethlinda to her feet. "We all were. Only what he doesn't seem to realise is that it is he who has failed!"

"Kryman, I have not failed. The Gifted One is in my possession, Carstan, bless his necromantic soul, is no longer guarding the weapon, shortly you will be no more and Elspeth is too much of a bleeding heart to fight her father, so I do believe that I have won! As for our people, Keeper, they had their chance. They chose Elder Oldershaw. Who, I would remind you, was an Elder as well. If anyone has damned Ostracia it is him! My plans…"

"Ostracia was damned from the moment you were born, father." Elspeth flinched as fire leapt from her fingers again. "I will fight you if I had to."

"We will both fight you," Kryman hissed, but not through anger or design – it was as loud as he could speak. Assundra couldn't understand what was happening – why was anybody fighting anybody?

"Elder Cairns will not let you do this," Bethlinda managed to get out, her words slightly garbled. Assundra pursed her lips – why was she drawing attention to them? "He will fight you if you try to take the power."

Cairns, or Lord North, whoever he was, just laughed. "I don't think so, Keeper, that is why I am here! Your precious Elder no longer cares! He knows our people have had three chances to save themselves and they took none! They followed Marchman in their greed, even after they were shown the errors of his thinking. They followed the Elders in childlike anger and impatient blind faith, when they were told they only had to be patient. Then they followed Oldershaw, in their craven fear and desperation, when they were told…"

"You told us nothing!" Assundra found herself screaming before she knew what she was doing. "You have lied to us for…for as long as I can remember! I…I don't even know your plan now! What did you expect us to do? We didn't have a choice, we didn't have anything!"

"Elder Oldershaw gave them something to focus on, something to want, something to need. You, as ever my father, gave them contempt and distrust! They did not follow you and your plan because they did not *know of your plan*!" Elspeth suddenly began to float, rising off the floor, her dress and hair billowing around her as if she was in a gale. Assundra took her cue, she wasn't going to wait any longer. Dragging Bethlinda to her feet, ignoring the burst of pain in her shoulder, Assundra dragged her along the gallery towards the opening.

"Stay where you are!" Cairns called out, but was cut off by Elspeth.

"Leave them be! They are mine to…"

"I grow tired of this." Cairns' limp, seemingly useless arm suddenly sprang into life, pulling something out of a fold of his robe and flinging it. Elspeth neatly pirouetted in the air with a sharp chuckle, but then hung suspended, a look of horror on her face as whatever Cairns had thrown plunged straight into Kryman.

Bethlinda gasped and stopped again as Assundra tried to pull her through the opening. "Beth come on," she urged, but there was no moving her.

"Sunny, look…" Beth whispered in awe. Assundra made a half-hearted attempt to pull Bethlinda through the smashed opening, but in truth she wanted to see as well. Kryman was slowly, but surely, dissolving. The spectre's legs were gone and his left arm was quickly following.

It was to Assundra that the spectre turned. "It's up to you now," was all he had time to say, then with a sigh of air, his body was gone, leaving only the eyes. Red eyes. Eyes that Assundra knew had been the ones watching her, knew had been the ones in her mind, not those of the beast Carstan. Or were they only after-effects? Were the red eyes just imprinted on her mind? Assundra blinked hard and when she opened her eyes, she saw nothing.

There was silence, but only for a moment as Elspeth screamed, lunging so quickly through the air it surprised Elder Cairns, who dropped Simon at once, raising his hands to protect himself. There was a loud crack in the air, almost like a sword striking a shield and both Cairns and Elspeth fell.

Then it was Beth who was pulling Assundra through the opening. "Beth, my father!" she cried, trying to pull her back, but Beth was too strong for her, pulling her down a steep flight of steps that ended abruptly in a wall. Gasping as she ran headlong into it, Bethlinda flicked her hand towards Assundra, who felt a wetness strike her face before the cellar they were in burst into light. Before she could look around Beth pulled her past the stairs they had just climbed down.

They were in a small, bare circular sandstone chamber. There were no adornments on the walls, there was no furniture, there was nothing but a slight dip in the centre of the floor to a grating.

Bethlinda was staring about her with a panicked look on her face. "It should be here! It should be here!" she cried, turning to look at Assundra.

Assundra didn't care. "What about my father, Beth? What are we going to do, Kryman said he could help him, what…"

"Nothing can help your father, Sunny, I'm sorry! It's too late now! Sunny, it's too late, what do I do? What do I do?"

There was a loud crash above them and the cellar shook, as if there had been an earthquake. Dust fell from above their heads, coating them. Neither of them moved for a second, fearing the ceiling was going to fall in, but there was nothing. No sound at all.

"Beth…"

"He was right, Sunny," Beth said quickly, rushing over to Assundra and planting a hard kiss on her lips, "it's up to you now. I don't know how to help you."

"Help me? Beth I have no idea what to do!"

A shrill, mad laugh floated slowly down the stairs. Slowly, a bedraggled, bleeding Elspeth limped into the light that Beth was somehow casting. Assundra, without thinking or knowing how she was doing it, pulled the green-hazed shield about them once more, but this time, with a wave of her hand, something struck it, sending it fizzing into nothingness. Assundra felt a stinging, tightening sensation stretch along her skin, everywhere, all over.

"You have no idea what to do," Elspeth laughed, staggering on one good leg. Blood started to collect in a pool at her feet. "As ever, you people know nothing. You fight us, you berate us for controlling you, yet when given your head, you make nothing but bad decisions, or worse, no decisions at all! You despise us for our greater wealth, our greater knowledge which you seem to think gives us a superior air, but in reality, you're just ashamed you have no idea what to do about any issue of any importance!"

"Release it," Bethlinda said calmly, spreading her hands wide of her body.

"No," Elspeth retorted strongly, flicking her hands at Bethlinda, who instantly collapsed, clutching her stomach. Assundra cried out for Beth and made to move to Beth's side, but Elspeth simply flicked one of her hands towards Assundra and her stomach began to burn. Assundra screamed as it felt like flesh was tearing inside her, as if two hands were pulling it apart.

Elspeth laughed again. "Pitiful! You people never cease to amaze me with your weakness! You, Assundra, the greatest sorceror born to this world and you know nothing of how to use it! Keeper, you are clearly the true Gifted One, I am aware Simon is little more than a creation of the Elders, for all his power!"

Something crashed hard on the ceiling again, shaking the cellar. Stone and dust fell in on the far side, distracting Elspeth for just a second. Assundra saw Beth fling out an arm and saw...something...created in the air. A ripple, little more, but it flew towards Elspeth. It was small, too small, it would do nothing. Assundra could see it in Beth's eyes, she was disappointed, sad. Something stirred in her. A symbol floated before her eyes and out of her mouth and Assundra saw the ripple in the air, saw how it moved, how it worked, how it would hurt...and she changed it.

She turned to Elspeth and smiled as the Gifted One's eyes widened as the ripple struck. Elspeth screamed as she fell backwards, coughing blood. For an instant Assundra felt guilty, but then the tearing in her stomach began again and took her attention. She was aware of Bethlinda standing near her, but her eyes were too watered to see.

"It won't help you," she heard Elspeth gasp and cough, "it's all been planned, there's nothing either of you can do now."

"Release it," Beth said again.

"No."

"Do as she says," a voice Assundra knew called but she could not see him. Another crash above them sent a large section of the ceiling crashing down, just missing Bethlinda, who staggered out of the way, lost her footing and fell on Assundra. Instinctively, Assundra raised an arm and put it around Beth, who just turned and stared at Assundra. Her face was full of pure horror.

"When I was a child," Elspeth gasped, "my father took great pains to tell me, along with my dearest siblings, how important we were and how we should do anything we could to make sure we succeeded. Our task was to take the Tower. Not because of its power, or ability to create power, or even because it was rightfully ours, but because it was better that we looked after it rather than somebody else."

Simon jumped down through the hole in the ceiling, smirking.

The pain lessened in Assundra's stomach, but she felt the tickle of blood at the back of her throat. "Beth," she tried to say, but nothing would come out. Beth, too, was mouthing words.

"Let her finish," Simon said simply, strolling over to Elspeth. He wasn't even hurt!

"It had to be us that protected the weapon," Elspeth gasped on, "because my father knew that whilst the Elders might be able to control the power, they would not be able to control themselves. But my father was wrong. Not about the Elders, he was right about them, but he taught us nothing of how to control ourselves, assuming our breeding would see us through."

Assundra coughed a soundless cough as the blood filled her throat. Bethlinda was looking at her with concern, but Elspeth just went on.

"We mastered the powers of Stracathri far quicker and far more easily than any of the interns. We thought that made us special, that we were somehow better than everyone because we were artistically blessed. Stracathri had grown in power over the years and we believed that to be a result of the energies we ourselves were putting into it, we thought of it as a repository of our own artistic prowess. Then it struck me."

"Tell them," Simon said softly, stroking her hair.

"When my brother was to marry the outsider, none of us could understand why. We couldn't understand why he would want to share our power with anyone outside the family, especially with my father so close to perfecting the weapon. We had to stick together to stop him, but he was determined. Then I understood. Simon, what is the traditional wedding gift for Ostracians?"

"A small blue stone from Stracathri."

"Exactly. Had my brother married the outsider, the stone would have left Ostracia for the first time in history. It was what the Tower wanted. It was then I understood that it was not us that controlled the weapon, as my father would have us believe – it controlled us. Stracathri had grown bored with the simplicity of Ostracia. Even in those far more prosperous days we were never an adventurous or inventive people. All those fine fabrics you all wear, all of the tapestries, the jewels, none of them were designed or made in Ostracia. The Ten Villages were far greater innovators than us."

Assundra tried to speak, but was again stopped. The Ten Villages were surely part of the old legends! She had never regarded the stories with anything other than disdain; the same disdain that her subconscious was trying to force on her for actually being interested in what Elspeth was saying. She shouldn't care about any of this. Somehow, even though she knew what she was, Elspeth's shaken, broken beauty made Assundra want to make everything alright for the evil woman.

"They bordered Ostracia on all sides," Elspeth replied, almost in answer to Assundra's unspoken question. One of Assundra's eyes seemed to go slack as more blood fell from her lips. "For all I know they still do. We were one of the Ten Villages, although we grew rather larger than the rest. It was us that first attracted trade to the region from the rest of the Western Side and from the South and the new wealth made the villages stop their futile little battles and each started selling their wares. Their tithes to us, to the Norths, allowed us to make our town into what it deserved to be. The city. Only our city grew too big, too powerful to control and we lost it."

"I don't think she has long, my love," Simon said, looking at Assundra sadly. She looked up, trying to let him know she needed help, but he just smiled apologetically.

"The point is," Elspeth said, her voice breaking into a frenzied coughing fit before she could continue. "The point is, the outsiders attacked us for a reason. We had become slaves to the idea of artistic betterment rather than using that artistry to work for us and in the end the artistry itself outgrew us. The Tower wants to be free. It got inside my brother's head, and, in addition to seeing his bride-to-be beheaded by our father, drove him mad. He vowed to destroy Stracathri, but my father had plans of his own.

"He did not expect the plague." Elspeth's voice faded now. It seemed like she was fading. Even Bethlinda was staring at the Gifted One with something approaching sympathy. Elspeth was focused on Assundra. "We expected you, Assundra Franks. The descendant of the outsider line. The sorceress."

There was a crash above them, sounding like one of the already ruined doors collapsing to the floor and heavy, broken breathing reached their ears.

"Elspeth," Simon said, his voice full of warning, pulling Elspeth to her feet.

"I know," she replied. "Assundra, I can't say that I am sorry. This was always your purpose, since your ancestors gave birth to your line, there was no other choice. You couldn't have stood against any of this."

"I'm sorry, Assundra," Simon said softly in his nasal voice.

All at once she became drenched in sweat, her head pulsing with a scorching, tearing of something trying to get out and Assundra knew she was going to die. Her back arched, twisting and snapping, but now there was no pain. Her head rolled back on its own, her neck muscles useless as the burning took hold, burning away even the pain.

"Let it go, Assundra," Elspeth cooed softly, as if she was speaking directly in her ear. "Let it all out. Let it pass. Let it end."

"Not while I still draw breath!"

Cairns' arm draped over the hole in the ceiling and he dragged himself until what was left of his face could be seen. Flesh hung off in lumps and his mouth hung slack. "Keeper," he drawled, only just managing to form words, "help me."

At once, Bethlinda stood, the Gozon Stone pulsing brighter than Assundra had ever seen and, just as Elspeth had done earlier, began to float. Blood dripped from her hands and something fizzed and crackled in the air around Beth. She looked amazing! She looked so powerful, so in control, all traces of whatever had caused her pain gone, but Elspeth was soon rising to meet her, radiating a fierce impatience.

Assundra's eyes exploded with light as Elspeth and Bethlinda clashed. Heat crackled around the cellar and her mouth filled with the taste of nothing. Assundra was almost glad of it, as it took away the taste of the blood, but she wanted to see what was happening to Beth!

She tried to open her eyes, but the light was too fierce, too bright to see and she was forced to slam them shut once more. A ringing developed in her ears, rising to a pitch that made her cry out a scream she couldn't hear.

Then it was gone. It was all gone. Bethlinda, Elspeth and Simon, they were all gone. There was only Elder Cairns, leering, as far as his melted face would allow, over the hole in the ceiling.

"Did you expect something different?" Cairns laughed, but he was speaking in her head. Not like Bethlinda used to, not in a distant, half-heard whisper, but loud, clear and precise. "Your Keeper has done her job well, she has forced Elspeth to release the curbs on the power! The one final twist to my own plan. I'd forgotten how ignorantly precise I used to be!"

"Where is Bethlinda?" Assundra asked. "I don't care about the rest. I don't care about any of it, I just want to know if she's... ok."

"I don't know," the reply came into her mid. "It is possible she survived. I've never considered whether she would or not. And as for not caring, Assundra... how can you no t care? This has all been about you!"

"About me?"

"Why yes! You have been the key all along, just as your mother was before you and her mother before her. I would go on, but I heard my daughter's exposition. She always did love a story."

"Your daughter? How are you..."

"A simple...well, no, not simple at all, in truth. A transference. Discarding the shell of one for another. Only as this other was a child, I did not predict his nature would survive as far as it has. It has blinded me, delayed my progress, yet I have arrived here as I always should have."

"Half-dead?"

The voice in her head laughed. The mouth of the figure slumped over the hole in the ceiling just drooped. "This is a temporary inconvenience. Once you release the power, my dear, all things will heal. The game will be over. There will be something in it for you, of course."

"For me?"

"Naturally!" the voice cooed.

"I don't want anything from you!" she shouted without words. "You killed Bethlinda! You...did whatever you did to my father! You let them *drink from me!*"

"And what did you do to try and stop any of that? Nothing." Assundra blinked. "You opened your legs for Galvarin Jallel, hoping he would rescue you. You hid behind you father, hoping he would protect you. You spurned Simon because of how the villagers treated him when he was the one who could have helped you. You ignored your sorcery when it could have saved you, protected you, helped you. You did nothing."

"I couldn't have done anything!" she cried. "I did everything I could!"

"You did nothing!" the voice laughed back. "You sat back and hoped someone else would sort it out. Even when your father started getting ill, did you seek help? No, you pretended everything was fine for your own sake. Your father could have been saved, Assundra."

"Saved? You did this to him!"

"And I can undo it."

"Undo it?" Assundra gasped out loud.

"Of course. Once I have the power I will be able to do anything. All you have to do is let the sorcery out."

"I have," she replied, confused. She had let the sorcery release itself before, she had seen the symbols come through her, she had raised the shield. "What more can I do?"

The voice in her head laughed again. "Let me show you."

A single, complex symbol passed across her eyes. The only detail she could make out was a serpent. No, not just a serpent...half a serpent, half a woman. With burst eyes...just like the statue she had seen through the eyes of the guard! The symbol was of Lamia! Something in her stomach tightened and her throat contracted.

"Don't resist it," the voice encouraged and she saw the symbol again, closer, in more detail. She could see things in the arms of the woman, whose mouth was stretched wide in a toothy snarl, something dripping from her maw. "It will help you, it will help all of us! Let it out!"

Her throat went completely dry. Whatever was inside her didn't want to let this symbol shape it. It didn't want to be used.

"Think of your father," the voice went on. "You could save him! We could save him together! We could find Bethlinda!"

"Beth?"

"Of course! I'm sure she survived, she was special! That was why I chose her. I'm *sure* she survived. Once I have the power I promise we will find her! I can destroy Elspeth for you to make sure she never hurts Bethlinda again. I can heal you. I can heal your father. I can make it so your family's curse will not follow you any longer, you will be able to have children with no risk. I can make sure the outsiders never find any Ostracians who escape. If you like, I can even teach you how to master your sorcery so you never have to use it again. You'd like all of those things wouldn't you? I can make all of them happen. You just have to do this one thing, for me."

The symbol passed before her eyes again.

So much death for this. So much death because of her. Was it her, was it Lamia who could stop it too?

"I trusted you…" she managed to say, but her head wasn't really there. She felt a wetness at the back of her head.

"I know, I hoped you would. I'm sorry, truly I am, you are one of the few people I have met during my life that I admire, Assundra Franks, you are truly remarkable." He meant it as well. The bastard *truly* meant it. "You were never intended to win this game, none of you were. Nothing was ever going to stop me, even the two *Gifted* Ones couldn't stop me. Don't let them and their lies stop you getting what you want! I can give you all of that."

The symbol passed again and this time stopped before her eyes. Assundra felt her throat relax. Her mouth opened. The dryness turned to a stale, sickly taste as bile rose in a slow trickle from her gut. She felt it. She felt it happen. Her body contracted, with intense pleasure, pleasure she had never felt, then a stinging pain. The symbol began to dissolve. As it did so, Assundra saw that Lamia was holding her children.

As the symbol vanished, there was a complete absence of any sound, smell or sense of touch, of even the air against her skin. The world stilled and Cairns' mind met hers. The cellar shimmered, greying slightly around the edges. Cairns and Assundra too were still, their eyes unblinking, their gaze locked together. Then the voice came, not to her mind this time but carried over the air as if by an absent breeze.

"This is the only time in your life it will affect you."

"Affect me?"

Then she felt it. The surge through the veins, each pulse gripping her heart, making her aching muscles feel three times as strong as they were, her mind ten times calmer. This was artistry! Was this is how they all felt? Gods, did they feel like this all the time? Was that what Beth had been trying to tell her?

"It's good isn't it?"

And it was. She wanted to cry out loud how good it was, as good as when she had lain with Beth that first time, but no words came; she knew nothing of how to use this power, she could not make the words real. Then, all too soon, it began to fade. She looked down with her mind, where Cairns' mind gently showed her, to the large wound seeping blood from her gut. The artistry was leaving with it, the edges of the wound healing as it flowed out with the blood until, with a tiny flash of blue light, it was gone and she was just Assundra once more.

"That is what you will never know," the voice said.

She wanted to know it! Her body ached for it now, screamed for it! She had never felt anything so powerful, like she could stop anything! No man could have hurt her if she had that power!

"Things that come easily are rarely valued," the voice said. "Your path now will lead you to places Ostracians will never go. Once the power transfers to me, we will both be free of this place! It is finally over!"

Assundra couldn't move. The bleeding from her gut wasn't slowing. "You promised," she whispered, but as she could barely hear herself she doubted Lord North could. She wasn't sure she cared. He had been right, of course. She was nothing. She had none of their power or artistry. She had simply waited for Galvarin and then Bethlinda to sort out all of her problems. What had she actually done, what had she physically done to help he father or herself? Nothing.

"What is this delay?" Lord North hissed to her mind impatiently.

The broken masonry and timber above them rang with the sound of footsteps, stealthily making their way across towards them. Four footsteps.

"Where is the power? No! It is gone!"

A low growl accompanied the heavy, shadowy shape that walked to the still prone body of Lord North, placing its front paws on his shoulders. Assundra heard her breaths, panting and panicked, rattling with blood, and she tried to cry out.

"Father!" she screamed, so loud she thought her head would burst, but only a gurgle spurted from her lips. It was enough though, as what was above them roared.

Her father's broken, hairy, bloodstained face looked out from the muzzle of the animal that held him. His eyes flicked down to Assundra's stomach and with a plaintive howl Tom cried.

"I'm sorry father," she said, though she didn't know if she could be heard, her voice felt so weak, "I think you're too late."

Tom's howl turned into a growl and she saw his love turn to anger. As her father bared his jaws and snapped down onto Cairns' head, Assundra closed her eyes. She didn't want to remember her father that way. She wanted to remember the hard but kind man who always took care of her. Who showed her how to make cider, who loved her mother completely. Who always told his daughter to live her life.

There seemed little purpose to living now. Elder Cairns, or Lord North, whoever the man had actually been, Elspeth, Bethlinda, everyone here had lost. For she understood now. As Elspeth had said, Stracathri's power hadn't wanted to stay in Ostracia. It didn't want to be in an Ostracian. In releasing it, Assundra had inflicted Ostracia on the world once more. Elspeth, Beth and Simon were gone as the power was gone. Only she was left behind.

"Sunny, it's over! It's over! Sunny? Sunny, what's wrong? Sunny!" Beth was screaming near Assundra's head, only Assundra knew she couldn't be. The sound seemed to drive the world from her sight. The wound in her gut had not sealed. Too much was lost. In her mind, for that must be were she was, as Beth, her sweet Beth, screamed her name over and over, in an agony all of her own, Assundra saw her mother once more and she one final symbol. She didn't bother trying to stop this one leaving her. Her mother smiled.

"Sunny!" Beth screamed, but she, too, was now fading. "I will not let you die!"

"I'll be with you soon, Beth, don't fret so," she said softly,

It had all gone: her father, the pain in her stomach, the fear, the barriers, Galvarin, Simon, the Crafters, the Norths, the Elders and her sweet Bethlinda. As the incessant, nagging beating in her chest stilled, she flew to put her arms around her mother's neck. She was free.

CHAPTER 34

A WEEK LATER

Assundra awoke with a start, as she always did, clutching a hand to the poultice strapped to her stomach under which the dull pain throbbed. At once the stench of her body hit her and she swallowed back hard. She hadn't washed in days, maybe weeks. She couldn't tell if the wound smelt bad or if it was just her.

She also knew this was one of the old settlements. Bethlinda had said, sadly, that this was where it had all begun, but Assundra didn't know what she meant. The building no longer had much of a roof left and plants grew through much of the floor, but where Assundra sat now, on the one bed made of crushed undergrowth, was dry. It was not clean. Assundra had lain here for a week without really moving, covered in her own filth. Beth had washed her as best she could, but the nearby stream was too far for her to reach before the wound crippled her with the pain.

The wound was taking longer to heal than the entire sorry episode, Assundra thought as she stared up through the shutter-less window with teary eyes at the night sky. Bethlinda had said they must leave tomorrow, that their time had run out. Assundra presumed it was some artistic sense of hers that Assundra didn't have, could never have. Beth had told her it would be too late if they stayed another day. Assundra supposed it was because of the outsiders, though the soldiers seemed to leave them alone. They hadn't seen one for weeks now either, not since Beth had brought her to this place. Not since the patrol had walked right past them as the girls had stood, terrified, at the side of the road. None of the men had even turned their heads.

Beth was always turning her head to look at Assundra, only she noticed Beth looked at her strangely these days, as if she was worried. Every day she replaced the poultice on Assundra's wound, but every day, no matter how often Assundra asked, Beth wouldn't say if it was healing properly.

So she'd stopped asking. After she'd first awoken it had been three days before she had been able to look Bethlinda in the eye. The anger at the betrayal was gone now, replaced by a dull ache. She knew she didn't want Beth to leave. She didn't want Beth to ever leave, even if it was sometimes a struggle to look at her. Sometimes Assundra tried to tell herself that it was just because she had nobody else, that Bethlinda was the only person left. That was somehow better than the alternative, better than being in love with someone who had willingly used her, but she knew deep down that the need she had for Beth was more than just practical. Despite everything, she wanted Bethlinda with her all the time.

She sighed. Beth wasn't here now, but she never took long to return after Assundra woke. It was as if she knew. All she could do was sit and wait, wondering if Beth was going to try and forcer her to eat again.

Bethlinda never stayed in the shelter overnight with her. Assundra didn't know where she went, but it wasn't far; if she ever cried out in pain it didn't take Beth long to rush to her side and take care of whatever need she may have. The girl smiled, but Assundra could see the turmoil inside, behind the encouragement and the care, and she didn't know what to do.

Nobody else was left now, Beth said. Those who could leave, who hadn't been slaughtered by the outsiders, had left.

"Elspeth showed them the tunnels," Beth had said, "which was good of her I suppose. Only those that would follow her, of course. The rest are dead." Assundra had asked about Alice, about Galvarin, but Bethlinda didn't know who had survived. Whenever she mentioned her father or Elder Cairns, Bethlinda's mouth tightened and she looked like she might cry, so Assundra had stopped asking about that too.

Sometimes Assundra wondered where she was, exactly. She assumed, from the amount of guards that walked past during the day, that they were somewhere near the border, the wall the outsiders had built around the edge of the Forest. Every day more of them poured into Ostracia, for all Beth said there was nobody left. They had to be guarding something.

Assundra didn't care.

She knew her father was dead. Not for sure, but she knew it inside. When he had killed Elder Cairns, she had seen the wounds he'd already suffered. She had failed him. Cairns, or Lord North, she still didn't know what to call him, had been right, she hadn't even tried, she'd done nothing, just waited for someone else to help her, to do it for her.

Turning, she eyed the piles of leaves and stones that hid the bodies. She'd had to help herself when she'd awoken to find Young and Just Crafter leering over her in bed. Just Crafter was badly wounded, but it hadn't seemed to affect his manhood, which had been sticking out from his body like a mini version of Galvarin's.

"We'll be off soon," Just had spat into her ear, "but seeing as we found you, we thought we'd have a little fun with you first!"

It was the one time she'd screamed for Beth and she hadn't come. "Look, Young 'un, she's seeing things now! Nobody's going to come and help you, love!"

Young Crafter was holding back. "Let's just go before the soldiers come!"

"I don't know, Young 'un, I've heard sorcerers can be quite a ride. Know things other women don't. Knows how to take a man in hand, you know what I mean?"

He'd grabbed her hand and shoved his prick into it then. It was the last thing he'd done. She felt it leave her, what she now knew was sorcery, rushing through her hands, but this time she wanted it to. She knew it was coming. She told it to come. She knew the symbol she called to her mind and knew what it meant. She knew what it would do.

Strangely, it had been Young Crafter who had screamed when Just had backed away from Assundra in horror, the bloody, twisted stump that had once been his prick dropping to the floor as he did. He'd bled to death on the floor with Assundra and Young Crafter watching.

"I told him," Young Crafter had said, without a trace of emotion for his brother. "I told him not to do it."

Assundra hadn't replied. She knew, somehow, that Young Crafter wasn't going to hurt her and it wasn't just because Simon had been standing behind him, unseen. She shook her head ever so slightly as Simon raised a finger dripping with blood.

"Do you need anything?" Young Crafter had asked, shifting nervously, unable to meet her eyes. "Only I could send help…you know, on the outside. If I make it. They're everywhere out there, hundreds of them. Elder Oldershaw was wrong."

The man sounded bitter, as if he'd been lied to, but Elder Cairns had been telling them all for years that they couldn't withstand another outsider attack. It was why the fires had been extinguished, it was why they had left the old city. They had known. They had all known, they just chose to ignore it, pretending they knew better, overlaying their pathetic ideology over the world when they should have been focusing on the truth.

"I'll leave then," Young Crafter had said eventually, after standing for some time just looking at her sadly. "I'm going to Caraiza, if you want to…you know. Come back. Come and find me if, you know…I'll look after you, Assundra. I'm sorry. I'm sorry for everything." He half-turned and jumped as he saw the boy in the doorway. Assundra saw the yellowing whites of Simon's teeth as he smiled. She shook her head again.

A girlish scream bubbled from Young Crafter's mouth as he went for the knife at his belt. "I'm afraid it's not going to work like that!" Simon laughed and before Assundra could tell him not to, Simon had pulled Young Crafter to him, those yellowing teeth digging into his neck, drawing the blood from the wound and swallowing it down. In seconds and with nothing more than a curdled whimper, Young Crafter was dead. Simon dropped the body to the floor. It pained Assundra to see the dead treated with such disrespect. They were still people.

"Seriously, what did Cairns expect?" Simon grinned, falling to his knees, an expression of delight on his face. "This is really good you know Assundra, better than any of your ciders. Makes you feel so alive!"

Assundra looked down at the bodies. In the space of a few minutes she'd killed one man and Simon had killed another. What had happened to them? Only a few days ago she was trying to stop Simon stealing cider from the alehouse and telling him to stop staring at her breasts. Now they were killers.

And she didn't even care. "What are you doing here?" They were the first words she'd spoken since she'd awoken.

Simon dragged a shaking finger along his lips, before licking it slowly through his smile. "We're leaving," he said simply.

"We?" Assundra's heart raced in panic – did he mean to take her with him?

"Elspeth and I," he replied, giggling slightly. Assundra's heart slowed. She found herself looking at the body again. Just had tried to rape her. He had deserved it, but Young Crafter was going, Simon didn't need to have killed him. She looked down, curious that there was no blood on her hands. "She's amazing, Assundra," she realised Simon was saying. "I've never met a woman like her. The things she's shown me…"

He looked towards her with a dirty grin, but she wasn't interested. "So why are you here? After what you made me…" She couldn't finish.

Simon paused, then sighed. "Haven't you figured it out yet?" He shook his head. "None of us had any choice in this, Assundra. Elspeth has explained it all to me now. Did you know I had the power all along?"

Assundra shot Simon a blank look. "I don't care," she replied – and she really didn't. "How does that help me or my father?"

Simon sighed again. "It doesn't, Assundra, but it does mean it wasn't your fault. Your family was always destined for this, Elspeth explained. It's your blood, your…sorcery. You being an outsider. Lord North planned it all years ago, it was how he withheld the power fore a century, he used outsider sorcery. He used you. Clever bugger, really."

"Clever?" Assundra echoed in horror. "How is it clever to destroy your people? There's none of us left, Simon!"

"Do you care?"

She opened her mouth to say of course she did, of course she cared – how could she not? She loved Ostracia and whilst she might not have loved everyone in it, they didn't deserve to die or be scattered like flies fleeing as a predator approached.

"No," was what she found she said, not surprising herself that she said it. "They were awful people, all of them."

"Exactly," Simon said with a chuckle. "They weren't a century ago, though. That was the Elder Council's doing. They did this Assundra, all of it. For all his cleverness, Lord North hadn't counted on them being so stupid. None of us had a chance."

With a final suck of his finger, Simon held it up proudly, as if he'd done something amazing. Turning to leave, he said simply, "Goodbye, Assundra. Make the right choice. Oh," he added, already out of the door, "we buried your father. We thought it was the right thing to do. Found him just outside the Ostracian border. No sign of Lord North, in case your friend asks. I'm sorry."

Assundra felt numb all over. She'd known it. She had been prepared for the worst, but still she would have expected to feel more of a sense of loss than this. Her father, her real father, had died months ago, the day the thing inside him took over, she knew that now. He had even tried to tell her, to warn her, but it was only now she understood.

She felt nothing for the rest of the villagers. They had made their beds, as her mother would have said. In the end, only Kryman, the lying, murdering, evil bastard, had been true to her. The only one who had not been lying to her.

She sighed. Ostracia's chapter in history had finally closed. The plague…no, not the plague, the plague hadn't ended their civilisation, they had done it themselves. Their cowardice had done this. Their anger. The strength of the Ostracian people had finally ebbed away as Elder Oldershaw's one revolution too many had stuttered even as it had taken hold.

The memory seemed to force a strength of a different kind had left her.

She awoke later, how much later she wasn't sure, but it was daylight, to a delighted Bethlinda, who was leaning over her, gushing with relief. One day she knew she would forgive the girl, the hurt on Bethlinda's face when Assundra had turned away from the delighted kisses was already doing its work on her conscience, but she hadn't been ready.

"I brought you some berries." Assundra's stomach turned at the thought, making her stretch a hand in fear to the poultice. Each time she moved she felt like it would come off. "You should eat, Sunny, you'll need your strength for later."

The smile was gone from Beth's face. Se had been crying. Not meeting her eyes, the Keeper – was she still the Keeper, Assundra wondered, did the Transept Tower still need her? – set the berries down beside her and set to checking the wound. How could Beth have betrayed her? How could she have ruined this? Assundra knew, she could tell, that Beth loved her, so why had she tricked her? Beth had let her believe that the whole thing was about helping her get away from the Crafters. Instead, it had all been about nothing more than power. Only Beth didn't know that. Beth thought Elder Cairns had been trying to save the village, ending the plague that had taken Beth's parents, freeing all Ostracians. She hadn't known he was a reincarnated murderer and dictator. Beth had thought she was doing the right thing, just as Elder Cairns had, before he remembered who he was. Just as Elder Oldershaw thought he was. Just as they all thought they were doing. Which of them was right?

As Assundra watched, a small tear fall from her friend's face. The wrench it wrought inside her told her it was time.

"Thank you, Beth."

The little gasp before Beth spoke was the most beautiful sound Assundra had ever heard. "Oh, Sunny!" she exclaimed, resuming her kisses from where she had left off a few moments before, but Assundra didn't turn away this time. "I thought I'd lost you forever! I didn't want to talk, not until you were ready, but you have to know I'm so sorry, so sorry about it all, about everything! He said it was too important, that you couldn't know or it would ruin everything, that it wouldn't work, but I think…I think he was wrong. I'm sorry."

It took some time to calm Bethlinda down and stop speaking after that. The sun was had risen to its highest point when they finally let go of each other. Bethlinda became agitated again when she realised that meant it was after noon and leapt from the bed. "If we're going to leave, we have to go now, Sunny!"

Assundra didn't move. She needed answers before she would go anywhere.

Beth nonetheless started fussing around, still naked, packing up their meagre things – the few remaining poultices, the few books Beth had rescued from somewhere and some spare clothes – when she saw the berries, some of which had been crushed underneath their bodies, on the bed.

"Oh, Sunny! You must eat the berries I got for you! I told you, you have to eat to keep your strength up, who knows where the nearest town is! Mind you," Beth added, pocketing the berries in a pouch before Assundra had a chance to take one, "you didn't seem to need much energy after all." Assundra smiled, feeling the corners of her mouth pull and crack. She knew then that she wouldn't leave, that she never had any intention of leaving her friend. Her lover. Her love.

"Beth, there are some things I must know." Assundra tentatively moved, waving away Beth's proffered arm, and sat on the rough branch lying on the floor. She was feeling much better, but standing still caused her pain.

"What is it, Sunny?" Beth replied, speaking softly, the strain evident, as if she was afraid, but had been expecting this. She had somehow got dressed so quickly that Assundra hadn't noticed and was now wearing the same dress she had worn when they had been reunited in the Transept Tower.

Assundra pushed thoughts of sex aside, she had to know these things. "What happened?" she said, swallowing. "All of it, I mean," she added, seeing Beth's confusion. "Why now, why me? Simon said…"

Bethlinda sighed, and sat down next to her, holding each breath in the strange way Assundra herself did when she was trying to stop herself crying. "Because of who you are. You're special, Sunny, you always have been! And not just to me. You're the only one of your kind, the only one of your kind there will ever be! An outsider with a perfect sorceric nature, powered by Ostracian blood!"

"Perfect sorceric nature?" Assundra laughed in exasperation. "I don't have a clue what I'm doing! Everything I've done, it's like someone else is controlling me, like something is working through me. I keep seeing my mother…"

"That's part of what sorcery is, Sunny," Beth interrupted eagerly. "Channelling the dead. Necromancy, they call it I believe."

"Channelling the dead?" Assundra looked at her friend's matter-of-fact expression in horror. "So my mother was with me?"

Beth's eyes widened. "Oh no, Sunny, I didn't mean to suggest that! Just that…she left something behind. Something in you. All of our parents leave something in us, they leave their traces. Sorcerors, like you, can tap into that better than the rest of us. It's something Elder Cairns was terrified of because it was something he couldn't do."

Assundra looked at Beth curiously. "Beth, can you?"

For a moment her lover did nothing, but then, slowly, she began to nod.

Assundra frowned. "Elspeth said…" she stopped, struggling to remember the words. "She said you were the true Gifted One. Beth, is that true?"

Beth just nodded again. "Elder Cairns didn't know. He thought he'd made it happen, he thought he'd channelled the power into Simon, but he just created…well, you knew him." Assundra pursed her lips. Simon had just saved her. Again. "Sunny, we had to keep it from you. If you'd known…"

"I could have learned, Beth! I could have defended myself! My whole life would have been different!"

"I know, but Sunny, I'm sorry, that's the point!" Beth was clearly upset, but Assundra was getting angry again now and snatched her hand away. "None of us wanted you to suffer! But if you'd learned about your sorcery you wouldn't have been able to hide it! You saw what happened when Alice found out – she was terrified of you! That would have got much worse, very quickly if Elder Oldershaw hadn't distracted them! You would have released too much power, you wouldn't have been ready…"

"You used me!" Assundra interrupted, the anger rising suddenly from wherever she had put it. Beth hung her head. "You used me like I was nothing more than a means to an end, all of you! There's nothing else to say!"

"Sunny, if you hadn't released the sorcery at the right time you'd have destroyed yourself. Possibly all of us."

"I don't believe you," Assundra spat back, aware she was being spiteful but right at this moment she didn't care.

"It's true! The outsiders would have sensed it, Sunny. Even at the council chambers, when you broke the shield, we were worried they would have sensed even such a small display of power."

"Small?"

Bethlinda smiled a tired but sympathetic smile. Assundra forced herself not to be swayed by it. "You have no idea of the power inside you. Sunny, if you learn how to control it, how to use it properly, learned what all the ancient symbols mean and remembered them, there isn't a person in the world who could stand against you, even Simon."

"Simon? What's so special about him?"

"He has the power of Stracathri. All of it. He always did."

Assundra felt her stomach turn at a memory. "Beth, he was here. He…"

"He could see you?" Beth's eyes widened. "Sunny that's fantastic! That means…"

Assundra didn't understand, but she didn't want to talk about that anyway. "Listen, Beth, that's not the point! Young and Just Crafter, I think, I can't remember properly…"

"Sunny…"

"Beth, let me finish! They were here and Simon…he…he did what Mary and the others did to me! Only he killed Young Crafter. But he *drank* from him, Beth!"

"I know, Sunny. You were…asleep for a while. I thought you'd done what you'd done in your sleep, that you'd protected yourself, but if they all saw you Sunny that's great!"

"Great? He tried to rape me!" Assundra knew Beth didn't mean that, but something inside her wanted to hurt Bethlinda. At the same time she felt bad for doing it. She didn't understand what she was doing at all.

"I'm sorry, Sunny," Beth said, her eyes watering. "You know I wouldn't want that! I love you!" Beth reached out a hand to Assundra again and this time she let her take it. Bethlinda sighed in obvious relief.

Assundra waited for Beth to carry on speaking, but she was just staring in awe at Assundra's hand. "Beth, what did you mean Simon has Stracathri's power?"

Beth's smile faded. "It was all a game. None of us stood a chance."

"Because of Lord North? I still don't really understand…"

"No, not Lord North. Kryman. Elspeth and Kryman, they unlocked the power years ago. They knew what their father was planning, all of it, at least Kryman did. He knew his father was planning to transfer himself into another host, to be reborn and live again, but they hadn't counted on Elder Cairns being so strong." Beth looked up. "He really was a good man, Sunny. He wanted what was best, for all of us! He wanted to save us, I'm sure of it."

Assundra smiled, but didn't believe Beth. The way to go about saving someone wasn't to do it behind their back, it was to involve them, to trust them. Cairns had done neither with his people.

"Only when Kryman killed Elder Cairns…it stopped everything. Lord North could finally take control, only by then I think he'd forgotten who he was. It was all part of Kryman's plan. He knew his father would try to make a Gifted One he could mould to his own designs. Elspeth had always disappointed him, always going against her father's wishes, too powerful for him to stop with anything but an outsider invasion."

"He did all this just to get at his daughter?" Assundra cried, incredulous.

"Maybe not just because of that, but it was Lord North who initiated it. I think he really wanted to show the outsiders what he could do. He'd grown bored with Ostracia, there was little for him to do any more, he wanted more. He wanted the world."

"Typical aristocracy," Assundra said, a sadness creeping over her when she realised she was echoing her father's words.

Beth was just nodding again. "Kryman knew his father better than anyone. It was such a simple plan – get Elspeth to release the Withholdings Lord North had put on the weapon, the power, then put his own on. He knew his father would leave clues for his successors, Elder Oldershaw as it turned out, so all Kryman had to do was make sure his own instructions got through with his father's. As soon as Elder Oldershaw forced Simon to pull the first of the triggers to releasing Kryman and Elspeth, the power of the weapon began to seep into him."

"Why Simon?" Assundra was confused. "Why didn't he take the power for himself?"

"He's dead," Beth said simply. "Living artistry would destroy him. It doesn't matter that it was Simon, Sunny, it could have been anyone. Kryman just wanted to beat his father, that's all."

Assundra almost choked on her words. "So they destroyed our entire people for a squabble between father and son?" she screamed. Beth just nodded again, holding her hand tightly. "They did what they did to my father for this? I've suffered what the Crafters put me through for *this*?"

Beth had tears in her eyes again. "It wasn't supposed to be like this! Elder Cairns wanted to save the villagers, he really did! Nobody predicted the outsiders' plague, nobody though they would be so vindictive. Even without the weapon Lord North thought they'd at least drive the outsiders out, but…yes, Sunny. It was all for nothing."

"So the outsiders got what they wanted," Assundra hissed angrily. "Ostracia is dead."

They didn't say anything for a while. Assundra couldn't stop picturing what she'd do to Elspeth if she saw her again.

"Elspeth was as surprised as anyone, she didn't know," Beth said quietly, as if she could read Assundra's thoughts. "She thought she was fighting for the power. She really thought only a North could control it."

"Only a North could control it?" Assundra scoffed. "How do you know anyway? Beth, where did you go when you vanished? Cairns…Lord North didn't seem surprised, but one minute you were there and then…"

"We went…" Bethlinda seemed to think for a second, then Assundra got the impression she was shaking herself. "It doesn't matter, Sunny. We went somewhere we couldn't fight. Somewhere there was no fighting, there was just…nothing. Trust me, you don't want to know."

"Trust you," Assundra echoed sadly. "I want to, Beth. But you and Cairns have ruined my life. He made me…he made me forget you!"

"That's why he chose me!" Beth shifted to kneel in front of her. "Because I love you! Because he knew I loved you. I always have. When he took me away, he told me it was because of you, that you would be in danger if I stayed and one day we could be together again. When we…in my room, Sunny, you had all of my heart, you must believe me!"

She did believe her. And she knew Beth knew that from her smile, but it couldn't be said. Not yet.

"Sunny, we were trying to do a wonderful thing! Perhaps in the wrong way, but still wonderful. We wanted Ostracia to be free! The rest of them, they just couldn't wait. Maybe if they hadn't pushed Elder Cairns, if the Norths hadn't come back, then Lord North wouldn't have been able to take control. We could have saved them all. It's all over now."

"Oh, you are wrong!" she wanted to scream, but she couldn't. It was true, once, that leaving the village was her sole aim, to get away from the villagers, from the Crafters, and what they would have done to her. That was before she knew about this power she had. This sorcery. She knew something was waiting for her somewhere outside Ostracia.

It was why she hadn't decided whether to come back.

Assundra found she couldn't blame Bethlinda any more. Perhaps mainly because she didn't want to. She knew Cairns had probably told her that the villagers would harm them if they found out about them. He would have told her that if it all went to plan they could be together far away from the villagers, they could be free to be themselves. She told herself there was no way Beth could know what that freedom would lead to, but then even Assundra didn't really know that. Beth was all she had to help her through whatever was to come, as Cairns had told her she would. More than that, she did love the girl.

"Sunny, we have to go. You know that, don't you?"

Assundra didn't know anything. She wanted to stay here. They couldn't find her here. Simon had told her it was her choice. Now, for the first time with anything that had happened to her, she had a choice and she didn't know what to do.

"What will we do, Beth?" she asked simply.

Bethlinda blinked. "Sunny! We can find your father, we can heal him – we can find some way…" She stopped as she saw Assundra's face. "Sunny, what is it?"

"My father's dead, Beth," she said simply. "Simon told me. They even buried him, I don't know where. I'll never see him again."

Beth didn't even breathe. Tears streamed down her face slowly and silently. "Oh gods," she said eventually before her body erupted in sobs. "I'm so sorry, Sunny! I'm so sorry!"

Assundra held Beth close to her then. Part of her wanted to tell her it wasn't her fault, that there was nothing she could have done, but none of that was true. Another part of her wanted to pull away from Beth, even to hurt her, for what she and Cairns had done to her father. A bigger part of her than both wanted Beth next to her. At that moment Assundra made her choice.

On their way to their new life, they found her father's grave, at Bethlinda's insistence, and Assundra wept.

"She loved you very much, I know she did," Assundra said to the simple cairn of stones he laid around the patch of earth. "And so do I."

Soldiers were still prowling for any survivors, but they let the two lovers pass as if they weren't there. Animals paid them no heed. Nobody was waiting for them as they passed through the newly opened Yawning Maw, something Assundra had only heard about in tales. She thought it was nothing special as she passed, just a row of trees with a gap through which they passed.

Skirting around the camps, which Assundra could now see were entire villages, they walked for a few days, not stopping for sleep. Assundra couldn't remember if they'd eaten anything or not.

Eventually they reached rolling green fields, that spread out as far as they could see. There was a small, deserted hamlet. Just a few cottages. Assundra thought it curious that such a collection of small cottages, not unlike the one Assundra had grown up in, should be collected so far from anything else. A stream ran behind the hamlet, flowing down from the hills that bordered it on two sides.

The outside was curious to Assundra. There didn't seem to be any of the huge towns and cities she had been expecting. Somehow she had pictured places like the old city of Ostracia, littered all along the landscape, one next to another. The idea of such a wide expanse of what was virtually nothing had never entered her head. She liked it.

Assundra turned to Bethlinda and smiled. The beauty in the smile she received in return eased Assundra's heavy heart and without a word they locked hands.

"It was all so hopeless, wasn't it?"

"We did our best, Sunny. We just didn't have a chance," her friend replied, her eyes wide as she scanned the lands ahead of them.

"No, but…"

"But we'll never know now. I know."

"Do you think he's dead?"

"Cairns? I don't know. I can't feel him any more. Even when Lord North took over, I could feel him, I knew I had to obey him. I can feel the Transept Tower." A wistful tone entered Bethlinda's voice and Assundra looked up in slight alarm. "If he is alive I don't think he's an Elder now. Ostracia has played its part, Sunny. It's not our world out here."

"It will be soon. We'll make part of it ours, at least."

"Yes!"

"But…what about Simon and Elspeth? Don't you think we should warn them, try to help them?"

"No."

Beth's voice was hard. "But…"

"They destroyed us, Sunny. They destroyed us all! Their damned plague…they killed my parents! Let them deal with it now. I'm too tired."

"But if Simon's as powerful as you say…"

"It's not about us any more, Sunny. Besides, I don't exactly know what we could do."

Assundra took Beth's arm. "But Beth, they said you…aren't you the Gifted One?"

To her surprise, Bethlinda just shrugged. "I have some powers, some I didn't even know I had." Something in Beth seemed to change at the thought. The Gozon Stone glared bright blue for just a moment and light seemed to enter Beth's face. "Besides, do you remember the histories in the writings?" Beth skipped down the hill, dragging Assundra by the hand of her good arm as she shook her head, laughing at Assundra's confusion. "Oh, Sunny, you are a scatterbrain! The stories, you know, the ones with knights and battles. If Simon or Elspeth decide to take on the world then I'm sure the world has some heroes to take care of them!"

"We could have done with some heroes back there!" she replied, startled when Beth reeled around on her, almost making her slip.

"We had the best hero we could wish for, Sunny! You! You're the most powerful hero this world has ever seen!" She moved close to Assundra slowly, smiling, planting a kiss on her lips that to Assundra was sweeter than sugar cane. "And I'm going to protect you."

"Oh, Beth, you can't!" she wanted to say, but found herself smiling and nodding. She remembered Simon's face as he had drained Young Crafter of blood. No, this wasn't over, but it was for them. Maybe Beth was right. Maybe Assundra was worried about nothing. Maybe they could keep each other safe now. Maybe nobody would find them.

Assundra wanted to ask for the berries. All of a sudden she was ravenously hungry.

But Beth hadn't finished. "Heroism is coming through what you have to, Sunny, the way you have. It's standing against what you faced in the village. It's having the courage to love as we do, despite what people say. That's being a hero and you are one!"

"That makes you a hero too," she replied softly.

Beth just looked down. "I had no choice. I had to follow instructions, I did nothing. I almost lost you doing what I was told, doing what I did. I…because of me…"

Assundra pulled Beth closer. "You're my hero!" she said, kissing Bethlinda Mullard on the brow. "Let's let the world look after itself. I'm tired and so are you and if we don't stop to rest soon my arm is going to drop off! We deserve to just be with each other now. There's nobody and nothing to stop us." It was a lie, but one that could become truth. What was building inside her, what she just knew, somehow, was waiting for her, could go to the seven hells.

Beth was all she wanted.

As they kissed, a ewe, heavy with lamb, bleated pleadingly, having crept up silently to lie at their feet. The two girls helped the ewe give birth to a healthy lamb, speaking tenderly to her, encouraging the new mother.

They named the lamb Tom.

EPILOGUE

A sliver of light was piercing the dim pre-dawn darkness when the man awoke. Anna could see that he was shivering, having spent the whole night in the damp field. Anna and her brother thought they'd been seen by the people who came to take the body of the big dog away, so they'd left the man there until now in case it was a trap. Now Fredik was gone, though, Anna had got scared on her own and didn't want to stay hidden in the hedgerow any more.

She'd placed a blanket on him to keep him warm, but she knew it probably wouldn't be enough to keep the cold from creeping under the skin like it did if you didn't stay awake to fight it. She knew that when it got under there it stayed there until it froze you dead.

Her father had told her that before he had gone away to fight. "Your body falls asleep when you do, see," he'd said, "so the cold can get inside through the holes that sweat come out of and made your blood freeze." Anna hoped that wasn't happening to the man in the field, it didn't sound good.

As the light gained hold of the world, she began to look about her for Fredik. Her brother had gone to look for food, but he had been gone for a long time. Anna hoped he hadn't gone back to the village. Their mother would not let him come back, or if she did she would bring those new sorts of guards with her. They had been gone from home for five days now.

"What's your name little girl?"

Anna jumped, falling backwards as she did so, landing hard on her bum. "Ow," she said, immediately feeling foolish, but also pleased that the man was smiling. That might mean he wouldn't die. "Anna. What's yours?"

But the man appeared to be out of strength now. Where was Fredik with the food? Gingerly, Anna got to her feet and looked at the man in the new light. She ought to check his wounds first; she should be a good nurse like her mother had been to her father that time he had come back from the fighting covered in his own blood. Her father the hero – they had almost crossed the canyon that time! Lifting back the part of the man's tattered white robe that covered his belly, she saw that the wounds had frozen shut in the cold. She would have to do something soon, or when the sun came out, the wounds would melt and leak and go bad.

Replacing the robe carefully and laying the blanket back over the man who appeared to be asleep again, she looked round yet again for Fredik, beginning to get afraid. She didn't like being on her own. When Fredik had said they should leave, he said he'd take care of her. Why wasn't he taking care of her now?

For the next few hours the man drifted in and out of sleep, asking her questions each time he did. He asked quite a few times where he was, so Anna told him. He was in a field south of what had once been Vallan, near the Sands. No, she couldn't take him to the nearest village because the villages were gone. No, not all gone, but taken over by the strange soldiers. Yes, she'd run away. No, she couldn't take him to Caraiza because he was too heavy, he'd have to wait for her brother to come back. Yes, she was sure he was coming back, he wouldn't leave her.

Only she wasn't sure, not now. Maybe he'd gone back to the cave.

"I do think we should move," the man was saying now, "I was…attacked…you might not be able to see the wounds, but they are there. Should the beast come back…"

"The big dog thing?" Anna asked, getting bored of the man talking. The big dog was much more interesting to talk about than the boring rubbish he'd talked about so far.

"Yes, it would look like a big dog to you…have you seen it?"

"The people took it away," she replied, pleased to be able to help. "It was dead, you see. They took it away back over there." She pointed, but the man was already looking.

"That's good," the man said with a smile. Anna frowned – the smile wasn't quite right. It was like the smile of the man who'd asked her about her father that time in the village, before the solders came. He'd offered her these hard, sugary little things and used that smile. The smile that was a lie. He'd tried to make her tell him where her father was, but she hadn't told him. She'd snatched the sweets and kicked him in the goolies. He'd chased her for a bit, but she'd run to the blacksmith. She knew the blacksmith and she knew he'd see any man off who was after her. He was also hiding her father. She didn't know his name, her father said it was better that way.

"Anna," the man said harshly, as if she hadn't been paying attention.

"Sorry, I drift off like that," she said sadly. Her mother was always telling her off for it. She kept trying to focus on what people said to her, but there was always so much to think about, so much to get done and say, how could she spend time…

"Anna!"

He was shouting now and that made her cross. "Look, Mr, I don't have to help you, you know! I could just leave you here and then…then, where would you be?" She'd heard her mother say that once and thought it sounded good. "You never told me your name anyway, friends should know each other's names. Unless you don't want me to be your friend in which case I will just leave!"

She stood, folding her arms to emphasise her point. Her heart was beating quickly, she hoped the man wouldn't say she could go. She didn't know what to do. She wasn't even sure she could remember where the cave was now.

"Well?" she shouted back, hoping her voice wasn't shaking. "What's your name then?"

"I don't know my name. I can't remember. I was…someone else, but I think…I'm not sure any more."

"That doesn't make any sense!" she said, stamping her foot. "You just don't want to tell me!"

"I would tell you if I knew. I only remember…something about being old. Too old…"

"You don't look old," she replied. "You don't look more than forty and that's not old. My Daddy's older than that. He looks younger than you, though." The man smiled again. This time she was sure. "Look, Mr, what do you want? I've met men like you before and they have lying faces, just like you! Why are you lying?"

"I'm not…"

"Your face is lying!" she shouted. "You're smiling but it's not real! I think you're a bad man," she decided, snatching her blanket back, "and I'm going to go."

"Wait," he croaked, "please…don't go. I need your help. Look."

She turned back to the man and dropped her blanket, screaming. She screamed until she couldn't scream any more. The man just lay there, looking at her with his bent face, his melted face, waiting for her to stop.

"I can hide it again if you'd prefer," he said sadly.

"No," she said quickly. Now she could see properly, she could see that the man had been burned. Old Churn-Face in the village had been burned. His skin was all hard and twisty, like the man's face was. She knew from her mother that she wasn't supposed to make fun or be scared of men with burns. It was Bad.

"How did you hide it?" she asked, picking up her blanket. Dropping blankets on the floor was Bad too, they got dirty.

"I have some…special skills," the man replied, though it looked like he was getting sleepy again.

"Are you a sorceror?" she asked, wild-eyed.

"Certainly not!" the man shouted back. "I am…something else."

"I see," Anna lied. She didn't understand at all. If the man used magic he was a sorceror, surely?

"You need to get me some help, Anna. I need…can you catch an animal?"

"Of course!" She was sure she could. She'd seen her brother do it loads of times, she was sure she could copy what he did. She could copy anything any boy could do. "I could get you a rabbit, or…"

"I would need something the size of a cow," the man interrupted.

"It's rude to interrupt!" she shouted at him again. "I can't catch you a cow! How do you even catch a cow, it's impossible! They're too big!"

Anna saw lights flashing past the horizon. *Stupid* girl! They'd heard her scream! Fredik had told her to be quiet and she'd forgotten! "You have to use your magic!" she pleaded with the man, kneeling beside him. "They can't find us!"

"Let me talk to them," the man said, but he clearly didn't understand.

"They won't talk! They never talk, they just stab! Stab, stabby stab, with their swords!"

"I don't think a sword…"

"That's what our sorcerors said! That they didn't need to worry about swords, but when they hit them with the magic, it did nothing! They just kept coming!"

"I thought you said it was rude to interrupt?"

"You don't understand! They're going to kill us!" She was crying she knew, she could feel the wetness, but she didn't sob. "You have to do something!"

Then it was too late. The first soldier broke through the hedge as if it wasn't there, his face shrouded by a thick black helmet. Several more followed until about ten of them had them surrounded.

They all wore the same armour, or at least it looked the same. Anna hated them – they had plates, with slits that covered their faces, riveted onto helmets that the slits didn't match. They were covered in chain mail and a vest with a stupid logo on it, a backwards E next to a proper E on a star. Even she knew there wasn't a letter in any language that was a backwards E! If that wasn't enough, they only wore sheepskin leggings – none of it matched!

It didn't stop them killing though. Anna didn't want to die! "Fredik!" she screamed, then shook the man. "Help me! Do something!"

One of them soldiers stepped forwards. "We have found them," he hissed. Anna gasped – she'd never heard any of the soldiers speak before! She'd never seen them speak, eat or sleep. "We do not need the girl."

Anna screamed as another soldier unsheathed a long, black blade and strode towards her with it.

"No!" The soldier flew right back to the hedge as the man moved his hand. "She will not be harmed. I am weak, but still more than a match for you. You know this."

"Who are you?" the first soldier hissed again, as if he was whispering, but it was as loud as a shout.

"I don't know," the man said simply in reply, holding his hand out as if it were a sword, moving it from soldier to soldier as if it was threatening. None of them advanced. Anna was impressed, but she couldn't stop feeling terrified.

"Good!" The soldier took a step forward and reached up a hand to his helmet. Anna whimpered as he removed the helmet to reveal a grey, rotten mass of a face that was almost as melty as the man in the field. "We have need of you, Ostracian."

"Ostracian?" Anna leapt back from the man, but soon knelt back at his side when a soldier moved for his sword.

"She will not be harmed!" the man cried, his voice stronger than Anna remembered. "Who are you and what need do you have of me?"

The soldier smiled and Anna noticed that he had no upper lip, just flaps of skin hanging from under his nose.

"I have returned to right my wrongs. I have been brought back as punishment for my cowardice and greed. I have been brought back to ensure greater wrongs do not result from my errors. I have returned…for you."

Anna shrunk back from the dead man as he seemed to grow before her eyes. He spread his arms wide and she saw his armour was different to the rest. It was gold. Pure gold.

"Ostracian, I am King Daseae!" he roared, his voice whispered, but louder than any voice had a right to be. "And I," he added, more quietly, "am here to serve you. My Lord."

Anna looked at the man lying on the ground, whose face was twisted in horror. "Ah yes…I remember now."

ABOUT THE AUTHOR

I have been writing 'Withheld', on and off, for just over ten years, a journey that started and ended with similar struggles. I'd been toying with the idea of writing something for a while, having regularly kept a diary as well as writing many plays and stories as a child, but had never really done anything serious about it.

Just as I was starting my third year at university, I learned that my best friend was suffering from cancer. Knowing of my desire to write, when I asked if there was anything I could do for her, she asked if I could write her something to read in hospital. That something turned into me sending her a chapter a week of an ever-evolving story, a story that evolved even after I had 'finished' the first draft, some years later. Thankfully, my friend completely recovered and the story was forgotten about for a while, for the main part, while I started other projects, took a course in short story and novel writing and generally got on with life.

Then, as if creating a circle of events, I was myself diagnosed with cancer in the autumn of 2009. The ensuing treatment left me with a lot of time off work to do little but lie in bed and my thoughts turned back to my book, determined to make something positive come out of the experience. After an extensive editing period, including rewriting most of the book, I ended up with the finished product and, hopefully, a returning clean bill of health.

As a writer, I have, as yet, had nothing published. I unsuccessfully attempted to write short stories, finding the limit on words constricting. I have started several other novels but have so far completed none as I've always come back to 'Withheld'. I feel this book has something to offer, something from inside me that means something to me and that I want to share.

A lot has happened in the history of this book already and after a period of reflection and getting back into life I feel it's ready to be sent out into the world!

CPSIA information can be obtained at www.ICGtesting.com
Printed in the USA
LVOW090244210412

278583LV00002B/3/P

9 781466 466197